RECEIVED
JAN - - 2016
By ______

D1706298

NO LONGER PROPERTY OF
SEATTLE PUBLIC LIBRARY

Beneath An Oil-Dark Sea:

The Best of Caitlín R. Kiernan

(Volume Two)

Beneath An Oil-Dark Sea:

The Best of Caitlín R. Kiernan

(Volume Two)

Caitlín R. Kiernan

SUBTERRANEAN PRESS 2015

Beneath an Oil-Dark Sea Copyright © 2015 by Caitlín R. Kiernan.
All rights reserved.

Dust jacket illustration Copyright © 2015 by Lee Moyer.
All rights reserved.

Author photograph Copyright © 2014 by Kathryn A. Pollnac.
All rights reserved.

Black Helicopters illustration Copyright © 2013 by Vince Locke.
All rights reserved.

Interior design Copyright © 2015 by Desert Isle Design, LLC.
All rights reserved.

First Edition

ISBN
978-1-59606-706-6

Subterranean Press
PO Box 190106
Burton, MI 48519

subterraneanpress.com

Table of Contents

For my mother, Susan Ramey Cleveland,
and for my sister, Angela Wright Osborn.

And for William K. Schafer, who gets the word out.

And, lastly, for *Papavar somniferum*, the only vampire I'll ever need.

In memory of Elizabeth Tilman Aldridge
(1970 – 1995)

There's always a siren,
Singing you to shipwreck.

Radiohead,
"There There (The Boney
King of Nowhere)"

I don't like work – no man does – but I like what is in work – the chance to find yourself. Your own reality – for yourself, not for others – what no other man can ever know.

Joseph Conrad,
The Heart of Darkness

Eventually, all things merge into one, and a river runs through it. The river was cut by the world's great flood and runs over rocks from the basement of time. On some of the rocks are timeless raindrops. Under the rocks are the words, and some of the words are theirs. I am haunted by waters.

Norman Maclean,
"A River Runs Through It"

INTRODUCTION

If I were a creative writer (which, mercifully, I am not) and stumbled upon this volume, I would be inclined simply to give up and find another line of work. Caitlín R. Kiernan is so much better than anyone writing imaginative fiction today that it has become something of an embarrassment. She is the best in her field at so many things – best in the exquisite modulation of her prose; best in the sensitive portrayal of the complex and at times contradictory motivations of humans, quasi-humans, and non-humans; and, most of all, best in the compelling evocation of fear, terror, loneliness, pain, tragedy, and heartbreak. In little over two decades of writing she has generated ten or eleven novels and thirteen short story collections, along with several separately published short novels. So she combines a gratifying productivity along with an impeccable standard of merit, and we can expect her to maintain that fusion of quality and quantity for many years to come.

One of the many distinctive qualities of her work – perhaps more readily visible in her story collections than in her novels – is her effortless mastery of a multiplicity of genres. In this book we have stories of supernatural horror, science fiction, fantasy, even some noir or hard-boiled crime tales – and, more provocatively, a melding of these and other genres into something beyond description or classification. This wide range again distinguishes her from her peers. Who can match it? Strangely enough, the only writer I can think of is the venerable William F. Nolan, who in every other regard is about as antipodal to Kiernan as any writer can possibly be. Or perhaps we have to go all the way back to the *fons et origo* of weird fiction, Edgar Allan Poe, who revolutionised the tale of supernatural and psychological horror, who all but founded the detective story, and who even engaged in cosmic fantasy (if his nonfiction treatise *Eureka* can be so classified).

There is, in addition to a diversity of genres, a matching diversity of tone and ambiance. It may be true that, in general, an overriding atmosphere of melancholy pervades all her narratives, but she is eminently able to vary the mood when the opportunity arises. In part, this variation is the product of the shifting or blending of genres Kiernan effects. Who would have expected her to write in the tough, hard-boiled manner of Hammett and Chandler? But in "The Maltese Unicorn" she brilliantly turns the trick; and noir elements are also present, along with much else besides, in the short novel *Black Helicopters* and the noir/cyberpunk hybrid "Hydrarguros."

But it is those tales that touch on heartbreak and the regret for lost lives, lost loves, and lost happiness that most move us. "Pony" is a vignette dedicated to love, sex, apple orchards, and stone walls. It was later incorporated into what I still regard as her most accomplished and evocative novel, *The Red Tree* (2009), although the award-winning *The Drowning Girl: A Memoir* (2012) is a close second. A prose poem like "A Child's Guide to the Hollow Hills" can be contrasted with the brooding stream-of-consciousness of the science fiction tale "A Season of Broken Dolls," which in turn is contrasted with the steampunk mode of "The Steam Dancer (1896)."

This volume, perhaps more than many of its predecessors, also displays the dynamic and imaginative manner in which its author engages with the work of her predecessors. A critic once chastised H. P. Lovecraft for being "too well read," by which he meant that Lovecraft had absorbed so many of the great writers of weird fiction before and during his lifetime that it sometimes became difficult to know what was Lovecraft's own imaginative creation and what was some conscious or unconscious recollection of something he had read. The criticism is, to my mind, unjust; for, like Shakespeare, Handel, and so many other creative artists, Lovecraft almost always transmuted what he borrowed from others, so that it became distinctively his own.

And we can say very much the same, to an amplified degree, for Kiernan's work. The very title of this book looks back to Homer and his "wine-dark sea," perhaps by way of Robert Aickman, who used that phrase for the title of one of his more memorable stories. The opening story, "Bradbury Weather," trumpets itself as a homage to Ray

Bradbury, but it is so much more than that. Even the author of *The Martian Chronicles* might have been challenged to feature the extraordinary union of clutching horror and inexpressible poignancy that we find in this slowly building narrative. A later story, "The Melusine (1898)," may also betray a Bradbury influence in its use of the carnival theme – but of course that theme is not owned by Bradbury, and this tale is more an echo of Kiernan's own fascination with the figure of the mermaid and analogous entities.

Other tales make nods to other writers – but only as a way of acknowledging their work as a springboard for the release of Kiernan's own imagination. Are we to think of "In the Dreamtime of Lady Resurrection," with its vivid second-person narration, as an evocation of the Frankenstein motif? The author candidly acknowledges "Untitled 17" as a tribute to Angela Carter's *The Company of Wolves,* while "The Sea Troll's Daughter" harks all the way back to *Beowulf* – an offshoot of her writing the novelization of that ancient text following the 2007 film. "One Tree Hill," although vividly summoning up the spectral depths of New England history and topography, is a nod to T. E. D. Klein's expansive novel *The Ceremonies* (1984), itself an homage to Machen, Lovecraft, and other classic weird fictionists.

Lovecraft, indeed, is a writer to whom Kiernan has returned time and again – and her imaginative elaborations of this writer far predate her relocation from the South to Lovecraft's native city of Providence, R.I., in 2008, as attested by several short stories and the novel *The Daughter of Hounds* (2007), a riff on Lovecraft's concept of ghouls.

Pickman himself is the focus (even though he never actually appears in the narrative) of "Pickman's Other Model," whose deliberately old-fashioned prose and manner of narration, using Lovecraft's patented method of the documentary style, paradoxically reveals Kiernan's own sophistication – her awareness of the ambiguities inherent in the historical record and the mysteries that may lurk beyond and behind bland newspaper reports and film reviews.

There is a vaguely Lovecraftian air to "As Red as Red," a rumination on certain historical features found in "The Shunned House" (1924), while "Fish Bride" and "Houndwife" infuse Lovecraft's "The Shadow over Innsmouth" and "The Hound" with a plangency those narratives consciously lack, as Kiernan teases out the emotive ramifications of their horrific scenarios. But her tales are by no means lacking in terror; the single sentence "The hound bays." toward the end of the latter is balefully potent.

Literature is not the only fount of inspiration that Kiernan has drawn upon. "The Ape's Wife" is a half-parodic, half-touching tribute to the film *King Kong* – but here the inherent absurdity of that scenario is shorn away and the implacable plangency of the interspecies love story is brought to the fore. "In View of Nothing" is a science fiction tale that presents a tip of the hat to the music of David Bowie.

Kiernan's well-known scientific training – she was trained in vertebrate palaeontology and has written learned papers on the subject – infuses much of her work, but she is careful not to let pure science overwhelm any narrative, even those science fiction tales set in the far future where scientific advance has perhaps rendered the distinction between human and non-human ambiguous at best and meaningless at worst. In this sense, "The Ammonite Violin (Murder Ballad No. 4)" is representative. It is not, indeed, a science fiction tale – far from it. Instead, it features a complex interplay of science (ammonites – a kind of extinct mollusc – are inlaid into the wood of a violin), crime, loss, and art.

But, more than any other feature of her work, it is Kiernan's prose that keeps us coming back to her over and over again, like a crazed drug addict desperate for his daily fix. Her prose is *sensuous* in the best sense of the much-abused term. By this I do not refer to the frequent erotic episodes in Kiernan's work – episodes whose languorous panache make her one of the more stimulating sex writers of our time. Many of her sexual scenarios involve lesbianism, although there is some token heterosexual sex here and there; and Kiernan's penchant for depicting sexual congress with aliens, androids, and other anomalous entities adds a distinctive flavour to much of her writing.

But that is not what I mean by calling her prose sensuous. Even in those passages whose subject-matter is perfectly chaste, her prose beckons us with a lapidary manipulation of rhythm and sense that conveys so much more than what is written on the page. Consider a paragraph chosen almost at random from "Pony":

> A thousand variations on a single moment. It doesn't matter which one's for real, or at least it doesn't matter to me. I'm not even sure that I can remember anymore, not for certain. They've all bled together through days and nights and repetition, like sepia ink and cheap wine, and by the time I've finally caught up with you (because I always catch up with you, sooner or later), you're standing at the low stone wall dividing the orchard from the field. You're leaning forward

against the wall, one leg up and your knee pressed to the granite and slate as if you were about to climb over it but then forgot what you were doing. The field is wide, and I think it might go on forever, that the wall might be here to keep apart more than an old orchard and a fallow plot of land.

What a deft intertwining of topographical description, pensive reflections on past and present, and dreamlike wistfulness! And yet, how different is this prose-poeticism from the tough-guy (or tough-gal?) style of "The Maltese Unicorn" ("It's the sort of self-righteous bushwa so many grifters hide behind. They might stab their own mothers in the back if they see an angle in it, but, you ask them, that's jake, cause so would anyone else"). Again, diversity of genre produces diversity of style, tone, and mood.

In "Galápagos" Kiernan has written: "There are sights and experiences to which the blunt and finite tools of human language are not equal." This may be true, even a truism; but, just as Lovecraft, for all his use (and overuse) of words such as "unnamable" and "indescribable," sought to portray his outré images and conceptions to the best of his considerable ability, Kiernan uses all the rhetorical tools available to her to make the reader grasp the bizarre, terrifying, at times ineffable scenes she has so carefully orchestrated. I will cite only one example and let it serve for the whole. "Tidal Forces" is an incredible fusion of cosmicism and body horror, and the almost inconceivable nature of the weirdness of this scenario is summed up in one imperishable sentence: "I think there are galaxies trapped within her eyes."

The more we learn about Kiernan, the more we see that there is an inextricable fusion between her life and her work. This is no doubt true for any author, but in Kiernan's case there seems to be something more going on; and that is why readers will appreciate the story notes, brief and laconic as some of them are, found in this book. We learn, for example, that "And the Cloud That Took the Form" is an expression of her *ouranophobia* – a fear of the wide-open sky. It becomes evident that Kiernan's life experiences enter into, and even in some mysterious way engender, the most distinctive features of her work, and future biographers and critics will be kept busy tracing the interrelations between the two.

Caitlín R. Kiernan does not care to be called a "horror writer," and with good reason: that term is far too crude and blunt to convey even a fraction of all the diverse elements that make her work unique. Perhaps she wishes to be a writer of what Lovecraft called "weird fiction"; or maybe she prefers Aickman's coinage "strange stories." These terms seem sufficiently broad and ambiguous to encompass the multiplicity of tones, moods, manners, and motifs that make up Kiernan's short fiction, and in this volume you will find the full range of her work amply displayed. Her output to date has already placed her at the head of her field; she has nothing more to prove. Any subsequent work can only augment her achievement.

– S. T. Joshi

PART ONE

Atlanta

2004 – 2008

Bradbury Weather

1.

I still have all the old books that Sailor left behind when she finally packed up and went looking for the Fenrir temples. I keep them in a big cargo crate with most of her other things, all that shit I haven't been able to part with. One of the books, a collection of proverbs, was written more than two hundred years ago by a Gyuto monk. It was published after his death in a Chinese prison, the manuscript smuggled out by someone or another, translated into Spanish and English, and then published in America. The monk, who did not wish to be remembered by name, wrote: "No story has a beginning, and no story has an end. Beginnings and endings may be conceived to serve a purpose, to serve a momentary and transient intent, but they are, in their truer nature, arbitrary and exist solely as a construct of the mind of man."

Sometimes, very late at night, or very early in the morning, when I should be sleeping or meditating, I read from Sailor's discarded books, and I've underlined that passage in red. If what I'm about to write down here needs an epigraph, that's probably as good as any I'll ever find, just as this beginning is as arbitrary and suitable as any I could ever choose. She left me. I couldn't have stopped her, not that I ever would have tried. I'm not that sort of woman. It was her decision, and I believed then it would have been wrong for me to interfere. But six months later, after the nightmares began, and I failed a routine mental-health evaluation, I resigned my teaching post and council seat and left to chase rumors and the ghost of her across the Xanthe Terra and Lunae Planum.

In Bhopai, a pornography dealer sold me a peep stick of Sailor dancing in a brothel. And I was told that maybe the stick had been made at Hope VII, a slatternly, backdust agradome that had seen better days and then some. I'd been up there once, on council business, more than twenty years before; Hope's Heaven, as the locals like to call the place, sits like a boil in the steep basalt hills northwest of Tharsis Tholus. The dome has been breached and patched so many times it looks more like a quilt than a habitat.

I know a woman there. We worked together a few times, but that's ancient fucking history. These days, she runs a whorehouse, though everyone in Hope's Heaven calls her a mechanic, and who the hell am I to argue? Her bulls let me in the front door, despite my bureaucratic pedigree and the council brands on the backs on my hands. I played the stick for her, played it straight through twice, and Jun'ko Valenzuela shrugged her narrow, tattooed shoulders, shook her head once, and then went back to stuffing the bowl of her pipe with the skunky britch weed she buys cheap off the shiks down in New Riyadh.

I waited for her to finish, because I'd spent enough time in the mechanic's company to know that she talked when she was ready and fuck all if that wasn't good enough. If I got impatient, if I got pushy, she'd have one of her girls handing me my hat and hustling me straight back across town to the air station, no ifs, ands, buts, or maybes. So, I sat quietly in my chair and watched while she used an antique ivory tamper to get the weed just the way she wanted it, before lighting the pipe with a match. Jun'ko exhaled, and the smoke was the color of steel, almost the same color as her long dreadlocks.

"I don't do business with the law," she said. "Leastways, not if I have a choice. But you already *knew* that, didn't you, Dorry? You knew that before you came in here."

"I'm not police," I said, starting to feel like I was reading my lines from a script I'd rehearsed until the words had lost their meaning, going through motions designed to waste my time and amuse Jun'ko. "This isn't a criminal investigation," I assured her.

"It's bloody well close enough, *perra*. You're nothing but a bunch of goddamn witches, I say, badges or no badges, the whole lot of you Council rats."

"I don't work for any corporate agency or government corpus, nor do I – "

"Maybe not," she interrupted, "but you do work *with* them," and she squinted at me across the small table, her face wreathed in smoke. "Don't deny it. They say fuck, you ask who. You tell them whatever they need to know, whenever they come around asking questions, especially if there's a percentage for your troubles."

"I already told you, this is a personal matter. I told you that before I ran the stick."

"People tell me lots of things. Most times, turns out they're lying."

"Has it ever occurred to you that just might mean you're running in the wrong circles?" I asked, the question slipping out before I let myself think better of it. There she was trying to pick a fight, looking for any excuse to have me thrown out of her place, and there I was playing along, like I thought I'd ever get a second chance.

"Oh, the thought has crossed my mind," she said calmly around a mouthful of britch smoke, smiled, and the sinuous gold and crimson Chinese dragon tattooed on her left shoulder uncoiled and flashed its gilded eyes. "Why are you *asking* me if I've seen this little share crop of yours?" Jun'ko said, and she motioned at the peep stick with her pipe. "It's obvious that was scratched here, and nothing happens in my place I *don't* know about."

"Was she working for you?"

The dragon on Jun'ko's shoulder showed me teeth like daggers.

"Yeah, Dorry. She worked for me."

"When'd she leave?"

"I didn't say she had."

"But she's not here now – "

"No, she's not," Jun'ko Valenzuela said and stared into the softly glowing bowl of her pipe. "That one, *conchita* cashed out and bought herself a nook on a freighter that came through Heaven a couple months back. One of those big transpolar wagons, hauling ore down from the Acidalia."

"Did this freighter happen to have a name?"

"Oh, no damn doubt about it," she smiled and emptied the bowl of her pipe into an ashtray cut from cobalt-blue glass. "I just don't happen to remember what it was."

"Or where it was headed."

"Lots of places, most likely."

"She's looking for the Fenrir," I said, saying too much, and Jun'ko laughed and tapped her pipe against the edge of the ashtray.

"Jesus, Joseph, and Buddha, you know how to pick 'em, Dorry."

"She never told you that, that she was looking for the temples?"

"Hell, no. She kept to herself, mostly. And if I'd known she was hodging for the Wolf, I'd never have put her skinny ass on the menu. *Mierda*. You listen to me. *Sácate el dedo del culo,* and you get yourself right the fuck back to Herschel City. Count yourself slick all this Jane cadged was your heart."

"Is that what you'd do, Jun'ko?"

She looked up at me, her hard brown eyes almost black in the dim light, and the dragon on her shoulder closed its mouth. "I got better sense than to crawl in bed with grey pilgrims," she said. "And you're officially out of time, Dorry. I trust you know the way back down to the street?"

"I think I can figure it out."

"That's cause you're such a goddamn smart lady. Of course, maybe you'd like to have a drink and sample the product first," and she nodded towards a couple of girls standing at the bar. "I'll even see you get a little discount, just to show there's no hard feelings."

"Thanks, but – "

" – she took your *huevos* with her when she left."

"I suppose that's one way of putting it," I replied, and she laughed again and began refilling her pipe.

"That's a goddamn shame," Jun'ko said and struck a match. "But you watch yourself out there. Way I hear it told, the Fenrir got more eyes than God. And they say the Wolf, he never sleeps."

When I stood up, she pointed at the two girls again. They were both watching me now, and one of them raised her skirt to show me that she had a dick. Jun'ko Valenzuela puffed at her pipe and shook her head. When she talked, smoke leaked from her mouth and from the jaws of the dragon tattoo. "Things ain't always what they seem. You don't forget that, Dorry. Not if you want to find this little *coño* and live to regret it."

The sun was already starting to slip behind Tharsis Tholus by the time I got back to the dingy, dusty sleeper that I'd rented near the eastern locks. The storm that had begun just before dawn still howled down the slopes of the great volcano, extinct two billion years if you trust the geologists, and battered the walls of Hope's Heaven, hammering the thin foil skin of the dome. I've always hated the western highlands, and part of me wanted nothing more than to take the mechanic's advice and go home. I imagined hauling the crate full of Sailor's belongings down the hall to the lift, pictured myself leaving it all piled in the street. It'd be easy, I told myself. It would be the easiest thing I'd ever done.

I ate, and, when the night came, I sat a little while in the darkness – I hadn't paid for electric – gazing out the sleeper's tiny window at the yellow runner lights dotting the avenue below, the street that led back up to Jun'ko's whorehouse or down to the docks, depending whether you turned left or turned right, north or south. When I finally went to bed, the nightmares found me, as they almost always do, and for a while, at least, I wasn't alone.

Just before dawn, I was awakened by a knock at the door, and I lay staring up into the gloom, looking for the ceiling, trying to recall where the hell I was and how I'd gotten myself there. Then I remembered smirking Jun'ko and her kinetitatts, and I remembered Hope VII, and then I remembered everything else. Whoever was out in the corridor knocked again, harder than before. I reached for my pants and vest, lying together on the floor near the foot of the cot.

"Who's there?" I shouted, hoping it was nothing more than someone banging on the wrong door, a drunk or an honest mistake. The only person in town whom I'd had business with was the mechanic, and as far as I was concerned, that business was finished.

"My name is Mikaela," the woman on the other side of the door called back. "I have information about Sailor. I may be able to help you find her. Please, open the door."

I paused, my vest still unfastened, my pants half on, half off. I realized that my mouth had gone dry, and my heart was racing. Maybe I'd pissed old Jun'ko off just a little more than I'd thought. Perhaps, in return, I was about to get the worst beating of my life, or perhaps word had gotten around the dome that the stranger from the east was an easy mark.

"Is that so?" I asked. "Who sent you?" And when she didn't answer, I asked again. "Mikaela, *who* sent you here?"

"This would be easier, Councilor, if you'd open the door. I might have been followed."

"All the more reason for me to keep it shut," I told her, groping about in the dark for anything substantial enough to serve as a weapon, cursing myself for being too cheap to pay the five credits extra for electric.

"I'm one of the mechanic's girls," she said, almost whispering now, "but I swear she didn't send me. Please, there isn't time for this."

My right hand closed around an aluminum juice flask I'd bought in one of Heaven's market plazas the day before. It wasn't much, hardly better than nothing, but it'd have to do. I finished dressing, then crossed the tiny room and stood with my hand on the lockpad.

"I have a gun," I lied, just loud enough I was sure the woman would hear me.

"I don't," she replied. "Open the door. *Please.*"

I gripped the flask a little more tightly, took a deep breath, and punched in the twelve-digit security code. The door slid open immediately, whining on its rusty tracks, and the woman slipped past me while I was still half-blind and blinking at the flickering lamps set into the walls of the corridor.

"Shut the door," she said, and I did, then turned back to the darkened room, to the place where her voice was coming from. Yellow and white splotches drifted to and fro before my eyes, abstract fish in a lightless sea.

"Why is it so dark in here?" she asked, impatiently.

"Same reason I opened the door for you. I'm an idiot."

"Isn't there a window? All these nooks have windows," and I remembered that I'd closed and locked the shutters before going to bed, so the morning sun wouldn't wake me.

"There's a window, but you don't need to see me to explain why you're here," I said, figuring the darkness might at least even the odds if she were lying.

"Christ, you're a nervous nit."

"Why are you *here*?" I asked, trying to sound angry when I was mostly scared and disoriented, and I took a step backwards, setting my shoulders squarely against the door.

"I told you. Sailor and me, we was sheba, until she paid off Jun'ko and headed south."

"South?" I asked. "The freighter was traveling south?"

"That's what she told me. Sailor, I mean. But, look here, Councilor, before I say any more, that quiff left owing me forty creds, and I'm not exactly in a position to play grace and let it slip."

"And what makes you think I'm in a position to pay off her debts, Mikaela? What makes you think I *would*?"

"You're a *titled* woman," she replied, and the tone in her voice made her feelings about the Council perfectly clear. "You've got it. And if you don't, you can get it. And you'll pay me, because nobody comes all the way the hell to Hope's Heaven looking for someone unless they want to find that someone awfully fucking bad. Am I wrong?"

"No," I sighed, because I didn't feel like arguing with her. "You're not wrong. But that doesn't mean you're telling the truth, either."

"About Sailor?"

"About anything."

"She told me about the Fenrir," the woman named Mikaela said. "It's almost all she ever talked about."

"That doesn't prove anything. That's nothing you couldn't have overheard at Jun'ko's yesterday evening."

Mikaela sighed. "I'm going to open the damned window," she said. "I hope you don't mind," and a moment later I heard her struggling with the bolt, heard it turning, and then the shutters spiraled open to reveal the easy pinkish light of false dawn. Mikaela was prettier than I'd expected, and a little older. Her hair was pulled back in a long braid, and the light through the window revealed tiny wrinkles around her eyes. The face seemed familiar, and then I realized she was one of the women who'd been standing at the bar in Jun'ko's, the one who'd shown me that she had a penis. She sat down on the cot and pointed at the flask in my hand.

"Is *that* your gun?" she asked.

"I need to know whether or not you're telling me the truth," I said. "I don't think that's unreasonable, considering the circumstances."

"I'm a whore. That doesn't necessarily make me a thief and a liar."

"I need something, Mikaela. More than your word."

"I'm actually a pretty good fuck," she said, as though it was exactly what I was waiting for her to say, and lay down on the cot. "You know, I'd wager I'm a skid better fuck than Sailor Li ever was. We could be sheba, you and me, Councilor. I'd go back to Herschel City with you, and you could forget all about her. If she wants to commit suicide, then, hell – "

"Something you couldn't have gotten from Jun'ko," I pressed. She rolled her eyes, which I could see were blue. There aren't many women on Mars with blue eyes.

"Yeah," she said, almost managing to sound disappointed, and clicked her tongue once against the roof of her mouth. "How's this? Sailor was with you for five years, if you count the three months after you started fucking her before you asked her to move into your flat. You lost two teeth in a fight when you were still just a kid, because someone called your birth mother an offworlder bitch, and sometimes the implants ache before a storm. The first time Sailor brought up the Fenrir, you showed her a stick from one of the containment crews and told her if she ever mentioned the temples again, you'd ask her to leave. When she *did* mention them again, you hit her so hard you almost – "

"You've made your point," I said, cutting her off. She smiled, a smug, satisfied smile, and nodded her head.

"I usually do, Dorry." She patted the edge of the cot with her left hand. "Why don't you come back to bed."

"I'm not going to fuck you," I replied and set the aluminum flask down on a shelf near the door. "I'll pay off whatever she owes you. You'll tell me what you know. But that's as far as it goes."

"Sure, if that's the way you want it." Mikaela shut her eyes. "Just thought I'd be polite and offer you a poke."

"You said the freighter was headed south."

"No. I said *Sailor* said it was headed south. And before I say more, I want half what I'm owed."

My eyes were beginning to adjust to the dim light getting in through the window, and I had no trouble locating the hook where I'd left my jacket hanging the night before. I removed my purse from an inside pocket, unfastened the clasp, and took out my credit tab. "How do you want to do this?" I asked, checking my balance, wondering how many more months I could make the dwindling sum last.

"Subdermal," she said. "Nobody out here carries around tabs, especially not whores."

I keyed in the amount, setting the exchange limit at twenty, and handed Mikaela the tab. She pressed it lightly to the inside of her left forearm, and the chip beneath her flesh subtracted twenty credits from my account. Then she handed the tab back to me, and I tried not to notice how warm it was.

"So, she told you the freighter was headed south," I said, anxious to have this over and done with and get this girl out of the sleeper.

"Yeah, that's what she said." Mikaela rolled over onto her right side, and her face was lost in the shadows. "The freighter's a Shimizu-Mochizuki ship, one of the old 500-meter ore buckets. You don't see many of those anymore. This one was hauling ice from a mine in the Chas Boreale to a refinery in Dry Lake, way the hell out on the Solis Planum."

"I know where Dry Lake is," I said, wondering how much of this she was inventing, and I sat down on the floor by the sleeper's door. "You've got an awfully good memory."

"Yes," she replied. "I do, don't I?"

"Do you also remember the freighter's name?"

"The *Oryoku Maru,* as a matter of fact."

"I can check these things out."

"I fully expect you to."

I watched her a minute or more, the angles and curves of her silhouette, wishing I had a pipe full of something strong, though I hadn't smoked in years. The shadows and thin wash of dawn between us seemed thicker than mere light and the absence of light.

"Does she know where she's going?" I asked, wishing I could have kept those words back.

"She *thinks* so. Anyhow, she heard there'd be a Fenrir priest on the freighter. She thought she could get it to talk with her."

"Why did she think that?"

"Sailor can be a very persuasive woman," Mikaela said and laughed. "Hell, I don't know. Ask her that when you find her."

"She thinks there's a temple somewhere on the Solis?"

"She wouldn't have told me that, and I never bothered to ask. I don't have the mark," and Mikaela held out her left arm for me to see. "She fucked me, and she liked to talk, but she's a pilgrim now, and I'm not."

"Did you try to stop her?"

"Not really. I told her she was fucking gowed, looking for salvation with that bunch of devils, but we're all free out here, Councilor. We choose our own fates."

Down on the street, something big roared and rattled past, its engines sounding just about ready for the scrapyard. Probably a harvester drone on its way to the locks and the fields beyond the dome. The sun was rising, and Hope VII was waking up around us.

"There's something else," Mikaela said, "something she wanted me to show you."

"She knew that I was coming?"

"She *hoped* you were coming. I should have hated her for that, but, like I said – "

" – you're all free out here."

"Bloody straight. Free as the goddamned dust," she replied. There was a little more light coming in the window now, morning starting to clear away the dregs of night, and I could see that Mikaela was smiling despite the bitterness in her voice.

"Did you want to go with her?"

"Are you fucking cocked? I wouldn't have gotten on that freighter with her for a million creds, not if she was right about there being a fucking Fenny priest aboard."

"So, what did she want you to show me?"

"Are you going after her?" Mikaela asked, ignoring my question, offering her own instead, and she sat up and turned her face towards the open window.

"Yes," I told her. "That's why I'm here."

"Then you *must* be cocked. You must be mad as a wind shrake."

"I'm starting to think so. What did she want you to show me, Mikaela?"

"Most people call me Mickie," she said.

And I thought about paying her the other twenty and letting her go back to Jun'ko's or wherever it was she slept. There wasn't much of her street-smart bluster left, and it was easy enough to see that she was scared. It was just as easy to figure out why.

"My mum, she was a good left-footer," Mikaela said. "God, Baby Jesus, the Pope and St. Teresa, all that tieg crap. And she used to tell me and my sisters that only the *evil* people have any cause to *fear* evil, but what'd she know? She never even left the dome where she was born. She never spent time out on the frontiers, never saw the crazy shit goes off out here. All the evil *she* ever imagined could be chased away with rosary beads and a few Hail Marys."

"Is it something you're afraid to show me, Mickie?" I asked, and she laughed and quickly hid her face in her hands. I didn't say anything else for a while, just sat there with my back to the door of the sleeper, watching the world outside the window grow brighter by slow degrees, waiting until she stopped crying.

I wish I could say that Sailor had lied, or at least exaggerated, when she told Mikaela that I'd beaten her. I wish it with the last, stingy speck of my dignity, the last vestiges of my sense of self-loathing. But if what I'm writing down here is to be the truth, the truth as complete as I might render it, then that's one of the things I have to admit, to myself, to whoever might someday read this. To God, if I'm so unfortunate and the universe so dicked over that she or he or it actually exists.

So, yes, I beat Sailor.

She'd been gone for several days, which wasn't unusual. She would do that sometimes, if we seemed to be wearing on one another. And it was mid-Pisces, deep into the long season of dust storms and endless wind, and we were both on edge. That time of year, just past the summer solstice, all of Herschel seems set on edge, the air ripe with static and raw nerves. I was busy with my duties at the university and, of course, with council business, and I doubt that I even took particular notice of her absence. I've never minded sleeping alone or taking my meals by myself. If I missed her, then I missed the conversation, the sex, the simple contact with another human body.

She showed up just after dark one evening, and I could tell from the way she was dressed that she hadn't been at her mothers' or at the scholars' hostel near the north gate, the two places she usually went when we needed time apart. She was dirty, her hair coppery and stiff with dust, and she was wearing her long coat and heavy boots. So I guessed she'd been traveling outside the dome; maybe she'd taken the tunnel sled up to Gale or all the way down to Molesworth. I was in my study, going over notes for the next day's lectures, and she came in and kissed me. Her lips were chapped and rough, faintly gritty, and I told her she needed a shower.

"Yeah, that'd be nice," she said. "If you stuck me right now, I think I'd bleed fucking dust."

"You were outside?" I asked, turning back to my desk. "That's very adventuresome of you."

"Did you miss me?"

"They've had me so busy, I hardly even noticed you were gone."

She laughed, the way she laughed whenever she wasn't sure that I was joking. Then I heard her unbuckling her boots, and afterwards she was quiet for a bit. Two or three minutes, maybe. When I glanced up, she'd taken off her coat and gloves and rolled her right shirt sleeve up past the elbow.

"Don't be angry," she said. "Please."

"What are you on about now?" I asked, and then I saw the fevery red marks on the soft underside of her forearm. It might have only been a rash, except for the almost perfect octagon formed by the intersection of welts or the three violet pustules at the center of it all. I'd seen the mark before, and I knew exactly what it meant.

"At least hear me out," she said. "I had to know – "

"*What?*" I demanded, getting to my feet, pushing the chair roughly across the floor. "*What* precisely did you have to fucking *know,* Sailor?"

"If it's true. If there's something more – "

"More than *what?* Jesus fucking Christ. You let them touch you. You let those sick fucks *inside* of you."

"More than *this,*" she said, retreating a step or two towards the doorway and the hall, retreating from me. "More than night and goddamn day. More than getting old and dying and no one even giving a shit that I was ever alive."

"How long's it been?" I asked, and she shook her head and flashed me a look like she didn't understand what I meant. "Since contact, Sailor. How long has it been since *contact*?"

"That doesn't matter. I wouldn't take the serum."

"We're not going to fucking argue about this. *Yes,* you're going to take the serum. We're going to the clinic right now, and you're going to start the serum *tonight.* If you're real bloody lucky, it might not be too late – "

"*Stop it!*" she hissed. "This isn't your decision, Dorry. It's my body. It's my goddamn life," and that's when she started crying. And that's when I hit her.

That's when I started hitting her.

There's no point pretending that I remember how many times I struck her. I only stopped when I saw the blood from her broken nose, splattered on the wall of my study. I like to believe that it wouldn't have happened if she hadn't started crying, those tears like a shield, like a weapon she'd fashioned from her weakness. I've always loathed the sight of tears, for no sane reason, and I like to think everything would have played out some other way if she just hadn't started crying. But that's probably bullshit, and even if it isn't, it wouldn't matter, would it? So, whatever I said earlier about not being the sort of woman to interfere in another's decisions, forget that. Remember this, instead.

Sailor left that night, and I haven't seen or heard from her since. I waited for a summons to appear before the quarter magistrate on charges of assault, but the summons never came, and one day I returned home from my morning classes to find that most of her clothes were gone. I never found out if she retrieved them herself or if someone did it for her. A couple of weeks later, I learned that three Fenrir priests had been arrested near Kepler City, and that the district marshals suspected they'd passed near Molesworth and Herschel earlier in Pisces, that they'd been camped outside Mensae sometime back in Capricorn.

And that morning in Hope VII, all those months later, I sat and listened to Jun'ko's billygirl sobbing because she was afraid, and I dug my nails into my palms until the pain was all that mattered.

"I think you must miss her," Mikaela said, looking back over her left shoulder at me, answering a question I hadn't asked. "To have left

Herschel and come all the way out here, to go poking around Jun'ko's place. Lady, no one comes to Heaven, not if she can help it."

"I've been here before," I said. "When I was young, about your age."

"Yeah, that's what Jun'ko was telling me," she replied, and I wanted to ask what else the mechanic might have told her, but I didn't. I was following Mikaela down a street so narrow it might as well have been an alleyway, three or four blocks over from the dome's main thoroughfare. Far above us, sensors buried in the framework of the central span were busy calibrating the skylights to match the rising sun outside. But some servo or relay-drive bot responsible for this sector of Hope VII had been down for the last few months, according to Mikaela. So we walked together in the lingering gloom, the patchy frost crunching softly beneath our feet, while the rest of the dome brightened and warmed. Once or twice, I noticed someone watching us through a smudgy window, suspicious eyes set in wary, indistinct faces, but there was no one on the street yet. The lack of traffic added to my unease and the general sense of desolation and decay; this was hardscrabble, even by the standards of Hope's Heaven. That far back from town center, almost everything was adobe brick and pressed sand-tile, mostly a jumble of warehouses, garages, and machine shops, with a shabby handful of old-line modular residential structures stacked about here and there. If Mikaela were leading me into an ambush, she couldn't have chosen a better setting.

"You hang close to me, Councilor," she said. "People around here, they don't care so much for outsiders. It's a bad part of town."

"You mean to say there's a *good* part?" I asked, and she laughed, then stopped and peered down a cross street, rubbing her hands together for warmth. Her breath steamed in the morning air.

"No," she said. "I sure wouldn't go so far as to say that. But there's bad and there's worse." She frowned and looked back the way we'd come.

"Is something wrong?" I asked. She shook her head, then pointed east, towards the cross street.

"It's that way, just a little piece farther," she said, and then she changed the subject. "Is it true you've been offworld? That's what Jun'ko said, that you've been up to Eos Station, that you've seen men. Men from Earth."

I nodded my head, still looking in the direction she'd pointed. "It's true. But that was a long time ago."

"What were they like?" she asked, and I shrugged.

"Different," I replied, "but not half so different as most of us think. Two eyes, two hands, one mouth, a dick," and I jabbed a thumb at her skirt. "More like some of us than others."

It was a crude comment, one I never would have made if I hadn't been so nervous, and I half expected her to get pissed or something. But Mikaela only kicked at a loose paving tile and rubbed her hands together a little harder, a little faster.

"Yeah, well, that was Jun'ko's idea," she said. "She even paid the surgeon. Claimed I wasn't pretty enough, that I needed something special, you know, something exotic, if I was gonna work out of her place. It's not so bad. Like I said, I'm a pretty good fuck. Better than I was before."

"No regrets, then?"

She made a half-amused, snorting noise, wiped her nose on the sleeve of her jacket, and stared at her shoes. "I was born here," she said. "What the hell would I do with a thing like regret?"

"When are you going to tell me what's waiting for me down there, Mickie?" I asked, and she almost smiled.

"Sailor said you'd be like this."

"Like what?"

"She said you weren't a very trusting person. She said you had a nasty habit of stabbing people in the back before they could beat you to it."

I suppose that was payback for the remark about her penis, nothing I didn't have coming, but it made me want to slap her. Before I could think of a reply, she was moving again, walking quickly away from me down the side street. I thought about turning around and heading straight back to the station. It was still three long hours until the next zep, but I could try to get a secure uplink and see what there was to learn about the *Oryoku Maru*. Following the whore seemed like a lazy way to commit suicide.

I followed her, anyway.

A couple of minutes later, we ducked through a low archway into what appeared to be an abandoned repair shop. It was dark inside, almost too dark to see, and even colder than it had been out on the street. The air stank of spent engine oil and hydrosol, dust and mildew and rat shit, and the place was crowded with the disassembled, rusting skeletons of harvesters and harrow rigs. They loomed around us and hung from ceiling hoists, broken, forgotten beasts with sickle teeth.

"Watch your step, Councilor," Mikaela warned, calling back to me after I tripped over some piece of machinery or another and almost stumbled into an open garage pit. I paused long enough to catch my breath, long enough to whisper a thankful prayer and be sure I hadn't broken my ankle.

"We need a fucking torch," I muttered, my voice much louder than I'd expected, magnified and thrown back at me by the darkness pressing in around us.

"Well, I don't have one," she said, "so you'll just have to be more careful."

She took my hand and guided me out of the repair bay, along a pitch-black corridor that turned left, then right, then left again, before finally ending in a dim pool of light spilling in through a number of ragged, fist-sized holes in the roof. I imagined it was sunlight, though it wasn't, of course, imagined it was warm against my upturned face, though it wasn't that, either.

"Down here," she said, and I turned towards her voice, blinking back orange and violet afterimages. We were standing at the top of a stairwell.

"I hid it when Sailor left," Mikaela said. "Jun'ko has our rooms tossed once or twice a month, regular as clockwork, so I couldn't leave it in the house. But I figured it'd be safe here. When I was a kid, my sister and I used to play hide-and-seek in this place."

"You have a sister?" I asked, and she started down the stairs without me, taking them two at a time despite the dark. I hurried to catch up, more afraid of being left alone in this place than wherever she might be leading me.

"Yeah," she called back. "I've got a little sister. She's out there somewhere. Sheba'd up with a guild mason down in Arsia Mons, last I heard. But we don't talk much these days. She got sick on Allah and doesn't approve of whoring anymore."

We reached the bottom of the stairs, and I glanced back up at the patch of imitation daylight we'd left at the top. "How much farther, Mickie?" I asked, trying hard to sound calm, trying to sound confident, trying desperately to bury my anxiety in a pantomime of equipoise. But the darkness was quickly becoming more than I could handle, so much darkness crammed into the gap between the walls and floor and ceiling. It was becoming inconceivable that this place might somehow simultaneously contain so much darkness and ourselves. *I'm a little claustrophobic,* I pretended to have said, so that the mechanic's girl would understand and get this the hell over and done with. Past the bottom of the stairs, the air was damp and smelled of mold and stagnant water, mushrooms and rotting cardboard. I was sweating now, despite the cold.

"She made me promise that I'd keep it safe," Mikaela said, as if she hadn't heard my question or had simply chosen to ignore it. "I'm not really used to people trusting me with things. Not with things that matter to – "

"How much *farther*?" I asked again, more insistent than before. "We need to hurry this up, or I'll miss my flight."

"Here," she said. "Right there, on your left," and when I turned my head that way, there was the faintest chartreuse glow, like some natural fungal phosphorescence, a glow that I could have sworn hadn't been there only a few seconds before. "Just inside the doorway, on the table," Mikaela said.

I took a deep breath of the fetid air and stepped past her through an opening leading into what might once have been a storeroom or maintenance locker. The glow became much brighter than it had been out in the corridor, illuminating the bare concrete walls, an M5 proctor droid that had been stripped raw and left for dead, and the intestine tangle of sagging pipes above my head. The yellow-green light was coming from a five- or six-liter translucent plastic catch cylinder, something that had probably been manufactured as part of a dew-farm's cistern. And I stood staring at the pale thing floating inside the cylinder – not precisely dead because it had probably never been precisely alive – a wad of hair and mottled flesh, bone and the scabby shell of a half-formed exoskeleton.

"She said it was yours, Dorry," Mikaela whispered from somewhere behind me. "She said she didn't know, when she took the mark, didn't know she was pregnant."

I said something. I honestly can't remember what.

It hardly matters.

The thing in the cylinder twitched and opened what I hadn't realized was an eye. It was all pupil, that eye, and blacker than space.

"She lost it before she even got here," the whore said, "when she was working up in Sytinskakya. She couldn't have taken it with her to the temples, and I promised her that I'd keep it safe. She thought you might want to take it back with you."

I turned away from the unborn thing, which might or might not have seen my face, pushing my way roughly past Mikaela and back out into the corridor. The darkness there seemed almost kind after the light from the catch cylinder, and I let it swallow me whole as I ran. I only fell twice or maybe three times, tripping over my own feet and sprawling hard on sand-tile or steel, then right back up in an instant, blindly making my way to the stairwell and the cluttered repair shop above, and, finally, to the perpetually shadowed street. I stopped and looked back then, breathless and faint and sick to my belly, pausing only long enough to see that Jun'ko's girl hadn't followed me. By the time I reached the transfer station at the lower end of Avenue South Eight, the morning was fading towards noon, and what I'd seen below Hope's Heaven seemed hardly as substantial, hardly as thinkable, as any woman's guilty dreams of Hell.

I have Sailor's book of proverbs from the cargo crate open on the table in front of me, the one written by the twentieth-century Tibetan monk. There's a passage here on dreams, one of the passages I've underlined in red, which reads, "The pathway to Nirvana is a road along which the traveler penetrates the countless illusions of his waking mind, his dreams and dreamless sleep. There must be a full and final awakening from all illusion, waking and dreaming. By many forms of meditation a man may at last achieve this necessary process of waking up in his life and in his dreams and nightmares. He may follow Vipassanâ in search of lasting, uninterrupted self-awareness, finally catching himself in the very act of losing himself in the cacophonous labyrinth of his thoughts and fantasies and the obscuring tides of emotion and sexual impulse that work to impede awakening."

I like to think that I know what most of that means, but, then again, I'm an arrogant woman, and admitting ignorance galls me. I may not have the faintest clue.

On the long flight from Hope VII, from the ages-dead caldera of Tharsis Tholus towards the greater, but equally spent, craters of Pavonis Mons and Arsia Mons, skirting the sheer, narrow fissures of the Noctis Fossae and the dismal mining operations scattered like old scabs out along the edges of that district, as the zep drifted high above the rust-colored world, I dozed, losing myself in those obscuring tides. It's not the same dream every time. I'm not sure I believe in dreams which recur with such absolute perfection that they're always the same dream. So, then, this is a collective caricature of the dreams that I've had since Sailor left, an approximation of the dream I must have had as the drone of the zep's engines answered my exhaustion and dragged me down to sleep.

I'm standing outside the vast, impenetrable dome of Herschel City, locked safely inside my pressure suit, breathing clean, fresh air untainted by the fine red dust blowing down from Elysium. I can hear the wind through my comms, wild and terrible as any mythological banshee long since exiled here from Earth. In the distance, far across the plain, I can see a procession, a single-file line of robed figures and their cragged assortment of sandrovers and skidwagons. A great cloud of dust rises up behind them and hangs like a caul, despite the wind. *Impervious* to the wind. And I am filled with such complete dread, a fear like none that I have never known, but I take one step forward. There's music coming through my helmet, flutes and violins and the *thump-thump-thump* of drums. I know that music at once, though I've never heard it before. I know that music instinctively.

"They're not for you, Dorry," Sailor says, and I turn, turning my back on the procession, and she's standing there with her left hand on the shoulder of my suit. She isn't wearing one herself. She isn't wearing much of anything, and the dust has painted her skin muted shades of terra-cotta. She might be another race entirely, another species, something alien or angelic or ghostly that I have fucked and loved thinking she was only a human girl.

"They would never let you follow," she says. "Not as you are now."

I don't wonder how she can breathe, or how her body is enduring the bitter cold or the low pressure or radiation. I only want to hold her, because it's been so long, and I never imagined I would really see her again. But then she pushes me away, frowning, that look she used to get whenever she thought I was being particularly stupid. She licks her red-brown lips, and her tongue is violet.

"No," she says, sounding almost angry, almost hateful. "You *hit* me, Dorry. And I don't need that shit. If I needed that shit, I'd have stayed with fucking Erin Antimisiaris. If I needed to be someone's punch hound, I'd go hunt up my asshole swap-mother and let *her* have another go at me."

She says other, more condemning things, and I say nothing at all in my defense, because I *know* she's telling the truth, laying it all out for me as the sun crawls feebly across the wide china sky. And then, slowly, grain by grain, the wind takes her apart, weathers her away until her face is hardly recognizable, a granite statue that might have stood at this spot a thousand years; her body has begun to crumble, too, reclaimed by the ground beneath our feet. I turn once more towards the procession, but it has passed beyond the range of my vision.

And then we are lying in my bed, and the air smells like fresh cinnamon and clean linen, a musky, faint hint of sweat and sex, and Sailor lights her pipe. I wonder how long I've been sleeping, how long the dream could have lasted, and as I turn to tell her about it all – an act of sharing secrets to rob the nightmare of its claws – the room dissolves around me, and I'm standing alone at the edge of a crater so wide I can see only a little ways across it. I'm facing west, I think, and the sky is a roiling kaleidoscope of clotted, oily grays and blues, blacks and deep purples, no sky that any woman has ever seen on Mars. *That's the color of nausea,* I think. *That's the color of plague and decay.*

I hear the music again, then. The pipes. The bows drawn across taut strings. The drums sounding out loudly across the flat, monotonous floor of the impact crater. A billion years ago, something fell screaming from the sky and buried itself here, broke apart in a storm of fire and vaporized stone, and here it has been waiting. It was here when the progenitors of humankind were mere protoplasmic slime clinging desperately to the sanctuary of abyssal hydrothermal vents. It was waiting when our australopithecine foremothers first looked up and noticed the red star hanging above African skies. It was here when men finally began to send their probes and landers, waiting while the human invasion was planned and executed. But not waiting patiently, because nothing so burned and shattered and hungry can wait patiently, but waiting all the same; it has been left no choice. It has been cast down, gravity's prisoner, and I look back once, looking back at the wastes stretching out behind me, before I begin the long, painful climb down to the place where the music is coming from.

2.

I was having a bowl of sage tea, the strong stuff the airlines serve, when I first noticed the journalist. She was sitting across the aisle from me, a few rows nearer the front of the passenger cabin, and she made no attempt to hide the fact that she was watching me. Her red hair was tied back in the high, braided topknot that has become so fashionable in the eastern cities, held up with an elaborate array of hematite and onyx pins. She was wearing a stiff brown MBS uniform, and when she saw me looking at her, she nodded and stood up.

"Fuck me," I muttered and then turned to stare out the portal, through thin, hazy clouds at the barren landscape fifteen hundred feet below the zep. We'd already made the stop at the new Keeslar-Nguyen depot near Arsia Mons and, afterwards, the airship had turned east, heading out across the Solis Planum.

"May I sit with you, Councilor?" the journalist asked a few moments later, and when I looked up, she was pointing at the empty seat opposite me. She was smiling, that practiced smile to match the casual tone of her voice, all of it meant to put me at ease and none of it doing anything of the sort.

"Do I really have any say in the matter?"

Her smile almost faded; not quite, but it faltered just enough that I could see she was nervous, her confidence a thin act, and I wondered how long it had been since the net had given this one her implants and press docs and sent her off into the world. I think I was even a little insulted that I didn't rate someone more seasoned.

"You must have known I was coming," she said. "You must have known *someone* would come."

"I know I'm going to die one day, and I'm not so happy about that, either."

"Why don't we skip this part, Councilor?" she asked, sitting down. "I'm just doing my job. I only want to ask you a few questions."

"Even though you know ahead of time that I don't want to answer them." I sipped at my tea, which was growing cold, and looked out the portal again.

"Yes. Something like that," she replied, and I knew that the cameras floating on her corneas, jacked into her forebrain and the MBS satellites, were relaying every word that passed between us, every move I made, to the network's clearcast facilities in Herschel. The footage would be trawled, filtered, and edited as we spoke and then broadcast seconds after our conversation ended.

"Have you ever been out this far?" I asked.

"No," she said, and I allowed myself to be impressed that the question hadn't thrown her. "Before this jaunt, I've never been any farther west than the foundries at Ma'adim Vallis."

"And how are you liking it so far, the frontiers?"

"It's big," she said, and cleared her throat. "Too damned big."

I drank the last of my tea and set the bowl down on the empty seat to my right; one of the attendants would be along soon to take it away.

"You were at that whorehouse in Hope VII," she said, "looking for your lover, Sailor Li."

"Is that so? Tell me, whoever the hell you are, is this what's passing for investigative work at MBS these days?" I asked and laughed. It felt good to laugh, and I tried to remember the last time I'd done it. I couldn't.

"My name is Ariadne," she said and sighed. "Ariadne Vaughn. You know, it might be in your best interest to try not to be such an asshole."

"And why is that, Ariadne?"

She stared at me a long second or two, then rubbed hard at the bridge of her nose like maybe it had started to itch. She sighed again and glanced at the portal. She couldn't have been much older than thirty, thirty-five at the outside, and I realized I wanted to fuck her. I suppose that should have elicited in me some sort of shame or disgust with myself, but it didn't.

"I asked you a simple question, Ariadne. Why might it be in my best interest not to be such an asshole."

"Because I might know where Sailor is," she said. "All we want is the story. You're the first council member known to have involvement with the Fenrir. Answer a few questions, and I'll tell you what I know."

My mouth had gone dry, and I wished I had another bowl of the hot, too-strong tea. "Sailor's the pilgrim here," I told the journalist, "not me. If you think otherwise, you're sorely mistaken."

"The way the network sees it, if your lover's chasing the Wolf and *you're* chasing your lover, that places you pretty damned close to – "

"I can have you put off at the next port," I said, interrupting her. "I still have that much authority."

"And how's that going to look, Councilor?" she asked, beginning to sound more confident now, and she leaned towards me and lowered her voice. I caught the sour-sweet scent of slake on her breath and realized why she'd been rubbing her nose. "I mean, unless this little walkabout of yours is some sort of suicide slag," she said, almost whispering.

"You're a junkie," I replied, as indifferently, as matter-of-factly, as I could manage. "Does the network buy it for you, the slake? With that much circuitry in your skull, I know *they* must know you're dragging."

Ariadne Vaughn blinked her left eye, shutting down the feed.

"I'm just wondering how it all works out," I continued. "Does the MBS have a special arrangement with the cops to protect junky remotes from prosecution?"

"They warned me you were a cunt," she said.

"They did their homework. Good for them."

Then she didn't say anything for a minute or two. One of the attendants came by, took my empty bowl, and I ordered another, this time with a shot of brandy.

"Are you lying to me about Sailor?" I asked the journalist, and she narrowed her dark eyes, eyes the color of polished agate, then shook her head and tried to look offended. "Because if you *are,*" I said, "after what I've been through and seen the past eight months, you ought to understand that I'd have no problem whatsoever with making a few calls that'll land you in flush so fast you won't even have time for one last fix before they plug you into scrub." I stabbed an index finger at her nostrils, and she flinched.

"That's a fact, little girl. You fuck me on this, and once the plumbers are finished, there won't be enough of you left for the network gats to bother salvaging the hardware. Are we absolutely clear?"

"Yes, Councilor," she said very softly, rubbing at her nose again. "I understand you very well."

I looked down the long aisle towards the zeppelin's small kitchen, wishing the attendant would hurry up with my tea and brandy. "Then ask me your questions, Ariadne Vaughn," and I glanced at my watch. "You have ten minutes."

"Ten *minutes?*" she balked. "No, Councilor, I'm afraid I'll need quite a bit more than that if – "

"Nine minutes and fifty-four seconds," I replied, and she nodded and blinked her agate-colored camera eyes on again.

Sometimes, in the dreams, I actually reach the floor of the crater. And I see it all with such clarity, a clarity that doesn't fade upon waking, a clarity such that I have sometimes been tempted to identify the crater as a real place, existing beyond the limits of my recurring nightmares. I take down a chart or my big globe and put a finger *there,* or *there,* or *there.* It might be Lomonosov, far out and alone on the Vastitas Borealis. Or it might be Kunowsky farther to the south, smaller, but just as desolate. I was once almost certain that it was the vast, weathered scar of Huygens. No one ever goes there, that pockmarked wasteland laid out above the dead inland sea of the Hellas Planitia. Not even the prospectors and dirt mags make it that far west, and if they do, they don't make it back. *Anything* at all might be hiding in a place like that. Anything. But I know that it *isn't* Huygens, and it isn't Lomonosov or Kunowsky, either, and, in the end, I always set the globe back in its place on my shelf and return the charts to their drawers.

Sometimes, I make it all the way down to the bottom.

The music rises and swells around me like a dust storm, like all the dust storms that have ever scrubbed the raw face of this god-forsaken planet. I stand there, wrapped in a suffocating melody that is almost cacophony, melody to drown me, trying to remember where I've heard this music before, knowing only that I have. I gaze back up at the rim of the crater, so sharp against the star-filled night sky, and trace my footprints and the displaced stones and tiny avalanches that mark the zigzag path of my descent.

I know full well that I'm being watched – some vestigial, primitive lobe of my brain pricked by that needling music, pricked by a thousand alien eyes – and I turn and begin the long march into the crater, towards its distant central peak and the place where the music might be coming from. I know that she's out there somewhere – Sailor – not waiting for me. I know that she's already given herself over to the Fenrir, and that means she's something worse than dead now. But I also know that doesn't mean I'm not supposed to find her.

The sky is full of demons.

Blood falls from Heaven.

I was sent to the containment facility just north of Apollinaris Patera only three months after my election to the Council. On all the fedstat grids it's marked as IHF21, a red biohazard symbol at Latitude -9.8, Longitude 174.4E to scar the northern slope of the volcano. But the physicians and epidemiologists, virologists and exobiologists and healers who work and live there call it something else, something I'd rather not write down just now. The patients or detainees or whatever you might choose to call them, if *they* have a name for the place, then I've never learned it. I'd never want to.

That was seventeen years ago, not long after a pharmaceutical multinational working with the Asian umbrella came up with the serum, the toxic antiviral cocktail that either kills you or slows down the Fenrir contagion and sometimes even stops it cold, but never reverses the alterations already made to the genome of the infected individual. So, there was something like hope in IHF21 when I arrived. That is, there was hope among the staff, not the inmates, who were each and every one being administered the serum against their will. The scientists reasoned that if a serum that inhibited the contagion had been found, a genuine cure might not be far behind it. But by the time I left, almost four years later, with no cure in sight and a resistance to the serum manifesting in some of the infected, that hope had been replaced by something a lot more like resignation.

The blood from Heaven is black and hisses when it strikes the hard, dusty ground. I step over and around the accumulated carcasses of creatures I know no names for, the hulks of other things I'm not even sure were ever alive. Corpses that might have belonged to organisms or machines or some perverse amalgam of the two. With every step, the plain before me seems ever more littered with these bodies, if they are, indeed, dead things. Some of them are so enormous that I step easily between ebony ribs and follow hallways roofed by fossilized vertebrae and scales like the hull plating of starships. The music is growing louder, yet through it I can hear the whisperers, the mumbling phantoms that I've never once glimpsed.

Three days after I arrived at IHF21, a senior physician, an earthborn woman named Zyra McNamara, led me on a tour of the Primary Ward, where the least advanced cases were being tended. The *least* advanced cases. There was hardly anything human left among them. I spent the better part of half an hour in a lavatory, puking up my lunch and breakfast and anything else that would come. Then I sat with Dr. McNamara in a staff lounge, a small room with a view of the mountain, sipping sour, hot coffee and listening to her talk.

"Is it true that they're not dying?" I asked, and she shrugged her shoulders.

"Yes. Strictly speaking, it's true that no one's died of the contagion, so far. But, you have to understand, we're dealing with such fundamental questions of organismal integrity – " and then she paused to stare out the window for a moment. There was a strong wind from the east, and it howled around the low plastic tower that held the lounge, rattled the windowpane, roared around the ancient ash and lava dome of Apollinaris Patera rising more than five kilometers above datum.

"It's now my belief," she said, "that we have to stop thinking of this thing as a disease. If I'm right, it's really much more like a parasite. Or rather, it's a viroid that reduces its victims to obligate parasites." And she was silent for a moment then, as though giving me a chance to reply or ask a question. When I didn't, because I was much too busy trying to calm my stomach for questions, she went on.

"On Earth, there are a number of species of fish that live in the deepest parts of the oceans. They're commonly, collectively, called anglerfish, and in these anglerfish, the males are very much smaller than the females. The males manage to locate the female fish in total darkness by honing in on the light from bioluminescent organs which the females possess."

"We're talking about *fish*?" I asked. "After what you just showed me, those things lying in there, we're sitting here talking about fucking fish?"

Dr. McNamara took a deep breath and let it out slowly. "Yes, Councilor. We're talking about fish. You see, the anglerfish males begin their lives as autonomous organisms, but when they finally locate a female, which must be an almost impossible task given the environmental conditions involved, they attach themselves to her body with their jaws and become parasitic. In time, they completely fuse with the female's body, losing much of their skeletal structure, sharing a common circulatory system, becoming, in essence, no more than reproductive organs. The question is, do the males, in some sense, *die*? They can no longer live free of the host female. They receive all of their nutrients via her bloodstream and – "

"I don't understand what you're saying," I told her, and looked down at the floor between my feet, starting to think I was going to vomit again.

"Don't worry about it, Councilor. We'll talk again later, when you're feeling better. There's no hurry."

There's no hurry.

But in my dreams, as I make my way across that corpse-strewn crater, my head and lungs and soul filled to bursting with the Fenrir's music, I am seized by an urgency beyond anything that I've ever known before. My feet cannot move quickly enough, and, after a while, I realize that it's not even Sailor that I'm looking for, not her that I'm navigating this terrible, impossible graveyard to find.

I have never reached the center.

I have never reached the center yet.

Since I was a child, I've loved the zeps. When I was four or five, my mothers took me to the Carver Street transfer station, and we watched together as one enormous gray airship docked and another departed. There was even a time when I fantasized that I might someday become a pilot, or an engineer. I read books on general aerodynamics and the development of Martian zeps, technical manuals on hybrid tricyclohydrazine/solar fuel cells and prop configuration and the problems of achieving low-speed lift in a thin CO_2-heavy atmosphere. I built plastic models that my mothers had bought for me in Earthgoods shops. And then, at some point, I moved on to other, less-remarkable things. Puberty. Girls. And my mathematics and low-grade psi aptitude scores that eventually led to my seat on the Council. But I still love the zeps, and I love traveling on them. They are elegant things in a world where we have created very little elegance and much ugliness. They drift regally above Mars like strange helium-filled animals, almost like the gigantic floaters that evolved some three hundred and fifty million miles away in the Jovian atmosphere. I'd been praying that the long flight from Hope VII to the military port at the eastern edge of the Claritas Fossae might be some small relief after the horror that Jun'ko's billygirl had shown me. But first there'd been the nightmare, and now this network *mesuinu* and her camera eyes and questions I'd agreed to hear.

"How do you spell 'anglerfish'?" she asked, scribbling something on a pad she'd pulled from the breast pocket of her brown jacket.

"*What?*"

"Anglerfish. Is it one word or two? I've never heard it before."

"How the hell would I know? What the fuck difference does it make? You're doing this on short delay, right?"

She frowned and wrote something on the pad. It was somehow sickeningly quaint, watching a cyborg with an eight-petabyte recall chip making handwritten notes.

"Do you think you'll forget?" I asked and sipped my second bowl of tea. The brandy was strong and better than I'd expected, the steam from the tea filling my head and making Ariadne Vaughn's questions a little easier to endure.

She laughed and thumped the pad with one end of her stylus. 'Oh, that. It's just an old habit. I don't think I'll ever quite get over it."

"I don't know how to spell 'anglerfish'," I lied.

"Jun'ko Valenzuela told me that you were trailing a freighter, that one of her girls said Sailor Li had booked passage on a freighter named *Oryoku Maru*."

"How much did you have to pay her to tell you that?" I asked. "Or did you find that threats were more effective with Jun'ko?"

"Are there currently any plans to allow civilian press into the containment facilities?"

"No," I said, watching her over the rim of my bowl. "The Council's public affairs office could have told you that."

"They did," she replied. "But I wanted to hear it from you. Now, there are rumors that you physically abused Sailor Li before she left you. Is that true, Councilor?"

I didn't answer right away. I sipped at my tea, glaring at her through the steam, trying to grasp the logic behind her seemingly random list of questions. The progression from one topic to another escaped me, and I wondered if something in her head was malfunctioning.

"Councilor, did you ever *beat* your lover?" she asked again and chewed at her lower lip.

I thought about lying, and then I said, "I hit her."

"After she took the mark?"

"Yes. I hit her after she took the mark."

"But no charges were ever filed with the magistrate's office in Herschel. Why do you think that is?"

I smiled and set my bowl down on the portal ledge. Vibrations through the wall of the airship sent tiny concentric ripples across the surface of the dark liquid.

"There have been allegations that the Council saw to it that no charges were filed against you," the journalist said. "Are you aware of that?"

"Sailor never brought charges against me because she knew if the case went to trial that I'd confess, and if I were in jail, I couldn't follow her. And, besides, she didn't have time left to waste on trials, Ms. Vaughn. The clock was ticking. She had more pressing matters to attend to."

"You mean the Fenrir?"

"No, Ms. Vaughn, I mean making a fortune as a whore in Hope VII."

She laughed, the comfortable sort of laugh she might have laughed if we were old, close friends and what I'd just said was no more than a joke. Once, not long after I returned to Herschel City from IHF21, one of the members of the Council's Board of Review and Advancement told me that she was deeply disturbed at my cynicism, my propensity for hatred, and that I was so quick to judge and anger. I admitted the fault and promised to meditate twice daily towards freeing myself of these shortcomings. I might as well have promised to raise the dead or make Mars safe for the XY chromo crowd. And now, sitting there on the *Barsoom XI,* facing this woman for whom my life and Sailor's life and the Fenrir contagion were together no more than a chance for early promotion and a fat bonus from the network snigs, I realized that I cherished my ability to hate.

I cherished it as surely as I'd cherished Sailor. As surely as I'd once stood in the shadows of docking zeppelins, joyful and dizzy with the bottomless wonder of childhood.

I could have killed the smiling bitch then and there, could have slammed her head against the aluminum-epoxy alloy wall of the zep's cabin until there was nothing left to shatter, and my fingers were slick and sticky with her blood and brains and the yellowish lube and cooling fluids of her ruptured optical and superpalatal implants.

I could have done it in an instant, with no regrets. But there was still Sailor and the Fenrir's music, that beckoning anglerfish bioluminescence shining brightly through absolute blackness and cold, leading me to a different and more unthinkable end than the sanctuary of a prison cell.

"Do you really think you'll find her?" Ariadne Vaughn asked.

"If I live long enough," I replied, turning to the portal again. The sun was beginning to set.

"There are rumors, Councilor, that you've already been infected, that the contagion was passed to you by Sailor."

I slowly, noncommittally, nodded my head for her, for everyone at MBS studios and everyone who would soon be seeing this footage, and watched as the western sky turned the color of bruises. I didn't bother telling her what she already knew, repeating data stored in her pretty patchwork skull, that the viroid can only be contracted directly from specialized delivery glands inside the cloaca of a Fenrir drone. The infected aren't contagious. She knew that.

"That's fifteen," I said instead, glancing from the portal to my watch, even though it had actually been more like twenty minutes since she'd started asking me questions. "Time's all up."

"Well then, we wish you luck," she said, mock cheerfully, ending the rambling interview, "and Godspeed in your return to Herschel City."

"Bullshit," I said quickly, before she had a chance to blink the o-feed down. She frowned and shook her head.

"You know that's going to be edited out," she said, returning the pad and stylus to her breast pocket. "You *know* that, Councilor."

"Yeah, I know that. But it felt good, anyway. Now, Ms. Vaughn, you tell me where you think she is," I said and smiled at the flight attendant as she passed our seats.

"I assume you've had a look at the *Oryoku Maru's* route db," she said, rubbing at her itching nose again. I wondered how long it would be before the acidic slake necessitated reconstructive rhinoplasty, or, if perhaps, it already had. "So you know its last refueling stop before the south polar crossing is at Lowell Station."

"Yes," I told her. "I know that. But I don't think Sailor will go that far. I think she'll get off before Lowell. I'm guessing Bosporos."

"Then you're guessing wrong, Councilor."

"And just what the hell makes you think that?" I asked. Ariadne Vaughn cocked her head ever so slightly to one side, raised her left eyebrow, and I imagined her rehearsing this moment in front of mirrors and prompts and vidloops, working to get that ah-see-this-is-what-I-know-that-you-*don't* expression just exactly fucking right. I began to suspect there were other cameras planted in the cabin, that we were still being pixed for MBS. "There's nothing in Lowell. There hasn't been since the war."

"We have some reliable contacts in the manifest dep and hanger crews down there," she replied, leaning back in her seat, either putting distance between us or playing out another part of the pantomime. "The last couple of years, Fenrir cultists have been moving in, occupying the old federal complex and some of the adjacent buildings. All the company people stay away from the place, of course, but they've seen some things. Some of them even think it's a temple."

There was an excited prickling at the back of my neck, a dull but hopeful flutter deep in my chest and stomach, but I did my best not to give anything away. The journalist knew too much already. She certainly didn't need me giving her more. "That's interesting" I said. "But the Council has a complete catalog of possible temple locations, as does the MCDC, and there's nothing in either of them about Lowell."

"Which means what, Councilor? That the Council's omniscient now? That it's infallible? That the MCDC never fucks shit up? I think we both know that none of those things are true."

As she talked, I tried to recall what little I knew about Lowell Crater. It was an old settlement, one of the first, but a couple of fusion warheads dropped from orbit just after the start of the war had all but destroyed it. When the dust settled, after treaties had been signed and the plagues had finally burned themselves out, the Transit Authority had decided what was left at Lowell would make a good last stop before the South Pole. And that's about all that I could recall, and none of it suggested that the Fenrir would choose Lowell as a temple site.

"Assuming you're not just yanking this out of your ass, Ms. Vaughn, why hasn't MBS released this information? Why hasn't the TA already filed disclosure reports with the MCDC and Offworld Control?"

"Ask them," she said, staring up at the ceiling of the cabin now. *Maybe that's where they hid the other cameras,* I thought, not caring how paranoid I'd become. "My guess," she continued, "they're afraid the military's gonna come sweeping in to clear the place out, and they'll lose a base they can't afford to lose, the economy being what it is. It'd cost them a fortune to relocate."

"And what about the network?"

"The network?" she asked, looking at me again. "Well, we just want to be sure of our sources. No sense broadcasting stories that might cause a panic and have severe pecuniary consequences, if there's a chance it's all just something dreamed up by a few bored mechs stuck in some shithole at the bottom of the world. MBS will release the story, when we're ready. Maybe you'll be a part of it, Councilor, before this thing is done."

And then she stood up, thanked me for my time, and walked back to her assigned seat nearer the front of the passenger cabin. I sat alone, silently repeating all the things she'd said, hearing her voice in my head – *But they've seen some things. Some of them even think it's a temple.* Outside the airship's protective womb, night was quickly claiming the high plains of the Sun, and I could just make out the irregular red-orange silhouette of Phobos rising – or so it seemed that illusion of ascension – above the western horizon.

It took me another two weeks to reach Lowell. The commercial airships don't run that far south, and I deplaned at Holden (noting that Ariadne Vaughn did not) and then spent four days trying to find someone willing to transport me the two thousand-plus kilometers south and west to Bosporos City. From there, I hoped to buy a nook on the TA line the rest of the way down to Lowell.

Finally, I paid a platinum prospector half of what was left in my accounts to make the trip. She grumbled endlessly about pirates and dust sinks, about the wear and mileage the trip would put on her rusted-out crawler. But it was likely more money than she'd see in the next three or four years cracking rocks and tagging cores, and we only broke down once, when the aft sediment filter clogged and the engine overheated. I had a narrow, filthy bunk behind the Laskar coils, and spent much of the trip asleep or watching the monotonous terrain roll by outside the windows. To the east, there were occasional, brief glimpses of shadowed canyonlands which I knew lead down to the wide, empty expanse of the Argyre Planitia laid out almost six klicks below the surrounding plains. I considered the possibility that it might be the corpse-strewn crater from my dreams, this monstrous wound carved deep into the face of Mars almost four thousand million years ago during the incessant bombardments of the Noachian Age, when the solar system was still young and hot and violent.

That thought only made the nightmares worse, of course. I considered asking the prospector to find another route, one not so near the canyons, but I knew she'd only laugh her bitter laugh, start in on dust sinks again, and tell me to go to hell. So I didn't say anything. Instead, I lay listening to the stones being ground to powder beneath the crawler's treads, to the wind battering itself against the hull, to the old-womanish wheeze of the failing Laskar coils, trying not to remember the thing Mikaela had shown me beneath Hope VII or what I might yet find in the ruins of Lowell. I slept, and I dreamed.

And on the final afternoon before we reached Bosporos City, dreaming, I made my way at last to the center of the crater. There was a desperate, lightless crawl through the mummified intestines of some leviathan while the Fenrir's pipes and strings and drums pounded at my senses. My ears and nose were bleeding when I emerged through a gaping tear in the creature's gut and stood, half-blind, blinking up at towering ebony spires and soaring arches and stairways that seemed to reach almost all the way to the stars. The music poured from this black city, gushed from every window and open doorway, and I sank to my knees and cried.

"You weren't ever meant to come here," Sailor said, and I realized she was standing over me. "You weren't invited."

"I can't *do* this shit anymore," I sobbed, for once not caring if she saw my weakness. "I can't."

"You never should have started."

My tears turned to crystal and fell with a sound like wind chimes. My heart turned to cut glass in my chest.

"Is this what you were looking for?" I asked her, gazing up at the spires and arches, hating that cruel, singing architecture, even as my soul begged it to open up and swallow me alive.

"No. This is only a dream, Dorry," she said, speaking to me as she might a child. "*You* made this place. You've been building it all your life."

"No. That's not true," I replied, though I understood perfectly well that it was, that it *must* be. The distance across the corpse-littered crater was only half the diameter of my own damnation, nothing more.

"If I let you see, will you go back?" she asked. "Will you go back and forget me?" She was speaking very softly, but I had no trouble hearing her over the wind and the music and the wheezing Laskar coils. I must have answered, must have said yes, because she took my hand in hers, and the black city before us collapsed and dissolved, taking the music with it, and I stood, instead, on a low platform in what I at first mistook for a room. But then I saw the fleshy, pulsing walls, the purple-green interlace of veins and capillaries, the massive supporting ribs or ridges, blacker than the vanished city, dividing that place into seven unequal crescent chambers. I stood somewhere within a living thing, within something that dwarfed even the fallen giants from the crater.

And each of the crescent chambers contained the remains of a single gray pilgrim, their bodies metamorphosed over months or years or decades to serve the needs of this incomplete, demonic biology. They were each no more than appendages now, human beings become coalesced obligate parasites or symbiotes, their glinting, chitinous bodies all but lost in a labyrinth of mucosal membranes, buried by the array of connective tissues and tubes that sprouted from them like cancerous umbilical cords.

Anglerfish. Is it one word or two?

And there, half buried in the chamber walls, was what remained of Sailor, just enough left of her face that I could be sure it was her. Something oily and red and viscous that wasn't blood leaked from the hole that had been her mouth, from the wreck of her lips and teeth, her mouth become only one more point of exit or entry for the restless, palpitating cords connecting her with this enormous organism. Her eyes opened partway, those atrophied slits parting to reveal bright, wet orbs like pools of night, and the fat, segmented tube emerging from the gap of her thighs began to quiver violently.

Can you see me now, Dorry? she whispered, her voice burrowing in behind my eyes, filled with pain and joy and regret beyond all comprehension. *Have you seen enough? Or do you need to see more?*

"No," I told her, waking up, opening my eyes wide and vomiting onto the floor beneath my bunk. The Laskar coils had stopped wheezing, and the crawler was no longer moving. I rolled over and lay very still, cold and sick and sweating, staring up at the dingy, low ceiling until the prospector finally came looking for me.

When I left home back in Aries, I brought the monk's book with me, the book from Sailor's crate of discards. I sit here on my bedroll in one corner of one room inside the concrete and steel husk of a bombed-out federal compound in Lowell. I have come this far, and I am comforted by the knowledge that there's only a little ways left to go. I open the book and read the words aloud again, the words underlined in red ink, that I might understand how not to lose my way in this tale which is almost all that remains of me: "No story has a beginning, and no story has an end. Beginnings and endings may be conceived to serve a purpose, to serve a momentary and transient intent, but they are, in their truer nature, arbitrary and exist solely as a construct of the mind of man."

I think this means I can stop when I'm ready.

I've been in Lowell for almost a full week now, writing all this shit down. Today is Monday, Libra 17th. We are deep in winter, and I have never been this far south.

There is a silence here, in this dead city, that seems almost as solid as the bare concrete around me. I'm camped far enough in from the transfer station that the hanger noise, the comings and goings of the zeps and spinners, the clockwork opening and closing of the dome, seem little more than a distant, occasional thunder. I'm not sure I've ever known such a profound silence as this. Were I sane, it might drive me mad. There *are* sounds, sounds other than the far-off noise of the station, but they are petty things that only seem to underscore the silence. They're more like the too-often recollected *memory* of sound, an ancient woman deaf since childhood remembering what sound was like before she lost it forever.

Last night, I lay awake, fighting sleep, listening to my heart and all those other petty sounds. I dozed towards dawn, and when I woke there was a woman crouched a few feet from my bedroll. She was reading the monk's book, flipping the pages in the dark, and, at first, I thought I was dreaming again, that this was another dream of Sailor. But then she closed the book and looked at me. Even in the dark, I could tell she wasn't as young as Sailor, and I saw that her head was shaved down to the skin. Her eyes were iridescent and flashed blue-green in the gloom.

"May I switch on the light?" I asked, pointing towards the travel lamp near my pillow.

"If you wish," she replied and set the book back down among my things. "If you need it."

I touched the lamp, and it blinked obediently on, throwing long shadows against the walls and floor and ceiling of the room where I was sleeping. The woman squinted, cursed, and turned her face away. I rubbed at my own eyes and sat up.

"What do you want?" I asked her.

"We saw you, yesterday. You were watching."

The woman was a Fenrir priest. She wore the signs on her skin and ragged clothing. Her feet were bare, and there was a simple onyx ring on each of her toes. I could tell that she'd been very beautiful once.

"Yes," I told her. "I was watching."

"But you didn't come for the mark," she said, not asking because she already knew the answer. "You came to find someone."

"Does that happen very often?"

She turned her face towards me again, shading her eyes with her left hand. "Do you think you will find her, Dorry? Do you think you'll take her back?"

It hadn't been hard to locate the temple. The old federal complex lies near the center of the dome, what the bombs left of it, anyway, and finding it was really no more than a matter of walking. The day that I arrived in Lowell City, one of the Transfer Authority's security agents had detained and questioned me for an hour or so, and I'd assured her that I was there as a scholar, looking for records that might have survived the war. I'd shown her the paper map that I'd purchased at a bookshop in Bosporos and pointed out the black X I'd made about half a mile north of the feddy, near one of the old canals. She'd looked at the map two or three times, asked me a few questions about the journey down from Holden, and then made a call to her senior officer before releasing me.

"You don't want to go down that way," she'd told me, tapping the map with an index finger. "I can't hold you here or deport you, Councilor. But you better trust me on this. You don't want to go down there."

"You've been chasing her such a long time," the woman crouched on the floor before me said, speaking more quietly now and smiling. Her teeth were filed to sharp points, and she licked at them with the tip of her violet tongue. "You must have had a lot of chances to give up. There must have been so much despair."

"Is she dead?" I asked, the words slipping almost nonsensically from my lips.

"No one *dies*. You know that. You've known that since the camp. No one ever dies."

"You know where she is?"

"She's with the Wolf," the woman whispered. "Three weeks now, she's with the Wolf. You came too late, Dorry. You came to her too late," and she drew a knife from her belt, something crude and heavy fashioned from scrap metal. "She isn't waiting anymore."

I kicked her hard, the toe of my right boot catching her in the chest just below her collar bone, and the priest cried out and fell over backwards. The knife slipped from her fingers and skittered away across the concrete.

"Did the Wolf tell *you* that you'd never die?" I demanded, getting to my feet and aiming the pistol at her head. I'd bought that in Bosporos, as well, the same day I'd bought the map, black-market military picked up cheap in the backroom of a britch bar. The blinking green ready light behind the sight assured me that the safety was off, that the trip cells were hot, and there was a live charge in the chamber. The woman coughed and clutched at her chest, then spat something dark onto the floor.

"That's what I want to know, bitch," I said, "what I want you to *tell* me," and I kicked her in the ribs. She grunted and tried to crawl away, so I kicked her again, harder than before, and she stopped moving. "I want you to tell me if that's what it *promised* you, that you'd fucking get to live forever if you brought it whatever it needed. Because I want you to know that it fucking lied."

And she opened her mouth wide, then, and I caught a glimpse of the barbed thing uncoiling from the hollow beneath her tongue, and I squeezed the trigger.

I suspect that one gunshot was the loudest noise anyone's heard here since the day bombs fell on Lowell. It echoed off the thick walls, all that noise trapped in such a little room, and left my ears ringing painfully. The priest was dead, and I sat down on my bedroll again. I'd never imagined that there would be so much blood or that killing someone could be so very simple. No, that's not true. That's a goddamn lie. I've imagined it all along.

I've been sitting here on the roof for the last hour, watching as the domeworks begin to mimic the morning light, shivering while the frost clinging to the old masonry melts away as the solar panels warm the air of Lowell. I brought the monk's book with me and half a bottle of whiskey and the gun. And my notebook, to write the last of it down.

When the bottle is empty, maybe then I'll make a decision. Maybe then I'll know what comes next.

BRADBURY WEATHER

My love affair with Mars goes back to my childhood, to the seventies, to the Viking landers, to my discovery of Barsoom and *The Martian Chronicles,* and to Elton John's "Rocket Man." Knowing full well I'll never walk those rusty red plains, I hope my ashes might someday be scattered throughout the channels of the Kasei Valles or across the dry-ice glaciers of the north polar cap. We earthbound creatures can always dream. Along with *The Dry Salvages* (2003), "Bradbury Weather" marks the beginning of my trusting myself with first-person narratives.

Pony

1. The Window (April)

Helen opens a window, props it open with a brick, and in a moment I can smell the Chinese wisteria out in the garden. The first genuinely warm breezes of spring spilling across the sill, filled with the smells of drooping white blossoms and a hundred other growing things. The sun is so warm on my face, and I lie on the floor and watch the only cloud I can see floating alone in a sky so blue it might still be winter out there. She was reading her poetry to me. I've been drinking cheap red wine from a chipped coffee cup with an Edward Gorey drawing printed on one side, and she's been reading me her poetry and pausing to talk about the field. At that moment, I still think that neither of us has been back to the field in years, and it's surprisingly easy to fool myself into believing that my memories are only some silly ghost story Helen's been slipping in between the stanzas. Not the vulgar sort of spook story that people write these days. More like something an Arthur Machen or an Algernon Blackwood might have written, something more mood and suggestion than anything else, and I congratulate myself on feeling so removed from that night in the field and take another sip of the bitter wine. Helen's been drinking water, only bottled water from a ruby-stemmed wine glass, because she says wine makes her slur.

I open my bathrobe, and the sun feels clean and good across my breasts and belly. I'm very proud of my belly, that it's still flat and hard this far past thirty. Helen stops reading her poem again and squeezes my left nipple until I tell her to quit it. She pretends to pout until I tell her to stop that, too.

"I went back," she says, and I keep my eyes on that one cloud, way up there where words and bad memories can't ever reach it. Helen's quiet for almost a full minute, and then she says, "Nothing happened. I just walked around for a little while, that's all. I just wanted to see."

"That last line seemed a bit forced," I say. "Maybe you should read it to me again," and I shut my eyes, but I don't have to see her face to know the sudden change in her expression or to feel the chill hiding just underneath the warm breeze getting in through the window. It must have been there all along, the chill, but I was too busy with the sun and my one cloud and the smell of Chinese wisteria to notice. I watch a scatter of orange afterimages floating in the darkness behind my eyelids and wait for Helen to bite back.

"I need a cigarette," she says, and I start to apologize, but it would be a lie, and I figure I've probably done enough damage for one afternoon. I listen to her bare feet on the hardwood as she crosses the room to the little table near her side of the bed. The table with her typewriter. I hear her strike a match and smell the sulfur.

"Nothing happened," she says again. "You don't have to be such a cunt about it."

"If nothing happened," I reply, "then there's no need for this conversation, is there?" And I open my eyes again. My cloud has moved along an inch or so towards the right side of the window frame, which would be east, and I can hear a mockingbird singing.

"Someone fixed the lock on the gate," she says. "I had to climb over. They put up a sign, too. Posted. No trespassing."

"But you climbed over anyway?"

"No one saw me."

"I don't care. It was still illegal."

"I went all the way up the hill," she tells me. "I went all the way to the stone wall."

"How many times do I have to tell you I don't want to talk about this," I say and roll over on my left side, rolling towards her, rolling away from the window and the cloud, the wisteria smell and the chattering mockingbird, and my elbow hits the Edward Gorey cup and it tips over. The wine almost looks like blood as it flows across the floor and the handwritten pages Helen's left lying there. The burgundy undoes her words, her delicate fountain-pen cursive, and the ink runs and mixes with the wine.

"Fuck you," she says and leaves me alone in the room, only a ragged, fading smoke ghost to mark the space she occupied a few seconds before. I pick up the empty cup, cursing myself, my carelessness and the things I've said because I'm scared and too drunk not to show it, and somewhere in the house a door slams. Later on, I think, Helen will believe it was only an accident, and I'm not so drunk or scared or stupid to know I'm better off not going after her. Outside, the mockingbird's stopped singing, and when I look back at the window, I can't find the white cloud anywhere.

2. The Field (October)

This is not the night. This is only a *dream* of the night, only my incomplete, unreliable memories of a dream, which is as close as I can come on paper. The dream I've had more times now than I can recall, and it's never precisely the truth of things, and it's never the same twice. I have even tried putting it down on canvas, again and again, but I can hardly stand the sight of them, those damned absurd paintings. I used to keep them hidden behind the old chifforobe where I store my paints and brushes and jars of pigment, kept them there until Helen finally found them. Sometimes, I still think about burning them.

The gate with the broken padlock, the gate halfway between Exeter and Nooseneck, and I follow you down the dirt road that winds steeply up the hill through the old apple orchard, past trees planted and grown before our parents were born, trees planted when our grandparents were still young. And the moon's so full and bright I can see everything – the ground-fall fruit rotting in the grass, your eyes, a fat spider hanging in her web. I can see the place ahead of us where the road turns sharply away from the orchard towards a field no one's bothered to plow in half a century or more, and you stop and hold a hand cupped to your right ear.

"No," I reply, when you tell me that you can hear music and ask if I can hear it, too. I'm not lying. I can't hear much of anything but the wind in the limbs of the apple trees and a dog barking somewhere far away.

"Well, I can. I can hear it clear as anything," you say, and then you leave the dirt road and head off through the trees.

Sometimes I yell for you to wait, because I don't want to be left there on the road by myself, and sometimes I follow you, and sometimes I just stand there in the moonlight and branch shadows listening to the night, trying to hear whatever it is you think you've heard. The air smells sweet and faintly vinegary, and I wonder if it's the apples going soft and brown all around me. Sometimes you stop and call for me to hurry.

A thousand variations on a single moment. It doesn't matter which one's for real, or at least it doesn't matter to me. I'm not even sure that I can remember anymore, not for certain. They've all bled together through days and nights and repetition, like sepia ink and cheap wine, and by the time I've finally caught up with you (because I always catch up with you, sooner or later), you're standing at the low stone wall dividing the orchard from the field. You're leaning forward against the wall, one leg up and your knee pressed to the granite and slate as if you were about to climb over it but then forgot what you were doing. The field is wide, and I think it might go on forever, that the wall might be here to keep apart more than an old orchard and a fallow plot of land.

"Tell me that you can see her," you say, and I start to tell you that I don't see anything at all, that I don't know what you're talking about and we really ought to go back to the car. Sometimes, I try to remember why I let you talk me into pulling off the road and parking in the weeds and wandering off into the trees.

We cannot comprehend even the edges of the abyss.
So we don't try.
We walk together on warm silver nights,
And there is cider in the air and
Someone has turned the ponies out again.

It's easier to steal your thoughts than make my own.

"Please, tell me you can see her."

And I can, but I don't tell you that. I have never yet told you that. Not in so many words. But I can see her standing there in the wide field, the tall, tall girl and the moon washing white across her wide shoulders and full breasts and Palomino hips, and then she sees us and turns quickly away. There are no clouds, and the moon's so bright that there's no mistaking the way her black hair continues straight down the center of her back like a horse's mane or the long tail that swats nervously from one side of her ass to the other as she begins to run. Sometimes I take your arm and hold you tight and stop you from going over the stone wall after her. Sometimes you stand very still and only watch. Sometimes you call out for her to please come back to you, that there's nothing to be afraid of because we'd never hurt her. Sometimes there are tears in your eyes, and you call me names and beg me to please, please let you run with her.

The cold iron flash from her hooves,
And that's my heart lost in the night.
I know all the lies. I know all the lies.

I know the ugly faces the moon makes when it thinks
No one is watching.

And we stand there a very long time, until there's nothing more to see or say that we haven't seen. You're the first to head back down the hill towards the car, and sometimes we get lost and seem to wander for hours and hours through the orchard, through tangles of creeper vines and wild grapes that weren't there before. And other times, it seems to take no time at all.

3. The Pantomime (January – February)

This is almost five months later, five months after that night at the edge of the field halfway between Exeter and Nooseneck. We never really talked about it. Helen would bring it up, and I would always, always immediately change the subject. I didn't tell her about the dreams I'd started having, living it over and over again in my sleep. And then one night we were fucking – not having sex, not making love – *fucking,* hammering our bodies one against the other, fucking so hard we'd both be bruised and sore the next day, as if this were actually some argument we lacked the courage to ever have aloud, so fucking instead of screaming at one another. And she began to whisper, details of what we'd seen or only thought we'd seen, what we'd seen re-imagined and embellished and become some sick fantasy of Helen's. I pushed her away from me, disgusted, angry, and so I pushed too hard, harder than I'd meant to push her. She slipped off the side of the bed and struck her chin against the floor. She bit her tongue, and there was blood on her lips and her chin, and then she *was* screaming at me, telling me I was a coward, telling me I was a bitch and a coward and a liar, and I lay still and stared at the ceiling and didn't say a single word in my defense. Most of what she said was true or very nearly true, but hearing it like that couldn't change anything. A few minutes later she was crying and went off to the bathroom to wipe the blood off her face, and I took my pillow and a blanket from the closet and spent the night downstairs on the sofa.

And this is another month after that, so late in February that it's almost March. I'd done nothing worth the price of the canvas it was painted on in months. Helen's been away in the city, a writer's workshop, and I take long walks late in the day, trying to clear my head with the cold air and the smell of woodsmoke. Sometimes I only walk as far as the garden, and sometimes I walk all the way down to the marshy place where our property ends and the woods begin. And I come back from an especially long walk one night, and Helen's car is in the garage. I have an owl skull I found lying among the roots of a hemlock, and I'm thinking it's the missing piece of the painting I haven't been able to finish. In through the kitchen, and I call her name, call her name three times, but no one answers me. I hear voices, Helen's voice and another woman's, and I climb the stairs and stop outside the bedroom door, which has been left open just wide enough that it's almost shut but I can still see what's going on in there. And I understand that I'm *meant* to see this. Helen isn't trying to hide anything. She could have stayed an extra night or two or three in the city, and I never would have asked why. This is being done for me almost as much as it's being done for her.

I sit down in the hallway, the owl skull cradled in my hands, and I watch them. I wonder how long Helen's been home, how long I must have lingered at the marshy place and the hemlock. I wonder what would have happened if I'd come back sooner, or if I'd never gone out at all.

The other woman is pretty – prettier than me, I think – and her blonde hair's pulled back into a tight bun. She's dressed in a dark green riding jacket, white jodhpurs, and tall black boots with neat little spurs on them. Helen's naked, or nearly so. She's wearing a bridle, an elaborate thing of black leather straps and stainless steel. She has a curb bit clenched tightly between her teeth, and her legs have been laced into tall leather boots that come up past her knees and end in shaggy fetlocks and broad wooden hooves. No heels, just the hooves, so she's balanced somehow on the balls of her feet. The pretty blonde woman whispers something in her ear and smiles. Helen nods once and then bends over the edge of the bed, leaning on her elbows now as the woman smears her right hand with KY and works her fingers slowly into Helen's ass.

And I'm watching this, all of it. I'm watching this because I know that I'm meant to see it, that it's a performance, and I can at least not be such a goddamn, ungrateful coward that I refuse to simply *see*. I watch this because I know I have it coming. This is Helen pushing *me* off the bed. This is Helen making me bite my tongue. This is me forced to share my dreams.

The blonde woman is holding something like a severed horse's tail, glossy chestnut strands hanging all the way down to the floor and attached to a thick rubber plug which has also been smeared with KY. She eases the rubber plug deep into Helen, who doesn't flinch or try to pull away, who doesn't make any sound at all, who remains perfectly still and perfectly quiet until the tail is firmly in place. The blonde woman is wiping her hands clean on a white bath towel, and then she takes Helen's reins and gives them a firm tug. Helen stands up straight again, not wobbling in those boots, not seeming even the least bit unsteady on her wooden hooves.

"You know what comes next?" the woman asks her, and Helen nods. "That's because you're a good girl," the pretty blonde woman tells her. "You're such a good, good pony."

And Helen leans across the bed again. But this time she raises her left leg and rests her knee on the mattress, and I can't help but be reminded of the way she leaned against the stone wall at the edge of the orchard.

The cold iron flash from her hooves,

And that's my heart lost in the night.

I watch from my spot on the floor while the woman uses a small ball-peen hammer to nail shiny new horseshoes onto Helen's hooves, first the left and then the right. And I watch almost everything that comes afterwards. I look away just once and then only for a few seconds, because I thought I might have heard someone else in the hall with me, someone walking towards me, someone who isn't there, and that's when I realize that the owl skull's gone. So I tell myself I must have only thought I brought it upstairs, that I must have absentmindedly set it down somewhere in the kitchen or on the table at the foot of the stairs. And then I go back to watching Helen and the pretty blonde woman in riding clothes.

4. The Paintings (May)

And this last part, this is only a week ago.

I wake up from a dream of that night, a dream of wild things running on two legs, wild things in moonlit pastures that seem to stretch away forever. I wake up sweating and breathless and alone. *She's gone to take a piss, that's all,* I think, blinking at the clock on the dresser. It's almost three in the morning, and for a while I lie there, listening to the secret, settling noises the house makes at three a.m., the noises no one's supposed to hear. I'm lying there listening and trying too hard not to remember the dream when I hear Helen crying, and I get up and follow the sound down the hall to the spare bedroom that I've taken for my studio.

Helen's found the canvases I hid behind the old chifforobe and pulled them all out into the light. She's lined them up, indecently, these things no one else was ever meant to see, lined them up along two of the walls, pushing other things aside to make space for them. I stand there in the doorway, knowing I should be angry and knowing, too, that I have no *right* to be angry. Knowing that somehow all my lies to her about that night at the edge of the field have forfeited my right to feel violated. Some lies are that profound, that cruel, and I understand this. I do, and so I stand there, silently wondering what she's going to say when she realizes I'm watching her.

Helen glances at me over her shoulder, her eyes red and swollen and her face streaked with snot and tears. "You saw what I saw," she says, the same way she might have said she was leaving me. And then she looks back at the paintings, each one only slightly different from the others, and shakes her head.

"You asshole," she says. "You fucking cunt. I thought I was losing my mind. Did you even know that? Did you know I thought that I was going crazy?"

"No," I lie. "I didn't know."

"How long have you been painting these?" she asks me, and I tell her the truth, that I painted the first one only a week after the night we walked through the orchard.

"I ought to have them framed and put them on the walls," she says and wipes at her eyes. "I ought to hang them all through the fucking house, so you have to see them wherever you go. That's what I ought to do. Would you like that?"

I tell her that I wouldn't, and she laughs and sits down on the floor with her back to me.

"Go to bed," she says.

"I wasn't trying to hurt you," I tell her. "I wasn't ever trying to hurt you."

"No. Don't you *dare* fucking say anything else to me. Go back to bed and leave me alone."

"I promise I'll get rid of them," I tell her, and Helen laughs again.

"No you won't," she says, almost whispering. "These are mine now. I need them, and you're not ever going to get rid of any them. Not tonight and not ever."

"I was scared, Helen."

"I told you to go back to bed," she says again, and I ask her to come with me.

"I'll come when I'm ready. I'll come when I'm done here."

"There's nothing else to see," I say, but then she looks at me again, her eyes filled with resentment and fury and bitterness, and I don't say anything else. I leave her alone with the paintings and walk back to the bedroom. Maybe, I think, she'll change her mind and destroy them. Maybe she'll take a knife to the paintings or burn them, the way I should have done months ago. I sit down on the edge of the bed, wishing I had a drink, thinking about going downstairs for a glass of whiskey or a brandy, or maybe going to the medicine cabinet for a couple of Helen's Valium. And that's when I see the owl skull, sitting atop the stack of books beside her typewriter. Bone bleached white by sun and weather, rain and snow and frost, those great empty, unseeing eye sockets, the yellow-brown sheath still covering that hooked beak. I looked for it after that night in February, three months ago, the night Helen brought the blonde woman home, but I never found it. So maybe, I told myself, maybe that was just some other part of the dreams. I lie down and do my best not to think about Helen, all alone in my studio with those terrible paintings of the thing from the field. And I try not to think about the owl skull; too, too many pieces to a puzzle I never want to solve. And before Helen comes back to bed, as the sky outside the window begins to go dusky shades of grey and purple with the deceits of false dawn, I drift back down to the orchard and the stone wall and someone has turned the ponies out again.

PONY

Written in January 2006, "Pony" unexpectedly ended up playing an important role in my novel *The Red Tree* (2009). "Pony" is an ode to a little apple orchard in Saunderstown, Rhode Island, and to countless dry stone walls, and all those pretty girls with hooves.

Untitled 17

For him I am a slim fay boy, a *fairy,* translucent wasp wings and yellow eyes, and for him I am a young man lost in the deepest part of the forest, trailing breadcrumbs behind me that I might ever find my way home again. For him. For him I am sliding through looking-glass doorways and shut away in high tower prisons, and for him I am cursed to dance until my feet are bloody and bruised and *still* I dance for him. He tells me that I am his, that I am a fancy which has been conjured by and for his imagination, birthed for his pleasure and discretion and innumerable indiscretions and, perhaps, in time, disposal, if that's what it comes to, ultimately. Once a month, only when the moon is full, only when I would bleed if I were but a woman as he sometimes dreams I am. Once a month. And he comes to me then. Or I to him. It hardly seems to matter. He smells of autumn and sunlight and mountain pools so deep even fish don't try to reach the bottom. He smells of sex and sweat and bitter lies and decay. And it all begins with the merest whisper, the game, the pantomime, the odyssey...he calls it many things. I open my eyes, and he's crouched there beneath my windowsill, the King of Appetites, wrapped in borrowed flesh to disguise the fires within. Sometimes, I think he's holding a thick book bound in leather as dark and sweet as licorice, and my name is written in that book, mine and maybe a billion more besides mine. But other times, I know the book is only some bit of make-believe spun from my dizzy head that I might find a way to understand so perfectly inexplicable a thing as the creature who looks and talks like a man but smells like clear streams and leaves gone brown and gold and some shade that's almost purple. I may as well give any random god a name and a form. I may as well try to hold the intangible vastness of an idea in the palm of my hand. I open my eyes, and he's there, because tonight the moon is lying low and cheese yellow white and full in its terrible circumference. It shines through my window, and he squats there in that light the moon has pissed down upon all the world or at his bidding. And he says, "Girl," and so I cover myself that my body will not pose any insult or argument or contradiction. For him I have spent long years learning to be a daughter or a wife or some whore caught out alone on a foggy Whitechapel night. For him, I have become another sort of chameleon. He's taught me that one need not shed his skin to become some other thing for a time. So, tonight I will be his bitch, in one sense or some other. Tonight the moon is full and there are no questions, only the contrivances of my best masks. He laughs, oh what stormy skies in that laugh oh what thunder and fire and he laughs so that I know the game has started. I pull on the crimson cape lying at the foot of my bed, and there's a hood to cover my face. Heavy wool lined with fine linen, and all of it might have been dipped in blood just five minutes before, there is so much *red* to this particular red. I know this story, though it's somewhere we've never once been before. I'm certain that he's been here a hundred, hundred thousand nights. And I'm certain, too, that he was here when it was first dreamt up, this old tale, because he happened then and now to need a story with a little lost girl and a wicker basket and a narrow trail winding through impenetrable forest shades, because he needed to be a wolf that night. He is always and forever a wolf, if a wolf is only appetite, if a wolf is only ribs showing through taut skin and only hollow, starveling eyes in winter snow. Tonight, I need him to be a wolf for me as he needs me to be lost and making deals with wolves to find my way home again. He laughs, and this time it's only a dry twig snapping loud beneath my bare feet, and I look fearfully back the way I've come, gazing between the parallel lines of trees and night like the iron bars of a cell I've closed myself inside. There's a fat owl somewhere nearby, its eyes filled up with avarice and lust and thoughts of a pussycat and a jar of honey and a beautiful pea-green boat, and it hoots indifferently and spares no thought for me. The foxes and the stoats cover their eyes. All the animals in the forest know this story, because he whispers it to them on cold November nights with cracked lips and frozen fingers. I pull the cape closed about me, a bunched handful of slaughterhouse wool as though I can ever place anything palpable between him and me and the story. I am running, breathless, and I hear him following after, coming swift on velvet pads and wolf claws in my footsteps, the chase only a game within the game. The owl hoots half a warning, as owls are fickle and always changing sides, and a sleeping squirrel makes a small, nervous sound while bloody droplets fall from the hem of my cape and stain its simpler dreams. And then there is a fallen tree, some great grandfather oak or birch or elm that has been brought down by time and its own weight, calendars and hubris, and the wolf who is my lover is waiting there for me. He squats atop the fallen log, staring ruefully down at me, and he smiles to show off sterling-silver steak knives set into black licorice, book-bound gums. What big teeth, what goddamn big teeth, I whisper, because knowing one's lines is as much a part of it all as knowing the art of disguise and narrative threads and stage direction. And nothing except him could ever smile so very wide a smile, so pleased and famished a smile for me. There's a compliment paid by his lolling tongue, and I sink to my knees in the litter of leaves and mold and spiderlings and mushrooms. I kneel, and the night waits and watches and wonders at even the smallest of variations on a theme. My basket has fallen over and a stale bit of bread has tumbled out, a roll or a slice of pumpernickel, and I hold my breath as the wolf descends on steps carved rough from darkness and desire, coming down to me from his lofty place upon the dead tree's corpse. "I know where you're bound," he growls and presses his muzzle to my throat. "I have always, always known. Were you aware of that? The sky has told me all your secrets, *girl.*" And what big ears you have, I reply, and the wolf laughs again, the way that wolves can laugh, and he laps at my face to remember the secret taste of me. I lie upon his mottled tongue, a lozenge dissolving there as my soul dissolves into the forest and the places the moonlight cannot reach and doesn't try to go. "You're a pretty girl," the wolf says, proud of his choice, and I am proud, too, but I dare not show him anything except the fear in my script. With one massive paw he forces me down onto, down *into* rotting leaf litter, down on my bare belly, and he strips away the red, red cape and casts it aside, only a prop and now its part in the production is done. He makes a careless gift of it to a bramble thicket, and the vines are at once all gratitude and thorns. "Are you lost?" he asks me. "Have you been foolish and left the path and lost your way?" And oh I am lost, I am lost beyond all recall, and I feel the weight of a wolf pressing down upon me. Weight that might crush me until I am as thin and brittle as the leaves, until I am only some meal for grubs and iridescent beetles and earthworm mouths. He growls and nips at the back of my neck. The steam of his breath against my skin, and I'm getting hard now, hard enough to give the game away, to spoil his sacred masquerade, and I imagine his anger and the rage as he plays critic to tear away my dick and my balls with his steak-knife teeth, and he would say, there, there now, that's better, and where was I? What was I saying before you interrupted me? He bites down harder, and I imagine the tearing, crunching sound he would draw from me as he ripped through muscle and bone and tore my head away. But that's not next. Not in the script, not this time, and he spreads my legs with his hind paws oh what nimble claws for such a brute and enters me. Divided, there is no divide then, at that moment, no him and I, only the conjunction of desire and desired, hunger and prey, and I stuff my mouth with a corner of the woolen cape that I will not scream this time. The ragged fur of his belly scraping against my back, nails digging at my shoulders, and his voice is every night thing which has ever waited in the shadows for lost girls and rabbits and stray sheep and anything else so raw and inviting and easy to bring down. Easy to take. His voice shatters me, as it shatters the indigo, star-scabbed sky. His voice and his cock sliding so deeply into me, and there will be spatters of crimson on the leaves to match my discarded cape. There will be wasted scraps of my body sacrificed to the forest, which is ever his ally and business associate. *Only* scraps, though, because I am so very, very good at this, my practiced talent, or there might be a heart left behind, a heart or a kidney or one third a liver given to the greedy roots of trees and the scuttling, restless life beneath dead leaves. When he comes, I fill my mouth with loam and filth to stifle a scream, and I remind myself that in the morning I'll have the marks to show for this. The marks his claws leave as silent testimony that I am not a dreamer in this instance. The welts and weeping violations to say that I am as sane as any haunted man. And the wolf leans close to my right ear and whispers words I cannot write because they were spoken in the savage tongue of all predators, and words will always be insufficient to that transcription. "Run away," he says a little later, when I have curled into a shivering hedgehog knot at his feet. Only feet again, his splayed toes and dirty nails where there were paws a moment before, and the transformation is the curtain falling, sweeping across footlight shadows and the moon and all will bow all will bow all will bow and cast roses upon the stage. And

UNTITLED 17

I am *alone,* having run away, having been gobbled up and shat out again into the waiting night, having died and been reborn in his ebony pupils. Knowing when to run as I do, knowing well my part, and I shut my eyes and hear his hard shoes against the street beneath my window.

UNTITLED 17

I could have titled this story "Love Letter to Angela Carter," but I didn't. Still and all, there's no use in my denying that's exactly what it is. Written in October 2006, I read it aloud at KGB Bar in Manhattan, on November 9, 2008. One of the best readings I've ever done.

A Child's Guide to the Hollow Hills

Beneath the low leaf-litter clouds, under endless dry monsoons of insect pupae, strangling rains of millipede droppings and noxious fungal spores, in this muddy, thin land pressed between soil and bedrock foundations, the fairie girl awakens in the bed of the Queen of Decay. She opens her violet eyes and sees, again, that it was not only some especially unpleasant dream or nightmare, her wild descent, her pell-mell tumble from light and day and stars and moonshine, down, down, down to this mouldering domain of shadow walls and gnarly taproot obelisks. She is *here,* after all. She is *still* here, and slowly she sits up, pushing away those clammy spider-spun sheets that slip in and tangle themselves about her whenever she dares to sleep. And what, she thinks, is sleep, but admitting to myself this is no dream? Admitting that she has been snared and likely there will be no escape from out this unhappy, foetid chamber. Always she has been afraid of falling, deathly frightened of great heights and holes and wells and all the very deep places of the world. Always she has watched so carefully where fell her feet, and never was she one to climb trees or walls, not this cautious fairie girl. When her bolder sisters went to bathe where the brook grows slow and wide beneath drooping willow boughs, she would venture no farther in than the depth of her ankles. They laughed and taunted her with impromptu fictions of careless, drowning children and hungry snapping turtle jaws and also an enormous catfish that might swallow up any careless fairie girl in a single lazy gulp of its bristling, barbeled lips. *And you only looked beneath a stone,* the Queen sneers, reminding her that she is never precisely alone here, that her thoughts are never only *her* thoughts. *Your own mother, she told you that your sisters were but wicked liars, and there was no monster catfish or snapping turtles waiting in the brook. But, she said, do not go turning over stones.* And the fairie girl would shut her violet eyes now, but knows too well she'd still hear that voice, which is like unto the splintering of granite by frost, the ceaseless tunneling noises of earthworms and moles, the crack of a goblin's whip in air that has never once seen the sky. *Don't you go looking under stones,* the Queen says again and smiles to show off a hundred rusted-needle teeth. *In particular, said she – your poor, unheeded mother – beware the great flat stones that lie in the oldest groves, scabbed over with lichens and streaked with the glinting trails of slugs, the flat stones that smell of salamanders and moss, for these are sometimes doorways, child.* The Queen laughs, and her laughter is so terrible that the fairie girl cringes and *does* close her eyes. *Disobedient urchin, you knew better.* "I was following the green lizard," she whispers, as though this might be some saving defence or extenuation, as if the Queen of Decay has not already heard it from her countless times before. "The green lizard crawled beneath the stone – " – *which you knew damn well not to lift and look beneath. So, here now. Stop your whimpering. You were warned; you knew better.* "I wanted only to find the lizard again. I never meant to – " *You only came knocking at my door, dear sweet thing. I only answered and showed you in. You'd have done well not to entrust your well-being to a fascination with such lowly, squamous things – serpents and lizards and the dirty, clutching feet of birds.* The fairie girl opens her eyes again, trying not to cry, because she almost always cries, and her tears and sobs so delight the Queen. She sees herself staring back with watery sapphire eyes, reflected in the many mirrors hanging from these filthy walls, mirrors which her captor ordered hung all about the chamber so that the girl might also witness the stages of her gradual dissolution. The fracturing and wearing away of her glamour, even as water etches at the most indurate stone. Her eyes have not yet lost their colour, but they have lost their inner light. In the main, her skin is still the uncorrupted white of fresh milk caught inside a milkmaid's pail, but there are ugly, parchment splotches that have begun to spread across her face and arms and chest. And her hair, once so full and luminous, has grown flat and devoid of lustre, without the sympathetic light of sun or moon, wilting even as her soul wilts. She is drinking me, the girl thinks, and, *Yes,* the Queen replies. *I have poured you into my silver cup, and I am drinking you down, mouthful by mouthful. You have a disagreeable taste upon my tongue, but it is a sacred duty, to consume anything so frail as you. I choke you down, lest your treacle and the radiance of you should spread and spoil the murk.* And all around them the walls, wherever there are not mirrors, twitch and titter, and fat trolls and raw-boned redcaps with phosphorescent skins and hungry, bulging eyes watch the depredations of their queen. This is rare sport, and the Queen is not so miserly or selfish that she will not share the spectacle with her subjects. *See,* she says, *but do not touch. Her flesh is deadly as cold iron to the likes of us. I alone have the strength to lay my hands upon so foul a being and live.* In the mirrors hung on bits of root and bone and the fishhook mandibles of beetles, the fairie girl sits on the black bed far below the forest floor, and the Queen of Decay moves across her like an eclipse of the sun. *Do not go looking under stones, your poor mother said. I have heard from the pillbugs and termites that she is a wise woman. You'd have done well to heed her good advices.* It is hard for the girl to see the Queen, for she is mostly fashioned of some viscous, shapeless substance that is not quite flesh, but always there is the dim impression of leathery wings, as if from some immense bat, and wherever the Queen brushes against the girl, there is the sensation of touching, or being touched by, matted fur and the blasted bark of dying, lightning-struck trees. The day the girl chased the quick green lizard through the forest, she was still whole, her maidenhead unbroken, the task of her deflowering promised – before her birth – to a nobleman, an elfin duke who held his court on the shores of a sparkling lake and was long owed a considerable debt by her father. The marriage would settle that account. Would *have* settled that account, for the Queen took the fairie girl's virginity almost at once. *We'll have none of that here,* she said, slipping a sickle thumb between the girl's pale thighs and pricking at her sex. There was only as much pain as she'd always expected, and hardly any blood, but the certain knowledge, too, that she had been undone, ruined, despoiled, and if ever she found some secret stairway leading up and out of the Queen's thin lands, her escape would only bring shame to her family. *Better a daughter lost and dead and picked clean by the ants and crows,* the Queen of Decay told her, *than one who's given herself to me, who's soiled my bedclothes with her body's juices and played my demimondaine.* "Nothing was given," replied the fairie girl, and how long ago *was* that? A month? A season? Only a single night? There is no time in the land of the Queen of Decay. There is no need of time when despair would serve so well as the past and all possible futures. Mark it all the present and be done. *What next?* the Queen asks, mocking the laws of her own timeless realm. *Have you been lying here, child, asking yourself, what is next in store for me?* "No," said the girl, refusing to admit the truth aloud, even if the Queen could hear it perfectly well unspoken. "I do not dwell on it," the girl lies. "You will do as you will, and neither my fear nor anticipation will stay your hand or teach you mercy." And then the Queen swelled and rose up around her like a glistening, alveolate wreath of ink and sealing wax, and the spectators clinging to the walls or looking out from their nooks and corners held their breath, collectively not breathing as though in that moment they had become a single beast divided into many bodies. *I only followed the lizard,* the fairie girl thinks, trying not to hear the wet and stretching noises leaking from the Queen's distorted form, trying not to think what will happen one second later, or two seconds after that. *It was so pretty in the morning sun. Its scales were a rainbow fashioned all of shades of green, a thousand shades of green,* and she bows her head and strains to recall the living warmth of sunlight on her face. *Show me your eyes, child,* growls the Queen of Decay. *We will not do this thing halfway.* And, reminded now of details she'd misplaced, the girl replies, "*Its* eyes were like faraway red stars twinkling in its skull. I'd never before seen such a lizard – verdant, iridian, gazing out at me with crimson eyes." The moldy air trapped within the chamber seems to shudder then, and the encircling mesh that the Unseelie queen has made of herself draws tighter about the girl from the bright lands that are ever crushing down upon those who must dwell below. *I have not taken everything,* the Queen says. *Not yet. We've hardly begun,* and the fairie girl remembers that she is not chasing a green lizard with red eyes on a summer's morning, that she has finally fallen into that abyss – the razor jaws of a granddaddy snapping turtle half buried in silt and waterlogged poplar leaves, or the gullet of a catfish that has waited long years in the mud and gloom to make a meal of her. There is always farther to fall. This pool has no bottom. She will sink until she at last forgets herself, and still she will go on sinking. She glances up into the void that the Queen of Decay has not bothered to cover with a mask, and something which has hidden itself under the black bed begins to snicker loudly. *You are mine, Daughter,* says the Queen. *And a daughter of loam and toadstools should not go about so gaudily attired. It is indecent,* and, with that, her claws move swiftly and snip away the girl's beautiful dragonfly wings. They slip from off her shoulder, falling from ragged stumps to lie dead upon the spider sheets. "My wings," the girl whispers, unsurprised and yet also disbelieving, this new violation and its attendant hurt seeming hardly more real than the bad dreams she woke from some short time ago (if there *were* time here). "You've taken my wings from me," and she reaches for them, meaning to hide them away beneath a pillow or within the folds of her stained and tattered shift before any greater harm is done to those delicate, papery mosaics. But the Queen, of course, knows the girl's will and is far faster than she; the amputated wings are snatched up by clicking, chitinous appendages which sprout suddenly from this or that dank and fleshy recess, then ferried quickly to the sucking void where a face should be. The Queen of Decay devours the fairie girl's wings in an instant, less than half an instant. And there below the leaf-litter clouds and the rustling, grub-haunted roof of this thin, thin world, the Queen, unsated, draws tight the quivering folds of her honeycomb skin and falls upon the screaming, stolen child…

…and later, the girl is shat out again, – that indigestible, fecal lump of her which the Queen's metabolism has found no use for, whatever *remains* when the glamour and magick have been stripped away by acid and cruel enzymes and a billion diligent intestinal cilia. This dull, undying scat which can now recall only the least tangible fragments of its life before the descent, before the fall, before the millennia spent in twisting, turning passage through the Queen's gut, and it sits at one of the mirrors which its mistress has so kindly, so thoughtfully, provided and watches its own gaunt face. On the bed behind it, there is a small green lizard with ruby eyes, and the lizard blinks and tastes the stale, forest-cellar air with a forked tongue the colour of ripe blackberries. *Perhaps,* thinks the thing that is no longer sprite nor nymph nor pixie, that is only this naked stub of gristle, *perhaps you were once a dragon, and then she swallowed you, as she swallowed me, and all that is left now is a little green lizard with red eyes*. The lizard blinks again, neither confirming nor denying the possibility, and the thing staring back at itself from the mirror considers conspiracy and connivance, the lovely little lizard only bait to lead her astray, that she might wander alone into a grove of ancient oaks and lift a flat, slug-streaked stone and…fall. The thing in the mirror is only the wage of its own careless, disobedient delight, and with one skeletal hand, it touches wrinkled fingertips to the cold, unyielding surface of the looking glass, reaching out to that *other* it. There is another green lizard, trapped there inside the mirror, and while the remains of the feast of the Queen of Decay tries to recall what might have come before the grove and the great flat stone and the headlong plunge down the throat of all the world, the tiny lizard slips away, vanishing into the shadows that hang everywhere like murmuring shreds of midnight.

A CHILD'S GUIDE TO THE HOLLOW HILLS

Jeff VanderMeer's introduction to *The Ammonite Violin & Others* (2009) is, in large part, an appreciation of this story. He wrote, "Here, then, is the true terrible *unknowableness* of that which is often sanitized or only brought forward for our amusement, revealed as terrible because we cannot truly fathom it." Of all my tales of Faerie, this is probably my favorite. And there's autobiography here, too, though I'm not the Queen, as some might think. I'm the stolen faerie girl.

The Cryomancer's Daughter

(Murder Ballad No. 3)

I.

"And then," she says, as though she still imagines that I've somehow never heard this story before, "the demons tried to carry the looking glass all the way up to Heaven, that they might even mock the angels." *But it shattered,* I cut in, trying to sound sober, and she smiles a vitreous sort of smile for me. I catch a glimpse of her uneven bluish teeth, set like mismatched pegs of lazulite into gums the colour of a stormy autumn sky. If I were but a stronger woman – a woman of uncommon courage and resolve – I might now use all my geologist's rambling vocabulary to describe the physical and optical properties of that half-glimpsed smile, to determine its electron density and Fermion index, the axial ratios and x-ray diffraction, diaphaneity, fracture, and et cetera. and et cetera , and on and on and on. I would take up my fountain pen and put it all down on paper, and there would be no mention anywhere of her tiresome fairy stories or my deceitful, subjective desires. I would reduce her to the driest of crystallographies. And then she says, as though I never interrupted her, "Every tiny sliver of the broken looking glass retained the full power of the whole, and they rained down over the entire world." *I'm tired,* I say. *I'm very tired, and now I want to sleep.* So she sighs, exasperated, impatient, exhaling the very breath of Boreas, and a ragged bouquet of frost blooms across the tiny window looking down on the nub end of Gar Fish Street. I've never seen her sleep. Not even once in the long three weeks since she came to the decrepit boarding house where I live, bearing a peculiar stone and a threadbare carpetbag and asking after me. Oh, sometimes she yawns or her eyes flutter in a way as to suggest the dimmest memory of sleep. Her eyes flutter, and those pale lashes scatter snowflakes across my bed, but I've never seen her asleep. Perhaps she sleeps only when *I'm* asleep; I can't prove otherwise. "Most of the bits of the looking glass were so small they were like dust or grains of sand," she says, still gazing down at the dim and gas-lit cobblestones. "But there were a few fragments large enough to be found and polished flat and smooth and fashioned into windowpanes." It sounds like a threat, the way she puts it, and also the way she's staring at the window, and then she turns her pretty head and looks at me, instead. "I should never have come to this terrible old house," she tells me. "I should have gone to some other town, farther inland, over and across the Klamath Mountains, and we should never have met." But I know this is a game, not so different from the stories she tells again and again, and I don't reply. I roll over and bury my face in my pillow. "It's a wicked, filthy place, this town," she continues, "a sodden ghetto, fit only for leprous fishmongers and ten-cent Jezebel's and –" *And what?* I ask her, my words muffled by the pillow. So here I am playing after all. Here I am dancing for her, and I know without turning to see that she's wearing that smug lazulite smile again. *Just what else is this filthy old town fit for?* She doesn't answer me right away, because now I'm dancing, and so she has all the time she needs. I open my eyes and stare at the wall, the peeling ribbons of pin-striped wallpaper, the books stacked high on my rented chifforobe. I put out the lamp some time ago, so the only light in the room is coming from the window, and now she's gone and blocked half that with the frost from her sigh. "My father," she says, beginning this *other* lie, "he said that I should find you, that I must seek out the Sapphic professor so recently disgraced and duly dismissed from her lofty post at University and fallen low and holed up in this squalid abode, drinking herself halfway to death and maybe then back again. He said you know all the deepest secrets of the earth, the mysteries of the ages, and that you even speak with her, the earth, in your dreams. He said I should show you the stone, that only you would know it for what it is." *But you have no father,* I say, playing the good and faithless heretic, stumbling through my part like the puppet she's made of me. *You're merely another wandering war orphan, an urchin whoring her way down the coast. And that precious rock of yours is nothing more than a cast-off ballast stone which you picked up on the beach the morning you crawled off that tramp steamer and first set foot in this wicked, filthy place. You're an orphan, my dear, and the rock is no more than a gastrolith puked forth from the overfull craw of some whaling ship or another.* She listens silently. She has never interrupted me, as that would be not so very different from interrupting herself. I can remember when there was some force behind these words, before I caught on. Before I wised up. I can remember when they had weight and anger. When I meant them, because I mistakenly believed that they were my own.

"My father..." she begins, then trails off, and I feel the temperature in my dingy little fourth-floor room at the end of Gar Fish Street plummet ten or fifteen degrees.

– *was likely a Russian foot soldier,* I continue for her on cue, *bound for some flea-ridden Kamchatkan hellhole, when he met up with whichever Koryak witch-sow you would have called your mother, had she ever given you the chance.* And yes, these are words from my mouth, spoken by my tongue and passing between my lips, but still they are always *her* words. I shut my eyes, willing silence upon myself (which is easy, as this particular soliloquy has come to its end), and she reaches out and brushes frozen fingertips across the space between my shoulder blades. I gasp, and at least it is *me* gasping, an *honest* gasp at the pain and cold flowing out of her and into me. All the breath driven from my lungs in that instant, and now I must surely look like some gulping, fish-eyed thing hauled up from the briny sea, my lips going a cyanotic tint and my mouth opening and closing, closing and opening, suffocating on this thin air I coughed out and can't seem to remember how to breathe back in. Then she presses her palm flat against my back and the chill doubles, trebles, expands tenfold and tenfold again between one gasp and the next. She draws the warmth from me, because she can manufacture none of her own, because, she says, she has been cursed by her own father, a man who conjures blizzards from clear summer skies and commands the grinding courses of mighty glaciers. A wizard king of snow and ice who has so condemned his own daughter because she would not be his consort in some unnatural and incestuous liaison. It's as good an explanation as any for what she is and what she's done to me, again and again and again, though I can believe it no more than I can believe that six and three are ten or that the sun and moon move round about the Earth. I am unaccustomed and unreceptive to *phantasia* and make-believe, even when I find myself trapped hopelessly within it. Perhaps my disbelief can be a prison as surely as this room, as surely as her wintry hand pressed against my spine, but I've little enough remaining of my former life, those vanished years when there was still camaraderie and purpose and dignity, and by all the gods in which I have never sought comfort I will cling to Reason, no matter how useless it may prove before she is done with me. She leans near, and her breath spills across my face like Arctic waters. "I am alone," she says sweetly and with a brittle edge of loss. "I have no one now but you, no one and nothing, only you and that damned stone. You will love me. You will love me as you have never comprehended love before. And your love will be the furnace to finally melt the sorcery that binds me." I would laugh at her, at these preposterous lines she might have ripped from the pages of some penny dreadful or stolen from a bit of low burlesque, but my throat has frozen over. I might as well be stone now. She has made of me the very thing I've spent my life researching and cataloging, for what is ice but water assuming a solid mineral form? I am made her petrifaction, and she leans nearer still and kisses me upon my icy lips. I wish that she'd at least allowed me to shut my eyes this time, just this once, that I would not now be forced to *see* her, to stare back into the daemon lover who is staring into me. That too-round, china-doll face and the wild, tumbling cataract of hair as white as snow spun into silk, her bitter lazulite grin, her own eyes the colour of a living oyster pulled from out its bivalve shell. In this moment, I could almost believe her tales of broken mirrors and snow queens, lost children and cruel magician fathers. And then she touches me, her hands seeking out the frigid gash of my sex, and I am no longer even granted the tethered freedoms of a marionette. I am at best a chiseled pagan idol to polar bears and hungry killer whales, a statue upon which she will prostrate herself, stealing from me such pleasures as she might wish and can yet endure.

II.

Later, long hours later, after she's grown bored with me and after dawn and sunrise and after my blood has thawed to slush and I'm left shivering and fevery, I sit naked at the foot of the bed in the boarding-house room on Gar Fish Street and sip the cheapest available gin from a tin cup. She's gone out. I can not say with any certainty *where* she goes, but she disappears from time to time. It's not unusual if she doesn't return for days, and I can not help but to imagine that she must have other unfortunates trapped in other dingy rooms scattered throughout the city. I stare back at my reflection, watching myself from the cracked mirror mounted crookedly on the dressing table. Perhaps, I think, she is gathering to her an *army* of puppets, and at the last she will have us take up flaming brands and march against her wizard father locked in his palace of ice and baling wire. I raise the cup to my lips, and the woman in the mirror obligingly does the same. I've seen corpses floating in the harbour that looked more alive than her, more alive than me. I could have aged ten years in these three few weeks. My lover has stolen more from me than simple warmth, of that I *am* certain. She's diminished me with every successive freeze and thaw, and this reflection is little more than a ghost of the woman who arrived here from San Francisco last summer. I came to hide and drink and maybe die, for there would never be any return to that former life of privilege and reward which had been so hastily, so thoughtlessly, traded for a hurried tryst with one of my first-year students, a yellow-haired girl whose name I can hardly now recollect. I only came here to be a drunkard and, in time, a suicide, to drift farther and farther away from the world which would have no more of me. I thought surely that would be penance enough for all my sins. I never dared conceive of any punishment so sublime as the wizard's daughter. No, I do not believe she is the daughter of a wizard, but how else would I name her? One night, I tried to make a game of guessing at some other appellation, whether Christian or heathen, but she waved away every suggestion I made. Hundreds or thousands of names dismissed, and there was never anything in her wet oyster eyes but truth. But I may be a poor, poor judge of truth, and we should keep that in mind. After all, remember, some fraction of me *believed* the yellow-haired girl in San Francisco when she promised that she'd never so much as whisper even the most nebulous hint of our nights together to another living soul. Indeed, I may be no fit judge of truth at all. The woman in the mirror who looks exactly like my corpse takes another sip of gin, realizes the cup is almost empty, and reaches for the quart bottle on the floor. She fills my cup halfway, and I thank her for such boundless generosity. The wizard's daughter, she won't ever deign to drink with me, though she sometimes returns from her disappearances with the gift of a fresh bottle – gin or rye whiskey or the peaty brown ale they brew down by the waterfront. She says she doesn't drink with anyone or alone, so I don't take it personally.

"Aren't you a sorry sight," the woman in the mirror says to me. "A shame the way you've let yourself go. Can you even remember the last time you bathed? Or took a comb to your hair, perhaps?" And so I tell her to go fuck herself.

Then there are footsteps in the hallway, and I listen, expecting them to stop outside my door, expecting the dry rattle of a key in the lock and then the cut-glass knob will turn and –

"The Tolowa Indians have a story about a crazy woman who talks to her reflection –"

Shut up, I hiss at my own face in the dressing-table mirror and almost drop the tin cup, my heart pounding and hands shaking so badly that no small measure of gin splashes over the rim and darkens the grimy floor at my feet. *Such a waste,* I think, *such a pointless, god-damned waste,* and by then the footsteps in question have come and gone, and it isn't the wizard's daughter, after all. Only another lodger or someone else, a prostitute or sneak thief or a dutiful officer of the law, coming to call upon another lodger. I reach for the gin bottle before the woman in the mirror does it for me. *She gives me dreams,* I say and, having refilled my cup, shove the cork firmly back into the mouth of the bottle. I can not afford another spill today, for I am in no condition to dress myself and descend the stairs to the smoky lobby and the narrow street beyond and still have to walk the two blocks (uphill) from the boarding house on Gar Fish Street to the Gramercy Digs Saloon on the corner of Muskie and Walleye. And I have no guarantee that she will bring me another bottle, either, as her small mercies and smaller kindnesses are, at best, capricious and wholly unpredictable. *She gives me dreams,* I say again, because I do not think the mirror woman heard me the first time.

"Does she?" the doppelgänger asks. It's grinning at me now, only that is not *my* grin, those rotting lazulite pegs in swollen stormy gums, but its is still my face. "I was until this moment quite unaware that any among the Oneiroi concealed a cunt between its legs."

I shut my eyes, praying to no one and nothing that I'll stop shaking and my teeth with stop chattering, wishing for warmth and sunlight and wishing, too, that I had even half the strength I'd need to get to my feet and stand and walk the five or six steps to the three-legged chair where my overcoat and gloves are lying in a careless heap. But I am too sick and much too drunk to try. I would wind up on the floor, and that's where she would find me when she returns. I would rather suffer this chill in my veins and my bones than have her find me sprawled naked upon the floor, unconscious in a pool of spilled gin and my own piss. Behind my eyelids, the dreams she has given unfold like flickering cinematograph projections. And I keep my eyes tightly closed, lest these Lumière images escape from out the windows of my blighted soul and fall upon the silvered glass, for I have no mind to share them with that grinning fiend behind the mirror. The wizard's daughter has given them to me, and so they are mine and mine alone – this clouded, snow-dimmed sky spread wide above a winter forest of blue spruce and fir and pine, the uneasy shadows huddled beneath the sagging boughs. I have been walking all my life, it seems, or, more precisely, all my *afterlife,* those many long months since my abrupt departure from San Francisco. The howling, wolf-throated wind stings, then numbs, my bare face, and I stumble blindly forward through snow piled almost as high as my knees. I can not feel my feet. I am become no more or less than a phantom of frostbite and rags, lost and certain that I will never again be anything but lost. I know what lies ahead of me, what she brings me here to see, again and again and again. It was only a surprise that first time I walked these woods, and also the second time, as I've never suffered from recurring dreams. My lungs ache, filled as they are with the thin air which, paradoxically, seems heavy and thick as lead, and then I've reached the place where the trees end, opening onto a high alpine meadow. In summer, the ground here would be resplendent in green and splashed with the gay blooms of black-eyed susans and Joe-Pye weed, columbine and parry clover, but this is a dead month, a smothered month – December or January, the ending or beginning of the year – and perhaps all months are dead here. Perhaps every word she's told me is the truth, plain and simple, and this *is* truly a blasted land which will never again know spring grasses nor the quickening hues of wildflowers. *Do not show me this,* I plead, but I can not ever say whether these are words spoken or merely words thought. Either way, they tumble from me, silently or whispered from my cracked and bleeding lips. *Do not show me this. Don't make me see. I know, I know already what happened here, because I've seen it all before, and there is no profit in seeing it ever again.* She does not answer me. Only the wind speaks to me here, as it rushes down from the raw charcoal-coloured peaks, the sky's breath pouring out across splintered metamorphic teeth and over the meadow. And this is what I behold: a great crimson sleigh with gilded rails and runners drawn by Indian ponies, like something a red-skinned Father Christmas might command; a single granite standing stone or menhir of a sort not known to exist in the Americas – there are glyphs or pictographs graven upon the stone, which I can never quite see clearly; and in the lee of the menhir, there is an enormously obese man wrapped in bearskin robes and a naked girl child kneeling in the snow at his feet. The man holds a four-gallon metal pail over her, and the furs which the girl must have worn only moments before are spread out very near the crimson sleigh. The man and the girl can not be more than fifty feet away from me, and every time I have tried to cry out, to draw his attention towards myself, to forestall what I know is coming next. And I have tried, too, to leave the shelter of the tree line and cross the meadow to the spot where he stands and she kneels and the granite menhir looms threatfully above them both. From the first time I beheld it with my dreaming eyes, I have understood that there is more to this awful standing stone than its constituent molecules, far more than mere chemistry and mineralogy can fathom. It is an evil thing, and the man in the bearskin robes is somehow in its service or its debt. It has stood a thousand years, perhaps, demanding offerings and forfeiture – and no, it matters not that I do not even now believe in the existence of evil beyond a shorthand phrase for the cruelties and insanity of human beings. It matters not in the least, for in the dream the menhir or something trapped within the stone *glances* towards the edge of the forest, and it *sees* me there. And I can feel its delight, that there is an audience to this atrocity, and I feel its perfect hatred, deeper and blacker than the submarine canyons out beyond the harbour. "Are you cold, my darling," the enormous man growls, and then he spits on the shivering girl at his feet. "Would you have me build for you a lovely roaring fire to chase the frostnip from your toes and fingertips?"

But she was not the same girl, my reflection calmly professes from its place behind the dressing table. *Not the same girl as your visitor.*

She was, I reply through gritted teeth and without opening my eyes. *She was that very same girl.*

But the girl in your dream – her hair is red as a sunset and her eyes blue as lapis lazuli. So, you see, she can not possibly be your pale companion.

The Tolowa Indians have a story about a crazy woman who talks to her reflection, I say, and at that the mirror falls silent again, but I know it wears a smirking satisfaction on its borrowed face. And there in the high meadow, the man wrapped in bearskins slowly pours water from his pail over the naked body of the red-haired girl. She screams, but only once, and makes no attempt whatsoever to escape. Her cry startles the ponies, and they neigh and stamp their hooves. "Is that better?" the man asks her, and already the water has begun to freeze on her skin, before the pail is even empty. "Are you warmer now?" I can hear the menhir laughing behind his back, an ancient, ugly sound which I could never hope to describe, the laughter of granite which isn't granite at all. For a moment it seems somehow less solid, and in my horror I imagine the menhir bending down low over the man and the dying girl. "See there?" the fat man cackles and tosses his pail away. "You are *mine,* child. You were mine from the start, from the day you slithered from twixt your momma's nethers, and you'll never be anyone else's." But she can no longer hear him. I am certain of that, for the cold mountain air has turned the water solid, sealing and stealing her away, and I can not help but think of the fossils of prehistoric flies and ants which I've seen encased in polished lumps of Baltic amber. The man spits on her again, spits at the crust of new ice concealing her, and then he turns and trudges away through the snow to the sleigh and the two waiting ponies. "Let her lie there till the spring," he bellows, taking up the leather reins and giving them a violent shake. "Let her lie there seven winters and another after that!" And then the sleigh is racing away, those golden runners not slicing through the snow, but seeming instead to float somehow an inch or so above it. And then I feel the ground fall away beneath my feet, in this nightmare which she has given to me that I might witness her desecration and murder a hundred, hundred times. The day vanishes, and I drop feet-first into an abyss, through the hollow, rotten heart of the world, and for a time I am grateful my eyes can no longer see and that the only sound is the air rushing past my ears as I fall.

III.

She comes back early the next morning, shortly after I have risen and had my first drink of the day and managed to dress in my slovenly, mannish best, feeling just a little more myself for her time away from me. The night before, I hardly slept, tossing and turning, starting awake at every sound, no matter how far off or insignificant it might have been. Towards dawn there was a foreboding, melancholy sort of dream in which I watched a waxing quarter moon sinking into the Pacific and the sun coming up over the town where it huddles at the crumbling western edge of the continent. This cluttered grotesquerie of winding lanes and leaning clapboard cottages, chimneys and cisterns and rusting corrugated tin roofs, and the few brick-and-mortar buildings so scabbed with mosses and ferns and such other local flora that one might easily mistake them for some natural part of the landscape, only lately and incompletely modified to the needs of men. The morning washed away the night, finishing off the drowning moon, and the motley assortment of boats and small ships moored along the wharves seemed no more than bobbing toys awaiting the hands of children. The morning light snagged in their sails and rigging, and a grey flock of gulls arising from the narrow, mussel-littered beach screeched out her name, which I heard clearly, but knew I would forget immediately upon waking. It was a peaceable scene, in its way, and I thought perhaps this is as good a place to lie down and die as any other. But, even so, I could not shake the sense that something immeasurably old and malign watched the town from the redwood forests crowding in on every side. Something that had trailed her here, possibly. Or something that had been here all along, something that was already here aeons before the mountains were heaved up from a sea swarming with great reptiles and ammonites and archaic species of gigantic predatory fish. Either way, they were in league now, the wizard's wayward daughter and this unseen watcher in the trees, and I alone knew of their alliance. The dream ended as a velvet curtain was drawn suddenly closed to hide what I realized had only been the most elaborate set arranged upon a theatre stage, a cleverly lit and orchestrated miniature to fool my sleeping eyes, and then there was vaudeville and then opera, and I woke to Verdi from a phonograph playing loudly across the hallway from my room.

"We should go for a walk together," she says and half fills my tin cup with gin. "Hand in hand, yes? Brazen in our forbidden love for one another."

I don't love you, I tell her. *I have never loved you,* but I can see from the knowing glimmer in her oyster eyes that she recognizes my lie at once. *Besides,* I add, *nothing which is properly depraved or deviant is forbidden here, unless it be some arcane offence to the patron saints of kelp and syphilitic mariners which I've yet to stumble upon. Why else would we be so tolerated here, you and I?* And, at that, she puts the cork back into the bottle and scowls at me. "Speak for yourself," she says. "I go where I like. I do as I wish." I laugh at her and sip my gin. She stands up, her petticoats rustling like snowy boughs, and I wonder what the townspeople descry when they look at her. Do they see her breath fog on balmy summer afternoons? Do they notice the scum of frost left behind on anything she's touched? Do they ever detect the faint auroral flicker from her pupils, a momentary glint of brilliant reds or greens or blues from her otherwise lifeless eyes? Or are they so accustomed to minding their own affairs – for I *am* convinced this town is a refuge for the damned and cast-away – that they see only some shabby girl too plain for even the most unpretentious sporting house? I'll never know, for I'll never have the courage to ask them. Secretly, I fear I am the only one who can see her, and I am possessed of no pressing desire to have this irrational dread confirmed. "Oh, they see well enough," she says, and I am not surprised. Puppets have no private thoughts. She lingers before the dressing table mirror, straightening the folds of her skirt. "They see and stay awake nights, wishing they could forget the sight of me." This seems to please her, and so she smiles, and I have another drink from my dented tin cup. "Or they long for my embrace," she continues. "They pine for my attentions. They can think of naught else save the torment of my cold hand about their prick or pressed tight to their windward passage. Some have been driven nigh unto *seppuku* or have learned to tie a hangman's noose, should the longing grow more than merely unbearable." And I reply that I can believe that part, at least, though myself I would prefer a bullet in the brain. "No, that's a *real* man's death," she says and turns to face me. "Now, have you figured out my stone? Last night, a magpie found me behind the livery and brought word from my father who wishes me home at the earliest possible date. But *not* without your learn'd observations, my sweet professor." I stare silently into my cup for a moment, my stomach sour and cramping, and I tell that her I'm in no mood for the game today. Tomorrow, maybe. Maybe the day after, and, in the meantime, she should haunt some other poor bitch or bastard. "But the magpie was quite insistent," she says. "You know by now that my father is not a patient man, even at his best, and he has long since tired of waiting on your verdict." And she holds the peculiar stone out to me as she has done so many times before. *But what of the curse?* I ask her, resigned that there will be no allowances today for hangovers and sour stomachs. I know all these lines by heart. *What of winning my love, the furnace to finally melt the sorcery that binds you? Has someone gone and changed the rules? Do you begin to miss the old man's cock between you legs?* She smiles her vitreous smile once more to flash those bluish pegs she wears for teeth and closes her fingers around the stone resting in her palm. "Surely you didn't take me *seriously?*" she scoffs. "My father is a proud man, a man of principles and lofty morals, and he would *never* permit me to take a lesbian dipsomaniac for my husband."

You have no father, I remind her, because I know all these lines by heart, and she would have me say nothing more or less. *You were born into a brothel but a few miles farther up the coast, the albino child of a half-nigger whore and a chink from a medicine show. Fortunately, your mother sold you to a kind-hearted merchant marine for two-pints and a black pearl broach, saving you from a life spent peddling pussy and Clark Stanley's snake oil liniment. Sadly, though, your adoptive father soon perished at sea when his ship was pulled down by the arms of a giant cephalopod.* She smiles again, licks her lips, and asks eagerly, "The Kraken of Norwegian legend?" *One and the same, I have no doubt about it. But you survived,* and I pause to drain and then refill my cup. *You were discovered in a leaky wicker basket one midsummer eve, carried in on the high tide.* And she tells me she'd almost forgotten that story, but I know that she's lying, that it's her most-favored of the lot. "That's so much better than the one in which I'm a Cossack's illegitimate daughter on the run from Czarist spies, or the other one, where we're actually half sisters, but I have been stricken with an hysterical amnesia beyond the curative powers of even the most accomplished alienists." Her voice rattles inside my skull like dice, like razor shards of ice. It is slicing apart my brain, and soon my thoughts will be little more than tatters. No, they were tattered long ago, if truth be told. I place three fingers against the soft spot at my left temple, as if this mere laying on of hands would alone would be enough to still the mad somersault of her words. "Though I was only an infant," she says, "I can almost recall my valiant, grief-stricken father swaddling me in his pea jacket and placing me inside that basket as the sea monster wailed and gnawed at the bowsprit." *No,* I reply, *you never had a father,* and for the briefest fraction of a moment I see (or only *wish* I'd see) the dull gleam of disappointment in her damp oyster eyes, as though she's begun to believe (or at least *wishes* to believe) in her own canard. "No matter," she sighs. "As I was saying, the snowflakes grew bigger and bigger until they resembled nothing so much as fat white geese." *That's not what you were saying,* I tell her. *You were reminding me of the stone and your father's impatient need to know its provenance.* But she ignores me, already deep into the middle of a story she's told so many times it hardly matters where she begins the tale. "The big sled stopped, and the child saw then that it was driven by a tall and upright lady, all shining white – the Snow Queen herself. 'It is cold enough to kill one,' she said. 'Creep inside my bearskin.'" *But you've never had a mother, either,* I say, and then, before she can reply or withdraw any deeper into that moth-eaten narrative, Kay and Gerda and the Snow Queen, the demons and their grinning looking glass, I ask to see the stone.

"Again? But I should think you'd have the damned thing memorized by now."

I stop rubbing at my aching head and hold out my left hand to her. *Give it to me,* I say, and she narrows her grey eyes suspiciously, as I've never once before *asked* to see the stone, and it isn't like me to deviate from the confines of the events and dialogue which she has scripted so meticulously. Possibly, she begins to suspect the unthinkable, rebellion from her wooden puppet, and must wonder if she's allowed me too much string, too much slack upon my tethers. I half expect her to turn away again, to seek such refuge as might be had in the cracked dressing-table mirror or to walk out the door and leave me alone in my dingy room. Instead, she nods her head and places the peculiar stone into my outstretched hand.

...and there would be no mention anywhere of her tiresome fairy stories or my deceitful, subjective desires.

I would reduce her to the driest of crystallographies.

The stone is not quite round and is somewhat flattened side to side, the approximate colour of licorice, and I tell her what I've already told her before, that it's only a beach cobble, a bit of Mesozoic slate fallen from the headlands or the high cliffs surrounding the harbour, then polished smooth by time and the ocean. I describe its mineral composition for her – muscovite and quartz, with small quantities of biotite, pyrite, and hematite, and perhaps also traces of kaolin and tourmaline. But I have said repeatedly that it is a *peculiar* stone, have I not, and none of these things make it peculiar in the least. "What else?" she asks. A flurry of minute snowflakes escapes her lips, borne upon her voice and blown towards me on her Siberian breath, and they look nothing at all like fat white geese. "What is there about it that I *couldn't* learn from the pages of one of your schoolbooks?" It grows so heavy in my hand then, her stone, as though it has suddenly trebled or quadrupled in size while appearing just exactly the same as always. *It is a sympathetic stone,* I say to her, surprising myself, and she takes a quick step backwards and bumps hard against a corner of the dressing table. *What?* I ask. *Did you believe we'd never get this far?* But she only looks afraid and doesn't answer me. And I understand now, at last, that the wizard's daughter is as surely a puppet as am I. She is frozen to her core, kneeling in an alpine meadow, trapped forever in the icy shadow of an old man's despite. It does not matter whether these things are literally true or only figurative. It does not matter, either, what I can and can not believe, or whether I am sane.

A sympathetic stone, I say again, and the snow from her lips settles in my hair and on the harsh angles of my face. *These markings scratched into its surface, I can't read those, but I suspect that's not important. It isn't what we can see in this stone, but what this stone can see in us. Are you following me?* She licks her lips nervously, and they sparkle with the thinnest sheen of frozen saliva. *That's its genius, you see. It truly is a looking glass.* She rubs at her hip where it struck the dressing table and laughs the driest, most unconvincing laugh that I have ever heard. "You think me simple, an imbecile, is that it? Do you think you might gain the upper hand, and your freedom, too, with only a quick-witted riddle and a straight face? My father –" *But that was such a very long time ago,* I say, interrupting her. *Long ago and far away, in a country I have never visited outside your dreams.*

"One day, the old hobgoblin invented a mirror," she says, and those cold auroral fires burn brightly in the twin voids of her pupils. Red, then blue, then green, and then back to red again; I can plainly hear them crackle in the sky above the boarding house on Gar Fish Street. "A mirror with this peculiarity – that every good thing reflected in its surface shrank away almost to nothing."

I set the tin cup down upon my bed, and for the third time I say to her, *It is a sympathetic stone,* as I have always heard there is magic contained within the number three. In my palm, the licorice-coloured cobble quivers and transforms into a crude sort of dagger. Many days or nights later, when these grim and fabulous events have run their course and I have weighted her corpse with an anvil and a burlap bag filled with rusted horseshoes, I shall ponder the question of her relationship with the stone. Or the stone's relationship with her. If, for instance, it is as Coleridge's murdered albatross, some cross she has been condemned to bear in penance for all eternity, acting out this marionette performance down countless centuries. I will draw no conclusions to satisfy me, nor will I find any sense in any fraction of it, but, still, I will lay awake nights, turning the question over and over in my persistent, gin-addled mind. But I think, in contradiction to the evidence of her fear, the tremble in her snowy voice, the northern lights blazing in her eyes, that she was *glad* when we were done (and here I surrender to more a truthful, more comforting *past* tense, for that day *has* come and gone). Perhaps she was permitted some brief period of oblivion between one haunting and the next, and so I'd granted her exhausted spirit an interval of rest, a respite from the trials and horrors of her damnation. Without speaking another word, I rose from the bed and drove the stone dagger deep into her chest just beneath the sternum, then twisted it sharply up and to the right, that the blade might find and pierce her heart. Her lips parted and a trickle of something dark which was not blood leaked from her mouth and spattered on my hand and the floor between us. In her grey eyes, the polar fires were extinguished, and she did not so much seem to fall at my feet as *flow* downward, as though her body had never been anything more substantial than water held forever but one degree below freezing. In my hand, the stone was only a stone again, still bearing those indecipherable runes or glyphs, the same ones I might have glimpsed, dreaming, carved into a granite menhir. And for the first time since she came to me, all those months ago, I felt warm, genuinely warm. But it is late, and the candle by which I have put down on paper these strange occurrences – being possibly nothing greater than a confession or the ramblings of a lunatic – has melted to little more than a puddle of beeswax and a guttering scrap of blackened wick. So I will not trouble myself with the details of how it was I removed her body from my room and the boarding house. However, I will add that I placed the peculiar, *sympathetic* stone inside her mouth, which was then sewn shut with a needle and thread I borrowed from the wife of my landlord. I told her simply that my socks had worn almost through and needed darning. I have considered leaving this place, before I am utterly bereft of even the price of a train ticket. I've looked at my maps and considered traveling north to Coos Bay, or inland to Salem or Pendleton. I might even go so far as Seattle. I have thought, too, that I might find gainful employment as a geologist in a mining camp. In the wild places, men are not so concerned with a woman's indiscretions, or so I have been led to believe.

THE CRYOMANCER'S DAUGHTER (MURDER BALLAD NO. 3)

The story presages many stories I'd yet to write, including the Cherry Creek tales and even *The Drowning Girl: A Memoir*. Its obvious inspiration is Hans Christian Andersen's "The Snow Queen." I'd intended to set several stories in the town where all the streets are named for fish, but, so far, there's only this one.

The Ammonite Violin
(Murder Ballad No. 4)

If he were ever to try to write this story, he would not know where to begin. It's that sort of a story, so fraught with unlikely things, so perfectly turned and filled with such wicked artifice and contrivances that readers would look away, unable to suspend their disbelief even for a page. But he will never try to write it, because he is not a poet, or a novelist, or a man who writes short stories for the newsstand pulp magazines. He is a collector. Or, as he thinks of himself, a Collector. He has never dared to think of himself as *The* Collector, as he is not without an ounce or two of modesty, and there must surely be those out there who are far better than he, shadow men, and maybe shadow women, too, haunting a busy, forgetful world that is only aware of its phantoms when one or another of them slips up and is exposed to flashing cameras and prison cells. Then people will stare, and maybe, for a time, there is horror and fear in their dull, wet eyes, but they soon enough forget again. They are busy people, after all, and they have lives to live, and jobs to show up for five days a week, and bills to pay, and secret nightmares all their own, and in their world there is very little *time* for phantoms.

He lives in a small house in a small town near the sea, for the only time the Collector is ever truly at peace is when he is in the presence of the sea. Even collecting has never brought him to that complete and utter peace, the quiet which finally fills him whenever there is only the crash of waves against a granite jetty and the saltwater mists to breathe in and hold in his lungs like opium fumes. He would love the sea, were she a woman. And sometimes he imagines her so, a wild and beautiful woman clothed all in blue and green, trailing sand and mussels in her wake. Her grey eyes would contain hurricanes, and her voice would be the lonely toll of bell buoys and the cries of gulls and a December wind scraping itself raw against the shore. But, he thinks, were the sea but a women, and were she his lover, then he would *have* her, as he is a Collector and *must* have all those things he loves, so that no one else might ever have them. He must draw them to him and keep them safe from a blind and busy world that cannot even comprehend its phantoms. And having her, he would lose her, and he would never again know the peace which only she can bring.

He has two specialties, this Collector. There are some who are perfectly content with only one, and he has never thought any less of them for it. But he has two, because, so long as he can recall, there has been this dual fascination, and he never saw the point in forsaking one for the other. Not if he might have them both and yet be a richer man for sharing his devotion between the two. They are his two mistresses, and neither has ever condemned his polyamorous heart. Like the sea, who is *not* his mistress, but only his constant savior, they understand who and what and *why* he is, and that he would be somehow diminished, perhaps even undone, were he forced to devote himself wholly to the one or the other. The first of the two is his vast collection of fossilized ammonites, gathered up from the quarries and ocean-side cliffs and the stony, barren places of half the globe's nations. The second are all the young women he has murdered by suffocation, *always* by suffocation, for that is how the sea would kill, how the sea *does* kill, usually, and in taking life he would ever pay tribute and honor that first mother of the world.

That first Collector.

He has never had to explain his collecting of suffocations, of the deaths of suffocated girls, as it is such a commonplace thing, and a secret collection, besides. But he has frequently found it necessary to explain to some acquaintance or another, someone who thinks that she or he *knows* the Collector, about the ammonites. The ammonites are not a secret and, it would seem, neither are they commonplace. It is simple enough to say that they are mollusks, a subdivision of the Cephalopoda, kin to the octopus and cuttlefish and squid, but possessing exquisite shells, not unlike another living cousin, the chambered nautilus. It is less easy to say that they became extinct at the end of the Cretaceous, along with most dinosaurs, or that they first appear in the fossil record in early Devonian times, as this only leads to the need to explain the Cretaceous and Devonian. Often, when asked that question, *What is an ammonite?,* he will change the subject. Or he will sidestep the truth of his collection, talking only of mathematics, and the geometry of the ancient Greeks, and how one arrives at the Golden Curve. Ammonites, he knows, are one of the sea's many exquisite expressions of that logarithmic spiral, but he does not bother to explain that part, keeping it back for himself. And, sometimes, he talks about the horns of Ammon, an Egyptian god of the air, or, if he is feeling especially impatient and annoyed by the question, he limits his response to a description of the Ammonites from the *Book of Mormon*, how they embraced the god of the Nephites and so came to know peace. He is not a Mormon, of course, as he has use of only a single deity, who is the sea and who kindly grants him peace when he can no longer bear the clamor in his head or the far more terrible clamor of mankind.

On this hazy winter day, he has returned to his small house from a very long walk along a favorite beach, as there was a great need to clear his head. He has made a steaming cup of Red Zinger tea with a few drops of honey and sits now in the room that has become the gallery for the best of his ammonites, oak shelves and glass display cases filled with their graceful planispiral or heteromorph curves, a thousand fragile aragonite bodies transformed by time and geochemistry into mere silica or pyrite or some other permineralization. He sits at his desk, sipping his tea and glancing occasionally at some beloved specimen or another –*this* one from South Dakota, or *that* one from the banks of the Volga River in Russia, or one of the *many* that have come from Whitby, England. And then he looks back to the desktop and the violin case lying open in front of him, crimson silk to cradle this newest and perhaps most precious of all the items which he has yet collected in his lifetime, the single miraculous piece which belongs strictly in neither one gallery nor the other. The piece which will at last form a bridge, he believes, allowing his two collections to remain distinct, but also affording a tangible transition between them.

The keystone, he thinks. *Yes, you will be my keystone.* But he knows, too, that the violin will be something more than that, that he has devised it to serve as something far grander than a token unification of the two halves of his delight. It will be a tool, a mediator or go-between in an act which may, he hopes, transcend collecting in its simplest sense. It has only just arrived today, special delivery, from the Belgian luthier to whom the Collector had hesitantly entrusted its birth.

"It must be done *precisely* as I have said," he told the violin-maker, four months ago, when he flew to Hotton to hand-deliver a substantial portion of the materials from which the instrument would be constructed. "You may not deviate in any significant way from these instructions."

"Yes," the luthier replied, "I understand. I understand completely." A man who appreciates discretion, the Belgian violin-maker, so there were no inconvenient questions asked, no prying inquiries as to *why,* and what's more, he'd even known something about ammonites beforehand.

"No substitutions," the Collector said firmly, just in case it needed to be stated one last time.

"No substitutions of any sort," replied the luthier.

"And the back must be carved – "

"I understand," the violin-maker assured him. "I have the sketches, and I will follow them exactly."

"And the pegs – "

"Will be precisely as we have discussed."

And so the collector paid the luthier half the price of the commission, the other half due upon delivery, and he took a six a.m. flight back across the wide Atlantic to New England and his small house in the small town near the sea. And he has waited, hardly daring to *half* believe that the violin-maker would, in fact, get it all right. Indeed – for men are ever at war with their hearts and minds and innermost demons – some infinitesimal scrap of the Collector has even *hoped* that there *would* be a mistake, the most trifling portion of his plan ignored, or the violin finished and perfect but then lost in transit, and so the whole plot ruined. For it is no small thing, what the Collector has set in motion, and having always considered himself a very wise and sober man, he suspects that he understands fully the consequences he would suffer should he be discovered by lesser men who have no regard for the ocean and her needs. Men who cannot see the flesh and blood phantoms walking among them in broad daylight, much less be bothered to pay tithes which are long overdue to a goddess who has cradled them all, each and every one, through the innumerable twists and turns of evolution's crucible, for three and a half thousand million years.

But there has been no mistake, and, if anything, the violin-maker can be faulted only in the complete sublimation of his craft to the will of his customer. In every way, this is the instrument the Collector asked him to make, and the varnish gleams faintly in the light from the display cases. The top is carved from spruce, and four small ammonites have been set into the wood – *Xipheroceras* from Jurassic rocks exposed along the Dorset Coast at Lyme Regis – two inlaid on the upper bout, two on the lower. He found the fossils himself, many years ago, and they are as perfectly preserved an example of their genus as he has yet seen anywhere, for any price. The violin's neck has been fashioned from maple, as is so often the tradition, and, likewise, the fingerboard is the customary ebony. However, the scroll has been formed from a fifth ammonite, and the Collector knows it is a far more perfect logarithmic spiral than any volute that could have ever been hacked from out a block of wood. In his mind, the five ammonites form the points of a pentacle. The luthier used maple for the back and ribs, and when the Collector turns the violin over, he's greeted by the intricate bas-relief he requested, faithfully reproduced from his own drawings – a great octopus, the ravenous devilfish of so many sea legends, and the maze of its eight tentacles makes a looping, tangled interweave.

As for the pegs and bridge, the chinrest and tailpiece, all these have been carved from the bits of bone he provided the luthier. They seem no more than antique ivory, the stolen tusks of an elephant, say, or a walrus, or the tooth of a sperm whale, perhaps. The Collector also provided the dried gut for the five strings, and when the violin-maker pointed out that they would not be nearly so durable as good stranded steel, that they would be much more likely to break and harder to keep in tune, the Collector told him that the instrument would be played only once and so these matters were of very little concern. For the bow, the luthier was given strands of hair which the Collector told him had come from the tail of a gelding, a fine grey horse from Kentucky thoroughbred stock. He'd even ordered a special rosin, and so the sap of an Aleppo pine was supplemented with a vial of oil he'd left in the care of the violin-maker.

And now, four long months later, the Collector is rewarded for all his painstaking designs, rewarded or damned, if indeed there is some distinction between the two, and the instrument he holds is more beautiful than he'd ever dared to imagine it could be.

The Collector finishes his tea, pausing for a moment to lick the commingled flavors of hibiscus and rosehips, honey and lemon-grass, from his thin, chapped lips. Then he closes the violin case and locks it, before writing a second, final check to the Belgian luthier. He slips it into an envelope bearing the violin-maker's name and the address of the shop on the rue de Centre in Hotton. The check will go out in the morning's mail, along with other checks for the gas, telephone, and electric bills, and a handwritten letter on lilac-scented stationary, addressed to a Brooklyn violinist. When he is done with these chores, the Collector sits there at the desk in his gallery, one hand resting lightly on the violin case, his face marred by an unaccustomed smile and his eyes filling up with the gluttonous wonder of so many precious things brought together in one room, content in the certain knowledge that they belong to him and will never belong to anyone else.

The violinist would never write this story, either. Words have never come easily for her. Sometimes, it seems she does not even think in words, but only in notes of music. When the lilac-scented letter arrives, she reads it several times over, then does what it asks of her, because she can't imagine what else she would do. She buys a ticket, and the next day she takes the train through Connecticut and Rhode Island and Massachusetts until, finally, she comes to a small town on a rocky spit of land very near the sea. She has never cared for the sea, as it has seemed always to her some awful, insoluble mystery, not so very different from the awful, insoluble mystery of death. Even before the loss of her sister, the violinist avoided the sea when possible. She loathes the taste of fish and lobster and of clams, and the smell of the ocean, too, which reminds her of raw sewage. She has often dreamt of drowning and of slimy things with bulging black eyes, eyes as empty as night, that have slithered up from abyssal depths to drag her back down with them to lightless plains of silt and diatomaceous ooze or to the ruins of haunted, sunken cities. But those are *only* dreams, and they do her only the bloodless harm that comes from dreams, and she has lived long enough to understand that she has worse things to fear than the sea.

She takes a taxi from the train depot, and it ferries her through the town and over a murky river winding between empty warehouses and rotting docks, a few fishing boats stranded at low tide, and then to a small house painted the color of sunflowers or canary feathers. The address on the mailbox matches the address on the lilac-scented letter, so she pays the driver, and he leaves her there. Then she stands in the driveway, watching the yellow house, which has begun to seem a disquieting shade of yellow, or only a shade of yellow made disquieting because there is so much of it all in one place. It's almost twilight, and she shivers, wishing she'd thought to wear a cardigan under her coat, and then a porch light comes on and there's a man waving to her.

He's the man who wrote the letter, she thinks. *The man who wants me to play for him.* For some reason she had expected him to be a great deal younger and not so fat. He looks a bit like Captain Kangaroo, this man, and he waves and calls her name and smiles. And the violinist wishes that the taxi were still waiting there to take her back to the station, that she didn't need the money the fat man in the yellow house had offered her, that she'd had the good sense to stay in the city where she belongs. *You could still turn and walk away,* she reminds herself. *There's nothing at all stopping you from just turning right around, and walking away, and never once looking back, and you could still forget about this whole ridiculous affair.*

And maybe that's true, and maybe it isn't, but there's more than a month's rent on the line, and the way work's been lately, a few students and catch-as-catch-can, she can't afford to find out. She nods and waves back at the smiling man on the porch, the man who told her not to bring her own instrument because he'd prefer to hear her play a particular one that he'd just brought back from a trip to Europe.

"Come on inside. You must be freezing out there," he calls from the porch, and the violinist tries not to think about the sea all around her or that shade of yellow, like a pool of melted butter, and goes to meet the man who sent her the lilac-scented letter.

The Collector makes a steaming-hot pot of Red Zinger, which the violinist takes without honey, and they each have a poppy-seed muffin, which he bought fresh that morning at a bakery in the village. They sit across from one another at his desk, surrounded by the display cases and the best of his ammonites, and she sips her tea and picks at the muffin and pretends to be interested while he explains the importance of recognizing sexual dimorphism when distinguishing one species of ammonite from another. The shells of females, he says, are often the larger, and so are called macroconchs by paleontologists. The males may have much smaller shells, called microconchs, and one must always be careful not to mistake the microconchs and macroconchs for two distinct species. He also talks about extinction rates, and the utility of ammonites as index fossils, and *Parapuzosia bradyi,* a giant among ammonites and the largest specimen in his collection, with a shell measuring only slightly under six feet in diameter, a Kraken of the warm Cretaceous seas.

"They're all quite beautiful," she says, and the violinist doesn't tell him how much she hates the sea and everything that comes from the sea, or that the thought of all the fleshy, tentacled creatures that once lived stuffed inside those pretty spiral shells makes her skin crawl. She sips her Red Zinger and smiles and nods her head whenever it seems appropriate to do so, and when he asks if he can call her Ellen, she says yes, of course.

"You won't think me too familiar?"

"Don't be silly," she replies, half charmed at his manners and wondering if he's gay or just a lonely old man who's grown a bit peculiar because he has nothing but his rocks and the yellow house for company. "That's my name. My name is Ellen."

"I wouldn't want to make you uncomfortable or take liberties that are not mine to take," the Collector says and clears away their china cups and saucers, the crumpled paper napkins and a few uneaten crumbs, and then he asks if she's ready to see the violin.

"If you're ready to show it to me," she tells him.

"It's just that I don't want to rush you," he says. "We could always talk some more, if you'd like."

And so the violinist explains to him that she's never felt comfortable with conversation, or with language in general, and that she's always suspected she was much better suited to speaking through her music. "Sometimes, I think it speaks for me," she tells him and apologizes, because she often apologizes when she's actually done nothing wrong. The Collector grins and laughs softly and taps the side of his nose with his left index finger.

"The way I see it, language is language is language," he says. "Words or music, bird songs or all the fancy, flashing colors made by chemoluminescent squids, what's the difference? I'll take conversation however I can wrangle it." And then he unlocks one of the desk drawers with a tiny brass-colored key and takes out the case containing the Belgian violin.

"If words don't come when you call them, then, by all means, please, talk to me with this," and he flips up the latches on the side of the case and opens it so she can see the instrument cradled inside.

"Oh my," she says, all her awkwardness and unease forgotten at the sight of the ammonite violin. "I've never seen anything like it. Never. It's lovely. No, it's much, *much* more than lovely."

"Then you will play it for me?"

"May I touch it?" she asks, and he laughs again.

"I can't imagine how you'll play it otherwise."

Ellen gently lifts the violin from its case, the way that some people might lift a newborn child, or a Minoan vase, or a stoppered bottle of nitroglycerine, the way the Collector would lift a particularly fragile ammonite from its bed of excelsior. It's heavier than any violin she's held before, and she guesses that the unexpected weight must be from the fossil shells set into the instrument. She wonders how they will affect the sound, those five ancient stones, how they might warp and alter this violin's voice.

"It's never been played, except by the man who made it, and that hardly seems to count. You, my dear, will be the very first."

And she almost asks him why *her,* because surely, for what he's paying, he could have lured some other, more talented player out here to his little yellow house. Surely someone a bit more celebrated, more accomplished, someone who doesn't have to take in students to make the rent, but would still be flattered and intrigued enough by the offer to come all the way to this squalid little village by the sea and play the fat man's violin for him. But then she thinks it would be rude, and she almost apologizes for a question she hasn't even asked.

As if he might have read her mind, and so maybe she should have apologized after all, the Collector shrugs his shoulders and dabs at the corners of his mouth with a white linen handkerchief he's pulled from a shirt pocket. "The universe is a marvelously complex bit of craftsmanship," he says. "And sometimes one must look very closely to even begin to understand how a given thing connects with another. Your late sister, for instance – "

"My *sister?*" she asks and looks up, surprised and glancing away from the ammonite violin and into the friendly, smiling eyes of the Collector. All at once, there's a cold knot deep in her belly and an unpleasant pricking sensation along her forearms and the back of her neck, goose bumps and histrionic ghost-story clichés, and now the violin feels unclean and dangerous, and she wants to return it to its case. "What do you know about my sister?"

The Collector blushes and peers down at his hands, folded there in front of him on the desk. He begins to speak and stammers, as if, possibly, he's really no better with words than she.

"What do you know about my sister?" Ellen asks again. "How do you know about her?"

The Collector frowns and licks nervously at his chapped lips. "I'm sorry," he says. "That was terribly tactless of me. I should not have brought it up."

"*How* do you know about my sister?"

"It's not exactly a secret, is it?" the Collector asks, letting his eyes drift by slow, calculated degrees from his hands and the desktop to her face. "I do read the newspapers. I don't usually watch television, but I imagine it was there, as well. She was murdered – "

"They don't *know* that. No one knows that for sure. She is *missing,*" the violinist says, hissing the last word between clenched teeth.

"Well, then she's been missing for quite some time," the Collector replies, feeling the smallest bit braver now and beginning to suspect he hasn't quite overplayed his hand.

"But they do not know that she's been murdered. They don't know that. No one ever found her body," and then Ellen decides that she's said far too much and stares down at the fat man's violin. She can't imagine how she ever thought it a lovely thing, only a moment or two before, this grotesque *parody* of a violin resting in her lap. It's more like a gargoyle, she thinks, or a sideshow freak, or a sick, sick joke, and suddenly she wants very badly to wash her hands.

"Please forgive me," the Collector says, sounding as sincere and contrite as any lonely man in a yellow house by the sea has ever sounded. "I am unaccustomed to company. I forget myself and say things I shouldn't. Please, Ellen. Play it for me. You've come all this way, and I would so love to hear you play. It would be such a pity if I've gone and spoiled it all with a few inconsiderate words. I so admire your work."

"No one *admires* my work," she replies, wondering how long it would take the taxi to show up and carry her back over the muddy, murky river, past the rows of empty warehouses to the depot, and how long she'd have to wait for the next train to New York. "I still don't even understand how you found me."

And at this opportunity to redeem himself, the Collector's face brightens, and he leans across the desk towards her. "Then I will tell you, if that will put your mind at ease. I saw you play at an art opening in Manhattan, you and your sister, a year or so back. At a gallery on Mercer Street. It was called…damn, it's right on the tip of my tongue."

"Eyecon," Ellen says, almost whispering. "The name of the gallery is Eyecon."

"Yes, yes, that's it. Thank you. I thought it was such a very silly name for a gallery, but then I've never cared for puns and wordplay. It was at a reception for a French painter, Albert Perrault, and I confess I found him quite completely hideous, and his paintings were dreadful, but I loved listening to the two of you play. I called the gallery, and they were nice enough to tell me how I could contact you."

"I didn't like his paintings, either. That was the last time we played together, my sister and I," Ellen says, and she presses a thumb to the ammonite shell that forms the violin's scroll.

"I didn't know that. I'm sorry, Ellen. I wasn't trying to dredge up bad memories."

"It's not a *bad* memory," she says, wishing it were all that simple and that were exactly the truth, and then she reaches for the violin's bow, which is still lying in the case lined with silk dyed the color of ripe pomegranates.

"I'm sorry," the Collector says again, certain now that he hasn't frightened her away, that everything is going precisely as planned. "Please, I only want to hear you play again."

"I'll need to tune it," Ellen tells him, because she's come this far, and she needs the money, and there's nothing the fat man has said that doesn't add up.

"Naturally," he replies. "I'll go to the kitchen and make us another pot of tea, and you can call me whenever you're ready."

"I'll need a tuning fork," she says, because she hasn't seen any sign of a piano in the yellow house. "Or if you have a metronome that has a tuner, that would work."

The Collector promptly produces a steel tuning fork from another of the drawers, and slides it across the desk to the violinist. She thanks him, and when he's left the room and she's alone with the ammonite violin and all the tall cases filled with fossils and the amber wash of incandescent bulbs, she glances at a window and sees that it's already dark outside. *I will play for him,* she thinks. *I'll play on his violin, and drink his tea, and smile, and then he'll pay me for my time and trouble. I'll go back to the city, and tomorrow or the next day, I'll be glad that I didn't chicken out. Tomorrow or the next day, it'll all seem silly, that I was afraid of a sad old man who lives in an ugly yellow house and collects rocks.*

"I will," she says out loud. "That's exactly how it will go," and then Ellen begins to tune the ammonite violin.

And after he brings her a rickety old music stand, something that looks like it has survived half a century of high-school marching bands, he sits behind his desk, sipping a fresh cup of tea, and she sits in the overlapping pools of light from the display cases. He asked for Paganini; specifically, he asked for Paganini's Violin Concerto No. 3 in E. She would have preferred something contemporary – Górecki, maybe, or Philip Glass, a little something she knows from memory – but he had the sheet music for Paganini, and it's his violin, and he's the one who's writing the check.

"Now?" she asks, and he nods his head.

"Yes, please," he replies and raises his tea cup as if to toast her.

So Ellen lifts the violin, supporting it with her left shoulder, bracing it firmly with her chin, and studies the sheet music a moment or two more before she begins. *Introduzione, allegro marziale,* and she wonders if he expects to hear all three movements, start to finish, or if he'll stop her when he's heard enough. She takes a deep breath and begins to play.

From his seat at the desk, the Collector closes his eyes as the lilting voice of the ammonite violin fills the room. He closes his eyes tightly and remembers another winter night, almost an entire year come and gone since then, but it might only have been yesterday, so clear are his memories. His collection of suffocations may indeed be more commonplace, as he has been led to conclude, but it is also the less frequently indulged of his two passions. He could never name the date and place of each and every ammonite acquisition, but in his brain the Collector carries a faultless accounting of all the suffocations. There have been sixteen, sixteen in twenty-one years, and now it has been almost one year to the night since the most recent. Perhaps, he thinks, he should have waited for the anniversary, but when the package arrived from Belgium, his enthusiasm and impatience got the better of him. When he wrote the violinist his lilac-scented note, he wrote "at your earliest possible convenience" and underlined "earliest" twice.

And here she is, and Paganini flows from out the ammonite violin just as it flowed from his car stereo that freezing night, one year ago, and his heart is beating so fast, so hard, racing itself and all his bright and breathless memories.

Don't let it end, he prays to the sea, whom he has faith can hear the prayers of all her supplicants and will answer those she deems worthy. *Let it go on and on and on. Let it never end.*

He clenches his fists, digging his short nails deep into the skin of his palms, and bites his lip so hard that he tastes blood. And the taste of those few drops of his own life is not so very different from holding the sea inside his mouth.

At last, I have done a perfect thing, he tells himself, himself and the sea and the ammonites and the lingering souls of all his suffocations.

So many years, so much time, so much work and money, but finally I have done this one perfect thing. And then he opens his eyes again, and also he opens the top middle drawer of his desk and takes out the revolver that once belonged to his father, who was a Gloucester fisherman who somehow managed never to collect anything at all.

Her fingers and the bow dance wild across the strings, and in only a few minutes Ellen has lost herself inside the giddy tangle of harmonics and drones and double stops, and if ever she has felt magic – *true* magic – in her art, then she feels it now. She lets her eyes drift from the music stand and the printed pages, because it is all right there behind her eyes and burning on her fingertips. She might well have written these lines herself and then spent half her life playing at nothing else, they rush through her with such ease and confidence. This is ecstasy, and this is abandon, and this is the tumble and roar of a thousand other emotions she seems never to have fully felt before this night. The strange violin no longer seems unusually heavy; in fact, it hardly seems to have any weight at all.

Perhaps there is no violin, she thinks. *Perhaps there never was a violin, only my hands and empty air, and that's all it takes to make music like this.*

Language is language is language, the fat man said, and so these chords have become her words. No, not words, but something so much less indirect than the clumsy interplay of her tongue and teeth, larynx and palate. They have become, simply, her language, as they ever have been. Her soul speaking to the world, and all the world need do in return is *listen.*

She shuts her eyes, no longer requiring them to grasp the progression from one note to the next, and at first there is only the comfortable darkness behind her lids, which seems better matched to the music than all the distractions of her eyes.

Don't let it stop, she thinks, not praying, unless this is a prayer to herself, for the violinist has never seen the need for gods. *Please, let it be like this forever. Let this moment never end, and I will never have to stop playing, and there will never again be silence or the noise of human thoughts and conversation.*

It can't be that way, Ellen, her sister whispers, not whispering in her ear, but from somewhere within the Paganini concerto, or from within the ammonite violin, or both at once. *I wish I could give you that. I would give you that, if it were mine to give.*

And then Ellen sees, or hears, or simply *understands* in this language which is *her* language, as language is language is language, the fat man's hands about her sister's throat. Her sister dying somewhere cold near the sea, dying all alone except for the company of her murderer, and there is half an instant when she almost stops playing.

No, her sister whispers, and that one word comes like a blazing gash across the concerto's whirl. Ellen doesn't stop playing, and she doesn't open her eyes, and she watches as her lost sister slowly dies.

The music is a typhoon gale flaying rocky shores to gravel and sand, and the violinist lets it spin and rage, and she watches as the fat man takes four of her sister's fingers and part of a thighbone, strands of her ash-blonde hair, a vial of oil boiled and distilled from the fat of her breasts, a pink-white section of small intestine – all these things and the five fossils from off an English beach to make the instrument he wooed her here to play for him. And now there are tears streaming hot down her cheeks, but still Ellen plays the violin that was her sister, and still she doesn't open her eyes.

The single gunshot is very loud in the room, and the display cases rattle, and a few of the ammonites slip off their Lucite stands and clatter against wood or glass or other spiraled shells.

And finally the violinist opens her eyes.

And the music ends as the bow slides from her fingers and falls to the floor at her feet.

"No," she says, "please don't let it stop, please," but the echo of the revolver and the memory of the concerto are so loud in her ears that her own words are almost lost to her.

That's all, her sister whispers, louder than any suicide's gun, soft as a midwinter night coming on, gentle as one unnoticed second bleeding into the next. *I've shown you, and now there isn't any more.*

Across the room, the Collector still sits at his desk, but now he's slumped a bit in his chair, and his head is thrown back so that he seems to be staring at something on the ceiling. Blood spills from the black cavern of his open mouth and drips to the floor.

There isn't any more.

And when she's stopped crying and is quite certain that her sister will not speak to her again, that all the secrets she has any business seeing have been revealed, the violinist retrieves the dropped bow and stands, then walks to the desk and returns the ammonite violin to its case. She will not give it to the police when they arrive, after she has gone to the kitchen to call them, and she will not tell them that it was the fat man who gave it to her. She will take it back to Brooklyn, and they will find other incriminating things in another room in the yellow house and so have no need of the violin and these stolen shreds of her sister. The Collector has kindly written everything down in three books bound in red leather, all the names and dates and places, and there are other souvenirs, besides. And she will never try to put this story into words, for words have never come easily to her, and like the violin, the story is hers now and hers alone.

For Robin Hazen

THE AMMONITE VIOLIN (MURDER BALLAD NO. 4)

Sometimes we wear our inspirations on our sleeve, and they are not the least bit cryptic. That's surely the case with this story, a retelling of a classic murder ballad, "The Twa Sisters," the earliest known variant of which appears in 1656. My childhood in the foothills of the Appalachians was filled with murder ballads, what my mother called dead-baby songs. As an adult, they inform my fiction. Special thanks to Indrid Em (Robin Hazen), a luthier who gave me invaluable technical advice while I was writing "The Ammonite Violin."

A Season of Broken Dolls

August 14, 2027

Sabit's the one with a hard-on for stitchwork, not me. It is not exactly (or at all) my particular realm of expertise, not my cuppa, not my *scene* – as the beatniks used to say, back there in those happy Neolithic times. I mean the plethora of Lower Manhattan flesh-art dives like Guro/Guro or Twist or that pretentious little shitstain way down on Pearl – *Corpus Ex Machina* – the one that gets almost as much space in the police blotters as in the glossy snip-art rags. Me, I'm still laboring alone or nearly so in the Dark Ages, and she never lets me forget it. My unfashionable and unprofitable preoccupation with mere canvas and paint, steel and plaster, all that which has been deemed *démodé, passé,* Post-Relevant, all that which is fit only to fill up musty old museum vaults and public galleries, gathering more dust even than my career. *You still write on a goddamn keyboard, for chris'sakes,* she laughs. *You're the only woman I ever fucked made being a living fossil a goddamn point of pride.* And then Sabit checks for my pulse – two fingers pressed gently to a wrist or the side of my throat – bcause, hey, maybe I'm not a living fossil at all. Maybe I'm that other kind, like Pollack and Mondrian, Henry Moore and poor old Man Ray. *No, no, no, the blood's still flowing sluggishly along,* she smiles and lights a cigarette. *Too bad. Maybe there's hope for you yet, my love.* Sabit likes to talk almost as much as she likes to watch. It's not as though the bitch has a mark on her hide anywhere, not as though she's anything but a tourist with a hard-on, a fetishist who cannot ever get enough of her kink. Prick her for a crimson bead and the results would come back same as mine, 98% the same as any chimpanzee. She knows how much contempt is reserved in those quarters for tourists and trippers, but I think that only makes her more zealous. She exhales, and smoke lingers like a unearned halo about her face. I should have dumped her months ago, but I'm not as young as I used to be, and I'm just as addicted to sex as she is to nicotine and pills and vicarious stitchwork. She calls herself a poet, but she has never let me read a word she's written, if she's ever written a word. I found her a year ago, almost a year ago, found her in a run-down titty bar getting fucked up on vodka and laudanum and speed and the too-firm silicone breasts of women who might have been the real thing – even if their perfect boobs were not – or might only have been cheap japandroids. She followed me home, fifteen years my junior, and the more things change, the more things stay the way they were day before day before yesterday, day before I met Sabit and her slumberous Arabian eyes. My sloe-eyed stitch-fiend of a girlfriend, and I have her, and she has me, and we're as happy as happy can be, and I pretend it means something more than orgasms and not being alone, something more than me annoying her and her taunting ~~and insulting~~ me. Now she's telling me there's a new line-up down @ *Corpus Ex Machina* (hereafter known simply as *CeM*), and we have to be there tomorrow night. *We have to be there*, she says. *The Trenton Group is showing, and last time the Trenton Group showed, there was almost a riot, so we have to be there.* I have deadlines that have nothing whatsoever to do with that constantly revolving meat-market spectacle, and in a moment I'll finish this entry & then I'll tell her that, and she'll tell me we have to be there, we have to be there, & there will be time to finish my articles later. There always is, & I'm never late. Never late enough to matter. I'll go with her, bcause I do not trust her to go alone – not go alone *and* come back here again – she'll tell me that, and she'll be right as fucking rain. Her smug triumph, well that's a given. Just as my obligatory refusal followed by inevitable, reluctant acquiescence is also a given. We play by the same rules every time. Now she's on about some scandal @ Guro/Guro – chicanery and artifice, prosthetics, and she says, *They're all a bunch of gidding poseurs, the shitheels run that sorry dump. Someone ought to burn it to the ground for this.* You know how to light a match, I reply, & she rolls her dark eyes @ me. No rain today. No rain since…June. The sky at noon is the color of rust, and I wish it were winter. Enough for now. Maybe she'll shut up for 10 or 15 if I fuck her.

August 16, 2027

"You're into that whole *scene,* right?" Which only shows to go once again that my editor still has her head rammed so far up her ass that her farts smell like toothpaste. But I said yeah, sure, bcause she wanted someone with cred on the Guro/Guro story, the stitch chicanery, allegations of fraud among the freaks, & what else was I supposed to say? I can't remember the last time I had the nerve to turn down a paying assignment. Must have been years before I met Sabit, at least. So, yeah, I tagged along last night, just like she wanted – both of them wanted – she & she, but @ least I can say it's work, and Berlin picked up the tab. Sabit's out, so I don't have her yammering in my goddamn ear, an hour to myself, perhaps, half an hour, however long it takes her to get back with dinner. I wanted to put something down, something that isn't in the notes and photos I've already filed with the pre-edit gleets. Fuck. I've been popping caps from Sabit's pharmacopoeia all goddamn day long, I don't even know what, the baby-blue ones she gets $300/two dozen from Peru, the ones she says calm her down but they're not calming me down. They haven't even dulled the edge, so far as I can tell. But, anyway, there we were @ *CeM,* in the crowded Pearl St. warehouse passing itself off as a *slaughter*house or a zoo or an exhibition or what the fuck ever, and there's this bird from Tokyo, and I never got her name, but she had eyes all the colors of peacock feathers, iridescent eyes, and she recognized me. Some monied bird with pretty peacock eyes. She'd read the series I wrote in '21 when the city finally gave up and let the sea have the subway. *I read a lot,* she said. *I might have been a journalist myself,* she said. That sort of shit. Thought she was going to ask me to sign a goddamn cocktail napkin. And I'm smiling & nodding yes, bcause that's agency policy, be nice to the readers, don't feed the pigeons, whatever. But I can't take my eyes off the walls. The walls are new. They were just walls last time Sabit dragged me down to one of her snip affairs. Now they're alive, every square inch, mottled shades of pink and gray and whatever you call that shade between pink and gray. Touch them (Sabit must have touched them a hundred times) and they twitch or sprout goose bumps. They sweat, those walls. And the peacock girl was in one ear, and Sabit was in the other, the music so loud I was already getting a headache before my fourth drink, and I was trying to stop looking at those walls. *Pig,* Sabit told me later in the evening. *It's all just pig,* and she sounded disappointed. Most of this is in the notes, though I didn't say how unsettling I found those walls of skin. I save the revulsion for my own dime. Sabit says they're working on adding functional genitalia and…fuck. I hear her at the door. Later, then. She has to shut up and go to sleep eventually.

August 16, 2027 (later, 11:47 p.m.)

Sabit came back with a bag full of Indian takeaway, when she'd gone out for sushi. I really couldn't care less, one way or the other, these days food is only fucking food – curry or wasabi, but when I *asked* why she'd changed her mind, she just stared at me, eyes blank as a goddamn dead codfish, & shrugged. Then she was quiet all night long, & the last thing I need just now is Sabit Abbasi going all silent and creepy on me. She's asleep, snoring bcause her sinuses are bad bcause she smokes too much. & I'm losing the momentum I needed to say *anything* more about what happened @ *CeM* on Sat. night. It's all fading, like a dream. I've been reading one of Sabit's books, *The Breathing Composition* (Welleran Smith, 2025), something from those long-ago days when the avant-garde abomination of stitch & snip was still hardly more than nervous rumor & theory & the wishful thinking of a handful of East Coast art pervs. I don't know what I was looking for, if it was just research for the article, don't know what I thought I might find – or what any of this has to do with Sat. nite. Am I afraid to write it down? That's what Sabit would say. But I won't ask Sabit. What do *you* dream, Sabit, my dear sadistic plaything? Do you *dream* in installations, muscles and tendons, gallery walls of sweating pig flesh, living bone exposed for all to see, vivisection as not-quite still life, portrait of the artist as a young atrocity? Are your sweet dreams the same things keeping me awake, making me afraid to sleep? There was so goddamn much @ *CeM* to turn my fucking stomach, but just this one thing has me jigged and sleepless and popping your blue Peruvian bon bons. Just this one thing. I'm not the squeamish sort, and everyone knows it. That's one reason the agency tossed the Guro/Guro story at me. Gore & sex and mutilation? Give it to Schuler. She's seen the worst and keeps coming back for more. Wasn't she one of the first into Brooklyn after the bomb? & she did that crazy whick out on the Stuyvesant rat attacks. How many murders and suicides and serial killers does that make for Schuler now? 9? Fourteen? 38? That kid in the Bronx, the Puerto Rican bastard who sliced up his little sister & then fed her through a food processor, that was one of Schuler's, yeah? *Ad infinitum, ad nauseam,* hail Mary, full of beans. Cause they know I won't be on my knees puking up lunch when I should be making notes & getting the vid or asking questions. But now, *now* Sabit, I'm dancing round this one thing. This one little thing. So, here there's a big ol' chink in these renowned nerves of steel. Maybe I've got a weak spot after fucking all. Rings of flesh, towers of iron – oh yeah, sure – fucking corpses heaped in dumpsters and rats eating fucking babies alive & winos & don't forget the kid with the Cuisinart – sure, fine – but that one labeled #17, oh, now *that's* another goddamn story. She saw something there, & ol' Brass-Balls Schuler was never quite the same again, isn't that the way it goes?

Are you laughing in your dreams, Sabit? Is that why you're smiling next to me in your goddamn sleep? I've dog-eared a page in your book, Sabit, a page with a poem written in a New Jersey loony bin by a woman, & Welleran Smith just calls her Jane Doe so I do not know her name. But Welleran Smith & that mangy bunch of stitch prophets called her a visionary, & I'm writing it down here, while I try to find the nerve to say whatever it is I'd wanted to say about #17:

spines and bellies knitted & proud and all open
all watching spines and bellies and the three;
triptych & buckled, ragdoll fusion
3 of you so conjoined, my eyes from yours,
arterial hallways knitted red proud flesh
Healing and straining for cartilage & epidermis
Not taking, we cannot imagine
So many wet lips, your sky Raggedy alchemy
And all expecting Jerusalem

And Welleran Smith, he proclaims Jane Doe a "hyperlucid transcendent schizo-oracle," a "visionary calling into the maelstrom." & turns out, here in the footnotes, they put the bitch away bcause she'd drugged her lover – she was a lesbian; of course, she had to be a lesbian – she drugged her lover and used surgical thread to sew the woman's lips & nostrils closed, *after* performing a crude tracheotomy so she wouldn't suffocate. Jane Doe sewed her own vagina shut, and she removed her own nipples & then tried grafting them onto her gf's belly. She kept the woman (not named, sorry, lost to anonymity) cuffed to a bed for almost 6 weeks before someone finally came poking around & jesus fucking christ, Sabit, this is the sort of sick bullshit set it all in motion. Jane Doe's still locked away in her padded cell, I'm guessing – *hyperlucid* & worshipped by the snips – & maybe the woman she mutilated is alive somewhere, trying to forget. Maybe the doctors even patched her up (ha, ha fucking ha). Maybe even made her good as new again, but I doubt it. I need to sleep. I need to lie down & close my eyes & not see #17 and sweating walls and Sabit ready to fucking cum bcause she can never, ever get enough. It's half an hour after midnight, & they expect copy from me tomorrow night, eight sharp, when I haven't written a goddamn word about the phony stitchwork @ Guro/Guro. Fuck you, Sabit, and fuck Jane Doe & that jackoff Welleran Smith and the girl with peacock eyes that I should have screwed just to piss you off, Sabit. I should have brought her back here and fucked her in our bed, let her use your toothbrush, & maybe you'd have found some other snip tourist & even now I could be basking in the sanguine cherry glow of happily ever fucking after.

August 18, 2027

I'm off the Guro/Guro story. Missed the *extended* DL tonight, no copy, never even made it down to the gallery. Just my notes and photos from *CeM* for someone else to pick up where I left off. Lucky the agency didn't let me go. Lucky or unlucky. But they can't can me, not for missing a deadline or two. I have rep, I have creds, I have awards & experience & loyal goddamn readers. Hell, I still get a byline on this thing; it's in my contract. Fuck it. Fuck it all.

August 19, 2027

Welleran Smith's "Jane Doe" died about six months ago, back in March. I asked some questions, said it was work for the magazine, tagged some people who know people who could get to the files. It was a suicide – oh, and never you mind that she'd been on suicide watch for years. This one was a certified trooper, a bona-fide martyr in the service of her own undoing. She chewed her tongue in half & choked herself on it. She had a name, too. Don't know if Smith knew it & simply withheld it, or if he never looked that far. Maybe he only prigged the bits he needed to put the snips in orbit & disregarded the rest. "Jane Doe" was Judith Louise Darger, born 1992, Ph.D. in Anthropology from Yale, specialized in urban neomythology, syncretism, etc. & did a book with HarperC back in '21 – *Bloody Mary, La Llorona, and the Blue Lady: Feminine Icons in a Fabricated Child's Apocalypse*. Sold for shit, out of print by 2023. But found a battered copy cheap uptown @ Paper Museum. Darger's gf and victim, she's dead, too. Another suicide, not long after they put Darger away. Turns out, she had a history of neurosis and *self*-mutilation going back to high school, & there was all sorts of shit there I'm not going to get into, but she told the courts that what Darger did to her, and to herself, they'd planned the whole thing for months. So, why the fuck did good old Welleran Smith leave *that* part out? It was in the goddamn press, no secret. I have a photograph of Judith Darger, right here on the dj of her book. She could not look less remarkable. Sabit says there's another Trenton Group show this weekend & don't I wanna to go? She's hardly said three words to me the last couple of days, but she told me this. Get another look at #17, she said, & I almost fucking hit her. No more pills, Schuler. No more pills. You're frying.

August 20, 2027

No sleep last night. Today, I filed for my next assignment, but so far the green bin's still empty. Maybe I'm being punished for blowing the DL on Weds. night, some sort of pass-ag bullshit bcause that's the best those weasels in senior edit can ever seem to manage. Or maybe it's only a sloooowwww week. I am having a hard time caring, either way. No sleep last night. No, I said that already. Time on my hands and that's never a good thing. Insomnia and black coffee and gin, takeaway and durian Pop-Tarts and a faint throb that wants to be a headache (how long since one of those?), me locked in my office last night reading a few chapters of Darger's grand flop, but there's nothing in there – fascinating and I don't know why it wasn't better received, but still leading me nowhere, nowhere at all (where did I *think* it would lead?). This bit re: La Llorona ("Bloody Mary") from Ch. 3 – "Some girls with no home feel claws scratching under the skin on their arms. Their hand [sic] looks like red fire." And this one, from a *Miami New Times* article: "When a child says he got the story from the spirit world, as homeless children do, you've hit the ultimate *non sequitur.*" Homeless kids and demons and angels, street gangs, drugs, the socioeconomic calamities of thirty goddamn years ago. News articles from 1997. A journalistic scam. None of this is gonna answer any of my questions, if I truly have questions to be answered. But this is "Jane Doe's" magnum opus, and there is some grim fascination I can't shake – How did she get from *there* to *there,* from phony diy street myths to sewing her gf's mouth shut? Maybe it wasn't such a short goddamn walk. Maybe, one night, she stood before a dark mirror in a darkened room, the mirror coated with dried saltwater – going native or just too fucking curious, whatever – and maybe she *stood* there chanting *Bloody Mary, Bloody Mary,* over and over and over and La Llorona scratched her way out through the looking glass, scarring the anthropologist's soul with her rosary beads. Maybe that's where this began, the snips and stitches, #17. Maybe it all goes back to those homeless kids in Miami, back before the flood, before the W. Antarctic ice sheet melted and Dade County FL sank like a stone, and all along it was the late Dr. J. L. Darger let this djinn out of its gin bottle in ways people like Sabit have not yet begun to suspect and never will. I'm babbling, and if that's the best I can do, I'm going to stop keeping a damned journal. I've agreed to be @ *CeM* tomorrow night with Sabit. I'm a big girl. I can sip my shitty Merlot and nibble greasy orange cheese and stale crackers with the best of them. I can bear the soulless conversation and the sweating porcine walls. I can look at #17 and see nothing there but bad art, fucked-up artless crap, pretentious carnage and willful suffering. Maybe then I can put *all* this shit behind me. Who knows, maybe I can even put Sabit behind me, too.

August 20, 2027 (later, p.m.)

Sabit says the surgeon on #17 will be at the show t'morrow night. I think maybe it's someone Sabit was screwing before she started screwing me. Oh, & this, from *The Breathing Composition,* which I've started reading again & frankly wish I had not. Seems Welleran Smith somehow got his paws on Darger's diary, or one of her diaries, & he quotes it at length (& no doubt there are contextual issues; don't know the fate of the original text):

"We are all alone on a darkling plain, precisely as Matt. Arnold said. We are so very alone here, and we yearn each day for the reunification promised by priests and gurus and by some ancient animal instinct. We are evolution's grand degenerates, locked away forever in the consummate prison cells of our conscious minds, each divided always from the other. I met a man from Spain, and he gave me a note card with the number seventeen written on it seventeen times. He thought that surely I would understand right away, and he was heartbroken when I did not. When I asked, he would not explain. I've kept the card in my files, and sometimes I take it out and stare at it, hoping that I will at last discern its message. But it remains perfectly opaque, bcause my eyes are the eyes of the damned."

& I'm looking thru the program for the Trenton Show on the 15th, last Sun., & only one piece is *numbered,* only 1 piece w/a # for a title – #17. Yes, I know. I'm going in circles here. Chasing my own ass. Toys in the attic. Nutters as the goddamn snips if I don't watch myself. If I don't get some sleep. I haven't seen Sabit all evening, just a call in this afternoon.

August 21, 2027 (Saturday, 10:12 a.m.)

Four whole hours sleep last night. & the hangover is not so bad that coffee and aspirin isn't helping. My head feels clearer than it has in days. Sabit came home sometime after I nodded off & I woke with her snoring next to me. When I asked if maybe she wanted breakfast, she smiled, so I made eggs & cut a grapefruit in half. Perhaps I can persuade her to stay home tonight, that we should *both* stay home tonight. There is nothing down there I need to see again.

August 21, 2027 (2:18 p.m.)

No, she says. *We are expected,* she says, & what the fuck is that supposed to mean, anyway? So there was a fight, bcause there always has to be a fight with Sabit, a real 4-alarm screamer this time, & I have no idea where she's run off to but she swore she'd be back by *five* & I better be sober, she said, & I better be dressed & ready for the show. So, yeah, fuck it. I'll go to the damn show with her. I'll rub shoulders with the stitch freaks this one last time. Maybe I'll even have a good long look at #17 (tho' now, I should add, now Sabit says the surgeon won't be there after all). Maybe I'll stand & stare until it's only flesh & wires & hooks & fancy lighting. Sidonie-Gabrielle Colette wrote somewhere, "Look for a long time at what pleases you, and for a longer time at what pains you." Maybe I'll shame them all with my staring. They only feel as much pain as they *want* to feel – isn't that what Sabit is always telling me? The stitchworks, they get all the best painkillers, ever since the Supreme Ct. wigs decided this sick shit constitutes Art – so long as certain lines are not crossed. They bask in glassy-eyed morphine hazes, shocked cold orange on neuroblocks & Fibrodene & Elyzzium, exotic transdermals & maybe all that shit's legal & maybe it ain't, but 2380 no one's asking too many questions as the City of NY has enough on its great collective plate these days w/out stitch-friendly lawyers raising a holy funk about censorship and freedom of expression and 1st Amendment violations. The cops hate the fuckers, but none of the arrests have had jack to do with drugs, just disorderly conduct, riots after shows, shit like that. But yeah, t'morrow night I'll go back to *CeM* with Sabit, my heart's damned desire, my cunt's lazy love, & I will look until they want to fucking charge me extra.

August 21, 2027

So Sabit shows up an hour or so after dark...she's gone now, gone again bcause I suppose I have chased her away, again. That's what she would say, I am sure. I have chased her away again. But, as I was saying, she shows up, & I can tell she's been drinking bcause she has that smirk and that swagger she gets when she's been drinking, & I can tell she's still pissed. I'm waiting for the other shoe. I'm waiting, bcause I fucking know whatever's coming next is for my benefit. & I'm thinking, screw it, get it over with, don't let her have the satisfaction of getting in the first blow. I'm thinking, this is where it ends. Tonight. No more of her bullshit. It's been a grandiose act of reciprocal masochism, Sabit, & it's been raw & all, but enough's enough. @ least the sex was good, so let's remember that & move on. & that's when I notice the gauze patch taped to her back, centered between her shoulder blades just so, placed *just so* there between her scapulae, centered on the smooth brown plain of her trapezius (let me write this the way a goddamn snip would write it, cluttered with an anatomist's Latin). & when I ask her what the fuck, she just shrugs, & that swatch of gauze goes up & then down again. But I know. I know whatever it is she's done, whatever comes next, this is it. This is her preemptive volley, so I can just forget all about landing the first punch this time, baby. Sabit knows revenge like a drunk knows an empty bottle, & I should have given up while I was ahead. *I've been wanting some ink,* she says. *You helped me to finally make up my mind, that's all.* & before she can say anything else, I rip away the bandage. She does not even fucking flinch, even though the tattoo can't be more than a couple hrs old, still seeping & puffy and red, & all I can hear is her laughing. Bcause there on her back is the Roman numeral XVII, & when she asks for the bandage back, I slap her. I *slapped* her. This use of present tense, what's that but keeping the wound open & fresh, keeping the scabs at bay just like some goddamn pathetic stitchwork would do. I *slapped* her. The sound of my hand against her cheek was so loud, crack like a goddamn firecracker, & in the silence afterwards (just as fucking loud) she just smiled & smiled & smiled for me. & then I started yelling – I don't know exactly what – accusations that couldn't possibly have made sense, slurs and insinuation, and truthfully I knew even then none of it was anything but bitterness & disappointment that she'd not only managed to draw first blood (hahaha) this round, she'd finally pushed me far enough to hit her. I'd never hit her before. I had never hit *anyone* before, not since some bullshit high school fights, &, at last, she did not even need to raise her voice. & then she just smiled @ me, & I think I must have finally told her to say something, bcause I was puking sick to death of that smug smile. *I'm glad you approve,* she said. Or maybe she said, *I'm glad you understand.* In this instance, the meanings would be the same somehow. Somehow interchangeable. But I did not apologize. That's the sort of prick I am. I sat down on the kitchen floor & stared @ linoleum Rorschach patterns & when I looked up again she was gone. I don't know if she's *gone,* gone, or if Sabit has merely retreated until she decides it's time for another blitz. Rethinking her maneuvers, the ins & outs of this campaign, logistics and field tactics & what the fuck ever. Cards must be played properly. I know Sabit, & she will never settle for Pyrrhic victory, no wars of attrition, no winner's curse. I sat on the floor until I heard the door shut & so knew I was alone again. I would say at least this gets me out of *CeM* on Sun. night, but I may go alone. Even though I know she'll be there. Clearly, I can hurt some more. Tonight I will get drunk, & that is all.

August 22, 2027 (2:56 a.m.)

Always have I been a sober drunk. I've finished the gin & started on an old bottle of rye whisky – gift from some former lover I won't name here – bcause I didn't feel like walking through the muggy, dusty evening, risking life and limb & lung for another pretty blue bottle of Bombay. A sober & lazy drunk, adverse to taking *unnecessary* risks. Sabit has not yet reappeared, likely she will not. I suspect she believes she has won not only the battle, but the war, as well. Good for her. May she go haunt some other sad fuck's life. Of course, the apt. is still awash in her junk, her clothes, her stitch lit, the hc zines and discs & her txtbooks filled with diagrams, schematics of skeletons & musculature, neuroanatomy, surgical technique, organic chem and pharmacology, immunology, all that crap. Snip porn. I should dump it all. I should call someone 2830 to cart it all away so I don't have to fucking look at it anymore. The clothes, her lucite ashtrays, the smoky, musky, spicy smell of her, bottles of perfume, cosmetics, music, Sanrio vibrators, jewelry, deodorant, jasmine soap, baby teeth & jesus all the *CRAP* she's left behind to keep me company. I don't know if I'll sleep tonight. I don't want to. I don't want to be awake anymore ever again. Why did she want to rub my nose in #17? Just that she's finally found a flaw, a goddamn weakness, & she has to make the most of it? A talkative, sober drunk. But wait – there is something. There is something else I found in Welleran Smith, & I'm gonna write it down. Something more from the diary/ies of Dr. Judith Darger, unless it's only something Smith concocted to suit his own ends. More & more I consider that likelihood, that Darger is only some lunatic just happened to be where these people needed her to be, but isn't that how it always is with saints and martyrs? Questions of victimhood arise. Who's exploiting who? Who's exploiting whom? Christ I get lost in all these words. I don't *need* words. I'm strangling on words. I need to see Sabit & end this mess & be done with her. According to Welleran Smith, Darger writes (none of the "entries" are dated): "I would not tell a child that it isn't going to hurt. I wouldn't lie. It is going to hurt, and it is going to hurt forever or as long as human consciousness may endure. It is going to hurt until it doesn't hurt anymore. That is what I would tell a child. That is what I tell myself, and what am I but my own child? So, I will not lie to any of you. Yes, there will be pain, and at times the pain will seem unbearable. But the pain will open doorways. The pain *is* a doorway, as is the scalpel and as are the sutures and each and every incision. Pain is to be thrown open wide that all may gaze at the wonders which lie beyond. Why is it assumed this flesh must not be cut? Why is it assumed this is my final corporeal form? What is it we cannot yet see for all our fear of pain and ugliness and disfiguration? I would not tell a child that it isn't going to hurt. I would teach a child to live in pain." Is that what I am learning from you, Sabit? Is that the lesson of #17 and the glassy stare of those six eyes? Would you, all of you, teach me to live with pain?

August 23, 2027

It's almost dawn, that first false dawn & just a bit of hesitant purple where the sky isn't quite night anymore. As much as I have ever seen false dawn in the city, where we try so hard to keep the night away forever. If I had a son, or a daughter, I would tell them a story, how people are @ war with night, & the city – like all cities – is only a fortress built to hold back the night, even though all the world is just a bit of grit floating in a sea of night that might go on almost forever. I'm on the roof. I've never been up here before. Sabit & I never came up here. Maybe another three hours left before it's too hot & bright to sit up here, only 95F now if my watch is telling me the truth. My face & hair are slick with sweat, sweating out the booze & pills, sweating out the sweet & sour memory of Sabit. It feels good to sweat. I went to Pearl St. & the Trenton reveal @ *Corpus ex Machina,* but apparently she did not. Maybe she had something better to do & someone better to be doing it with. I flashed my press tag @ the door, so at least I didn't have to pay the $47 cover. I was not the only pundit in attendance. I saw Kline, who's over @ the Voice these days (that venerable old whore) & I saw Garrison, too. Buzzards w/their beaks sharp, stomachs empty, mouths watering. No, I do not know if birds salivate, but reporters sure fucking do. None of them spoke to me, & I exchanged the favor. The place was *replete,* as the dollymops are wont to say, chock-full, standing room only. I sipped dirty martinis and licorice shides & looked no one in the eye, no one who was not on exhibit. #17 was near the back, not as well lit as some of the others, & I stood there & stared, bcause that is what I'd come for. Sometimes it gazed back @ me, or *they* gazed @ me – I am uncertain of the proper idiom or parlance or phrase. Is *it* One or are *they* 3? I stared & stared & stared, like any good voyeur would do, any dedicated peeper, bcause no clips are allowed, so you stand & drink it all in there the same way the Neanderthals did it or pony up the fat spool of cash for one of the Trenton chips or mnemonic lozenges ("all proceeds for R&D, promo, & ongoing medical expenses," of course). I looked until all I saw was all I was *meant* to see – the sculpted body(ies), living & breathing & conscious – the perpetually hurting realization of all Darger's nightmares. If I saw beauty there, it was no different from the *beauty* I saw in Brooklyn after the New Konsojaya Trading Co. popped their micro-nuke over on Tillary St. No different from the hundred lingering deaths I've witnessed. Welleran Smith said this was to be "the soul's terrorism against the tyranny of genes & phenotype." I stood there & I saw everything there was to see. Maybe Sabit would have been proud. Maybe she would have been disappointed @ my resolve. It hardly matters, either way. A drop of sweat dissolving on my tongue & I wonder if that's the way the ocean used to taste, when it wasn't suicide to taste the ocean? When I had seen all I had come to see, my communion w/#17, I found an empty stool @ the bar. I thought you might still put in an appearance, Sabit, so I got drunker & waited for a glimpse of you in the crowd. & there was a man sitting next to me, Harvey somebody or another from Chicago, gray-haired with a mustache, & he talked & I listened, as best I could hear him over the music. I think the music was suffocating me. He said, *That's my granddaughter over there, what's left of her,* & he pointed thru the crush of bodies toward a stitchwork hanging from the warehouse ceiling, a dim chandelier of circuitry & bone & muscles flayed & rearranged. I'd looked at the piece on the way in – *The Lighthouse of Francis Bacon,* it was called. The old man told me he'd been following the show for months, but now he was almost broke & would have to head back to Chicago soon. He was only drinking ginger ale. I bought him a ginger ale & listened, leaning close so he didn't have to shout to be heard. The chandelier had once been a student @ the Pritzker School of Medicine, but then, he said, "something happened." I did not ask what. I decided if he wanted me to know, he would tell me. He didn't. Didn't tell me, I mean. He tried to buy me a drink, but I wouldn't let him. The grandfather of the *Lighthouse of Francis Bacon* tried to buy me a drink, & I realized I was thinking like a journalist again, thinking *you dumb fucks – here's your goddamn story – not some bullshit hearsay about chicanery among the snips, no, this old man's your goddamn story, this poor guy probably born way the fuck back before man even walked on the goddamn moon & now he's sitting here at the end of the world, this anonymous old man rubbing his bony shoulders with the tourists and art critics & stitch fiends and freaks because his granddaughter decided she'd rather be a fucking light fixture than a gynecologist.* Oh god, Sabit. If you could have shown him your brand-new tattoo. I left the place before midnight, paid the hack extra to go farther south, to get me as near the ruins as he dared. I needed to see them, that's all. Rings of flesh & towers of iron, right, rust-stained granite and the empty eye sockets where once were windows. The skyscraper stubs of Old Downtown, Wall St. and Battery Park City, all hurricane aftermaths of it inundated by the rising waters there @ the confluence of the Hudson & the E. River. And then I came home, & now I am sitting here on the roof, getting less & less drunk, sweating & listening to traffic & the city waking up around me – the living fossil with her antique keyboard. If you do come back here, Sabit, if that's whatever happens next, you will not find me intimidated by your XVII or by #17, either, but I don't think you ever will. You've moved on. & if you send someone to pack up your shit, I'll probably already be in Bratislava by then. After *CeM*, there were 2 good assigns waiting for me in the green bin, & I'm taking the one that gets me far, far, farthest away from here for 3 weeks in Slovakia. But right now I'm just gonna sit here on the roof & watch the sun come up all swollen & lobster red over this rotten, drowning city, over this rotten fucking world. I think the pigeons are waking up.

A SEASON OF BROKEN DOLLS

During the winter of 2007, I was plagued by a terrible recurring dream. It came almost every night, and I'd spend the days in between the dream's recurrence in a foggy state I have called *dreamsickness*. The dream, recorded in my LiveJournal (December 18, 2006 – March 11, 2007) and in the chapbook *B is for Beginnings* (Subterranean Press, 2009), left me with two short stories. I needed the dream visitation of what felt like a thoroughly authentic parallel life to end, and I meant to kill it with a short story. Two were required. "A Season of Broken Dolls" is the first, and is far less literal than the second, "In View of Nothing." At the time I chided myself for abstracting the dream so entirely in "A Season of Broken Dolls," but now I consider it one of my best pieces of science fiction.

In View of Nothing

Oh, pity us here, we angels of lead.
We're dead, we're sick, hanging by thread...
David Bowie ("Get Real," 1995)

02. The Bed

My breasts ache.

I have enough trouble just remembering the name of this city, and I have yet to be convinced that the name remains the same from one day to the next, one night to the next night. Or even that the city itself remains the same. These are the very sorts of details that will be my undoing someday, someday quite soon, if I am anything less than mindful. Today, I believe that I have awakened in Sakyo-ku, in the Kyoto Prefecture, but lying here staring up at the bright banks of fluorescent lights on the ceiling, I might be anywhere. I might well be in Boston or Johannesburg or Sydney, and maybe I've never even been to Japan. Maybe I have lived my entire life without setting foot in Kyoto.

From where I lie, almost everything seems merely various shades of unwelcome conjecture. Almost everything. I think about getting up and going to the window, because from there I might confirm or deny my Kyoto hypothesis. I might spy the Kamo River, flowing down from its source on Mount Sajikigatake, or the withered cherry trees that did not blossom last year and perhaps will not blossom this spring, either. I might see the silver-grey ribbon of the Kamo, running between the neon-scarlet flicker of torii gates at the Kamigamo and Shimogamo shrines. Maybe that window looks eastward, towards the not-so-distant ocean, and I would see Mount Daimonji. Or I might see only the steel and glass wall of a neighboring skyscraper.

I lie where I am and do not go to the window, and I stare up at the low plaster ceiling, the ugly water stains spread out there like bruises or melanoma or concentric geographical features on an ice moon of Saturn or Jupiter or Neptune. This whole goddamn building is rotten; I recall that much clearly enough. The ceiling of my room – if it *is* my room – has more leaks than I can count, and I think it's not even on the top floor. The rain is loud against the window, but the dripping ceiling seems to my ears much louder, as each drop grows finally too heavy and falls to the ceramic tiles. I hear a distinct *plink* for each and every drop that drips down from the motel ceiling, and that *plink* does not quite seem to match what I recall about the sound of water dripping against tile.

The paler-than-oyster sheets are damp, too. As are the mattress and box springs underneath. Why there are not mushrooms, I can't say. There is mold, mold or mildew if there's some difference between the two, because I can smell it, and I can see it. I can taste it.

I lie here on my back and stare up at the leaky ceiling, listening to the rain, letting these vague thoughts ricochet through my incontinent skull. My mind leaks, too, I suspect, and in much the same way that this ceiling leaks. My thoughts and memories have stained the moldering sheets, discrete units of me drifting away in a slow flood of cerebrospinal fluid, my ears for sluice gates – or my eyes – *Liquor cerebrospinalis* draining out a few precious milliliters per day or hour, leaving only vast echoes in emptied subarachnoid cavities.

She looks at me over her left shoulder, her skin as white as snow that never falls, her hair whiter still, her eyes like broken sapphire shards, and she frowns, knitting her white eyebrows. She is talking into the antique black rotary telephone, but looking at me, disapproving of these meandering, senseless thoughts when I have yet to answer her questions to anyone's satisfaction. I turn away – the exact wrong thing to do, and yet I do it, anyway. I wish she would put some clothes on. Her robe is hanging on a hook not far away. I would get it for her, if she would only ask. She lights a cigarette, and that's good, because now the air wrapped all about the bed smells less like the mold and poisonous rainwater.

"We do the best we can," she tells the telephone, whoever's listening on the other end of the line, "given what we have to work with."

Having turned away, I lie on my left side, my face pressed into those damp sheets, shivering and wondering how long now since I have been genuinely warm. Wondering, too, if this season is spring or winter or autumn. I am fairly certain it is not summer. She laughs, but I don't shut my eyes. I imagine that the folds and creases of the sheets are ridges and valleys, and I am the slain giant of some creation myth. My cerebrospinal fluid will form lakes and rivers and seas, and trees will sprout, and grass and ferns and lichen, and all that vegetation shall be imbued with my lost, or merely forfeited, memories. The birds will rise up from fancies that have bled from me.

My breasts ache.

Maybe that has some role to play in this cosmogony, the aching, swollen breasts of the fallen giantess whose mind became the wide white-grey world.

"I need more time, that's all," the naked snow-coloured woman tells the black Bakelite handset. "There were so many more layers than we'd anticipated."

With an index finger I trace the course of one of the V-shaped sheet valleys. It gradually widens towards the foot of the bed, towards my *own* feet, and I decide that I shall arbitrarily call that direction *south,* as I arbitrarily think this motel might exist somewhere in Kyoto. Where it ends, there is a broad alluvial fan, this silk-cotton blend splaying out into flat deltas where an unseen river at last deposits its burden of mnemonic silt and clay and sand – only the finest particles make it all the way over the far away edge of the bed to the white-tile sea spread out below. Never meaning to, I have made a *flat* white-grey world. Beyond the delta are low hills, smooth ridges in the shadow of my knees. Call it an eclipse, that gloom; *any* shadow in this stark room is Divine.

These thoughts are leading me nowhere, and I think now that they must exist only to erect a defence, this complete absence of direction. She has pried and stabbed and pricked that fragile innermost stratum of the meningeal envelope, the precious pia matter, and so triggered inside me these meandering responses. She thought to find only pliable grey matter waiting underneath, and maybe the answers to her questions – tap in, cross ref, download – but, no, here's this damned firewall, instead. But I did not put it there. I am holding nothing back by choice. I know she won't believe that, though it is the truth.

"Maybe another twelve hours," she tells the handset.

I must be a barren, pitiless goddess, to have placed all those fluorescent tubes for a sun and nothing else. They shed no warmth from out that otherwise starless ivory firmament. Heaven drips to make a filthy sea, and she rings off and places the handset back into its

Bakelite cradle. It is all a cradle, I think, this room in this motel in this city I cannot name with any certainty. Perhaps I never even left Manhattan or Atlanta or San Francisco.

"I'm losing patience," she says and sighs impatiently. "More importantly, they're losing patience with me."

And I apologise again, though I am not actually certain this statement warrants an apology. I turn my head and watch as she leans back against her pillow, lifting the stumps of her legs onto the bed. She once told me how she lost them, and it was not so very long ago when she told me, but I can no longer remember that, either.

She smokes her cigarette, and her blue eyes seem fixed on something beyond the walls of the motel room.

"Maybe I should look at the book again," I suggest.

"Maybe," she agrees. "Or maybe I should put a bullet in your skull and say it was an accident."

"Or that I was trying to escape."

She nods and takes another drag off her cigarette. "If you are a goddess," she asks, "what the fuck does that make me?"

But I have no response for that. No response whatsoever. The smoke from her lips and nostrils hangs above our damp bed like the first clouds spreading out above my flat creation of sheets and fallen giants. Her skin is milk, and my breasts ache.

I close my eyes, and possibly I smell cherry blossoms behind her smoke and the stink of mildew, and I try hard to recollect when I first walked the avenues of Kyoto's Good Luck Meadow – Yoshiwara – the green houses and courtesans, boy whores and tea-shop girls, kabuki and paper dragons.

"You have never left this room," she tells me, and I have no compelling reason either to believe her or to suspect that she's lying.

"We could shut off the lights," I say. "It could be dark for at least a little while."

"There isn't time now," she replies and stubs out her cigarette on the wall beside the bed, then drops the butt to the floor, and I think I hear a very faint hiss when it hits the damp tiles. She's left an ashen smudge on the wall near the plastic headboard, and that, I think, must be how evil enters the world.

04. The Book (1)

This is the very first time that she will show me the scrapbook. I *call* it a scrapbook, because I don't know what else to call it. Her robotic knees whir and click softly as she leans forward and snaps open the leather attaché case. She takes the scrapbook out and sets it on the counter beside the rust-streaked sink. This is an hour or so after the first time we made love, and I'm still in bed, watching her and thinking how much more beautiful she is without the ungainly chromium-plated prosthetics. The skin around the external fix posts and neural ports is pink and inflamed, and I wonder if she even bothers to keep them clean. I wonder how much it must hurt, being hauled about by those contraptions. She closes the lid of the briefcase, her every move deliberate, somehow calculated without seeming stiff, and the ankle joints purr like a tick-tock cat as she turns towards me. She is still naked, and I marvel again at the pallid thatch of her pubic hair. She retrieves the scrapbook from the sink.

"You look at the photographs," she says, "and tell me what you see there. This is what matters now, your impressions. We know the rest already."

"I need a hot shower," I tell her, but she shakes her head, and the robotic legs whir and move her towards the bed on broad tridactyl feet.

"Later," she says. "Later, you can have a hot shower, after we're done here."

And so I take the scrapbook from her when she offers it to me – a thick sheaf of yellowed pages held between two sturdy brown pieces of cardstock, the whole thing bound together with a length of brown string. The string has been laced through perforations in the pages and through small silver grommets set into the cardstock covers, and each end of the string is finished with black aiglets to keep it from fraying. The string has been tied into a sloppy sort of reef knot. There is nothing printed or written on the cover.

"Open it," she says, and her prosthetics whine and hiss pneumatic laments as she sits down on the bed near me. The box springs creak.

"What am I supposed to see?" I ask her.

"You are not *supposed* to see anything."

I open the scrapbook, and inside each page displays four black-and-white photographs, held in place by black metal photo corners. And at once I see, as it is plainly obvious, that all the photographs in the book are of the same man. Page after page after page, the same man, though not always the same photograph. They look like mug shots. The man is Caucasian, maybe forty-five years old, maybe fifty. His eyes are dark, and always he is staring directly into the camera lens. There are deep creases in his forehead, and his skin is mottled, large pored, acne scarred, pockmarked. His lips are very thin, and his nose large and hooked. There are bags beneath his eyes.

"Who is he?" I ask.

"That's not your problem," she replies. "Just look at the pictures and tell me what you see."

I turn another page, and another, and another after that, and on every one that haggard face glares back at up me. "They're all the same."

"They are not," she says.

"I mean, they're all of the same man. Who is he?"

"I said that's not your problem. And surely you must know I haven't brought you here to tell me what I can see for myself."

So, I want to ask why she has brought me here, only I cannot recall being brought here. I am not certain I can recall anything before this white dripping room. It seems in this moment to be all I have ever known. I turn more pages, some so brittle they flake at my touch. But there is nothing to see here but the man with the shaved head and the hooked nose.

"Take your time," she says and lights another cigarette. "Just don't take too much of it."

"If this is about the syringes – "

"This isn't about the syringes. But we'll come to that later, trust me. And that Taiwanese chap, too, the lieutenant. What's his name?"

"The war isn't going well, is it?" I ask her, and now I look up from the scrapbook lying open in my lap and watch the darkness filling the doorway to our room. Our room or her room or my room, I cannot say which. That darkness seems as sticky and solid as hot asphalt.

"That depends whose side you're on," she says and smiles and flicks ash onto the floor.

It occurs to me for the first time that someone might be watching from that darkness, getting everything on tape, making notes, waiting and biding their time. I think I might well go mad if I stare too long into that impenetrable black. I look back down at the book, trying to see whatever it is she wants me to see on those pages, whatever it is she needs to know.

03. The Dream

The night after I lost the girl who lost the syringe – if any of that did in fact occur – I awoke in the white room on the not-quite-oyster sheets, gasping and squinting at those bare fluorescent tubes. My mouth so dry, my chest hurting, and the dream already beginning to fade. There was a pencil and a legal pad on the table beside the bed, and I wrote this much down:

This must have been near the end of it all, just before I finally woke. Being on the street of an Asian city, maybe Tokyo, I don't know. Possibly an analym of every Asian city I have ever visited. Night. Flickering neon and cosplay girls and noodle shops. The commingled smells of car exhaust and cooking and garbage. And I'm late for an appointment in a building I can see, an immaculate tower of shimmering steel. I can't read any of the street signs, because they're all Japanese or Mandarin or whatever. I'm lost. Men mutter as they pass me. The cosplay girls laugh and point. There's an immense animatronic Ganesh-like thing directing traffic (and I suppose this is foreshadowing). I finally find someone who doesn't speak English, but she speaks German, and she shows me where to cross the street to reach the steel tower.

There might have been a lobby and an elevator ride, or I may only be filling in a jump cut. But then I was in the examination room of what seemed to be something very like a dentist's office. Only there wasn't that dentist-office smell. There was some other smell that only added to my unease and disorientation. I was asked to take a seat, please, in this thing that wasn't quite a dentist's chair. There was a woman with a British accent asking me questions, checking off items on a form of some sort.

She kept asking about my memory, and if I were comfortable. And then the woman with the British accent placed her thumb beneath my jaw, and I began to feel cold and fevery. She said something like, *We'll be as gentle as we can.* That's when I saw that she was holding my detached jaw in her hands. And I could see my tongue and teeth and gums and lower lip and everything else. The sensation of cold grew more intense, and she told me to please remain calm, that it would all be over soon. Then she pressed something like a dental drill to my forehead, and there was a horrible whine and a burring sort of pain. She set the drill aside and plugged a jack into the roof of my mouth, something attached to an assortment of coaxial cables, and there was a suffocating blackness that seemed to rush up all around me.

I stare for a few moments at what I've written, then return the pencil and the pad to the table. My mouth tastes like onions and curry and aluminum foil, a metallic tang like a freshly filled molar, and I lie back down and shut my eyes tightly, wondering if the throbbing in my chest is the beginning of a heart attack or only indigestion. I'm sick to my stomach and dizzy, and I know that lying down and closing my eyes is the worst thing I could do for either. But I cannot bear the white glare of those bulbs. I will vomit, or it will pass without my having vomited, but I won't look up into that cold light. I do not know where I am or how I got here. I cannot recall ever having seen this dingy room before. No, not dingy – squalid. The sound of dripping water is very loud, a leaky ceiling, so at least maybe the damp sheets do not mean that I've pissed myself in my sleep. I lie very still, listening to the dripping water and to my pounding heart and to a restless sound that might be automobiles on the street outside.

05. The White Woman

She leans close, and her lips brush the lobe of my right ear, her tepid breath on my cheek, breath that smells of tobacco and more faintly of Indian cooking (cardamom, tamarind, fenugreek, cloves). She whispers, and her voice is *so* soft, so soft that she might in this moment have become someone else entirely.

"Nothing to be desired anymore," she whispers. "*Nichts gewünscht zu werden.*"

I don't argue. In this place and time, these are somehow words of kindness, words of absolution, and within them seems to rest the vague hope of release. Her body is warm against mine, her flat belly pressed against mine which is not so flat as it once was, her strong thighs laid against my thighs and her small breasts against my breasts. Together, we have formed an improbable binary opposition, lovers drawn from a deck of cards, my skin so pink and raw and hers so chalky and fine.

"*Gelassen gehen Sie,*" she whispers, and I open my eyes and gaze up into hers, those dazzling, broken blue gems. Her beauty is unearthly, and I might almost believe her an exile from another galaxy, a fallen angel, the calculated product of biotech and genetic alchemy. She lifts herself, rising up on those muscular arms, my hips seized firmly and held fast between the stumps of her transfemoral amputations. There was an accident when she was only a child, but that's all I can now recall. *This is how a mouse must feel,* I think, *in the claws of a cat, or a mouse lost in a laboratory maze*. She smiles, and that expression could mean so many different things.

She leans down again and kisses me, her tongue sliding easily between my teeth.

The room is filled with music, which I am almost certain wasn't there only a moment before. The scratchy, brittle tones of a phonograph recording, something to listen to besides the goddamn rain and the leaking ceiling and the creaking bed springs. And then she enters me, and it comes as no surprise that the robotic legs are not the full extent of her prosthetics. She slips her left arm beneath me, pulling me towards her, and I arch my back, finding her rhythm and the more predictable rhythm of the mechanical cock working its way deeper inside me.

In all the universe, there might be nothing but this room. In all the world, there might only be the two of us.

She kisses me again, but this time it is not a gentle act. This time, there is force and a violence only half-repressed, and I think of cats again. I do not want to think of cats, but I do. She will suck my breath, will draw my soul from me through my nostrils and lips to get at whatever it is she needs to know. How many souls would a woman like her have swallowed in her lifetime? She must be filled with ghosts, a gypsum alabaster bottle stoppered with two blue stones – lapis lazuli or chalcedony – cleverly shaped to resemble the eyes of a woman and not a cat and not an alabaster bottle filled with devoured souls.

Our lips part, and if she has taken my soul, it's nothing I ever needed, anyway.

My mouth wanders across the smooth expanse above and between her breasts, and then I find her right nipple, and my tongue traces a mandala three times about her areola. Perhaps I have sorceries all my own.

"No, you don't," she says and thrusts her hips hard against mine.

And maybe I remember something then, so maybe this room is not all there is in all the world. Maybe I recall a train rushing along through long darknesses and brief puddles of mercury-vapour light, barreling forward, floating on old maglev tracks, and all around me are the cement walls of a narrow tunnel carved out deep below a city whose name I *cannot* recollect. But cities might not have names – I presently have no evidence that they do – and so perhaps this is not exactly forgetfulness or amnesia. I turn my head and look out the window as the train races past a ruined and deserted station. I'm gripping a semi-automatic the way some women would hold onto a rosary or a string of tasbih beads. My forefinger slips through the familiar ring of the trigger guard…

"You still with me, sister?" the albino woman asks, and I nod as the memory of the train and the gun dissolves and is forgotten once again. I am sweating now, even in this cold, dank room on these sodden not-quite-oyster sheets, I am sweating. I could not say if it is from fear or exertion or from something else entirely.

And she comes then, her head bending back so far I think her neck will snap, the taut V of her clavicles below her delicate throat, and if only I had the teeth to do the job. She comes with a shudder and a gasp and a sudden rush of profanity in some odd, staccato language that I do not speak, have never even heard before, but still I know that those words are profane. I see that she is sweating, too, brilliant drops standing out like nectar on her too-white skin, and I lick away a salty trickle from her chest. So there's another way that she is in me now. Her body shudders again, and she releases me, withdrawing and rolling away to lie on her back. She is breathing heavily and grinning, and it is a perfectly merciless sort of grin, choked with triumph and bitter guile. I envy her that grin and the callous heart in back of it. Then my eyes go to that space between her legs, that fine white thatch of hair, and for a moment I only imagine the instrument of my seduction was not a prosthesis. For a moment, I watch the writhing, opalescent thing, still glistening and slick with me. Its body bristles with an assortment of fleshy spines, and I cannot help but ponder what venoms or exotic nanorobotic or nubot serums they might contain.

"Only a fleeting trick of the light, my love," she says, still grinning that brutal grin of hers. And I blink, and now there is only a dildo there between her legs, four or five inches of beige silicone molded into an erect phallus. I close my eyes again and listen to the music and the rain tapping against the windowpane.

01. The Train

The girl is sitting across the aisle and only three rows in front of me, and there's almost no one else riding the tube this late, just a very old man reading a paperback novel. But he's seated far away, many rows ahead of us, and only has eyes for his book, which he holds bent double in trembling, liver-spotted hands. The girl is wearing a raincoat made of lavender vinyl, the collar turned up high so it's hard for me to get a good look at her face. Her hair is long and black and oily, and her hands are hidden inside snug leather gloves that match her raincoat. She's younger than I expected, maybe somewhere in her early twenties, maybe younger still, and a few years ago that might have made what I have to do next a lot harder. But running wet dispatch for the Greeks, you get numb to this sort of shit quick or you get into some other line of work. It doesn't matter how old she is or that she might still have a mother and a father somewhere who love her, sisters or brothers, or that skimming parcels is the only thing keeping her from a life of whoring or selling herself off bit by bit to the carrion apes. These are most emphatically not my troubles. And soon, they will no longer be hers, either.

I glance back down the aisle towards the geezer, but he's still lost in the pages of his paperback.

The girl in the lavender coat is carrying, concealed somewhere on her person, seven 3/10ths cc syringes, and if I'm real goddamn fortunate, I'll never find out what's in them. It is not my job to know. It is my job to retrieve the package with as little fuss and fanfare and bloodshed as possible and then get it back across the border to the spooks in Alexandroupoli.

She wipes at her nose and stares out the window at the tube walls hidden in the darkness.

I take a deep breath and glance back towards the old man. He hasn't moved a muscle, unless it's been to flip a page or two.

Mister, I think, *you just stay absolutely goddamn still, and maybe you'll get to find out how it ends.*

Then I check my gun again, to be double fucking sure the safety's off. With any sort of half-assed luck, I won't need the M9 tonight, but you live by better safe than sorry – if you live at all. The girl wipes her nose a second time and sniffles. Then she leans forward, resting her forehead against the back of the seat in front of her.

There's no time left to worry about whether or not the surveillance wasps are still running, taking it all in from their not-so-secret nooks and crannies, taking it all down. Another six minutes and we'll be pulling into the next terminal, and I have no intention of chasing this bitch in her lavender mack all over Ankara.

I stand and move quickly down the aisle towards her, flexing my left wrist to extend the niobium barb implanted beneath my skin. The neurotoxin will stop her heart before she even feels the prick, or so they tell me. Point is, she won't make a sound. It'll look like a heart attack, if anyone bothers with an autopsy, which I suspect they won't. I've been up against the Turks enough times now to know they only recruit the sort no one's ever going to miss.

But then she turns and looks directly at me, and I've never seen eyes so blue. Or I've never seen eyes that *shade* of blue. Eyes that are both so terribly empty and so filled to bursting, and I know that something's gone very, very goddamn wrong. I know someone somewhere's lied to me, and this isn't just some kid plucked from the slums to mule pilfered load. She sits there, staring up at me, and I reach for the 9mm, shit-sure that's exactly the wrong thing to do, knowing that I've panicked even if I can't quite fathom *why* I've panicked. I'm close enough to get her with the barb, though now there might be a struggle, and then I'd have to deal with the antique bookworm up front. I've hesitated, allowed myself to be distracted, and there's no way it's not gonna go down messy.

She smiles, a voracious, carnivorous smile.

"Nothing to be desired anymore," she says, and I feel the muscles in my hand and wrist relax, feel the barb retracting. I feel the gun slip from my slack fingers and hear it clatter to the floor.

"Go back to your seat," she tells me, but I've fallen so far into those eyes – those eyes that lead straight down through endless electric blue chasms, and I almost don't understand what she means. She leans over and picks my gun up off the floor of the maglev and hands it back to me.

"Go back to your seat," she says again, and I do. I turn and go back to my seat, returning the M9 to its shoulder holster, and sit staring at my hands or staring out the train window for what seems hours and hours and hours and…

06. Marlene Dietrich

I sit alone at the foot of the bed, "south" of that sprawling river delta and the low damp-sheet hills beyond, all rearranged now by the geological upheaval of my movements. I sit there smoking and shivering and watching the dirty rainwater dripping onto the white tiles covering the floor of the room. The phonograph is playing "I May Never Go Home Anymore," and I know all the words, though I cannot remember ever having heard the song before.

"I have always loved her voice," the albino woman says from her place at the window, behind me and to my left.

"It's Marlene Dietrich, isn't it?" I ask, wishing I could say if I have always been afflicted with this patchwork memory. Perhaps this is merely the *nature* of memory, and that's something else I've forgotten.

"That wasn't her birth name," the white woman replies. "But it wasn't a stage name, either. Her parents named her Marie Magdalene – "

"Just like Jesus' whore," I say, interrupting. She ignores me.

"I read somewhere that Dietrich changed it, when she was still a teenager in Schöneberg. Marlene is a contraction of Marie

Magdalene. Did you know that? I always thought that was quite clever of her."

I shrug and take a long drag on my cigarette, then glance at the scrapbook lying open on the bed next to me. The black-and-white photographs are all numbered, beginning with .0001, though I'm not at all sure they were the last time I went through it. The voice of the long dead actress fills the room, making it seem somehow warmer.

Don't ever think about tomorrow.

For tomorrow may never come.

"You should have another good look at the book," the albino woman suggests.

"I don't know what you expect me to see there. I don't understand what it is you want me to *tell* you. I've never *seen* that man before. I don't *remember* ever having seen that man before."

"Of course you don't. But you need to realise, we're running out of time. You're running out of time, love."

Time is nothing as long as I'm living it up this way.

I may never go home anymore.

I turn my head and watch her watching whatever lies on the other side of the windowpane. I still have not had the nerve to look for myself. Some part of me does not want to know, and some part of me still suspects there may be no more to the world than this room. If I look out that window, I might see nothing at all, because nothing may be all there is to see. When I fashioned the flat, rectangular world of the bed, and then this white room which must be the vault of the heavens which surrounds it, perhaps I stopped at the room's four walls. Plaster painted the same white as the floor tiles and the ceiling and the light shining down from those bare fluorescent stars. Beyond that, there is no more, the edges of my universe, the practical boundaries of my cosmic bubble.

"She really did a number on your skull," the albino says. "I don't know how they expect me to get anything, between the goddamn firewall and what she did."

"What *did* she do?" I ask, not really wanting to know that, either, but it doesn't matter, because the albino woman does not answer me. She's still naked, as am I. I still do not know her name. "Are we in Kyoto?" I ask.

"Why the hell would they bother slinging a wog sniper all the way the fuck to Japan?" she wants to know, and I have no answer for that. I seem to have no answers at all.

I've got kisses and kisses galore,
That have never been tasted before.

"Just be a good little girl and look at the book again," she says to me. "Maybe this time you'll see something that you've missed."

I breathe a grey cloud of smoke out through my nostrils, then pick the scrapbook up off the bed. The covers are very slightly damp from lying there on the damp sheets. I don't suppose it matters. I turn the pages and smoke my cigarette. The same careworn, hollow-eyed, middle-aged face looking back at me as before, staring back at whomever took all these pictures. I turn another page, coming to page number nine, the four photos designated .0033 through .0036, and none of it means any more to me than it did the last time through.

"I think that I may remember a good deal about Kyoto," I say. "But I don't remember anything at all about Greece. And I don't look Greek, do I?"

"You don't look Japanese, either."

One last puff, then I drop the butt of my cigarette to the wet tiles, and it sizzles there for half a moment. I run my fingers slowly over the four glossy photographs on the page, as if touching them might make some sort of difference. And, as it happens, I do see a scar on the man's chin I hadn't noticed before. I examine some of the other pages, and the scar is there on every single one of them.

"If I don't find it, whatever it is you want me to find in here – "

" – there are going to be a lot of disappointed people, Sunshine, and you'll be the first."

"Can I have another cigarette?" I ask her.

"Just look at the damned book," she replies, so that's what I do. It's open to page fifteen, .0057–.0060. I try focusing on what the man's wearing instead of his face, but all I can see is the collar of a light-coloured T-shirt, and it's the same in every photograph. My eyes are so tired, and I shut them for a moment. I can almost imagine that the flat illumination from the fluorescent bulbs is draining me somehow, diminishing me, both body and soul. But then I remember that the white woman took my soul when she fucked me, so never mind. I sit there with my eyes shut, listening to the dripping water and listening to Marlene Dietrich and wishing I could at least remember if I've ever had a name.

If you treat me right, this might be the night.
I may never go home, I may never go home.
I may never go home anymore.
I may never go home anymore.

08. The Fire Escape

When I found the umbrella leaning in one corner of the room and opened the window and climbed out onto the fire escape, she didn't try to stop me. She did not even say a word. And there is a world beyond the white room, after all. But it isn't Kyoto. It is no city that I have seen or even dreamt of before. It must *be* a city, because I cannot imagine what else it could possibly be. I'm sitting with the window and the redbrick wall of the motel on my right, my naked ass against the icy steel grating, and the falling rain is very loud on the clear polyvinyl canopy of the umbrella. I think I might never have been this cold in all my life, and I don't know why I didn't take her robe, as well. If I have clothes of my own they are not anywhere to be found in the room.

I peer through the rain-streaked umbrella and try to find words that would do justice to the intricate, towering structures rising up all around me and the motel (that it is a motel, I will readily admit, is only a working assumption, and why motel and not hotel?) But I know I don't possess that sort of vocabulary. Maybe the peculiar staccato language the albino woman spoke when she came, maybe it contains nouns and verbs equal to these things I see.

They are both magnificent and terrible, these edifices that might be buildings and railways, smokestacks and turbines, streets and chimneys and great glass atriums. They are awful. That word might come the closest, in all its connotations. I will not say they are beautiful, for there is something *loathsome* about these bizarre structures. At least, to me they seem bizarre; I cannot say with any certainty that they are in an absolute, objective sense. Possibly, I am the alien here, me and this unremarkable redbrick motel. Thinking through this amnesiac mist locked up inside my head, there is no solid point of reference left to me, no external standard by which I may judge. There is only gut reaction, and my gut reaction is that they are bizarre and loathsome things.

The air out here smells like rain and ozone, carbon monoxide and other chemicals I do not know the names for, and yet it still smells very much cleaner than the white room with its soggy miasma of mold and slow decay.

These spiraling, jointed, ribsy things which *might* be the skyscrapers of an unnamed or unnamable city, they are as intricate as the calcareous or chitinous skeletons of deep-sea creatures. There. I *do* have a few words, though they are utterly insufficient. They are mere *approximations* of what I see. So, yes, they seem organic, these towers, as though they are the product not of conscious engineering and construction but of evolution and ontogeny. They have *grown* here, I think – all of them – and I wonder if the men and women who planted the necessary seeds or embryos, however many ages ago, are anything like the albino who took my soul away.

And then I hear the noise of vast machineries…no, I have been *hearing* this noise all along, but only now has my amazement or apprehension or awe at the sight of this city dimmed enough that I look for the source of the sounds. And I see, not far away, there is a sort of clearing in this urban, industrial carapace. And I can see the muddy earth ripped open there, red as a wound in any living creature. There are great indescribable contraptions busy making the wound much larger, gouging and drilling out buckets or mouthfuls of mud and meat to be dumped upon steaming spoilage heaps or fed onto conveyer belts that stretch away into the foggy distance.

And there is something in that hole, something still only partly exposed by the exertions of these machines that might not be machines at all. Something I know (and no, I cannot say how I could ever *know* such a thing) has lain there undisturbed and sleeping for millennia, and now they mean to wake it up.

I look away. I've seen too much already.

Something is creeping slowly along the exterior of one of the strange buildings, and it might be a living tumor – a malignant mass of tissue and corruption and ideas – and, then again, it might be nothing more than an elevator.

I hear knuckles rapping a windowpane, and when I turn my head back towards the motel, the albino woman is watching me with her bright blue eyes.

07. The Book (II)

Don't ever think about tomorrow.

For tomorrow may never come.

And then the albino woman lifts the phonograph needle from the record and, instantly, the music goes away. I wish she had let it keep on playing, over and over and over, because now the unceasing *drip, drip, drip* from the ceiling to the tiles seems so much louder than when I had the song and Marlene Dietrich's voice to concentrate on. The woman turns my way on her whirring robotic legs and stares at me.

"You never did tell me what happened to your arm," she says and smiles.

"Did you ask?"

"I believe that I did, yes."

I am sitting there at the foot of the bed with the scrapbook lying open on my lap, my shriveled left arm held close to my chest. And it occurs to me that I do not *know* what happened to my arm, and also it occurs to me that I have no recollection whatsoever of there being anything at all wrong with it before she asked how it got this way. And then this *third* observation, which seems only slightly less disconcerting than having forgotten that I'm a cripple (like her), and that I must have been a cripple for a very long time: the book is open to photos .0705–.0708, page 177, and I notice that beside each photo's number are distinct and upraised dimples, like Braille, though I do not know for certain this *is* Braille. I flip back a few pages and see that, yes, the dimples are there on every page.

"That's very thoughtful," I say, so softly that I am almost whispering. "I might have been blind, after all."

"You might be yet," the white woman says.

"If I were," I reply without looking up from the book, "I couldn't even see the damned photographs, much less find whatever it is you *think* I can find in here."

"You don't get off that easily," she laughs, and her noisy mechanical legs carry her from the table with the phonograph to the bed, and she begins the arduous and apparently painful process of detaching herself from the contraptions. I try to focus on the book, trying not to watch her or hear the dripping ceiling or smell the dank stench of the room. Trying only to see the photographs. I don't ask why anyone would bother to provide Braille numbers for photographs that a blind person could not see. And this time, she kindly does not answer my unasked question. I return to page 177, then proceed to 178, then on to 179.

"Shit," the albino woman hisses, forcing her curse out through clenched teeth as she disconnects the primary neural lead to her right thigh. There's thick, dark pus and a bead of fresh blood clinging to the plug. More pus leaks from the port and runs down the stump of her leg.

"Is it actually worth all that trouble and discomfort?" I ask. "Wouldn't a wheelchair be – "

"Why don't you try to mind your own goddamn business," she barks at me, and so I do. I go back to the scrapbook, back to photos .0713-.0716 and that face I know I will be seeing for a long time to come, whenever I shut my eyes. I will see him in my sleep, if I am allowed to live long enough to ever sleep again.

The woman sighs a halting, painful sort of sigh and eases herself back onto the sheets, freed now from the prosthetics, which are left standing side by side at the foot of the bed.

"I picked up a patch bug a while back," she says. "Some sort of cross-scripting germ, a quaint little XSSV symbiote. But it's being treated. It's nothing lethal."

And that's when I see it. She's stretched out there next to me talking about viruses and slow-purge reboots, and I notice the puffy reddish rim surrounding photograph number .0715. This *page* is infected, like the albino woman and her robotic legs, and the *site* of the infection is right here beneath .0715.

"I think I've found it," I say and press the pad of my thumb gently to the photograph. It's hot to the touch, and I can feel something moving about beneath the haggard face of the man with the shaved head and the scar on his chin.

She props herself up on her elbows when I hold the scrapbook out so that she can see. "Well, well," she says. "Maybe you have, and maybe you haven't. Either way, Sunshine, it's going to hurt when you pull that scab away."

"Is that what I'm supposed to do?" I ask her, laying the heavy scrapbook back across my lap. Even as I watch, the necrosis has begun to spread across the page towards the other three photographs.

"Do it quickly," she says, and I can hear the eagerness in her voice. "Like pulling off a sticky plaster. Do it fast, and maybe it'll hurt less."

"Is *this* what you wanted me to find? Is this *it*?"

"You're stalling," she says. "Just fucking do it."

And then the black telephone begins to ring again.

09. Exit Music (The Gun)

Sitting beneath the transparent canopy of the borrowed umbrella, sitting naked in the rain on the fire escape, and now she's standing over me, held up by all those shiny chrome struts and gears and pistons. She did not even have to open the window or climb out over the sill, but I cannot ever explain, in words, how it was she exited the room. It only matters that she did. It only matters that she's standing over me holding the Beretta 9mm, aiming it at my head.

"I never made any promises," she tells me, and I nod (because that's true) and lower the umbrella and fold it shut. I support my useless left arm with my right and stare directly up into the cold rain, wishing there were anything falling from that leaden sky clean enough to wash away the weight of all these things I cannot remember or will never be permitted to remember.

"The war isn't going well," she says. "We've lost Hsinchu and Changhua. I think we all know that Taipei can't be far behind. Too many feedback loops. Way too many scratch hits."

"Nothing to be desired anymore," I say and taste the bitter, toxic raindrops on my tongue.

"Nothing at all," she tells me, setting the muzzle of the M9 to my right temple. I am already so chilled I do not feel the cold steel, only the pressure of the gun against my skin. The rain stings my eyes, and I blink. I take a deep breath and try not to shiver.

"Whatever they're digging up over there," and I nod towards the excavations, "they should stop. You should tell them that soon, before they wake it up."

"You think they'd listen…to someone like me?" she asks. "Is that what you think?"

"I don't know what I think anymore."

Above me and all around me this lifeless, living husk that might be a city or only the mummified innards of some immense biomechanoid crustacean goes on about its clockwork day-to-day affairs, all its secret metabolisms, its ancient habits. It does not see me – or seeing me, it shows even less regard for me than I might show a single mite nestled deep within a single eyelash follicle. I gaze up at that inscrutable tangle of spires and flying buttresses, rotundas and acroterion flourishes and all the thousands of solemn gushing rainspouts.

"Do not feel unloved," she says, and I shut my eyes and sense all the world move beneath me.

IN VIEW OF NOTHING

Take two. And this is the better-written of the two attempts at banishing the dream, I think. It was composed linearly, but when I was finished I placed a number representing each section of the story in a hat, and the order in which I drew the numbers determined the order in which they appeared in the finalized narrative. Both this story and "A Season of Broken Dolls" owe no small debt to David Bowie's *Outside* (1995). In some ways, "In View of Nothing" feels like a dry run for my novella *Black Helicopters*.

The Ape's Wife

Neither yet awake nor quite still asleep, she pauses in her dreaming to listen to the distant sounds of the jungle approaching twilight. They are each balanced now between one world and another – she between sleep and waking and the jungle between day and night. Dreaming, she is once again the woman she was before she came to the island, the starving woman on that *other* island, that faraway island that was not warm and green, but had come to seem to her always cold and grey, stinking of dirty snow and the exhaust of automobiles and buses. She stands outside a lunch room on Mulberry Street, her empty belly rumbling as she watches other people eat. The evening begins to fill up with the raucous screams of nocturnal birds and flying reptiles and a gentle tropical wind rustling through the leaves of banana and banyan trees, through cycads and ferns grown as tall or taller than the brick and steel and concrete canyon that surrounds her.

She leans forward, and her breath fogs the lunch room's plate-glass window, but none of those faces turn to stare back at her. They are all too occupied with their meals, these swells with their forks and knives and china platters buried under mounds of scrambled eggs or roast beef on toast or mashed potatoes and gravy. They raise china cups of hot black coffee to their lips and pretend she isn't there. This winter night is too filled with starving, tattered women on the bum. There is not time to notice them all, so better to notice none of them, better not to allow the sight of real hunger to spoil your appetite. A little farther down the street there is a Greek who sells apples and oranges and pears from a little sidewalk stand, and she wonders how long before he catches her stealing, him or someone else. She has never been a particularly lucky girl.

Somewhere close by, a parrot shrieks and another parrot answers it, and finally she turns away from the people and the tiled walls of the lunch room and opens her eyes; the Manhattan street vanishes in a slushy, disorienting flurry and takes the cold with it. She is still hungry, but for a while she is content to lie in her carefully woven nest of rattan, bamboo, and ebony branches, blinking away the last shreds of sleep and gazing deeply into the rising mists and gathering dusk. She has made her home high atop a weathered promontory, this charcoal peak of lava rock and tephra a vestige of the island's fiery origins. It is for this summit's unusual shape – not so unlike a human skull – that white men named the place. And it is here that she last saw the giant ape, before it left her to pursue the moving-picture man and Captain Englehorn, the first mate and the rest of the crew of the *Venture,* left her alone to get itself killed and hauled away in the rusty hold of that evil-smelling ship.

At least, that is one version of the story she tells herself to explain why the beast never returned for her. It may not be the truth. Perhaps the ape died somewhere in the swampy jungle spread out below the mountain, somewhere along the meandering river leading down to the sea. She has learned that there is no end of ways to die on the island and that nothing alive is so fierce or so cunning as to be entirely immune to those countless perils. The ape's hide was riddled with bullets, and it might simply have succumbed to its wounds and bled to death. Time and again she has imagined this, the ape only halfway back to the wall but growing suddenly too weak to continue the chase, and perhaps it stopped, surrendering to pain and exhaustion, and sat down in a glade somewhere below the cliffs, resting against the bole of an enormous tree. Maybe it sat there, peering through a break in the perpetual mist and the forest canopy, gazing forlornly back up at the skull-shaped mountain. It would have been a terrible, lonely death, but not so terrible an end as the beast might have met had it managed to gain the ancient aboriginal gates and the sandy peninsula beyond.

She has, on occasion, imagined another outcome, one in which the enraged god-thing overtook the men from the steamer, either in the jungle or somewhere out beyond the wall, in the village or on the beachhead. And though the ape was killed by their gunshots and gas bombs (for surely he would have returned, otherwise), first they died screaming, every last mother's son of them. She has taken some grim satisfaction in this fantasy, on days when she has had need of grim satisfaction. But she knows it isn't true, if only because she watched with her own eyes the *Venture* sailing away from the place where it had anchored out past the reefs, the smoke from its single stack drawing an ashen smudge across the blue morning sky. They escaped, at least enough of them to pilot the ship, and left her for dead or good as dead.

She stretches and sits up in her nest, watching the sun as it sinks slowly into the shimmering, flat monotony of the Indian Ocean, the dying day setting the western horizon on fire. She stands, and the red-orange light paints her naked skin the color of clay. Her stomach growls again, and she thinks of her small hoard of fruit and nuts, dried fish, and a couple of turtle eggs she found the day before, all wrapped up safe in banana leaves and hidden in amongst the stones and brambles. Here, she need only fear nightmares of hunger and never hunger itself. There is the faint, rotten smell of sulfur emanating from the cavern that forms the skull's left eye socket, as the mountain's malodorous breath wafts up from bubbling hot springs deep within the grotto. She has long since grown accustomed to the stench and has found that the treacherous maze of bubbling lakes and mud helps to protect her from many of the island's predators. For this reason, more than any other, more even than the sentimentality that she no longer denies, she chose these steep volcanic cliffs for her eyrie.

Stepping from her bed, the stones warm against the thickly calloused soles of her feet, she remembers a bit of melody, a ghostly snatch of lyrics that has followed her up from the dream of the city and the woman she will never be again. She closes her eyes, shutting out the jungle noises for just a moment, and listens to the faint crackle of a half-forgotten radio broadcast.

Once I built a tower up to the sun,
Brick and rivet and lime.
Once I built a tower,
Now it's done.
Brother, can you spare a dime?

And when she opens her eyes again, the sun is almost gone, just a blazing sliver remaining now above the sea. She sighs and reminds herself that there is no percentage in recalling the clutter and racket of that lost world. Not now. Not here. Night is coming on, sweeping in fast and mean on leathery pterodactyl wings and the wings of flying foxes and the wings of ur-birds, and like so many of the island's inhabitants, she puts all else from her mind and rises to meet it. The island has made of her a night thing, has stripped her of old diurnal ways. Better to sleep through the stifling equatorial days than to lie awake through the equally stifling nights; better the company of the sun for her uneasy dreams than the moon's cool, seductive glow and her terror of what might be watching hungrily from the cover of darkness.

When she has eaten, she sits awhile near the cliff's edge, contemplating what month this might be, what month in which year. It is a futile, but harmless, pastime. At first, she scratched marks on stone to keep track of the passing time, but after only a few hundred marks she forgot one day, and then another, and when she finally remembered again, she found she was uncertain how many days had come and gone during her forgetfulness. It was then that she came to understand the futility of counting days in this place – indeed, the futility of the very concept of time. She has thought often that the island must be time's primordial orphan, a castaway, not unlike herself, stranded in some nether region, this sweltering antediluvian limbo where there is only the rising and setting of the sun, the phases of the moon, the long rainy season which is hardly less hot or less brutal than the longer dry. Maybe the men who built the wall long ago were a race of sorcerers, and in their arrogance they committed a grave transgression against time, some unspeakable contravention of the sanctity of months and hours. And so Chronos cast this place back down into the gulf of Chaos, and now it is damned to exist forever apart from the tick-tock, calendar-page blessings of Aion.

Sure, she still recalls a few hazy scraps of Greek mythology, and Roman, too, this farmer's only daughter who always got good marks and waited until school was done before leaving the cornfields of Indiana to go east to seek her fortune in New York and New Jersey. All her girlhood dreams of the stage, the silver screen, and her name on theater marquees, but by the time she reached Fort Lee, most of the studios were relocating west to California, following the promise of a more hospitable, more profitable climate. Black Tuesday had left its stain upon the country, and she never found more than extra work at the few remaining studios, happy just to play anonymous faces in crowd scenes and the like, but finally she could not even find that. Finally, she was fit only for the squalor of bread lines and mission soup kitchens and flop houses, until the night she met a man who promised to make her a star, who, chasing dreams of his own, dragged her halfway round the world and then abandoned her here in this serpent-haunted and time-forsaken wilderness. The irony is not lost on her. Seeking fame and adoration, she has found, instead, what might well be the ultimate obscurity.

Below her, some creature suddenly cries out in pain from the forest tangle clinging to the slopes of the mountain, and she squints into the darkness. She knows that hers are only one of a hundred – or a thousand – pairs of eyes that have stopped to see, to try and catch a glimpse of whatever bloody panoply is being played out among the vines and undergrowth, and that this is only one of the innumerable slaughters to come before sunrise. Something screams and so all eyes turn to see, for every thing that creeps or crawls, flits or slithers upon the island will fall prey, one day or another. And she is no exception.

One day, perhaps, the island itself will fall, not so unlike the dissatisfied angels in Milton or in Blake.

Ann Darrow opens her eyes, having nodded off again, and she is once more only a civilized woman not yet grown old, but no longer young. One who has been taken away from the world and touched, then returned and set adrift in the sooty gulches and avenues and asphalt ravines of this modern, electric city. But that was such a long time ago, before the war that proved the Great War was not so very great after all, that it was not the war to end all wars. Japan has been burned with the fire of two tiny manufactured suns. Europe lies in ruins, and already the fighting has begun again and young men are dying in Korea. History is a steamroller. History is a litany of war.

She sits alone in the Natural History Museum off Central Park West, a bench all to herself in the alcove where the giant ape's broken skeleton was mounted for public exhibition after the creature tumbled from the top of the Empire State, plummeting more than twelve hundred feet to the frozen streets below. There is an informative placard (white letters on black) declaring it *Brontopithecus singularis* Osborn (1934), the only known specimen, now believed extinct. *So there,* she thinks. Denham and his men dragged it from the not-quite-impenetrable sanctuary of its jungle and hauled it back to Broadway; they chained it and murdered it and, in that final act of desecration, they *named* it. The enigma was dissected and quantified, given its rightful place in the grand analytic scheme, in the Latinized order of things, and that's one less blank spot to cause the mapmakers and zoologists to scratch their heads. Now, Carl Denham's monster is no threat at all, only another harmless, impressive heap of bones shellacked and wired together in this stately, static mausoleum. And hardly anyone remembers or comes to look upon these bleached remains. The world is a steamroller. The Eighth Wonder of the World was old news twenty years ago, and now it is only a chapter in some dusty textbook devoted to anthropological curiosities.

He was the king and the god of the world he knew, but now he comes to civilization, merely a captive, a show to gratify your curiosity. Curiosity killed the cat, and it slew the ape, as well, and that December night hundreds died for the price of a theater ticket, the fatal price of *their* curiosity and Carl Denham's hubris. By dawn, the passion play was done, and the king and god and son of Skull Island lay crucified by biplanes, by the pilots and trigger-happy Navy men borne aloft in Curtis Helldivers armed with .50 caliber machine guns. A tiered Golgotha skyscraper, one hundred and two stories of steel and glass and concrete, a dizzying Art-Deco Calvary, and no chance of resurrection save what the museum's anatomists and taxidermists might in time effect.

Ann Darrow closes her eyes, because she can only ever bear to look at the bones for just so long and no longer. Henry Fairfield Osborn, the museum's former president, had wanted to name it after her, in her *honour – Brontopithecus darrowii,* "Darrow's thunder ape" – but, for his trouble, she'd threatened a lawsuit against him *and* his museum, and so he'd christened the species *singularis,* instead. She'd played her Judas role, delivering the jungle god to Manhattan's Roman holiday, and wasn't that enough? Must she also have her name forever nailed up there with the poor beast's corpse? Maybe she deserved as much or far worse, but Osborn's "honour" was poetic justice she managed to evade.

There are voices now, a mother and her little girl, so Ann knows that she's no longer alone in the alcove. She keeps her eyes tightly shut, wishing she could shut her ears as well and not hear the things that are being said.

"Why did they kill him?" asks the little girl.

"It was a very dangerous animal," her mother replies sensibly. "It got loose and hurt people. I was just a child then, about your age."

"They could have put him in a zoo," the girl protests. "They didn't have to kill him."

"I don't think a zoo would ever have been safe. It broke free and hurt a lot of innocent people."

"But there aren't any more monkeys like him."

"There are still plenty of gorillas in Africa," the mother replies.

"Not that big," says the little girl. "Not as big as an elephant."

"No," the mother agrees. "Not as big as an elephant. But then we hardly need gorillas as big as elephants, now do we?"

Ann clenches her jaws, grinding her teeth together, biting her tongue (so to speak), and gripping the edge of the bench with nails chewed down to the quick.

They'll leave soon, she reminds herself. *They always do, get bored and move along after only a minute or so. It won't be much longer.*

"What does *that* part say?" the child asks, so her mother reads to her from the text printed on the placard.

"Well, it says, 'Kong was not a true gorilla, but a close cousin, and belongs in the Superfamily Hominoidea with gorillas, chimpanzees, orang-utans, gibbons, and human beings. His exceptional size might have evolved in response to his island isolation.'"

"What's a *super* family?"

"I don't really know, dear."

"What's a gibbon?"

"Another sort of monkey, I suppose."

"But we don't believe in evolution, do we?"

"No, we don't."

"So God made Kong, just like he made us?"

"Yes, honey. God made Kong, but not like he made us. He gave us a soul. Kong was an animal."

And then there's a pause, and Ann holds her breath, wishing she were still dozing, still lost in her terrible dreams, because this waking world is so much more terrible.

"I want to see the *Tyrannosaurus* again," says the little girl, "and the *Brontosaurus* and *Triceratops,* too." Her mother says okay, there's just enough time to see the dinosaurs again before we have to meet your Daddy, and Ann sits still and listens to their footsteps on the polished marble floor, growing fainter and fainter until silence has at last been restored to the alcove. But now the sterile, drab museum smells are gone, supplanted by the various rank odors of the apartment Jack rented for the both of them before he shipped out on a merchant steamer, the *Polyphemus,* bound for the Azores and then Lisbon and the Mediterranean. He never made it much farther than São Miguel, because the steamer was torpedoed by a Nazi U-boat and went down with all hands onboard. Ann opens her eyes, and the strange dream of the museum and the ape's skeleton has already begun to fade. It isn't morning yet, and the lamp beside the bed washes the tiny room with yellow-white light that makes her eyes ache.

She sits up, pushing the sheets away, exposing the ratty grey mattress underneath. The bedclothes are damp with her sweat and with radiator steam, and she reaches for the half-empty gin bottle there beside the lamp. The booze used to keep the dreams at bay, but these last few months, since she got the telegram informing her that Jack Driscoll was drowned and given up for dead and she would never be seeing him again, the nightmares have seemed hardly the least bit intimidated by alcohol. She squints at the clock, way over on the chifforobe, and sees that it's not yet even four a.m. Still hours until sunrise, hours until the bitter comfort of winter sunlight through the bedroom curtains. She tips the bottle to her lips, and the liquor tastes like turpentine and regret and everything she's lost in the last three years. Better she would have never been anything more than a starving woman stealing apples and oranges and bread to try to stay alive, better she would have never stepped foot on the *Venture*. Better she would have died in the green hell of that uncharted island. She can easily imagine a thousand ways it might have gone better, all grim, but better than *this* drunken half-life. She does not torture herself with fairy-tale fantasies of happy endings that never were and never will be. There's enough pain in the world without that luxury.

She takes another swallow from the bottle, then reminds herself that it has to last until morning and sets it back down on the table. But morning seems at least as far away as that night on the island, as far away as the carcass of the sailor she married. Often, she dreams of him, mangled by shrapnel and gnawed by the barbed teeth of deep-sea fish, burned alive and rotted beyond recognition, tangled in the wreckage and ropes and cables of a ship somewhere at the bottom of the Atlantic Ocean. He peers out at her with eyes that are no longer eyes at all, but only empty sockets where hagfish and spiny albino crabs nestle. She usually wakes screaming from those dreams, wakes to the bastard next door pounding on the wall with the heel of a shoe or just his bare fist and shouting how he's gonna call the cops if she can't keep it down. He has a job and has to sleep, and he can't have some goddamn rummy broad half the bay over or gone crazy with the DTs keeping him awake. The old Italian cunt who runs this dump, she says she's tired of hearing the complaints, and either the hollering stops or Ann will have to find another place to flop. She tries not to think about how she'll have to leave soon, anyway. She had a little money stashed in the lining of her coat, from all the interviews she gave the papers and magazines and the newsreel people, but now it's almost gone. Soon, she'll be back out on the bum, sleeping in mission beds or worse places, whoring for the sauce and as few bites of food as she can possibly get by on. She has another month before that, at most, and isn't that what they mean by coming full circle?

She lies down again, trying not to smell herself or the pillowcase or the sheets, thinking about bright July sun falling warm between green leaves. And soon she drifts off once more, listening to the rumble of a garbage truck down on Canal Street, the rattle of its engine and the squeal of its breaks not so very different from the primeval grunts and cries that filled the torrid air of the ape's profane cathedral.

And perhaps now she is lying safe and drunk in a squalid Bowery tenement and only dreaming away the sorry dregs of her life, and it's not the freezing morning when Jack led her from the skyscraper's spire down to the bedlam of Fifth Avenue. Maybe these are nothing more than an alcoholic's fevered recollections, and she is not being bundled in wool blankets and shielded from reporters and photographers and the sight of the ape's shattered body.

"It's over," says Jack, and she wants to believe that's true, by all the saints in Heaven and all the sinners in Hell, wherever and whenever she is, she wants to believe that it is finally and irrevocably over. There is not one moment to be relived, not ever again, because it has *ended,* and she is rescued, like Beauty somehow delivered from the clutching paws of the Beast. But there is so much commotion, the chatter of confused and frightened bystanders, the triumphant, confident cheers and shouting of soldiers and policemen, and she's begging Jack to get her out of it, away from it. It *must* be real, all of it, real and here and now, because she has never been so horribly cold in her dreams. She shivers and stares up at the narrow slice of sky visible between the buildings. The summit of that tallest of all tall towers is already washed with dawn, but down here on the street it may as well still be midnight.

Life is just a bowl of cherries.
Don't take it serious; it's too mysterious.
At eight each morning I have got a date,
To take my plunge 'round the Empire State.
You'll admit it's not the berries,
In a building that's so tall...

"It's over," Jack assures her for the tenth or twentieth or fiftieth time. "They got him. The airplanes got him, Ann. He can't hurt you, not anymore."

And she's trying to remember through the clamor of voices and machines and the popping of flash bulbs – *Did he hurt me? Is that what happened?* – when the crowd divides like the holy winds of Jehovah parting the waters for Moses, and for the first time she can see what's left of the ape. She screams, and they all *think* she's screaming in terror at the sight of a monster. They do not know the truth, and maybe she does not yet know herself, and it will be weeks or months before she fully comprehends why she is standing there screaming, unable to look away from the impossible, immense mound of black fur and jutting white bone and the dark rivulets of blood leaking sluggishly from the dead and vanquished thing.

"Don't," Jack says, and he covers her eyes. "It's nothing you need to see."

So she does *not* see, shutting her bright blue eyes and all the eyes of her soul, the eyes without and those other eyes within. Shutting *herself,* slamming closed doors and windows of perception, and how could she have known that morning that she was locking in more than she was locking out. *Don't look at it,* he said, much too late, and these images are burned forever into her lidless, unsleeping mind's eye.

A sable hill from which red torrents flow.

Ann kneels in clay and mud the colour of a slaughterhouse floor, all the shades of shit and blood and gore, and dips her fingertips into the stream. She has performed this simple act of prostration times beyond counting, and it no longer holds for her any revulsion. She comes here from her nest high in the smoldering ruins of Manhattan and places her hand inside the wound, like St. Thomas fondling the pierced side of Christ. She comes down to remember, because there is an unpardonable sin in forgetting such a forfeiture. In this deep canyon molded not by geologic upheaval and erosion but by the tireless, automatic industry of man, she bows her head before the black hill. God sleeps there below the hill, and one day he will awaken from his slumber, for all those in the city are not faithless. Some still remember and follow the buckled blacktop paths, weaving their determined pilgrims' way along decaying thoroughfares and between twisted girders and the tumbledown heaps of burnt-out rubble. The city was cast down when God fell from his throne (or was pushed, as some have dared to whisper), and his fall broke apart the ribs of the world and sundered even the progression of one day unto the next so that time must now spill backwards to fill in the chasm. Ann leans forward, sinking her hand in up to the wrist, and the steaming crimson stream begins to clot and scab where it touches her skin.

Above her, the black hill seems to shudder, to shift almost imperceptibly in its sleep.

She has thought repeatedly of drowning herself in the stream, has wondered what it would be like to submerge in those veins and be carried along through silent veils of silt and ruby-tinted light. She might dissolve and be no more than another bit of flotsam, unburdened by bitter memory and self-knowledge and these rituals to keep a comatose god alive. She would open her mouth wide, and as the air rushed from her lungs and across her mouth, she would fill herself with His blood. She has even entertained the notion that such a sacrifice would be enough to wake the black sleeper, and as the waters that are not waters carried her away, the god beast might stir. As she melted, He would open His eyes and shake Himself free of the holdfasts of that tarmac and cement and sewer-pipe grave. It *could* be that simple. In her waking dreams she has learned there is incalculable magic in sacrifice.

Ann withdraws her hand from the stream, and blood drips from her fingers, rejoining the whole as it flows away north and east towards the noxious lake that has formed where once lay the carefully landscaped and sculpted conceits of Mr. Olmsted and Mr. Vaux's Central Park. She will not wipe her hand clean as would some infidel, but rather permit the blood to dry to a claret crust upon her skin, for she has already committed blasphemy enough for three lifetimes. The shuddering black hill is still again, and a vinegar wind blows through the tall grass on either side of the stream.

And then Ann realizes that she's being watched from the gaping brick maw that was a jeweler's window long ago. The frame is still rimmed round about with jagged crystal teeth waiting to snap shut on unwary dreamers, waiting to shred and pierce, starved for diamonds and sapphires and emeralds, but more than ready to accept mere meat. In dusty shafts of sunlight, Ann can see the form of a young girl gazing out at her.

"What do you want?" Ann calls to her, and a moment or two later, the girl replies.

"You have become a goddess," she says, moving a little nearer the broken shop window so that Ann might have a better look at her. "But even a goddess cannot dream forever. I have come a long way and through many perils to speak with you, Golden Mother, and I did not expect to find you sleeping and hiding in the lies told by dreams."

"I'm not hiding," Ann replies very softly, so softly she thinks surely the girl will not have heard.

"Forgive me, Golden Mother, but you are. You are seeking refuge in guilt that is not your guilt."

"I am not your mother," Ann tells her. "I have never been anyone's mother."

A branch whips around and catches her in the face, a leaf's razor edge to draw a nasty cut across her forehead. But the pain slices cleanly through exhaustion and shock and brings her suddenly back to herself, back to *this* night and *this* moment, hers and Jack's mad, headlong dash from the river to the gate. The Cyclopean wall rises up before them, towering above the tree tops. There cannot now be more than a hundred yards remaining between them and the safety of the gate, but the ape is so very close behind. A fire-eyed demon who refuses to be so easily cheated of his prize by mere mortal men. The jungle cringes around them, flinching at the cacophony of Kong's approach, and even the air seems to draw back from that typhoon of muscle and fury, his angry roars and thunderous footfalls to divide all creation. Her right hand is gripped tightly in Jack's left, and he's all but dragging her forward. Ann can no longer feel her bare feet, which have been bruised and gouged and torn, and it is a miracle she can still run at all. Now, she can make out the dim silhouettes of men standing atop the wall, white men with guns and guttering torches, and, for a moment, she allows herself to hope.

"You are needed, Golden Mother," the girl says, and then she steps through the open mouth of the shop window. The blistering sun shimmers off her smooth, dark skin. "You are needed *here* and *now,*" she says. "That night and every way that it might have gone, but did not, are passed forever beyond your reach."

"You don't see what I can see," Ann tells the girl, hearing the desperation and resentment in her own voice.

And what she sees is the wall and that last barrier of banyan figs and tree ferns. What she sees is the open gate and the way out of this nightmare; she sees the road home.

"Only dreams," the girl says, not unkindly, and she takes a step nearer the red stream. "Only the phantoms of things that have never happened and never will."

"No," says Ann, and she shakes her head. "We *made* it to the gate. Jack and I both, together. We ran and we ran and we ran, and the ape was right there on top of us all the way, so close that I could smell his rancid breath. But we didn't look back, not even once. We *ran,* and, in the end, we made it to the gate."

"No, Golden Mother. It did not happen that way."

One of the sailors on the wall is shouting a warning now, and at first, Ann believes it's only because he can see Kong behind them. But then something huge lunges from the underbrush, all scales and knobby scutes, scrabbling talons and the blue-green iridescent flash of eyes fashioned for night hunting. The high, sharp quills sprouting from the creature's backbone clatter one against the other like bony castanets, and it snatches Jack Driscoll in its saurian jaws and drags him screaming into the reedy shadows. On the wall, someone shouts, and she hears the staccato report of rifle fire.

The brown girl stands on the far side of the stream flowing along Fifth Avenue, the tall grass murmuring about her knees. "You have become lost in All-At-Once time, and you must find your way back from the Everywhen. I can help, if you'll let me."

"I do not *need* your help," Ann snarls. "You keep away from me, you goddamn, filthy heathen."

Beneath the vast, star-specked Indonesian sky, Ann Darrow stands alone. Jack is gone, taken by some unnamable abomination, and in another second the ape will be upon her. This is when she realizes that she's bleeding, a dark bloom unfolding from her right breast, staining the gossamer rags that are all that remain of her dress and underclothes. She doesn't yet feel the sting of the bullet, a single shot gone wild, intended for Jack's reptilian attacker, but finding her, instead. *I do not blame you,* she thinks, slowly collapsing, going down onto her knees in the thick carpet of moss and bracken. *It was an accident, and I do not blame anyone.*

"That is a lie," the girl says from the other side of the red stream. "You *do* blame them, Golden Mother, and you blame yourself, most of all."

Ann stares up at the dilapidated skyline of a city as lost in time as she, and the Vault of Heaven turns above them like a dime-store kaleidoscope.

Once I built a railroad, I made it run, made it race against time. Once I built a railroad; now it's done. Brother, can you spare a dime? Once I built a tower, up to the sun, brick, and rivet, and lime; Once I built a tower, now it's done. Brother, can you spare a dime?

"When does this end?" she asks, asking the girl or herself or no one at all. "*Where* does it end?"

"Take my hand," the girl replies and reaches out to Ann, a bridge spanning the rill and time and spanning all these endless possibilities. "Take my hand and come back over. Just step across and stand with me."

"No," Ann hears herself say, though it isn't at all what she *wanted* to say or what she *meant* to say. "No, I can't do that. I'm sorry."

And the air around her reeks of hay and sawdust, human filth and beer and cigarette smoke, and the sideshow barker is howling his line of ballyhoo to all the rubes who've paid their two-bits to get a seat under the tent. All the yokels and hayseeds who have come to point and whisper and laugh and gawk at the figure cowering inside the cage.

"Them bars there, they are solid carbon *steel,* mind you," the barker informs them. "Manufactured special for us by the same Pittsburgh firm that supplies prison bars to Alcatraz. Ain't nothing else known to man strong enough to contain *her,* and if not for them iron bars, well...rest assured, my good people, we have not in the *least* exaggerated the threat she poses to life and limb in the absence of such precautions."

Inside the cage, Ann squats in a corner, staring out at all the faces staring in. Only she has not been Ann Darrow in years – just ask the barker or the garish canvas flaps rattling in the chilly breeze of an Indiana autumn evening. She is the Ape Woman of Sumatra, captured at great personal risk by intrepid explorers and hauled out into the incandescent light of the Twentieth Century. She is naked, except for the moth-eaten scraps of buffalo and bear pelts they have given her to wear. Every inch of exposed skin is smeared with dirt and offal and whatever other filth has accumulated in her cage since it was last mucked out. Her snarled and matted hair hangs in her face, and there's nothing the least bit human in the guttural serenade of growls and hoots and yaps that escapes her lips.

The barker slams his walking cane against the iron bars, and she throws her head back and howls. A woman in the front row faints and has to be carried outside.

"She was the queen and the goddess of the strange world she knew," bellows the barker, "but now she comes to civilization, merely a captive, a show to gratify your curiosity. Learned men at colleges – forsaking the words of the Good Book – proclaim that we are *all* descended from monkeys. And, I'll tell you, seeing this wretched bitch, I am *almost* tempted to believe them, and also to suspect that in dark and far-flung corners of the globe there exist to this day beings *still* more simian than human, lower even than your ordinary niggers, hottentots, negritos, and lowly African pygmies."

Ann Darrow stands on the muddy bank of the red stream, and the girl from the ruined and vine-draped jewelry shop holds out her hand, the brown-skinned girl who has somehow found her way into the most secret, tortured recesses of Ann's consciousness.

"The world is still here," the girl says, "only waiting for you to return."

"I have heard tell another tale of her origin," the barker confides. "But I must *warn* you, it is not fit for the faint of heart or the ears of decent Christian women."

There is a long pause, while two or three of the women rise from their folding chairs and hurriedly leave the tent. The barker tugs at his pink suspenders and grins an enormous, satisfied grin, then glances into the cage.

"As I was saying," he continues, "there is *another* story. The Chinaman who sold me this pitiful oddity of human *de*volution said that its mother was born of French aristocracy, the lone survivor of a calamitous shipwreck, cast ashore on black volcanic sands. There, in the hideous misery and perdition of that tropical wilderness, the poor woman was *defiled* by some lustful species of jungle imp, though whether it were chimp or baboon I cannot say."

There is a collective gasp from the men and women inside the tent, and the barker rattles the bars again, eliciting another irate howl from its occupant.

"And here before you is the foul *spawn* of that unnatural union of anthropoid and womankind. The aged Celestial confided to me that the mother expired shortly after giving birth, God rest her immortal soul. Her death was a mercy, I should think, as she would have lived always in shame and horror at having borne into the world this shameful, misbegotten progeny."

"Take my hand," the girl says, reaching into the iron cage. "You do not have to stay here. Take my hand, Golden Mother, and I will help you find the path."

There below the hairy black tumulus, the great slumbering titan belching forth the headwaters of all the earth's rivers, Ann Darrow takes a single hesitant step into the red stream. *This is the most perilous part of the journey,* she thinks, reaching to accept the girl's outstretched hand. *It wants me, this torrent, and if I am not careful, it will pull me down and drown me for my trespasses.*

"It's only a little ways more," the girl tells her and smiles. "Just step across to me."

The barker raps his silver-handled walking cane sharply against the bars of the cage, so that Ann remembers where she is and when, and doing so, forgets herself again. For the benefit of all those licentious, ogling eyes, all those slack jaws that have paid precious quarters to be shocked and titillated, she bites the head off a live hen, and when she has eaten her fill of the bird, she spreads her thighs and masturbates for the delight of her audience with filthy, bloodstained fingers.

Elsewhen, she takes another step towards the girl, and the softly gurgling stream wraps itself greedily about her calves. Her feet sink deeply into the slimy bottom, and the sinuous, clammy bodies of conger eels and giant axolotl salamanders wriggle between her ankles and twine themselves about her legs. She cannot reach the girl, and the opposite bank may as well be a thousand miles away.

I'm only going over Jordan...

In a smoke-filled screening room, Ann Darrow sits beside Carl Denham while the footage he shot on the island almost a year ago flickers across the screen at twenty-four frames per second. They are not alone, the room half-filled with low-level studio men from RKO and Paramount and Universal and a couple of would-be financiers lured here by the Hollywood rumor mill. Ann watches the images revealed in grainy shades of grey, in overexposed whites and underexposed smudges of black.

"What exactly are we supposed to be looking at?" someone asks, impatiently.

"We shot this from the top of the wall, once Englehorn's men had managed to frighten away all the goddamn tar babies. Just wait. It's coming."

"Denham, we've already been sitting here half an hour. This shit's pretty underwhelming, you ask me. You're better off sticking to the safari pictures."

"It's *coming,*" Denham insists and chomps anxiously at the stem of his pipe.

And Ann knows he's right, that it's coming, because this is not the first time she's seen the footage. Up there on the screen, the eye of the camera looks out over the jungle canopy, and it always reminds her of Gustave Doré's visions of Eden from her mother's copy of *Paradise Lost,* or the illustrations of lush Pre-Adamite landscapes from a geology book she once perused while seeking shelter in the New York Public Library.

"Honestly, Mr. Denham," the man from RKO sighs. "I've got a meeting in twenty minutes."

"*There,*" Denham says, pointing at the screen. "There it is. Right fucking *there*. Do you see it?"

And the studio men and the would-be financiers fall silent as the beast's head and shoulders emerge from the tangle of vines and orchid-encrusted branches and wide palm fronds. It stops and turns its mammoth head towards the camera, glaring hatefully up at the wall and directly into the smoke-filled room, across a million years and nine thousand miles. There is a dreadful, unexpected intelligence in those dark eyes as the creature tries to comprehend the purpose of the weird, pale men and their hand-crank contraption perched there on the wall above it. The ape's lips fold back, baring gigantic canines, eyeteeth longer than a grown man's hand, and there is a low, rumbling sound, then a screeching sort of yell, before the thing the natives called *Kong* turns and vanishes back into the forest.

"Great god," the Universal man whispers.

"Yes, gentlemen," says Denham, sounding very pleased with himself and no longer the least bit anxious, certain that he has them all right where he wants them. "That's just *exactly* what those tar babies think. They worship it and offer up human sacrifices. Why, they wanted Ann here. Offered us six of their women so she could become the *bride* of Kong. And *there's* our story, gentlemen."

"Great *god,*" the Universal man says again, louder than before.

"But an expedition like this costs money," Denham tells them, getting down to brass tacks as the reel ends and the lights come up. "I mean to make a picture the whole damn *world's* gonna pay to see, and I can't do that without committed backers."

"Excuse me," Ann says, rising from her seat, feeling sick and dizzy and wanting to be away from these men and all their talk of profit and spectacle, wanting to drive the sight of the ape from her mind, once and for all.

"I'm fine, really," she tells them. "I just need some fresh air."

On the far side of the stream, the brown girl urges her forward; no more than twenty feet left to go, and Ann will have reached the other side.

"You're waking up," the girl says. "You're almost there. Give me your hand."

I'm only going over Jordan
I'm only going over home...

And the moments flash and glimmer as the dream breaks apart around her, and the barker rattles the iron bars of a stinking cage, and her empty stomach rumbles as she watches men and women bending over their plates in a lunch room, and she sits on a bench in an alcove on the third floor of the American Museum of Natural History. Crossing the red stream, Ann Darrow hemorrhages time and possibility, all these seconds and hours and days vomited forth like a bellyful of tainted meals. She shuts her eyes and takes another step, sinking even deeper in the mud, the blood risen now as high as her waist. Here is the morning they brought her down from the Empire State Building, and the morning she wakes in her nest on Skull Mountain, and the night she watched Jack Driscoll devoured well within sight of the archaic gates. Here's the Bowery tenement, and here the screening room, and here a fallen Manhattan, crumbling and lost in the storm-tossed gulf of eons, set adrift no differently than she has set herself adrift. Every moment, all at once, each as real as every other; never mind the contradictions; each moment damned and equally inevitable, all following from a stolen apple and the man who paid the Greek a dollar to look the other way.

The world is a steamroller.

Once I built a railroad; now it's done.

She stands alone in the seaward lee of the great wall and knows that its gates have been forever shut against her *and* all the daughters of men yet to come. This hallowed, living wall of human bone and sinew erected to protect what scrap of Paradise lies inside, not the dissolute, iniquitous world of men sprawling beyond its borders. Winged Cherubim stand guard on either side, and in their leonine forepaws they grasp flaming swords forged in unknown furnaces before the coming of the World, fiery brands that reach all the way to the sky and about which spin the hearts of newborn hurricanes. The molten eyes of the Cherubim watch her every move, and their indifferent minds know her every secret thought, these dispassionate servants of the vengeful god of her father and her mother. Neither tears nor all her words will ever wring mercy from these sentinels, for they know precisely what she is, and they know her crimes.

I am she who cries out,
and I am cast forth upon the face of the earth.

The starving, ragged woman who stole an apple. Starving in body and in mind, starving in spirit, if so base a thing as she can be said to possess a soul. Starving and ragged in all ways.

I am the members of my mother.
I am the barren one
and many are her sons.
I am she whose wedding is great,
and I have not taken a husband.

And as is the way of all exiles, she cannot kill hope that her exile will one day end. Even the withering gaze of the Cherubim cannot kill that hope, and so hope is the cruelest reward.

Brother, can you spare a dime?

"Take my hand," the girl says, and Ann Darrow feels herself grown weightless and buoyed from that foul brook, hauled free of the morass of her own nightmares and regret onto a clean shore of verdant mosses and zoysiagrass, bamboo and reeds, and the girl leans down and kisses her gently on the forehead. The girl smells like sweat and nutmeg and the pungent yellow pigment dabbed across her cheeks. The girl is salvation.

"You have come *home* to us, Golden Mother," she says, and there are tears in her eyes.

"You don't see," Ann whispers, the words slipping out across her tongue and teeth and lips like her own ghost's death rattle. If the jungle air were not so still and heavy, not so turgid with the smells of living and dying, decay and birth and conception, she's sure it would lift her as easily as it might a stray feather and carry her away. She lies very still, her head cradled in the girl's lap, and the stream flowing past them is only water and the random detritus of any forest stream.

"The world blinds those who cannot close their eyes," the girl tells her. "You were not always a god and have come here from some outer, fallen world, so it may be you were never taught how to travel that path and not become lost in All-At-Once time."

Ann Darrow digs her fingers into the soft, damp earth, driving them into the loam of the jungle floor, holding on and still expecting this scene to shift, to unfurl, to send her tumbling pell-mell and head over heels into some other *now,* some other *where.*

And sometime later, when she's strong enough to stand again, and the sickening vertiginous sensation of fluidity has at last begun to ebb, the girl helps Ann to her feet, and together they follow the narrow dirt trail leading back up this long ravine to the temple. Like Ann, the girl is naked save a leather breechcloth tied about her waist. They walk together beneath the sagging boughs of trees that must have been old before Ann's great-great grandmothers were born, and here and there is ample evidence of the civilization that ruled the island in some murky, immemorial past – glimpses of great stone idols worn away by time and rain and the humid air, disintegrating walls and archways leaning at such precarious angles Ann cannot fathom why they have not yet succumbed to gravity. Crumbling bas-reliefs depicting the loathsome gods and demons and the bizarre reptilian denizens of this place. As they draw nearer to the temple, the ruins are somewhat more intact, though even here the splayed roots of the trees are slowly forcing the masonry apart. The roots put Ann in mind of the tentacles of gargantuan octopuses or cuttlefish, and that is how she envisions the spirit of the jungles and marshes fanning out around this ridge – grey tentacles advancing inch by inch, year by year, inexorably reclaiming what has been theirs all along.

As she and the girl begin to climb the steep, crooked steps leading up from the deep ravine – stones smoothed by untold generations of footsteps – Ann stops to catch her breath and asks the brown girl how she knew where to look, how it was she found her at the stream. But the girl only stares at her, confused and uncomprehending, and then she frowns and shakes her head and says something in the native tongue. In Anne's long years on the island, since the *Venture* deserted her and sailed away with what remained of the dead ape, she has never learned more than a few words of that language, and she has never tried to teach this girl, nor any of her people, English. The girl looks back the way they've come; she presses the fingers of her left hand against her breast, above her heart, then uses the same hand to motion towards Ann.

Life is just a bowl of cherries.

Don't take it serious; it's too mysterious.

By sunset, Ann has taken her place on the rough-hewn throne carved from beds of coral limestone thrust up from the seafloor in the throes of the island's cataclysmic genesis. As night begins to gather once again, torches are lit, and the people come bearing sweet-smelling baskets of flowers and fruit, fish and the roasted flesh of gulls and rats and crocodiles. They lay multicolored garlands and strings of pearls at her feet, a necklace of ankylosaur teeth, rodent claws, and monkey vertebrae, and she is only the Golden Mother once again. They bow and genuflect, and the tropical night rings out with joyous songs she cannot understand. The men and woman decorate their bodies with yellow paint in an effort to emulate Ann's blonde hair, and a sort of pantomime is acted out for her benefit, as it is once every month, on the night of the new moon. She does not *need* to understand their words to grasp its meaning – the coming of the *Venture* from somewhere far away, Ann offered up as the bride of a god, her marriage and the death of Kong, and the obligatory ascent of the Golden Mother from a hellish underworld to preside in his stead. She who steals a god's heart must herself become a god.

The end of one myth and the beginning of another, the turning of a page. *I am not lost,* Ann thinks. *I am right here, right now – here and now where, surely, I must belong,* and she watches the glowing bonfire embers rising up to meet the dark sky. She knows she will see that terrible black hill again, the hill that is not a hill and its fetid crimson river, but she knows, too, that there will always be a road back from her dreams, from that All-At-Once tapestry of possibility and penitence. In her dreams, she will be lost and wander those treacherous, deceitful paths of Might-Have-Been, and always she will wake and find herself once more.

THE APE'S WIFE

A simple question of "what if's," all the ways a story might have gone. And, in the end, what if THIS, instead? I'm a serial speculator on unrealized realities. See "Emptiness Spoke Eloquent," for example. And "From Cabinet 34, Drawer 6." And, too, I wanted to permit Ann Darrow to exist as something more than a shrieking rag doll. "The Ape's Wife" was voted the *Clarkesworld* reader's favorite for 2007.

The Steam Dancer (1896)

1.

Missouri Banks lives in the great smoky city at the edge of the mountains, here where the endless yellow prairie laps gently with grassy waves and locust tides at the exposed bones of the world jutting suddenly up towards the western sky. She was not born here, but came to the city long ago, when she was still only a small child and her father traveled from town to town in one of Edison's electric wagons selling his herbs and medicinals, his stinking poultices and elixirs. This is the city where her mother grew suddenly ill with miner's fever and where all her father's liniments and ministrations could not restore his wife's failing health or spare her life. In his grief, he drank a vial of either antimony or arsenic a few days after the funeral, leaving his only daughter and only child to fend for herself. And so she grew up here, an orphan, one of a thousand or so dispossessed urchins with sooty bare feet and sooty faces, filching coal with sooty hands to stay warm in winter, clothed in rags, and eating what could be found in trash barrels and what could be begged or stolen.

But these things are only her past, and she has a bit of paper torn from a lending-library book of old plays which reads *What's past is prologue,* which she tacked up on the wall near her dressing mirror in the room she shares with the mechanic. Whenever the weight of Missouri's past begins to press in upon her, she reads those words aloud to herself, once or twice or however many times is required, and usually it makes her feel at least a little better. It has been years since she was alone and on the streets. She has the mechanic, and he loves her, and most of the time she believes that she loves him, as well.

He found her when she was nineteen, living in a shanty on the edge of the colliers' slum, hiding away in amongst the spoil piles and the rusting ruin of junked steam shovels, hydraulic pumps, and bent bore-drill heads. He was out looking for salvage, and salvage is what he found, finding her when he lifted a broad sheet of corrugated tin, uncovering the squalid burrow where she lay slowly dying on a filthy mattress. She'd been badly bitten during a swarm of red-bellied bloatflies, and now the hungry white maggots were doing their work. It was not an uncommon fate for the likes of Missouri Banks, those caught out in the open during the spring swarms, those without safe houses to hide inside until the voracious flies had come and gone, moving on to bedevil other towns and cities and farms. By the time the mechanic chanced upon her, Missouri's left leg, her right hand, and right forearm, were gangrenous, seething with the larvae. Her left eye was a pulpy, painful boil, and he carried her to the charity hospital on Arapahoe where he paid the surgeons who meticulously picked out the parasites and sliced away the rotten flesh and finally performed the necessary amputations. Afterwards, the mechanic nursed her back to health, and when she was well enough, he fashioned for her a new leg and a new arm. The eye was entirely beyond his expertise, but he knew a Chinaman in San Francisco who did nothing but eyes and ears, and it happened that the Chinaman owed the mechanic a favour. And in this way was Missouri Banks made whole again, after a fashion, and the mechanic took her as his lover and then as his wife, and they found a better, roomier room in an upscale boarding house near the Seventh Avenue irrigation works.

And today, which is the seventh day of July, she settles onto the little bench in front of the dressing-table mirror and reads aloud to herself the shred of paper.

"What's past is prologue," she says, and then sits looking at her face and the artificial eye and listening to the oppressive drone of cicadas outside the open window. The mechanic has promised that someday he will read her *The Tempest* by William Shakespeare, which he says is where the line was taken from. She can read it herself, she's told him, because she isn't illiterate. But the truth is she'd much prefer to hear him read, breathing out the words in his rough, soothing voice, and often he does read to her in the evenings.

She thinks that she has grown to be a very beautiful woman, and sometimes she believes the parts she wasn't born with have only served to make her that much more so and not any the less. Missouri smiles and gazes back at her reflection, admiring the high cheekbones and full lips (which were her mother's before her), the glistening beads of sweat on her chin and forehead and upper lip, the way her left eye pulses with a soft turquoise radiance. Afternoon light glints off the Galvanized plating of her mechanical arm, the sculpted steel rods and struts, the well-oiled wheels and cogs, all the rivets and welds and perfectly fitted joints. For now, it hangs heavy and limp at her side, because she hasn't yet cranked its tiny double-acting Trevithick engine. There's only the noise of the cicadas and the traffic down on the street and the faint, familiar, comforting chug of her leg.

Other women are only whole, she thinks. *Other women are only born, not made. I have been crafted.*

With her living left hand, Missouri wipes some of the sweat from her face and then turns towards the small electric fan perched on the chifforobe. It hardly does more than stir the muggy summer air about, and she thinks how good it would be to go back to bed. How good to spend the whole damned day lying naked on cool sheets, dozing and dreaming and waiting for the mechanic to come home from the foundry. But she dances at Madam Ling's place four days a week, and today is one of those days, so soon she'll have to get dressed and start her arm – and her leg, too – , then make her way to the trolley and on down to the Asian Quarter. The mechanic didn't want her to work, but she told him she owed him a great debt and it would be far kinder of him to allow her to repay it. And, being kind, he knew she was telling the truth. Sometimes, he even comes down to see, to sit among the coolies and the pungent clouds of opium smoke and watch her on the stage.

2.

The shrewd old woman known in the city only as Madam Ling made the long crossing to America sometime in 1861, shortly after the end of the Second Opium War. Missouri has heard that she garnered a tidy fortune from smuggling and piracy, and maybe a bit of murder, too, but that she found Hong Kong considerably less amenable to her business ventures after the treaty that ended the war and legalized the import of opium to China. She came ashore in San Francisco and followed the railroads and airships east across the Rockies, and when she reached the city at the edge of the prairie, she went no farther. She opened a saloon and whorehouse, the Nine Dragons, on a muddy, unnamed thoroughfare, and the mechanic has explained to

Missouri that in China nine is considered a very lucky number. The Nine Dragons is wedged in between a hotel and a gambling house, and no matter the time of day or night seems always just as busy. Madam Ling never wants for trade.

Missouri always undresses behind the curtain, before she takes the stage, and so presents herself to the sleepy-eyed men wearing only a fringed shawl of vermilion silk, her corset and sheer muslin shift, her white linen pantalettes. The shawl was a gift from Madam Ling, who told her in broken English that it came all the way from Beijing. Madam Ling of the Nine Dragons is not renowned for her generosity towards white women, or much of anyone else, and Missouri knows the gift was a reward for attracting a certain clientele, the men who come here just to watch her. She does not have many belongings, but she treasures the shawl as one of her most prized possessions and keeps it safe in a cedar chest at the foot of the bed she shares with the mechanic, and it always smells of the camphor-soaked cotton balls she uses to keep the moths at bay.

There is no applause, but she knows that most eyes have turned her way now. She stands sweating in the flickering gaslight glow, the open flames that ring the small stage, and listens to the men muttering in Mandarin amongst themselves and laying down mahjong tiles and sucking at their pipes. And then her music begins, the negro piano player and the woman who plucks so proficiently at a guzheng's twenty-five strings, the thin man at his xiao flute, and the burly Irishman who keeps the beat on a goatskin bodhrán and always takes his pay in celestial whores. The smoky air fills with a peculiar, jangling rendition of the final aria of Verdi's *La traviata,* because Madam Ling is a great admirer of Italian opera. The four musicians huddle together, occupying the space that has been set aside especially for them, crammed between the bar and the stage, and Missouri breathes in deeply, taking her cues as much from the reliable metronome rhythms of the engines that drive her metal leg and arm as from the music.

This is her time, her moment as truly as any moment will ever belong to Missouri Banks.

And her dance is not what men might see in the white saloons and dance halls and brothels strung out along Broadway and Lawrence, not the schottisches and waltzes of the ladies of the line, the uptown sporting women in their fine ruffled skirts made in New Amsterdam and Chicago. No one has ever taught Missouri how to dance, and these are only the moves that come naturally to her, that she finds for herself. This is the interplay and synthesis of her body and the mechanic's handiwork, of the music and her own secret dreams. Her clothes fall away in gentle, inevitable drifts, like the first snows of October. Steel toe to flesh-and-bone heel, the graceful arch of an iron calf and the clockwork motion of porcelain and nickel fingers across her sweaty belly and thighs. She spins and sways and dips, as lissome and sure of herself as anything that was ever only born of Nature. And there is such joy in the dance that she might almost offer prayers of thanks to her suicide father and the bloatfly maggots that took her leg and arm and eye. There is such joy in the dancing, it might almost match the delight and peace she's found in the arms of the mechanic. There is such joy, and she thinks this is why some men and women turn to drink and laudanum, tinctures of morphine and Madam Ling's black tar, because they cannot dance.

The music rises and falls, like the seas of grass rustling to themselves out beyond the edges of the city, and the delicate mechanisms of her prosthetics clank and hum and whine. Missouri weaves herself through this landscape of sound with the easy dexterity of pronghorn antelope and deer fleeing the jaws of wolves or the hunters' rifles, the long haunches and fleet paws of jackrabbits running out before a wildfire. For this moment, she is lost, and, for this moment, she wishes never to be found again. Soon, the air has begun to smell of the steam leaking from the exhaust ports in her leg and arm, an oily, hot sort of aroma that is as sweet to Missouri Banks as rosewater or honeysuckle blossoms. She closes her eyes – the one she was born with and the one from San Francisco – and feels no shame whatsoever at the lazy stares of the opium smokers. The piston rods in her left leg pump something more alive than blood, and the flywheels turn on their axels. She is muscle and skin, steel and artifice. She is the woman who was once a filthy, ragged guttersnipe, and she is Madam Ling's special attraction, a wondrous child of Terpsichore and Industry. Once she overheard the piano player whispering to the Irishman, and he said, "You'd think she emerged outta her momma's womb like that," and then there was a joke about screwing automata and the offspring that could ensue. But, however it might have been meant, she took it as praise and confirmation.

Too soon the music ends, leaving her gasping and breathless, dripping sweat and an iridescent sheen of lubricant onto the boards, and she must sit in her room backstage and wait out another hour before her next dance.

3.

And after the mechanic has washed away the day's share of grime and they're finished with their modest supper of apple pie and beans with thick slices of bacon, after his evening cigar and her cup of strong black Indian tea, after all the little habits and rituals of their nights together are done, he follows her to bed. The mechanic sits down and the springs squeak like stepped-on mice; he leans back against the tarnished brass headboard, smiling his easy, disarming smile while she undresses. When she slips the stocking off her right leg, he sees the gauze bandage wrapped about her knee, and his smile fades to concern.

"Here," he says. "What's that? What happened there?" and he points at her leg.

"It's nothing," she tells him. "It's nothing much."

"That seems an awful lot of dressing for nothing much. Did you fall?"

"I didn't fall," she replies. "I never fall."

"Of course not," he says. "Only us mere mortal folk fall. Of course you didn't fall. So what is it? It ain't the latest goddamn fashion."

Missouri drapes her stocking across the footboard, which is also brass, and turns her head to frown at him over her shoulder.

"A burn," she says, "that's all. One of Madam Ling's girls patched it for me. It's nothing to worry over."

"How bad a burn?"

"I said it's nothing, didn't I?"

"You did," says the mechanic and nods his head, looking not the least bit convinced. "But that secondary sliding valve's leaking again, and that's what did it. Am I right?"

Missouri turns back to her bandaged knee, wishing that there'd been some way to hide it from him, because she doesn't feel like him fussing over her tonight. "It doesn't hurt much at all. Madam Ling had a salve."

"Haven't I been telling you that seal needs to be replaced?"

"I know you have."

"Well, you just stay in tomorrow, and I'll take that leg with me to the shop, get it fixed up tip-top again. Have it back before you know."

"It's *fine.* I already patched it. It'll hold."

"Until the *next* time," he says, and she knows well enough from the tone of his voice that he doesn't want to argue with her about this, that he's losing patience. "You go and let that valve blow out, and you'll be needing a good deal more doctoring than a chink whore can provide. There's a lot of pressure builds up inside those pistons. You know that, Missouri."

"Yeah, I know that," she says.

"Sometimes you don't *act* like you know it."

"I can't stay in tomorrow. But I'll let you take it the next day, I swear. I'll stay in Thursday, and you can take my leg then."

"Thursday," the mechanic grumbles. "And so I just gotta keep my fingers crossed until then?"

"It'll be fine," she tells him again, trying to sound reassuring and reasonable, trying not to let the bright rind of panic in her head show in her voice. "I won't push so hard. I'll stick to the slow dances."

And then a long and disagreeable sort of silence settles over the room, and for a time she sits there at the edge of the bed, staring at both her legs, at injured meat and treacherous, unreliable metal. *Machines break down,* she thinks, *and the flesh is weak. Ain't nothing yet conjured by God nor man won't go and turn against you, sooner or later.* Missouri sighs and lightly presses a porcelain thumb to the artificial leg's green release switch; there's a series of dull clicks and pops as it comes free of the bolts set directly into her pelvic bones.

"I'll stay in tomorrow," she says and sets her left leg into its stand near the foot of their bed. "I'll send word to Madam Ling. She'll understand."

When the mechanic doesn't tell her that it's really for the best, when he doesn't say anything at all, she looks and sees he's dozed off sitting up, still wearing his trousers and suspenders and undershirt.

"You," she says quietly, then reaches for the release switch on her right arm.

4.

When she feels his hands on her, Missouri thinks at first that this is only some new direction her dream has taken, the rambling dream of her father's medicine wagon and of buffalo, of rutted roads and a flaxen Nebraska sky filled with flocks of automatic birds chirping arias from *La traviata.* But there's something substantial about the pale light of the waxing moon falling though the open window and the way the curtains move in the midnight breeze that convinces her she's awake. Then he kisses her, and one hand wanders down across her breasts and stomach and lingers in the unruly thatch of hair between her legs.

"Unless maybe you got something better to be doing," he mutters in her ear.

"Well, now that you mention it, I *was* dreaming," she tells him, "before you woke me up," and the mechanic laughs.

"Then maybe I should let you get back to it," but when he starts to move his hand away from her privy parts, she takes hold of it and rubs his fingertips across her labia.

"So, what exactly were you dreaming about that's got you in such a cooperative mood, Miss Missouri Banks?" he asks and kisses her again, the dark stubble on his cheeks scratching at her face.

"Wouldn't you like to know," she says.

"I figure that's likely why I inquired."

His face is washed in the soft blue-green glow of her San Francisco eye, which switched on as soon as she awoke, and times like this it's hard not to imagine all the ways her life might have gone, but didn't, how very unlikely that it went this way, instead. And she starts to tell him the truth, her dream of being a little girl and all the manufactured birds, the shaggy herds of bison, and how her father kept insisting he should give up peddling his herbs and remedies and settle down somewhere. But at the last, and for no particular reason, she changes her mind, and Missouri tells him another dream, just something she makes up off the top of her sleep-blurred head.

"You might not like it," she says.

"Might not," he agrees. "Then again, you never know," and the first joint of an index finger slips inside her.

"Then again," she whispers, and so she tells him a dream she's never dreamt. How there was a terrible fire, and before it was over and done with, the flames had claimed half the city, there where the grass ends and the mountains start. And at first, she tells him, it was an awful, awful dream, because she was trapped in the boarding house when it burned, and she could see him down on the street, calling for her, but, try as they may, neither could reach the other.

"Why you want to go and have a dream like that for?" he asks.

"You wanted to hear it. Now shut up and listen."

So he does as he's bidden, and she describes to him seeing an enormous airship hovering above the flames, spewing its load of water and sand into the ravenous inferno.

"There might have been a dragon," she says. "Or it might have only been started by lightning."

"A dragon," he replies, working his finger in a little deeper. "Yes, I think it must definitely have been a dragon. They're so ill-tempered this time of year."

"Shut up. This is my dream," she tells him, even though it isn't. "I almost died, so much of me got burned away, and they had me scattered about in pieces in the Charity Hospital. But you went right to work, putting me back together again. You worked night and day at the shop, making me a pretty metal face and a tin heart, and you built my breasts – "

" – from sterling silver," he says. "And your nipples I fashioned from out pure gold."

"And just how the sam hell did you know *that?*" she grins. Then Missouri reaches down and moves his hand, slowly pulling his finger out of her. Before he can protest, she's laid his palm over the four bare bolts where her leg fits on. He smiles and licks at her nipples, then grips one of the bolts and gives it a very slight tug.

"Well, while you were sleeping," he says, "I made a small window in your skull, only just large enough that I can see inside. So, no more secrets. But don't you fret. I expect your hair will hide it quite completely. Madam Ling will never even notice, and nary a Chinaman will steal a glimpse of your sweet, darling brain."

"Why, I never even felt a thing."

"I was very careful not to wake you."

"Until you did."

And then the talk is done, without either of them acknowledging that the time has come, and there's no more of her fiery, undreamt dreams or his glib comebacks. There's only the mechanic's busy, eager hands upon her, only her belly pressed against his, the grind of their hips after he has entered her, his fingertips lingering at the sensitive bolts where her prosthetics attach. She likes that best of all, that faint electric tingle, and she knows *he* knows, though she has never had to tell him so. Outside and far away, she thinks she hears an owl, but there are no owls in the city.

5.

And when she wakes again, the boarding-house room is filled with the dusty light of a summer morning. The mechanic is gone, and he's taken her leg with him. Her crutches are leaned against the wall near her side of the bed. She stares at them for a while, wondering how long it's been since the last time she had to use them, then deciding it doesn't really matter, because however long it's been, it hasn't been long enough. There's a note, too, on her nightstand, and the mechanic says not to worry about Madam Ling, that he'll send one of the boys from the foundry down to the Asian Quarter with the news. Take it easy, he says. Let that burn heal. Burns can be bad. Burns can scar, if you don't look after them.

When the clanging steeple bells of St. Margaret of Castello's have rung nine o'clock, she shuts her eyes and thinks about going back to sleep. St. Margaret, she recalls, is a patron saint of the crippled, an Italian woman who was born blind and hunchbacked, lame and malformed. Missouri envies the men and women who take comfort in those bells, who find in their tolling more than the time of day. She has never believed in the Catholic god or any other sort, unless perhaps it was some capricious heathen deity assigned to watch over starving, maggot-ridden guttersnipes. She imagines what form that god might assume, and it is a far more fearsome thing than any hunchbacked crone. A wolf, she thinks. Yes, an enormous black wolf – or coyote, perhaps – all ribs and mange and a distended, empty belly, crooked ivory fangs and burning eyes like smoldering embers glimpsed through a cast-iron grate. *That* would be her god, if ever she'd been blessed with such a thing. Her mother had come from Presbyterian stock somewhere back in Virginia, but her father believed in nothing more powerful than the hand and intellect of man, and he was not about to have his child's head filled up with Protestant superstition and nonsense, not in a Modern age of science and enlightenment.

Missouri opens her eyes again, her green eye – all cornea and iris, aqueous and vitreous humours – and the ersatz one designed for her in San Francisco. The crutches are still right there, near enough that she could reach out and touch them. They have good sheepskin padding and the vulcanized rubber tips have pivots and are filled with some shock-absorbing gelatinous substance, the name of which she has been told but cannot recall. The mechanic ordered them for her special from a company in some faraway Prussian city, and she knows they cost more than he could rightly afford, but she hates them anyway. And lying on the sweat-damp sheets, smelling the hazy morning air rustling the gingham curtains, she wonders if she built a little shrine to the wolf god of all collier guttersnipes, if maybe he would come in the night and take the crutches away so she would never have to see them again.

"It's not that simple, Missouri," she says aloud, and she thinks that those could have been her father's words, if the theosophists are right and the dead might ever speak through the mouths of the living.

"Leave me alone, old man" she says and sits up. "Go back to the grave you yearned for, and leave me be."

Her arm is waiting for her at the foot of the bed, right where she left it the night before, reclining in its cradle, next to the empty space her leg *ought* to occupy. And the hot breeze through the window, the street- and coal smoke-scented breeze, causes the scrap of paper tacked up by her vanity mirror to flutter against the wall. Her proverb, her precious stolen scrap of Shakespeare: *What's past is prologue.*

Missouri Banks considers how she can keep herself busy until the mechanic comes back to her. There's a torn shirt sleeve that needs mending, and she's no slouch with a needle and thread. Her good stockings could use a rinsing. The dressing on her leg should be changed; Madam Ling saw to it she had a small tin of the pungent salve to reapply when Missouri changed the bandages. Easily half a dozen such mundane tasks, any woman's work, any woman who is not a dancer, and nothing that won't wait until the bells of St. Margaret's ring ten or eleven. And so she watches the window, the sunlight and flapping gingham, and it isn't difficult to call up with almost perfect clarity the piano and the guzheng and the Irishman thumping his bodhrán, the exotic, festive trill of the xiao. And with the music swelling loudly inside her skull, she can then recall the dance. And she is not a cripple in need of patron saints or a guttersnipe praying to black wolf gods, but Madam Ling's specialty, the steam- and blood-powered gem of the Nine Dragons. She moves across the boards, and men watch her with dark and drowsy eyes as she pirouettes and prances through grey opium clouds.

THE STEAM DANCER (1896)

I'm fairly sure this has become the most reprinted steampunk story ever. It's also a story that seems especially prone to misreading, especially by people with political agendas that are not necessarily my own. For me, it's a joyful, triumphant story, and I don't write many of those. This was the first of my Cherry Creek stories, though the city is never named.

In the Dreamtime of Lady Resurrection

How I, then a young girl, came to think of, and to dilate upon, so very hideous an idea?

Mary Wollstonecraft Godwin Shelley
(October 15th, 1831)

"Wake up," she whispers, as ever she is always whispering with those demanding, ashen lips, but I do not open my eyes. I do not wake up, as she has bidden me to do, but, instead, lie drifting in this amniotic moment, unwilling to move one instant forward and incapable of retreating by even the scant breadth of a single second. For now, there is *only* now; yet, even so, an infinity stretches all around, haunted by dim shapes and half-glimpsed phantasmagoria, and if I named this time and place, I might name it Pluto or Orcus or Dis Pater. But never would I name it purgatorial, for here there are no purging flames, nor trials of final purification from venial transgressions. I have not arrived here by any shade of damnation and await no deliverance, but scud gently through Pre-Adamite seas, and so might I name this wide pacific realm *Womb,* the uterus common to all that which has ever risen squirming from mere insensate earth. I might name it *Mother.* I might best call it nothing at all, for a name may only lessen and constrain this inconceivable vastness.

"Wake up now," she whispers, but I shall rather seek these deeper currents.

No longer can I distinguish that which is *without* from that which is *within.* In ocher and loden green and malachite dusks do I dissolve and somehow still retain this flesh and this unbeating heart and this blood grown cold and stagnant in my veins. Even as I slip free, I am constrained, and in the eel-grass shadows do I descry her desperate, damned form bending low above this warm and salty sea where she has lain me down. She is Heaven, her milky skin is star-pierced through a thousand, thousand times to spill forth droplets of the dazzling light which is but one half of her unspeakable art. She would have me think it the totality, as though a dead woman is blind merely because her eyes remain shut. Long did I suspect the whole of her. When I breathed and had occasion to walk beneath the sun and moon, even then did I harbour my suspicions and guess at the blackness fastidiously concealed within that blinding glare. And here, at this moment, she is to me as naked as in the hour of her birth, and no guise nor glamour would ever hide from me that perpetual evening of her soul. At this moment, all and everything is laid bare. I am gutted like a gasping fish, and she is flayed by revelation.

She whispers to me, and I float across endless plains of primordial silt and gaping hadopelagic chasms where sometimes I sense the awful minds of other sleepers, ancient before the coming of time, waiting alone in sunken temples and drowned sepulchers. Below me lies the grey and glairy mass of Professor Huxley's *Bathybius haeckelii,* the boundless, wriggling sheet of *Urschleim* that encircles all the globe. Here and there do I catch sight of the bleached skeletons of mighty whales and ichthyosauria, their bones gnawed raw by centuries and millennia and aeons, by the busy proboscides of nameless invertebrata. The struts of a Leviathan's ribcage rise from the gloom like a cathedral's vaulted roof, and a startled retinue of spiny crabs wave threatful pincers that I might not forget I am the intruder. For this I *would* forget, and forswear that tattered life she stole and now so labours to restore, were that choice only mine to make.

I know this is no ocean, and I know there is no firmament set out over me. But I am sinking, all the same, spiraling down with infinite slowness towards some unimaginable beginning or conclusion (as though there is a difference between the two). And you watch on worriedly, and yet always that devouring curiosity to defuse any fear or regret. Your hands wander impatiently across copper coils and spark tungsten filaments, tap upon sluggish dials and tug so slightly at the rubber tubes that enter and exit me as though I have sprouted a bouquet of umbilici. You mind the gate and the road back, and so I turn away and would not see your pale, exhausted face.

With a glass dropper, you taint my pool with poisonous tinctures of quicksilver and iodine, meaning to shock me back into a discarded shell.

And I misstep, then, some fraction of a footfall this way or that, and now somehow I have not yet felt the snip that divided *me* from *me.* I sit naked on a wooden stool near *Der Ocean auf dem Tische,* the great vivarium tank you have fashioned from iron and plate glass and marble.

You will be my goldfish, you laugh. *You will be my newt. What better part could you ever play, my dear?*

You kiss my bare shoulders and my lips, and I taste brandy on your tongue. You hold my breasts cupped in your hands and tease my nipples with your teeth. And I know none of this is misdirection to put my mind at ease, but rather your delight in changes to come. The experiment is your bacchanal, and the mad glint in your eyes would shame any maenad or rutting satyr. I have no delusions regarding what is soon to come. I am the sacrifice, and it matters little or none at all whether the altar you have raised is to Science or Dionysus.

"Oh, if I could stand in your place," you sigh, and again your lips brush mine. "If I could *see* what you will see and *feel* what you will feel!"

"I will be your eyes," I say, echoing myself. "I will be your curious, probing hands." These might be wedding vows that we exchange. These might be the last words of the condemned on the morning of her execution.

"Yes, you shall, but I would make this journey myself and have need of no surrogate." Then and now, I wonder in secret if you mean everything you say. It is easy to declare envy when there is no likelihood of exchanging places. "Where you go, my love, all go in due time, but you may be the first ever to return and report to the living what she has witnessed there."

You kneel before me, as if in awe or gratitude, and your head settles upon my lap. I touch your golden hair with fingers that have scarcely begun to feel the tingling and chill, the numbness that will consume me soon enough. You kindly offered to place the lethal preparation in a cup of something sweet that I would not taste its bitterness, but I told you how I preferred to know my executioner and would not have his grim face so pleasantly hooded. I took it in a single acrid spoonful, and now we wait, and I touch your golden hair.

"When I was a girl," I begin, then must pause to lick my dry lips.

"You have told me this story already."

"I would have you hear it once more. Am I not accorded some last indulgence before the stroll to the gallows?"

"It will not be a gallows," you reply, but there is a sharp edge around your words, a brittle frame and all the gilt flaking free. "Indeed, it will be little more than a quick glance stolen through a window before the drapes are drawn shut against you. So, dear, you do not stand to *earn* some final coddling, not this day, and so I would not hear that tale repeated, when I know it as well as I know the four syllables of my own beloved's name."

"You *will* hear me," I say, and my fingers twine and knot themselves tightly in your hair. A few flaxen strands pull free, and I hope I can carry them down into the dark with me. You tense, but do not pull away, or make any further protest. "When I was a girl, my own brother died beneath the wheels of an ox cart. It was an accident, of course. But still his skull was broken and his chest all staved in. Though, in the end, no one was judged at fault."

I sit on my stool, and you kneel there on the stone floor, waiting for me to be done, restlessly awaiting my passage and the moment when I have been rendered incapable of repeating familiar tales you do not wish to hear retold.

"I held him, what remained of him. I felt the shudder when his child's soul pulled loose from its prison. His blue eyes were as bright in that instant as the glare of sunlight off freshly fallen snow. As for the man who drove the cart, he committed suicide some weeks later, though I did not learn this until I was almost grown."

"There is no ox cart here," you whisper. "There are no careless hooves and no innocent drover."

"I did not say he was a drover. I have never said that. He was merely a farmer, I think, on his way to market with a load of potatoes and cabbages. My brother's entire unlived life traded for a only few bushels of potatoes and cabbages. That must be esteemed a bargain, by any measure."

"We should begin now," you say, and I don't disagree, for my legs are growing stiff and an indefinable weight has begun to press in upon me. I was warned of these symptoms, and so there is not surprise, only the fear that I have prayed I would be strong enough to bear. You stand and help me to my feet, then lead me the short distance to the vivarium tank. Suddenly, I cannot escape the fanciful and disagreeable impression that your mechanical apparatuses and contraptions are watching on. Maybe, I think, they have been watching all along. Perhaps, they were my jurors, an impassionate, unbiased tribunal of brass and steel and porcelain, and now they gaze out with automaton eyes and exhale steam and oily vapours to see their sentence served. You told me there would be madness, that the toxin would act upon my mind as well as my body, but in my madness I have forgotten the warning.

"Please, I would not have them see me, not like this," I tell you, but already we have reached the great tank that will only serve as my carriage for these brief and extraordinary travels – if your calculations and theories are proved correct – or that will become my deathbed, if, perchance, you have made some critical error. There is a stepladder, and you guide me, and so I endeavor not to feel their enthusiastic, damp-palmed scrutiny. I sit down on the platform at the top of the ladder and let my feet dangle into the warm liquid, both my feet and then my legs up to the knees. It is not an objectionable sensation and promises that I will not be cold for much longer. Streams of bubbles rise slowly from vents set into the rear wall of the tank, stirring and oxygenating this translucent primal soup of viscous humours, your painstaking brew of protéine and hæmatoglobin, carbamide resin and cellulose, water and phlegm and bile. All those substances believed fundamental to life, a recipe gleaned from out dusty volumes of Medieval alchemy and metaphysics, but also from your own researches and the work of more modern scientific practitioners and professors of chemistry and anatomy. Previously, I have found the odor all but unbearable, though now there seems to be no detectable scent at all.

"Believe me," you say, "I will have you back with me in less than an hour." And I try hard then to remember how long an hour is, but the poison leeches away even the memory of time. With hands as gentle as a midwife's, you help me from the platform and into my strange bath, and you keep my head above the surface until the last convulsions have come and gone, and I am made no more than any cadaver.

"Wake up," she says – *you* say – but the shock of the mercury and iodine you administered to the vivarium have rapidly faded, and once more there is but the absolute and inviolable present moment, so impervious and sacrosanct that I can not even imagine conscious action, which would require the concept of an apprehension of some future, that time is somehow more than this static aqueous matrix surrounding and defining me.

"Do you hear me? Can you not even *hear* me?"

All at once, and with a certitude almost agonizing in its omneity, I am aware that I am being watched. No, that is not right. That is not precisely the way of it. All at once, I know that I am being watched by eyes which have not heretofore beheld me; all along there have been *her* eyes, as well as the stalked eyes of the scuttling crabs I mentioned and other such creeping, slithering inhabitants of my mind's ocean as have glommed the dim pageant of my voyage. But *these* eyes, and this spectator – my love, nothing has ever seen me with such complete and merciless understanding. And now the act of *seeing* has ceased to be a passive action, as the act of being *seen* has stopped being an activity that neither diminishes nor alters the observed. I would scream, but dead women do not seem to be permitted that luxury, and the scream of my soul is as silent as the moon. And in another place and in another time where *past* and *future* still hold meaning, you plunge your arms into the tank, hauling me up from the shallow deep and moving me not one whit. I am fixed by these eyes, like a butterfly pinned after the killing jar.

It does not speak to me, for there can be no need of speech when vision is so thorough and so incapable of misreckoning. Plagues need not speak, nor floods, nor the voracious winds of tropical hurricanes. A thing with eyes for teeth, eyes for its tongue and gullet. A thing which has been waiting for me in this moment that has no antecedents and which can spawn no successors. Maybe it waits here for every dying man and woman, for every insect and beast and falling leaf, or maybe some specific quality of my obliteration has brought me to its attention. Possibly, it only catches sight of suicides, and surely I have become that, though *your* Circean hands poured the poison draught and then held the spoon. There is such terrible force in this gaze that it seems not implausible that I am the first it has ever beheld, and now it will know all, and it shall have more than knowledge for this opportunity might never come again.

"Only tell me what happened," you will say, in some time that cannot ever be, not from *when* I lie here in the vivarium you have built for me, not from this occasion when I lie exposed to a Cosmos hardly half considered by the mortal minds contained therein. "Only put down what seems most significant, in retrospect. Do not dwell upon everything you might recall, every perception. You may make a full accounting later."

"Later, I might forget something," I will reply. "It's not so unlike a dream." And you will frown and slide the inkwell a little ways across the writing desk towards me. On your face I will see the stain of an anxiety that has been mounting down all the days since my return.

That will be a lie, of course, for nothing of this will I ever forget. Never shall it fade. I will be taunting you, or through me *it* will be taunting your heedless curiosity, which even then will remain undaunted. This hour, though, is far, far away. From when I lie, it is a fancy that can never come to pass – a unicorn, the roaring cataract at the edge of a flat world, a Hell which punishes only those who deserve eternal torment. Around me flows the sea of all beginnings and of all conclusion, and through the weeds and murk, from the peaks of submarine mountains to the lowest vales of Neptune's sovereignty, benighted in perpetuum – horizon to horizon – does its vision stretch unbroken. And as I have written already, observing me it takes away, and observing me it adds to my acumen and marrow. I am increased as much or more than I am consumed, so it must be a *fair* encounter, when all is said and done.

Somewhen immeasurably inconceivable to my present-bound mind, a hollow needle pierces my flesh, there in some unforeseeable aftertime, and the hypodermic's plunger forces into me your concoction of caffeine citrate, cocaine, belladonna, epinephrine, foxglove, etcetera & etcetera. And I think you will be screaming for me to come back, then, to open my eyes, to wake up as if you had only given me over to an afternoon catnap. I would not answer, even now, even with its smothering eyes upon me, in me, performing their metamorphosis. But you are calling (*wake up, wake up, wake up*), and your chemicals are working upon my traitorous physiology, and, worst of all, *it* wishes me to return whence and from when I have come. It has infected me, or placed within me some fraction of itself, or made from my sentience something suited to its own explorations. Did this never occur to you, my dear? That in those liminal spaces, across the thresholds that separate life from death, might lurk an inhabitant supremely adapted to those climes, and yet also possessed of its own questions, driven by its own peculiar acquisitiveness, seeking always some means to penetrate the veil. I cross one way for you, and I return as another's experiment, the vessel of another's inquisition.

"Breathe, goddamn you!" you will scream, screaming that seems no more or less disingenuous or melodramatic than any actor upon any stage. With your fingers you will clear, have cleared, are evermore clearing my mouth and nostrils of the thickening elixir filling the vivarium tank. "You won't leave me. I will not let you go. There are no ox carts here, no wagon wheels."

But, also, you have, or you will, or at this very second you are placing that fatal spoon upon my tongue.

And when it is done – if I may arbitrarily use that word here, *when* – and its modifications are complete, it shuts its eyes, like the sun tumbling down from the sky, and I am tossed helpless back into the rushing flow of time's river. In the vivarium, I try to draw a breath and vomit milky gouts. At the writing desk, I take the quill you have provided me, and I write – *"Wake up," she whispers*. There are long days when I do not have the strength to speak or even sit. The fears of pneumonia and fever, of dementia and some heretofore unseen necrosis triggered by my time *away*. The relief that begins to show itself as weeks pass and your fears fade slowly, replaced again by that old and indomitable inquisitiveness. The evening that you drained the tank and found something lying at the bottom which you have refused to ever let me see, but keep under lock and key. And this night, which might be *now,* in our bed in the dingy room above your laboratory, and you hold me in your arms, and I lie with my ear against your breast, listening to the tireless rhythm of your heart winding down, and *it* listens through me. You think me still but your love, and I let my hand wander across your belly and on, lower, to the damp cleft of your sex. And there also is the day I hold my dying brother. And there are my long walks beside the sea, too, with the winter waves hammering against the Cobb. That brine is only the faintest echo of the tenebrous kingdom I might have named *Womb*. Overhead, the wheeling gulls mock me, and the freezing wind drives me home again. But always it watches, and it waits, and it studies the intricacies of the winding avenue I have become.

She rolls through an ether of sighs –
She revels in a region of sighs…
Edgar Allan Poe (December 1847)

IN THE DREAMTIME OF LADY RESURRECTION

In my mind, this is an intensely erotic story. However, I don't expect anyone else to feel that way about it. For me, it's the ultimate *ménage à trois*.

Pickman's Other Model (1929)

1.

I have never been much for the movies, preferring, instead, to take my entertainment in the theater, always favoring living actors over those flickering, garish ghosts magnified and splashed across the walls of dark and smoky rooms at twenty-four frames per second. I've never seemed able to get past the knowledge that the apparent motion is merely an optical illusion, a clever procession of still images streaming past my eye at such a rate of speed that I only perceive motion where none actually exists. But in the months before I finally met Vera Endecott, I found myself drawn with increasing regularity to the Boston movie houses, despite this longstanding reservation.

I had been shocked to my core by Thurber's suicide, though, with the unavailing curse of hindsight, it's something I should certainly have had the presence of mind to have seen coming. Thurber was an infantryman during the war – *La grande Guerre pour la civilisation,* as he so often called it. He was at the Battle of Saint-Mihiel when Pershing failed in his campaign to seize Metz from the Germans, and he survived only to see the atrocities at the Battle of the Argonne Forest less than two weeks later. When he returned home from France early in 1919, Thurber was hardly more than a fading, nervous echo of the man I'd first met during our college years at the Rhode Island School of Design, and, on those increasingly rare occasions when we met and spoke, more often than not our conversations turned from painting and sculpture and matters of aesthetics to the things he'd seen in the muddy trenches and ruined cities of Europe.

And then there was his dogged fascination with that sick bastard Richard Upton Pickman, an obsession that would lead quickly to what I took to be no less than a sort of psychoneurotic fixation on the man and the blasphemies he committed to canvas. When, two years ago, Pickman vanished from the squalor of his North End "studio," never to be seen again, this fixation only worsened, until Thurber finally came to me with an incredible, nightmarish tale which, at the time, I could only dismiss as the ravings of a mind left unhinged by the bloodshed and madness and countless wartime horrors he'd witnessed along the banks of the Meuse River and then in the wilds of the Argonne Forest.

But I am not the man I was then, that evening we sat together in a dingy tavern near Faneuil Hall (I don't recall the name of the place, as it wasn't one of my usual haunts). Even as William Thurber was changed by the war and by whatever it is he may have experienced in the company of Pickman, so too have I been changed, and changed *utterly,* first by Thurber's sudden death at his own hands and then by a film actress named Vera Endecott. I do not believe that I have yet lost possession of my mental faculties, and if asked, I would attest before a judge of law that my mind remains sound, if quite shaken. But I cannot now see the world around me the way I once did, for having beheld certain things there can be no return to the unprofaned state of innocence or grace that prevailed before those sights. There can be no return to the sacred cradle of Eden, for the gates are guarded by the flaming swords of cherubim, and the mind may not – excepting in merciful cases of shock and hysterical amnesia – simply forget the weird and dismaying revelations visited upon men and women who choose to ask forbidden questions. And I would be lying if I were to claim that I failed to comprehend, to suspect, that the path I was setting myself upon when I began my investigations following Thurber's inquest and funeral would lead me where they have. I knew, or I knew well enough. I am not yet so degraded that I am beyond taking responsibility for my own actions and the consequences of those actions.

Thurber and I used to argue about the validity of first-person narration as an effective literary device, him defending it and me calling into question the believability of such stories, doubting both the motivation of their fictional authors and the ability of those character narrators to accurately recall with such perfect clarity and detail specific conversations and the order of events during times of great stress and even personal danger. This is probably not so very different from my difficulty appreciating a moving picture because I am aware it is *not,* in fact, a moving picture. I suspect it points to some conscious unwillingness or unconscious inability, on my part, to effect what Coleridge dubbed the "suspension of disbelief." And now I sit down to write my own account, though I attest there is not a word of *intentional* fiction to it, and I certainly have no plans of ever seeking its publication. Nonetheless, it will undoubtedly be filled with inaccuracies following from the objections to a first-person recital that I have already belabored above. What I am putting down here is my best attempt to recall the events preceding and surrounding the murder of Vera Endecott, and it should be read as such.

It is my story, presented with such meager corroborative documentation as I am here able to provide. It is some small part of her story, as well, and over it hang the phantoms of Pickman and Thurber. In all honesty, already I begin to doubt that setting any of it down will achieve the remedy which I so desperately desire – the dampening of damnable memory, the lessening of the hold that those memories have upon me, and, if I am most lucky, the ability to sleep in dark rooms once again and an end to any number of phobias which have come to plague me. Too late do I understand poor Thurber's morbid fear of cellars and subway tunnels, and to that I can add my own fears, whether they might ever be proven rational or not. "I guess you won't wonder now why I have to steer clear of subways and cellars," he said to me that day in the tavern. I *did* wonder, of course, at that and at the sanity of a dear and trusted friend. But, in this matter, at least, I have long since ceased to wonder.

The first time I saw Vera Endecott on the "big screen," it was only a supporting part in Josef von Sternberg's *A Woman of the Sea,* at the Exeter Street Theater. But that was not the first time I saw Vera Endecott.

2.

I first encountered the name and face of the actress while sorting through William's papers, which I'd been asked to do by the only surviving member of his immediate family, Ellen Thurber, an older sister. I found myself faced with no small or simple task, as the close, rather shabby room he'd taken on Hope Street in Providence after leaving Boston was littered with a veritable bedlam of correspondence, typescripts, journals, and unfinished compositions, including the monograph on weird art that had played such a considerable role in his taking up with Richard Pickman three years prior. I was only mildly surprised to discover, in the midst of this disarray, a number of

Pickman's sketches, all of them either charcoal or pen and ink. Their presence among Thurber's effects seemed rather incongruous, given how completely terrified of the man he'd professed to having become. And even more so given his claim to have destroyed the one piece of evidence that could support the incredible tale of what he purported to have heard and seen and taken away from Pickman's cellar studio.

It was a hot day, so late into July that it was very nearly August. When I came across the sketches, seven of them tucked inside a cardboard portfolio case, I carried them across the room and spread the lot out upon the narrow, swaybacked bed occupying one corner. I had a decent enough familiarity with the man's work, and I must confess that what I'd seen of it had never struck me quite so profoundly as it had Thurber. Yes, to be sure, Pickman was possessed of a great and singular talent, and I suppose someone unaccustomed to images of the diabolic, the alien, or monstrous, would find them disturbing and unpleasant to look upon. I always credited his success at capturing the weird largely to his intentional juxtaposition of phantasmagoric subject matter with a starkly, painstakingly realistic style. Thurber also noted this, and, indeed, had devoted almost a full chapter of his unfinished monograph to an examination of Pickman's technique.

I sat down on the bed to study the sketches, and the mattress springs complained loudly beneath my weight, leading me to wonder yet again why my friend had taken such mean accommodations when he certainly could have afforded better. At any rate, glancing over the drawings, they struck me, for the most part, as nothing particularly remarkable, and I assumed that they must have been gifts from Pickman, or that Thurber might even have paid him some small sum for them. Two I recognized as studies for one of the paintings mentioned that day in the Chatham Street tavern, the one titled *The Lesson,* in which the artist had sought to depict a number of his subhuman, doglike ghouls instructing a young child (a *changeling,* Thurber had supposed) in their practice of necrophagy. Another was a rather hasty sketch of what I took to be some of the statelier monuments in Copp's Hill Burying Ground, and there were also a couple of rather slapdash renderings of hunched gargoyle-like creatures.

But it was the last two pieces from the folio that caught and held my attention. Both were very accomplished nudes, more finished than any of the other sketches, and given the subject matter, I might have doubted they had come from Pickman's hand had it not been for his signature at the bottom of each. There was nothing that could have been deemed pornographic about either, and considering their provenance, this surprised me, as well. Of the portion of Richard Pickman's *oeuvre* that I'd seen for myself, I'd not once found any testament to an interest in the female form, and there had even been whispers in the Art Club that he was a homosexual. But there were so many rumors traded about the man in the days leading up to his disappearance, many of them plainly spurious, that I'd never given the subject much thought. Regardless of his own sexual inclinations, these two studies were imbued with an appreciation and familiarity with a woman's body that seemed unlikely to have been gleaned entirely from academic exercises or mooched from the work of other, less-eccentric artists.

As I inspected the nudes, thinking that these two pieces, at least, might bring a few dollars to help Thurber's sister cover the unexpected expenses incurred by her brother's death, as well as his outstanding debts, my eyes were drawn to a bundle of magazine and newspaper clippings that had also been stored inside the portfolio. There were a goodly number of them, and I guessed then, and still suppose, that Thurber had employed a clipping bureau. About half were write-ups of gallery showings that had included Pickman's work, mostly spanning the years from 1921 to 1925, before he'd been so ostracized that opportunities for public showings had dried up. But the remainder appeared to have been culled largely from tabloids, sheetlets, and magazines such as *Photoplay* and The *New York Evening Graphic,* and every one of the articles was either devoted to or made mention of a Massachusetts-born actress named Vera Marie Endecott. There were, among these clippings, a number of photographs of the woman, and her likeness to the woman who'd modeled for the two Pickman nudes was unmistakable.

There was something quite distinct about her high cheekbones, the angle of her nose, an undeniable hardness to her countenance despite her starlet's beauty and "sex appeal." Later, I would come to recognize some commonality between her face and those of such movie "vamps" and *femmes fatales* as Theda Bara, Eva Galli, Musidora, and, in particular, Pola Negri. But, as best as I can now recollect, my first impression of Vera Endecott, untainted by film personae (though undoubtedly colored by the association of the clippings with the work of Richard Pickman, there among the belongings of a suicide) was of a woman whose loveliness might merely be a glamour concealing some truer, feral face. It was an admittedly odd impression, and I sat in the sweltering boarding-house room, as the sun slid slowly towards dusk, reading each of the articles, and then reading some over again. I suspected they must surely contain, somewhere, evidence that the woman in the sketches was, indeed, the same woman who'd gotten her start in the movie studios of Long Island and New Jersey, before the industry moved west to California.

For the most part, the clippings were no more than the usual sort of picture-show gossip, innuendo, and sensationalism. But, here and there, someone, presumably Thurber himself, had underlined various passages with a red pencil, and when those lines were considered together, removed from the context of their accompanying articles, a curious pattern could be discerned. At least, such a pattern might be imagined by a reader who was either *searching* for it, and so predisposed to discovering it whether it truly existed or not, or by someone, like myself, coming to these collected scraps of yellow journalism under such circumstances and such an atmosphere of dread as may urge the reader to draw parallels where, objectively, there are none to be found. I believed, that summer afternoon, that Thurber's *idée fixe* with Richard Pickman had led him to piece together an absurdly macabre set of notions regarding this woman, and that I, still grieving the loss of a close friend and surrounded as I was by the disorder of that friend's unfulfilled life's work, had done nothing but uncover another of Thurber's delusions.

The woman known to moviegoers as Vera Endecott had been sired into an admittedly peculiar family from the North Shore region of Massachusetts, and she'd undoubtedly taken steps to hide her heritage, adopting a stage name shortly after her arrival in Fort Lee in February of 1922. She'd also invented a new history for herself, claiming to hail not from rural Essex County, but from Boston's Beacon Hill. However, as early as '24, shortly after landing her first substantial role – an appearance in Biograph Studios' *Sky Below the Lake* – a number of popular columnists had begun printing their suspicions about her professed background. The banker she'd claimed as her father could not be found, and it proved a straightforward enough matter to demonstrate that she'd never attended the Winsor School for girls. By '25, after her starring role in Robert G. Vignola's *The Horse Winter,* a reporter for The *New York Evening Graphic* claimed Endecott's actual father was a man named Iscariot Howard Snow, the owner of several Cape Anne granite quarries. His wife, Make-peace, had come either from Salem or Marblehead and had died in 1902 while giving birth to their only daughter, whose name was not Vera, but Lillian Margaret. There was no evidence in any of the clippings that the actress had ever denied or even responded to these allegations, despite the fact that the Snows, and Iscariot Snow in particular, had a distinctly unsavory reputation in and around Ipswich. Regardless of the family's wealth and prominence in local business, it was notoriously secretive, and there was no want for back-fence talk concerning sorcery and witchcraft, incest and even cannibalism. In 1899, Make-peace Snow had also borne twin sons, Aldous and Edward, though Edward had been a stillbirth.

But it was a clipping from *Kidder's Weekly Art News* (March 27th, 1925), a publication I was well enough acquainted with, that first tied the actress to Richard Pickman. A "Miss Vera Endecott of Manhattan" was listed among those in attendance at the premiere of an exhibition that had included a couple of Pickman's less provocative paintings, though no mention was made of her celebrity. Thurber had circled her name with red pencil and drawn two exclamation points beside it. By the time I came across the article, twilight had descended upon Hope Street, and I was having trouble reading. I briefly considered the old gas lamp near the bed, but then, staring into the shadows gathering amongst the clutter and threadbare furniture of the seedy little room, I was gripped by a sudden, vague apprehension – by what, even now, I am reluctant to name *fear.* I returned the clippings and the seven sketches to the folio, tucked it under my arm and quickly retrieved my hat from a table buried beneath a typewriter, an assortment of paper and library books, unwashed dishes and empty soda bottles. A few minutes later, I was outside again and clear of the building, standing beneath a streetlight, staring up at the two darkened windows opening into the room where, a week before, William Thurber had put the barrel of a revolver in his mouth and pulled the trigger.

3.

I have just awakened from another of my nightmares, which become ever more vivid and frequent, ever more appalling, often permitting me no more than one or two hours' sleep each night. I'm sitting at my writing desk, watching as the sky begins to go the grey violet of false dawn, listening to the clock ticking like some giant wind-up insect perched upon the mantel. But my mind is still lodged firmly in a dream of the musty private screening room near Harvard Square, operated by a small circle of aficionados of grotesque cinema, the room where first I saw "moving" images of the daughter of Iscariot Snow.

I'd learned of the group from an acquaintance in acquisitions at the Museum of Fine Arts, who'd told me it met irregularly, rarely more than once every three months, to view and discuss such fanciful and morbid fare as Benjamin Christensen's *Häxen*, Rupert Julian's *The Phantom of the Opera,* Murnau's *Nosferatu, eine Symphonie des Grauens,* and Todd Browning's *London After Midnight*. These titles and the names of their directors meant very little to me, since, as I have already noted, I've never been much for the movies. This was in August, only a couple of weeks after I'd returned to Boston from Providence, having set Thurber's affairs in order as best I could. I still prefer not to consider what unfortunate caprice of fate aligned my discovery of Pickman's sketches of Vera Endecott and Thurber's interest in her with the group's screening of what, in my opinion, was a profane and a deservedly unheard-of film. Made sometime in 1923 or '24, I was informed that it had achieved infamy following the director's death (another suicide). All the film's financiers remained unknown, and it seemed that production had never proceeded beyond the incomplete rough cut I saw that night.

However, I did not sit down here to write out a dry account of my discovery of this untitled, unfinished film, but rather to try and capture something of the dream that is already breaking into hazy scraps and shreds. Like Perseus, who dared to view the face of the Gorgon Medusa only indirectly, as a reflection in his bronze shield, so I seem bound and determined to reflect upon these events, and even my own nightmares, as obliquely as I may. I have always despised cowardice, and yet, looking back over these pages, there seems in it something undeniably cowardly. It does not matter that I intend that no one else shall ever read this. Unless I write honestly, there is hardly any reason in writing it at all. If this is a ghost story (and, increasingly, it feels that way to me), then let it *be* a ghost story and not this rambling reminiscence.

In the dream, I am sitting in a wooden folding chair in that dark room, lit only by the single shaft of light spilling forth from the projectionist's booth. And the wall in front of me has become a window, looking out upon or into another world, one devoid of sound and almost all color, its palette limited to a spectrum of somber blacks and dazzling whites and innumerable shades of grey. Around me, the others who have come to see smoke their cigars and cigarettes, and they mutter among themselves. I cannot make out anything they say, but, then, I'm not trying particularly hard. I cannot look away from that silent, grisaille scene, and little else truly occupies my mind.

"Now, do you understand?" Thurber asks from his seat next to mine, and maybe I nod, and maybe I even whisper some hushed affirmation or another. But I do *not* take my eyes from the screen long enough to glimpse his face. There is too much there I might miss, were I to dare look away, even for an instant, and, moreover, I have no desire to gaze upon the face of a dead man. Thurber says nothing else for a time, apparently content that I have found my way to this place, to witness for myself some fraction of what drove him, at last, to the very end of madness.

She is there on the screen – Vera Endecott, Lillian Margaret Snow – standing at the edge of a rocky pool. She is as naked as in Pickman's sketches of her and is positioned, at first, with her back to the camera. The gnarled roots and branches of what might be ancient willow trees bend low over the pool, their whip-like branches brushing the surface and moving gracefully to and fro, disturbed by the same breeze that ruffles the actress' short, bob-cut hair. And though there appears to be nothing the least bit sinister about this scene, it at once inspires in me the same sort of awe and uneasiness as Doré's engravings for *Orlando Furioso* and the *Divine Comedy*. There is about the tableau a sense of intense foreboding and anticipation, and I wonder what subtle, clever cues have been placed just so that this seemingly idyllic view would be interpreted with such grim expectancy.

And then I realize that the actress is holding in her right hand some manner of phial, and she tilts it just enough that the contents, a thick and pitchy liquid, drip into the pool. Concentric ripples spread slowly across the water, much *too* slowly, I'm convinced, to have followed from any earthly physics, and so I dismiss it as merely trick photography. When the phial is empty, or has, at least, ceased to taint the pool (and I am quite sure that it *has* been tainted), the woman kneels in the mud and weeds at the water's edge. From somewhere overhead, there in the room with me, comes a sound like the wings of startled pigeons taking flight, and the actress half turns towards the audience, as if she has also somehow heard the commotion. The fluttering racket quickly subsides, and once more there is only the mechanical noise from the projector and the whispering of the men and women crowded into the musty room. Onscreen, the actress turns back to the pool, but not before I am certain that her face is the same one from the clippings I found in Thurber's room, the same one sketched by the hand of Richard Upton Pickman. The phial slips from her fingers, falling into the water, and this time there are no ripples whatsoever. No splash. Nothing.

Here, the image flickers before the screen goes blinding white, and I think, for a moment, that the filmstrip has, mercifully, jumped one sprocket or another, so maybe I'll not have to see the rest. But then she's back, the woman and the pool and the willows, playing out frame by frame by frame. She kneels at the edge of the pool, and I think of Narcissus pining for Echo or his lost twin, of jealous Circe poisoning the spring where Scylla bathed, and of Tennyson's cursed Shalott, and, too, again I think of Perseus and Medusa. I am not seeing the thing itself, but only some dim, misguiding counterpart, and my mind grasps for analogies and signification and points of reference.

On the screen, Vera Endecott, or Lillian Margaret Snow – one or the other, the two who were always only one – leans forward and dips her hand into the pool. And again, there are no ripples to mar its smooth obsidian surface. The woman in the film is speaking now, her lips moving deliberately, making no sound whatsoever, and I can hear nothing but the mumbling, smoky room and the sputtering projector. And this is when I realize that the willows are not precisely willows at all, but that those twisted trunks and limbs and roots are actually the entwined human bodies of both sexes, their skin painted and perfectly mimicking the scaly bark of a willow. I understand that these are no wood nymphs, no daughters of Hamadryas and Oxylus. These are prisoners, or condemned souls bound eternally for their sins, and for a time I can only stare in wonder at the confusion of arms and legs, hips and breasts and faces marked by untold ages of the ceaseless agony of this contortion and transformation. This is William Blake's Wood of Self-Murderers, Dante's Forest of Suicides. I want to turn and ask the others if they see what I see, and how the deception has been accomplished, for surely these people know more of the prosaic magic of filmmaking that do I. Worst of all, the bodies have not been rendered entirely inert, but writhe ever so slightly, helping the wind to stir the long, leafy branches first this way, then that.

Then my eye is drawn back to the pool, which has begun to steam, a grey-white mist rising languidly from off the water (if it still is water). The actress leans yet farther out over the strangely quiescent mere, and I find myself eager to look away. Whatever being the cameraman has caught her in the act of summoning or appeasing, I do not want to *see,* do not want to *know* its daemonic physiognomy. Her lips continue to move, and her hands stir the waters that remain smooth as glass, betraying no evidence that they have been disturbed in any way.

At Rhegium she arrives; the ocean braves,
And treads with unwet feet the boiling waves...

But desire is not enough, nor trepidation, and I do not look away, either because I have been bewitched along with all those others who have come to see her, or because some deeper, more disquisitive facet of my being has taken command and is willing to risk damnation in the seeking into this mystery.

"It is only a moving picture," dead Thurber reminds me from his seat beside mine. "Whatever else she would say, you must never forget it is only a dream."

And I want to reply, "Is that what happened to you, dear William? Did you forget it was never anything more than a dream and find yourself unable to waken to lucidity and life?" But I do not say a word, and Thurber does not say anything more.

But yet she knows not, who it is she fears;
In vain she offers from herself to run,
And drags about her what she strives to shun.

"Brilliant," whispers a woman in the darkness at my back, and "Sublime," mumbles what sounds to be a very old man. My eyes do not stray from the screen. The actress has stopped stirring the pool, has withdrawn her hand from the water, but still she kneels there, staring at the sooty stain it has left on her fingers and palm and wrist. *Maybe,* I think, *that is what she came for, that mark, that she will be known,* though my dreaming mind does not presume to guess what or whom she would have recognize her by such a bruise or blotch. She reaches into the reeds and moss and produces a black-handled dagger, which she then holds high above her head, as though making an offering to unseen gods, before she uses the glinting blade to slice open the hand she previously offered to the waters. And I think perhaps I understand, finally, and the phial and the stirring of the pool were only some preparatory wizardry before presenting this far more precious alms or expiation. As her blood drips to spatter and *roll* across the surface of the pool like drops of mercury striking a solid tabletop, something has begun to take shape, assembling itself from those concealed depths, and, even without sound, it is plain enough that the willows have begun to scream and to sway as though in the grip of a hurricane wind. I think, perhaps, it is a mouth, of sorts, coalescing before the prostrate form of Vera Endecott or Lillian Margaret Snow, a mouth or a vagina or a blind and lidless eye, or some versatile organ that may serve as all three. I debate each of these possibilities, in turn.

Five minutes ago, almost, I lay my pen aside, and I have just finished reading back over, aloud, what I have written, as false dawn gave way to sunrise and the first uncomforting light of a new October day. But before I return these pages to the folio containing Pickman's sketches and Thurber's clippings and go on about the business that the morning demands of me, I would confess that what I have dreamed and what I have recorded here are not what I saw that afternoon in the screening room near Harvard Square. Neither is it entirely the nightmare that woke me and sent me stumbling to my desk. Too much of the dream deserted me, even as I rushed to get it all down, and the dreams are never exactly, and sometimes not even remotely, what I saw projected on that wall, that deceiving stream of still images conspiring to suggest animation. This is another point I always tried to make with Thurber, and which he never would accept, the fact of the inevitability of unreliable narrators. I have not lied; I would not say that. But none of this is any nearer to the truth than any other fairy tale.

4.

After the days I spent in the boarding house in Providence, trying to bring some semblance of order to the chaos of Thurber's interrupted life, I began accumulating my own files on Vera Endecott, spending several days in August drawing upon the holdings of the Boston Athenaeum, the Public Library, and the Widener Library at Harvard. It was not difficult to piece together the story of the actress' rise to stardom and the scandal that led to her descent into obscurity and alcoholism late in 1927, not so very long before Thurber came to me with his wild tale of Pickman and subterranean ghouls. What was much more difficult to trace was her movement through certain theosophical and occult societies, from Manhattan to Los Angeles, circles to which Richard Upton Pickman was, himself, no stranger.

In January '27, after being placed under contract to Paramount Pictures the previous spring, and during production of a film adaptation of Margaret Kennedy's novel, *The Constant Nymph,* rumors began surfacing in the tabloids that Vera Endecott was drinking heavily and, possibly, using heroin. However, these allegations appear at first to have caused her no more alarm or damage to her film career than the earlier discovery that she was, in fact, Lillian Snow, or the public airing of her disreputable North Shore roots. Then, on May 3rd, she was arrested in what was, at first, reported as merely a raid on a speakeasy somewhere along Durand Drive, at an address in the steep, scrubby canyons above Los Angeles, not far from the Lake Hollywood Reservoir and Mulholland Highway. A few days later, after Endecott's release on bail, queerer accounts of the events of that night began to surface, and by the 7th, articles in the *Van Nuys Call, Los Angeles Times,* and the *Herald-Express* were describing the gathering on Durand Drive not as a speakeasy, but as everything from a "witches' Sabbat" to "a decadent, sacrilegious, orgiastic rite of witchcraft and homosexuality."

But the final, damning development came when reporters discovered that one of the many women found that night in the company of Vera Endecott, a Mexican prostitute named Ariadna Delgado, had been taken immediately to Queen of Angels-Hollywood Presbyterian, comatose and suffering from multiple stab wounds to her torso, breasts, and face. Delgado died on the morning of May 4th, without ever having regained consciousness. A second "victim" or "participant" (depending on the newspaper), a young and unsuccessful screenwriter listed only as Joseph E. Chapman, was placed in the psychopathic ward of LA County General Hospital following the arrests.

Though there appear to have been attempts to keep the incident quiet by both studio lawyers and also, perhaps, members of the Los Angeles Police Department, Endecott was arrested a second time on May 10th and charged with multiple counts of rape, sodomy, second-degree murder, kidnapping, and solicitation. Accounts of the specific charges brought vary from one source to another, but regardless, Endecott was granted and made bail a second time on May 11th, and four days later, the office of Los Angeles District Attorney Asa Keyes abruptly and rather inexplicably asked for a dismissal of all charges against the actress, a motion granted in an equally inexplicable move by the Superior Court of California, Los Angeles County (it bears mentioning, of course, that District Attorney Keyes was, himself, soon thereafter indicted for conspiracy to receive bribes, and is presently awaiting trial). So, eight days after her initial arrest at the residence on Durand Drive, Vera Endecott was a free woman, and, by late May, she had returned to Manhattan, after her contract with Paramount was terminated.

Scattered throughout the newspaper and tabloid coverage of the affair are numerous details which take on a greater significance in light of her connection with Richard Pickman. For one, some reporters made mention of "an obscene idol" and "a repellent statuette carved from something like greenish soapstone" recovered from the crime scene, a statue which one of the arresting officers is purported to have described as a "crouching, dog-like beast." One article listed the item as having been examined by a local (unnamed) archaeologist, who was supposedly baffled at its origins and cultural affinities. The house on Durand Drive was, and may still be, owned by a man named Beauchamp who'd spent time in the company of Aleister Crowley during his four-year visit to America (1914–1918) and who had connections with a number of hermetic and theurgical organizations. And finally, the screenwriter Joseph Chapman drowned himself in the Pacific somewhere near Malibu only a few months ago, shortly after being discharged from the hospital. The one short article I could locate regarding his death made mention of his part in the "notorious Durand Drive incident" and printed a short passage reputed to have come from the suicide note. It reads, in part, as follows:

Oh God, how does a man forget, deliberately and wholly and forever, once he has glimpsed such sights as I have had the misfortune to have seen? The awful things we did and permitted to be done that night, the events we set in motion, how do I lay my culpability aside? Truthfully, I cannot and am no longer able to fight through day after day of trying. The Endecotte [sic] *woman is back East somewhere, I hear, and I hope to hell she gets what's coming to her. I burned the abominable painting she gave me, but I feel no cleaner, no less foul, for having done so. There is nothing left of me but the putrescence we invited. I cannot do this anymore.*

Am I correct in surmising, then, that Vera Endecott made a gift of one of Pickman's paintings to the unfortunate Joseph Chapman, and that it played some role in his madness and death? If so, how many others received such gifts from her, and how many of those canvases yet survive so many thousands of miles from the dank cellar studio near Battery Street where Pickman created them? It's not something I like to dwell upon.

After Endecott's reported return to Manhattan, I failed to find any printed record of her whereabouts or doings until October of that year, shortly after Pickman's disappearance and my meeting with Thurber in the tavern near Faneuil Hall. It's only a passing mention from a society column in the *New York Herald Tribune,* that "the actress Vera Endecott" was among those in attendance at the unveiling of a new display of Sumerian, Hittite, and Babylonian antiquities at the Metropolitan Museum of Art.

What is it I am trying to accomplish with this catalog of dates and death and misfortune, calamity and crime? Among Thurber's books, I found a copy of Charles Hoy Fort's *The Book of the Damned* (Boni and Liveright; New York, December 1, 1919). I'm not even sure why I took it away with me, and having read it, I find the man's writings almost hysterically belligerent and constantly prone to intentional obfuscation and misdirection. Oh, and wouldn't that contentious bastard love to have a go at this tryst with "the damned"? My point here is that I'm forced to admit that these last few pages bear a marked and annoying similarity to much of Fort's first book (I have not read his second, *New Lands,* nor do I propose ever to do so). Fort wrote of his intention to present a collection of data which had been excluded by science (*id est,* "damned"):

Battalions of the accursed, captained by pallid data that I have exhumed, will march. You'll read them – or they'll march. Some of them livid and some of them fiery and some of them rotten.

Some of them are corpses, skeletons, mummies, twitching, tottering, animated by companions that have been damned alive. There are giants that will walk by, though sound asleep. There are things that are theorems and things that are rags: they'll go by like Euclid arm in arm with the spirit of anarchy. Here and there will flit little harlots. Many are clowns. But many are of the highest respectability. Some are assassins. There are pale stenches and gaunt superstitions and mere shadows and lively malices: whims and amiabilities. The naïve and the pedantic and the bizarre and the grotesque and the sincere and the insincere, the profound and the puerile.

And I think I have accomplished nothing more *than* this, in my recounting of Endecott's rise and fall, drawing attention to some of the more melodramatic and vulgar parts of a story that is, in the main, hardly more remarkable than numerous other Hollywood scandals. But also, Fort would laugh at my own "pallid data," I am sure, my pathetic grasping at straws, as though I might make this all seem perfectly reasonable by selectively quoting newspapers and police reports, straining to preserve the fraying infrastructure of my rational mind. It's time to lay these dubious, slipshod attempts at scholarship aside. There are enough Forts in the world already, enough crackpots and provocateurs and intellectual heretics without my joining their ranks. The files I have assembled will be attached to this document, all my "battalions of the accursed," and if anyone should ever have cause to read this, they may make of those appendices what they will. It's time to tell the truth, as best I am able, and be done with this.

5.

It is true that I attended a screening of a film, featuring Vera Endecott, in a musty little room near Harvard Square. And that it still haunts my dreams. But as noted above, the dreams rarely are anything like an accurate replaying of what I saw that night. There was no black pool, no willow trees stitched together from human bodies, no venomous phial emptied upon the waters. Those are the embellishments of my dreaming, subconscious mind. I could fill several journals with such nightmares.

What I *did* see, only two months ago now, and one month before I finally met the woman for myself, was little more than a grisly, but strangely mundane, scene. It might have only been a test reel, or perhaps 17,000 or so frames, some twelve minutes, give or take, excised from a far longer film. All in all, it was little more than a blatantly pornographic pastiche of the widely circulated 1918 publicity stills of Theda Bara lying in various risqué poses with a human skeleton (for J. Edward Gordon's *Salomé*).

The print was in very poor condition, and the projectionist had to stop twice to splice the film back together after it broke. The daughter of Iscariot Snow, known to most of the world as Vera Endecott, lay naked upon a stone floor with a skeleton. However, the human skull had been replaced with what I assumed then (and still believe) to have been a plaster or papier-mâché prop that more closely resembled the cranium of a mandrill, baboon, or some malformed, macrocephalic dog. The wall or backdrop behind her was a stark matte-grey, and the scene seemed to me purposefully under-lit in an attempt to bring more atmosphere to a shoddy production. The skeleton (and its ersatz skull) were wired together, and Endecott caressed all the osseous angles of its arms and legs and lavished kisses upon its lipless mouth, before masturbating, first with the bones of its right hand and then by rubbing herself against the crest of an ilium.

The reactions from the others who'd come to see the film that night ranged from bored silence to rapt attention to laughter. My own reaction was, for the most part, merely disgust and embarrassment to be counted among that audience. I overheard, when the lights came back up, that the can containing the reel bore two titles, *The Necrophile* and *The Hound's Daughter,* and also bore two dates – 1923 and 1924. Later, from someone who had a passing acquaintance with Richard Pickman, I would hear a rumor that he'd worked on scenarios for a filmmaker, possibly Bernard Natan, the prominent Franco-Romanian director of blue movies, who recently acquired Pathé and merged it with his own studio, Rapid Film. I cannot confirm or deny this, but certainly, I imagine what I saw that evening would have delighted Pickman no end.

However, what has lodged that night so firmly in my mind, and what I believe is the genuine author of those among my nightmares featuring Endecott in an endless parade of nonexistent, horrific pictures transpired only in the final few seconds of the film. Indeed, it came and went so quickly, the projectionist was asked by a number of those present to rewind and play the ending over four times, in an effort to ascertain whether we'd seen what we *thought* we had seen.

Her lust apparently satiated, the actress lay down with her skeletal lover, one arm about its empty ribcage, and closed her kohl-smudged eyes. And in that last instant, before the film ended, a shadow appeared, something passing slowly between the set and the camera's light source. Even after five viewings, I can only describe that shade as having put me in mind of some hulking figure, something considerably farther down the evolutionary ladder than Piltdown or Java man. And it was generally agreed among those seated in that close and musty room that the shadow was possessed of an odd sort of snout or muzzle, suggestive of the prognathous jaw and face of the fake skull wired to the skeleton.

There, then. *That* is what I actually saw that evening, as best I now can remember it. Which leaves me with only a single piece of this story left to tell, the night I finally met the woman who called herself Vera Endecott.

6.

"Disappointed? Not quite what you were expecting?" she asked, smiling a distasteful, wry sort of smile, and I think I might have nodded in reply. She appeared at least a decade older than her twenty-seven years, looking like a woman who had survived one rather tumultuous life already and had, perhaps, started in upon a second. There were fine lines at the corners of her eyes and mouth, the bruised circles below her eyes that spoke of chronic insomnia and drug abuse, and, if I'm not mistaken, a premature hint of silver in her bobbed black hair.

What had I anticipated? It's hard to say now, after the fact, but I was surprised by her height, and by her irises, which were a striking shade of grey. At once, they reminded me of the sea, of fog and breakers and granite cobbles polished perfectly smooth by ages in the surf. The Greeks said that the goddess Athena had "sea-grey" eyes, and I wonder what they would have thought of the eyes of Lillian Snow.

"I have not been well," she confided, making the divulgence sound almost like a *mea culpa,* and those stony eyes glanced towards a chair in the foyer of my flat. I apologized for not having already asked her in, for having kept her standing in the hallway. I led her to the davenport sofa in the tiny parlor off my studio, and she thanked me. She asked for whiskey or gin, and then laughed at me when I told her I was a teetotaler. When I offered her tea, she declined.

"A painter who doesn't drink?" she asked. "No wonder I've never heard of you."

I believe that I mumbled something then about the Eighteenth Amendment and the Volstead Act, which earned from her an expression of commingled disbelief and contempt. She told me that was strike two, and if it turned out that I didn't smoke, either, she was leaving, as my claim to be an artist would have been proven a bald-faced lie, and she'd know I'd lured her to my apartment under false pretenses. But I offered her a cigarette, one of the *brun* Gitanes I first developed a taste for in college, and at that she seemed to relax somewhat. I lit her cigarette, and she leaned back on the sofa, still smiling that wry smile, watching me with her sea-grey eyes, her thin face wreathed in gauzy veils of smoke. She wore a yellow felt cloche that didn't exactly match her burgundy silk chemise, and I noticed there was a run in her left stocking.

"You knew Richard Upton Pickman," I said, blundering much too quickly to the point, and, immediately, her expression turned somewhat suspicious. She said nothing for almost a full minute, just sat there smoking and staring back at me, and I silently cursed my impatience and lack of tact. But then the smile returned, and she laughed softly and nodded.

"Wow," she said. "There's a name I haven't heard in a while. But, yeah, sure, I knew the son of a bitch. So, what are you? Another of his protégés, or maybe just one of the three-letter-men he liked to keep handy?"

"Then it's true Pickman was light on his feet?" I asked.

She laughed again, and this time there was an unmistakable edge of derision there. She took another long drag on her cigarette, exhaled, and squinted at me through the smoke.

"Mister, I have yet to meet the beast – male, female, or anything in between – that degenerate fuck wouldn't have screwed, given half a chance." She paused, here, tapping ash onto the floorboards. "So, if you're not a fag, just what are you? A kike, maybe? You sort of look like a kike."

"No," I replied. "I'm not Jewish. My parents were Roman Catholic, but me, I'm not much of anything, I'm afraid, but a painter you've never heard of."

"Are you?"

"Am I what, Miss Endecott?"

"Afraid," she said, smoke leaking from her nostrils. "And do *not* dare start in calling me 'Miss Endecott.' It makes me sound like a goddamned schoolteacher or something equally wretched."

"So, these days, do you prefer Vera?" I asked, pushing my luck. "Or Lillian?"

"How about Lily?" she smiled, completely nonplussed, so far as I could tell, as though these were all only lines from a script she'd spent the last week rehearsing.

"Very well, Lily," I said, moving the glass ashtray on the table closer to her. She scowled at it, as though I were offering her a platter of some perfectly odious foodstuff and expecting her to eat, but she stopped tapping her ash on my floor.

"Why am I here?" she demanded, commanding an answer without raising her voice. "Why have you gone to so much trouble to see me?"

"It wasn't as difficult as all that," I replied, not yet ready to answer her question, wanting to stretch this meeting out a little longer and understanding, expecting, that she would likely leave as soon as she had what she'd come for. In truth, it had been quite a lot of trouble, beginning with a telephone call to her former agent, and then proceeding through half a dozen increasingly disreputable and uncooperative contacts. Two I'd had to bribe, and one I'd had to coerce with a number of hollow threats involving nonexistent contacts in the Boston Police Department. But, when all was said and done, my diligence had paid off, because here she sat before me, the two of us, alone, just me and the woman who'd been a movie star and who had played some role in Thurber's breakdown, who'd posed for Pickman and almost certainly done murder on a spring night in Hollywood. Here was the woman who could answer questions I did not have the nerve to ask, who knew what had cast the shadow I'd seen in that dingy pornographic film. Or, at least, here was all that remained of her.

"There aren't many left who would have bothered," she said, gazing down at the smoldering tip-end of her Gitane.

"Well, I have always been a somewhat persistent sort of fellow," I told her, and she smiled again. It was an oddly bestial smile that reminded me of one of my earliest impressions of her – that oppressive summer's day, now more than two months past, studying a handful of old clippings in the Hope Street boarding house. That her human face was nothing more than a mask or fairy glamour conjured to hide the truth of her from the world.

"How did you meet him?" I asked, and she stubbed out her cigarette in the ashtray.

"Who? How did I meet who?" She furrowed her brow and glanced nervously towards the parlor window, which faces east, towards the harbor.

"I'm sorry," I replied. "Pickman. How is it that you came to know Richard Pickman?"

"Some people would say that you have very unhealthy interests, Mr. Blackman," she said, her peculiarly carnivorous smile quickly fading, taking with it any implied menace. In its stead, there was only this destitute, used-up husk of a woman.

"And surely they've said the same of you, many, many times, Lily. I've read all about Durand Drive and the Delgado woman."

"Of course, you have," she sighed, not taking her eyes from the window. "I'd have expected nothing less from a persistent fellow such as you."

"How did you meet Richard Pickman?" I asked for the third time.

"Does it make a difference? That was so very long ago. Years and years ago. He's dead and buried. "

"No body was ever found."

And, here, she looked from the window to me, and all those unexpected lines on her face seemed to have abruptly deepened; she might well have been twenty-seven, by birth, but no one would have argued if she laid claim to forty.

"The man is dead," she said flatly, then added, cryptically. "And if by chance he's *not,* well, we should all be fortunate enough to find our heart's desire, whatever it might be." Then she went back to staring at the window, and, for a minute or two, neither of us said anything more.

"You told me that you have the sketches," she said, finally. "Was that a lie, just to get me up here?"

"No, I have them. Two of them, anyway," and I reached for the folio beside my chair and untied the string holding it closed. "I don't know, of course, how many you might have posed for. There were more?"

"More than two," she replied, almost whispering now.

"Lily, you still haven't answered my question."

"And you are a persistent fellow."

"Yes," I assured her, taking the two nudes from the stack and holding them up for her to see, but not yet touch. She studied them a moment, her face remaining slack and dispassionate, as if the sight of them elicited no memories at all.

"He needed a model," she said, turning back to the window and the blue October sky. "I was up from New York, staying with a friend who'd met him at a gallery or lecture or something of the sort. My friend knew that he was looking for models, and I needed the money."

I glanced at the two charcoal sketches again, at the curve of those full hips, the round, firm buttocks, and the tail – a crooked, malformed thing sprouting from the base of the spine and reaching halfway to the bend of the subject's knees. As I have said, Pickman had a flair for realism, and his eye for human anatomy was almost as uncanny as the ghouls and demons he painted. I pointed to one of the sketches, to the tail.

"That isn't artistic license, is it?"

She did not look back to the two drawings, but simply, slowly, shook her head. "I had the surgery done in Jersey, back in '21," she said.

"Why did you wait so long, Lily? It's my understanding that such a defect is usually corrected at birth, or shortly thereafter."

And she almost smiled that smile again, that hungry, savage smile, but it died, incomplete, on her lips.

"My father, he has his own ideas about such things," she said quietly. "He was always so proud, you see, that his daughter's body was blessed with evidence of her heritage. It made him very happy."

"Your heritage – " I began, but Lily Snow held up her left hand, silencing me.

"I believe, sir, I've answered enough questions for one afternoon. Especially given that you have only the pair, and that you did not tell me that was the case when we spoke."

Reluctantly, I nodded and passed both the sketches to her. She took them, thanked me, and stood up, brushing at a bit of lint or dust on her burgundy chemise. I told her that I regretted that the others were not in my possession, that it had not even occurred to me she would have posed for more than these two. The last part was a lie, of course, as I knew Pickman would surely have made as many studies as possible when presented with so unusual a body.

"I can show myself out," she informed me when I started to rise from my chair. "And you will not disturb me again, not ever."

"No," I agreed. "Not ever. You have my word."

"You're lying sons of bitches, the whole lot of you," she said, and with that, the living ghost of Vera Endecott turned and left the parlor. A few seconds later, I heard the door open and slam shut again, and I sat there in the wan light of a fading day, looking at what grim traces remained in Thurber's folio.

7. (October 24th, 1929)

This is the last of it. Just a few more words, and I will be done. I know now that having attempted to trap these terrible events I have not managed to trap them at all, but merely given them some new, clearer focus.

Four days ago, on the morning of October 20th, a body was discovered dangling from the trunk of an oak growing near the center of King's Chapel Burial Ground. According to newspaper accounts, the corpse was suspended a full seventeen feet off the ground, bound round about the waist and chest with interwoven lengths of jute rope and baling wire. The woman was identified as a former screen actress, Vera Endecott, née Lillian Margaret Snow, and much was made of her notoriety and her unsuccessful attempt to conceal connections to the wealthy but secretive and ill-rumored Snows of Ipswich, Massachusetts. Her body had been stripped of all clothing, disemboweled, her throat cut, and her tongue removed. He lips had been sewn shut with cat-gut stitches. About her neck hung a wooden placard, on which one word had been written in what is believed to be the dead woman's own blood: *apostate.*

This morning I almost burned Thurber's folio, along with all my files. I went so far as to carry them to the hearth, but then my resolve faltered, and I just sat on the floor, staring at the clippings and Pickman's sketches. I'm not sure what stayed my hand, beyond the suspicion that destroying these papers would not save my life. If they want me dead, then dead I'll be. I've gone too far down this road to spare myself by trying to annihilate the physical evidence of my investigation.

I will place this manuscript, and all the related documents I have gathered, in my safe deposit box, and then I will try to return to the life I was living before Thurber's death. But I cannot forget a line from the suicide note of the screenwriter Joseph Chapman – *how does a man forget, deliberately and wholly and forever, once he has glimpsed such sights*. How, indeed. And, too, I cannot forget that woman's eyes, that stony, sea-tumbled shade of grey. Or a rough shadow glimpsed in the final moments of a film that might have been made either in 1923 or 1924, that may have been titled *The Hound's Daughter* or *The Necrophile*.

I know the dreams will not desert me, not now nor at some future time, but I pray for such fortune as to have seen the last of the waking horrors that my foolish, prying mind has called forth.

PICKMAN'S OTHER MODEL (1929)

Here's another example of my obsession with lost films and films that never were made. Also, it always bugged the hell out of me that we don't know to whom Lovecraft's narrator is speaking. This is one of those rare stories that was enjoyable to write despite being very difficult.

PART TWO

Providence

2008 – 2012

Galápagos

March 17, 2037 (Wednesday)

Whenever I wake up screaming, the nurses kindly come in and give me the shiny yellow pills and the white pills flecked with grey; they prick my skin with hollow needles until I grow quiet and calm again. They speak in exquisitely gentle voices, reminding me that I'm home, that I've been home for many, many months. They remind me that if I open the blinds and look out the hospital window, I will see a parking lot, and cars, and a carefully tended lawn. I will only see California. I will see only Earth. If I look up, and it happens to be day, I'll see the sky, too, sprawled blue above me and peppered with dirty-white clouds and contrails. If it happens to be night, instead, I'll see the comforting pale orange skyglow that mercifully hides the stars from view. I'm home, not strapped into *Yastreb-4*'s taxi module. I can't crane my neck for a glance at the monitor screen displaying a tableau of dusty volcanic wastelands as I speed by the Tharsis plateau, more than four hundred kilometers below me. I can't turn my head and gaze through the tiny docking windows at *Pilgrimage's* glittering alabaster hull, quickly growing larger as I rush towards the aft docking port. These are merely memories, inaccurate and untrustworthy, and may only do me the harm that memories are capable of doing.

Then the nurses go away. They leave the light above my bed burning and tell me if I need anything at all to press the intercom button. They're just down the hall, and they always come when I call. They're never anything except prompt and do not fail to arrive bearing the chemical solace of pharmaceuticals, only half of which I know by name. I am not neglected. My needs are met as well as anyone alive can meet them. I'm too precious a commodity not to coddle. I'm the woman who was invited to the strangest, most terrible rendezvous in the history of space exploration. The one they dragged all the way to Mars after *Pilgrimage* abruptly, inexplicably, diverged from its mission parameters, when the crew went silent and the AI stopped responding. I'm the woman who stepped through an airlock hatch and into that alien Eden; I'm the one who spoke with a goddess. I'm the woman who was the goddess' lover, when she was still human and had a name and a consciousness that could be comprehended.

"Are you sleeping better?" the psychiatrist asks, and I tell him that I sleep just fine, thank you, seven to eight hours every night now. He nods and patiently smiles, but I know I haven't answered his question. He's actually asking me if I'm still having the nightmares about my time aboard *Pilgrimage,* if they've decreased in their frequency and/or severity. He doesn't want to know *if* I sleep or how *long* I sleep, but if my sleep is still haunted. Though he'd never use that particular word, *haunted.*

He's a thin, balding man, with perfectly manicured nails and an unremarkable mid-Atlantic accent. He dutifully makes the commute down from Berkeley once a week, because those are his orders, and I'm too great a puzzle for his inquisitive mind to ignore. All in all, I find the psychiatrist far less helpful than the nurses and their dependable drugs. Whereas they've been assigned the task of watching over me, of soothing and steadying me and keeping me from harming myself, he's been given the unenviable responsibility of discovering what happened during the comms blackout, those seventeen interminable minutes after I boarded the derelict ship and promptly lost radio contact with *Yastreb-4* and Earth. Despite countless debriefings and interviews, NASA still thinks I'm holding out on them. And maybe I am. Honestly, it's hard for me to say. It's hard for me to keep it all straight anymore: what happened and what didn't, what I've said to them and what I've only thought about saying, what I genuinely remember and what I may have fabricated wholesale as a means of self-preservation.

The psychiatrist says it's to be expected, this sort of confusion from someone who's survived very traumatic events. *He* calls the events very traumatic, by the way. I don't; I'm not yet sure if I think of them that way. Regardless, he's diagnosed me as suffering from Survivor Syndrome, which he also calls K-Z Syndrome. There's a jack in my hospital room with filtered and monitored web access, but I was able to look up "K-Z Syndrome." It was named for a Nazi concentration camp survivor, an Israeli author named Yehiel De-Nur. De-Nur published under the pseudonym Ka-Tzetnik 135633. That was his number at Auschwitz, and K-Z Syndrome is named after him. In 1956, he published *House of Dolls,* describing the Nazi "Joy Division," the *Freudenabteilung*, a system that utilized Jewish women as sex slaves.

The psychiatrist is the one who asked if I would at least try to write it down, what happened, what I saw and heard (and smelled and felt) when I entered the *Pilgrimage* a year and a half ago. He knows, of course, that there have already been numerous written and vidded depositions and affidavits for NASA and the CSS/NSA, the WHO, the CDC, and the CIA and, to tell the truth, I don't *know* who requested and read and then filed away all those reports. He knows about them, though, and that, by my own admission, they barely scratched the surface of whatever happened out there. He knows, but I reminded him, anyway.

"This will be different," he said. "This will be more subjective." And the psychiatrist explained that he wasn't looking for a blow-by-blow linear narrative of my experiences aboard *Pilgrimage,* and I told him that was good, because I seem to have forgotten how to think or relate events in a linear fashion, without a lot of switchbacks and digressions and meandering.

"Just write," he said. "Write what you can remember, and write until you don't want to write anymore."

"That would be now," I said, and he silently stared at me for a while. He didn't laugh, even though I'd thought it was pretty funny.

"I understand that the medication makes this sort of thing more difficult for you," he said, sometime later. "But the medication helps you reach back to those things you don't want to remember, those things you're trying to forget." I almost told him that he was starting to sound like a character in a Lewis Carroll story – riddling and contradicting – but I didn't. Our hour was almost over, anyway.

So, after three days of stalling, I'm trying to write something that will make you happy, Dr. Ostrowski. I know you're trying to do your job, and I know a lot of people must be peering over your shoulder, expecting the sort of results they've failed to get themselves. I don't want to show up for our next session empty-handed.

The taxi module was on autopilot during the approach. See, I'm not an astronaut or mission specialist or engineer or anything like that. I'm a anthropologist, and I mostly study the Middle Paleolithic of Europe and Asia Minor. I have a keen interest in tool use and manufacture by the Neanderthals. Or at least that's who I used to be. Right now, I'm a madwoman in a psych ward at a military hospital in San Jose, California. I'm a case number and an eyewitness who has proven less than satisfactory. But, what I'm *trying* to say, Doctor, the module *was* on autopilot, and there was nothing for me to do but wait there inside my encounter suit and sweat and watch the round screen divided by a Y-shaped reticle as I approached the derelict's docking port, the taxi barreling forward at 0.06 meters per second. The ship grew so huge so quickly, looming up in the blackness, and that only made the whole thing seem that much more unreal.

I tried hard to focus, to breathe slowly, and follow the words being spoken between the painful, bright bursts of static in my ears, the babble of sound trapped inside the helmet with me. *Module approaching 50-meter threshold. On target and configuring KU-band from radar to comms mode. Slowing now to 0.045 meters per second. Decelerating for angular alignment, extending docking ring,* nine meters, three meters, a whole lot of noise and nonsense about latches and hooks and seals, capture and final position, and then it seemed like I wasn't moving anymore. Like the taxi wasn't moving anymore. We were, of course, the little module and I, only now we were riding piggyback on *Pilgrimage*, locked into geosynchronous orbit, with nothing but the instrument panel to remind me I wasn't sitting still in space. Then the mission commander was telling me I'd done a great job, congratulations, they were all proud of me, even though I hadn't done anything except sit and wait.

But all this is right there in the mission dossiers, Doctor. You don't need me to tell you these things. You already know that *Pilgrimage's* AI would allow no one but me to dock and that MS Lowry's repeated attempts to hack the firewall failed. You know about the nurses and their pills, and Yehiel De-Nur and *House of Dolls*. You know about the affair I had with the Korean payload specialist during the long flight to Mars. You're probably skimming this part, hoping it gets better a little farther along.

So, I'll try to tell you something you don't know. Just one thing, for now.

Hanging there in my tiny, life-sustaining capsule, suspended two hundred and fifty miles above extinct Martian volcanoes and surrounded by near vacuum, I had two recurring thoughts, the only ones that I can now clearly recall having had. First, the grim hope that, when the hatch finally opened – *if* the hatch opened – they'd all be dead. All of them. Every single one of the men and women aboard *Pilgrimage,* and most especially her. And, secondly, I closed my eyes as tightly as I could and wished that I would soon discover there'd been some perfectly mundane accident or malfunction, and the bizarre, garbled transmissions that had sent us all the way to Mars to try and save the day meant nothing at all. But I only hoped and wished, mind you. I haven't prayed since I was fourteen years old.

March 19, 2037 (Friday)

Last night was worse than usual. The dreams, I mean. The nurses and my physicians don't exactly approve of what I've begun writing for you, Dr. Ostrowski. Of what you've asked me to do. I suspect they would say there's a conflict of interest at work. They're supposed to keep me sane and healthy, but here you are, the latest episode in the inquisition that's landed me in their ward. When I asked for the keypad this afternoon, they didn't want to give it to me. Maybe tomorrow, they said. Maybe the day *after* tomorrow. Right now, you need your rest. And sure, I know they're right. What you want, it's only making matters worse, for them *and* for me, but when I'd finally had enough and threatened to report the hospital staff for attempting to obstruct a federal investigation, they relented. But, just so you know, they've got me doped to the gills with an especially potent cocktail of tranquilizers and antipsychotics, so I'll be lucky if I can manage more than gibberish. Already, it's taken me half an hour to write (and repeatedly rewrite) this one paragraph, so who gets the final laugh?

Last night I dreamed of the cloud again.

I dreamed I was back in Germany, in Darmstadt, only this time, I wasn't sitting in that dingy hotel room near the Luisenplatz. This time it wasn't a phone call that brought me the news, or a courier. And I didn't look up to find *her* standing there in the room with me, which, you know, is how this one usually goes. I'll be sitting on the bed, or I'll walk out of the bathroom, or turn away from the window, and there she'll be. Even though *Pilgrimage* and its crew is all those hundreds of millions of kilometers away, finishing up their experiments at Ganymede and preparing to begin the long journey home, she's standing there in the room with me. Only not this time. Not last night.

The way it played out last night, I'd been cleared for access to the ESOC central control room. I have no idea why. But I was there, standing near one wall with a young French woman, younger than me by at least a decade. She was blonde, with green eyes, and she was pretty; her English was better than my French. I watched all those men and women, too occupied with their computer terminals to notice me. The pretty French woman (sorry, but I never learned her name) was pointing out different people, explaining their various roles and responsibilities: the ground operations manager, the director of flight operations, a visiting astrodynamics consultant, the software coordinator, and so forth. The lights in the room were almost painfully bright, and when I looked up at the ceiling I saw it wasn't a ceiling at all, but the night sky, blazing with countless fluorescent stars.

And then that last transmission from *Pilgrimage* came in. We didn't realize it would be the last, but everything stopped, and everyone listened. Afterwards, no one panicked, as if they'd expected something of this sort all along. I understood that it had taken the message the better part of an hour to reach Earth, and that any reply would take just as long, but the French woman was explaining the communications delay, anyway.

"We can't know what that means," somebody said. "We can't *possibly* know, can we?"

"Run through the telemetry data again," someone else said, and I think it was the man the French woman had told me was the director of flight operations.

But it might have been someone else. I was still looking at the ceiling composed of starlight and planets and the emptiness between starlight and planets, and I knew exactly what the transmission meant. It was a suicide note, of sorts, streamed across space at three hundred kilometers per second. I knew, because I plainly saw the mile-long silhouette of the ship sailing by overhead, only a silvery speck against the roiling backdrop of Jupiter. I saw that cloud, too, saw *Pilgrimage* enter it and exit a minute or so later (and I think I even paused to calculate the width of the cloud, based on the vessel's speed).

You know as well as I what was said that day, Dr. Ostrowski, the contents in that final broadcast. You've probably even committed it to memory, just as I have. I imagine you've listened to the tape more times than you could ever recollect, right? Well, what was said in my dream last night was almost verbatim what Commander Yun said in the actual transmission. There was only one difference. The part right at the end, when the commander quotes from Chapter 13 of the *Book of Revelation*, that didn't happen. Instead, he said:

"Lead us from the unreal to real,
Lead us from darkness to light,
Lead us from death to immortality,
Om Shanti, Shanti, Shanti."

I admit I had to look that up online. It's from the Hindu *Bṛhadāraṇyaka* Upanishad. I haven't studied Vedic literature since a seminar in grad school, and that was mostly an excuse to visit Bangalore. But the unconscious doesn't lose much, does it, Doctor? And you never know what it's going to cough up, or when.

In my dream, I stood staring at the ceiling that was really no ceiling at all. If anyone else could see what I was seeing, they didn't act like it. The strange cloud near Ganymede made me think of an oil slick floating on water, and when *Pilgrimage* came out the far side, it was like those dying sea birds that wash up on beaches after tanker spills. That's exactly how it seemed to me, in the dream last night. I looked away, finally, looked down at the floor, and I was trying to explain what I'd seen to the French woman. I described the ruined plumage of ducks and gulls and cormorants, but I couldn't make her understand. And then I woke up. I woke up screaming, but you'll have guessed that part.

I need to stop now. The meds have made going on almost impossible, and I should read back over everything I've written, do what I can to make myself clearer. I feel like I ought to say more about the cloud, because I've never seen it so clearly in any of the other dreams. It never before reminded me of an oil slick. I'll try to come back to this. Maybe later. Maybe not.

March 20, 2037 (Saturday)

I don't have to scream for the nurses to know that I'm awake, of course. I don't have to scream, and I don't have to use the call button, either. They get everything relayed in real-time, directly from my cerebral cortex and hippocampus to their wrist tops, via the depth electrodes and subdural strips that were implanted in my head a few weeks after the crew of *Yastreb-4* was released from suborbital quarantine. The nurses see it all, spelled out in the spikes and waves of electrocorticography, which is how I know *they* know that I'm awake right now, when I should be asleep. Tomorrow morning, I imagine there will be some sort of confab about adjusting the levels of my benzo and nonbenzo hypnotics to ensure the insomnia doesn't return.

I'm not sure why I'm awake, really. There wasn't a nightmare, at least none I can recall. I woke up and simply couldn't get back to sleep. After ten or fifteen minutes, I reached for the keypad. I find the soft cobalt-blue glow from the screen is oddly soothing, and it's nice to find comfort that isn't injected, comfort that I don't have to swallow or get from a jet spray or IV drip. And I want to have something more substantial to show the psychiatrist come Tuesday than dreams about Darmstadt, oil slicks, and pretty French women.

I keep expecting the vidcom beside my bed to buzz and wink to life, and there will be one of the nurses looking concerned and wanting to know if I'm all right, if I'd like a little extra coby to help me get back to sleep. But the box has been quiet and blank so far, which leaves me equal parts surprised and relieved.

"There are things you've yet to tell anyone," the psychiatrist said. "Those are the things I'm trying to help you talk about. If they've been repressed, they're the memories I'm trying to help you access." That is, they're what he's going to want to see when I give him my report on Tuesday morning.

And if at first I don't succeed…

So, where was I?

The handoff.

I'm sitting alone in the taxi, waiting, and below me, Mars is a sullen, rusty cadaver of a planet. I have the distinct impression that it's watching as I'm handed off from one ship to the other. I imagine those countless craters and calderas have become eyes, and all those eyes are filled with jealousy and spite. The module's capture ring has successfully snagged *Pilgrimage's* aft PMA, and it only takes a few seconds for the ring to achieve proper alignment. The module deploys twenty or so hooks, establishing an impermeable seal, and, a few seconds later, the taxi's hatch spirals open, and I enter the airlock. I feel dizzy, slightly nauseous, and I almost stumble, almost fall. I see a red light above the hatch go blue and realize that the chamber has pressurized, which means I'm subject to the centripetal force that generates the ship's artificial gravity. I've been living in near zero-g for more than eleven months, and nothing they told me in training or aboard the *Yastreb-4* could have prepared me for the return of any degree of gravity. The EVA suit's exoskeleton begins to compensate. It keeps me on my feet, keeps my atrophied muscles moving, keeps me breathing.

"You're doing great," Commander Yun assures me from the bridge of *Yastreb-4,* and that's when my comms cut out. I panic and try to return to the taxi module, but the hatchway has already sealed itself shut again. I have a go at the control panel, my gloved fingers fumbling clumsily at the unfamiliar switches, but I can't get it to respond. The display on the inside of my visor tells me that my heart rate's jumped to 186 BPM, my blood pressure's in the red, and oxygen consumption has doubled. I'm hyperventilating, which has my CO_2 down and is beginning to affect blood oxygen levels. The medic on my left wrist responds by secreting a relatively mild anxiolytic compound directly into the radial artery. Milder, I might add, than the shit they give me here.

And yes, Dr. Ostrowski, I know that you've read all this before. I know that I'm trying your patience, and you're probably disappointed. I'm doing this the only way I know how. I was never any good at jumping into the deep end of the pool.

But we're almost there, I promise.

It took me a year and a half to find the words to describe what happened next, or to find the courage to say it aloud, or the resignation necessary to let it out into the world. Whichever. They've been *my* secrets and almost mine alone. And soon, now, they won't be anymore.

The soup from the medic hits me, and I begin to relax. I give up on the airlock and shut my eyes a moment, leaning forward, my helmet resting against the closed hatch. I'm almost certain my eyes are still shut when the *Pilgrimage's* AI first speaks to me. And here, Doctor, right *here,* pay attention, because this is where I'm going to come clean and tell you something I've never told another living soul. It's not a repressed memory that's suddenly found its way to the surface. It hasn't been coaxed from me by all those potent psychotropics. It's just something I've managed to keep to myself until now.

"Hello," the computer says. Only, I'd heard recordings of the mainframe's NLP, and this isn't the voice it was given. This is, unmistakably, *her* voice, only slightly distorted by the audio interface. My eyes are shut, and I don't open them right away. I just stand there, my head against the hatch, listening to that voice and to my heart. The sound of my breath is very loud inside the helmet.

"We were not certain our message had been received, or, if it had been, that it had been properly understood. We did not expect you would come so far."

"Then why did you call?" I ask and open my eyes.

"We were lonely," the voice replies. "We have not seen you in a very long time now."

I don't turn around. I keep my faceplate pressed to the airlock, some desperate, insensible part of me willing it to reopen and admit me once more to the sanctuary of the taxi. Whatever I should say next, of all the things I might say, what I *do* say is, simply, "Amery, I'm frightened."

There's a pause before her response, five or six or seven seconds, I don't know, and my fingers move futilely across the control pad again. I hear the inner hatch open behind me, though I'm fairly certain I'm not the one who opened it.

"We see that," she says. "But it wasn't our intent to make you afraid, Merrick. It was never our intent to frighten you."

"Amery, what's happened here?" I ask, speaking hardly above a whisper, but my voice is amplified and made clearer by the vocal modulator in my EVA helmet. "What happened to the ship, back at Jupiter? To the rest of the crew? What's happened to you?"

I expect another pause, but there isn't one.

"The most remarkable thing," she replies. And there's a sort of elation in her voice, audible even through the tinny flatness of the NLP relay. "You will hardly believe it."

"Are they dead, the others?" I ask her, and my eyes wander to the external atmo readout inside my visor. Argon's showing a little high, a few tenths of a percent off earth normal, but not enough to act as an asphyxiant. Water vapor's twice what I'd have expected, anywhere but the ship's hydroponics lab. Pressure's steady at 14.2 psi. Whatever happened aboard *Pilgrimage,* life support is still up and running. All the numbers are in the green.

"That's not a simple question to answer," she says, Amery or the AI or whatever it is I'm having this conversation with. "None of it is simple, Merrick. And yet, it is so elegant."

"Are they *dead*?" I ask again, resisting the urge to flip the release toggle beneath my chin and raise the visor. It stinks inside the suit, like sweat and plastic, urine and stale, recycled air.

"Yes," she says. "It couldn't be helped."

I lick my lips, Dr. Ostrowski, and my mouth has gone very, very dry. "Did you kill them, Amery?"

"You're asking the wrong questions," she says, and I stare down at my feet, at the shiny white toes of the EVA's overshoes.

"They're the questions we've come all the way out here to have answered," I tell *her*, or I tell *it*. "What questions would you have me ask, instead?"

"It may be, there is no longer any need for questions. It may be, Merrick, that you've been called to see, and seeing will be enough.

The force that through the green fuse drives the flower, drives my green age, that blasts the roots of trees, is my destroyer."

"I've been summoned to Mars to listen to you quote Dylan Thomas?"

"You're *not* listening, Merrick. That's the thing. And that's why it will be so much easier if we show you what's happened. What's begun."

"And I am dumb to tell the lover's tomb," I say as softly as I can, but the suit adjusts the volume so it's just as loud as everything else I've said.

"We have not died," she replies. "You will find no tomb here," and, possibly, this voice that wants me to believe it is only Amery Domico has become defensive, and impatient, and somehow this seems the strangest thing so far. I imagine Amery speaking through clenched teeth. I imagine her rubbing her forehead like a headache's coming on, and it's my fault. "I am very much alive," she says, "and I need you to pay attention. You cannot stay here very long. It's not safe, and I will see no harm come to you."

"Why?" I ask her, only half expecting a response. "Why isn't it safe for me to be here?"

"Turn around, Merrick," she says. "You've come so far, and there is so little time." I do as she says. I turn towards the voice, towards the airlock's open inner hatch.

It's almost morning. I mean, the sun will be rising soon. Here in California. Still no interruption from the nurses. But I can't keep this up. I can't do this all at once. The rest will have to wait.

March 21, 2037 (Sunday)

Dr. Bernardyn Ostrowski is no longer handling my case. One of my physicians delivered the news this morning, bright and early. It came with no explanation attached. And I thought better of asking for one. That is, I thought better of wasting my breath asking for one. When I signed on for the *Yastreb-4* intercept, the waivers and NDAs and whatnot were all very, very clear about things like the principle of least privilege and mandatory access control. I'm told what they decide I need to know, which isn't much. I *did* ask if I should continue with the account of the mission that Dr. O asked me to write, and the physician (a hematologist named Prideaux) said he'd gotten no word to the contrary, and if there would be a change in the direction of my psychotherapy regimen, I'd find out about it when I meet with the new shrink Tuesday morning. Her name is Teasdale, by the way. Eleanor Teasdale.

I thanked Dr. Prideaux for bringing me the news, and he only shrugged and scribbled something on my chart. I suppose that's fair, as it was hardly a sincere show of gratitude on my part. At any rate, I have no idea what to expect from this Teasdale woman, and I appear to have lost the stingy drab of momentum pushing me recklessly towards full disclosure. That in and of itself is enough to set me wondering what my keepers are up to now, if the shrink switch is some fresh skullduggery. It seems counterintuitive, given they were finally getting the results they've been asking for (and I'm not so naïve as to assume that this pad isn't outfitted with a direct patch to some agency goon or another). But then an awful lot of what they've done seems counterintuitive to me. And counterproductive.

Simply put, I don't know what to say next. No, strike that. I don't know what I'm *willing* to say next.

I've already mentioned my indiscretion with the South Korean payload specialist on the outbound half of the trip. Actually, *indiscretion* is hardly accurate, since Amery explicitly gave me her permission to take other lovers while she was gone, because, after all, there was a damned decent chance she wouldn't make it back alive. Or make it back at all. So, *indiscretion* is just my guilt talking. Anyway, her name was Bae Jin-ah – the *Yastreb-4* PS, I mean – though everyone called her Sam, which she seemed to prefer. She was born in Incheon and was still a kid when the war started. A relative in the States helped her parents get Bae on one of the last transports out of Seoul before the bombs started raining down. But we didn't have many conversations about the past, mine or hers. She was a biochemist obsessed with the structure-function relationships of peptides, and she liked to talk shop after we fucked. It was pretty dry stuff – the talk, not the sex – and I admit I only half listened and didn't understand all that much of what I heard. But I don't think that mattered to Sam. I have a feeling she was just grateful that I bothered to cover my mouth whenever I yawned.

She only asked about Amery once.

We were both crammed into the warm cocoon of her sleeping bag, or into mine; I can't recall which. Probably hers, since the micrograv restraints in my bunk kept popping loose. I was on the edge of dozing off, and Sam asked me how we met. I made up some half-assed romance about an academic conference in Manhattan, and a party, a formal affair at the American Museum of Natural History. It was love at first sight, I said (or something equally ridiculous), right there in the Roosevelt Rotunda, beneath the rearing *Barosaurus* skeleton. Sam thought it was sweet as hell, though, and I figured lies were fine, if they gave us a moment's respite from the crowded day-to-day monotony of the ship, or from our (usually) unspoken dread of all that nothingness surrounding us and the uncertainty we were hurdling towards. I don't even know if she believed me, but it made her smile.

"You've read the docs on the cloud?" she asked, and I told her yeah, I had, or at least the ones I was given clearance to read. And then Sam watched me for while without saying anything. I could feel her silently weighing options and consequences, duty and need and repercussion.

"So, you *know* it's some pretty hinky shit out there," she said, finally, and went back to watching me, as if waiting for a particular reaction. And, here, I lied to her again.

"Relax, Sam," I whispered, then kissed her on the forehead. "I've read most of the spectroscopy and astrochem profiles. Discussing it with me, you're not in danger of compromising protocol or mission security or anything."

She nodded once and looked slightly relieved.

"I've never given much credence to the exogenesis crowd," she said, "but, Jesus, Mary, and Joseph...glycine, DHA, adenine, cytosine, et cetera and fucking et cetera. When – or, rather, *if* this gets out – the panspermia guys are going to go monkey shit. And rightly so. No one saw this coming, Merrick. No one you'd ever take seriously."

I must have managed a fairly convincing job of acting like I knew what she was talking about, because she kept it up for the next ten or fifteen minutes. Her voice assumed that same sort of jittery, excited edge Amery's used to get whenever she'd start in on the role of Io in the Jovian magnetosphere or any number of other astronomical phenomena I didn't quite understand, and how much the *Pilgrimage* experiments were going to change this or that model or theory. Only, unlike Amery, Sam's excitement was tinged with fear.

"The inherent risks," she said, and then trailed off and wiped at her forehead before starting again. "When they first showed me the back-contamination safeguards for this run, I figured no way, right. No way are NASA and the ESA going to pony up the budget for that sort of overkill. But this was *before* I read Murchison's reports on the cloud's composition and behavior. And afterwards, the thought of intentionally sending a human crew anywhere near that thing, or, shit, anything that had been *exposed* to it? I couldn't believe they were serious. It's fucking crazy. No, it's whatever comes *after* fucking crazy.

They should have cut their losses..." and then she trailed off again and went back to staring at me.

"You shouldn't have come," she said.

"I had to," I told her. "If there's any chance at all that Amery's still alive, I had to come."

"Of course. Yeah, of course you did," Sam said, looking away.

"When they asked, I couldn't very well say no."

"But do you honestly believe we're going to find any of them alive, that we'll be docking with anything but a ghost ship?"

"You're really not into pulling punches, are you?"

"You read the reports on the cloud."

"I had to come," I told her a third time.

Then we both let the subject drop and neither of us ever brought it up again. Indeed, I think I probably would have forgotten most of it, especially after what I saw when I stepped through the airlock and into *Pilgrimage.* That whole conversation might have dissolved into the tedious grey blur of outbound and been forgotten, if Bae Jin-ah hadn't killed herself on the return trip, just five days before we made Earth orbit.

March 23, 2037 (Tuesday)

Tuesday night now, and the meds are making me sleepy and stupid, but I wanted to put some of this down, even if it isn't what they want me to be writing. I see how it's all connected, even if they never will, or, if seeing, they simply do not care. *They,* whoever, precisely, they may be.

This morning I had my first session with you, Dr. Eleanor Teasdale. I never much liked that bastard Ostrowski, but at least I was moderately certain he was who and what he claimed to be. Between you and me, Eleanor, I think you're an asset, sent in because someone somewhere is getting nervous. Nervous enough to swap an actual psychiatrist for a bug dressed up to pass for a psychiatrist. Fine. I'm flexible. If these are the new rules, I can play along. But it does leave me pondering what Dr. O was telling his superiors (whom I'll assume are also your superiors, Dr. T). It couldn't have been anything so simple as labeling me a suicide risk; they've known that since I stepped off *Pilgrimage,* probably before I even stepped on.

And yes, I've noticed that you bear more than a passing resemblance to Amery. That was a bold and wicked move, and I applaud these ruthless shock tactics. I do, sincerely. This merciless Blitzkrieg waltz we're dancing, coupled with the drugs, it shows you're in this game to win, and if you *can't* win, you'll settle for the pyrrhic victory of having driven the enemy to resort to a scorched-earth retreat. Yeah, the pills and injections, they don't mesh so well with extended metaphor and simile, so I'll drop it. But I can't have you thinking all the theater has been wasted on an inattentive audience. That's all. You wear that rough facsimile of her face, Dr. T. And that annoying habit you have of tap-tap-tapping the business end of a stylus against your lower incisors, that's hers, too. And half a dozen carefully planted turns of phrase. The smile that isn't quite a smile. The self-conscious laugh. You hardly missed a trick, you and the agency handlers who sculpted you and slotted you and packed you off to play havoc with a lunatic's fading will.

My mouth is so dry.

Eleanor Teasdale watches me from the other side of her desk, and behind her, through the wide window twelve stories up, I can see the blue-brown sky, and, between the steel and glass and concrete towers, I can just make out the scrubby hills of the Diablo Range through the smog. She glances over her shoulder, following my gaze.

"Quite a view, isn't it?" she asks, and maybe I nod, and maybe I agree, and maybe I say nothing at all.

"When I was a little girl," she tells me, "my father used to take me on long hikes through the mountains. And we'd visit Lick Observatory, on the top of Mount Hamilton."

"I'm not from around here," I reply. But, then, I'd be willing to bet neither is she.

Eleanor Teasdale turns back towards me, silhouetted against the murky light through that window, framed like a misplaced Catholic saint. She stares straight at me, and I do not detect even a trace of guile when she speaks.

"We all want you to get better, Miss Merrick. You know that, don't you?"

I look away, preferring the oatmeal-colored carpet to that mask she wears.

"It's easier if we don't play games," I say.

"Yes. Yes, it is. Obviously."

"What I saw. What it meant. What she said to me. What I think it means."

"Yes, and talking about those things, bringing them out into the open, it's an important part of you *getting* better, Miss Merrick. Don't you think that's true?"

"I think..." and I pause, choosing my words as carefully as I still am able. "I think you're afraid, all of you, of never knowing. None of this is about my getting better. I've understood that almost from the start." And my voice is calm, and there is no hint of bitterness for her to hear; my voice does not betray me.

Eleanor Teasdale's smile wavers, but only a little and for only an instant or two.

"Naturally, yes, these matters are interwoven," she replies. "Quite intricately so. Almost inextricably, and I don't believe anyone has ever tried to lie to you about that. What you witnessed out there, what you seem unable, or unwilling, to share with anyone else – "

I laugh, and she sits, watching me with Amery's pale blue eyes, tapping the stylus against her teeth. Her teeth are much whiter and more even than Amery's were, and I draw some dim comfort from that incongruity.

"Share," I say, very softly, and there are other things I *want* to say to her, but I keep them to myself.

"I want you to think about that, Miss Merrick. Between now and our next session, I need you to consider, seriously, the price of your selfishness, both to your own well being and to the rest of humanity."

"Fine," I say, because I don't feel like arguing. Besides, manipulative or not, she isn't entirely wrong. "And what I was writing for Dr. Ostrowski, do I keep that up?"

"Yes, please," she replies and glances at the clock on the wall, as if she expects me to believe she'll be seeing anyone else today, that she even has other patients. "It's a sound approach, and, reviewing what you've written so far, it feels to me like you're close to a breakthrough."

I nod my head, and I also look at the clock.

"Our time's almost up," I say, and she agrees with me, then looks over her shoulder again at the green-brown hills beyond San Jose.

"I have a question," I say.

"That's why I'm here," Dr. Eleanor Teasdale tells me, imbuing the words with all the false veracity of her craft. Having affected the role of the good patient, I pretend that she isn't lying, hoping the pretense lends weight to my question.

"Have they sent a retrieval team yet? To Mars, to the caverns on Arsia Mons?"

"I wouldn't know that," she says. "I'm not privileged to such information. However, if you'd like, I can file an inquiry on your behalf. Someone with the agency might get back to you."

"No," I reply. "I was just curious if you knew," and I almost ask her another question, about Darwin's finches, and the tortoises and mockingbirds and iguanas that once populated the Galápagos Islands. But then the black minute hand on the clock ticks forward, deleting another sixty seconds from the future, converting it to past, and I decide we've both had enough for one morning.

Don't fret, Dr. T. You've done your bit for the cause, swept me off my feet, and now we're dancing. If you were here, in the hospital room with me, I'd even let you lead. I really don't care if the nurses mind or not. I'd turn up the jack, find just the right tune, and dance with the ghost you've let them make of you. I can never be too haunted, after all. Hush, hush. It's just, they give me these drugs, you see, so I need to sleep for a while, and then the waltz can continue. Your answers are coming.

March 24, 2037 (Wednesday)

It's raining. I asked one of the nurses to please raise the blinds in my room so I can watch the storm hammering the windowpane, pelting the glass, smudging my view of the diffident sky. I count off the moments between occasional flashes of lightning and the thunderclaps that follow. Storms number among the very few things remaining in all the world that can actually soothe my nerves. They certainly beat the synthetic opiates I'm given, beat them all the way to hell and back. I haven't ever bothered to tell any of my doctors or the nurses this. I don't know why; it simply hasn't occurred to me to do so. I doubt they'd care, anyway.

I've asked to please not be disturbed for a couple of hours, and I've been promised my request will be honored. That should give me the time I need to finish this.

Dr. Teasdale, I will readily confess that one of the reasons it's taken me so long reach this point is the fact that words fail. It's an awful cliché, I know, but also a point I cannot stress strongly enough. There are sights and experiences to which the blunt and finite tool of human language are not equal. I know this, though I'm no poet. But I want that caveat understood. This is not what happened aboard *Pilgrimage*; this is the sky seen through a window blurred by driving rain. It's the best I can manage, and it's the best you'll ever get. I've said all along, if the technology existed to plug in and extract the memories from my brain, I wouldn't deign to call it rape. Most of the people who've spent so much time and energy and money trying to prise from me the truth about the fate of *Pilgrimage* and its crew, they're only scientists, after all. They have no other aphrodisiac *but* curiosity. As for the rest, the spooks and politicians, the bureaucrats and corporate shills, those guys are only along for the ride, and I figure most of them know they're in over their heads.

I could make of it a fairy tale. It might begin:

Once upon a time, there was a woman who lived in New York. She was an anthropologist and shared a tiny apartment in downtown Brooklyn with her lover. And her lover was a woman named Amery Domico, who happened to be a molecular geneticist, exobiologist, and also an astronaut. They had a cat and a tank of tropical fish. They always wanted a dog, but the apartment was too small. They could probably have afforded a better, larger place to live, a loft in midtown Manhattan, perhaps, north and east of the flood zone, but the anthropologist was happy enough with Brooklyn, and her lover was usually on the road, anyway. Besides, walking a dog would have been a lot of trouble.

No. That's not working. I've never been much good with irony. And I'm better served by the immediacy of present tense. So, instead:

"Turn around, Merrick," she says. "You've come so far, and there is so little time."

And I do as she tells me. I turn towards the voice, towards the airlock's open inner hatch. There's no sign of Amery, or anyone else, for that matter. The first thing I notice, stepping from the brightly lit airlock, is that the narrow heptagonal corridor beyond is mostly dark. The second thing I notice is the mist. I know at once that it *is* mist, not smoke. It fills the hallway from deck to ceiling, and, even with the blue in-floor path lighting, it's hard to see more than a few feet ahead. The mist swirls thickly around me, like Halloween phantoms, and I'm about to ask Amery where it's coming from, what it's doing here, when I notice the walls.

Or, rather, when I notice what's growing *on* the walls. I'm fairly confident I've never seen anything with precisely that texture before. It half reminds me (but only half) of the rubbery blades and stipes of kelp. It's almost the same color as kelp, too, some shade that's not quite brown, nor green, nor a very dark purple. It also reminds me of tripe. It glimmers wetly, as though it's sweating, or secreting, mucus. I stop and stare, simultaneously alarmed and amazed and revolted. It *is* revolting, extremely so, this clinging material covering over and obscuring almost everything. I look up and see that it's also growing on the ceiling. In places, long tendrils of it hang down like dripping vines. Dr. Teasdale, I *want* so badly to describe these things, this waking nightmare, in much greater detail. I want to describe it perfectly. But, as I've said, words fail. For that matter, memory fades. And there's so much more to come.

A few thick drops of the almost colorless mucus drip from the ceiling onto my visor, and I gag reflexively. The sensors in my EVA suit respond by administering a dose of a potent antiemetic. The nausea passes quickly, and I use my left hand to wipe the slime away as best I can.

I follow the corridor, going very slowly because the mist is only getting denser and, as I move farther away from the airlock, I discover that the stuff growing on the walls and ceiling is also sprouting from the deck plates. It's slippery and squelches beneath my boots. Worse, most of the path lighting is now buried beneath it, and I switch on the magspots built into either side of my helmet. The beams reach only a short distance into the gloom.

"You're almost there," Amery says, Amery or the AI speaking with her stolen voice. "Ten yards ahead, the corridor forks. Take the right fork. It leads directly to the transhab module."

"You want to tell me what's waiting in there?" I ask, neither expecting, nor actually desiring, an answer.

"Nothing is waiting," Amery replies. "But there are many things we would have you see. There's not much time. You should hurry."

And I do try to walk faster, but, despite the suit's stabilizing exoskeleton and gyros, almost lose my footing on the slick deck. Where the corridor forks, I go right, as instructed. The habitation module is open, the hatch fully dilated, as though I'm expected. Or maybe it's been left open for days or months or years. I linger a moment on the threshold. It's so very dark in there. I call out for Amery. I call out for anyone at all, but this time there's no answer. I try my comms again, and there's not even static. I fully comprehend that in all my life I have never been so alone as I am at this moment, and, likely, I never will be again. I know, too, with a sudden and unwavering certainty, that Amery Domico is gone from me forever, and that I'm the only human being aboard *Pilgrimage*.

I take three or four steps into the transhab, but stop when something pale and big around as my forearm slithers lazily across the floor directly in front of me. If there was a head, I didn't see it. Watching as it slides past, I think of pythons, boas, anacondas, though, in truth, it bears only a passing similarity to a snake of any sort.

"You will not be harmed, Merrick," Amery says from a speaker somewhere in the darkness. The voice is almost reassuring. "You must trust that you will not be harmed, so long as you do as we say."

"What was that?" I ask. "On the floor just now. What was that?"

"Soon now, you will see," the voice replies. "We have ten million children. Soon, we will have ten million more. We are pleased that you have come to say goodbye."

"They want to know what's happened," I say, breathing too hard, much too fast, gasping despite the suit's ministrations. "At Jupiter, what happened to the ship? Where's the crew? Why is *Pilgrimage* in orbit around Mars?"

I turn my head to the left, and where there were once bunks, I can only make out a great swelling or clot of the kelp-like growth. Its surface swarms with what I briefly mistake for maggots.

"I didn't *come* to say goodbye," I whisper. "This is a retrieval mission, Amery. We've come to take you..." and I trail off, unable to complete the sentence, too keenly aware of its irrelevance.

"Merrick, are you beginning to see?"

I look away from the not-kelp and the wriggling things that aren't maggots and take another step into the habitation module.

"No, Amery. I'm not. Help me to see. Please."

"Close your eyes," she says, and I do. And when I open them again, I'm lying in bed with her. There's still an hour or so left before dawn, and we're lying in bed, naked together beneath the blankets, staring up through the apartment's skylight. It's snowing. This is the last night before Amery leaves for Cape Canaveral, the last time I see her, because I've refused to be present at the launch or even watch it online. She has her arms around me, and one of the big, ungainly hovers is passing low above our building. I do my best to pretend that its complex array of landing beacons are actually stars.

Amery kisses my right cheek, and then her lips brush lightly against my ear. "We could not understand, Merrick, because we were too far and could not remember," she says, quoting Joseph Conrad. The words roll from her tongue and palate like the spiraling snowflakes tumbling down from that tangerine sky. "We were traveling in the night of first ages, of those ages that are gone, leaving hardly a sign, and no memories."

Once, Dr. Teasdale, when Amery was sick with the flu, I read her most of *The Heart of Darkness*. She always liked when I read to her. When I came to that passage, she had me press highlight, so that she could return to it later.

"The earth seemed unearthly," she says, and I blink, dismissing the illusion. I'm standing near the center of the transhab now, and in the stark white light from my helmet I see what I've been brought here to see. Around me, the walls leak, and every inch of the module seems alive with organisms too alien for any earthborn vernacular. I've spent my adult life describing artifacts and fossil bones, but I will not even attempt to describe the myriad of forms that crawled and skittered, flitted and rolled through the ruins of *Pilgrimage.* I would fail if I did, and I would fail utterly.

"We want you to know we had a choice," Amery says. "We want you to know that, Merrick. And what is about to happen, when you leave this ship, we want you to know that is also of our choosing."

I see her, then, all that's left of her, or all that she's become. The rough outline of her body, squatting near one of the lower bunks. Her damp skin shimmers, all but indistinguishable from the rubbery substance growing throughout the vessel. Only, no, her skin is not so smooth as that, but pocked with countless oozing pores or lesions. Though the finer features of her face have been obliterated – there is no mouth remaining, no eyes, only a faint ridge that was her nose – I recognize her beyond any shadow of a doubt. She is rooted to that spot, her legs below the knees, her arms below the elbow, simply vanishing into the deck. There is constant, eager movement from inside her distended breasts and belly. And where the cleft of her sex once was...I don't have the language to describe what I saw there. But she bleeds life from that impossible wound, and I know that she has become a daughter of the oily black cloud that *Pilgrimage* encountered near Ganymede, just as she is mother and father to every living thing trapped within the crucible of that ship, every living thing but me.

"There isn't any time left," the voice from the AI says calmly, calmly but sternly. "You must leave now, Merrick. All available resources on this craft have been depleted, and we must seek sanctuary or perish."

I nod and turn away from her, because I understand as much as I'm ever going to understand, and I've seen more than I can bear to remember. I move as fast as I dare across the transhab and along the corridor leading back to the airlock. In less than five minutes, I'm safely strapped into my seat on the taxi again, decoupling and falling back towards *Yastreb-4.* A few hours later, while I'm waiting out my time in decon, Commander Yun tells me that *Pilgrimage* has fired its main engines and broken orbit. In a few moments, it will enter the thin Martian atmosphere and begin to burn. Our AI has plotted a best-guess trajectory, placing the point of impact within the Tharsis Montes, along the flanks of Arsia Mons. He tells me that the exact coordinates, -5.636°S, 241.259°E, correspond to one of the collapsed cavern roofs dotting the flanks of the ancient volcano. The pit named Jeanne, discovered way back in 2007.

"There's not much chance of anything surviving the descent," he says. I don't reply, and I never tell him, nor anyone else aboard the *Yastreb-4,* what I saw during my seventeen minutes on *Pilgrimage.*

And there's no need, Dr. Teasdale, for me to tell you what you already know. Or what your handlers know. Which means, I think, that we've reached the end of this confession. Here's the feather in your cap. May you choke on it.

Outside my hospital window, the rain has stopped. I press the call button and wait on the nurses with their shiny yellow pills and the white pills flecked with grey, their jet sprays and hollow needles filled with nightmares and, sometimes, when I'm very lucky, dreamless sleep.

GALÁPAGOS

The 2009 James Tiptree Award jurors recognized "Galápagos," placing it on the Honor List "of science fiction and fantasy stories that explore and expand gender roles." The Tiptree press release said of the story, "A mysterious space disaster, a terrifying alien reproductivity, a story reminiscent of the work of Octavia Butler. There can be no higher praise." I was pleasantly surprised and very flattered, so thank you Secret Feminist Cabal. In 2013, my novel *The Drowning Girl: A Memoir* won the Tiptree outright, and I was just as surprised, all over again. And thank you, Jonathan Strahan.

The Melusine (1898)

1.

In this blistering, midsummer month of bloatflies and thunder without so much as a drop of rain, the traveling show rolls into the great smoky burg spread out at the foot of the Chippewan Mountains. By some legerdemain unknown to the people of the city, the carnival's prairie schooners and Bollée carriages declare its name in letters five-stories high – Othniel Z. Bracken's Transportable Marvels – shaped from out of nothing but the billowing clouds of red dust raised by those rolling broad steel and vulcanized rims. The traveling show arrives at midday, as if to spite the high white eye of the summer sun glinting off tin roofs and factory windows and the acetate-aluminum envelopes of the zeppelins moored at Arapahoe Station. "Only mad dogs and Englishmen," as the saying goes, but apparently also this rattling, clanking hullabaloo of steam organs and barkers and pounding bass drums.

And the townspeople, confused and taken off their guard, peer from the sweltering shadows of their homes, from shop windows, from all those places where shade offers some negligible shelter from the July sky. They gaze in wonder, annoyance, or simple, speechless bafflement at this unexpected parade spilling along East Evens Avenue, led by an assortment of automaton mastodons, living elephants and rhinoceri, and a dozen white and prancing Percherons with braided manes. There are twirling, somersaulting women on the horses' backs, scantily clad after the fashion of Arabian harem girls; from the distance of only a few feet, it's difficult to tell if these acrobats are mechanical or the real thing.

Soon, there is an impromptu assortment of street urchins and drunkards trailing alongside the parade, coming as near as they dare to wheels and stamping hooves and stomping brass feet, and clowns with gaudy faces toss candy and squibs from the wagons, delighting the ragged children and frustrating the drunks, who might have wished for just a little more than sweets. And a man in a long black duster, his face half as red as ripe cherries, stands on a wooden platform mounted precariously atop one of the schooners. He bellows a command through a shining silver speaking-trumpet, and at once a flock of clockwork doves erupts from some hidden recess to flutter and cavort beneath the merciless sun.

"A long, long way have we come!" he shouts, the trumpet magnifying his voice until it can be plainly heard even above the noise of the parade and the clatter of the ironworks two streets over. "From the Cossack-haunted steppes of Siberia to the deadly forests of French Equatorial Africa, from the celestial palaces of the Qing Dynasty to the farthest wild shores of both polar climes, we arrive, bearing the perplexing fruits of all our intrepid journeys!"

The barker pauses, taking a breath or pausing for effect or both, and from his high perch he watches the peering, upturned faces, the thousand flavors of skepticism and dismay, anticipation and surprise. The clockwork doves circle him again, then suddenly retreat into whatever cage released them a few moments before.

"Yes! It's true!" he continues, wielding the trumpet the way, two decades earlier, before the Great Depredations, a buffalo hunter would have wielded his Spencer repeating spark rifle. "In these very wagons, the treasures of the wide, wide world, the secrets of the globe that have so entertained crowned pates and bewildered men of science and philosophy! Here, presented for each and every one among you to look upon and draw your own conclusions!"

And now, there is a hesitant smattering of applause, a handful of wolf whistles and catcalls, and the barker leans out over the railing of his platform, risking a dreadful tumble (or so it surely seems).

"And lest any there among ye lot think us mere profiteers and scalawags," he bellows through the speaking trumpet, "unscrupulous purveyors of humbuggery or chicanery, let me please assure you otherwise! A *small* return, yes, yes, astonishments for a most nominal and reasonable fee, *only* to cover our not-inconsiderable expenses in wending our way about the fearsome world. *But,* by the sacred horns of Moses, *not one copper more!*" And at this, on cue, or by providence, one of the elephants splinters the already cacophonous air with a trumpeting of her own. There is laughter from the crowd, and the tension breaks, and some of the onlookers' hesitant skepticism dissolves. The barker grins his wide grin, knowing half the battle's as good as won (and making a mental note to reward that particular elephant later on), and he sets the silver megaphone against his lips again.

"For, indeed, it is to the *betterment* and general *erudition* of all mankind – even savages in their mud huts and wigwams – that the men and women of Othniel Z. Bracken's Transportable Marvels have devoted themselves!" And though, at this point, he knows it's unnecessary, the barker adds the customary, "Come one! Come all! Come and see! Come and be *astounded!*" Then the agreeable elephant raises her trunk and lets out a blast that would have shamed even the troops of Jehoshuah during his blaring seven-day march about the walls of ill-fated Jericho. The animal's cry echoes down the slatternly, riveted canyon of thoroughfares and alleyways. Below the chandeliered ceiling of the Grand Chagrin, the dancers and sporting girls stop flirting and fanning themselves. In basements and backrooms, rapscallions and reprobates pause at their games of *crapaud* and poker, at the cutting of purse strings and throats. The air thrums and crackles, transformed, as if by the sizzling tendrils of an electrical storm. The choking, obscuring cloud of red dust streams out behind the wagons and automobiles.

And the barker, almost whispering through his trumpet, ends his soliloquy with a tipping of his tall black top hat, a bow, and, finally, a single, pregnant word – "Miracles." – and the show rolls on, triumphant, through the smoky, industrious city.

2.

At the southernmost edge of the city, just before the crooked, tumbledown shacks of Collier's Row, in the lee of the towering gob piles stripped of their lustrous anthracitic treasures, the carnival has unfolded across the dusty., disused cavalry training grounds. Like an inconceivable bird fashioned all of canvas and tent poles, the show has spread itself wide, unfurling beneath the vast western sky. And by dusk, there are what seems veritable miles of Chinese lanterns and gas lamps and Edison carbon-filament bulbs strung gaily, gaudily, here and yon. You might think, spying down upon the city from the windy crevice of Genessee Pass or Kittredge Point, that the very stars of Heaven had been lured down to Earth to light these delirious festivities. All those who can have come, and the air is filled with laughter and conversation, and it smells of sawdust and confections, incense and the exotic dung of at least a hundred species of animals.

Here are aisle after aisle of flapping, painted broadsides depicting the most fearsome and obscene and unlikely beings. And a gigantic, revolving iron wheel crafted by G. W. G. Ferris & Co. of Pittsburgh, Pennsylvania; just one thin Liberty dime buys a ten-minute ride in its rocking, colorful gondolas. There's a musical carousel fitted with all manner of saddled clockwork beasts – horses, humped camels, giraffes, a pair of snarling iguanodons, roaring lions, and even an ostrich. All around the cavalry grounds, there are fire-eaters and fakirs, tattooed women and a legion of wind-up Roman Praetorians, unicyclists and jugglers and a trio of sword-swallowing Malays not content with swords, but, contrarily, busy swallowing Nantucket harpoons and living rattlesnakes (headfirst, naturally). And rising lofty and somehow yet more unreal above all this orchestrated madness and phantasmagoria stands the great main tent, a red, white, and blue octagon fringed with golden tassels and the twinkle of ten thousand artificial fireflies.

Her name is Cala – Cala Monroe Weatherall – this tall, freckled, straw-haired woman who has come alone to answer the barker's battle cry, and, also, a more urgent, secret calling. All day, every day but Sundays, she sees to the production of valves at Jackson-Merritt Manufacturing, steel valves designed and tooled to the most exacting specifications for such august clients as the Colorado and Northern Kansas Railway, the new Colorado Central Railroad, and the Front Range and West Coast divisions of the Gesellschaft zur Förderung der Luftschiffahrt. Cala Weatherall is a learned woman of industry and science, a rationalist and an engineer with a hard-earned diploma on her office wall, received a decade earlier from the Missouri School of Mines and Metalliferous Arts. Unmarried and generally disinterested in such flitting, womanly pursuits as matrimony and men, hers is a life of math and precision, of slide rules and difference engines, logarithms and trigonometric functions. She does her small (and well-paid) part to keep the trains running and the zeppelins aloft, and she sees no shame or sin in the pride she feels at her modest accomplishments in an arena still dominated by men.

But, this night is not any usual night for Miss Cala Weatherall, who rarely spares even the strayest thought for such oddities and amusements as those offered up by Othniel Z. Bracken's Transportable Marvels. Any other night, if asked, she might have laughed or snorted and dismissed the whole, seedy affair as only so much brummagem, silly distractions best left to those *without* the responsibilities she shoulders every single day, excepting Sundays (and even then, she usually works from her room at Jane Smithson's boarding house on the lower end of Downing Street). Last night, however, and for each of the three proceeding nights, she's had a dream, a dream so vivid and bizarre that she might almost name it a nightmare. But Cala doesn't have nightmares, and, for that matter, she only rarely ever remembers her dreams upon waking. But *this* dream, this dream spoke of the imminent coming of a traveling show, and of many, many other things, besides. Though she sets no store in the fashionable delusions of spiritualism, mysticism, and theosophy promulgated by the likes of Madame Helena Blavatsky and the Hermetic Order of the Golden Dawn – charlatans and liars and fools, every one – she *has* had this dream, this dream that was *almost* a nightmare, if there had not been such beauty and longing to it. And so, uneasy and reluctant, embarrassed at herself, she has come to the old cavalry training grounds, to the traveling show, to face this rutting coincidence and be done with it, once and for always.

So, this is how she finds herself outside the sideshow tent, heavy canvas painted in a garish riot of blues and greens, whites and greys, as though some impossible Artesian well leading all the way to the sea has sprung up, suddenly from this very spot. Above the entrance is a wooden placard that reads *Poseidon's Abyss Revealed!* In her dream, there was this selfsame tent, or one near enough to raise goose bumps on her arms. And there was a placard, too, though she is not able to recollect the lettering she saw there. She pays her fifteen cents to the black man outside the tent flap – the "talker" in his scuffed-up bowler and red suspenders, busy enticing the crowd with promises of the mysteries that lie within, the *arcanum arcanorum* of the Seven Seas and any number of lakes, fjords, fens, wells, bogs, rivers, and the most desolate of great dismal swamps. Another man pushes open the flap for her, and a stream of cool air rushes out into the muggy summer night. Air so cold and damp it seems to seep forth and wrap itself about her, air that smells of low-tide along an Oregonian shore or icy slime dredged from the supposedly lifeless bottom of the Atlantic.

"Good evening, Miss," the second man – an Oriental – says, beckoning her inside. And then he winks and adds in a conspiratorial whisper, "She'll be glad to see you've come."

Cala Weatherall almost turns back then, at the man's peculiar confidence and, too, at the memory of that chill, dank smell from her dream. But now there's someone very close behind her, pushing, hurrying her forward, some other rube who's paid his money and is chomping at the bit to look upon whatever hoaxes and half truths the carnies keep hidden in this place.

"Please, sir," she grumbles. "No shoving, *please,*" but then she's inside the tent, and when Cala Weatherall glances over her left shoulder, the fellow's attention has already been seized by a desiccated "Feejee mermaid," and by the dim gaslight she can read the plaque mounted below the pathetic, shriveled thing – "Formerly of PHINEAS T. BARNUM'S AMERICAN MUSEUM, prior to that Grand Institution's DESTRUCTION on the night 8 October 1871, a CASUALTY of the GREAT CHICAGO and PESHTIGO FIRESTORM, following this Earth's COLLISION with parts of the Comet BIELA." And for a moment, Cala Weatherall forgets the dream and her trepidations, and she almost steps over to explain to the man that this purported "mermaid" is no more than the upper portion of a monkey sewn onto the rear portions of a fish, the seams concealed, no doubt, with putty or papier-mâché. And, while she's at it, also inform him that no reputable scientist anywhere accepts that the terrible fires in Chicago and Peshtigo were in any way connected, one to the other, much less the result of a collision with any ethereal object.

But then she hears a loud splash, and turning about, squinting into the gloom of the tent, through murk interrupted only by the unsteady light of the gas jets, her eyes fall upon a tremendous, roughly rectilinear slab of white marble. Stepping nearer, she sees that its surface is inscribed with all manner of pictogrammes or hieroglyphics. This time, the accompanying plaque reads, "IRREFUTABLE PROOF of the ANCIENT & SUBMERGED realm of LOST LEMURIA, dredged by BRAVE SEAMEN off the coast of PERU, from a depth of more than 2100 FATHOMS!" Cala shakes her head ruefully, noting that the glyphs are a nonsensical hodge-podge, vaguely resembling something Egyptian, and that the chisel marks appear quite fresh. There is certainly no evidence that this stone was ever long subjected to the rigors of the sea's abyssopelagic plains or hadopelagic trenches. She laughs to herself and *at* herself, laughing at having paid good, hard-earned coin and to have come this far, suckered in with all the others. The anxiety borne of her dreams, and the coincidence of the traveling show's arrival, and the existence of this sideshow tent begin to release their hold upon her, and she laughs again, louder than before, and shakes her head at the blatant forgery.

"I should ask for a refund of the price of admission," she mutters. Then, rather more loudly, so that anyone else nearby might hear, she says, "You should *all* ask for your money back." And, to herself, Cala adds, "I should notify the law, that's what I *should* do."

Increasingly embarrassed that she, even for one moment, feared her vivid dreams were anything more tangible than any dream, or the arrival of the carnival any more than a coincidence, she walks past a number of other "exhibits" arranged beneath the tent. There is a fossilized whale vertebra, almost big as a pickle barrel, of the sort long known to anatomists and students of bygone eras as *Zeuglodon cetoides,* generally found by cotton farmers while plowing their fields in Alabama and Mississippi. Here, though, the backbone is claimed to have come from the GREAT AMERICAN SEA SERPENT "HYDRARCHOS," sighted in Gloucester, Massachusetts in 1817, and, earlier, in the cold waters off Cape Ann in 1639. Farther along, past the vertebra and any number of peculiar fishes and invertebrata floating in corked jars of formaldehyde, and protected inside a locked display case, is something like a golden tiara or crown, tall towards the front, and with a very pronounced and curiously irregular periphery, as if designed for a freakishly elliptical skull. Adorned with an assortment of geometrical and marine designs, the tiara's plaque reports that it was recovered from a now-extinct cannibal tribe at some undisclosed location in the South Seas. And all this time, there are other men and women (though mostly men), and occasionally she speaks to one of them, explaining the more likely identity or origin of some specimen or artefact. Cala Weatherall has never thought that a lack of education or of a well-nurtured intellect should be an excuse for gullibility. From time to time, her whispered explanations (whispered, for several people have dared to *shush* her) are interrupted by sudden splashing sounds, like water sloshing about in a container of some sort or the tail of an otter or beaver slapping the surface of a pond. And that sound is something else from her four-times recurrent dream, the dream which was emphatically not a nightmare, and even as the sound seems to draw her forward through the ill-lit maze of this rough and mismatched collection, she pushes her *conscious* awareness of the splashing away, away and down.

"If they are all fakes," one man asks her, "why hasn't someone put a stop to this?"

"Likely as not, Sir," she replies, ignoring another of the sudden swashing noises, "whoever runs this racket paid off the relevant authorities well ahead of time, to prevent just such an interruption of commerce."

The man cocks one bushy greying eyebrow, at least appearing to look shocked at what she's just said. "My word, woman," he scowls. "We *elect* these people. Our taxes pay their salaries. We must surely not be quite so cynical as all that." And then he goes back to examining the barnacle-encrusted iron anchor supposed to have come from the *Argo* of Grecian myth. She patiently explains to the gentleman that the barnacles are of a genus not found anywhere in the Mediterranean, though quite common along the western coasts of Mexico, but he only harrumphs and says something rude about women no longer knowing their proper place. Cala lets it go, as she's heard far worse in her days, and is accustomed and, to a degree, dulled to the narrow opinions of such men.

"I only *thought* – mistakenly, I will concede – that you'd want to know the truth of the matter," she murmurs, and quickly steps past the *Argo* anchor exhibit and through yet another curtain, this one comprised of innumerable small glass beads the colour of sea foam and thunderstorms, strung along dangling lengths of silk twine. This area seems even colder than those previous sections of the labyrinth, but somewhat brighter, too, and she pauses, waiting for her eyes to adjust to the unexpected glare. The air here is markedly more dank, and smells particularly, almost overwhelmingly, briny. So strong is the odor, Cala might be standing at the very edge of the sea. Around her, the canvas walls are washed with a reflected, coruscating light, and in only a few seconds more she sees the source of both the saltwater smell and the constantly shifting rays playing across the tent's walls. At first, squinting at and into the enormous aquarium standing before her – thick glass and a rusty cast-iron framework, a chugging pump to keep the water oxygenated and filtered of detritus – she expects to see nothing more remarkable than a pair of trained seals or, possibly instead, some grim variety of devilfish or giant squid to appall and startle these people who have never known the ocean and its inhabitants.

But the tank does not contain trained seals.

Nor an octopus or squid.

For a time, Cala stands quite still, staring, disbelieving the evidence of her own eyes, willing herself not to draw any obvious conclusions or connections with the dreams, for too frequently, she knows, are we deceived by that which seems so perfectly obvious to our senses.

The thing in the tank, she reasons, must certainly be an automaton, an admirably cunning clockwork, impermeable to moisture, but not so unlike the mastodons and doves in the afternoon's parade along East Evens Avenue. The acquisition of such a device is clearly not beyond the resources of the carnival, and if it *is* only mechanical, then there remains but the niggling issue of coincidence to address. Despite her pounding heart and the sweat slicking her palms and upper lip, she is very near to dismissing it, this absurd fairy-tale chimera peering back at her from the aquarium, its head and shoulders held above the slopping surface, the rest coiled below the waterline. But then it opens its mouth and speaks, and that voice is so exquisite, and so familiar, that Cala Weatherall believes she might well scream, and never mind who would hear or what they would think.

"So long, girl," the thing in the tank sighs, its voice rolling, tumbling, rushing through the tent like breakers before an incoming tide. "So very, very long have I waited for this night, hauled across time and these death-dry lands, through arid wilderness and the smoldering, unseeing cities of men."

"No," Cala says, but the word is not meant as a response, only as a personal statement of her disbelief, spoken aloud for her own benefit. There is still no reason, beyond the coincidence of her recurring dream, to suppose the thing in the tank is not a hoax, and that its voice does not originate, for instance, from a woman sequestered somewhere behind the tank. Probably, she speaks into a small brass horn attached to a length of tubing, and her voice emerges from the mechanized rubber lips of the melusine.

"They *said* that you would be the Skeptic," the thing responds, not knowing that Cala was not speaking to it (for what sane woman *talks* to an automaton).

"They," Cala says, repeating what the thing has said, though still not speaking *to* it.

"My dear sisters," it replies, "Palatyne and Melior. They each, in turn, warned that, in the end, all my searching would yield only so much dubiety and fleer."

"I have seen many a clever puppet show," Cala says, and this time she realizes that she is answering the thing in the tank. "I did not always see the strings or the puppeteers, but I never doubted the performers were only marionettes."

"You do not strike me as the sort to attend a puppet show," the melusine replies. "Which is a shame, I think."

Cala Weatherall glances uneasily back the way she's come, and there's the curtain of glass beads, still swaying slightly, softly clicking and clacking against each other. She looks back at the aquarium tank, still clinging as ferociously to her disbelief as any caterwauling Baptist minister ever clung to his King James Bible. The thing in the tank has the appearance of a very pale and beautiful woman from the hips up. Its skin has a disquieting iridescent quality, almost opalescent in this light. Its perfectly wrought hands have no nails, but end in sharp, recurved, and chitinous claws at the tip of each long finger, and its eyes are the yellow of the yolk from a chicken's egg. Its small breasts are shamelessly bare, though Cala notes that it has no visible nipples, and so she wonders, absently, at the utility of breasts so ill-equipped for nursing. A sculptor's fancy or accidental imperfection, and likely nothing more. She dares to take one step nearer, seeking other flaws in the design. The melusine's long straight hair hangs in sodden strands about its mother-of-pearl shoulders, black as a freshly-exposed vein of coal. Only, on closer inspection, there are what appear to be dozens of fleshy tendrils writhing within those sable tresses, no bigger around than a lead pencil. Its sharp teeth flash when it mimics speech, and they are almost identical to those of certain lamniform sharks known to ichthyologists as sand tigers, row upon row anchored in gums the bruised colour of ripening elderberries.

"I know your lonely nights, Cala," the melusine tells her. "I have watched you, at your window, envying the couples passing by."

"Enough," Cala replies angrily, for there are limits to what any woman must endure, even in well-meaning jest, and this jest has long since transcended the boundaries of propriety. "I do not know how you people learned my name," she says, not speaking to the thing in the tank, but to whatever unseen actress speaks its lines. "Though I doubt it was so very difficult. You must have numerous marks each time you enter a new town."

"And we know your dreams?" the melusine asks, as its scaly, serpentine tails coil and uncoil beneath that human torso. It cocks its head to one side, waiting for an answer, and the small flukes at the ends of its tails slap the surface of the water. "Pray thee, tell how it is we might accomplish that feat?"

For the span of several heartbeats, Cala does not reply, transfixed not only by the power of the thing's question, but by the rhythmic, almost hypnotic, smack of those silvery-green flukes. *Yes,* she thinks. *Hypnosis, mesmerism, autosuggestion, these must be part of the deception. Turning my own mind against me to achieve this effect.*

"Yes," the melusine says. "Hypnosis, mesmerism, autosuggestion, these must be part of the deception. Turning your own mind against you to achieve this effect."

Cala Weatherall gasps, and takes another step towards the tank. "It cannot be," she says. "It's impossible."

"Why?" asks the thing in the tank. "Because you have not been taught that it is so? I have not come so far, across gulfs of time and space, merely to deceive a lonely, dissatisfied woman. What bitter daemon has taken hold of the world of men that it no longer trusts its own eyes and its own ears?"

"Ours is an enlightened age," Cala says, but her voice is hardly audible now, a half whisper as she steps still nearer to the aquarium tank. "Not an age of ignorance and superstition. Not an age of sirens and mermaids and sea monsters."

"And neither is it an age in which a woman who is brilliant and enterprising, but whose heart does not seek a *man,* can hope for the balm of love or even of a soul mate's companionship? Did you also sell your heart, Cala Weatherall, when you sold off your imagination? Is there remaining now no way ever that I may comfort thee?"

"It simply is not *possible,*" Cala whispers, meaning only the existence of this creature and not to answer its question. And she realizes, if only distantly, that she has begun to weep, and, whether from sympathy or mockery, the melusine has begun to weep as well.

"It says, you must be brilliant, indeed, if your mind contains a catalog of all those things possible and all those things that are not."

"They were dreams. *Only* dreams. I have never even dared to hope."

"A mighty daemon, indeed, that it leads a woman to fear even the meager solace of *hope.*"

Now Cala is standing so near the tank that she might easily extend a hand to reach out and touch the melusine's strange, restless hair and pearly skin. And she sees, for the first time, a small and tarnished brass plaque bolted to the tank, which reads simply *Le Fontaine de Soif.*

"It *is* so, is it not?" the melusine asks, seeing that Cala's read the plaque on the aquarium. "You are so terribly thirsty, like a woman lost and wandering in an endless desert." And then the creature ventures the faintest of smiles, and one glistening arm slides out over the rim of the tank towards her.

"It *is* so," Cala confesses to the beast. "I am so alone. I am so lost, so terribly alone. And you...you are more beautiful times ten than anything I have ever looked upon with waking eyes." She starts to take the melusine's hand, recalling again details of her vivid dreams – the wordless embraces in lightless, submerged halls formed of coral and the carved ribs of leviathans. Already, she knows the taste of the melusine's thin pink lips, the feel of those vicious teeth upon her skin, the unspeakable pleasure of the faerie's mouth and hands and those appendages for which men have not ever devised names moving upon her and probing deeply within her.

"It is such a small thing, belief," the melusine tells her. "It is no more than taking my hand."

And then, in the last fraction of an instant before Cala *does* accept that proffered hand, there is a violent hissing, and a loud *pop,* and all at once the smell of ozone and hot metal, of stripped gears and melting polymers fills the air inside the tent, pushing back the salty, primordial smells of the ocean and of birth and death and love. The thing in the tank shudders and then goes limp, and steam begins to rise from the water in the aquarium. Somewhere nearby, she hears a woman, a woman with a voice like the melusine's, cursing, and a man begins to shout. Cala lets her arm drop to her side, and her eyes linger only a few seconds longer on the ruined automaton, before she turns and silently makes her way out of the tent and back out into the muggy summer night and the hullabaloo of Othniel Z. Bracken's Transportable Marvels. The next day, after a few hours of fitful sleep, she will discover the jimmied lock on her dresser drawer and the missing diary wherein she recorded all her secret thoughts and desires and dreams. And there will remain unanswered questions, but she will not ever ask them. There is too much work to be done, a job that fifty men, fifty men easy, would be happy to take if she were to fail. There are calculations to make and orders to be filled, and if in the empty stretches of her nights, she sometimes finds herself far below the churning surface of the sea, beloved and belonging in those sunken corridors, these are things she keeps forever to herself and never again commits to the fickle confidences of ink and paper.

THE MELUSINE (1898)

It will be obvious to anyone who's read my story "Postcards from the King of Tides" that there's significant reworking going on here, although I wasn't aware I'd done it until years later. I suppose this story could be said to be a rationalist response to "Postcards from the King of Tides," but, if so, it was my rational subconscious responding, which is odd as I tend to suspect my subconscious mind of being embarrassingly superstitious. Of my five Cherry Creek stories, this is my second favorite, after "The Steam Dancer (1896)".

As Red as Red

1.

"So, you believe in vampires?" she asks, then takes another sip of her coffee and looks out at the rain pelting Thames Street beyond the café window. It's been pissing rain for almost an hour, a cold, stinging shower on an overcast afternoon near the end of March, a bitter Newport afternoon that would have been equally at home in January or February. But at least it's not pissing snow.

I put my own cup down – tea, not coffee – and stare across the booth at her for a moment or two before answering. "No," I tell Abby Gladding. "But, quite clearly, those people in Exeter who saw to it that Mercy Brown's body was exhumed, the ones who cut out her heart and burned it, clearly *they* believed in vampires. And that's what I'm studying, the psychology behind that hysteria, behind the superstitions."

"It was so long ago," she replies and smiles. There's no foreshadowing in that smile, not even in hindsight. It surely isn't a predatory smile. There's nothing malevolent, or hungry, or feral in the expression. She just watches the rain and smiles, as though something I've said amuses her.

"Not really," I say, glancing down at my steaming cup. "Not so long ago as people might *like* to think. The Mercy Brown incident, that was in 1892, and the most recent case of purported vampirism in the Northeast I've been able to pin down dates from sometime in 1898, a mere hundred and eleven years ago."

Her smile lingers, and she traces a circle in the condensation on the plate-glass window, then traces another circle inside it.

"We're not so far removed from the villagers with their torches and pitchforks, from old Cotton Mather and his bunch. That's what you're saying."

"Well, not exactly, but..." and when I trail off, she turns her head towards me, and her blue-grey eyes seem as cold as the low-slung sky above Newport. You could almost freeze to death in eyes like those, I think, and I take another sip of my lukewarm Earl Grey with lemon. Her eyes seem somehow brighter than they should in the dim light of the coffeehouse, so there's your foreshadowing, I suppose, if you're the sort who needs it.

"You're pretty far from Exeter, Ms. Howard," she says and takes another sip of her coffee. And me, I'm sitting here wishing we were talking about almost anything but Rhode Island vampires and the madness of crowds, tuberculosis and the Master's thesis I'll be defending at the end of May. It has been months since I've had anything even resembling a date, and I don't want to squander the next half hour or so talking shop.

"I think I've turned up something interesting," I tell her, because I can't think of any subtle way to steer the conversation in another direction. "A case no one's documented before, right here in Newport."

She smiles that smile again.

"I got a tip from a folklorist up at Brown," I say. "Seems like maybe there was an incident here in 1785 or thereabouts. If it checks out, I might be onto the oldest case of suspected vampirism resulting in an exhumation anywhere in New England. So, now I'm trying to verify the rumors. But there's precious little to go on. Chasing vampires, it's not like studying the Salem witch trials, where you have all those court records, the indictments and depositions and what have you. Instead, it's necessary to spend a lot of time sifting and sorting fact from fiction, and, usually, there's not much of either to work with."

She nods, then glances back towards the big window and the rain. "Be a feather in your cap, though. If it's not just a rumor, I mean."

"Yes," I reply. "Yes, it certainly would."

And here, there's an unsettling wave of not-quite déjà vu, something closer to dissociation, perhaps, and for a few dizzying seconds I feel as if I'm watching this conversation, a voyeur listening in, or as if I'm only remembering it, but in no way actually, presently, taking part in it. And, too, the coffeehouse and our talk and the rain outside seem no more concrete – no more *here and now* – than does the morning before. One day that might as well be the next, and it's raining, either way.

I'm standing alone on Bowen's Warf, staring out past the masts crowded into the marina at sleek white sailboats skimming over the glittering water, and there's the silhouette of Goat Island, half hidden in the fog. I'm about to turn and walk back up the hill to Washington Square and the library, about to leave the gaudy Disney World concessions catering to the tastes of tourists and return to the comforting maze of ancient gabled houses lining winding, narrow streets. And that's when I see her for the first time. She's standing alone near the "seal safari" kiosk, staring at a faded sign, at black-and-white photographs of harbor seals with eyes like the puppies and little girls from those hideous Margaret Keane paintings. She's wearing an old pea coat and shiny green galoshes that look new, but there's nothing on her head, and she doesn't have an umbrella. Her long black hair hangs wet and limp, and when she looks at me, it frames her pale face.

Then it passes, the blip or glitch in my psyche, and I've snapped back, into myself, into *this* present. I'm sitting across the booth from her once more, and the air smells almost oppressively of freshly roasted and freshly ground coffee beans.

"I'm sure it has a lot of secrets, this town," she says, fixing me again with those blue-grey eyes and smiling that irreproachable smile of hers.

"Can't swing a dead cat," I say, and she laughs.

"Well, did it ever work?" Abby asks. "I mean, digging up the dead, desecrating their mortal remains to appease the living. Did it tend to do the trick?"

"No," I reply. "Of course not. But that's beside the point. People do strange things when they're scared."

And there's more, mostly more questions from her about Colonial-era vampirism, Newport's urban legends, and my research as a folklorist. I'm grateful that she's kind or polite enough not to ask the usual "you mean people get paid to do this sort of thing" questions. Instead, she tells me a werewolf story dating back to the 1800's, a local priest supposedly locked away in the Portsmouth Poor Asylum after he committed a particularly gruesome murder, how he was spared the gallows because people believed he was a werewolf and so not in control of his actions. She even tells me about seeing his nameless grave in a cemetery up in Middletown, his tombstone bearing the head of a wolf. And I'm polite enough not to tell her that I've heard this one before.

Finally, I notice that it's stopped raining.

"I really ought to get back to work," I say, and she nods and suggests that we should have dinner sometime soon. I agree, but we don't set a date. She has my number, after all, so we can figure that out later. She also mentions a movie playing at Jane Pickens that she hasn't seen and thinks I might enjoy. I leave her sitting there in the booth, in her pea coat and green galoshes, and she orders another cup of coffee as I'm exiting the café. On the way back to the library, I see a tree filled with noisy, cawing crows, and for some reason it reminds me of Abby Gladding.

2.

That was Monday, and there's nothing the least bit remarkable about Tuesday. I make the commute from Providence to Newport, crossing the West Passage of Narragansett Bay to Conanicut Island, and then the East Passage to Aquidneck Island and Newport. Most of the day is spent at the Redwood Library and Athenaeum on Bellevue, shut away with my newspaper clippings and microfiche, with frail yellowed books that were printed before the Revolutionary War. I wear the white cotton gloves they give me for handling archival materials and make several pages of handwritten notes, pertaining primarily to the treatment of cases of consumption in Newport during the first two decades of the Eighteenth Century.

The library is open late on Tuesdays, and I don't leave until sometime after seven p.m. But nothing I find gets me any nearer to confirming that a corpse believed to have belonged to a vampire was exhumed from the Common Burying Ground in 1785. On the long drive home, I try not to think about the fact that she hasn't called, or my growing suspicion that she likely never will. I have a can of ravioli and a beer for dinner. I half watch something forgettable on television. I take a hot shower and brush my teeth. If there are any dreams – good, bad, or otherwise – they're nothing I recall upon waking. The day is sunny, and not quite as cold, and I do my best to summon a few shoddy scraps of optimism, enough to get me out the door and into the car.

But by the time I reach the library in Newport, I've got a headache, what feels like the beginnings of a migraine, railroad spikes in both my eyes, and I'm wishing I'd stayed in bed. I find a comfortable seat in the Roderick Terry Reading Room, one of the armchairs upholstered with dark green leather, and leave my sunglasses on while I flip through books pulled randomly from the shelf on my right. Novels by William Kennedy and Elia Kazan, familiar, friendly books, but trying to focus on the words only makes my head hurt worse. I return *The Arrangement* to its slot on the shelf, and pick up something called *Thousand Cranes* by a Japanese author, Yasunari Kawbata. I've never heard of him, but the blurb on the back of the dust jacket assures me he was awarded the Nobel Prize for Literature in 1968, and that he was the first Japanese author to receive it.

I don't open the book, but I don't reshelve it, either. It rests there in my lap, and I sit beneath the octagonal skylight with my eyes closed for a while. Five minutes maybe, maybe more, and the only sounds are muffled footsteps, the turning of pages, an old man clearing his throat, a passing police siren, one of the librarians at the front desk whispering a little more loudly than usual. Or maybe the migraine magnifies her voice and only makes it seem that way. In fact, all these small, unremarkable sounds seem magnified, if only by the quiet of the library.

When I open my eyes, I have to blink a few times to bring the room back into focus. So I don't immediately notice the woman standing outside the window, looking in at me. Or only looking *in*, and I just happen to be in her line of sight. Maybe she's looking at nothing in particular, or at the bronze statue of Pheidippides perched on its wooden pedestal. Perhaps she's looking for someone else, someone who isn't me. The window is on the opposite side of the library from where I'm sitting, forty feet or so away. But even at that distance, I'm almost certain that the pale face and lank black hair belong to Abby Gladding. I raise a hand, half waving to her, but if she sees me, she doesn't acknowledge having seen me. She just stands there, perfectly still, staring in.

I get to my feet, and the copy of *Thousand Cranes* slides off my lap; the noise the book makes when it hits the floor is enough that a couple of people look up from their magazines and glare at me. I offer them an apologetic gesture – part shrug and part sheepish frown – and they shake their heads, almost in unison, and go back to reading. When I glance at the window again, the black-haired woman is no longer there. Suddenly, my headache is much worse (probably from standing so quickly, I think), and I feel a sudden, dizzying rush of adrenalin. No, it's more than that. I feel afraid. My heart races, and my mouth has gone very dry. Any plans I might have harbored of going outside to see if the woman looking in actually was Abby vanish immediately, and I sit down again. If it was her, I reason, then she'll come inside.

So I wait, and, very slowly, my pulse returns to its normal rhythm, but the adrenaline leaves me feeling jittery, and the pain behind my eyes doesn't get any better. I pick the novel by Yasunari Kawbata up off the floor and place it back upon the shelf. Leaning over makes my head pound even worse, and I'm starting to feel nauseous. I consider going to the restrooms, near the circulation desk, but part of me is still afraid, for whatever reason, and it seems to be the part of me that controls my legs. I stay in the seat and wait for the woman from the window to walk into the Roderick Terry Reading Room. I wait for her to be Abby, and I expect to hear her green galoshes squeaking against the lacquered hardwood. She'll say that she thought about calling, but then figured that I'd be in the library, so of course my phone would be switched off. She'll say something about the weather, and she'll want to know if I'm still up for dinner and the movie. I'll tell her about the migraine, and maybe she'll offer me Excedrin or Tylenol. Our hushed conversation will annoy someone, and he or she will shush us. We'll laugh about it later on.

But Abby doesn't appear, and so I sit for a while, gazing across the wide room at the window, a tree *outside* the window, at the houses lined up neat and tidy along Redwood Street. On Wednesday, the library is open until eight, but I leave as soon as I feel well enough to drive back to Providence.

3.

It's Thursday, and I'm sitting in that same green armchair in the Terry Roderick Reading Room. It's only 11:26 a.m., and already I understand that I've lost the day. I have no days to spare, but already I know that the research that I should get done today isn't going to happen. Last night was too filled with uneasy dreaming, and this morning I can't concentrate. It's hard to think about anything but the nightmares and the face of Abby Gladding at the window, her blue eyes, her black hair. And yes, I have grown quite certain that it *was* her face I saw peering in and that she was peering in *at* me.

She hasn't called (and I didn't get her number, assuming she has one). An hour ago, I walked along the Newport waterfront looking for her, but to no avail. I stood a while beside the "seal safari" kiosk, hoping, irrationally I suppose, that she might turn up. I smoked a cigarette and stood there in the cold, watching the sunlight on the bay, listening to traffic and the wind and a giggling flock of grey seagulls. Just before I gave up and made my way back to the library, I noticed dog tracks in a muddy patch of ground near the kiosk. I thought that they seemed unusually large, and I couldn't help but recall the café on Monday and Abby relating the story of the werewolf priest buried in Middletown. But lots of people in Newport have big dogs, and they walk them along the wharf.

I'm sitting in the green leather chair, and there's a manila folder of photocopies and computer printouts in my lap. I've been picking through them, pretending this is work. It isn't. There's nothing in the folder I haven't read five or ten times over, nothing that hasn't been cited by other academics chasing stories of New England vampires. On top of the stack is "The 'Vampires' of Rhode Island," from *Yankee* magazine, October 1970. Beneath that, "They Burned Her Heart...Was Mercy Brown a Vampire?" from the *Narragansett Times,* October 25th 1979, and from the *Providence Sunday Journal,* also October 1979, "Did They Hear the Vampire Whisper?" So many of these popular pieces have October dates, a testament to journalism's attitude towards the subject, which it clearly views as nothing more than a convenient skeleton to pull from the closet every Halloween, something to dust off and trot out for laughs.

Salem has its witches. Sleepy Hollow its headless Hessian mercenary. And Rhode Island has its consumptive, consuming phantoms – Mercy Brown, Sarah Tillinghast, Nellie Vaughn, Ruth Ellen Rose, and all the rest. Beneath the *Providence Sunday Journal* piece is a black-and-white photograph I took a couple of years ago, Nellie Vaughn's vandalized headstone with its infamous inscription: "I am waiting and watching for you." I stare at the photograph for a moment or two and set it aside. Beneath it there's a copy of another October article, "When the Wind Howls and the Trees Moan," also from the *Providence Sunday Journal.* I close the manila folder and try not to stare at the window across the room.

It is only a window, and it only looks out on trees and houses and sunlight.

I open the folder again and read from a much older article, "The Animistic Vampire in New England" from *American Anthropologist,* published in 1896, only four years after the Mercy Brown incident. I read it silently, to myself, but catch my lips moving:

In New England the vampire superstition is unknown by its proper name. It is believed that consumption is not a physical but spiritual disease, obsession, or visitation; that as long as the body of a dead consumptive relative has blood in its heart it is proof that an occult influence steals from it for death and is at work draining the blood of the living into the heart of the dead and causing his rapid decline.

I close the folder again and return it to its place in my book bag. And then I stand and cross the wide reading room to the window and the alcove where I saw, or only thought I saw, Abby looking in at me. There's a marble bust of Cicero on the window ledge, and I've been staring out at the leafless trees and the brown grass, the sidewalk and the street, for several minutes before I notice the smudges on the pane of glass, only inches from my face. Sometime recently, when the window was wet, a finger traced a circle there, and then traced a circle within that first circle. When the glass dried, these smudges were left behind. And I remember Monday afternoon at the coffeehouse, Abby tracing an identical symbol (if "symbol" is the appropriate word here) in the condensation on the window while we talked and watched the rain.

I press my palm to the glass, which is much colder than I'd expected.

In my dream, I stood at another window, at the end of a long hallway, and looked down at the North Burial Ground. With some difficulty, I opened the window, hoping the air outside would be fresher than the stale air in the hallway. It was, and I thought it smelled faintly of clover and strawberries. And there was music. I saw, then, Abby standing beneath a tree, playing a violin. The music was very beautiful, though very sad, and completely unfamiliar. She drew the bow slowly across the strings, and I realized that somehow the music was shaping the night. There were clouds sailing past above the cemetery, and the chords she drew from the violin changed the shapes of those clouds and also seemed to dictate the speed at which they moved. The moon was bloated and shone an unhealthy shade of ivory, and the whole sky writhed like a Van Gogh painting. I wondered why she didn't tell me that she plays the violin.

Behind me, something clattered to the floor, and I looked over my shoulder. But there was only the long hallway, leading off into perfect darkness, leading back the way I'd apparently come. When I turned again to the open window and the cemetery, the music had ceased, and Abby was gone. There was only the tree and row after row of tilted headstones, charcoal-colored slate, white marble, a few cut from slabs of reddish sandstone mined from Massachusetts or Connecticut.

I was reminded of a platoon of drunken soldiers, lined up for a battle they knew they were going to lose.

I have never liked writing my dreams down.

It is late Thursday morning, almost noon, and I pull my hand back from the cold, smudged windowpane. I have to be in Providence for an evening lecture, and I gather my things and leave the Redwood Library and Athenaeum. On the drive back to the city, I do my best to stop thinking about the nightmare, my best not to dwell on what I saw sitting beneath the tree, after the music stopped and Abby Gladding disappeared. My best isn't good enough.

4.

The lecture goes well, quite a bit better than I'd expected it would, better, probably, than it had a right to, all things considered. "Mercy Brown as Inspiration for Bram Stoker's *Dracula,*" presented to the Rhode Island Historical Society, and, somehow, I even manage not to make a fool of myself answering questions afterwards. It helps that I've answered these same questions so many times in the past. For example:

"I'm assuming you've also drawn connections between the Mercy Brown incident and Sheridan Le Fanu's 'Carmilla?'"

"There are similarities, certainly, but so far as I know, no one has been able to demonstrate conclusively that Le Fanu knew of the New England phenomena. And, more importantly, the publication of 'Carmilla' predates the exhumation of Mercy Brown's body by twenty years."

"Still, he might have known of the earlier cases."

"Certainly. He may well have. However, I have no evidence that he did."

But, the entire time, my mind is elsewhere, back across the water in Newport, in that coffeehouse on Thames, and the Redwood Library, and standing in a dream hallway, looking down on my subconscious rendering of the Common Burying Ground. A woman playing a violin beneath a tree. A woman with whom I have only actually spoken once, but about whom I cannot stop thinking.

It is believed that consumption is not a physical but spiritual disease, obsession, or visitation…

After the lecture, and the questions, after introductions are made and notable, influential hands are shaken, when I can finally slip away without seeming either rude or unprofessional, I spend an hour or so walking alone on College Hill. It's a cold, clear night, and I follow Benevolent Street west to Benefit and turn north. There's comfort in the uneven, buckled bricks of the sidewalk, in the bare limbs of the trees, in all the softly glowing windows. I pause at the granite steps leading up to the front door of what historians call the Stephen Harris House, built in 1764. One hundred and sixty years later, H. P. Lovecraft called this the "Babbitt House" and used it as the setting for an odd tale of lycanthropy and vampirism. I know this huge yellow house well. And I know, too, the four hand-painted signs nailed up on the gatepost, all of them in French. From the sidewalk, by the electric glow of a nearby street lamp, I can only make out the top half of the third sign in the series; the rest are lost in the gloom – *Oubliez le Chien*. Forget the Dog.

I start walking again, heading home to my tiny, cluttered apartment, only a couple of blocks east on Prospect. The side streets are notoriously steep, and I've been in better shape. I haven't gone twenty-five yards before I'm winded and have a nasty stitch in my side. I lean against a stone wall, cursing the cigarettes and the exercise I can't be bothered with, trying to catch my breath. The freezing air makes my sinuses and teeth ache. It burns my throat like whiskey.

And this is when I glimpse a sudden blur from out the corner of my right eye, hardly *more* than a blur. An impression or the shadow of something large and black, moving quickly across the street. It's no more than ten feet away from me, but downhill, back towards Benefit. By the time I turn to get a better look, it's gone, and I'm already beginning to doubt I saw anything, except, possibly, a stray dog.

I linger here a moment, squinting into the darkness and the yellow-orange sodium-vapor pool of streetlight that the blur seemed to cross before it disappeared. I want to laugh at myself, because I can actually feel the prick of goose bumps along my forearms, and the short, fine hairs at the nape of my neck standing on end. I've blundered into a horror-movie cliché, and I can't help but be reminded of Val Lewton's *Cat People,* the scene where Jane Rudolph walks quickly past Central Park, stalked by a vengeful Simone Simon, only to be rescued at the last possible moment by the fortuitous arrival of a city bus. But I know there's no helpful bus coming to intervene on my behalf, and, more importantly, I understand full fucking well that this night holds in store nothing more menacing than what my over-stimulated imagination has put there. I turn away from the street light and continue up the hill towards home. And I do not have to *pretend* that I don't hear footsteps following me, or the clack of claws on concrete, because I *don't*. The quick shadow, the peripheral blur, it was only a moment's misapprehension, no more than a trick of my exhausted, preoccupied mind, filled with the evening's morbid banter.

Oubliez le Chien.

Fifteen minutes later, I'm locking the front door of my apartment behind me. I make a hot cup of chamomile tea, which I drink standing at the kitchen counter. I'm in bed shortly after ten o'clock. By then, I've managed to completely dismiss whatever I only thought I saw crossing Jenckes Street.

5.

"Open your eyes, Ms. Howard," Abby Gladding says, and I do. Her voice does not in any way command me to open my eyes, and it is perfectly clear that I have a choice in the matter. But there's a certain *je ne sais quoi* in the delivery, the inflection and intonation, in the measured conveyance of these seven syllables, that makes it impossible for me to keep my eyes closed. It's not yet dawn, but sunrise cannot be very far away, and I am lying in my bed. I cannot say whether I am awake or dreaming or if possibly I am stranded in some liminal state that is neither one nor the other. I am immediately conscious of an unseen weight bearing down painfully upon my chest, and I am having difficulty breathing.

"I promised that I'd call on you," she says, and, with great effort, I turn my head towards the sound of her voice, my cheek pressing deeply into my pillow. I am aware now that I am all but paralyzed, perhaps by the same force pushing down on my chest, and I strain for any glimpse of her. But there's only the bedside table, the clock radio and reading lamp and ashtray, an overcrowded bookcase with sagging shelves, and the floral calico wallpaper that came with the apartment. If I could move my arms, I would switch on the lamp. If I could move, I'd sit up, and maybe I would be able to breathe again.

And then I think that she must surely be singing, though her song has no words. There is no need for mere lyrics, not when texture and timbre, harmony and melody, are sufficient to unmake the mundane artifacts that comprise my bedroom, wiping aside the here and now that belie what I am meant to see in this fleeting moment. And even as the wall and the bookshelf and the table beside my bed dissolve and fall away, I understand that her music is drawing me deeper into sleep again, though I must have been very nearly awake when she told me to open my eyes. I have no time to worry over apparent contradictions, and I can't move my head to look away from what she means for me to see.

There's nothing to be afraid of, I think. *No more here than in any bad dream.* But I find the thought carries no conviction whatsoever. It's even less substantial than the dissolving wallpaper and bookcase.

Now I'm looking at the weed-choked shore of a misty pond or swamp, a bog or tidal marsh. The light is so dim it might be dusk, or it might be dawn, or merely an overcast day. There are huge trees bending low near the water, water which seems almost perfectly smooth and the green of polished malachite. I hear frogs, hidden among the moss and reeds, the ferns and skunk cabbages, and now the calls of birds form a counterpoint to Abby's voice. Except, seeing her standing ankle deep in that stagnant green pool, I also see that she isn't singing. The music is coming from the violin braced against her shoulder, from the bow and strings and the movement of her left hand along the fingerboard of the instrument. She has her back to me, but I don't need to see her face to know it's her. Her black hair hangs down almost to her hips. And only now do I realize that she's naked.

Abruptly, she stops playing, and her arms fall to her sides, the violin in her left hand, the bow in her right. The tip of the bow breaks the surface of the pool, and ripples in concentric rings race away from it.

"I wear this rough garment to deceive," she says, and, at that, all the birds and frogs fall silent. "Aren't you the clever girl? Aren't you canny? I would not think appearances would so easily lead you astray. Not for long as this."

No words escape my rigid, sleeping jaws, but she hears me all the same, my answer that needs no voice, and she turns to face me. Her eyes are golden, not blue. And in the low light, they briefly flash a bright, iridescent yellow. She smiles, showing me teeth as sharp as razors, and then she quotes from the *Gospel of Matthew*.

"Inwardly, they were ravening wolves," she says to me. "You've seen all that you need to see, and probably more, I'd wager." With this, she turns away again, turning to face the fog shrouding the wide green pool. As I watch, helpless to divert my gaze or even shut my eyes, she lets the violin and bow slip from her hands; they fall into the water with quiet splashes. The bow sinks, though the violin floats. And then she goes down on all fours. She laps at the pool, and her hair has begun to writhe like a nest of serpents.

And now I'm awake, disoriented and my chest aching, gasping for air as if a moment before I was drowning and have only just been pulled to the safety of dry land. The wallpaper is only dingy calico again, and the bookcase is only a bookcase. The clock radio and the lamp and the ashtray sit in their appointed places upon the bedside table.

The sheets are soaked through with sweat, and I'm shivering. I sit up, my back braced against the headboard, and my eyes go to the second-story window on the other side of the small room. The sun is still down, but it's a little lighter out there than it is in the bedroom. And for a fraction of a moment, clearly silhouetted against that false dawn, I see the head and shoulders of a young woman. I also see the muzzle and alert ears of a wolf and that golden eyeshine watching me. Then it's gone, she or it, whichever pronoun might best apply. It doesn't seem to matter. Because now I do know exactly what I'm looking for, and I know that I've seen it before, years before I first caught sight of Abby Gladding standing in the rain without an umbrella.

6.

Friday morning I drive back to Newport, and it doesn't take me long at all to find the grave. It's just a little ways south of the chain-link fence dividing the North Burial Ground from the older Common Burying Ground and Island Cemetery. I turn off Warner Street onto the rutted, unpaved road winding between the indistinct rows of monuments. I find a place that's wide enough to pull over and park. The trees have only just begun to bud, and their bare limbs are stark against a sky so blue-white it hurts my eyes to look directly into it. The grass is mostly still brown from long months of snow and frost, though there are small clumps of new green showing here and there.

The cemetery has been in use since 1640 or so. There are three Colonial-era governors buried here (one a delegate to the Continental Congress), along with the founder of Freemasonry in Rhode Island, a signatory to the Declaration of Independence, various Civil War generals, lighthouse keepers, and hundreds of African slaves stolen from Gambia and Sierra Leone, the Gold and Ivory coasts, and brought to Newport in the heyday of whaling and the Rhode Island rum trade. The grave of Abby Gladding is marked by a weathered slate headstone, badly scabbed over with lichen. But, despite the centuries, the shallow inscription is still easy enough to read:

HERE LYETH INTERED Y^{e} BODY
OF ABBY MARY GLADDING
DAUGHTER OF SOLOMON GLADDING ^{esq}
& MARY HIS WYFE WHO
DEPARTED THIS LIFE Y^{e} 2^{d} DAY OF
SEPT 1785 AGED 22 YEARS
SHE WAS DROWN'D & DEPARTED & SLEEPS
$^{ZECH\ 4:1}$ NEITHER SHALL THEY WEAR
A HAIRY GARMENT TO DECEIVE

Above the inscription, in place of the usual death's head, is a crude carving of a violin. I sit down in the dry, dead grass in front of the marker, and I don't know how long I've been sitting there when I hear crows cawing. I look over my shoulder, and there's a tree back towards Farewell Street filled with the big black birds. They watch me, and I take that as my cue to leave. I know now that I have to go back to the library, that whatever remains of this mystery is waiting for me there. I might find it tucked away in an old journal, a newspaper clipping, or in crumbling church records. I only know I'll find it, because now I have the missing pieces. But there is an odd reluctance to leave the grave of Abby Gladding. There's no fear in me, no shock or stubborn disbelief at what I've discovered or at its impossible ramifications. And some part of me notes the oddness of this, that I am not afraid. I leave her alone in that narrow house, watched over by the wary crows, and go back to my car. Less than fifteen minutes later I'm in the Redwood Library, asking for anything they can find on a Solomon Gladding and his daughter, Abby.

"Are you okay?" the librarian asks, and I wonder what she sees in my face, in my eyes, to elicit such a question. "Are you feeling well?"

"I'm fine," I assure her. "I was up a little too late last night, that's all. A little too much to drink, most likely."

She nods, and I smile.

"Well, then. I'll see what we might have," she says, and, cutting to the chase, it ends with a short article that appeared in the *Newport Mercury* early in November 1785, hardly more than two months after Abby Gladding's death. It begins, "We hear a ſtrange account from laſt Thursday evening, the Night of the 3rd of November, of a body diſinterred from its Grave and coffin. This most peculiar occurrence was undertaken at the beheſt of the father of the deceaſed young woman therein buried, a circumſtance making the affair even ſtranger ſtill." What follows is a description of a ritual which will be familiar to anyone who has read of the 1892 Mercy Brown case from Exeter, or the much earlier exhumation of Nancy Young (summer of 1827), or other purported New England "vampires."

In September, Abby Gladding's body was discovered in Newport Harbor by a local fisherman, and it was determined that she had drowned. The body was in an advanced state of decay, leading me to wonder if the date on the headstone is meant to be the date the body was found, not the date of her death. There were persistent rumors that the daughter of Solomon Gladding, a local merchant, had taken her own life. She is said to have been a "child of ſingular and morbid temperament," who had recently refused a marriage proposal by the eldest son of another Newport merchant, Ebenezer Burrill. There was also back-fence talk that Abby had practiced witchcraft in the woods bordering the town and that she would play her violin (a gift from her mother) to summon "voraciouſ wolveſ and other ſuch dæmonſ to do her bidding."

Very shortly after her death, her youngest sister, Susan, suddenly fell ill. This was in October, and the girl was dead before the end of the month. Her symptoms, like those of Mercy Brown's stricken family members, can readily be identified as late-stage tuberculosis. What is peculiar here is that Abby doesn't appear to have suffered any such wasting disease herself, and the speed with which Susan became ill and died is also atypical of consumption. Even as Susan fought for her life, Abby's mother, Mary, fell ill, and it was in hope of saving his wife that Solomon Gladding agreed to the exhumation of his daughter's body. The article in the *Newport Mercury* speculates that he'd learned of this ritual and folk remedy from a Jamaican slave woman.

At sunrise, with the aid of several other men, some apparently family members, the grave was opened, and all present were horrified to see "the body freſh as the day it waſ conſigned to God," her cheeks "fluſhed with colour and luſterous." The liver and heart were duly cut out, and both were discovered to contain clotted blood, which Solomon had been told would prove that Abby was rising from her grave each night to steal the blood of her mother and sister. The heart was burned in a fire kindled in the cemetery, the ashes mixed with water, and the mother drank the mixture. The body of Abby was turned facedown in her casket, and an iron stake was driven through her chest, to insure that the restless spirit would be unable to find its way out of the grave. Nonetheless, according to parish records from

Trinity Church, Mary Gladding died before Christmas. Her father fell ill a few months later and died in August of 1786.

And I find one more thing that I will put down here. Scribbled in sepia ink in the left-hand margin of the newspaper page containing the account of the exhumation of Abby Gladding is the phrase *Jé-rouge,* or "red eyes," which I've learned is a Haitian term denoting werewolfery and cannibalism. Below that word, in the same spidery hand, is written "As white as snow, as red as red, as green as briers, as black as coal." There is no date or signature accompanying these notations.

Now it is almost Friday night, and I sit alone on a wooden bench at Bowen's Wharf, not too far from the kiosk advertising daily boat tours to view fat, doe-eyed seals sunning themselves on the rocky beaches ringing Narragansett Bay. I sit here and watch the sun going down, shivering because I left home this morning without my coat. I do not expect to see Abby Gladding, tonight or ever again. But I've come here, anyway, and I may come again tomorrow evening.

I will not include the 1785 disinterment in my thesis, no matter how many feathers it might earn for my cap. I mean never to speak of it again. What I have written here, I suspect I'll destroy it later on. It has only been written for me and for me alone. If Abby was trying to speak *through* me to find a larger audience, she'll have to find another mouthpiece. I watch a lobster boat heading out for the night. I light a cigarette and eye the herring gulls wheeling above the marina.

AS RED AS RED

This story earned me my first nomination for the Shirley Jackson Award. I've called it a footnote to my novel *The Red Tree,* and it is that, a repository for a haunting which didn't quite fit into that book. It's a story that I walked through, from Bowen's Wharf to the Roderick Terry Reading Room, from Benefit Street to Newport's North Burial Ground, because I believe that Hemingway was absolutely correct in saying we must write what we know. It's just that fantasists have to go an extra mile and include that which we know only from our restless mind's eye, which may only be visited in fits of subjective, secret tourism. I thank my late grandfather, Gordon Monroe Ramey, for this title.

Fish Bride (1970)

We lie here together, naked on her sheets which are always damp, no matter the weather, and she's still sleeping. I've lain next to her, watching the long cold sunrise, the walls of this dingy room in this dingy house turning so slowly from charcoal to a hundred successively lighter shades of grey. The weak November morning has a hard time at the window, because the glass was knocked out years ago and she chose as a substitute a sheet of tattered and not-quite-clear plastic she found washed up on the shore, now held in place with mismatched nails and a few thumbtacks. But it deters the worst of the wind and rain and snow, and she says there's nothing out there she wants to see, anyway. I've offered to replace the broken glass, a couple of times I've said that, but it's just another of the hundred or so things that I've promised I would do for her and haven't yet gotten around to doing; she doesn't seem to mind. That's not why she keeps letting me come here. Whatever she wants from me, it isn't handouts and pity and someone to fix her broken windows and leaky ceiling. Which is fortunate, as I've never fixed anything in my whole life. I can't even change a flat tire. I've only ever been the sort of man who does harm and leaves it for someone else to put right again or simply sweep beneath a rug where no one will have to notice the damage I've done. So, why should she be any different? And yet, to my knowledge, I've done her no harm so far.

I come down the hill from the village on those interminable nights and afternoons when I can't write and don't feel like getting drunk alone. I leave that other world, that safe and smothering kingdom of clean sheets and typescript, electric lights and indoor plumbing and radio and window frames with windowpanes, and I follow the sandy path through gale-stunted trees and stolen, burned-out automobiles, smoldering trash-barrel fires and suspicious, under-lit glances.

They all know I don't belong here with them, all the other men and women who share her squalid existence at the edge of the sea, the ones who have come down and never gone back up the hill again. When I call them her apostles, she gets sullen and angry.

"No," she says, "it's not like that. They're nothing of the sort."

But I understand well enough that's exactly what they are, even if she doesn't want to admit it, either to herself or to me. And so they hold me in contempt, because she's taken me into her bed – me, an interloper who comes and goes, who has some choice in the matter, who has that option because the world beyond these dunes and shanty walls still imagines it has some use for me. One of these nights, I think, her apostles will do murder against me. One of them alone or all of them together. It may be stones or sticks or an old filleting knife. It may even be a gun. I wouldn't put it past them. They are resourceful, and there's a lot on the line. They'll bury me in the dog roses, or sink me in some deep place among the tide-worn rocks, or carve me up like a fat sow and have themselves a feast. She'll likely join them, if they are bold enough and offer her a few scraps of my charred, anonymous flesh to complete the sacrifice. And later, much, much later, she'll remember and miss me, in her sloppy, indifferent way, and wonder whatever became of the man who brought her beer and whiskey, candles and chocolate bars, the man who said he'd fix the window, but never did. She might recall my name, but I wouldn't hold it against her if she doesn't.

"This used to be someplace," she's told me time and time again. "Oh, sure, you'd never know it now. But when my mother was a girl, this used to be a town. When I was little, it was still a town. There were dress shops, and a diner, and a jail. There was a public park with a bandshell and a hundred-year-old oak tree. In the summer, there was music in the park, and picnics. There were even churches, *two* of them, one Catholic and one Presbyterian. But then the storm came and took it all away."

And it's true, most of what she says. There was a town here once. A decade's neglect hasn't quite erased all signs of it. She's shown me some of what there's left to see – the stump of a brick chimney, a few broken pilings where the waterfront once stood – and I've asked questions around the village. But people up there don't like to speak openly about this place or even allow their thoughts to linger on it very long. Every now and then, usually after a burglary or before an election, there's talk of cleaning it up, pulling down these listing, clapboard shacks and chasing away the vagrants and squatters and winos. So far, the talk has come to nothing.

A sudden gust of wind blows in from off the beach, and the sheet of plastic stretched across the window flaps and rustles, and she opens her eyes.

"You're still here," she says, not sounding surprised, merely telling me what I already know. "I was dreaming that you'd gone away and would never come back to me again. I dreamed there was a boat called the *Silver Star*, and it took you away."

"I get seasick," I tell her. "I don't like boats. I haven't been on a boat since I was fifteen."

"Well, you got on this one," she insists, and the dim light filling up the room catches in the facets of her sleepy grey eyes. "You said that you were going to seek your fortune on the Ivory Coast. You had your typewriter, and a suitcase, and you were wearing a brand new suit of worsted wool. I was standing on the dock, watching as the *Silver Star* got smaller and smaller."

"I'm not even sure I know where the Ivory Coast is supposed to be," I say.

"Africa," she replies.

"Well, I know that much, sure. But I don't know where in Africa. And it's an awfully big place."

"In the dream, you knew," she assures me, and I don't press the point further. It's her dream, not mine, even if it's not a dream she's actually ever had, even if it's only something she's making up as she goes along. "In the dream," she continues, undaunted, "you had a travel brochure that the ticket agent had given you. It was printed all in color. There was a sort of tree called a bombax tree, with bright red flowers. There were elephants and a parrot. There were pretty women with skin the color of roasted coffee beans."

"That's quite a brochure," I say, and for a moment I watch the plastic tacked over the window as it rustles in the wind off the bay. "I wish I could have a look at it right now."

"I thought what a warm place it must be, the Ivory Coast," and I glance down at her, at those drowsy eyes watching me. She lifts her right hand from the damp sheets, and patches of iridescent skin shimmer ever so faintly in the morning light. The sun shows through the thin, translucent webbing stretched between her long fingers. Her sharp nails brush gently across my unshaven cheek, and she smiles. Even I don't like to look at those teeth for very long, and I let my eyes wander back to the flapping plastic. The wind is picking up, and I think maybe this might be the day when I finally have to find a hammer, a few ten-penny nails, and enough discarded pine slats to board up the hole in the wall.

"Not much longer before the snow comes," she says, as if she doesn't need to hear me speak to know my thoughts.

"Probably not for a couple of weeks yet," I counter, and she blinks and turns her head towards the window.

In the village, I have a tiny room in a boardinghouse on Darling Street, and I keep a spiral-bound notebook hidden between my mattress and box springs. I've written a lot of things in that book that I shouldn't like any other human being to ever read – secret desires, things I've heard, and read; things she's told me, and things I've come to suspect all on my own. Sometimes, I think it would be wise to keep the notebook better hidden. But it's true that the old woman who owns the place, and who does all the housekeeping herself, is afraid of me, and she never goes into my room. She leaves the clean linen and towels in a stack outside my door. Months ago, I stopped taking my meals with the other lodgers, because the strained silence and fleeting, leery glimpses that attended those breakfasts and dinners only served to give me indigestion. I expect the widow O'Dwyer would ask me to find a room elsewhere, if she weren't so intimidated by me. Or, rather, if she weren't so intimidated by the company I keep.

Outside the shanty, the wind howls like the son of Poseidon, and, for the moment, there's no more talk of the Ivory Coast or dreams or sailing gaily away into the sunset aboard the *Silver Star.*

Much of what I've secretly scribbled there in my notebook concerns that terrible storm that she claims rose up from the sea to steal away the little park and the bandshell, the diner and the jail and the dress shops, the two churches, one Presbyterian and the other Catholic. From what she's said, it must have happened sometime in September of '57 or '58, but I've spent long afternoons in the small public library, carefully poring over old newspapers and magazines. I can find no evidence of such a tempest making landfall in the autumn of either of those years. What I can verify is that the village once extended down the hill, past the marshes and dunes to the bay, and there was a lively, prosperous waterfront. There was trade with Gloucester and Boston, Nantucket and Newport, and the bay was renowned for its lobsters, fat black sea bass, and teeming shoals of haddock. Then, abruptly, the waterfront was all but abandoned sometime before 1960. In print, I've found hardly more than scant and unsubstantiated speculations to account for it, that exodus, that strange desertion. Talk of overfishing, for instance, and passing comparisons with Cannery Row in faraway California and the collapse of the Monterey Bay sardine canning industry back in the 1950's. I write down everything I find, no matter how unconvincing, but I permit myself to believe only a very little of it.

"A penny for your thoughts," she says, then shuts her eyes again.

"You haven't got a penny," I reply, trying to ignore the raw, hungry sound of the wind and the constant noise at the window.

"I most certainly do," she tells me and pretends to scowl and look offended. "I have a few dollars, tucked away. I'm not an indigent."

"Fine, then. I was thinking of Africa," I lie. "I was thinking of palm trees and parrots."

"I don't remember any palm trees in the travel brochure," she says. "But I expect there must be quite a lot of them, regardless."

"Undoubtedly," I agree. I don't say anything else, though, because I think I hear voices coming from somewhere outside her shack – urgent, muttering voices that reach me despite the wind and the flapping plastic. I can't make out the words, no matter how hard I try. It ought to scare me more than it does. Like I said, one of these nights, they'll do murder against me. One of them alone, or all of them together. Maybe they won't even wait for the conspiring cover of nightfall. Maybe they'll come for me in broad daylight. I begin to suspect my murder would not even be deemed a crime by the people who live in those brightly painted houses up the hill, back beyond the dunes. On the contrary, they might consider it a necessary sacrifice, something to placate the flotsam and jetsam huddling in the ruins along the shore, an oblation of blood and flesh to buy them time.

Seems more likely than not.

"They shouldn't come so near," she says, acknowledging that she too hears the whispering voices. "I'll have a word with them later. They ought to know better."

"They've more business being here than I do," I reply, and she silently watches me for a moment or two. In the last month, her grey eyes have gone almost entirely black, and I can no longer distinguish the irises from the pupils.

"They ought to know better," she says again, and this time her tone leaves me no room for argument.

There are tales that I've heard, and bits of dreams I sometimes think I've borrowed — from her or one of her apostles – that I find somewhat more convincing than either newspaper accounts of depleted fish stocks or rumors of a cataclysmic hurricane. There are the spook stories I've overheard, passed between children. There are yarns traded by the half dozen or so grizzled old men who sit outside the filling station near the widow's boardinghouse, who seem possessed of no greater ambition than checkers and hand-rolled cigarettes, cheap gin and gossip. I have begun to believe the truth is not something that was entrusted to the press, but, instead, an ignominy the town has struggled, purposefully, to forget, and which is now recalled dimly or not at all. There is remaining no consensus to be had, but there *are* common threads from which I have woven rough speculation.

Late one night, very near the end of summer or towards the beginning of fall, there was an unusually high tide. It quickly swallowed the granite jetty and the shingle, then broke across the seawall and flooded the streets of the harbor. There was a full moon that night, hanging low and ripe on the eastern horizon, and by its wicked reddish glow men and women saw the things that came slithering and creeping and lurching out of those angry waves. The invaders cast no shadow, or the moonlight shone straight through them, but was somehow oddly distorted. Or, perhaps, what came out of the sea that night glimmered faintly with an eerie phosphorescence of its own.

I know that I'm choosing lurid, loaded words here – *wicked, lurching, hungry, eerie* – hoping, I suppose, to discredit all the cock and bull I've heard, trying to neuter those schoolyard demons. But, in my defense, the children and the old men whom I've overheard were quite a bit less discreet. They have little use, and even less concern, for the sensibilities of people who aren't going to believe them, anyway. In some respects, they're almost as removed as she, as distant and disconnected as the shanty dwellers here in the rubble at the edge of the bay.

"I would be sorry," she says, "if you were to sail away to Africa."

"I'm not going anywhere. There isn't anywhere I want to go. There isn't anywhere I'd rather be."

She smiles again, and this time I don't allow myself to look away. She has teeth like those of a very small shark, and they glint wet and dark in healthy pink gums. I have often wondered how she manages not to cut her lips or tongue on those teeth, why there are not always trickles of drying blood at the corners of her thin lips. She's bitten into me enough times now. I have ugly crescent scars across my shoulders and chest and upper arms to prove that we are lovers, stigmata to make her apostles hate me that much more.

"It's silly of you to waste good money on a room," she says, changing the course of our conversation. "You could stay here with me. I hate the nights when you're in the village, and I'm alone."

"Or you could go back with me," I reply. It's a familiar sort of futility, this exchange, and we both know our lines by heart, just as we both know the outcome.

"No," she says, her shark's smile fading. "You know that I can't. You know they'd never have me up there," and she nods in the general direction of the town.

And yes, I do know that, but I've never yet told her that I do.

The tide rose up beneath a low red moon and washed across the waterfront. The sturdy wharf was shattered like matchsticks, and boats of various shapes and sizes – dories and jiggers, trollers and Bermuda-rigged schooners – were torn free of their moorings and tossed onto the shivered docks. But there was no storm, no wind, no lashing rain. No thunder and lightning and white spray off the breakers. The air was hot and still that night, and the cloudless sky blazed with the countless pin-prick stars that shine brazenly through the punctured dome of Heaven.

"They say the witch what brought the trouble came from someplace up Amesbury way," I heard one of the old men tell the others, months and months ago. None of his companions replied, neither nodding their heads in agreement, nor voicing dissent. "I heard she made offerings every month, on the night of the new moon, and I heard she had herself a daughter, though I never learned the girl's name. Don't guess it matters, though. And the name of her father, well, ain't nothing I'll ever say aloud."

That night, the cobbled streets and alleyways were fully submerged for long hours. Buildings and houses were lifted clear of their foundations and dashed one against the other. What with no warning of the freakish tide, only a handful of the waterfront's inhabitants managed to escape the deluge and gain the safety of higher ground. More than two hundred souls perished, and for weeks afterwards the corpses of the drowned continued to wash ashore. Many of the bodies were so badly mangled that they could never be placed with a name or a face and went unclaimed, to be buried in unmarked graves in the village beyond the dunes.

I can no longer hear the whisperers through the thin walls of her shack, so I'll assume that they've gone or have simply had their say and subsequently fallen silent. Possibly, they're leaning now with their ears pressed close to the corrugated aluminum and rotting clapboard, listening in, hanging on her every syllable, even as my own voice fills them with loathing and jealous spite.

"I'll have a word with them," she tells me for the third time. "You should feel as welcome here as any of us."

The sea swept across the land, and, by the light of that swollen, sanguine moon, grim approximations of humanity moved freely, unimpeded, through the flooded thoroughfares. Sometimes they swam, and sometimes they went about deftly on all fours, and sometimes they shambled clumsily along, as though walking were new to them and not entirely comfortable.

"They weren't men," I overheard a boy explaining to his friends. The boy had ginger-colored hair, and he was nine, maybe ten years old at the most. The children were sitting together at the edge of the weedy vacant lot where a traveling carnival sets up three or four times a year.

"Then were they women?" one of the others asked him.

The boy frowned and gravely shook his head. "No. You're not listening. They weren't women, neither. They weren't anything human. But, what I heard said, if you were to take all the stuff gets pulled up in trawler nets – all the hauls of cod and flounder and eel, the dogfish and the skates, the squids and jellyfish and crabs, all of it and whatever else you can conjure – if you took those things, still alive and wriggling, and could mush them up together into the shapes of men and women, *that's* exactly what walked out of the bay that night."

"That's not true," a girl said indignantly, and the others stared at her. "That's not true at all. God wouldn't let things like that run loose."

The ginger-haired boy shook his head again. "They got different gods than us, gods no one even knows the names for, and that's who the Amesbury witch was worshipping. Those gods from the bottom of the ocean."

"Well, I think you're a liar," the girl told him. "I think you're a blasphemer *and* a liar, and, also, I think you're just making this up to scare us." And then she stood and stalked away across the weedy lot, leaving the others behind. They all watched her go, and then the ginger-haired boy resumed his tale.

"It gets worse," he said.

A cold rain has started to fall, and the drops hitting the tin roof sound almost exactly like bacon frying in a skillet. She's moved away from me and is sitting naked at the edge of the bed, her long legs dangling over the side, her right shoulder braced against the rusted iron headboard. I'm still lying on the damp sheets, staring up at the leaky ceiling, waiting for the water tumbling from the sky to find its way inside. She'll set jars and cooking pots beneath the worst of the leaks, but there are far too many to bother with them all.

"I can't stay here forever," she says. It's not the first time, but, I admit, those words always take me by surprise. "It's getting harder being here. Every day, it gets harder on me. I'm so awfully tired, all the time."

I look away from the ceiling, at her throat and the peculiar welts just below the line of her chin. The swellings first appeared a few weeks back, and the skin there has turned dry and scaly, and has taken on a sickly greyish-yellow hue. Sometimes, there are boils or seeping blisters. When she goes out among the others, she wears the silk scarf I gave her, tied about her neck so that they won't have to see. So they won't ask questions she doesn't want to answer.

"I don't have to go alone," she says, but doesn't turn her head to look at me. "I don't want to leave you here."

"I can't," I say.

"I know," she replies.

And this is how it almost always is. I come down from the village, and we make love, and she tells me her dreams, here in this ramshackle cabin out past the dunes and dog roses and the gale-stunted trees. In her dreams, I am always leaving her behind, buying tickets on tramp steamers or signing on with freighters, sailing away to the Ivory Coast or Portugal or Singapore. I can't begin to recall all the faraway places she's dreamt me leaving her for. Her nightmares have sent me round and round the globe. But the truth is, *she's* the one who's leaving, and soon, before the first snows come.

I know it (though I play her games of transference), and all her apostles know it, too. The ones who have come down from the village and never gone back up the hill again. The vagrants and squatters and winos, the lunatics and true believers, who have turned their backs on the world, but only after it turned its back on them. Destitute and cast away, they found the daughter of the sea, each of them, and the shanty town is dotted with their tawdry, makeshift altars and shrines.

She knows precisely what she is to them, even if she won't admit it. She knows that these lost souls have been blinded by the trials and tribulations of their various, sordid lives, and *she* is the soothing darkness they've found. She is the only genuine balm they've ever known against the cruel glare of the sun and the moon, which are the unblinking eyes of the gods of all mankind.

She sits there, at the edge of the bed. She is always alone, no matter how near we are, no matter how many apostles crowd around and eavesdrop and plot my demise. She stares at the flapping sheet of plastic tacked up where the windowpane used to be, and I go back to watching the ceiling. A single drop of rainwater gets through the layers of tin and tarpaper shingles and lands on my exposed belly.

She laughs softly. She doesn't laugh very often anymore, and I shut my eyes and listen to the rain.

"You can really have no notion how delightful it will be, when they take us up and throw us, with the lobsters, out to sea," she whispers, and then laughs again.

I take the bait, because I almost always take the bait.

"But the snail replied 'Too far, too far!' and gave a look askance," I say, quoting Lewis Carroll, and she doesn't laugh. She starts to scratch at the welts below her chin, then stops herself.

"In the halls of my mother," she says, "there is such silence, such absolute and immemorial peace. In that hallowed place, the mind can be still. There is serenity, finally, and an end to all sickness and fear." She pauses and looks at the floor, at the careless scatter of empty tin cans and empty bottles and bones picked clean. "But," she continues, "it will be lonely down there, without you. It will be something even worse than lonely."

I don't reply, and in a moment, she gets to her feet and goes to stand by the door.

FISH BRIDE (1970)

Readers and reviewers have considered this an Innsmouth story, and I suppose that's reasonable. It even appeared in Steve Jones' *Weirder Shadows Over Innsmouth* (2013). However, I would argue that the greater inspiration was Lovecraft's 1936 "collaboration" with R. H. Barlow, "The Night Ocean." In the end, though, it's a love story for Panthalassa's changelings, and I dedicate it to everyone who was unable to follow me down.

The Mermaid of the Concrete Ocean

The building's elevator is busted, and so I've had to drag my ass up twelve flights of stairs. Her apartment is smaller and more tawdry than I expected, but I'm not entirely sure I could say what I thought I'd find at the top of all those stairs. I don't know this part of Manhattan very well, this ugly wedge of buildings one block over from South Street and Roosevelt Drive and the ferry terminal. She keeps reminding me that if I look out the window (there's only one), I can see the Brooklyn Bridge. It seems a great source of pride, that she has a view of the bridge and the East River. The apartment is too hot, filled with soggy heat pouring off the radiators, and there are so many unpleasant odors competing for my attention that I'd be hard pressed to assign any one of them priority over the rest. Mildew. Dust. Stale cigarette smoke. Better I say the apartment smells shut away, and leave it at that. The place is crammed wall to wall with threadbare, dust-skimmed antiques, the tattered refuse of Victorian and Edwardian bygones. I have trouble imagining how she navigates the clutter in her wheelchair, which is something of an antique itself. I compliment the Tiffany lamps, all of which appear not to be reproductions and are in considerably better shape than most of the other furnishings. She smiles, revealing dentures stained by nicotine and neglect. At least, I assume they're dentures. She switches on one of the table lamps, its shade a circlet of stained-glass dragonflies, and tells me it was a Christmas gift from a playwright. He's dead now, she says. She tells me his name, but it's no one I've ever heard of, and I admit this to her. Her yellow-brown smile doesn't waver.

"Nobody remembers him. He was *very* avant-garde," she says. "No one understood what he was trying to say. But obscurity was precious to him. It pained him terribly, that so few ever understood that about his work."

I nod, once or twice or three times, I don't know, and it hardly matters. Her thin fingers glide across the lampshade, leaving furrows in the accumulated dust, and now I can see that the dragonflies have wings the color of amber, and their abdomens and thoraces are a deep cobalt blue. They all have eyes like poisonous crimson berries. She asks me to please have a seat and apologizes for not having offered one sooner. She motions to an armchair near the lamp, and also to a chaise lounge a few feet farther away. Both are upholstered with the same faded floral brocade. I choose the armchair and am hardly surprised to discover that all the springs are shot. I sink several inches into the chair, and my knees jut upwards, towards the water-stained plaster ceiling.

"Will you mind if I tape our conversation?" I ask, opening my briefcase, and she stares at me for a moment, as though she hasn't quite understood the question. By way of explanation, I remove the tiny Olympus digital recorder and hold it up for her to see. "Well, it doesn't actually use audio tapes," I add.

"I don't mind," she tells me. "It must be much simpler than having to write down everything you hear, everything someone says. Probably, you do not even know shorthand."

"Much simpler," I say and switch the recorder on. "We can shut it off anytime you like, of course. Just say the word." I lay the recorder in the table, near the base of the dragonfly lamp.

"That's very considerate," she says. "That's very kind of you."

And it occurs to me how much she, like the apartment, differs from whatever I might have expected to find. This isn't *Sunset Boulevard,* Norma Desmond and her shuffling cadre of "waxwork" acquaintances. There's nothing of the grotesque or Gothic – even that *Hollywood* Gothic – about her. Despite the advance and ravages of ninety-four years, her green eyes are bright and clear. Neither her voice nor hands tremble, and only the old wheelchair stands as any indication of infirmity. She sits up very straight, and whenever she speaks, tends to move her hands about, as though possessed of more energy and excitement than words alone can convey. She's wearing only a little makeup, some pale lipstick and a hint of rouge on her high cheekbones, and her long grey hair is pulled back in a single braid. There's an easy grace about her. Watching by the light of the dragonfly lamp and the light coming in through the single window, it occurs to me that she is showing me *her* face and not some mask of counterfeit youth. Only the stained teeth (or dentures) betray any hint of the decay I'd anticipated and steeled myself against. Indeed, if not for the rank smell of the apartment, and the oppressive heat, there would be nothing particularly unpleasant about being here with her.

I retrieve a stenographer's pad from my briefcase, then close it and set it on the floor near my feet. I tell her that I haven't written out a lot of questions, that I prefer to allow interviews to unfold more organically, like conversations, and this seems to please her.

"I don't go in for the usual brand of interrogation," I say. "Too forced. Too weighted by the journalist's own agenda."

"So, you think of yourself as a journalist?" she asks, and I tell her yes, usually.

"Well, I haven't done this in such a very long time," she replies, straightening her skirt. "I hope you'll understand if I'm a little rusty. I don't often talk about those days, or the pictures. It was all so very long ago."

"Still," I say, "you must have fond memories."

"Must I now?" she asks, and before I can think of an answer, she says, "There are only memories, young man, and, yes, most of them are not so bad, and some are even rather agreeable. But there are many things I've tried to forget. Every life must be like that, wouldn't you say?"

"To some extent," I reply.

She sighs, as if I haven't understood at all, and her eyes wander up to a painting on the wall behind me. I hardly noticed it when I sat down, but now I turn my head for a better view.

When I ask, "Is that one of the originals?" she nods, her smile widening by almost imperceptible degrees, and she points at the painting of a mermaid.

"Yes," she says. "The only one I have. Oh, I've got a few lithographs. I have prints or photographs of them all, but this is the only one of the genuine paintings I own."

"It's beautiful," I say, and that isn't idle flattery. The mermaid paintings are the reason that I've come to New York City and tracked her to the tawdry little hovel by the river. This isn't the first time I've seen an original up close, but it is the first time outside a museum gallery. There's one hanging in Newport, at the National Museum of American Illustration. I've seen it, and also the one at the Art Institute of Chicago, and one other, the mermaid in the permanent collection of the Society of Illustrators here in Manhattan. But there are more than thirty documented, and most of them I've only seen reproduced in books and folios. Frankly, I wonder if this painting's existence is very widely known, and how long it's been since anyone but the model, sitting here in her wheelchair, has admired it. I've read all the artist's surviving journals and correspondence (including the letters to his model), and I know that there are at least ten mermaid paintings that remain unaccounted for. I assume this must be one of them.

"Wow," I gasp, unable to look away from the painting. "I mean, it's amazing."

"It's the very last one he did, you know," she says. "He wanted me to have it. If someone offered me a million dollars, I still wouldn't part with it."

I glance at her, then back to the painting. "More likely, they'd offer you ten million," I tell her, and she laughs. It might easily be mistaken for the laugh of a much younger woman.

"Wouldn't make any difference if they did," she says. "He gave it to me, and I'll never part with it. Not ever. He named this one *Regarding the Shore from Whale Rock,* and that was my idea, the title. He often asked me to name them. At least half their titles, I thought up for him." And I already know this; it's in his letters.

The painting occupies a large, narrow canvas, easily four feet tall by two feet wide – somewhat too large for this wall, really – held inside an ornately carved frame. The frame has been stained dark as mahogany, though I'm sure it's made from something far less costly; here and there, where the varnish has been scratched or chipped, I can see the blond wood showing through. But I don't doubt that the painting is authentic, despite numerous compositional deviations, all of which are immediately apparent to anyone familiar with the mermaid series. For instance, in contravention to his usual approach, the siren has been placed in the foreground, and also somewhat to the right. And, more importantly, she's facing away from the viewer. Buoyed by rough waves, she holds her arms outstretched to either side, as if to say, "Let me enfold you," while her long hair flows around her like a dense tangle of kelp, and the mermaid gazes towards land and a whitewashed lighthouse perched on a granite promontory. The rocky coastline is familiar, some wild place he'd found in Massachusetts or Maine or Rhode Island. The viewer might be fooled into thinking this is only a painting of a woman swimming in the sea, as so little of her is showing above the waterline. She might be mistaken for a suicide, taking a final glimpse of the rugged strand before slipping below the surface. But, if one looks only a little closer, the patches of red-orange scales flecking her arms are unmistakable, and there are living creatures caught up in the snarls of her black hair: tiny crabs and brittle stars, the twisting shapes of strange oceanic worms and a gasping, wide-eyed fish of some sort, suffocating in the air.

"That was the last one he did," she says again.

It's hard to take my eyes off the painting, and I'm already wondering if she will permit me to get a few shots of it before I leave.

"It's not in any of the catalogs," I say. "It's not mentioned anywhere in his papers or the literature."

"No, it wouldn't be. It was our secret," she replies. "After all those years working together, he wanted to give me something special, and so he did this last one and then never showed it to anyone else. I had it framed when I came back from Europe in forty-six, after the war. For years, it was rolled up in a cardboard tube, rolled up and swaddled in muslin, kept on the top shelf of a friend's closet. A mutual friend, actually, who admired him greatly, though I never showed her this painting."

I finally manage to look away from the canvas, turning back towards the woman sitting up straight in her wheelchair. She looks very pleased at my surprise, and I ask her the first question that comes to mind.

"Has *anyone* else ever seen it. Besides me?"

"Certainly," she says. "It's been hanging right there for the past twenty years, and I *do* occasionally have visitors, every now and then. I'm not a complete recluse. Not quite yet."

"I'm sorry. I didn't mean to imply that you were."

And she's still staring up at the painting, and the impression I have is that she hasn't paused to *look* at it closely for a long time. It's as though she's suddenly *noticing* it and probably couldn't recall the last time that she did. Sure, it's a fact of her everyday landscape, another component of the crowded reliquary of her apartment. But, like the Tiffany dragonfly lamp given her by that forgotten playwright, I suspect she rarely ever pauses to consider it.

Watching her as she peers so intently at the painting looming up behind me and the threadbare brocade chair where I sit, I'm struck once more by those green eyes of hers. They're the same green eyes the artist gave to every incarnation of his mermaid, and they seem to me even brighter than they did before, and not the least bit dimmed by age. They are like some subtle marriage of emerald and jade and shallow saltwater, brought to life by unknown alchemies. They give me a greater appreciation of the painter, that he so perfectly conveyed her eyes, deftly communicating the complexities of iris and sclera, cornea and retina and pupil. That anyone could have the talent required to transfer these precise and complex hues into mere oils and acrylics.

"How did it begin?" I ask, predictably enough. Of course, the artist wrote repeatedly of the mermaids' genesis. I even found a 1967 dissertation on the subject hidden away in the stacks at Harvard. But I'm pretty sure no one has ever bothered to ask the model. Gradually, and, I think, reluctantly, her green eyes drift away from the canvas and back to me.

"It's not as if that's a secret," she says. "I believe he even told a couple of the magazine reporters about the dreams. One in Paris, and maybe one here in New York, too. He often spoke with me about his dreams. They were always so vivid, and he wrote them down. He painted them, whenever he could. Just as he painted the mermaids."

I glance over at the recorder lying on the table and wish that I'd waited until later on to ask that particular question. It should have been placed somewhere towards the end, not right at the front. I'm definitely off my game today, and it's not only the heat from the radiators making me sweat. I've been disarmed, unbalanced, first by *Regarding the Shore from Whale Rock,* and then by having looked so deeply into her eyes. I clear my throat, and she asks if I'd like a glass of water or maybe a cold A & W cream soda. I thank her, but shake my head no.

"I'm fine," I say, "but thank you."

"It can get awfully stuffy in here," she says and glances down at the dingy Persian rug that covers almost the entire floor. This is the first time since she let me through the door that I've seen her frown.

"Honestly, it's not so bad," I insist, failing to sound the least bit honest.

"Why, there are days," she says, "it's like being in a sauna. Or a damned tropical jungle, Tahiti or Brazil or someplace like that, and it's a wonder I don't start hearing parrots and monkeys. But it helps with the pain, usually more than the pills do."

And here's the one thing she was adamant that we not discuss, the childhood injury that left her crippled. She's told me how she has always loathed writers and critics who tried to draw a parallel between the mermaids and her paralysis. "Don't even bring it up," she warned on the phone, almost a week ago, and I assured her that I wouldn't. Only, now *she's* brought it up. I sit very still in the broken-down armchair, there beneath the last painting, waiting to see what she'll say next. I try hard to clear my head and focus and to decide what question on the short list scribbled in my steno pad might steer the interview back on course.

"There *was* more than his dreams," she admits, almost a full minute later. The statement has the slightly abashed quality of a confession. And I have no idea how to respond, so I don't. She blinks, and looks up at me again, the pale ghost of that previous smile returning to her lips. "Would it bother you if I smoke?" she asks.

"No," I reply. "Not at all. Please, whatever makes you comfortable."

"These days, well, it bothers so many people. As though the Pope had added smoking to the list of venial sins. I get the most awful glares, sometimes, so I thought I'd best ask first."

"It's your home," I tell her, and she nods and reaches into a pocket of her skirt, retrieving a pack of Marlboro Reds and a disposable lighter.

"To some, that doesn't seem to matter," she says. "There's a woman comes around twice a week to attend to the dusting and trash and whatnot, a Cuban woman, and if I smoke when she's here, she always complains and tries to open the window, even though I've told her time and time again it's been painted shut for ages. It's not like I don't pay her."

Considering the thick and plainly undisturbed strata of dust, and the odors, I wonder if she's making this up, or if perhaps the Cuban woman might have stopped coming around a long time ago.

"I promised him, when he told me, I would never tell anyone else this," she says, and here she pauses to light her cigarette, then return the rest of the pack and her lighter to their place in her skirt pocket. She blows a gray cloud of smoke away from me. "Not another living soul. It was a sort of pact between us, you understand. But, lately, it's been weighing on me. I wake up in the night, sometimes, and it's like a stone around my neck. I don't think it's something I want to take with me to the grave. He told me the day we started work on the second painting."

"That would have been in May 1939, yes?"

And here she laughs again and shakes her head. "Hell if I know. Maybe you have it written down somewhere in that pad of yours, but I don't remember the date. Not anymore. But…I *do* know it was the same year the World's Fair opened here in New York, and I know it was after Amelia Earhart disappeared. He knew her, Amelia Earhart. He knew so many interesting people. But I'm rambling, aren't I?"

"I'm in no hurry," I answer. "Take your time." But she frowns again and stares at the smoldering tip of her cigarette for a moment.

"I like to think, sir, that I am a practical woman," she says, looking directly at me and raising her chin an inch or so. "I have always wanted to be able to consider myself a practical woman. And now I'm very old. Very, *very* old, yes, and a practical woman must acknowledge the fact that women who *are* this old will not live much longer. I know I'll die soon, and the truth about the mermaids, it isn't something I want to take with me to my grave. So, I'll tell you and betray his confidence. If you'll listen, of course."

"Certainly," I reply, struggling not let my excitement show through, but feeling like a vulture, anyway. "If you'd prefer, I can shut off the recorder," I offer.

"No, no...I want you to put this in your article. I want them to print it in that magazine you write for, because it seems to me that people ought to know. If they're still so infatuated with the mermaids after all this time, it doesn't seem fitting that they *don't* know. It seems almost indecent."

I don't remind her that I'm a freelance and the article's being done on spec, so there's no guarantee anyone's going to buy it, or that it will ever be printed and read. And withholding that information feels indecent, too, but I keep my mouth shut and listen while she talks. I can always nurse my guilty conscience later on.

"The summer before I met him, before we started working together," she begins and then pauses to take another drag on her cigarette. Her eyes return to the painting behind me. "I suppose that would have been the summer of 1937. The Depression was still on, but his family, out on Long Island, they'd come through it better than most. He had money. Sometimes he'd take commissions from magazines, if the pay was decent. *The New Yorker,* that was one he did some work for, and *Harper's Bazaar,* and *Collier's,* but I guess you know this sort of thing, having done so much research on his life."

The ash on her Marlboro is growing perilously long, though she seems not have noticed. I glance about and spot an ashtray, heavy lead glass, perched on the edge of a nearby coffee table. It doesn't look as though it's been emptied in days or weeks, another argument against the reality of the Cuban maid. My armchair squeaks and pops angrily when I lean forward to retrieve it. I offer it to her, and she takes her eyes off the painting just long enough to accept it and to thank me.

"Anyway," she continues, "mostly he was able to paint what he wanted. That was a freedom that he never took for granted. He was staying in Atlantic City that summer, because he said he liked watching the people on the boardwalk. Sometimes, he'd sit and sketch them for hours, in charcoal and pastels. He showed quite a lot of the boardwalk sketches to me, and I think he always meant to do paintings from them, but, to my knowledge, he ever did.

"That summer, he was staying at the Traymore, which I never saw, but he said was wonderful. Many of his friends and acquaintances would go to Atlantic City in the summer, so he never lacked for company if he wanted it. There were the most wonderful parties, he told me. Sometimes, in the evenings, he'd go down onto the beach alone, onto the sand, I mean, because he said the waves and the gulls and the smell of the sea comforted him. In his studio, the one he kept on the Upper West Side, there was a quart mayonnaise jar filled with seashells and sand dollars and the like. He'd picked them all up at Atlantic City, over the years. Some of them we used as props in the paintings, and he also had a cabinet with shells from Florida and Nassau and the Cape and I don't know where else. He showed me conchs and starfish from the Mediterranean and Japan, I remember. Seashells from all over the world, easily. He loved them, and driftwood, too."

She taps her cigarette against the rim of the ashtray and stares at the painting of the mermaid and the lighthouse, and I have the distinct feeling that she's drawing some sort of courage from it, the requisite courage needed to break a promise she's kept for seventy years. A promise she made three decades before my own birth. And I know now how to sum up the smell of her apartment. It smells like time.

"It was late July, and the sun was setting," she says, speaking very slowly now, as though every word is being chosen with great and deliberate care. "And he told me that he was in a foul temper that evening, having fared poorly at a poker game the night before. He played cards. He said it was one of his only weaknesses.

"At any rate, he went down onto the sand, and he was barefoot, he said. I remember that, him telling me he wasn't wearing shoes." And it occurs to me then that possibly none of what I'm hearing is the truth, that she's spinning a fanciful yarn so I won't be disappointed, lying for my benefit, or because her days are so filled with monotony and she is determined this unusual guest will be entertained. I push the thoughts away. There's no evidence of deceit in her voice. Art journalism hasn't made me rich or well known, but I have gotten pretty good at knowing a lie when I hear one.

"He said to me, 'The sand was so cool beneath my feet.' He walked for a while, and then, just before dark, came across a group of young boys, eight or nine years old, and they were crowded around something that had washed up on the beach. The tide was going out, and what the boys had found, it had been stranded by the retreating tide. He recalled thinking it odd that they were all out so late, the boys, that they were not at dinner with their families. The lights were coming on along the boardwalk."

Now she suddenly averts her eyes from the painting on the wall of her apartment, *Regarding the Shore from Whale Rock,* as though she's taken what she needs and it has nothing left to offer. She crushes her cigarette out in the ashtray and doesn't look at me. She chews at her lower lip, chewing away some of the lipstick. The old woman in the wheelchair does not appear sad nor wistful. I think it's anger, that expression, and I want to ask her *why* she's angry. Instead, I ask what it was the boys found on the beach, what the artist saw that evening. She doesn't answer right away, but closes her eyes and takes a deep breath, exhaling slowly, raggedly.

"I'm sorry," I say. "I didn't mean to press you. If you want to stop–"

"I do *not* want to stop," she says, opening her eyes again. "I have not come this far, and said this much, only to *stop.* It was a woman, a very *young* woman. He said that she couldn't have been much more than nineteen or twenty. One of the children was poking at her with a stick, and he *took* the stick and shooed them all away."

"She was drowned?" I ask.

"Maybe. Maybe she drowned first. But she was bitten in half. There was nothing much left of her below the ribcage. Just bone and meat and a big hollowed-out place where all her organs had been, her stomach and lungs and everything. Still, there was no blood anywhere. It was like she'd never had a single drop of blood in her. He told me, 'I never saw anything else even half that horrible.' And, you know, that wasn't so long after he'd come back to the States from the war in Spain, fighting against the fascists, the Francoists. He was at the Siege of Madrid and saw awful, awful things there. He said to me, 'I saw *atrocities,* but this was worse...'"

And then she trails off and glares down at the ashtray in her lap, at a curl of smoke rising lazily from her cigarette butt.

"You don't have to go on," I say, almost whispering. "I'll understand – "

"Oh hell," she says and shrugs her frail shoulders. "There isn't that much left to tell. He figured that a shark did it, maybe one big shark or several smaller ones. He took her by the arms, and he hauled what was left of her up onto the dry sand, up towards the boardwalk, so she wouldn't be swept back out to sea. He sat down beside the body, because at first he didn't know what to do, and he said he didn't want to leave her alone. She was dead, but he didn't want to leave her alone. I don't know how long he sat there, but he said it was dark when he finally went to find a policeman.

"The body was still there when they got back. No one had disturbed it. The little boys had not returned. But he said the whole affair was hushed up, because the chamber of commerce was afraid that a shark scare would frighten away the tourists and ruin the rest of the season. It had happened before. He said he went straight back to the Traymore and packed his bags, got a ticket on the next train to Manhattan. And he never visited Atlantic City ever again, but he started painting the mermaids, the very next year, right after he found me. Sometimes," she says, "I think maybe I should have taken it as an insult. But I didn't, and I still don't."

And then she falls silent, the way a storyteller falls silent when a tale is done. She takes another deep breath, rolls her wheelchair back about a foot or so, until it bumps hard against one end of the chaise lounge. She laughs nervously and lights another cigarette. And I ask her other questions, but they have nothing whatsoever to do with Atlantic City or the dead woman. We talk about other painters she's known, and jazz musicians, and writers, and she talks about how much New York's changed, how much the whole world has changed around her. As she speaks, I have the peculiar, disquieting sensation that, somehow, she's passed the weight of that seventy-year-old secret on to me, and I think even if the article sells (and now I don't doubt that it will) and a million people read it, a hundred million people, the weight will not be diminished.

This is what it's like to be haunted, I think, and then I try to dismiss the thought as melodramatic, or absurd, or childish. But her jade-and-surf green eyes, the mermaids' eyes, are there to assure me otherwise.

It's almost dusk before we're done. She asks me to stay for dinner, but I make excuses about needing to be back in Boston. I promise to mail her a copy of the article when I've finished, and she tells me she'll watch for it. She tells me how she doesn't get much mail anymore, a few bills and ads, but nothing she ever wants to read.

"I am so very pleased that you contacted me," she says, as I slip the recorder and my steno pad back into the briefcase and snap it shut.

"It was gracious of you to talk so candidly with me," I reply, and she smiles.

I only glance at the painting once more, just before I leave. Earlier, I thought I might call someone I know, an ex who owns a gallery in the East Village. I owe him a favor, and the tip would surely square us. But standing there, looking at the pale, scale-dappled form of a woman bobbing in the frothing waves, her wet black hair tangled with wriggling crabs and fish, and nothing at all but a hint of shadow visible beneath the wreath of her floating hair, *seeing* it as I've never before seen any of the mermaids, I know I won't make the call. Maybe I'll mention the painting in the article I write, and maybe I won't.

She follows me to the door, and we each say our goodbyes. I kiss her hand when she offers it to me. I don't believe I've ever kissed a woman's hand, not until this moment. She locks the door behind me, two deadbolts and a chain, and then I stand in the hallway. It's much cooler here than it was in her apartment, in the shadows that have gathered despite the windows at either end of the corridor. There are people arguing loudly somewhere in the building below me, and a dog barking. By the time I descend the stairs and reach the sidewalk, the streetlamps are winking on.

THE MERMAID OF THE CONCRETE OCEAN

There are natural and man-made calamities and anomalies with which I become fascinated: the Peshtigo Fire (October 8, 1871), *La Bête du Gévaudan* (1764-1767), the Johnstown Flood (May 31, 1889), the Tunguska event (June 30, 1908), the lion attacks at Tsavo (March–December 1898), et cetera. Among the more obscure of my fascinations are the 1916 Jersey Shore and Matawan Creek shark attacks, one of many inspirations for "The Mermaid of the Concrete Ocean." This story eventually found a place in *The Drowning Girl: A Memoir,* which also drew inspiration, repeatedly, from the 1916 shark attacks.

The Sea Troll's Daughter

1.

It had been three days since the stranger returned to Invergó, there on the muddy shores of the milky blue-green bay where the glacier met the sea. Bruised and bleeding, she'd walked out of the freezing water. Much of her armor and clothing were torn or altogether missing, but she still had her spear and her dagger, and claimed to have slain the demon troll that had for so long plagued the people of the tiny village.

Yet, she returned to them with no *proof* of this mighty deed, except her word and her wounds. Many were quick to point out that the former could be lies, and that she could have come by the latter in any number of ways that did not actually involve killing the troll, or anything else, for that matter. She might have been foolhardy and wandered up onto the wide splay of the glacier, then taken a bad tumble on the ice. It might have happened just that way. Or she might have only slain a bear, or a wild boar or auroch, or a walrus, having mistook one of these beasts for the demon. Some even suggested it may have been an honest mistake, for bears and walrus, and even boars and aurochs, can be quite fearsome when angered, and if encountered unexpectedly in the night, may have easily been confused with the troll.

Others among the villagers were much less gracious, such as the blacksmith and his one-eyed wife, who went so far as to suggest the stranger's injuries may have been self-inflicted. She had bludgeoned and battered herself, they argued, so that she might claim the reward, then flee the village before the creature showed itself again, exposing her deceit. This stranger from the south, they argued, thought them all feebleminded. She intended to take their gold and leave them that much poorer and still troubled by the troll.

The elders of Invergó spoke with the stranger, and they relayed these concerns, even as her wounds were being cleaned and dressed. They'd arrived at a solution by which the matter might be settled. And it seemed fair enough, at least to them.

"Merely deliver unto us the body," they told the stranger. "Show us this irrefutable testament to your handiwork, and we will happily see that you are compensated with all that has been promised to whomsoever slays the troll. All the monies and horses and mammoth hides, for ours was not an idle offer. We would not have the world thinking we are liars, but neither would we have it thinking we can be beguiled by make-believe heroics."

But, she replied, the corpse had been snatched away from her by a treacherous current. She'd searched the murky depths, all to no avail, and had been forced to return to the village empty-handed, with nothing but the scars of a lengthy and terrible battle to attest to her victory over the monster.

The elders remained unconvinced, repeated their demand, and left the stranger to puzzle over her dilemma.

So, penniless and deemed either a fool or a charlatan, she sat in the moldering, broken-down hovel that passed for Invergó's one tavern, bandaged and staring forlornly into a smoky sod fire. She stayed drunk on whatever mead or barley wine the curious villagers might offer to loosen her tongue, so that she'd repeat the tale of how she'd purportedly bested the demon. They came and listened and bought her drinks, almost as though they believed her story, though it was plain none among them did.

"The fiend wasn't hard to find," the stranger muttered, thoroughly dispirited, looking from the fire to her half-empty cup to the doubtful faces of her audience. "There's a sort of reef, far down at the very bottom of the bay. The troll made his home there, in a hall fashioned from the bones of great whales and other such leviathans. How did I learn this?" she asked, and when no one ventured a guess, she continued, more dispirited than before.

"Well, after dark, I lay in wait along the shore, and there I spied your monster making off with a ewe and a lamb, one tucked under each arm, and so I trailed him into the water. He was bold, and took no notice of me, and so I swam down, down, down through the tangling blades of kelp and the ruins of sunken trees and the masts of ships that have foundered – "

"Now, exactly how did you hold your breath so long?" one of the men asked, raising a skeptical eyebrow.

"Also, how did you not succumb to the chill?" asked a woman with a fat goose in her lap. "The water is so dreadfully cold, and especially – "

"*Might* it be that someone here knows this tale *better* than I?" the stranger growled, and when no one admitted they did, she continued. "Now, as *I* was saying, the troll kept close to the bottom of the bay, in a hall made all of bones, and it was there that he retired with the ewe and the lamb he'd slaughtered and dragged into the water. I drew my weapon," and here she quickly slipped her dagger from its sheath for effect. The iron blade glinted dully in the firelight. Startled, the goose began honking and flapping her wings.

"I *still* don't see how you possibly held your breath so long as that," the man said, raising his voice to be heard above the noise of the frightened goose. "Not to mention the darkness. How did you see anything at all down there, it being night and the bay being so silty?"

The stranger shook her head and sighed in disgust, her face half hidden by the tangled black tresses that covered her head and hung down almost to the tavern's dirt floor. She returned the dagger to its sheath and informed the lot of them they'd hear not another word from her if they persisted with all these questions and interruptions. She also raised up her cup, and the woman with the goose nodded to the barmaid, indicating a refill was in order.

"I *found* the troll there inside its lair," the stranger continued, "feasting on the entrails and viscera of the slaughtered sheep. Inside, the walls of its lair glowed, and they glowed rather *brightly*, I might add, casting a ghostly phantom light all across the bottom of the bay."

"Awfully bloody convenient, that," the woman with the goose frowned, as the barmaid refilled the stranger's cup.

"*Sometimes,* the Fates, they do us a favorable turn," the stranger said and took an especially long swallow of barley wine. She belched, then went on. "I watched the troll, I did, for a moment or two, hoping to discern any weak spots it might have in its scaly, knobby hide. That's when it espied me, and straightaway the fiend released its dinner and rushed towards me, baring a mouth filled with fangs longer even than the tusks of a bull walrus."

"Long as that?" asked the woman with the goose, stroking the bird's head.

"Or longer," the stranger told her. "Of a sudden, it was upon me, all fins and claws, and there was hardly time to fix every detail in my memory. As I said, it *rushed* me, and bore me down upon the muddy belly of that accursed hall with all its weight. I thought it might crush me, stave in my skull and chest, and soon mine would count among the jumble of bleached skeletons littering that floor. There were plenty enough human bones, I *do* recall that much. Its talons sundered my armor, and sliced my flesh, and soon my blood was mingling with that of the stolen ewe and lamb. I almost despaired, then and there, and I'll admit that much freely and suffer no shame in the admission."

"Still," the woman with the goose persisted, "awfully damned convenient, all that light."

The stranger sighed and stared sullenly into the fire.

And for the people of Invergó, and also for the stranger who claimed to have done them such a service, this was the way those three days and those three nights passed. The curious came to the tavern to hear the tale, and most of them went away just as skeptical as they'd arrived. The stranger only slept when the drink overcame her, and then she sprawled on a filthy mat at one side of the hearth; at least no one saw fit to begrudge her that small luxury.

But then, late on the morning of the fourth day, the troll's mangled corpse fetched up on the tide, not far distant from the village. A clam-digger and his three sons had been working the mudflats where the narrow aquamarine bay meets the open sea, and they were the ones who discovered the creature's remains. Before midday, a group had been dispatched by the village constabulary to retrieve the body and haul it across the marshes, delivering it to Invergó, where all could see and judge for themselves. Seven strong men were required to hoist the carcass onto a litter (usually reserved for transporting strips of blubber and the like), which was drawn across the mire and through the rushes by a team of six oxen. Most of the afternoon was required to cross hardly a single league. The mud was deep and the going slow, and the animals strained in their harnesses, foam flecking their lips and nostrils. One of the cattle perished from exhaustion not long after the putrefying load was finally dragged through the village gates and dumped unceremoniously upon the flagstones in the common square.

Before this day, none among them had been afforded more than the briefest, fleeting glimpse of the sea devil. And now, every man, woman, and child who'd heard the news of the recovered corpse crowded about, able to peer and gawk and prod the dead thing to their hearts' content. The mob seethed with awe and morbid curiosity, apprehension and disbelief. For their pleasure, the enormous head was raised up and an anvil slid underneath its broken jaw, and, also, a fishing gaff was inserted into the dripping mouth, that all could look upon those protruding fangs, which did, indeed, put to shame the tusks of many a bull walrus.

However, it was almost twilight before anyone thought to rouse the stranger, who was still lying unconscious on her mat in the tavern, sleeping off the proceeds of the previous evening's storytelling. She'd been dreaming of her home, which was very far to the south, beyond the raw black mountains and the glaciers, the fjords and the snow. In the dream, she'd been sitting at the edge of a wide green pool, shaded by willow boughs from the heat of the noonday sun, watching the pretty women who came to bathe there. Half a bucket of soapy, lukewarm seawater was required to wake her from this reverie, and the stranger spat and sputtered and cursed the man who'd doused her (he'd drawn the short straw). She was ready to reach for her spear when someone hastily explained that a clam-digger had come across the troll's body on the mudflats, and so the people of Invergó were now quite a bit more inclined than before to accept her tale.

"That means I'll get the reward and can be shed of this sorry one-whore piss-hole of a town?" she asked. The barmaid explained how the decision was still up to the elders, but that the scales *did* seem to have tipped somewhat in her favor.

And so, with help from the barmaid and the cook, the still half-drunken stranger was led from the shadows and into what passed for bright daylight, there on the gloomy streets of Invergó. Soon, she was pushing her way roughly through the mumbling throng of bodies that had gathered about the slain sea troll, and when she saw the fruits of her battle – when she saw that everyone *else* had seen them – she smiled broadly and spat directly in the monster's face.

"Do you doubt me *still*?" she called out and managed to climb onto the creature's back, slipping off only once before she gained secure footing on its shoulders. "Will you continue to ridicule me as a liar, when the evidence is right here before your own eyes?"

"Well, it *might* conceivably have died some other way," a peat-cutter said without looking at the stranger.

"Perhaps," suggested a cooper, "it swam too near the glacier, and was struck by a chunk of calving ice."

The stranger glared furiously and whirled about to face the elders, who were gathered together near the troll's webbed feet. "Do you truly mean to *cheat* me of the bounty?" she demanded. "Why, you ungrateful, two-faced gaggle of sheep-fuckers," she began, then almost slipped off the cadaver again.

"Now, now," one of the elders said, holding up a hand in a gesture meant to calm the stranger. "There will, of course, be an inquest. Certainly. But, be assured, my fine woman, it is only a matter of formality, you understand. I'm sure not one here among us doubts, even for a moment, it was *your* blade returned this vile, contemptible spirit to the nether pits that spawned it."

For a few tense seconds, the stranger stared warily back at the elder, for she'd never liked men, and especially not men who used many words when only a few would suffice. She then looked out over the restless crowd, silently daring anyone present to contradict him. And, when no one did, she once again turned her gaze down to the corpse, laid out below her feet.

"I cut its throat, from ear to ear," the stranger said, though she was not entirely sure the troll *had* ears. "I gouged out the left eye, and I expect you'll come across the tip end of my blade lodged somewhere in the gore. I am Malmury, daughter of my Lord Gwrtheyrn the Undefeated, and before the eyes of the gods do I so claim this as *my* kill, and I know that even *they* would not gainsay this rightful averment."

And with that, the stranger, whom they at last knew was named Malmury, slid clumsily off the monster's back, her boots and breeches now stained with blood and the various excrescences leaking from the troll. She returned immediately to the tavern, as the salty evening air had made her quite thirsty. When she'd gone, the men and women and children of Invergó went back to examining the corpse, though a disquiet and guilty sort of solemnity had settled over them, and what was said was generally spoken in whispers. Overhead, a chorus of hungry gulls and ravens cawed and greedily surveyed the troll's shattered body.

"Malmury," the cooper murmured to the clam digger who'd found the corpse (and so was, himself, enjoying some small degree of celebrity). "A *fine* name, that. And the daughter of a lord, even. Never questioned her story in the least. No, not me."

"Nor I," whispered the peat-cutter, leaning in a little closer for a better look at the creature's warty hide. "Can't imagine where she'd have gotten the notion any of us distrusted her."

Torches were lit and set up round about the troll, and much of the crowd lingered far into the night, though a few found their way back to the tavern to listen to Malmury's tale a third or fourth time, for it had grown considerably more interesting, now that it seemed to be true. A local alchemist and astrologer, rarely seen by the other inhabitants of Invergó, arrived and was permitted to take samples of the monster's flesh and saliva. It was he who located the point of the stranger's broken dagger, embedded firmly in the troll's sternum, and the artifact was duly handed over to the constabulary. A young boy in the alchemist's service made highly detailed sketches from numerous angles, and labeled anatomical features as the old man had taught him. By midnight, it became necessary to post a sentry to prevent fisherman and urchins slicing off souvenirs. But only half an hour later, a fishwife was found with a horn cut from the sea troll's cheek hidden in her bustle, and a second sentry was posted.

In the tavern, Malmury, daughter of Lord Gwrtheyrn, managed to regale her audience with increasingly fabulous variations of her battle with the demon. But no one much seemed to mind the embellishments, or that, partway through the tenth retelling of the night, it was revealed that the troll had summoned a gigantic, fire-breathing worm from the ooze that carpeted the floor of the bay, which Malmury also claimed to have dispatched in short order.

"Sure," she said, wiping at her lips with the hem of the barmaid's skirt. "And now, there's something *else* for your muck-rakers to turn up, sooner or later."

By dawn, the stench wafting from the common was becoming unbearable, and a daunting array of dogs and cats had begun to gather round about the edges of the square, attracted by the odor, which promised a fine carrion feast. The cries of the gulls and the ravens had become a cacophony, as though all the heavens had sprouted feathers and sharp, pecking beaks and were descending upon the village. The harbormaster, two physicians, and a cadre of minor civil servants were becoming concerned about the assorted noxious fluids seeping from the rapidly decomposing carcass. This poisonous concoction spilled between the cobbles and had begun to fill gutters and strangle drains as it flowed downhill, towards both the waterfront and the village well. Though there was some talk of removing the source of the taint from the village, it was decided, rather, that a low bulwark or levee of dried peat would be stacked around the corpse.

And, true, this appeared to solve the problem of seepage, for the time being, the peat acting both as a dam and serving to absorb much of the rot. But it did nothing whatsoever to deter the cats and dogs milling about the square, or the raucous cloud of birds that had begun to swoop in, snatching mouthfuls of flesh before they could be chased away by the two sentries, who shouted at them and brandished brooms and long wooden poles.

Inside the smoky warmth of the tavern – which, by the way, was known as the Cod's Demise, though no sign had ever borne that title – Malmury knew nothing of the trouble and worry her trophy was causing in the square or the talk of having the troll hauled back into the marshes. But neither was she any longer precisely carefree, despite her drunkenness. Even as the sun was rising over the village and peat was being stacked about the corpse, a stooped and toothless old crone of a woman had entered the Cod's Demise. All those who'd been enjoying the tale's new wrinkle of a fire-breathing worm turned towards her. Not a few of them uttered prayers and clutched tightly to the fetishes they carried against the evil eye and all manner of sorcery and malevolent spirits. The crone stood near the doorway, and she leveled a long, crooked finger at Malmury.

"*Her,*" she said ominously, in a voice that was not unlike low tide swishing about rocks and rubbery heaps of bladder wrack. "She is the stranger? The one who has murdered the troll who for so long called the bay his home?"

There was a brief silence as eyes drifted from the crone to Malmury, who was blinking and peering through a haze of alcohol and smoke, trying to get a better view of the frail, hunched woman.

"That I am," Malmury said at last, confused by this latest arrival and the way the people of Invergó appeared to fear her. Malmury tried to stand, then thought better of it and stayed in her seat by the hearth, where there was less chance of tipping over.

"Then she's the one I've come to see," said the crone, who seemed less like a living, breathing woman and more like something assembled from bundles of twigs and scraps of leather, sloppily held together with twine, rope, and sinew. She leaned on a gnarled cane, though it was difficult to be sure if the cane were wood or bone or some skillful amalgam of the two. "She's the interloper who has doomed this village and all those who dwell here."

Malmury, confused and growing angry, rubbed at her eyes, starting to think this was surely nothing more than an unpleasant dream, born of too much drink and the boiled mutton and cabbage she'd eaten for dinner.

"How *dare* you stand there and speak to me this way?" she barked back at the crone, trying hard not to slur as she spoke. "Aren't I the one who, only five days ago, *delivered* this place from the depredations of that demon? Am I not the one who risked her *life* in the icy brine of the bay to keep these people safe?"

"*Oh,* she thinks much of herself," the crone cackled, slowly bobbing her head, as though in time to some music nobody else could hear. "Yes, she thinks herself gallant and brave and favored by the gods of her land. And who can say? Maybe she is. But she should know, this is not *her* land, and we have our *own* gods. And it is one of *their* children she has slain."

Malmury sat up as straight as she could manage, which wasn't very straight at all, and, with her sloshing cup, jabbed fiercely at the old woman. Barley wine spilled out and spattered across the toes of Malmury's boots and the hard-packed dirt floor.

"Hag," she snarled, "how dare you address me as though I'm not even present. If you have some quarrel with me, then let's hear it spoken. Else, crab, scuttle away and bother this good house no more."

"This good *house*?" the crone asked, feigning dismay as she peered into the gloom, her stooped countenance framed by the morning light coming in through the opened door. "Beg pardon. I thought possibly I'd wandered into a rather ambitious privy hole, but that the swine had found it first."

Malmury dropped her cup and drew her chipped dagger, which she brandished menacingly at the crone. "You *will* leave now, and without another insult passing across those withered lips, or we shall be presenting you to the swine for their breakfast."

At this, the barmaid, a fair woman with blondish hair, bent close to Malmury and whispered in her ear, "Worse yet than the blasted troll, this one. Be cautious, my lady."

Malmury looked away from the crone, and, for a long moment, stared, instead, at the barmaid. Malmury had the distinct sensation that she was missing some crucial bit of wisdom or history that would serve to make sense of the foul old woman's intrusion and the villagers' reactions to her. Without turning from the barmaid, she furrowed her brow and again pointed at the crone with her dagger.

"This slattern?" she asked, almost laughing. "This shriveled harridan not even the most miserable of harpies would claim? I'm to *fear* her?"

"No," the crone said, coming nearer now. The crowd parted to grant her passage, one or two among them stumbling in their haste to avoid the witch. "*You* need not fear *me,* Malmury Trollbane. Not this day. But, you *would* do well to find some ounce of sobriety and fear the consequences of your actions."

"She's insane," Malmury sneered, than spat at the floor between herself and the crone. "Someone show her a mercy, and find the hag a root cellar to haunt."

The old woman stopped and stared down at the glob of spittle, then raised her head, flared her nostrils, and fixed Malmury in her gaze.

"There was a balance here, Trollbane, an equity, decreed when my great-grandmothers were still infants swaddled in their cribs. The debt paid for a grave injustice born of the arrogance of men. A tithe, if you will, and if it cost these people a few souls now and again, or thinned their bleating flocks, it also kept them safe from that greater wrath, which watches us always from the Sea at the Top of the World. But this selfsame balance have you undone, and, foolishly, they name you a hero for that deed. For their damnation and their doom."

Malmury cursed, spat again, and tried then to rise from her chair, but was held back by her own inebriation and by the barmaid's firm hand upon her shoulder.

The crone coughed and added a portion of her own jaundiced spittle to the floor of the tavern. "They will *tell* you, Trollbane, though the tales be less than half remembered among this misbegotten legion of cowards and imbeciles. You *ask* them, they will tell you what has not yet been spoken, what was never freely uttered for fear no hero would have accepted their blood-gold. Do not think *me* the villain in this ballad they are spinning around you."

"You would do well to *leave,* witch," answered Malmury, her voice grown low and throaty, as threatful as breakers before a storm tide or the grumble of a chained hound. "They might fear you, but I do not, and I'm in an ill temper to suffer your threats and intimations."

"Very well," the old woman replied, and she bowed her head to Malmury, though it was clear to all that the crone's gesture carried not one whit of respect. "So be it. But you *ask* them, Trollbane. You ask after the *cause* of the troll's coming, and you ask after his daughter, too."

And with that, she raised her cane, and the fumy air about her appeared to shimmer and fold back upon itself. There was a strong smell, like the scent of brimstone and of smoldering sage, and a sound, as well. Later, Malmury would not be able to decide if it was more akin to a distant thunderclap or the crackle of burning logs. And, with that, the old woman vanished, and her spit sizzled loudly upon the floor.

"Then she *is* a sorceress," Malmury said, sliding the dagger back into its sheath.

"After a fashion," the barmaid told her and slowly removed her grip upon Malmury's shoulder. "She's the last priestess of the Old Ways and still pays tribute to those beings who came before the gods. I've heard her called Grímhildr, and also Gunna, though none among us recall her right name. She is powerful and treacherous, but know that she has also done great *good* for Invergó and all the people along the coast. When there was plague, she dispelled the sickness – "

"What did she *mean*, to ask after the coming of the troll and its daughter?"

"These are not questions I would answer," the barmaid replied and turned suddenly away. "You must take them to the elders. They can tell you these things."

Malmury nodded and sipped from her cup, her eyes wandering about the tavern, which she saw was now emptying out into the morning-drenched street. The crone's warnings had left them in no mood for tales of monsters and had ruined their appetite for the stranger's endless boasting and bluster. No matter, Malmury thought. They'd be back come nightfall, and she was weary, besides, and needed sleep. There was now a cot waiting for her upstairs, in the loft above the kitchen, a proper bed complete with mattress and pillows stuffed with the down of geese, even a white bearskin blanket to guard against the frigid air that blew in through the cracks in the walls. She considered going before the council of elders, after she was rested and merely hungover, and pressing them for answers to the crone's questions. But Malmury's head was beginning to ache, and she entertained the proposition only in passing. Already, the appearance of the old woman and what she'd said was beginning to seem less like something that had actually happened, and Malmury wondered, dimly, if she were having trouble discerning where the truth ended and her own generous embroidery of the truth began. Perhaps she'd invented the hag, feeling the tale needed an appropriate epilogue, and then, in her drunkenness, forgotten that she'd invented her.

Soon, the barmaid – whose name was Dóta – returned to lead Malmury up the narrow, creaking stairs to her small room and the cot, and Malmury forgot about sea trolls and witches and even the gold she had coming. For Dóta was a comely girl, and free with her favors, and the stranger's sex mattered little to her.

2.

The daughter of the sea troll lived among the jagged, windswept highlands that loomed above the milky blue-green bay and the village of Invergó. Here had she dwelt for almost three generations, as men reckoned the passing of time, and here did she imagine she would live until the long span of her days was at last exhausted.

Her cave lay deep within the earth, where once had been only solid basalt. But over incalculable eons, the glacier that swept down from the mountains, inching between high volcanic cliffs as it carved a wide path to the sea, had worked its way beneath the bare and stony flesh of the land. A ceaseless trickle of meltwater had carried the bedrock away, grain by grain, down to the bay, as the perpetual cycle of freeze and thaw had split and shattered the stone. In time (and then, as now, the world had nothing but time), the smallest of breaches had become cracks, cracks became fissures, and intersecting labyrinths of fissures collapsed to form a cavern. And so, in this way, had the struggle between mountain and ice prepared for her a home, and she dwelt there, alone, almost beyond the memory of the village and its inhabitants, which she despised and feared and avoided when at all possible.

However, she had not always lived in the cave, nor unattended. Her mother, a child of man, had died while birthing the sea troll's daughter, and, afterwards, she'd been taken in by the widowed conjurer who would, so many years later, seek out and confront a stranger named Malmury who'd come up from the southern kingdoms. When the people of Invergó had looked upon the infant, what they'd seen was enough to guess at its parentage. And they would have put the mother to death, then and there, for her congress with the fiend, had she not been dead already. And surely, likewise, would they have murdered the baby, had the old woman not seen fit to intervene. The villagers had always feared the crone, but also they'd had cause to seek her out in times of hardship and calamity. So it gave them pause, once she'd made it known that the infant was in her care, and this knowledge stayed their hand, for a while.

In the tumbledown remains of a stone cottage at the edge of the mudflats, the crone had raised the infant until the child was old enough to care for herself. And until even the old woman's infamy, and the prospect of losing her favors, was no longer enough to protect the sea troll's daughter from the villagers. Though more human than not, she had the creature's blood in her veins. In the eyes of some, this made her a greater abomination than her father.

Finally, rumors had spread that the girl was a danger to them all, and, after an especially harsh winter, many become convinced that she could make herself into an ocean mist and pass easily through windowpanes. In this way, it was claimed, had she begun feeding on the blood of men and women while they slept. Soon, a much-prized milking cow had been found with her udder mutilated, and the farmer had been forced to put the beast out of her misery. The very next day, the elders of Invergó had sent a warning to the crone, that their tolerance of the half-breed was at an end, and she was to be remanded to the constable forthwith.

But the old woman had planned against this day. She'd discovered the cave high above the bay, and she'd taught the sea troll's daughter to find auk eggs and mushrooms and to hunt the goats and such other wild things as lived among the peaks and ravines bordering the glacier. The girl was bright and had learned to make clothing and boots from the hides of her kills, and also she had been taught herb lore, and much else that would be needed to survive on her own in that forbidding, barren place.

Late one night in the summer of her fourteenth year, she'd fled Invergó, and made her way to the cave. Only one man had ever been foolish enough to go looking for her, and his body was found pinned to an iceberg floating in the bay, his own sword driven through his chest to the hilt. After that, they left her alone, and soon the daughter of the sea troll was little more than legend and a tale to frighten children. She began to believe, and to hope, that she would never again have cause to journey down the slopes to the village.

But then, as the stranger Malmury, senseless with drink, slept in the arms of a barmaid, the crone came to the sea troll's daughter in her dreams, as the old woman had done many times before.

"Your father has been slain," she said, not bothering to temper the words. "His corpse lies desecrated and rotting in the village square, where all can come and gloat and admire the mischief of the one who killed him."

The sea troll's daughter, whom the crone had named Sæhildr, for the ocean, had been dreaming of stalking elk and a shaggy herd of mammoth across a meadow. But the crone's voice had startled her prey, and the dream animals had all fled across the tundra.

The sea troll's daughter rolled over onto her back, stared up at the grizzled face of the old woman, and asked, "Should this bring me sorrow? Should I have tears, to receive such tidings? If so, I must admit it doesn't, and I don't. Never have I seen the face of my father, not with my waking eyes, and never has he spoken unto me, nor sought me out. I was nothing more to him than a curious consequence of his indiscretions."

"You and he lived always in different worlds," the old woman replied, but the one she called Sæhildr had turned back over onto her belly and was staring forlornly at the place where the elk and mammoth had been grazing, only a few moments before.

"It is none of my concern," the sea troll's daughter sighed, thinking she should wake soon, that then the old woman could no longer plague her thoughts. Besides, she was hungry, and there was fresh meat from a bear she'd killed only the day before.

"Sæhildr," the crone said, "I've not come expecting you to grieve, for too well do I know your mettle. I've come with a warning, as the one who slew your father may yet come seeking you."

The sea troll's daughter smiled, baring teeth that effortlessly cracked bone to reach the rich marrow inside. With the hooked claws of a thumb and forefinger, she plucked the yellow blossom from an arctic poppy, and held it to her wide nostrils.

"Old mother, knowing my mettle, you should know that I am not afraid of men," she whispered, then she let the flower fall back to the ground.

"The one who slew your father was not a man, but a woman, the likes of which I've never seen," the crone replied. "She is a warrior, of noble birth, from the lands south of the mountains. She came to collect the bounty placed upon the troll's head. Sæhildr, this one is strong, and I fear for you."

In the dream, low clouds the color of steel raced by overhead, fat with snow, and the sea troll's daughter lay among the flowers of the meadow and thought about the father she'd never met. Her short tail twitched from side to side, like the tail of a lazy, contented cat, and she decapitated another poppy.

"You believe this warrior will hunt *me* now?" she asked the crone.

"What I think, Sæhildr, is that the men of Invergó have no intention of honoring their agreement to pay this woman her reward. Rather, I believe they will entice her with even greater riches, if only she will stalk and destroy the bastard daughter of their dispatched foe. The woman is greedy, and prideful, and I hold that she will hunt you, yes."

"Then let her come to me, Old Mother," the sea troll's daughter said. "There is little enough sport to be had in these hills. Let her come into the mountains and face me."

The old woman sighed and began to break apart on the wind, like sea foam before a wave. "She's not a fool," the crone said. "A braggart, yes, and a liar, and also a drunk. But by her own strength and wits did she undo your father. I'd not see the same fate befall you, Sæhildr. She will lay a trap."

"Oh, I know something of traps," the troll's daughter replied, and then the dream ended. She opened her black eyes and lay awake in her freezing den, deep within the mountains. Not far from the nest of pelts that was her bed, a lantern she'd fashioned from walrus bone and blubber burned unsteadily, casting tall, writhing shadows across the basalt walls. The sea troll's daughter lay very still, watching the flame, and praying to all the beings who'd come before the gods of men that the battle with her father's killer would not be over too quickly.

3.

As it happened, however, the elders of Invergó were far too preoccupied with other matters to busy themselves trying to conceive of schemes by which they might cheat Malmury of her bounty. With each passing hour, the clam-digger's grisly trophy became increasingly putrid, and the decision not to remove it from the village's common square had set in motion a chain of events that would prove far more disastrous to the village than the *living* troll ever could have been. Moreover, Malmury was entirely too distracted by her own intoxication and with the pleasures visited upon her by the barmaid, Dóta, to even recollect she had the reward coming. So, while there can be hardly any doubt that the old crone who lived at the edge of the mudflats was, in fact, both wise and clever, she had little cause to fear for Sæhildr's immediate well-being.

The troll's corpse, hauled so triumphantly from the marsh, had begun to swell in the mid-day sun, distending magnificently as the gases of decomposition built up inside its innards. Meanwhile, the flock of gulls and ravens had been joined by countless numbers of fish crows and kittiwakes, a constantly shifting, swooping, shrieking cloud that, at last, succeeded in chasing off the two sentries who'd been charged with the task of protecting the carcass from scavengers and souvenir hunters. And, no longer dissuaded by the men and their jabbing sticks, the cats and dogs that had skulked all night about the edges of the common grew bold and joined in the banquet (though the cats proved more interested in seizing unwary birds than in the sour flesh of the troll). A terrific swarm of biting flies arrived only a short time later, and there were ants, as well, and voracious beetles the size of a grown man's thumb. Crabs and less savory things made their way up from the beach. An order was posted that the citizens of Invergó should retreat to their homes and bolt all doors and windows until such time as the pandemonium could be resolved.

There was, briefly, talk of towing the body back to the salt marshes from whence it had come. But this proposal was soon dismissed as impractical and hazardous. Even if a determined crew of men dragging a litter or wagon and armed with the requisite hooks and cables, the block and tackle, could fight their way through the seething, foraging mass of birds, cats, dogs, insects, and crustaceans, it seemed very unlikely that the corpse retained enough integrity that it could now be moved in a single piece. And just the thought of intentionally breaking it apart, tearing it open and thereby releasing whatever foul brew festered within, was enough to inspire the elders to seek some alternate route of ridding the village of the corruption and all its attendant chaos. To make matters worse, the peat levee that had been hastily stacked around the carcass suddenly failed partway through the day, disgorging all the oily fluid that had built up behind it. There was now talk of pestilence, and a second order was posted, advising the villagers that all water from the pumps was no longer potable, and that the bay, too, appeared to have been contaminated. The fish market was closed, and incoming boats forbidden to offload any of the day's catch.

And then, when the elders thought matters were surely at their worst, the alchemist's young apprentice arrived bearing a sheaf of equations and ascertainments based upon the samples taken from the carcass. In their chambers, the old men flipped through these pages for some considerable time, no one wanting to be the first to admit he didn't actually understand what he was reading. Finally, the apprentice cleared his throat, which caused them to look up at him.

"It's simple, really," the boy said. "You see, the various humors of the troll's peculiar composition have been demonstrated to undergo a predictable variance during the process of putrefaction."

The elders stared back at him, seeming no less confused by his words than by the spidery handwriting on the pages spread out before them.

"To put it more plainly," the boy said, "the creature's blood is becoming volatile. Flammable. Given significant enough concentrations, which must certainly exist by now, even explosive."

Almost in unison, the faces of the elders of Invergó went pale. One of them immediately stood and ordered the boy to fetch his master forthwith, but was duly informed that the alchemist had already fled the village. He'd packed a mule and left by the winding, narrow path that led west into the wilderness. He hoped, the apprentice told them, to observe for posterity the grandeur of the inevitable conflagration, but from a safe distance.

At once, a proclamation went out that all flames were to be extinguished, all hearths and forges and ovens, every candle and lantern, in Invergó. Not so much as a tinderbox or pipe must be left smoldering anywhere, so dire was the threat to life and property. However, most of the men dispatched to see that this proclamation was enforced, instead fled into the marshes, or towards the foothills, or across the milky blue-green bay to the far shore, which was reckoned to be sufficiently remote that sanctuary could be found there. The calls that rang through the streets of the village were not so much "Douse the fires," or "Mind your stray embers," as "Flee for your lives, the troll's going to explode."

In their cot, in the small but cozy space above the Cod's Demise, Malmury and Dóta had been dozing. But the commotion from outside, both the wild ruckus from the feeding scavengers and the panic that was now sweeping through the village, woke them. Malmury cursed and groped about for the jug of fine apple brandy on the floor, which Dóta had pilfered from the larder. Dóta lay listening to the uproar, and, being for the most part sober, began to sense that something, somewhere, somehow had gone terribly wrong, and that they might now be in very grave danger.

Dóta handed the brandy to Malmury, who took a long pull from the jug and squinted at the barmaid.

"They have no intention of paying you," Dóta said flatly, buttoning her blouse. "We've known it all along. All of us. Everyone who lives in Invergó."

Malmury blinked and rubbed at her eyes, not quite able to make sense of what she was hearing. She had another swallow from the jug, hoping the strong liquor might clear her ears.

"It was a dreadful thing we did," Dóta admitted. "I know that now. You're brave, and risked much, and – "

"I'll *beat* it out of them," Malmury muttered.

"That might have worked," Dóta said softly, nodding her head. "Only, they don't have it. The elders, I mean. In all Invergó's coffers, there's not even a quarter what they offered."

Beyond the walls of the tavern, there was a terrific crash, then, and, soon thereafter, the sound of women screaming.

"Malmury, listen to me. You stay here and have the last of the brandy. I'll be back very soon."

"I'll beat it out of them," Malmury declared again, though this time with slightly less conviction.

"Yes," Dóta told her. "I'm sure you will do just that. Only now, wait here. I'll return as quickly as I can."

"Bastards," Malmury sneered. "Bastards and ingrates."

"You finish the brandy," Dóta said, pointing at the jug clutched in Malmury's hands. "It's excellent brandy, and very expensive. Maybe not the same as gold, but…" and then the barmaid trailed off, seeing that Malmury had passed out again. Dóta dressed and hurried downstairs, leaving the stranger, who no longer seemed quite so strange, alone and naked, sprawled and snoring loudly on the cot.

In the street outside the Cod's Demise, the barmaid was greeted by a scene of utter chaos. The reek from the rotting troll, only palpable in the tavern, was now overwhelming, and she covered her mouth and tried not to gag. Men, women, and children rushed to and fro, many burdened with bundles of valuables or food, some on horseback, others trying to drive herds of pigs or sheep through the crowd. And, yet, rising above it all, was the deafening clamor of that horde of sea birds and dogs and cats squabbling amongst themselves for a share of the troll. Off towards the docks, someone was clanging the huge bronze bell reserved for naught but the direst of catastrophes. Dóta shrank back against the tavern wall, recalling the crone's warnings and admonitions, expecting to see, any moment now, the titanic form of one of those beings who came before the gods, towering over the rooftops, striding towards her through the village.

Just then, a tinker, who frequently spent his evenings and his earnings in the tavern, stopped and seized the barmaid by both shoulders, gazing directly into her eyes.

"You must *run!*" he implored. "Now, this very minute, you must get away from this place!"

"But why?" Dóta responded, trying to show as little of her terror as possible, trying to behave the way she imagined a woman like Malmury might behave. "What has happened?"

"It *burns,*" the tinker said, and before she could ask him *what* burned, he released her and vanished into the mob. But, as if in answer to that unasked question, there came a muffled crack and then a boom that shook the very street beneath her boots. A roiling mass of charcoal-colored smoke shot through with glowing red-orange cinders billowed up from the direction of the livery, and Dóta turned and dashed back into the Cod's Demise.

Another explosion followed, and another, and by the time she reached the cot upstairs, dust was sifting down from the rafters of the tavern, and the roofing timbers had begun to creak alarmingly. Malmury was still asleep, oblivious to whatever cataclysm was befalling Invergó. The barmaid grabbed the bearskin blanket and wrapped it about Malmury's shoulders, then slapped her several times, hard, until the woman's eyelids fluttered partway open.

"*Stop that,*" Malmury glowered, seeming now more like an indignant girl child than the warrior who'd swum to the bottom of the bay and slain their sea troll.

"We have to *go,*" Dóta said, almost shouting to be understood above the racket. "It's not safe here anymore, Malmury. We have to get out of Invergó."

"But I've done *killed* the poor, sorry wretch," Malmury mumbled, shivering and pulling the bearskin tighter about her. "Have you lot gone and found another?"

"Truthfully," Dóta replied, "I do not *know* what fresh devilry this is, only that we can't stay here. There is fire, and a roar like naval cannonade."

"I was sleeping," Malmury said petulantly. I was dreaming of – "

The barmaid slapped her again, harder, and this time Malmury seized her wrist and glared blearily back at Dóta. "I *told* you not to do that."

"Aye, and I told *you* to get up off your fat ass and get moving." There was another explosion then, nearer than any of the others, and both women felt the floorboards shift and tilt below them. Malmury nodded, some dim comprehension wriggling its way through the brandy and wine.

"My horse is in the stable," she said. "I cannot leave without my horse. She was given me by my father."

Dóta shook her head, straining to help Malmury to her feet. "I'm sorry," she said. "It's too late. The stables are all ablaze." Then neither of them said anything more, and the barmaid led the stranger down the swaying stairs and through the tavern and out into the burning village.

4.

From a rocky crag high above Invergó, the sea troll's daughter watched as the town burned. Even at this distance and altitude, the earth shuddered with the force of each successive detonation. Loose stones were shaken free of the talus and rolled away down the steep slope. The sky was sooty with smoke, and beneath the pall, everything glowed from the hellish light of the flames.

And, too, she watched the progress of those who'd managed to escape the fire. Most fled westward, across the mudflats, but some had filled the hulls of doggers and dories and ventured out into the bay. She'd seen one of the little boats lurch to starboard and capsize, and was surprised at how many of those it spilled into the icy cove reached the other shore. But of all these refugees, only two had headed south, into the hills, choosing the treacherous pass that led up towards the glacier and the basalt mountains that flanked it. The daughter of the sea troll watched their progress with an especial fascination. One of them appeared to be unconscious and was slung across the back of a mule, and the other, a woman with hair the color of the sun, held tight to the mule's reins and urged it forward. With every new explosion the animal bucked and brayed and struggled against her; once or twice, they almost went over the edge, all three of them. By the time they gained the wider ledge where Sæhildr crouched, the sun was setting and nothing much remained intact of Invergó, nothing that hadn't been touched by the devouring fire.

The sun-haired woman lashed the reigns securely to a boulder, then sat down in the rubble. She was trembling, and it was clear she'd not had time to dress with an eye towards the cold breath of the mountains. There was a heavy belt cinched about her waist and from it hung a sheathed dagger. The sea troll's daughter noted the blade, then turned her attention to the mule and its burden. She could see now that the person slung over the animal's back was also a woman, unconscious and partially covered with a moth-eaten bearskin. Her long black hair hung down almost to the muddy ground.

Invisible from her hiding place in the scree, Sæhildr asked, "Is the bitch dead, your companion?"

Without raising her head, the sun-haired woman replied. "Now, why would I have bothered to drag a dead woman all the way up here?"

"Perhaps she is dear to you," the daughter of the sea troll replied. "It may be you did not wish to see her corpse go to ash with the others."

"She's *not* a corpse," the woman said. "Not yet, anyway." And as if to corroborate the claim, the body draped across the mule farted loudly and then muttered a few unintelligible words.

"Your sister?" the daughter of the sea troll asked, and when the sun-haired woman told her no, Sæhildr said, "She seems far too young to be your mother."

"She's not my mother. She's...a friend. More than that, she's a hero."

The sea troll's daughter licked at her lips, then glanced back to the inferno by the bay. "A hero," she said, almost too softly to be heard.

"Well, that's the way it started," the sun-haired woman said, her teeth chattering so badly she was having trouble speaking. "She came here from a kingdom beyond the mountains, and, single-handedly, she slew the fiend that haunted the bay. But – "

" – then the fire came," Sæhildr said, and, with that, she stood, revealing herself to the woman. "My *father's* fire, the wrath of the Old Ones, unleashed by the blade there on your hip."

The woman stared at the sea troll's daughter, her eyes filling with wonder and fear and confusion, with panic and awe. Her mouth opened, as though she meant to say something or to scream, but she uttered not a sound. Her hand drifted towards the dagger's hilt.

"*That,* my lady, would be a very poor idea," Sæhildr said calmly. Taller by a head than even the tallest of tall men, she stood looking down at the shivering woman, and her skin glinted oddly in the half light. "Why do you think I mean you harm?"

"You," the woman stammered. "You're the troll's whelp. I have heard the tales. The old witch is your mother."

Sæhildr made an ugly, derisive noise that was partly a laugh. "Is that how they tell it these days, that Gunna is my mother?"

The sun-haired woman only nodded once and stared at the rocks.

"*My* mother is dead," the troll's daughter said, moving nearer, causing the mule to bray and tug at its reigns. "And now, it seems, my father has joined her."

"I cannot let you harm her," the woman said, risking a quick sidewise glance at Sæhildr. The daughter of the sea troll laughed again and dipped her head, almost seeming to bow. The distant firelight reflected off the small curved horns on either side of her head, hardly more than nubs and mostly hidden by her thick hair, and it shone off the scales dappling her cheekbones and brow, as well.

"What you *mean* to say is that you would have to *try* to prevent me from harming her."

"Yes," the sun-haired woman replied, and now she glanced nervously towards the mule and her unconscious companion.

"If, of course, I *intended* her harm."

"Are you saying that you don't?" the woman asked. "That you do not desire vengeance for your father's death?"

Sæhildr licked her lips again, then stepped past the seated woman to stand above the mule. The animal rolled its eyes, neighed horribly, and kicked at the air, almost dislodging its load. But then the sea troll's daughter gently laid a hand on its rump, and immediately the beast grew calm and silent once more. Sæhildr leaned forward and grasped the unconscious woman's chin, lifting it, wishing to know the face of the one who'd defeated the brute who'd raped her mother and made of his daughter so shunned and misshapen a thing.

"This one is drunk," Sæhildr said, sniffing the air.

"Very much so," the sun-haired woman replied.

"A *drunkard* slew the troll?"

"She was sober that day," said Dóta. "I think."

Sæhildr snorted and said, "Know that there was no bond but blood between my father and I. Hence, what need have I to seek vengeance upon his executioner? Though, I will confess, I'd hoped she might bring me some measure of sport. But even that seems unlikely in her current state." The troll's daughter released the sleeping woman's jaw, letting it bump roughly against the mule's ribs, and stood upright again. "No, I think you need not fear for your lover's life. Not this day. Besides, hasn't the utter destruction of your village counted as a more appropriate reprisal?"

The sun-haired woman blinked and said, "Why do you say that, that she's my lover?"

"Liquor is not the only stink on her," answered the sea troll's daughter. "Now, *deny* the truth of this, my lady, and I may yet grow angry."

The woman from doomed Invergó didn't reply, but only sighed and continued staring into the gravel at her feet.

"This one is practically naked," Sæhildr said. "And you're not much better. You'll freeze, the both of you, before morning."

"There was no time to find proper clothes," the woman protested, and the wind shifted then, bringing with it the cloying reek of the burning village.

"Not very much farther along this path, you'll come to a small cave," the sea troll's daughter said. "I will find you there, tonight, and bring what furs and provisions I can spare. Enough, perhaps, that you may yet have some slim chance of making your way through the mountains."

"I don't understand," Dóta said, exhausted and near to tears, and when the troll's daughter made no response, the barmaid discovered that she and the mule and Malmury were alone on the mountain ledge. She'd not heard the demon take its leave, so maybe the stories were true, and it could become a fog and float away whenever it so pleased. Dóta sat a moment longer, watching the raging fire spread out far below them. And then she got to her feet, took up the mule's reins, and began searching for the shelter that the troll's daughter had promised her she would discover. She did not spare a thought for the people of Invergó, not for her lost family, and not even for the kindly old man who'd owned the Cod's Demise and had taken her in off the streets when she was hardly more than a babe. They were the past, and the past would keep neither her nor Malmury alive.

Twice, she lost her way among the boulders, and by the time Dóta stumbled upon the cave, a heavy snow had begun to fall, large wet flakes spiraling down from the darkness. But it was warm inside, out of the howling wind. And, what's more, she found bundles of wolf and bear pelts, seal skins and mammoth hide, some sewn together into sturdy garments. And there was salted meat, a few potatoes, and a freshly killed rabbit spitted and roasting above a small fire. She would never again set eyes on the sea troll's daughter, but in the long days ahead, as Dóta and the stranger named Malmury made their way through blizzards and across fields of ice, she would often sense someone nearby, watching over them. Or only watching.

THE SEA TROLL'S DAUGHTER

In 2007, I was hired by HarperCollins to write a novelization for Robert Zemeckis' animated film adaptation of *Beowulf.* I was broke and badly needed the money. The film was utter shit, and my only consolation is that my novelization is just ever so slightly less shitty than the movie. Afterwards, I vowed never again to commit a novelization, a promise I have managed to keep despite the allure of decent paydays. "The Sea Troll's Daughter" is, in part, an apology to the unknown author of *Beowulf* and to *Beowulf* scholars everywhere for my part in promoting Zemeckis' abomination. That said, many of those same scholars would likely be appalled at my feminist-queer satirical approach to this retelling. So it goes. Only rarely do I make myself laugh, but I still laugh aloud whenever I have cause to revisit this story.

Hydrarguros

01.

The very first time I see silver, it's five minutes past noon on a Monday and I'm crammed into a seat on the Bridge Line, racing over the slate-grey Delaware River. Philly is crouched at my back, and a one o'clock with the Czech and a couple of his meatheads is waiting for me on the Jersey side of the Ben Franklin. I've been popping since I woke up half an hour late, the lucky greens Eli scores from his chemist somewhere in Devil's Pocket, so my head's buzzing almost bright and cold as the sun pouring down through the late January clouds. My gums are tingling, and my fucking fingertips, too, and I'm sitting there, wishing I was just about anywhere else but on my way to Camden, payday at journey's end or no payday at journey's end. I'm trying to look at nothing that isn't *out there,* on the opposite side of the window, because faces always make me jumpy when I'm using the stuff Eli assures me is mostly only methylphenidate with a little Phenotropil by way of his chemists' Russian connections. I'm in my seat, trying to concentrate on the shadow of the span and the Speedline on the water below, on the silhouettes of buildings to the south, on a goddamn flock of birds, anything out there to keep me focused, keep me awake. But then my ears pop, and there's a second or two of dizziness before I smell ozone and ammonia and something with the carbon stink of burning sugar.

We're almost across the bridge by then, and I tell myself not to look, not to dare fucking look, just mind my own business and watch the window, my sickly, pale reflection *in* the window, and the dingy winter scene the window's holding at bay. But I look anyhow.

There's a very pretty woman sitting across the aisle from me, her skin as dark as freshly ground coffee, her hair dreadlocked and pulled back away from her face. Her eyes are a brilliant, bottomless green. For a seemingly elastic moment, I am unable to look away from those eyes. They manage to be both merciful and fierce, like the painted eyes of Catholic saints rendered in plaster of Paris. And I'm thinking it's no big, and I'll be able to look back out the window; who gives a shit what that smell might have been. It's already starting to fade. But then the pretty woman turns her head to the left, towards the front of the car, and quicksilver trickles from her left nostril and spatters her jeans. If she felt it – if she's in any way aware of this strange excrescence – she shows no sign that she felt it. She doesn't wipe her nose or look down at her pants. If anyone else saw what I saw, they're busy pretending like they didn't. I call it quicksilver, though I know that's not what I'm seeing. Even this first time, I know it's only something that *looks* like mercury, because I have no frame of reference to think of it any other way.

The woman turns back towards me, and she smiles. It's a nervous, slightly embarrassed sort of smile, and I suppose I must have been sitting there gawking at her. I want to apologize. Instead, I force myself to go back to the window, and I curse that Irish cunt who's been selling Eli fuck knows what. I curse myself for being such a lazy asshole and popping whatever's at hand when I have access to good clean junk. And then the train is across that filthy, poisoned river and rolling past Campbell Field and Pearl Street. My heart's going a mile a minute, and I'm sweating like it's August. I grip the handle of the shiny aluminum briefcase I'm supposed to hand over to the Czech, assuming he has the cash, and do my best to push back everything but my trepidation of things I know I'm not imagining. You don't go into a face-to-face with one of El Diamante's bastards with a shake on, not if you want to keep the red stuff on the inside where it fucking belongs.

I don't look at the pretty black woman again.

02.

The very first thing you learn about the Czech is that he's not from the Czech Republic or the dear departed Czech Socialist Republic or, for that matter, Slovakia. He's not even European. He's just some Canuck motherfucker who used to haunt Montreal, selling cloned phones and heroin and whores. A genuine Renaissance crook, the

Czech. I have no idea where or when or why he picked up the nickname, but it stuck like shit on the wall of a gorilla's cage. The second thing you learn about the Czech is not to ask about the scars. If you're lucky, you've learned both these things before you have the misfortune of making his acquaintance up close and personal.

Anyway, he has a car waiting for me when the train dumps me out at Broadway Station, but I make the driver wait while I pay too much for bottled water at Starbucks. The lucky greens have me in such a fizz I'm almost seeing double, and there are rare occasions when a little H_20 seems to help bring me down again. I don't actually expect *this* will be one of those times, but I'm still a bit weirded out by what I think I saw on the Speedline, and I'm a lot pissed that the Czech's dragged me all the way over to Jersey at this indecent hour on a Monday. So, I let the driver idle for five while I buy a lukewarm bottle of Dasani that I know is just twelve ounces of Philly tap water with a fancy blue label slapped on it.

"Czech, he don't like to be kept waiting," says the skinny Mexican kid behind the wheel when I climb into the backseat. I show him my middle finger, and he shrugs and pulls away from the curb. I set the briefcase on the seat beside me, just wanting to be free of the package and on my way back to Eli and our cozy dump of an apartment in Chinatown. As the jet-black Lincoln MKS turns off Broadway onto Mickle Boulevard, heading west, carrying me back towards the river, I think how I'm going to have a chat with Eli about finding a better pusher. My gums feel like I've been chewing foil, and there are wasps darting about behind my eyes. At least the wasps are keeping their stingers to themselves.

"Just how late are we?" I ask the driver.

"Ten minutes," he replies.

"Blame the train."

"You blame the train, Mister. I don't talk to the Czech unless he talks to me, and he never talks to me."

"Fortunate you," I say and take another swallow of Dasani. It tastes more like the polyethylene terephthalate bottle than water, and I try not to think about toxicity and esters of phthalic acid, endocrine disruption and antimony trioxide, because that just puts me right back on the Bridge Line watching a pretty woman's silver nosebleed.

We stop at a red light, then turn left onto South Third Street, paralleling the waterfront, and I realize the drop's going to be the warehouse on Spruce. I want to close my eyes, but all those lucky green wasps won't let me. The sun is so bright it seems to be flashing off even the most nonreflective of surfaces. Vast seas of asphalt might as well be goddamn mirrors. I drum my fingers on the lid of the aluminum briefcase, wishing the driver had the radio on or a DVD playing, anything to distract me from the buzz in my skull and the noise the tires make against the pavement. Another three or four long minutes and we're bumping off the road into a parking lot that might have last been paved when Obama was in the White House. And the Mexican kid pulls up at the loading bay, and I open the door and step out into the cold, sunny day. The Lincoln has stirred up a shroud of red-grey dust, but all that sunlight doesn't give a shit. It shines straight on through the haze and almost lays me open, head to fucking toe. I cough a few times on my way from the car to the bald-headed gook in Ray-Bans waiting to usher me to my rendezvous with the Czech. However, the wasps do not take my cough as an opportunity to vacate my cranium, so maybe they're here to stay. The gook pats me down, and then double checks with a security wand. When he's sure I'm not packing anything more menacing than my phone, he leads me out of the flaying day and into merciful shadows and muted pools of halogen.

"You're late," the Czech says, just in case I haven't noticed, and he points at a clock on the wall. "You're almost twelve minutes late."

I glance over my shoulder at the clock, because it seems rude not to look after he's gone to the trouble to point. Actually, I'm almost eleven minutes late.

"You got some more important place to be, Czech?" I ask, deciding it's as good a day as any to push my luck a few extra inches.

"Maybe I do at that, you sick homo fuck. Maybe your ass is sitting at the very bottom of my to-do list this fine day. So, how about you zip it, and let's get this over with."

I turn away from the clock and back to the fold-out card table where the Czech's sitting in a fold-out chair. He's smoking a Parliament, and in front of him there's a half-eaten corned-beef sandwich cradled in white butcher's paper. I try not to stare at the scars, but you might as well try to make your heart stop beating for a minute or two. Way I heard it, the stupid son of a bitch got drunk and went bear-hunting in some Alaskan national park or another, only he tried to make do with a bottle of vodka and a .22 caliber pocket pistol, instead of a rifle. No, that's probably not the truth of it, but his face does look like something a grizzly's been gnawing at.

"You got the goods?" he asks, and I have the impression I'm watching Quasimodo quoting old Jimmy Cagney gangster films. I hold up the briefcase, and he nods and puffs his cigarette.

"But I am curious as hell why you went and switched the drop date," I say, wondering if it's really me talking this trash to the Czech or if maybe the lucky greens have hijacked the speech centers of my brain and are determined to get me shot in the face. "I might have had plans, you know. And El Diamante usually sticks to the script."

"What El Diamante does, that ain't none of your business, and that ain't my business, neither. Now, didn't I say zip it?" And then he jabs a thumb at a second folding metal chair, a few feet in front of the card table, and he tells me to give him the case and sit the fuck down. Which is what I do. Maybe the greens have decided to give me a break, after all. Or maybe they just want to draw this out as long as possible. The Czech dials the three-digit combination and opens the aluminum briefcase. He has a long look inside. Then he grunts and shuts it again. And that's when I notice something shimmering on the toe of his left shoe. It looks a lot like a few drops of spilled mercury. This is the second time I see silver.

03.

This is hours later, and I'm back in Philly, trying to forget all about the woman on the train and the Czech's shoes and whatever might have been in the briefcase I delivered. The sun's been down for hours. The city is dark and cold, and there's supposed to be snow before the sun comes up again. I'm lying in the bed I share with Eli, just lying there on my right side watching him read. There are things I want to tell him, but I know full fucking well that I won't. I won't because some of those things might get him killed if a deal ever goes sideways somewhere down the line (and it's only a matter of time) or if I should fall from grace with Her Majesty Madam Adrianne and all the powers that be and keep the axles upon which the world spins greased up and relatively friction-free. And other things I will not tell him because maybe it was only the pills, or maybe it's stress, or maybe I'm losing my goddamn mind, and if it's the latter, I'd rather keep that morsel to myself as long as possible, pretty please and thank you.

Eli turns a page and shifts slightly, to better take advantage of the reading lamp on the little table beside the bed. I scan the spine of the hardback, the words printed on the dust jacket, like I don't already know it by heart. Eli reads books, and I read their dust jackets. Catch me in just the right mood, I might read the flap copy.

"I thought you were asleep," Eli says without bothering to look at me.

"Maybe later, *chica,*" I reply, and Eli nods the way he does when he's far more interested in whatever he's reading than in talking to me. So, I read the spine again, aloud this time, purposefully mispronouncing the Korean author's name. Which is enough to get Eli to glance my way. Eli's eyes are emeralds, crossed with some less precious stone. Agate maybe. Eli's eyes are emerald and agate, cut and polished to precision, flawed in ways that only make them more perfect.

"Go to sleep," he tells me, pretending to frown. "You look exhausted."

"Yeah, sure, but I got this fucking hard-on like you wouldn't believe."

"Last time I checked, you also had two good hands and a more than adequate knowledge of how they work."

"That's cold," I say. "That is some cold shit to say to someone who had to go spend the day in Jersey."

Eli snorts, and his emerald and agate eyes, which might pass for only hazel-green if you haven't lived with them as long as I have lived with them, they drift back to the printed page.

"The lube warms up just fine," he says, "you hold it a minute or so first." He doesn't laugh, but I do, and then I roll over to stare at the wall instead of watching Eli read. The wall is flat and dull, and sometimes it makes me sleepy. I'd take something, but after the lucky greens, it's probably best if I forego the cocktail of pot and prescription benzodiazepines I usually rely on to beat my insomnia into submission. I don't masturbate, because, boner from hell or not, I'm not in the right frame of mind to give myself a hj. So, I lie and stare at the wall and listen to the soft sounds of Eli reading his biography of South Korean astronaut Yi So-Yeon, whom I do recall, and without having to read the book, was the first Korean in space. She might also have been the second Asian woman to slip the surly fucking bonds of Earth and dance the skies or what the hell ever.

"Why don't you take something if you can't sleep," Eli says after maybe half an hour of me lying there.

"I don't think so, *chica.* My brain's still rocking and rolling from the breath mints you been buying off that mick cocksucker you call a dealer. Me, I think he's using drain cleaner again."

"No way," Eli says, and I can tell from the tone of his voice he's only half interested, at best, in whether or not the mad chemist holed up in Devil's Pocket is using Drano to cut his shit. "Donncha's merchandise is clean."

"Maybe *Mr.* Clean," I reply, and Eli smacks me lightly on the back of the head with his book. He tells me to jack off and go to sleep. I tell him to blow me. We spar with the age-old poetry of true love's tin-eared wit. Then he goes back to reading, and I go back to staring at the bedroom wall.

Eli is the only guy I've ever been with more than a month, and here we are going on two years. I found him waiting tables in a noodle and sushi joint over on Race Street. Most of the waiters in the place were either drag queens or trannies, dressed up like geisha whores from some sort of post-apocalyptic Yakuza flick. He was wearing so much makeup, and I was so drunk on Sapporo Black Label and saki, I didn't even realize he was every bit *gai-ko* as me. That first night, back at Eli's old apartment not far from the noodle shop, we screwed like goddamn bunnies on crank. I must have walked funny for a week.

I started eating in that place every night, and almost every one of those nights we'd wind up in bed together, and that's probably the happiest I've ever been or ever will be. Sure, the sex was absolute supremo, standout – state of the fucking *art* of fucking – but it never would have been enough to keep things going after a few weeks. I don't care how sweet the cock, sooner or later, if that's all there is interest wanes and I start to drift. I used to think maybe my libido had ADD or something, or I'd convinced myself that commitment meant I might miss out on something better. What matters, though, there was more, and four months later Eli packed up his shit and moved in with me. He never asked what I do to pay the rent, and I've never felt compelled to volunteer that piece of intel.

"You're still awake," Eli says, and I hear him toss his book onto the table beside the bed. I hear him reach for a pill bottle.

"Yeah, I'm still awake."

"Good, 'cause there's something I meant to tell you earlier, and I almost forgot."

"And what is that, pray tell?" I ask, listening as he rattles a few milligrams of this or that out into his palm.

"This woman in the restaurant. It was the weirdest thing. I mean, I'd think maybe I was hallucinating or imagining crap, only Jules saw it, too. Think it scared her, to tell you the truth."

Jules is the noodle shop's post-op hostess, who sometimes comes over to play, when Eli and I find ourselves inclined for takeout of that particular variety. It happens. But, point here is, Eli says these words, words that ought to be nothing more than a passing fleck of conversation peering in on the edge of my not going to sleep, and I get goddamn goose bumps and my stomach does some sort of roll like it just discovered the pommel horse. Because I know what he's going to say. Not exactly, no, but close enough that I want to tell him to please shut the fuck up and turn off the light and never mind what it is he *thinks* he saw.

But I don't, and he says, "This woman came in alone and so Jules sat her at the bar, right? Total dyke, but she had this whole butch-glam demeanor working for her, like Nicole Kidman with a buzz cut."

"You're right," I mutter at the wall, as if it's not too late for intervention. "That's pretty goddamn weird."

"No, you ass. That's not the weird part. The weird part was when I brought her order out, and I noticed there was this shiny silver stuff dripping out of her left ear. At first, I thought it was only a tragus piercing or something, and I just wasn't seeing it right. But then…well, I looked again, and it had run down her neck and was soaking into the collar of her blouse. Jules saw it, too. Freaky, yeah?"

"Yeah," I say, but I don't say much more, and a few minutes later, Eli finally switches off the lamp, and I can stare at the wall without actually having to see it.

04.

It's two days later, as the crow flies, and I'm waiting on a call from one of Her Majesty's lieutenants. I'm holed up in the backroom of a meat market in Bella Vista, on a side street just off Washington, me and Joey the Kike. We're bored and second-guessing our daily marching orders from the pampered, privileged pit bulls those of us so much nearer the bottom of this miscreant food chain refer to as Carrion Dispatch. Not very clever, sure, but all too fucking often, it hits the nail on the proverbial head. I might not like having to ride the Speedline out to Camden for a handoff with the Czech, but it beats waiting, and it sure as hell beats scraping up someone else's road kill and seeing to its discrete and final disposition. Which is where I have a feeling today is bound. Joey keeps trying to lure me into a game of whiskey poker, even though he knows I don't play cards or dice or dominoes or anything else that might lighten my wallet. You work for Madam Adrianne, you already got enough debt stacked up without gambling, even if it's only penny-ante foolishness to make the time go faster.

Joey the Kike isn't the absolute last person I'd pick to spend a morning with, but he's just next door. Back in the Ohs, when he was still just a kid, Joey did a stint in Afghanistan and lost three fingers off his left hand and more than a few of his marbles. He still checks his shoes for scorpions. And most of us, we trust that whatever you hear coming out of his mouth is pure and unadulterated baloney. It's not that he lies, or even exaggerates to make something more interesting. It's more like he's a bottomless well of bullshit, and every conversation with Joey is another tour through the highways and byways of his shattered psyche. For years, we've been waiting for the bastard to get yanked off the street and sent away to his own padded rumpus room at Norristown, where he can while away the days trading his crapola with other guys stuck on that same ever-tilting mental plane of existence. Still, I'll be the first to admit he's ace on the job, and nobody ever has to clean up after Joey the Kike.

He lights a cigarette and takes off his left shoe, and his sock, too, because you never can tell where a scorpion might turn up.

"You didn't open the case?" he asks, banging the heel of his shoe against the edge of a shipping crate.

"Hell no, I didn't open the case. You think we'd be having this delightful conversation today if I'd delivered a violated parcel to the Czech? Or anybody else, for that matter. For pity's sake, Joey."

"You ain't sleeping," he says, not a question, just a statement of the obvious.

"I'm getting very good at lying awake," I reply. "Anyway, what's that got to do with anything?"

"Sleep deprivation makes people paranoid," he says, and bangs his loafer against the crate two or three more times. But if he manages to dislodge any scorpions, they're of the invisible brand. "Makes you prone to erratic behavior."

"Joey, please put your damn shoe back on."

"Hey, dude, you want to hear about the Trenton drop or not?" he asks, turning his sock wrong-side out for the second time. Ash falls from the cigarette dangling at the corner of his mouth.

I don't answer the question. Instead, I pick up my phone and stare at the screen, like I can will the thing to ring. All I really want right now is to get on with whatever inconvenience and unpleasantness the day holds in store, because Joey's a lot easier to take when confined spaces and the odor of raw pork fat aren't involved.

"Do you or don't you?" he prods.

Not that he needs my permission to keep going. Not that my saying no, I *don't* want to hear about the Trenton drop, is going to put an end to it.

"Well," he says, lowering his voice like he's about to spill a state secret, "what we saw when Tony Palamara opened that briefcase – and keep in mind, it was me *and* Jack on that job, so I've got backup corroboration if you need that sort of thing – what we saw was five or six of these silver vials. I'm not sure Tony realized we got a look inside or not, and, actually, it wasn't much more than a peek. It's not like either of us was *trying* to see inside. But, yeah, that's what we saw, these silver vials lined up neat as houses, each one maybe sixty or seventy milliliters, and they all had a piece of yellow tape or a yellow sticker on them. Jack, he thinks it was some sort of high-tech, next-gen explosive, maybe something you have to mix with something else to get the big bangola, right?"

And I stare at him for a few seconds, and he stares back at me, that one green-and-black argyle sock drooping from his hand like some giant's idea of a novelty prophylactic. Whatever he sees in my face, it can't be good, not if his expression is any indication. He takes the cigarette out of his mouth and balances it on the edge of the shipping crate.

"Joey, were the vials silver, or was the silver what was inside of the vials?"

And I can tell right away it hasn't occurred to him to wonder which. Why the hell would it? He asks me what difference it makes, sounding confused and suspicious and wary all at the same time.

"So you couldn't tell?"

"Like I said, it wasn't much more than a peek. Then Tony Palamara shut the case again. But if I had to speculate, if this was a wager, and there was money on the line? Was that the situation, I'd probably say the silver stuff was inside the vials."

"If you had to speculate?" I ask him, and Joey the Kike bobs his head and turns his sock right-side out again.

"What difference does it make?" he wants to know. "I haven't even gotten around to the interesting part of the story yet."

And then, before I can ask him what the interesting part might be, my phone rings, and it's dispatch, and I stand there and listen while the dog barks. Straightforward janitorial work, because some asshole decided to use a shotgun when a 9mm would have sufficed. Nothing I haven't had to deal with a dozen times or more. I tell the dog we're on our way, and then I tell Joey it's his balls on the cutting board if we're late because he can't keep his shoes and socks on his goddamn feet.

05.

Some nights, mostly in the summer, Eli and me, we climb the rickety fire escape onto the roof to try to see the stars. There are a couple of injection-molded plastic lawn chairs up there, left behind by a former tenant, someone who moved out years before I moved into the building. We sit in those chairs that have come all the way from some East Asian factory shithole in Hong Kong or Taiwan, and we drink beer and smoke weed and stare up at the night spread out above Philly, trying to see anything at all. Mostly, it's a white-orange sky-glow haze, the opaque murk of photopollution, and I suspect we imagine far more stars than we actually see. I tell him that some night or another we'll drive way the hell out to the middle of nowhere, someplace where the sky is still mostly dark. He humors me, but Eli is a city kid, born and bred, and I think his idea of a pastoral landscape is Marconi Plaza. We might sit there and wax poetic about planets and nebulas and shit, but I have a feeling that if he ever found himself standing beneath the real deal, with all those twinkling pinpricks scattered overhead and maybe a full moon to boot, it'd probably freak him right the fuck on out.

One night he said to me, "Maybe this is preferable," and I had to ask what he meant.

"I just mean, maybe it's better this way, not being able to see the sky. Maybe, all this light, it's sort of like camouflage."

I squinted back at Eli through a cloud of fresh ganja smoke, and when he reached for the pipe I passed it to him.

"I have no idea what you're talking about," I told him, and Eli shrugged and took a big hit of the 990 Master Kush I get from a grower whose well aware how much time I've spent in Amsterdam and Nepal, so she knows better than to sell me dirt grass. Eli exhaled and passed the pipe back to me.

"Maybe I don't mean anything at all," he said and gave me half a smile. "Maybe I'm just stoned and tired and talking out my ass."

I think that was the same night we might have seen a falling star, though Eli was of the opinion it wasn't anything but a pile of space junk burning up as it tumbled back to earth.

06.

I've been handling the consequences of other people's half-assed *mokroye delo* since I was sixteen going on forty-five. So, yeah, takes an awfully bad scene to get me to so much as flinch, which is not to say I *enjoy* the shit. Truth of it, nothing pisses me off worse or quicker than some bastard spinning off the rails, running around with that first-person shooter mentality that, more often than not, turns a simple, straight-up hit into a bloodbath. And that is precisely the brand of unnecessary sangre pageantry that me and Joey the Kike have just spent the last three hours mopping up. What's left of the recently deceased, along with a bin of crimson rags and sponges and the latex gloves and coveralls we wore, is stowed snugly in the trunk of the car. Another ten minutes, it won't be our problem anymore, soon as we make the scheduled meet and greet with one of Madam Adrianne's garbage men.

So, it's hardly business as usual that Joey's behind the wheel because my hands won't stop shaking enough that I can drive. They won't stop shaking long enough for me to even light a cigarette.

"You really aren't gonna tell me what it was happened back there?" he asks for, I don't know, the hundredth time in the last thirty or forty minutes. I glance at my watch, then the speedometer, making sure we're not late and he's not speeding. At least I have that much presence of mind left to me.

"Never yet known you to be the squeamish type with wet work," he says and stops for a red light.

Most of the snow from Tuesday night has melted, but there are still plenty of off-white scabs hiding in the shadows, and there's also the filthy mix of ice and sand and anonymous schmutz heaped at either side of the street. There are people out there shivering at a bus stop, people rushing along the icy sidewalk, a homeless guy huddled in the doorway of an abandoned office building. Every last bit of that tableau is as ordinary as it gets, the humdrum day to day of the ineptly named City of Brotherly Love, and that ought to help, but it doesn't. All of it comes across as window dressing, meticulously crafted misdirection meant to keep me from getting a good look at what's really going down.

"Dude, seriously, you're starting to give me the heebie-jeebies," Joey says.

"Why don't you just concentrate on getting us where we're going," I tell him. "See if you can do that, all right? 'Cause it's about the only thing in the world you have to worry about right now."

"We're not gonna be late," says Joey the Kike. "At this rate, we might be fucking early, but we sure as hell ain't gonna be late."

I keep my mouth shut. Out there, a thin woman with a purse Doberman on a pink rhinestone leash walks past. She's wearing galoshes and a pink wool coat that only comes down to her knees. At the bus stop, tucked safe inside that translucent half-shell, a man lays down a newspaper and answers his phone. The homeless guy scratches at his beard and talks to himself. Then the traffic light turns green, and we're moving again.

This is the day that I saw silver for the third time. But no way in hell I'm going to tell Joey that.

Just like the first time, sitting on the train as it barreled towards Camden and my tryst with the Czech, I felt my ears pop, and then there was the same brief dizziness, followed by the commingled reek of ammonia, ozone, and burnt sugar. Me and Joey, we'd just found the room with the body, some poor son of a bitch who'd taken both barrels of a Remington in the face. Who knows what he'd done, or if he'd done anything at all. Could have been over money or dope or maybe someone just wanted him out of the way. I don't let myself think too much about that sort of thing. Better not to even think of the body as *someone*. Better to treat it the way a stock boy handles a messy cleanup on aisle five after someone's shopping cart has careened into a towering display of spaghetti sauce.

"Sometimes," said Joey, "I wish I'd gone to college. What about you, man? Ever long for another line of work? Something that *don't* involve scraping brains off the linoleum after a throwdown."

But me, I was too busy simply trying to breathe to remind him that I *had* gone to college, too busy trying not to gag to partake in witty repartee. The dizziness had come and gone, but that acrid stench was forcing its way past my nostrils, scalding my sinuses and the back of my throat. And I knew that Joey didn't smell it, not so much as a whiff, and that his ears hadn't popped, and that he'd not shared that fleeting moment of vertigo. He stood there, glaring at me, his expression equal parts confusion and annoyance. Finally, he shook his head and stepped over the dead guy's legs.

"Jesus and Mary, we've both seen way worse than this," he said, and right then, that's when I caught the dull sparkle on the floor. The lower jaw was still in one piece, mostly, so for half a second or so I pretended I was only seeing the glint of fluorescent lighting off a filling or a crown. But then the silvery puddle, no larger than a dime, moved. It stood out very starkly against all that blood, against the soup of brain and muscle tissue punctuated by countless shards of human skull. It flowed a few inches before encountering a jellied lump of cerebellum, and then I watched as it slowly extended...what? What the fuck would you call what I saw? A *pseudopod*? Yeah, sure. Let's go for broke. I watched as it extended a pseudopod and began crawling *over* the obstacle in its path. That's when I turned away, and when I looked back, it wasn't there anymore.

Joey curses and honks the horn. I don't know why. I don't ask him. I don't care. I'm still staring out the passenger side window at this brilliant winter day that wants or needs me to believe it's all nothing more or less than another round of the same old same old. I'm thinking about the woman on the Speedline and about the scuffed toe of the Czech's shoe, about whatever Eli saw at the noodle shop and the silver vials Joey and Jack got a peep at when Tony Palamara opened the case they'd delivered to him. I'm drawing lines and making correlations, parsing best I can, dot-to-fucking-dot, right? Nothing it takes a genius to see, even if I've no idea whatsoever what it all adds up to in the end. I blink, and the sun sparks brutally off distant blue-black towers of mirrored glass. Joey hits the horn again, broadcasting his displeasure for all Girard Avenue to hear, and I shut my eyes.

07.

And it's a night or two later that I have the dream. That I have the dream for the first time.

I've never given much thought to nightmares. Sure, I rack up more than my fair share. I wake up sweating and the sheets soaked, Eli awake, too, and asking if I'm okay. But what would you fucking expect? That's how it goes when your life is a never-ending game of Stepin Fetchit and "Mistress may I have another," when you exist in the everlasting umbrage of Madam Adrianne's Grand Guignol of vice and crime and profit. No one lives this life and expects to sleep well – leastways, no one with walking-around sense. That's why white-coated bastards in pharmaceutical labs had to go and invent Zolpidem and so many other merciful soporifics, so the bad guys could get a little more shut-eye every now and again.

This is not my recollection of that first time. Hell, this is not my recollection of *any* single instance of the dream. It has a hundred subtle and not-so-subtle permutations, but always it stays the same. It wears a hundred gaudy masks to half conceal an immutable underlying face. So, take this as the amalgam or composite that it is. Take this as a rough approximation. Be smart, and take this with a goddamn grain of salt.

Let's say it starts with me and Eli in our plastic lawn chairs, sitting on the roof, gazing heavenward, like either one of us has half a snowball's chance at salvation. Sure. This is as good a place to begin as any other. There we sit, holding hands, scrounging mean comfort in one another's company – only, this time, some human agency or force of nature has intervened and swept back all that orange sky-glow. The stars are spread out overhead like an astronomer's banquet, and neither of us can look away. You see pictures like that online, sure, but you don't look up and expect to behold the dazzling entrails of the Milky Way draped above your head, fit to make the ghost of Neil deGrasse Tyson come. You don't live your whole life in the over-illuminated filth of cities and ever expect to glimpse all those stars arching pretty as you please across the celestial hemisphere.

We sit there, content and amazed, and I want to tell Eli those aren't stars. It's only fireworks on the Fourth of July or the moment the clock strikes the New Year. But he's too busy naming constellations to hear me. How Eli would know a constellation from throbbing gristle is beyond me. But there he sits, reciting them for my edification.

"That's Sagittarius," he says. "Right there, between Ophiuchus and Capricornus. The centaur, between the serpent in the west and the goat in the east." And he tells me that more extrasolar planets have been discovered in Sagittarius than in any other constellation. "*That's* why we should keep a close watch on it."

And I realize then, whiz-bang, presto, abracadabra, that the stars are wheeling overhead, exchanging positions in some crazy cosmic square dance, and Eli, *he* sees it too, and he laughs. I've never heard Eli laugh like this before, not while I was awake. It's the laughter of a child. It's a laughter filled with delight. There's innocence in a laugh like this.

And maybe, after that, I'm not on the roof anymore. Maybe, after that, I'm sitting in a crowded bar down on Locust Street. I know the place, but I can never remember its name, not in the dream. Nothing to write home about, one way or the other. Neither classy enough nor sleazy enough to be especially memorable. Just fags and dykes wall to fucking wall and lousy, ancient disco blaring through unseen speakers. There's a pint bottle of Wild Turkey sitting on the bar in front of me, and an empty shot glass. Someone's holding a gun to the back of my head. And, yeah, I know the feeling of having a gun to my head, because it happened this one time on a run to Atlantic City that went almost bad as bad can be. I also know that it's Joey the Kike holding the pistol, seeing as how there's a dead scorpion the color of pus lying right there on the bar beside the bottle of bourbon.

"This ain't the way it ought to be," he says, and I'm surprised I can hear his voice over the shitty music and all those queers trying to talk over the shitty music.

"Then how about we find some other way to work it out," I say, sounding lame as any asshole ever tried to talk his way out of a slug to the brain. "How about you sit down here next to me and we have a drink and make sure there are no more creepy-crawlies in your shoes."

"I shouldn't be seen in a place like this," he says, and I hear him pull the hammer back. "People talk, they see you hanging round a place like this."

"People do fucking talk," I agree. With my left index finger, I flick the dead scorpion off the bar. No one seems to notice. For that matter, no one seems to notice he's got a gun to my head. I say, "Maybe you should bounce before some hard-nosed bastard takes a notion to make you his bitch, yeah? You ever taken it up the ass, Joey?"

"You're such a smart guy," Joey replies, "you're still gonna be passing woof tickets when you're six feet under, ain't you? Expect you'll manage to smack-talk your way out of Hell, given half a chance."

"Well, you know me, Joey. Never let 'em see you sweat. *Veni, vedi, vici* and all that *hùnzhàng*."

And I'm sitting there waiting to die, when the music stops, and all eyes turn towards the rear of the bar. I look, too, though Joey's still got his 9mm parked on my scalp. A baby spot with a green gel is playing across a tiny stage, and there's Eli with a microphone. I'd think he was actual, factual fish if I didn't know better, that's how good Eli looks in a black evening gown and pumps and a wig that makes me think of Isabella Rossellini playing Dorothy Vallens in *Blue Velvet*. The din of voices is only a murmur now, only a gentle whisper of expectation as we all wait to see which way the wind's about to blow.

"Damn, she's hot," Joey says.

"Fuckin' A, she's hot," I tell him. "You should be so goddamn lucky to get a piece of ass like that one day."

He tells me to keep quiet, zip it and toss the key, that he wants to hear, but it's not *me* he wants to hear. So I make like a good boy and oblige. After all, I want to hear this nightingale, too. And then Eli begins to sing, a cappella and in Spanish, and everyone goes hushed as midnight after Judgment Day. His voice is his voice, not some dream impersonation, and I wonder why I never knew Eli could sing.

Bueno, ahora, pagar la atención
Sólo en caso de que no había oído...

And I'm still right there in the bar, but I'm somewhere else, as well. I'm walking in a desert somewhere, like something out of an old Wild and Woolly West flick, and the sun beats down on me from a sky so blue it's almost white. There are mountains far, far away, a hazy jagged line against the horizon, and I wonder if that's where I'm trying to get to. If there's something in the mountains that I need to see. The playa stretches out all around me, a lifeless plain of alkali flats and desiccation cracks. Maybe this was a lake or inland sea, long, long ago. Maybe the water still comes back, from time to time. Sweat runs into my eyes, and I squint against the sting.

On the little stage, Eli sings in Spanish, and I sit on my bar stool with the barrel of Joey's gun prodding my skull. I wish the shot glass weren't empty, 'cause the baking desert sun has me thirsty as a motherfucker. I keep my eyes on Eli, and I hear the parching salt wind whipping across the flats, and I hear that song in a language that I can only half understand.

Basta con mirar hacia el cielo
Y gracias al Gobierno por la nieve
Y cantar la baja hacia abajo...

"What's she sayin'?" Joey the Kike wants to know, and I ask him which part of me looks Mexican.

In the desert, I stop walking and peer up at the sun. High above me, there are contrails. And I know that's what Eli's singing about – those vaporous wakes – even if I have no idea why.

"It's a dream," I tell Joey the Kike, growing impatient with the gun. "Specifically, it's *my* dream. I come here all the time, and I don't remember ever inviting you."

The playa crunches loudly beneath my feet.

Tony Palamara opens a briefcase, and I see half a dozen silver vials marked with yellow tape.

A woman on a train wipes at her nose, and my ears pop.

Eli is no longer singing in Spanish, though I don't recall the transition to English. No one says a word. They're all much too busy watching him make love to the resonant phallus of his microphone.

Trying to make it rain.
So when you're out there in that blizzard,
Shivering in the cold,
Just look up to the sky...

I kneel on that plain and dig my fingers into the scorched saline crust. I crush the sandy dirt in my hand, and the wind sweeps it away.

And that's when I notice what looks like a kid's spinning top – only big around as a tractor-trailer's wheel – lying on the ground maybe twenty yards ahead of me. A tattered drogue parachute is attached to the enormous top by a tangled skein of nylon kernmantle cord. The wind ruffles wildly through the chute, and I notice the skid marks leading from the spinning top that isn't a spinning top, trailing away into the distance.

And sing the low-down experimental cloud-seeding
Who-needs-'em-baby? Silver-iodide blues.

I stand, and look back the way I've come. In the dream, I guess I've come from the south, walking north. So, looking south, the desert seems to run on forever, with no unobtainable mountainous El Dorado to upset the monotony. There's only the sky above, crisscrossed with contrails, and the yellow-brown playa below, the line drawn between them sharp as a paper cut. There's not even the mirage shimmer of heat I'd have expected, but, of course, this desert is only required to obey the dictates of my unconscious mind, not any laws of physical science. I stand staring at the horizon for a moment and then resume my northwards march. I know now I'm not trying to reach the mountains. No one reaches those mountains, not no way, not no how, right? I'm only trying to go as far as the kid's top that's not a top and its rippling nylon parachute. I understand that now, and I tell Joey to either pull the trigger or put his piece away. I don't have time for reindeer games tonight. And if I did, I still wouldn't be looking for action from the likes of him.

I stare at the bar, and the pus-colored scorpion's returned. This time, I don't bother to make it go away. I do wonder if dead scorpions can still kill a guy.

Was you ever bit by a dead bee?

All those people in the bar have begun applauding, and Eli takes a bow and sets his mike back into its stand.

"What you saw," Joey sneers, "I got as much right to know as you. We were both slopping about in that stiff's innards, and if something was wrong with him, I deserve to know. You got no place keepin' it from me."

"I didn't see anything," I tell him, wishing it were the truth. "Now, are you going to shoot me or put away the roscoe and make nice?"

"Making you nervous?" asks Joey.

"Not really, but the potential for injury is pissing me off righteously."

I reach the top that's not a top, and now I'm almost certain it's actually some sort of return capsule from a space probe. One side is scorched black, so I suppose that must be the heat shield. I stand three or four feet back, and I never, in any version of the dream, have touched the thing. It's maybe five feet in diameter, maybe a little less. I'm wondering how long its been out here, and where it might have traveled before hurtling back to earth, and, while I'm at it, why no retrieval team's come along to fetch the thing. I wonder if it's even a NASA probe, or maybe, instead, a chunk of foreign hardware that strayed from its target area. Either way, no one leaves shit like this lying around in the goddamn desert. I know *that* much.

"Yeah, you know it all," Joey says and jabs me a little harder with the muzzle of his gun. "You must be the original Doctor Albert Eisenstein, and me, I'm just some schmuck can't be trusted with the time of day."

Catch a falling star an' put it in your pocket...

And on the rooftop, Eli tells me, "The star at the centaur's knee is Alpha Sagittarii, or Rukbat, which means 'knee' in Arabic. Rukbat is a blue class B star, one hundred and eighteen light years away. It's twice as hot as the sun and forty times brighter."

"You been holding out on me, *chica*. Here I thought you were nothing but good looks and grace, and then you get all Wikipedia on me."

Eli laughs, and the crowded, noisy bar on Locust Street dissolves like fog, and the desert fades to half a memory. Joey the Kike and his pea-shooter, the dead scorpion and the bottle of Wild Turkey, every bit of it merely the echo of an echo now. I'm standing at the doorway of our bathroom, the tiny bathroom in mine and Eli's place in Chinatown. Regardless which rendition of the dream we're talking about, sooner or later they *all* end here. I'm standing in the open door of the bathroom, and Eli's in the old claw-foot tub. The air is thick with steam and condensation drips in crystal beads from the mirror on the medicine cabinet. Even the floor, that mosaic of white hexagonal tiles, is slick. I'm barefoot, and the ceramic feels slick beneath my feet. I swear and ask Eli if he thinks he got the water hot enough, and he asks me about the briefcase I delivered to the Czech. It doesn't even occur to me to ask how the hell he knows about the delivery.

"What about we don't talk shop just this once," I say, as though it's something we make a habit of doing. "And how about we most especially don't linger on the subject of the fucking Czech?"

"Hey, *you* brought it up, lover, not me," Joey says, returning the soap to the scallop-shaped soap dish. His hand leaves behind a smear of silver on the sudsy lavender bar. I stare at it, trying hard to recall something important that's teetering right there on the tip end of my tongue.

For love may come an' tap you on the shoulder, some starless night...

"Make yourself useful and hand me a towel," he says. "Long as you're standing there, I mean."

I reach into the linen closet for a bath towel, and when I turn back to pass it to Eli, he's standing, the water lapping about his lower calves. Only it's not water anymore. It's something that looks like mercury, and it flows quickly up his legs, his hips, his ass, and drips like cum from the end of his dick. Eli either isn't aware of what's going on, or he doesn't care. I hand him the towel as the silver reaches his smooth, hairless chest and begins to makes its way down both his arms.

"Anyway," he says, "we can talk about it or we can not talk about it. Either way's fine by me. So long as you don't start fooling yourself into thinking your hands are clean. I don't want to hear about how you were only following orders, you know?"

It's easy to forget them without tryin', with just a pocketful of starlight.

My ears haven't popped, and there's been no dizziness, but, all the same, the bathroom is redolent with those caustic triplets, ammonia and ozone, and, more subtly, sugar sizzling away to a carbon-black scum. The silver has reached Eli's throat and rushes up over his chin, finding its way into his mouth and nostrils. A moment more, and he stands staring back at me with eyes like polished ball bearings.

"You and your gangster buddies, you get it in your heads you're only blameless errand boys," Eli says, and his voice has become smooth and shiny as what the silver has made of his flesh. "You think ignorance is some kind of virtue, and none of the evil shit you do for your taskmasters is ever coming back to haunt you."

I don't argue with him, no matter whether Eli (or the sterling apparition standing where Eli stood a few moments before) is right or wrong or someplace in between. I could disagree, sure, but I don't. I'm reasonably fucking confident it no longer makes any difference. The towel falls to the floor, fluttering like a drogue parachute in a desert gale, and Eli steps out of the tub, spreading silver in his wake.

HYDRARGUROS

"Jason Statham stars in this near-future cybernoir thriller, soundtrack by Nick Cave and Warren Ellis, directed by..." Pretty much, yeah. And there's quite likely a nod to Kathe Koja in here that I was entirely unaware of until years after I'd written the story. To me, those are the best sorts of nods.

Houndwife

1.

Memory fails, moments bleeding one against and into the next or the one before, merging and diverging and commingling again farther along. Rain streaking glass, muddy rivers flowing to the sea, or blood on a slaughterhouse floor, wending its way towards a drain. There was a time, I am still reasonably certain, when all this might have been set forth as a mere *tale,* starting at some more or less arbitrary, but seemingly consequential, moment: the day I first met Isobel Endecott, the evening I boarded a train from Savannah to Boston, or the turning of frail yellowed pages in a black magician's grimoire and coming upon the graven image of a jade idol. But I am passed now so far out beyond the conveniences and conventions of chronology and narrative and gone down to some place so few (and so very many) women before me have ever gone. It cannot be a tale, any more than a crystal goblet dropped on a marble floor may ever again hold half an ounce of wine. I have been dropped, like that, from a great height, and I have shattered on a marble floor. I may not have been dropped. I may have only fallen, but that hardly seems to matter now. I may have been pushed, also. And, too, it might well be I was dropped, fell, *and* was pushed, none of these actions necessarily being mutually exclusive of the others. I am no different from the broken goblet, whose shards do not worry overly about how they came to be divided from some former whole.

Memory fails. I fall. Not one or the other, but both. I tumble through the vulgar, musty shadows of sepulchers. I lie in my own grave, dug by my own hands, and listen to hungry black beetles and maggots busy at my corporeal undoing. I am led to the altar on the dais in the sanctuary of the Church of Starry Wisdom, to be bedded and worshipped and bled dry. I look up from a hole in the earth and see the bloated moon. There is no ordering these events, no matter how I might try, if I even *cared* to try. They occurred, or I am yet rushing towards them. They are past and present and future, realized and unrealized and imagined and inconceivable; I would be a damned fool to worry over such trivialities. Better I be only damned.

"It was lost," Isobel tells me. "For a very long time it was lost. There were rumors it had gone to Holland, early in the Fifteenth Century, that it was buried there with one who'd worn it in life. Other stories say it was stolen from the grave of that man sometime in the 1920's and carried off to England."

I sip coffee while she talks.

"It's all bound up in irony and coincidence, and, really, I don't give that sort of prattle much credence," she continues. "The Dutchman who's said to have been buried with the idol, some claim he was a grave robber, that he fancied himself a proper ghoul. Charming fellow, sure, and then, five hundred years later, along come these two British degenerates – from somewhere in Yorkshire, I think. Supposedly, they dug him up and stole the idol, which they found hung around his neck."

"But before that…I mean, before the Dutchman, where might it have been?" I ask, and Isobel smiles. Her smile could melt ice, or freeze the blood, depending on one's perspective and penchant for hyperbole and metaphor. She shrugs and sets her coffee cup down on the kitchen table. We're sitting together in her loft on Atlantic Avenue. The building was constructed in the 1890's, as cold storage for the wares of fur merchants. The walls are thick and solid and keep our secrets. She lights a cigarette and watches me a moment.

My train is pulling into South Station; I've never visited Boston before, and I shall never leave. It's a rainy day, and I've been promised that Isobel will be waiting for me on the platform.

"Well, before Holland – assuming, of course, it was ever *in* Holland – I've spoken with a man who thinks it might have spent time in Greece, hidden at the Holy Trinity Monastry at Metéora, but the monastery wasn't built until 1475, so this really doesn't jibe with the story of the Dutch grave robber. Of course, the hound is mentioned in *Al Azif*. But you know that." And then the conversation shifts from the jade idol to archaeology in Damascus, and then Yemen, and, finally, the ruins of Babylon. In particular, I listen to Isobel describe the blue-glazed tiles of the Ishtar Gate, with their golden bas-reliefs of lions and auroch bulls and the strange, dragon-like *sirrush*. She saw a reconstructed portion of the gate at the Pergamon Museum when she was in Berlin, many years ago.

"In Germany, I was still a young woman," she says and glances at a window and the city lights, the Massachusetts night and the yellow-orange skyglow that's there so no one ever has to look too closely at the stars.

This is the night of the new moon, and Isobel kneels before me and bathes my feet. I'm naked save the jade idol on its silver chain, hung about my neck. The temple of the Starry Wisdom smells of frankincense, galbanum, sage, clove, myrrh, and saffron smoldering in iron braziers suspended from the high ceiling beams. Her ash-blonde hair is pulled back from her face, pinned into a neat chignon. Her robes are the color of raw meat. I don't want her to look me in the eyes, and yet I cannot imagine going up the granite stairs to the dais without first having done so, without that easy, familiar reassurance. Dark figures in robes of half a dozen other shades of red and black and grey press in close from all sides. The colors of their robes denote their rank. I close my eyes, though I have been forbidden to do so.

"This is our daughter," barks the High Priestess, the old one crouched near the base of the altar. Her voice is phlegm and stripped gears, discord and tumult. "Of her own will does she come, and of her own will and the will of the Nameless Gods will she make the passage."

And even in this instant – here at the end of my life *and* the beginning of my existence – I cannot help but smile at the High Priestess' choice of words, at force of habit, her calling them *the Nameless Gods,* when we have given them so very many names over the millennia.

"She will see what we cannot," the High Priestess barks. "She will walk unhindered where our feet will never tread. She will know their faces and their embrace. She will suffer fire and flood and the frozen wastes, and she will dine with the Mother and the Father. She will take a place at their table. She will know their blood, as they will know hers. She will fall and sleep, be raised and walk."

I am pulling into South Station.

I am drinking coffee with Isobel.

I am nineteen years old, dreaming of a Dutch churchyard and violated graves. My dream is filled with the rustle of leathery wings and the mournful baying of some great, unseen beast. I smell freshly broken earth. The sky glares down at all the world with a single cratered eye which humanity, in its merciful ignorance, would mistake for a full autumnal moon. There are two men with shovels and pick axes. Fascinated, I watch their grim, determined work, an unspeakable thievery done sixty-three years before my own birth. I hear the shovel scrape stone and wood.

In the temple, Isobel rises and kisses me. It's no more than the palest ghost of all the many kisses we've shared during our long nights of lovemaking, those afternoons and mornings spent exploring one another's bodies and desires and most taboo fancies.

The Hermit passes a jade cup to the Hierophant, who in turn passes it to Isobel. Though, in this place and in this hour, Isobel is *not* Isobel Endecott. She is the Empress, as I am here named the Wheel of Fortune. I have never seen this cup until now, but I know well enough that it was carved untold thousands of years before this night and from the same vein of leek-green *piedra de ijada* as the pendant I wear about my throat. The mad Arabian author of the *Al Azif* believed the jade to have come from the Plateau of Y'Pawfrm e'din Leng, and it may be he was correct. The Empress places the rim of the cup to my lips, and I drink. The bitter ecru tincture burns going down, and it kindles a fire in my chest and belly. I know this is the fire that will make ashes of me, and from those ashes will I rise as surely as any phoenix.

"She stands at the threshold," the High Priestess growls, "and soon will enter the Hall of the Mother and the Father." The crowd murmurs blessings and blasphemies. Isobel's delicate fingers caress my face, and I see the longing in her blue eyes, but the High Priestess may not kiss me again, not in this life.

"I will be waiting," she whispers.

My train leaves Savannah.

"Do you miss Georgia?" Isobel asks me, a week after I arrive in Boston, and I tell her yes, sometimes I do miss Georgia. "But it always passes," I say, and she smiles.

I am almost twenty years old, standing alone on a wide white beach where the tannin-stained Tybee River empties into the Atlantic Ocean, watching as a hurricane barrels towards shore. The outermost rain bands lash the sea, but haven't yet reached the beach. The sand around me is littered with dead fish and sharks, crabs and squid. On February 5th, 1958, a B-47 collided in midair with an F-86 Sabre fighter 7,200 feet above this very spot, and the crew of the B-47 was forced to jettison the Mark 15 hydrogen bomb it was carrying; the "Tybee bomb" was never recovered and lies buried somewhere in silt and mud below the brackish waters of Wassaw Sound, six or seven miles southwest of where I'm standing. I draw a line in the sand, connecting one moment to another, and the hurricane wails.

I am sixteen, and a high-school English teacher is telling me that if a gun appears at the beginning of a story, it should be fired by the end. If it's a bomb, the conscientious author should take care to be certain it explodes, so that the reader's expectations are not neglected. It all sounds very silly, and I cite several examples to the contrary. The English teacher scowls and changes the subject.

In the temple of the Church of Starry Wisdom, I walk through the flames consuming my soul and take my place on the altar.

2.

It's a sweltering day in late August 20__, and I walk from the green shade of Telfair Square, moving north along Barnard Street. I would try to describe here the violence of the alabaster sun on this afternoon, hanging so far above Savannah, but I know I'd never come close to capturing in words the sheer *spite* and *vehemence* of it. The sky is bleached as pallid as the cement sidewalk and the whitewashed bricks on either side of the street. I pass what was once a cotton and grain warehouse, when the New South was still the Old South, more than a century ago. The building has been "repurposed" for lofts and boutiques and a trendy soul-food restaurant. I walk, and the stillness of the summer afternoon makes my footsteps seem almost loud as thunderclaps. I can feel the dull beginnings of a headache and wish I had a Pepsi or an orange drink, something icy cold in a perspiring bottle. I glance through windows at the air-conditioned sanctuaries on the other side of the glass, but I don't stop and go inside.

The night before this day there were dreams I will never tell anyone until I meet Isobel Endecott, two years farther along. I had dreams of a Dutch graveyard, and of a baying hound, and awoke to find an address on West Broughton scribbled on the cover of a paperback book I'd been reading when I fell asleep. The handwriting was indisputably mine, though I have no memory of having picked up the ballpoint pen on my nightstand and writing the address. I did not get back to sleep until sometime after sunrise, and then there were only more dreams of that cemetery and the spire of a cathedral and the two men, busy with their picks and shovels.

I glance directly at the sun, daring it to blind me.

"You knew where to go," Isobel says, my first evening in Boston, my first evening with her, and already I felt as though I'd known her all my life. "The time was right, and you were chosen. I can't even imagine such an honor."

It is late August, and I sweat and walk north until I come to the intersection with West Broughton Street. I am clutching the paperback copy of *Absalom, Absalom!* in my left hand, and I pause to read the address again. Then I turn left, which also means I turn west.

"The stars were right," she says and pours me another brandy. "Which is really only another way of saying these events cannot occur until it is *time* for them to occur. That there is a proper sequence. A protocol."

I walk west down West Broughton until I come to the address that my sleeping self wrote on the Faulkner book. It's a shop (calling itself an "emporium") specializing in antique jewelry, porcelain figurines, and Oriental curios. Inside, after the scorching gaze of the sun, the dusty gloom seems almost frigid. I find what I did not even know I was looking for in a display case near the register. It is one of the most hideous things I've ever seen, and one of the most beautiful, too. I guess the stone is jade, but it's only a guess. I know next to nothing about gemstones and the lapidary arts. That day, I do not even know the word *lapidary*. I won't learn it until later, when I begin asking questions about the pendant.

There's a middle-aged man sitting on a stool behind the counter. He watches me through the lenses of his spectacles. He has about him a certain mincing fastidiousness. I notice the mole above his left eyebrow and that his clean nails are trimmed almost to the quick. I notice there's a hair growing from the mole. My mother always said I had an eye for detail.

"Anything I can show you today?" he wants to know, and I only *almost* hesitate before nodding and pointing to the jade pendant.

"Now, that is a very peculiar piece," he says, leaning forward and sliding the back of the case open. He reaches inside and lifts the pendant and its chain from a felt-lined tray. The felt is a faded shade of burgundy. He sits up again and passes the pendant across the counter to me. I'd not expected it to be so heavy or to feel so slick in my fingers, almost as though it were coated with oil or wax.

"Picked it up at an estate sale, a few years back," says the fastidious seller of antiques. "Never liked the thing myself, but different strokes, as they say. If I only stocked what I liked, wouldn't make much of a living, now would I?"

"No," I reply. "I don't suppose you would."

I stand alone on a beach at the south end of Tybee Island, watching the arrival of a hurricane. I've come to the beach to drown. However, I already know that's not what's going to happen, and the realization brings with it a faint pang of disappointment.

"Came from an old house down in Stephen's Ward," the man behind the counter says. "On East Hall Street, if memory serves. Strange bunch of women lived there, years ago, but then, one June, all of a sudden, the whole lot up and moved away. There were nine of them living in that house, and, well, you know how people talk."

"Yes," I say. "People talk."

"Might be better if we all tended to our own business and let others be," the man says and watches me as I examine the jade pendant. It looks a bit like a crouching dog, except for the wings, and it also puts me in mind of a sphinx. Its teeth are bared. Here, in my palm, carved from stone, is the countenance of every starving, tortured animal that has ever lived, and also the face of every madman, pure malevolence given form. I shiver, and the sensation is not entirely unpleasant. I realize that I am becoming aroused, that I am wet. There are letters from an alphabet I don't recognize inscribed about the base of the figurine, and a stylized skull has been etched into the bottom. The pendant is wholly repellent, and I know I cannot possibly leave the shop without it. It occurs to me that I might kill to own this thing.

"I think it would be," I tell him. "Be better if we all tended to our own business, I mean."

"Still, you can't change human nature," he says.

"No, you can't do that," I agree.

The train is pulling into South Station.

The hurricane bears down on Tybee Island.

And I'm only eleven and standing at a wrought-iron gate set into a brick wall, a wall that surrounds a decrepit mansion on East Hall Street. The wall is yellow, not because it has been painted yellow, but because all the bricks used in its construction have been glazed the color of goldenrods. They shimmer in the heat of a late May afternoon. On the other side of the gate is a woman named Maddy (which she says is short for Madeleine). Sometimes, like today, I walk past and find Maddy waiting, as though I'm expected. She never opens the gate; we only ever talk through the bars, there in the cool below the live oak branches and Spanish moss. Sometimes, she reads my fortune with a pack of Tarot cards. Other times, we talk about books. On this day, though, she's telling me about the woman who owns the house, whom she calls Aramat, a name I'm sure I've never heard before.

"Isn't that the mountain where the Bible says Noah's Ark landed after the flood?" I ask her.

"No, dear. That's Mount Ararat."

"Well, they *sound* very much alike, Ararat and Aramat," I say, and Maddy stares at me. I can tell she's thinking all sorts of things she's not going to say aloud, things I'm not meant to ever hear.

And then Maddy says, almost whispering, "Write her name backwards sometime. Very often, what seems unusual becomes perfectly ordinary, if we take care to look at it from another angle." She peers over her shoulder and tells me that she has to go and that I should be on my way.

I'm twenty-three, and this is the day I found the pendant in an antique shop on West Broughton Street. I ask the man behind the counter how much he wants for it, and after he tells me, I ask him if it's jade or if it only *looks* like jade.

"Seems like real jade to me," he replies, and I know from his expression that the question has offended him. "It's not glass or plastic, if that's what you mean. I don't sell costume jewelry, Miss. The chain, that's sterling silver. You want it, I'll take ten bucks off the price on the tag. Frankly, it gives me the creeps, and I'll be happy to be shed of it."

I pay him in twenty-five dollars, cash, and he puts the pendant into a small brown paper bag, and I go back out into the blazing sun.

I dream of a graveyard in Holland, and the October sky is filled with flittering bats. There is another sound, also of wings beating at the cold night air, but *that* sound is not being made by anything like a bat.

"This card," says Maddy, "is the High Priestess. She has many meanings, depending."

"Depending on what?" I want to know.

"Depending on many things," Maddy says and smiles. Her Tarot cards are spread out on the mossy paving stones on her side of the black iron gate. She taps at the High Priestess with an index finger. "In this instance, I'd suspect a future that has yet to be revealed, and duality, too, and also hidden influences at work in your life."

"I'm not sure what you *mean* by duality," I tell her, so she explains.

"The Empress, she sits there on her throne, with a pillar on either side. Some say, these are two pillars from the Temple of Solomon, king of the Israelites and a powerful mystic. And some say that the woman on the throne is Pope Joan."

"I never knew there was a woman pope," I say.

"There probably wasn't. It's just a legend from the Middle Ages." And then Maddy brushes a stray wisp of hair from her eyes before she goes back to explaining duality and the card's symbolism. "On the Empress' right hand is a dark pillar, which is called Boaz. It represents the negative life principle. On her left is a white pillar, Jakin, which represents the positive life principle. Positive and negative, that's duality, and because she sits here between them we know that the Empress represents balance."

Maddy turns over another card, the Wheel of Fortune, but it's upside down, reversed.

I am twenty-five years old, and Isobel Endecott is asleep in the bed we share in her loft on Atlantic Avenue. I lie awake, listening to her breathing and the myriad of noises from the street three stories below. It's four minutes after three a.m., and I briefly consider taking an Ambien. But I don't *want* to sleep. That's the truth of it. There's so little time left to me, and I'd rather not spend it in dreams. The night is fast approaching when the Starry Wisdom will meet on my behalf, because of what I've brought with me on that train from Savannah, and on that night I will slip this mortal coil (or be pushed, one or the other or both), and there'll be time enough for dreaming when I'm dead and in my grave, or during whatever's to come after my resurrection.

I find a pencil and a notepad. The latter has the name of the law firm that Isobel works for printed across the top of each page: Jackson, Monk, & Rowe, with an ampersand instead of "and" being written out. I don't bother to put on my robe. I go to the bathroom wearing only my panties and stand before the wide mirror above the sink and stare back at my reflection a few minutes. I've never thought of myself as pretty, and I still don't. Tonight, I look like someone who hasn't slept much in a while. My hazel eyes seem more green than brown, when it's usually the other way around. The tattoo between my breasts is beginning to heal, the ink worked into my skin by the thin, nervous man designated the Ace of Pentacles by the High Priestess of the Church of Starry Wisdom.

I write *Aramat* on the notepad, then hold it up to the mirror. I read it aloud, as it appears in the looking glass, and then I do the same with *Isobel Endecott,* speaking utter nonsense, my voice low so I won't wake Isobel. In the mirror, my jade amulet does its impossible trick, which I first noticed a few nights after I bought it from a fastidious man in a shop on West Broughton Street. The reflection of the letters carved around the base, beneath the claws of the winged dog-like beast, are precisely the same as when I look directly at them. The mirror does not reverse the image of the pendant. I have never yet found a mirror that will. I turn away from the sink, gazing into the darkness framed by the bathroom door.

I stand on a beach.

I sit on a sidewalk, eleven years old, and a woman named Maddy passes me the Wheel of Fortune between the bars of an iron gate.

3.

Memory fails, and my thoughts become an apparently disordered torrent. I'm a dead woman recalling the events of a life I have relinquished, a life I have repudiated. I sit in this chair at this desk and hold this pen in my hand because Isobel has asked it of me, not because I have any motivation of my own to speak of all the moments that have led me here. I'm helpless to deny her, so I didn't bother asking *why* she would have me write this. I did very nearly ask why she didn't request it *before,* when I was living and still bound by the beeline perception of time that marshals human recollection into more conventional recitals. But then an epiphany, or something like an epiphany, and I understood, without having asked. No linear account would ever satisfy the congregation of the Church of Starry Wisdom, for they seek more occult patterns, less intuitive paths, some alternate perception of the relationships between past and present, between one moment and the next (or, for that matter, one moment and the last). Cause and effect have not exactly been rejected, but have been found severely wanting.

"That *is* you," says Madeleine, passing me the Tarot card. "You *are* the Wheel of Fortune, an avatar of Tyche, the goddess of fate."

"I don't understand," I tell her, reluctantly accepting the card, taking it from her because I enjoy her company and don't wish to be rude.

"In time," she says, "it may make sense," then gathers her deck and hurries back inside that dilapidated house on East Hall Street, kept safe from the world behind its moldering yellow brick walls.

Burning, I lie down upon the cold granite altar. Soon, my lover, the Empress, climbs on top of me – straddling my hips – while the ragged High Priestess snarls her incantations, while the Major Arcana and the

Minor Arcana and all the members of the Four Suits (Pentacles, Cups, Swords, and Staves) chant mantras borrowed from the *Al Azif*.

The train rattles and sways and dips as it hurries me through Connecticut and then Rhode Island on my way to South Station. *Because I could not stop for Death, He kindly stopped for me…* The woman sitting next to me is reading a book by an author I've never heard of, and the man across the aisle is busy with his laptop.

I come awake to the dank embrace of the clayey soil that fills in my grave. It presses down on me, that astounding, unexpected weight, wishing to pin me forever to this spot. I am, after all, an abomination and an outlaw in the eyes of biology. I've cheated. The ferryman waits for a passenger who will never cross his river, or whose crossing has been delayed indefinitely. I lie here, not yet moving, marveling at every discomfort and at my collapsed lungs and the dirt filling my mouth and throat. I was not even permitted the luxury of a coffin.

"Caskets offend the Mother and the Father," said the High Priestess. "What use have they of an offering they cannot touch?"

I drift in a fog of pain and impenetrable night. I cannot open my sunken eyes. And even now, through this agony and confusion, I'm aware of the jade pendant's presence, icy against the tattoo on my chest.

I awaken in my bed, in my mother's house, a few nights after her funeral. I lie still, listening to my heartbeat and the settling noises that old houses make when they think no one will hear. I lie there, listening for the sound that reached into my dream of a Dutch churchyard and dragged me back to consciousness – the mournful baying of a monstrous hound.

On the altar, beneath those smoking braziers, the Empress has begun to clean the mud and filth and maggots from my body. The Priestess mutters caustic sorceries, invoking those nameless gods burdened with innumerable names. The congregation chants. I am delirious, lost in some fever that afflicts the risen, and I wonder if Lazarus knew it, or Osiris, or if it is suffered by Persephone every spring. I'm not certain if this is the night of my rebirth or the night of my death. Possibly, they are not even two distinct events, but only a single one, a serpent looping forever back upon itself, tail clasped tightly between venomous jaws. I struggle to speak, but my vocal cords haven't healed enough to permit more than the most incoherent, guttural croaking.

…I am Lazarus, come from the dead,
Come back to tell you all, I shall tell you all…

"Hush, hush," says the Empress, wiping earth and hungry larvae from my face. "The words *will* come, my darling. Be patient, and the words will come back to you. You didn't crawl into Hell and all the way up again to be struck mute. Hush." I know that Isobel Endecott is trying to console me, but I can also hear the fear and doubt and misgiving in her voice. "Hush," she says.

All around me, on the sand, are dead fish and crabs and the carcasses of gulls and pelicans.

It's summer in Savannah, and from the wide verandah of the house on East Hall Street, an older woman calls to Maddy, ordering her back inside. She leaves me holding that single card, *my* card, and I sit there on the sidewalk for another half hour, staring at it intently, trying to make sense of the card *and* what Maddy has told me. A blue sphinx squats atop the Wheel of Fortune, and below it there is the nude figure of a man with red skin and the head of a dog.

"You are *taking too long,*" snaps the High Priestess, and Isobel answers her in an angry burst of French. I cannot speak French, but I'm not so ignorant that I don't know it when I hear it spoken. I wonder dimly what Isobel has said, and I adore her for the outburst, for her brashness, for talking back. I begin to suspect something has gone wrong with the ritual, but the thought doesn't frighten me. Though I'm still more than half blind, my eyes still raw and rheumy, I strain desperately for a better view of Isobel. In all the wide world, at this instant, there is nothing I want but her and nothing else I can imagine needing.

This is a Saturday morning, and I'm a few weeks from my tenth birthday. I'm sitting in the swing on the back porch. My mother is just inside the screen door, in the kitchen, talking to someone on the telephone. I can hear her voice quite plainly. It's a warm day late in February, and the sky above our house is an immaculate and seemingly inviolable shade of blue. I've been daydreaming, woolgathering, staring up at that sky, past the sagging eaves of the porch, when I hear something and notice that there's a very large black dog only a few yards away from me. It's standing in the gravel alleyway that separates our tiny backyard from that of the next house over. I have no way of knowing how long the dog has been standing there. I watch it, and it watches me. The dog has bright amber eyes and isn't wearing a collar or tags. I've never before seen a dog smile, but *this* dog is smiling. After five minutes or so, it growls softly, then turns and trots away down the alley. I decide not to tell my mother about the smiling dog. She probably wouldn't believe me anyway.

"What was that you said to her?" I ask Isobel, several nights after my resurrection. We're sitting together on the floor of her loft on Atlantic, and there's a Beatles album playing on the turntable.

"What did I say to whom?" she wants to know.

"The High Priestess. You said something to her in French, while I was still on the altar. I'd forgotten about it until this morning. You sounded angry. I don't understand French, so I don't know what you said."

"It doesn't really matter what I said," she replies, glancing over the liner notes for *Hey Jude*. "It only matters that I said it. The old woman is a coward."

Somewhere in North Carolina, the rhythm of the train's wheels against the rails lulls me to sleep. I dream of a neglected Dutch graveyard and the amulet, of hurricanes and smiling black dogs. Maddy is also in my dreams, reading fortunes at a carnival. I can smell sawdust and cotton candy, horseshit and sweating bodies. Maddy sits on a milking stool inside a tent beneath a canvas banner emblazoned with the words *Lo! Behold! The Strikefire & Z. B. Harbinger Wonder Show!* in bold crimson letters fully five feet high.

She turns another card, the Wheel of Fortune.

I lie in my grave, fully cognizant but immobile, unable to summon the will or the physical strength to begin worming my way towards the surface, six feet overhead. I lie there, thinking of Maddy and the jade pendant. I lie there considering, in the mocking solitude of my burial place, what it does and does not mean that I've returned with absolutely no conscious knowledge of anything I may have experienced in death. Whatever secrets the Starry Wisdom sent me off to discover remain secrets. After all that has been risked and forfeited, I have no revelations to offer my fellow seekers. They'll ask their questions, and I'll have no answers. This should upset me, but it doesn't.

Now I can hear footsteps on the roof of my narrow house. Something is pacing heavily, back and forth, snuffling at the recently disturbed earth where I've been planted like a tulip bulb, like an acorn, like a seed that *will* unfold, but surely never sprout.

It goes about on four feet, I think, *not two.*

The hound bays.

I wonder, will it kindly dig me up, this restless visitor? And I wonder, too, about the rumors of the others who've worn the jade pendant before me, and the stories of their fates. Those two ghoulish Englishmen in 1922, for instance; they cross my reanimated mind. As does a passage from Francois-Honore Balfour's notorious grimoire, *Cultes des Goules,* and a few stray lines from the *Al Azif.* My bestial caller suddenly stops pacing and begins scratching at the soft dirt, urging me to move.

In the temple, as my lover takes my hand and I'm led towards the altar stone, through the fire devouring me from the inside out, the High Priestess of the Starry Wisdom reminds us all that only once in every thousand years does the hound choose a wife. Only once each millennium is any living woman accorded that privilege.

My train pulls into a depot somewhere in southern Rhode Island, grumbling to a slow stop, and my dreams are interrupted by other passengers bustling about around me, retrieving their bags and briefcases, talking too loudly. Or I'm jarred awake by the simple fact that the train is no longer moving.

After sex, I lie in bed with Isobel, and the only light comes from the television set mounted on the wall across the room. The sound is turned down, so the black-and-white world trapped inside that box exists in perfect grainy silence. I'm trying to tell her about the pacing thing from the night I awoke. I'm trying to describe the snuffling noises and the way it worried at the ground with its sharp claws. But she only scowls and shakes her head dismissively.

"No," she insists. "The hound is nothing but a metaphor. We weren't meant to take it literally. Whatever you heard that night, you imagined it, that's all. You heard what some part of you expected, and maybe even needed, to hear. But the hound, it's a superstition, and we're not superstitious people."

"Isobel, I fucking *died,*" I say, trying not to laugh, gazing across her belly towards the television. "And I came *back* from the dead. I tunneled out of my grave with my bare hands and then, blind, found my way to the temple alone. My flesh was already rotting, and now it's good as new. Those things actually happened, to *me,* and you don't *doubt* that they happened. You practice necromancy, but you want me to think I'm being superstitious if I believe that the hound is real?"

She's quiet for a long moment. Finally, she says, "I worry about you, that's all. You're so very precious to me, to all of us, and you've been through so much already." And she closes her hand tightly around the amulet still draped about my neck.

On a sweltering August day in Savannah, a fastidious man who sells antique jewelry and Chinese porcelain makes no attempt whatsoever to hide his relief when I tell him I've decided to buy the jade pendant. As he rings up the sale, he asks me if I'm a good Christian girl. He talks about Calvary and the Pentecost, then admits he'll be glad to have the pendant out of his shop.

I stand on a beach.

I board a train.

Maddy turns another card.

And on the altar of the Church of Starry Wisdom, I draw a deep, hitching breath. I smell incense burning and hear the lilting voices of all those assembled for my homecoming. My heart is a sledgehammer battering at my chest, and I would scream, but I can't even speak. Isobel Endecott is straddling me, and her right hand goes to my vagina. With her fingers, she scoops out the slimy plug of soil and minute branches of fungal hyphae that has filled my sex during the week and a half I've spent below. When the pad of her thumb brushes my clit every shadow and shape half glimpsed by my wounded eyes seems to glow, as if my lust is contagious, as though light and darkness have become sympathetic. I lunge for her, my jaws snapping like the jaws of any starving creature; there are tears in her eyes as I'm restrained by the Sun and the Moon. The Hanged Man dutifully places a leather strap between my teeth.

Madness rides on the star-wind…

"Hush," Isobel whispers. "Hush, hush," whispers the Empress. "It'll pass."

It's the day I leave Savannah for the last time. In the bedroom of the house where I grew up, I pack the few things that still hold meaning for me. These include a photo album, and tucked inside the album is the Tarot card that the woman named Madeleine gave me.

4.

Isobel is watching me from the other side of the dining room. She's been watching, while I write, for the better part of an hour. She asks, "How does it end? Do you even know?"

"Maybe it doesn't end," I reply. "I half think it's hardly even started."

"Then how will you know when to stop?" she asks. There's dread wedged in between every word she speaks, between every syllable.

"I don't think I will," I say, this thought occurring to me for the first time. She nods, then stands and leaves the room, and when she's gone, I'm glad. I can't deny that there is a certain solace in her absence. I've been trying not too look too closely at Isobel's eyes. I don't like what I see there anymore.

HOUNDWIFE

I should hope that not even the most die-hard admirer of H. P. Lovecraft's work would dare argue that "The Hound" (1922) is a well-written story. And yet I love it. Despite all it's garish purple-prose histrionics, the story pushes my buttons. So, it was probably inevitable that I would someday write a tribute to this minor Lovecraft tale, and in March 2010 that's exactly what I did. Also, there really is a Mark 15 hydrogen bomb slumbering beneath the waters of Wassaw Sound. That part isn't fiction.

The Maltese Unicorn

New York City (May 1935)

It wasn't hard to find her. Sure, she had run. After Szabó let her walk like that, I knew Ellen would get wise that something was rotten, and she'd run like a scared rabbit with the dogs hot on its heels. She'd have it in her head to skip town, and she'd probably keep right on skipping until she was out of the country. Odds were pretty good she wouldn't stop until she was altogether free and clear of this particular plane of existence. There are plenty enough fetid little hidey-holes in the universe, if you don't mind the heat and the smell and the company you keep. You only have to know how to find them, and the way I saw it, Ellen Andrews was good as Rand and McNally when it came to knowing her way around.

But first, she'd go back to that apartment of hers, the whole eleventh floor of the Colosseum, with its bleak westward view of the Hudson River and the New Jersey Palisades. I figured there would be those two or three little things she couldn't bear to leave the city without, even if it meant risking her skin to collect them. Only she hadn't expected me to get there before her. Word on the street was Harpootlian still had me locked up tight, so Ellen hadn't expected me to get there at all.

From the hall came the buzz of the elevator, then I heard her key in the lock, the front door, and her footsteps as she hurried through the foyer and the dining room. Then she came dashing into that French Rococo nightmare of a library and stopped cold in her tracks when she saw me sitting at the reading table with al-Jaldaki's grimoire open in front of me.

For a second, she didn't say anything. She just stood there, staring at me. Then she managed a forced sort of laugh and said, "I knew they'd send someone, Nat. I just didn't think it'd be you."

"After that gip you pulled with the dingus, they didn't really leave me much choice," I told her, which was the truth, or at least all the truth I felt like sharing. "You shouldn't have come back here. It's the first place anyone would think to check."

Ellen sat down in the arm chair by the door. She looked beat, like whatever comes after exhausted, and I could tell Szabó's gunsels had made sure all the fight was gone before they'd turned her loose. They weren't taking any chances, and we were just going through the motions now, me and her. All our lines had been written.

"You played me for a sucker," I said and picked up the pistol that had been lying beside the grimoire. My hand was shaking, and I tried to steady it by bracing my elbow against the table. "You played me, then you tried to play Harpootlian and Szabó both. Then you got caught. It was a bonehead move all the way round, Ellen."

"So, how's it gonna be, Natalie? You gonna shoot me for being stupid?"

"No, I'm going shoot you because it's the only way I can square things with Auntie H and the only thing that's gonna keep Szabó from going on the warpath. *And* because you played me."

"In my shoes, you'd have done the same thing," she said. And the way she said it, I could tell she believed what she was saying. It's the sort of self-righteous bushwa so many grifters hide behind. They might stab their own mothers in the back if they see an angle in it, but, you ask them, that's jake, cause so would anyone else.

"Is that really all you have to say for yourself?" I asked and pulled back the slide on the Colt, chambering the first round. She didn't even flinch…but, wait…I'm getting ahead of myself. Maybe I ought to begin nearer the beginning.

As it happens, I didn't go and name the place Yellow Dragon Books. It came with that moniker, and I just never saw any reason to change it. I'd only have had to pay for a new sign. Late in '28 – right after Arnie "The Brain" Rothstein was shot to death during a poker game at the Park Central Hotel – I accidentally found myself on the sunny side of the proprietress of one of Manhattan's more infernal brothels. I say *accidentally* because I hadn't even heard of Madam Yeksabet Harpootlian when I began trying to dig up a buyer for an antique manuscript, a collection of necromantic erotica purportedly written by John Dee and Edward Kelley sometime in the Sixteenth Century. Turns out, Harpootlian had been looking to get her mitts on it for decades.

Now, just how I came into possession of said manuscript, that's another story entirely, one for some other time and place. One that, with luck, I'll never get around to putting down on paper. Let's just say a couple of years earlier. I'd been living in Paris. Truthfully, I'd been doing my best, in a sloppy, irresolute way, to *die* in Paris. I was holed up in a fleabag Montmartre boarding house, busy squandering the last of a dwindling inheritance. I had in mind how maybe I could drown myself in cheap wine, bad poetry, Pernod, and prostitutes before the money ran out. But somewhere along the way, I lost my nerve, failed at my slow suicide, and bought a ticket back to the States. And the manuscript in question was one of the many strange and unsavory things I brought back with me. I'd always had a nose for the macabre and had dabbled – on and off – in the black arts since college. At Radcliffe, I'd fallen in with a circle of lesbyterians who fancied themselves witches. Mostly, I was in it for the sex...but I'm digressing.

A friend of a friend heard I was busted, down and out and peddling a bunch of old books, schlepping them about Manhattan in search of a buyer. This same friend, he knew one of Harpootlian's clients. One of her *human* clients, which was a pretty exclusive set (not that I knew that at the time). This friend of mine, he was the client's lover, and said client brokered the sale for Harpootlian – for a fat ten-percent finder's fee, of course. I promptly sold the Dee and Kelly manuscript to this supposedly notorious madam whom, near as I could tell, no one much had ever heard of. She paid me what I asked, no questions, no haggling, never mind it was a fairly exorbitant sum. And on top of that, Harpootlian was so impressed I'd gotten ahold of the damned thing, she staked me to the bookshop on Bowery, there in the shadow of the Third Avenue El, just a little ways south of Delancey Street. Only one catch: she had first dibs on everything I ferreted out, and sometimes I'd be asked to make deliveries. I should like to note that way back then, during that long-lost November of 1928, I had no idea whatsoever that her sobriquet, "the Demon Madam of the Lower East Side," was anything more than colorful hyperbole.

Anyway, jump ahead to a rainy May afternoon, more than six years later, and that's when I first laid eyes on Ellen Andrews. Well, that's what she called herself, though later on I'd find out she'd borrowed the name from Claudette Colbert's character in *It Happened One Night*. I was just back from an estate sale in Connecticut and was busy unpacking a large crate when I heard the bell mounted above the shop door jingle. I looked up, and there she was, carelessly shaking rainwater from her orange umbrella before folding it closed. Droplets sprayed across the welcome mat and the floor and onto the spines of several nearby books.

"Hey, be careful," I said, "unless you intend to pay for those." I jabbed a thumb at the books she'd spattered. She promptly stopped shaking the umbrella and dropped it into the stand beside the door. That umbrella stand has always been one of my favorite things about the Yellow Dragon. It's made from the taxidermied foot of a hippopotamus and accommodates at least a dozen umbrellas, although I don't think I've ever seen even half that many people in the shop at one time.

"Are you Natalie Beaumont?" she asked, looking down at her wet shoes. Her overcoat was dripping, and a small puddle was forming about her feet.

"Usually."

"Usually," she repeated. "How about right now?"

"Depends whether or not I owe you money," I replied and removed a battered copy of Blavatsky's *Isis Unveiled* from the crate. "Also, depends whether you happen to be *employed* by someone I owe money."

"I see," she said, as if that settled the matter, then proceeded to examine the complete twelve-volume set of *The Golden Bough* occupying a top shelf not far from the door. "Awful funny sort of neighborhood for a bookstore, if you ask me."

"You don't think bums and winos read?"

"You ask me, people down here," she said, "they panhandle a few cents, I don't imagine they spend it on books."

"I don't recall asking for your opinion" I told her.

"No," she said. "You didn't. Still, queer sort of a shop to come across in this part of town."

"If you must know," I said, "the rent's cheap," then reached for my spectacles, which were dangling from their silver chain about my neck. I set them on the bridge of my nose and watched while she feigned interest in Frazerian anthropology. It would be an understatement to say Ellen Andrews was a pretty girl. She was, in fact, a certified knockout, and I didn't get too many beautiful women in the Yellow

Dragon, even when the weather was good. She wouldn't have looked out of place in Flo Ziegfeld's follies; on the Bowery, she stuck out like a sore thumb.

"Looking for anything in particular?" I asked her, and she shrugged.

"Just you," she said.

"Then I suppose you're in luck."

"I suppose I am," she said and turned towards me again. Her eyes glinted red, just for an instant, like the eyes of a Siamese cat. I figured it for a trick of the light. "I'm a friend of Auntie H. I run errands for her, now and then. She needs you to pick up a package and see it gets safely where its going."

So, there it was. Madam Harpootlian, or Auntie H to those few unfortunates she called her friends. And suddenly it made a lot more sense, this choice bit of calico walking into my place, strolling in off the street like maybe she did all her shopping down on Skid Row. I'd have to finish unpacking the crate later. I stood up and dusted my hands off on the seat of my slacks.

"Sorry about the confusion," I said, even if I wasn't actually sorry, even if I was actually kind of pissed the girl hadn't told me who she was right up front. "When Auntie H wants something done she doesn't usually bother sending her orders around in such an attractive envelope."

The girl laughed, then said, "Yeah, she warned me about you, Miss Beaumont."

"Did she now. How so?"

"You know, your predilections. How you're not like other women."

"I'd say that depends on which other women we're discussing, don't you think?"

"*Most* other women," she said, glancing over her shoulder at the rain pelting the shop windows. It sounded like frying meat out there, the sizzle of the rain against asphalt and concrete and the roofs of passing automobiles.

"And what about you?" I asked her. "Are *you* like most other women?"

She looked away from the window, looking back at me, and she smiled what must have been the faintest smile possible.

"Are you always this charming?"

"Not that I'm aware of," I said. "Then again, I never took a poll."

"The job, it's nothing particularly complicated," she said, changing the subject. "There's a Chinese apothecary not too far from here."

"That doesn't exactly narrow it down," I said and lit a cigarette.

"65 Mott Street. The joint's run by an elderly Cantonese fellow name of Fong."

"Yeah, I know Jimmy Fong."

"That's good. Then maybe you won't get lost. Mr. Fong will be expecting you, and he'll have the package ready at five-thirty this evening. He's already been paid in full, so all you have to do is be there to receive it, right? And Miss Beaumont, please try to be on time. Auntie H said you have a problem with punctuality."

"You believe everything you hear?"

"Only if I'm hearing it from Auntie H."

"Fair enough," I told her, then offered her a Pall Mall, but she declined.

"I need to be getting back," she said, reaching for the umbrella she'd only just deposited in the stuffed hippopotamus foot.

"What's the rush? What'd you come after, anyway, a ball of fire?"

She rolled her eyes. "I got places to be. You're not the only stop on my itinerary."

"Fine. Wouldn't want you getting in dutch with Harpootlian on my account. Don't suppose you've got a name?"

"I might," she said.

"Don't suppose you'd share?" I asked her, and I took a long drag on my cigarette, wondering why in blue blazes Harpootlian had sent this smart-mouthed skirt instead of one of her usual flunkies. Of course, Auntie H always did have a sadistic streak to put de Sade to shame, and likely as not this was her idea of a joke.

"Ellen," the girl said. "Ellen Andrews."

"So, Ellen Andrews, how is it we've never met? I mean, I've been making deliveries for your boss lady now going on seven years, and if I'd seen you, I'd remember. You're not the sort I forget."

"You got the moxie, don't you?"

"I'm just good with faces is all."

She chewed at a thumbnail, as if considering carefully what she should or shouldn't divulge. Then she said, "I'm from out of town, mostly. Just passing through and thought I'd lend a hand. That's why you've never seen me before, Miss Beaumont. Now, I'll let you get back to work. And remember, don't be late."

"I heard you the first time, sister."

And then she left, and the brass bell above the door jingled again. I finished my cigarette and went back to unpacking the big crate of books from Connecticut. If I hurried, I could finish the job before heading for Chinatown.

She was right, of course. I did have a well-deserved reputation for not being on time. But I knew that Auntie H was of the opinion that my acumen in antiquarian and occult matters more than compensated for my not infrequent tardiness. I've never much cared for personal mottos, but maybe if I had one it might be, *You want it on time, or you want it done right?* Still, I honestly tried to be on time for the meeting with Fong. And still, through no fault of my own, I was more than twenty minutes late. I was lucky enough to find a cab, despite the rain, but then got stuck behind some sort of brouhaha after turning onto Canal, so there you go. It's not like the old man Fong had any place more pressing to be, not like he was gonna get pissy and leave me high and dry.

When I got to 65 Mott, the Chinaman's apothecary was locked up tight, all the lights were off, and the "Sorry, We're Closed" sign was hung in the front window. No big surprise there. But then I went around back, to the alley, and found a door standing wide open and quite a lot of fresh blood on the cinderblock steps leading into the building. Now, maybe I was the only lady bookseller in Manhattan who carried a gun, and maybe I wasn't. But times like that, I was glad to have the Colt tucked snugly inside its shoulder holster and happier still that I knew how to use it. I took a deep breath, drew the pistol, flipped off the safety catch, and stepped inside.

The door opened onto a stockroom, and the tiny nook Jimmy Fong used as his office was a little farther in, over on my left. There was some light from a banker's lamp, but not much of it. I lingered in the shadows a moment, waiting for my heart to stop pounding, for the adrenaline high to fade. The air was close and stunk of angelica root and dust, ginger and frankincense and fuck only knows what else. Powdered rhino horn and the pickled gallbladders of panda bears. What the hell ever. I found the old man slumped over at his desk.

Whoever knifed him hadn't bothered to pull the shiv out of his spine, and I wondered if the poor s.o.b. had even seen it coming. It didn't exactly add up, not after seeing all that blood back on the steps, but I figured, hey, maybe the killer was the sort of klutz can't spread butter without cutting himself. I had a quick look-see around the cluttered office, hoping I might turn up the package Ellen Andrews had sent me there to retrieve. But no dice, and then it occurred to me, maybe whoever had murdered Fong had come looking for the same thing I was looking for. Maybe they'd found it, too, only Fong knew better than to just hand it over, and that had gotten him killed. Anyway, nobody was paying me to play junior shamus, hence the hows, whys, and wherefores of the Chinaman's death were not my problem. *My* problem would be showing up at Harpootlian's cathouse empty-handed.

I returned the gun to its holster, then I started rifling through everything in sight – the great disarray of papers heaped upon the desk, Fong's accounting ledgers, sales invoices, catalogs, letters and postcards written in English, Mandarin, Wu, Cantonese, French, Spanish, and Arabic. I still had my gloves on, so it's not like I had to worry over fingerprints. A few of the desk drawers were unlocked, and I'd just started in on those, when the phone perched atop the filing cabinet rang. I froze, whatever I was looking at clutched forgotten in my hands, and stared at the phone.

Sure, it wasn't every day I blundered into the immediate aftermath of this sort of foul play, but I was plenty savvy enough I knew better than to answer that call. It didn't much matter who was on the other end of the line. If I answered, I could be placed at the scene of a murder only minutes after it had gone down. The phone rang a second time, and a third, and I glanced at the dead man in the chair. The crimson halo surrounding the switchblade's inlaid mother-of-pearl handle was still spreading, blossoming like some grim rose, and now there was blood dripping to the floor, as well. The phone rang a fourth time. A fifth. And then I was seized by an overwhelming compulsion to answer it, and answer it I did. I wasn't the least bit thrown that the voice coming through the receiver was Ellen Andrews'. All at once, the pieces were falling into place. You spend enough years doing the stepin fetchit routine for imps like Harpootlian, you find yourself ever more jaded at the inexplicable and the uncanny.

"Beaumont," she said, "I didn't think you were going to pick up."

"I wasn't. Funny thing how I did anyway."

"Funny thing," she said, and I heard her light a cigarette and realized my hands were shaking.

"See, I'm thinking maybe I had a little push," I said. "That about the size of it?"

"Wouldn't have been necessary if you'd have just answered the damn phone in the first place."

"You already know Fong's dead, don't you?" And, I swear to fuck, nothing makes me feel like more of a jackass than asking questions I know the answers to.

"Don't you worry about Fong. I'm sure he had all his ducks in a row and was right as rain with Buddha. I need you to pay attention – "

"Harpootlian had him killed, didn't she? And you *knew* he'd be dead when I showed up." She didn't reply straight away, and I thought I could hear a radio playing in the background. "You knew," I said again, only this time it wasn't a query.

"Listen," she said. "You're a courier. I was told you're a courier we can trust, elsewise I never would have handed you this job."

"You didn't hand me the job. Your boss did."

"You're splitting hairs, Miss Beaumont."

"Yeah, well, there's a fucking dead celestial in the room with me. It's giving me the fidgets."

"So, how about you shut up and listen, and I'll have you out of there in a jiffy." And that's what I did, I shut up, either because I knew it was the path of least resistance or because whatever spell she'd used to persuade me to answer the phone was still working.

"On Fong's desk there's a funny little porcelain statue of a cat."

"You mean the Maneki Neko?"

"If that's what it's called, that's what I mean. Now, break it open. There's a key inside."

I *tried* not to, just to see if I was being played as badly as I suspected I was being played. I gritted my teeth, dug in my heels, and tried *hard* not to break that damned cat.

"You're wasting time. Auntie H didn't mention you were such a crybaby."

"Auntie H and I have an agreement when it comes to free will. To *my* free will."

"*Break the goddamn cat,*" Ellen Andrews growled, and that's exactly what I did. In fact, I slammed it down directly on top of Fong's head. Bits of brightly painted porcelain flew everywhere, and a rusty barrel key tumbled out and landed at my feet. "Now pick it up," she said. "The key fits the bottom left-hand drawer of Fong's desk. Open it."

This time, I didn't even try to resist her. I was getting a headache from the last futile attempt. I unlocked the drawer and pulled it open. Inside, there was nothing but the yellowed sheet of newspaper lining the drawer, three golf balls, a couple of old racing forms, and a finely carved wooden box lacquered almost the same shade of red as Jimmy Fong's blood. I didn't need to be told I'd been sent to retrieve the box – or, more specifically, whatever was *inside* the box.

"Yeah, I got it," I told Ellen Andrews.

"Good girl. Now, you have maybe twelve minutes before the cops show. Go out the same way you came in." Then she gave me a Riverside Drive address and said there'd be a car waiting for me at the corner of Canal and Mulberry, a green Chevrolet coupe. "Just give the driver that address. He'll see you get where you're going."

"Yeah," I said, sliding the desk drawer shut again and locking it. I pocketed the key. "But sister, you and me are gonna have a talk."

"Wouldn't miss it for the world, Nat," she said and hung up. I shut my eyes, wondering if I really had twelve minutes before the bulls arrived, and if they were even on their way, wondering what would happen if I endeavored *not* to make the rendezvous with the green coupe. I stood there, trying to decide whether Harpootlian would have gone back on her word and given this bitch permission to turn her hoodoo tricks on me, and if aspirin would do anything at all for the dull throb behind my eyes. Then I looked at Fong one last time, at the knife jutting out of his back, his thin grey hair powdered with porcelain dust from the shattered "Lucky Cat." And then I stopped asking questions and did as I'd been told.

The car was there, just like she'd told me it would be. There was a young colored man behind the wheel, and when I climbed in the back, he asked me where we were headed.

"I'm guessing Hell," I said, "sooner or later."

"Got that right," he laughed and winked at me from the rearview mirror. "But I was thinking more in terms of the immediate here and now."

So I recited the address I'd been given over the phone, 435 Riverside.

"That's the Colosseum," he said.

"It is if you say so," I replied. "Just get me there."

The driver nodded and pulled away from the curb. As he navigated the slick, wet streets, I sat listening to the rain against the Chevy's hard top and the music coming from the Motorola. In particular, I can remember hearing the Dorsey Brothers' "Chasing Shadows." I suppose you'd call that a harbinger, if you go in for that sort of thing. Me, I do my best not to. In this business, you start jumping at everything that *might* be an omen or a portent, you end up doing nothing else.

Ironically, rubbing shoulders with the supernatural has made me a great believer in coincidence.

Anyway, the driver drove, the radio played, and I sat staring at the red lacquered box I'd stolen from a dead man's locked desk drawer. I thought it might be mahogany, but it was impossible to be sure, what with all that cinnabar-tinted varnish. I know enough about Chinese mythology that I recognized the strange creature carved into the top. It was a *qilin*, a stout, antlered beast with cloven hooves, the scales of a dragon, and a long leonine tail. Much of its body was wreathed in flame, and its gaping jaws revealed teeth like daggers. For the Chinese, the *qilin* is a harbinger of good fortune, though it certainly hadn't worked out that way for Jimmy Fong. The box was heavier than it looked, most likely because of whatever was stashed inside. There was no latch, and as I examined it more closely, I realized there was no sign whatsoever of hinges or even a seam to indicate it actually had a lid.

"Unless I got it backwards," the driver said, "Miss Andrews didn't say nothing about trying to open that box, now did she?"

I looked up, startled, feeling like the proverbial kid caught with her hand in the cookie jar. He glanced at me in the mirror, then his eyes drifted back to the road.

"She didn't say one way or the other," I told him.

"Then how about we err on the side of caution?"

"So you didn't know where you're taking me, but you know I shouldn't open this box? How's that work?"

"Ain't the world just full of mysteries," he said.

For a minute or so, I silently watched the headlights of the oncoming traffic and the metronomic sweep of the windshield wipers. Then I asked the driver how long he'd worked for Ellen Andrews.

"Not very," he said. "Never laid eyes on the lady before this afternoon. Why you want to know?"

"No particular reason," I said, looking back down at the box and the *qilin* etched in the wood. I decided I was better off not asking any more questions, better off getting this over and done with, and never mind what did and didn't quite add up. "Just trying to make conversation, that's all."

Which got him to talking about the Chicago stockyards and Cleveland and how it was he'd eventually wound up in New York City. He never told me his name, and I didn't ask. The trip uptown seemed to take forever, and the longer I sat with that box in my lap, the heavier it felt. I finally moved it, putting it down on the seat beside me. By the time we reached our destination, the rain had stopped and the setting sun was showing through the clouds, glittering off the dripping trees in Riverside Park and the waters of the wide grey Hudson. He pulled over, and I reached for my wallet.

"No ma'am," he said, shaking his head. "Miss Andrews, she's already seen to your fare."

"Then I hope you won't mind if I see to your tip," I said, and I gave him five dollars. He thanked me, and I took the wooden box and stepped out onto the wet sidewalk.

"She's up on the eleventh," he told me, nodding towards the apartments. Then he drove off, and I turned to face the imposing curved brick and limestone façade of the building the driver had called the Colosseum. I rarely find myself any farther north than the Upper West Side, so this was pretty much *terra incognita* for me.

The doorman gave me directions, *after* giving both me and Fong's box the hairy eyeball, and I quickly made my way to the elevators, hurrying through that ritzy marble sepulcher passing itself off as a lobby. When the operator asked which floor I needed, I told him the eleventh, and he shook his head and muttered something under his breath. I almost asked him to speak up, but thought better of it. Didn't I already have plenty enough on my mind without entertaining the opinions of elevator boys? Sure, I did. I had a murdered Chinaman, a mysterious box, and this pushy little sorceress calling herself Ellen Andrews. I also had an especially disagreeable feeling about this job, and the sooner it was settled, the better. I kept my eyes on the brass needle as it haltingly swung from left to right, counting off the floors, and when the doors parted she was there waiting for me. She slipped the boy a sawbuck, and he stuffed it into his jacket pocket and left us alone.

"So nice to see you again, Nat," she said, but she was looking at the lacquered box, not me. "Would you like to come in and have a drink? Auntie H says you have a weakness for rye whiskey."

"Well, she's right about that. But, just now, I'd be more fond of an explanation."

"How odd," she said, glancing up at me, still smiling. "Auntie said one thing she liked about you was how you didn't ask a lot of questions. Said you were real good at minding your own business."

"Sometimes I make exceptions."

"Let me get you that drink," she said, and I followed her the short distance from the elevator to the door of her apartment. Turns out, she had the whole floor to herself, each level of the Colosseum being a single apartment. Pretty ritzy accommodations, I thought, for someone who was *mostly* from out of town. But then I'd spent the last few years living in that one-bedroom cracker box above the Yellow Dragon, hot and cold running cockroaches and so forth. She locked the door behind us, then led me through the foyer to a parlor. The whole place was done up gaudy period French, Louis Quinze and the like, all floral brocade and Orientalia. The walls were decorated with damask hangings, mostly of ample-bosomed women reclining in pastoral scenes, dogs and sheep and what have you lying at their feet. Ellen told me to have a seat, so I parked myself on a récamier near a window.

"Harpootlian spring for this place?" I asked.

"No," she replied. "It belonged to my mother."

"So you come from money."

"Did I mention how you ask an awful lot of questions?"

"You might have," I said, and she inquired as to whether I liked my whiskey neat or on the rocks. I told her neat, and I set the red box down on the sofa next to me.

"If you're not *too* thirsty, would you mind if I take a peek at that first?" she asked, pointing at the box.

"Be my guest," I said, and Ellen smiled again. She picked up the red lacquered box, then sat next to me. She cradled it in her lap, and there was this goofy expression on her face, a mix of awe, dread, and eager expectation.

"Must be something extra damn special," I said, and she laughed. It was a nervous kind of a laugh.

I've already mentioned how I couldn't discern any evidence the box had a lid, and I'd supposed there was some secret to getting it open, a gentle squeeze or nudge in just the right spot. Turns out, all it needed was someone to say the magic words.

"*Pain had no sting, and pleasure's wreath no flower,*" she said, speaking slowly and all but whispering the words. There was a sharp *click* and the top of the box suddenly slid back with enough force that it tumbled over her knees and fell to the carpet.

"Keats," I said.

"Keats," she echoed, but added nothing more. She was too busy gazing at what lay inside the box, nestled in a bed of velvet the color of poppies. She started to touch it, then hesitated, her fingertips hovering an inch or so above the object.

"You're fucking kidding me," I said, once I saw what was inside.

"Don't go jumping to conclusions, Nat."

"It's a dildo," I said, probably sounding as incredulous as I felt. "Exactly which conclusions am I not supposed to jump to? Sure, I enjoy a good rub-off as much as the next girl, but...you're telling me Harpootlian killed Fong over a dildo?"

"I never said Auntie H killed Fong."

"Then I suppose he stuck that knife there himself."

And that's when she told me to shut the hell up for five minutes, if I knew how. She reached into the box and lifted out the phallus, handling it as gingerly as somebody might handle a sweaty stick of dynamite. But whatever made the thing special, it wasn't anything I could see.

"*Le godemichet maudit,*" she murmured, her voice so filled with reverence you'd have thought she was holding the devil's own wang. Near as I could tell, it was cast from some sort of hard black ceramic. It glistened faintly in the light getting in through the drapes. "I'll tell you about it," she said, "if you really want to know. I don't see the harm."

"Just so long as you get to the part where it makes sense that Harpootlian bumped the Chinaman for this dingus of yours, then sure."

She took her eyes off the thing long enough to scowl at me. "Auntie H didn't kill Fong. One of Szabó's goons did that, then panicked and ran before he figured out where the box was hidden."

(Now, as for Madam Magdalena Szabó, the biggest boil on Auntie H's fanny, we'll get back to her by and by.)

"Ellen, how can you *possibly* fucking know that? Better yet, how could you've known Szabó's man would have given up and cleared out by the time I arrived?"

"Why did you answer that phone, Nat?" she asked, and that shut me up, good and proper. "As for our prize here," she continued, "it's a long story, a long story with a lot of missing pieces. The dingus, as you put it, is usually called *le godemichet maudit.* Which doesn't necessarily mean it's actually cursed, mind you. Not literally. You *do* speak French, I assume?"

"Yeah," I said. "I do speak French."

"That's ducky, Nat. Now, here's about as much as anyone could tell you. Though, frankly, I'd have thought a scholarly type like yourself would know all about it."

"Never said I was a scholar," I interrupted.

"But you went to college. Radcliffe, Class of 1923, right? Graduated with honors."

"Lots of people go to college. Doesn't necessarily make them scholars. I just sell books."

"My mistake," she said, carefully returning the black dildo to its velvet case. "It won't happen again." Then she told me her tale, and I sat there on the récamier and listened to what she had to say. Yeah, it was long. There *were* certainly a whole lot of missing pieces. And as a wise man once said, this might not be schoolbook history, not Mr. Wells' history, but, near as I've been able to discover since that evening at her apartment, it's history, nevertheless. She asked me whether or not I'd ever heard of a Fourteenth-Century Persian alchemist named al-Jaldaki, Izz al-Din Aydamir al-Jaldaki, and I had, naturally.

"Well, he's sort of a hobby of mine," she said. "Came across his grimoire a few years back. Anyway, he's not where it begins, but that's where the written record starts. While studying in Anatolia, al-Jaldaki heard tales of a fabulous artifact that had been crafted from the horn of a unicorn at the behest of King Solomon."

"From a unicorn," I cut in. "So we believe in those now, do we?"

"Why not, Nat? I think it's safe to assume you've seen some peculiar shit in your time. That you've pierced the veil, so to speak. Surely a unicorn must be small potatoes for a worldly woman like yourself."

"So you'd think," I said.

"Anyhow," she went on, "the ivory horn was carved into the shape of a penis by the king's most skilled artisans. Supposedly, the result was so revered it was even placed in Solomon's temple, alongside the Ark of the Covenant and a slew of other sacred Hebrew relics. Records al-Jaldaki found in a mosque in the Taurus Mountains indicated that the horn had been removed from Solomon's temple when it was sacked in 587 BC by the Babylonians and that eventually it had gone to Medina. But it was taken from Medina during, or shortly after, the siege of 627, when the Meccans invaded. And it's at this point that the horn is believed to have been given its ebony coating of porcelain enamel, possibly in an attempt to disguise it."

"Or," I said, "because someone in Medina preferred swarthy cock. You mind if I smoke?" I asked her, and she shook her head and pointed at an ashtray.

"A Medinan rabbi of the Banu Nadir tribe was entrusted with the horn's safety. He escaped, making his way west across the desert to Yanbu' al Bahr, then north along the al-Hejaz all the way to Jerusalem. But two years later, when the Sassanid army lost control of the city to the Byzantine Emperor Heraclius, the horn was taken to a monastery in Malta, where it remained for centuries."

"That's quite the saga for a dildo. But you still haven't answered my question. What makes it so special? What the hell's it *do*?"

"Maybe you've heard enough," she said. The whole time she'd been talking, she hadn't taken her eyes off the thing in the box.

"Yeah, and maybe I haven't," I told her, tapping ash from my Pall Mall into the ashtray. "So, al-Jaldaki goes to Malta and finds the big black dingus."

She scowled again. No, it was more than a scowl; she *glowered,* and she looked away from the box just long enough to glower *at* me. "Yes," Ellen Andrews said. "At least, that's what he wrote. al-Jaldaki found it buried in the ruins of a monastery in Malta and then carried the horn with him to Cairo. It seems to have been in his possession until his death in 1342. After that it disappeared, and there's no word of it again until 1891."

I did the math in my head. "Five hundred and forty-nine years," I said. "So it must have gone to a good home. Must have lucked out and found itself a long-lived and appreciative keeper."

"The Freemasons might have had it," she went on, ignoring or oblivious to my sarcasm. "Maybe the Vatican. Doesn't make much difference."

"Okay. So what happened in 1891?"

"A party in Paris happened, in an old house not far from the Cimetière du Montparnasse. Not so much a party, really, as an out-and-out orgy, the way the story goes. This was back before Montparnasse became so fashionable with painters and poets and expatriate Americans. Verlaine was there, though. At the orgy, I mean. It's not clear what happened precisely, but three women died, and afterwards there were rumors of black magic and ritual sacrifice, and tales surfaced of a cult that worshipped some sort of daemonic *objet d'art* that had made its way to France from Egypt. There was an official investigation, naturally, but someone saw to it that *la préfecture de police* came up with zilch."

"Naturally," I said. I glanced at the window. It was getting dark, and I wondered if my ride back to the Bowery had been arranged. "So, where's Black Beauty here been for the past forty-four years?"

Ellen leaned forward, reaching for the lid to the red lacquered box. When she set it back in place, covering that brazen scrap of antiquity, I heard the *click* again as the lid melded seamlessly with the rest of the box. Now there was only the etching of the *qilin*, and I remembered that the beast has sometimes been referred to as the "Chinese unicorn." Yeah, it seemed odd I'd not thought of that before.

"I think we've probably had enough of a history lesson for now," she said, and I didn't disagree. Truth be told, the whole subject was beginning to bore me. It hardly mattered whether or not I believed in unicorns or enchanted dildos. I'd done my job, so there'd be no complaints from Harpootlian. I admit I felt kind of shitty about poor old Fong, who wasn't such a bad sort. But when you're an errand girl for the wicked folk, that shit comes with the territory. People get killed, and people get worse.

"Well, that's that," I said, crushing out my cigarette in the ashtray. "I should dangle."

"Wait. Please. I promised you a drink, Nat. Don't want you telling Auntie H I was a bad hostess, now do I?" And Ellen Andrews stood up, the red box tucked snugly beneath her left arm.

"No worries, kiddo," I assured her. "If she ever asks, which I doubt, I'll say you were a regular Emily Post."

"I insist," she replied. "I really, truly do," and before I could say another word, she turned and rushed out of the parlor, leaving me alone with all that furniture and the buxom giantesses watching me from the walls. I wondered if there were any servants, or a live-in beau, or if possibly she had the place all to herself, that huge apartment overlooking the river. I pushed the drapes aside and stared out at twilight gathering in the park across the street. Then she was back (minus the red box) with a silver serving tray, two glasses, and a virgin bottle of Sazerac rye.

"Maybe just one," I said, and she smiled. I went back to watching Riverside Park while she poured the whiskey. No harm in a shot or two. It's not like I had some place to be, and there were still a couple of unanswered questions bugging me. Such as why Harpootlian had broken her promise, the one that was supposed to prevent her underlings from practicing their hocus-pocus on me. That is, assuming Ellen Andrews had even bothered to ask permission. Regardless, she didn't need magic or a spell book for her next dirty trick. The Mickey Finn she slipped me did the job just fine.

So, I came to, four, perhaps five hours later – sometime before midnight. By then, as I'd soon learn, the shit had already hit the fan. I woke up sick as a dog and my head pounding like there was an ape with a kettledrum loose inside my skull. I opened my eyes, but it wasn't Ellen Andrews' Baroque clutter and chintz that greeted me, and I immediately shut them again. I smelled the hookahs and the smoldering *bukhoor*, the opium smoke and sandarac and, somewhere underneath it all, that pervasive brimstone stink that no amount of incense can mask. Besides, I'd seen the spiny ginger-skinned thing crouching not far from me, the eunuch, and I knew I was somewhere in the rat's maze labyrinth of Harpootlian's bordello. I started to sit up, but then my stomach lurched and I thought better of it. At least there were soft cushions beneath me, and the silk was cool against my feverish skin.

"You know where you are?" the eunuch asked; it had a woman's voice and a hint of a Russian accent, but I was pretty sure both were only affectations. First rule of demon brothels: Check your preconceptions of male and female at the door. Second rule: Appearances are fucking *meant* to be deceiving.

"Sure," I moaned and tried not to think about vomiting. "I might have a notion or three."

"Good. Then you lie still and take it easy, Miss Beaumont. We've got a few questions need answering." Which made it mutual, but I kept my mouth shut on that account. The voice was beginning to sound not so much feminine as what you might hear if you scraped frozen pork back and forth across a cheese grater. "This afternoon, you were contacted by an associate of Madam Harpootlian's, yes? She told you her name was Ellen Andrews. That's not her true name, of course. Just something she heard in a motion picture."

"Of course," I replied. "You sort never bother with your real names. Anyway, what of it?"

"She asked you to go see Jimmy Fong and bring her something, yes? Something very precious. Something powerful and rare."

"The dingus," I said, rubbing at my aching head. "Right, but… hey…Fong was already dead when I got there, scout's honor. Andrews told me one of Szabó's people did him."

"The Chinese gentleman's fate is no concern of ours," the eunuch said. "But we need to talk about Ellen Andrews. She has caused this house serious inconvenience. She's troubled us, and troubles us still."

"You and me both, bub," I said. It was just starting to dawn on me how there were some sizable holes in my memory. I clearly recalled the taste of rye, and gazing down at the park, but then nothing. Nothing at all. I asked the ginger demon, "Where is she? And how'd I get here, anyway?"

"We seem to have many of the same questions," it replied, dispassionate as a corpse. "You answer ours, maybe we shall find the answers to yours along the way."

I knew damn well I didn't have much say in the matter. After all, I'd been down this road before. When Auntie H wants answers, she doesn't usually bother with asking. Why waste your time wondering if someone's feeding you a load of baloney when all you gotta do is reach inside his brain and help yourself to whatever you need?

"Fine," I said, trying not to tense up, because tensing up only ever makes it worse. "How about let's cut the chit-chat and get this over with."

"Very well, but you should know," it said, "Madam regrets the necessity of this imposition." And then there were the usual wet, squelching noises as the relevant appendages unfurled and slithered across the floor towards me.

"Sure, no problem. Ain't no secret Madam's got a heart of gold," and maybe I shouldn't have smarted off like that, because when the stingers hit me, they hit hard. Harder than I knew was necessary to make the connection. I might have screamed. I know I pissed myself. And then it was inside me, prowling about, roughly picking its way through my conscious and unconscious mind – through my soul, if that word suits you better. All the heady sounds and smells of the brothel faded away, along with my physical discomfort. For a while I drifted nowhere and nowhen in particular, and then, then I stopped drifting…

…Ellen asked me, "You ever think you've had enough? Of the life, I mean. Don't you sometimes contemplate just up and blowing town, not even stopping long enough to look back? Doesn't that ever cross your mind, Nat?"

I sipped my whiskey and watched her, undressing her with my eyes and not especially ashamed of myself for doing so. "Not too often," I said. "I've had it worse. This gig's not perfect, but I usually get a fair shake."

"Yeah, usually," she said, her words hardly more than a sigh. "Just, now and then, I feel like I'm missing out."

I laughed, and she glared at me.

"You'd cut a swell figure in a breadline," I said and took another swallow of the rye.

"I hate when people laugh at me."

"Then don't say funny things," I told her.

And that's when she turned and took my glass. I thought she was about to tell me to get lost, blow, and don't let the door hit me in the ass on the way out. Instead, she set the drink down on the silver serving tray, and she kissed me. Her mouth tasted like peaches. Peaches and cinnamon. Then she pulled back, and her eyes flashed red, the way they had in the Yellow Dragon, only now I knew it wasn't an illusion.

"You're a demon," I said, not all that surprised.

"Only two bits. My grandmother...well, I'd rather not get into that, if it's all the same to you. Does my pedigree make you uncomfortable?"

"No, it's not a problem," I replied, and she kissed me again. Right about here, I started to feel the first twinges of whatever she'd put into the Sazerac, but, frankly, I was too horny to heed the warning signs.

"I've got a plan," she said, whispering, as if she were afraid someone were listening in. "I have it all worked out, but I wouldn't mind some company on the road."

"I have no...no idea...what you're talking about," and there was something else I wanted to say, but I'd begun slurring my words and decided against it. I put a hand on her left breast, and she didn't stop me.

"We'll talk about it later," she said, kissing me again, and right about then, that's when the curtain came crashing down, and the ginger-colored demon in my brain turned a page...

...I opened my eyes, and I was lying in a black room. I mean, a *perfectly* black room. Every wall had been painted matte black, and the ceiling, and the floor. If there were any windows, they'd also been painted over or boarded up. I was cold, and a moment later I realized that was because I was naked. I was naked and lying at the center of a wide white pentagram that had been chalked onto that black floor. A white pentagram held within a white circle. There was a single white candle burning at each of the five points. I looked up, and Ellen Andrews was standing above me. Like me, she was naked. Except she was wearing that dingus from the lacquered box, fitted into a leather harness strapped about her hips. The phallus drooped obscenely and glimmered in the candlelight. There were dozens of runic and Enochian symbols painted on her skin in blood and shit and charcoal. Most of them I recognized. At her feet, there was a small iron cauldron, and a black-handled dagger, and something dead. It might have been a rabbit, or a very small dog. I couldn't be sure which, because she'd skinned it.

Ellen looked down and saw me looking up at her. She frowned and tilted her head to one side. For just a second, there was something undeniably predatory in that expression, something murderous. All spite and not a jot of mercy. For that second, I was face-to-face with the one quarter of her bloodline that changed all the rules, the ancestor she hadn't wanted to talk about. But then that second passed, and she softly whispered, "I have a plan, Natalie Beaumont."

"What are you doing?" I asked her. But my mouth was so dry and numb, my throat so parched, it felt like I took forever to cajole my tongue into shaping those four simple words.

"No one will know," she said. "I promise. Not Harpootlian, not Szabó, not anyone. I've been over this a thousand times, worked all the angles." And she went down on one knee then, leaning over me. "But you're supposed to be asleep, Nat."

"Ellen, you don't cross Harpootlian," I croaked.

"Trust me," she said.

In that place, the two of us adrift on an island of light in an endless sea of blackness, she was the most beautiful woman I'd ever seen. Her hair was down now, and I reached up, brushing it back from her face. When my fingers moved across her scalp, I found two stubby horns, but it wasn't anything a girl couldn't hide with the right hairdo and a hat.

"Ellen, what are you doing?"

"I'm about to give you a gift, Nat. The most exquisite gift in all creation. A gift that even the angels might covet. You wanted to know what the Unicorn does. Well, I'm not going to tell you, I'm going to *show* you."

She put a hand between my legs and found I was already wet.

I licked at my chapped lips, fumbling for words that wouldn't come. Maybe I didn't know what she was getting at, this *gift,* but I had a feeling I didn't want any part of it, no matter how exquisite it might be. I knew these things, clear as day, but I was lost in the beauty of her, and whatever protests I might have uttered, they were about as sincere as ol' Brer Rabbit begging Brer Fox not to throw him into that briar patch. I could say I was bewitched, but it would be a lie.

She mounted me then, and I didn't argue.

"What happens now?" I asked.

"Now I fuck you," she replied. "Then I'm going to talk to my grandmother." And, with that, the world fell out from beneath me again. And the ginger-skinned eunuch moved along to the next tableau, that next set of memories I couldn't recollect on my own...

***

...Stars were tumbling from the skies. Not a few stray shooting stars here and there. No, *all* the stars were falling. One by one, at first, and then the sky was raining pitchforks, only it *wasn't* rain, see. It was light. The whole sorry world was being born or was dying, and I saw it didn't much matter which. Go back far enough, or far enough forward, the past and future wind up holding hands, cozy as a couple of lovebirds. Ellen had thrown open a doorway, and she'd dragged me along for the ride. I was *so* cold. I couldn't understand how there could be that much fire in the sky and me still be freezing my tits off like that. I lay there shivering as the brittle heavens collapsed. I could feel her inside me. I could feel *it* inside me, and same as I'd been lost in Ellen's beauty I was being smothered by that ecstasy. And then... then the eunuch showed me the gift, which I'd forgotten...and which I would immediately forget again.

How do you write about something, when all that remains of it is the faintest of impressions of glory? When all you can bring to mind is the empty place where a memory ought to be and isn't, and only that conspicuous absence is there to remind you of what cannot ever be recalled? Strain as you might, all that effort hardly adds up to a trip for biscuits. So, *how do you write it down?* You don't, *that's* how. You do your damnedest to think about what came next, instead, knowing your sanity hangs in the balance.

So, here's what came *after* the gift, since *le godemichet maudit* is a goddamn Indian giver if ever one were born. Here's the curse that rides shotgun on the gift, as impossible to obliterate from reminiscence as the other is to awaken.

There were falling stars, and that unendurable cold...and then the empty, aching socket to mark the countermanded gift...and *then* I saw the unicorn. I don't mean the dingus. I mean the *living creature*, standing in a glade of cedars, bathed in clean sunlight and radiating a light all its own. It didn't look much like what you see in story books or those medieval tapestries they got hanging in the Cloisters. It also didn't look much like the beast carved into the lid of Fong's wooden box. But I knew what it was, all the same.

A naked girl stood before it, and the unicorn kneeled at her feet. She sat down, and it rested its head on her lap. She whispered reassurances I couldn't hear, because they were spoken as softly as falling snow. And then she offered the unicorn one of her breasts, and I watched as it suckled. This scene of chastity and absolute peace lasted maybe a minute, maybe two, before the trap was sprung and the hunters stepped out from the shadows of the cedar boughs. They killed the unicorn, with cold iron lances and swords, but first the unicorn killed the virgin who'd betrayed it to its doom…

…and Harpootlian's ginger eunuch turned another page (a ham-fisted analogy if ever there were one, but it works for me), and we were back in the black room. Ellen and me. Only two of the candles were still burning, two guttering, half-hearted counterpoints to all that darkness. The other three had been snuffed out by a sudden gust of wind that had smelled of rust, sulfur, and slaughterhouse floors. I could hear Ellen crying, weeping somewhere in the darkness beyond the candles and the periphery of her protective circle. I rolled over onto my right side, still shivering, still so cold I couldn't imagine being warm ever again. I stared into the black, blinking and dimly amazed that my eyelids hadn't frozen shut. Then something snapped into focus, and there she was, cowering on her hands and knees, a tattered rag of a woman lost in the gloom. I could see her stunted, twitching tail, hardly as long as my middle finger, and the thing from the box was still strapped to her crotch. Only now it had a twin, clutched tightly in her left hand.

I think I must have asked her what the hell she'd done, though I had a pretty good idea. She turned towards me, and her eyes…well, you see that sort of pain and you spend the rest of your life trying to forget you saw it.

"I didn't understand," she said, still sobbing. "I didn't understand she'd take so much of me away."

A bitter wave of conflicting, irreconcilable emotion surged and boiled about inside me. Yeah, I knew what she'd done to me, and I knew I'd been used for something unspeakable. I knew *violation* was too tame a word for it, and that I'd been marked forever by this gold-digging half-breed of a twist. And part of me was determined to drag her kicking and screaming to Harpootlian. Or fuck it, I could kill her myself and take my own sweet time doing so. I could kill her the way the hunters had murdered the unicorn. But – on the other hand – the woman I saw lying there before me was shattered almost beyond recognition. There'd been a steep price for her trespass, and she'd paid it and then some. Besides, I was learning fast that when you've been to Hades' doorstep with someone, and the two of you've made it back more or less alive, there's a bond, whether you want it or not. So, there we were, a cheap, latter-day parody of Orpheus and Eurydice, and all

I could think about was holding her, tight as I could, until she stopped crying and I was warm again.

"She took *so much*," Ellen whispered. I didn't ask what her grandmother had taken. Maybe it was a slice of her soul or maybe a scrap of her humanity. Maybe it was the memory of the happiest day of her life or the ability to taste her favorite food. It didn't seem to matter. It was gone, and she'd never get it back. I reached for her, too cold and too sick to speak, but sharing her hurt and needing to offer my hollow consolation, stretching out to touch…

…and the eunuch said, "Madam wishes to speak with you now," and that's when I realized the parade down memory lane was over. I was back at Harpootlian's, and there was a clock somewhere chiming down to three a.m., the dead hour. I could feel the nasty welt the stingers had left at the base of my skull and underneath my jaw, and I still hadn't shaken off the hangover from that tainted shot of rye. But above and underneath and all about these mundane discomforts was a far more egregious pang, a portrait of that guileless white beast cut down and its blood spurting from gaping wounds. Still, I did manage to get myself upright without puking. Sure, I gagged once or twice, but I didn't puke. I pride myself on that. I sat with my head cradled in my hands, waiting for the room to stop tilting and sliding around like I'd gone for a spin on the Coney Island Wonder Wheel.

"Soon, you'll feel better, Miss Beaumont."

"Says you," I replied. "Anyway, give me a half fucking minute, will you please? Surely your employer isn't gonna cast a kitten if you let me get my bearings first, not after the work over you just gave me. Not after – "

"I will remind you, her patience is not infinite," the ginger demon said firmly, and then it clicked its long claws together.

"That so?" I asked. "Well, who the hell's is?" But I'd gotten the message, plain and clear. The gloves were off, and whatever forbearance Auntie H might have granted me in the past, it was spent, and now I was living on the installment plan. I took a deep breath and struggled to my feet. At least the eunuch didn't try to lend a hand.

I can't say for certain when Yeksabet Harpootlian set up shop in Manhattan, but I have it on good faith that Magdalena Szabó was here first. And anyone who knows her onions knows the two of them have been at each other's throats since the day Auntie H decided to claim a slice of the action for herself. Now, you'd think there'd be plenty enough of the hellion cock-and-tail trade to go around, what with all the netherworlders who call the Five Boroughs their home away from home. And likely as not you'd be right. Just don't try telling that to Szabó or Auntie H. Sure, they've each got their elite stable of "girls and boys," and they both have more customers than they know what to do with. Doesn't stop them from spending every waking hour looking for a way to banish the other once and for all – or at least find the unholy grail of competitive advantages.

Now, by the time the ginger-skinned eunuch led me through the chaos of Auntie H's stately pleasure dome, far below the subways and sewers and tenements of the Lower East Side, I already had a pretty good idea the dingus from Jimmy Fong's shiny box was meant to be Harpootlian's trump card. Only, here was Ellen Andrews, this mutt of a courier gumming up the works, playing fast and loose with the loving cup. And here was me, stuck smack in the middle, the unwilling stooge in her double-cross.

As I followed the eunuch down the winding corridor that ended in Auntie H's grand salon, we passed doorway after doorway, all of them opening onto scenes of inhuman passion and madness, the most odious of perversions and tortures that make short work of merely mortal flesh. It would be disingenuous to say I looked away. After all, this wasn't my first time. Here were the hinterlands of wanton physical delight and agony, where the two become indistinguishable in a rapturous *Totentanz*. Here were spectacles to remind me how Doré and Hieronymus Bosch never even came close and all of it laid bare for the eyes of any passing voyeur. You see, there are no locked doors to be found at Madam Harpootlian's. In fact, there are no doors at all.

"It's a busy night," the eunuch said, though it looked like business as usual to me.

"Sure," I muttered. "You'd think the Shriners were in town. You'd think Mayor La Guardia himself had come down off his high horse to raise a little hell."

And then we reached the end of the hallway, and I was shown into the mirrored chamber where Auntie H holds court. The eunuch told me to wait, then left me alone. I'd never seen the place so empty. There was no sign of the usual retinue of rogues, ghouls, and archfiends, only all those goddamn mirrors, because no one looks directly at Madam Harpootlian and lives to tell the tale. I chose a particularly fancy looking glass, maybe ten feet high and held inside an elaborate gilded frame. When Harpootlian spoke up, the mirror rippled like it were only water, and my reflection rippled with it.

"Good evening, Natalie," she said. "I trust you've been treated well?"

"You won't hear any complaints outta me," I replied. "I always say, the Waldorf-Astoria's got nothing on you."

She laughed then, or something that we'll call laughter for the sake of convenience.

"A crying shame we're not meeting under more amicable circumstances. Were it not for this unpleasantness with Miss Andrews, I'd offer you something – on the house, of course."

"Maybe another time," I said.

"So, you *know* why you're here?"

"Sure," I said. "The dingus I took off the dead Chinaman. The salami with the fancy French name."

"It has many names, Natalie. Karkadann's Brow, *El consolador sangriento,* the Horn of Malta – "

"*Le godemichet maudit,*" I said. "Me, I'm just gonna call it Ellen's cock."

Harpootlian grunted, and her reflection made an ugly dismissive gesture. "It is nothing of Miss Andrews. It is *mine*, bought and paid for. By my own sweat and blood did I track down the spoils of al-Jaldaki's long search. It's *my* investment, one purchased with so grievous a forfeiture this quadroon mongrel could not begin to appreciate the severity of her crime. But you, Natalie, you know, don't you? You've been privy to the wonders of Sulaymān's talisman, so I think, maybe, you are cognizant of my loss."

"I can't exactly say what I'm cognizant of," I told her, doing my best to stand up straight and not flinch or look away. "I saw the murder of a creature I didn't even believe in yesterday morning. That was sort of an eye opener, I'll grant you. And then there's the part I can't seem to conjure up, even after golden boy did that swell Roto-Rooter number on my head."

"Yes. Well, that's the catch," she said and smiled. There's no shame in saying I looked away then. Even in a mirror, the smile of Yeksabet Harpootlian isn't something you want to see straight on.

"Isn't there always a catch?" I asked, and she chuckled.

"True, it's a fleeting boon," she purled. "The gift comes, and then it goes, and no one may ever remember it. But always, *always* they will long for it again, even hobbled by that forgetfulness."

"You've lost me, Auntie," I said, and she grunted again. That's when I told her I wouldn't take it as an insult to my intelligence or expertise if she laid her cards on the table and spelled it out plain and simple, like she was talking to a woman who didn't regularly have tea and crumpets with the damned. She mumbled something to the effect that maybe she gave me too much credit, and I didn't disagree.

"Consider," she said, "what it *is*, a unicorn. It is the incarnation of purity, an avatar of innocence. And here is the *power* of the talisman, for that state of grace which soon passes from us each and every one is forever locked inside the horn, the horn become the phallus. And in the instant that it brought you, Natalie, to orgasm, you knew again that innocence, the bliss of a child before it suffers corruption."

I didn't interrupt her, but all at once I got the gist.

"Still, you are only a mortal woman, so what negligible, insignificant sins could you have possibly committed during your short life? Likewise, whatever calamities and wrongs have been visited upon your flesh *or* your soul, they are trifles. But say, instead, you survived the war in Paradise, if you refused the yoke and so are counted among the exiles, then you've persisted down all the long eons. You were already broken and despoiled billions of years before the coming of man. And your transgressions outnumber the stars.

"Now," she asked, "what would *you* pay, were you so cursed, to know even one fleeting moment of that stainless, former existence?"

Starting to feel sick to my stomach all over again, I said, "More to the point, if I *always* forgot it, immediately, but it left this emptiness I feel – "

"You would come back," Auntie H smirked. "You would come back again and again and again, because there would be no satiating that void, and always would you hope that maybe *this* time it would take and you might *keep* the memories of that former immaculate condition."

"Which makes it priceless, no matter what you paid."

"Precisely. And now Miss Andrews has forged a copy – an *identical* copy, actually – meaning to sell one to me, and one to Magdalena Szabó. That's where Miss Andrews is now."

"Did you tell her she could hex me?"

"I would never do such a thing, Natalie. You're much too valuable to me."

"*But* you think I had something to do with Ellen's mystical little counterfeit scheme."

"Technically, you did. The ritual of division required a supplicant, someone to *receive* the gift granted by the Unicorn, before the summoning of a succubus mighty enough to affect such a difficult twinning."

"So maybe, instead of sitting here bumping gums with me, you should send one of your torpedoes after her. And, while we're on the subject of how you pick your little henchmen, maybe – "

"*Natalie,*" snarled Auntie H from someplace not far behind me. "Have I failed to make myself *understood*? Might it be I need to raise my voice?" The floor rumbled, and tiny hairline cracks began to crisscross the surface of the looking glass. I shut my eyes.

"No," I told her. "I get it. It's a grift, and you're out for blood. But you *know* she used me. Your lackey, it had a good, long look around my upper story, right, and there's no way you can think I was trying to con you."

For a dozen or so heartbeats, she didn't answer me, and the mirrored room was still and silent, save all the moans and screaming leaking in through the walls. I could smell my own sour sweat, and it was making me sick to my stomach.

"There are some grey areas," she said finally. "Matters of sentiment and lust, a certain reluctant infatuation, even."

I opened my eyes and forced myself to gaze directly into that mirror, at the abomination crouched on its writhing throne. And all at once, I'd had enough, enough of Ellen Andrews and her dingus, enough of the cloak-and-dagger bullshit, and definitely enough kowtowing to the monsters.

"For fuck's sake," I said, "I only just met the woman this afternoon. She drugs and rapes me, and you think that means she's my sheba?"

"Like I told you, I think there are grey areas," Auntie H replied. She grinned, and I looked away again.

"Fine. You tell me what it's gonna take to make this right with you, and I'll do it."

"Always so eager to please," Auntie H laughed, and once again, the mirror in front of me rippled. "But, since you've asked, and as I do not doubt your *present* sincerity, I will tell you. I want her dead, Natalie. Kill her, and all will be...forgiven."

"Sure," I said, because what the hell else was I going to say. "But if she's with Szabó – "

"I have spoken already with Magdalena Szabó, and we have agreed to set aside our differences long enough to deal with Miss Andrews. After all, she has attempted to cheat us both, in equal measure."

"How do I find her?"

"You're a resourceful young lady, Natalie," she said. "I have faith in you. Now...if you will excuse me," and, before I could get in another word, the mirrored room dissolved around me. There was a flash, not of light, but a flash of the deepest abyssal darkness, and I found myself back at the Yellow Dragon, watching through the bookshop's grimy windows as the sun rose over the Bowery.

There you go, the dope on just how it is I found myself holding a gun on Ellen Andrews, and just how it is she found herself wondering if I were angry enough or scared enough or desperate enough to pull the trigger. And like I said, I chambered a round, but she just stood there. She didn't even flinch.

"I wanted to give you a gift, Nat," she said.

"Even if I believed that – and I don't – all I got to show for this *gift* of yours is a nagging yen for something I'm never going to get back. We lose our innocence, it stays lost. That's the way it works. So, all I got from you, Ellen, is a thirst can't ever be slaked. That and Harpootlian figuring me for a clip artist."

She looked hard at the gun, then looked harder at me.

"So what? You thought I was gonna plead for my life? You thought maybe I was gonna get down on my knees for you and beg? Is that how you like it? Maybe you're just steamed 'cause I was on top – "

"Shut up, Ellen. You don't get to talk yourself out of this mess. It's a done deal. You tried to give Auntie H the high hat."

"And you honestly think she's on the level? You think you pop me and she lets you off the hook, like nothing happened?"

"I do," I said. And maybe it wasn't as simple as that, but I wasn't exactly lying, either. I needed to believe Harpootlian, the same way old women need to believe in the infinite compassion of the little baby Jesus and Mother Mary. Same way poor kids need to believe in the inexplicable generosity of Popeye the Sailor and Santa Claus.

"It didn't have to be this way," she said.

"I didn't dig your grave, Ellen. I'm just the sap left holding the shovel."

And she smiled that smug smile of hers, and said, "I get it now, what Auntie H sees in you. And it's not your knack for finding shit that doesn't want to be found. It's not that at all."

"Is this a guessing game," I asked, "or do you have something to say?"

"No, I think I'm finished," she replied. "In fact, I think I'm done for. So let's get this over with. By the way, how many women *have* you killed?"

"You played me," I said again.

"Takes two to make a sucker, Nat," she smiled.

Me, I don't even remember pulling the trigger. Just the sound of the gunshot, louder than thunder.

THE MALTESE UNICORN

Ellen Datlow had asked me for a supernatural noir tale, and I was stumped. "The Maltese Unicorn" is the story that I swore I would *not* write for her. I even swore it publicly, in a May 6, 2010 entry to my online journal. A dildo carved from a unicorn's horn just seemed a bit much, even for me. Then I told the idea to Ellen, and she liked it, and so I wrote it anyway. And I'm very glad that I did. Of all my protagonists/narrators, Natalie Beaumont is one of my favorites. Originally, there was a frame set in a Nazi concentration camp; however, it was ponderous and unnecessary, and I made it go away. Thank you, Dashiell Hammett, and thank you, Raymond Chandler, and Polly Adler, and Howard Hawks, and Lauren Bacall, and Humphrey Bogart, and John Huston, and Mary Astor, and...well, you get the picture.

Tidal Forces

Charlotte says, "That's just it, Em. There wasn't any pain. I didn't feel anything much at all." She sips her coffee and stares out the kitchen window, squinting at the bright Monday morning sunlight. The sun melts like butter across her face. It catches in the strands of her brown hair, like a late summer afternoon tangling itself in dead cornstalks. It deepens the lines around her eyes and at the corners of her mouth. She takes another sip of coffee, then sets her cup down on the table. I've never once seen her use a saucer.

And the next minute seems to last longer than it ought to last, longer than the mere sum of the sixty seconds that compose it, the way time stretches out to fill in awkward pauses. She smiles for me, and so I smile back. I don't want to smile, but isn't that what you do? The person you love is frightened, but she smiles anyway. So you have to smile back, despite your own fear. I tell myself it isn't so much an act of reciprocation as an acknowledgement. I could be more honest with myself and say I only smiled back out of guilt.

"I *wish* it had hurt," she says, finally, on the other side of all that long, long moment. I don't have to ask what she means, though *I* wish that *I* did. I wish I didn't already know. She says the same words over again, but more quietly than before, and there's a subtle shift in emphasis. "I wish it *had* hurt."

I apologize and say I shouldn't have brought it up again, and she shrugs.

"No, don't be sorry, Em. Don't let's be sorry for anything."

I'm stacking days, building a house of cards made from nothing but days. Monday is the Ace of Hearts. Saturday is the Four of Spades.

Wednesday is the Seven of Clubs. Thursday night is, I suspect, the Seven of Diamonds, and it might be heavy enough to bring the whole precarious thing tumbling down around my ears. I would spend an entire hour watching cards fall, because time would stretch, the same way it stretches out to fill in awkward pauses, the way time is stretched thin in that thundering moment of a car crash. Or at the edges of a wound.

If it's Monday morning, I can lean across the breakfast table and kiss her, as if nothing has happened. And if we're lucky, that might be the moment that endures almost indefinitely. I can kiss her, taste her, savor her, drawing the moment out like a card drawn from a deck. But no, now it's Thursday night, instead of Monday morning. There's something playing on the television in the bedroom, but the sound is turned all the way down, so that whatever the something may be proceeds like a silent movie filmed in color and without intertitles. A movie for lip readers. There's no other light but the light from the television. She's lying next to me, almost undressed, asking me questions about the book I don't think I'm ever going to be able to finish. I understand she's not asking them because she needs to know the answers, which is the only reason I haven't tried to change the subject.

"The Age of Exploration was already long over with," I say. "For all intents and purposes, it ended early in the Seventeenth Century. Everything after that – reaching the north and south poles, for instance – is only a series of footnotes. There were no great blank spaces left for men to fill in. No more 'Here be monsters.'"

She's lying on top of the sheets. It's the middle of July and too hot for anything more than sheets. Clean white sheets and underwear. In the glow from the television, Charlotte looks less pale and less fragile than she would if the bedside lamp were on, and I'm grateful for the illusion. I want to stop talking, because it all sounds absurd, pedantic, all these unfinished, half-formed ideas that add up to nothing much at all. I want to stop talking and just lie here beside her.

"So writers made up stories about lost worlds," she says, having heard all this before and pretty much knowing it by heart. "But those made-up worlds weren't really *lost*. They just weren't *found* yet. They'd not yet been imagined."

"That's the point," I reply. "The value of those stories rests in their insistence that blank spaces still do exist on the map. They *have* to exist, even if it's necessary to twist and distort the map to make room for them. All those overlooked islands, inaccessible plateaus in South American jungles, the sunken continents and the entrances to a hollow earth, they were important psychological buffers against progress and certainty. It's no coincidence that they're usually places where time has stood still, to one degree or another."

"But not really so much time," she says, "as the processes of evolution, which require time."

"See? You understand this stuff better than I do," and I tell her she should write the book. I'm only half joking. That's something else Charlotte knows. I lay my hand on her exposed belly, just below the navel, and she flinches and pulls away.

"Don't do that," she says.

"All right. I won't. I wasn't thinking." I was thinking, but it's easier if I tell her that I wasn't.

Monday morning. Thursday night. This day or that. My own private house of cards, held together by nothing more substantial than balance and friction. And the loops I'd rather make than admit to the present. Connecting dot-to-dot, from here to there, from there to here. Here being half an hour before dawn on a Saturday, the sky growing lighter by slow degrees. Here, where I'm on my knees, and Charlotte is standing naked in front of me. Here, now, when the perfectly round hole above her left hip and below her ribcage has grown from a pinprick to the size of the saucers she never uses for her coffee cups.

"I don't think it will hurt," she tells me. And I can't see any point in asking whether she means, *I don't think it will hurt me,* or *I don't think it will hurt you.*

"Now?" I ask her, and she says, "No. Not yet. Wait."

So, handed that reprieve, I withdraw again to the relative safety of the Ace of Hearts – or Monday morning, call it what you will. In my mind's eye, I run back to the kitchen washed in warm yellow sunlight. Charlotte is telling me about the time, when she was ten years old, that she was shot with a BB gun, her brother's Red Ryder BB gun.

"It wasn't an accident," she's telling me. "He meant to do it. I still have the scar from where my mother had to dig the BB out of my ankle with tweezers and a sewing needle. It's very small, but it's a scar all the same."

"Is that what it felt like, like being hit with a BB?"

"No," she says, shaking her head and gazing down into her coffee cup. "It didn't. But when I think about the two things, it seems like there's a link between them, all these years apart. Like, somehow, this thing was an echo of the day he shot me with the BB gun."

"A meaningful coincidence," I suggest. "A sort of synchronicity."

"Maybe," Charlotte says. "But maybe not." She looks out the window again. From the kitchen, you can see the three oaks and her flower bed and the land running down to the rocks and the churning sea. "It's been an awfully long time since I read Jung. My memory's rusty. And, anyway, maybe it's not a coincidence. It could be something else. Just an echo."

"I don't understand, Charlotte. I really don't think I know what you mean."

"Never mind," she says, not taking her eyes off the window. "Whatever I do or don't mean, it isn't important."

The warm yellow light from the sun, the colorless light from a color television. A purplish sky fading towards the light of false dawn. The complete absence of light from the hole punched into her body by something that wasn't a BB. Something that also wasn't a shadow.

"What scares me most," she says (and I could draw *this* particular card from anywhere in the deck), "is that it didn't come back out the other side. So, it must still be lodged in there, *in* me."

I was watching when she was hit. I saw when she fell. I'm coming to that.

"Writers made up stories about *lost* worlds" she says again, after she's flinched, after I've pulled my hand back from the brink. "They did it because we were afraid of having found all there *was* to find. Accurate maps became more disturbing, at least unconsciously, than the idea of sailing off the edge of a flat world."

"I don't want to talk about the book."

"Maybe that's why you can't finish it."

"Maybe you don't know what you're talking about."

"Probably," she says, without the least bit of anger or impatience in her voice.

I roll over, turning my back on Charlotte and the silent television. Turning my back on what cannot be heard and doesn't want to be acknowledged. The sheets are damp with sweat, and there's the stink of ozone that's not *quite* the stink of ozone. The acrid smell that always follows her now, wherever she goes. No. That isn't true. The smell doesn't follow her, it comes *from* her. She radiates the stink that is almost, but not quite, the stink of ozone.

"Does *Alice's Adventures in Wonderland* count?" she asks me, even though I've said I don't want to talk about the goddamned book. I'm sure that she heard me, and I don't answer her.

Better not to linger too long on Thursday night.

Better if I return, instead, to Monday morning. Only Monday morning. Which I have carelessly, randomly, designated here as the Ace of Hearts, and hearts are cups, so Monday morning is the Ace of Cups. In four days more, Charlotte will ask me about Alice, and though I won't respond to the question (at least not aloud), I *will* recall that Lewis Carroll considered the *Queen* of Hearts – who rules over the Ace and is also the Queen of Cups – I will recollect that Lewis Carroll considered her the embodiment of a certain type of passion. That passion, he said, which is ungovernable, but which exists as an aimless, unseeing, furious thing. And he said, also, that the Queen of Cups, the Queen of Hearts, is not to be confused with the *Red* Queen, whom he named another brand of passion altogether.

Monday morning in the kitchen.

"My brother always claimed he was shooting at a blue jay and missed. He said he was aiming for the bird and hit me. He said the sun was in his eyes."

"Did he make a habit of shooting songbirds?"

"Birds and squirrels," she says. "Once he shot a neighbor's cat, right between the eyes." And Charlotte presses the tip of an index finger to the spot between her brows. "The cat had to be taken to a vet to get the BB out, and my mom had to pay the bill. Of course, he said he wasn't shooting at the cat. He was shooting at a sparrow and missed."

"What a little bastard," I say.

"He was just a kid, only a year older than I was. Kids don't mean to be cruel, Em, they just are sometimes. From our perspectives, they appear cruel. They exist outside the boundaries of adult conceits of morality. Anyway, after the cat, my dad took the BB gun away from him. So, after that, he always kind of hated cats."

But here I am neglecting Wednesday, overlooking Wednesday, even though I went to the trouble of drawing a card for it. And it occurs to me now I didn't even draw one for Tuesday. Or Friday, for that matter. It occurs to me that I'm becoming lost in this ungainly metaphor, that the tail is wagging the dog. But Wednesday was of consequence. More so than was Thursday night, with its mute TV and the Seven of Diamonds and Charlotte shying away from my touch.

The Seven of Clubs. Wednesday, or the Seven of Pentacles, seen another way round. Charlotte, wrapped in her bathrobe, comes downstairs after taking a hot shower, and she finds me reading Kip Thorne's *Black Holes and Time Warps*, the book lying lewdly open in my lap. I quickly close it, feeling like I'm a teenager again and my mother's just barged into my room to find me masturbating to the *Hustler* centerfold. Yes, your daughter is a lesbian, and yes, your girlfriend is reading quantum theory behind your back.

Charlotte stares at me awhile, staring silently, and then she stares at the thick volume lying on the coffee table, *Principles of Physical Cosmology*. She sits down on the floor, not far from the sofa. Her hair is dripping, spattering the hardwood.

"I don't believe you're going to find anything in there," she says, meaning the books.

"I just thought…" I begin, but let the sentence die unfinished, because I'm not at all sure *what* I was thinking. Only that I've always turned to books for solace.

And here, on the afternoon of the Seven of Pentacles, this Wednesday weighted with those seven visionary chalices, she tells me what happened in the shower. How she stood in the steaming spray watching the water rolling down her breasts and *across* her stomach and *up* her buttocks before falling into the hole in her side. Not in defiance of gravity, but in perfect accord with gravity. She hardly speaks above a whisper. I sit quietly listening, wishing that I could suppose she'd only lost her mind. Recourse to wishful thinking, the seven visionary chalices of the Seven of Pentacles, of the Seven of Clubs, or Wednesday. Running away to hide in the comfort of insanity, or the authority of books, or the delusion of lost worlds.

"I'm sorry, but what the fuck do I say to that?" I ask her, and she laughs. It's a terrible sound, that laugh, a harrowing, forsaken sound. And then she stops laughing, and I feel relief spill over me, because now she's crying, instead. There's shame at the relief, of course, but even the shame is welcome. I couldn't have stood that terrible laughter much longer. I go to her and put my arms around her and hold her, as if holding her will make it all better. The sun's almost down by the time she finally stops crying.

I have a quote from Albert Einstein, from sometime in 1912, which I found in the book by Kip Thorne, the book Charlotte caught me reading on Wednesday: "Henceforth, space by itself, and time by itself, are doomed to fade away into mere shadows, and only a kind of union of the two will preserve an independent reality."

Space, time, shadows.

As I've said, I was watching when she was hit. I saw when she fell. That was Saturday last, two days before the yellow morning in the kitchen and not to be confused with the *next* Saturday, which is the Four of Spades. I was sitting on the porch and had been watching two noisy grey-white gulls wheeling far up against the blue summer sky. Charlotte had been working in her garden, pulling weeds. She called out to me, and I looked away from the birds. She was pointing towards the ocean, and at first I wasn't sure what it was she wanted me to see. I stared at the breakers shattering themselves against the granite boulders and past that, to the horizon where the water was busy with its all but eternal task of shouldering the burden of the heavens. I was about to tell her that I didn't see anything. This wasn't true, of course. I just didn't see anything out of the ordinary, nothing special, nothing that ought not occupy that time and that space.

I saw nothing to give me pause.

But then I did.

Space, time, spacetime, shadows.

I'll call it a shadow, because I'm at a loss for any more appropriate word. It was spread out like a shadow rushing across the waves, though, at first, I thought I was seeing something dark moving *beneath* the waves. A very big fish, perhaps. Possibly a large shark or a small whale. We've seen whales in the bay before. Or it might have been caused by a cloud passing in front of the sun, though there were no clouds that day. The truth is I knew it was none of these things. I can sit here all night long, composing a list of what it *wasn't*, and I'll never come any nearer to what it might have been.

"Emily," she shouted. "Do you *see* it?" And I called back that I did. Having noticed it, it was impossible *not* to see that grimy, indefinite smear sliding swiftly towards the shore. In a few seconds more, I realized, it would reach the boulders, and if it wasn't something beneath the water, the rocks wouldn't stop it. Part of my mind still insisted it was only a shadow, a freakish trick of the light, a mirage. Nothing substantial, certainly nothing malign, nothing that could do us any mischief or injury. No need to be alarmed, and yet I don't ever remember being as afraid as I was then. I couldn't move, but I yelled for Charlotte to run. I don't think she heard me. Or if she heard me, she was also too mesmerized by the sight of the thing to move.

I was safe, there on the porch. It came no nearer to me than ten or twenty yards. But Charlotte, standing alone at the garden gate, was well within its circumference. It swept over her, and she screamed, and fell to the ground. It swept over her and then was gone, vanishing into the tangle of green briars and poison ivy and wind-stunted evergreens behind our house. I stood there, smelling something that almost smelled like ozone. And maybe it's an awful cliché to put to paper, but my mind *reeled*. My heart raced, and my mind reeled. For a fraction of an instant I was seized by something that was neither déjà vu nor vertigo, and I thought I might vomit.

But the sensation passed, like the shadow had, or the shadow of a shadow, and I dashed down the steps and across the grass to the place where Charlotte sat stunned among the clover and the dandelions. Her clothes and skin looked as though they'd been misted with the thinnest sheen of...what? Oil? No, no, no, not oil at all. But it's the closest I can come to describing that sticky brownish iridescence clinging to her dress and her face, her arms and the pickets of the garden fence and to every single blade of grass.

"It knocked me down," she said, sounding more amazed than hurt or frightened. Her eyes were filled with startled disbelief. "It wasn't *anything*, Em. It wasn't anything at all, but it knocked me right off my feet."

"Are you hurt?" I asked, and she shook her head.

I didn't ask her anything else, and she didn't say anything more. I helped her up and inside the house. I got her clothes off and led her into the downstairs shower. But the oily residue that the shadow had left behind had already begun to *evaporate* – and again, that's not the right word, but it's the best I can manage – before we began trying to scrub it away with soap and scalding clean water. By the next morning there would be no sign of the stuff anywhere, inside the house or out of doors. Not so much as a stain.

"It knocked me down. It was just a shadow, but it knocked me down." I can't recall how many times she must have said that. She repeated it over and over again, as though repetition would render it less implausible, less inherently ludicrous. "A shadow knocked me down, Em. A shadow knocked me down."

But it wasn't until we were in the bedroom, and she was dressing, that I noticed the red welt above her left hip, just below her ribs. It almost looked like an insect bite, except the center was...well, when I bent down and examined it closely, I saw there *was* no center. There was only a hole. As I've said, a pinprick, but a hole all the same. There wasn't so much as a drop of blood, and she swore to me that it didn't hurt, that she was fine, and it was nothing to get excited about. She went to the medicine cabinet and found a Band-Aid to cover the welt. And I didn't see it again until the next day, which as yet has no playing card, the Sunday before the warm yellow Monday morning in the kitchen.

I'll call that Sunday by the Two of Spades.

It rains on the Two of Spades. It rains cats and dogs all the damn day long. I spend the afternoon sitting in my study, parked there in front of my computer, trying to find the end to Chapter Nine of the book I can't seem to finish. The rain beats at the windows, all rhythm and no melody. I write a line, then delete it. One step forward, two steps back. Zeno's "Achilles and the Tortoise" paradox played out at my keyboard – "That which is in locomotion must arrive at the halfway stage before it arrives at the goal," and each halfway stage has it's own halfway stage, *ad infinitum*. These are the sorts of rationalizations that comfort me as I only pretend to be working. This is the *true* reward of my twelve years of college, these erudite excuses for not getting the job done. In the days to come, I will set the same apologetics and exculpations to work on the problem of how a shadow can possibly knock a woman down and how a hole can be explained away as no more than a wound.

Sometime after seven o'clock, Charlotte raps on the door to ask me how it's going and what I'd like for dinner. I haven't got a ready answer for either question, and she comes in and sits down on the futon near my desk. She has to move a stack of books to make a place to sit. We talk about the weather, which she tells me is supposed to improve after sunset, that the meteorologists are saying Monday will be sunny and hot. We talk about the book – my exploration of the phenomenon of the literary *Terrae Anachronismorum*, from 1714 and Simon Tyssot de Patot's *Voyages et Aventures de Jacques Massé* to 1918 and Edgar Rice Burroughs's *Out of Time's Abyss* (and beyond; see Aristotle on Zeno, above). I close Microsoft Word, accepting that nothing more will be written until at least tomorrow.

"I took off the Band-Aid," she says, reminding me of what I've spent the day trying to forget.

"When you fell, you probably jabbed yourself on a stick or something," I tell her, which doesn't explain *why* she fell, but seeks to dismiss the result of the fall.

"I don't think it was a stick."

"Well, whatever it was, you hardly got more than a scratch."

And that's when she asks me to look. I would have said no, if saying no were an option.

She stands and pulls up her T-shirt, just on the left side, and points at the hole, though there's no way I could ever miss it. On the rainy Two of Spades, hardly twenty-four hours after Charlotte was knocked off her feet by a shadow, it's already grown to the diameter and circumferance of a dime. I've never seen anything so black in all my life, a black so complete I'm almost certain I would go blind if I stared into it too long. I don't say these things. I don't remember what I say, so maybe I say nothing at all. At first, I think the skin at the edges of the hole is puckered, drawn tight like the skin at the edges of a scab. Then I see that's not the case at all. The skin around the periphery of the hole in her flesh is *moving*, rotating, swirling about that preposterous and undeniable blackness.

"I'm scared," she whispers. "I mean, I'm *really* fucking scared, Emily."

I start to touch the wound, and she stops me. She grabs hold of my hand and stops me.

"Don't," she says, and so I don't.

"You *know* that it can't be what it looks like," I tell her, and I think maybe I even laugh.

"Em, I don't know anything at all."

"You damn well know *that* much, Charlotte. It's some sort of infection, that's all, and – "

She releases my hand, only to cover my mouth before I can finish. Three fingers to still my lips, and she asks me if we can go upstairs, if I'll please make love to her.

"Right now, that's all I want," she says. "In all the world, there's nothing I want more."

I almost make her promise that she'll see our doctor the next day, but already some part of me has admitted to myself this is nothing a physician can diagnose or treat. We have moved out beyond medicine. We have been pushed down into these nether regions by the shadow of a shadow. I have stared directly into that hole, and already I understand it's not merely a hole in Charlotte's skin, but a hole in the cosmos. I could parade her before any number of physicians and physicists, psychologists and priests, and not a one would have the means to seal that breach. In fact, I suspect they would deny the evidence, even if it meant denying all their science and technology and faith. There are things worse than blank spaces on maps. There are moments when certitude becomes the greatest enemy of sanity. Denial becomes an antidote.

Unlike those other days and those other cards, I haven't chosen the Two of Spades at random. I've chosen it because on Thursday she asks me if Alice counts. And I have begun to assume that everything counts, just as everything is claimed by that infinitely small, infinitely dense point beyond the event horizon.

"Would you tell me, please," said Alice, a little timidly, "why you are painting those roses?"

Five and Seven said nothing, but looked at Two. Two began, in a low voice, "Why, the fact is, you see, Miss, this here ought to have been a red rose-tree, and we put a white one in by mistake..."

On that rainy Sunday, that Two of Spades with an incriminating red brush concealed behind its back, I do as she asks. I cannot do otherwise. I bed her. I fuck her. I am tender and violent by turns, as is she. On that stormy evening, that Two of Pentacles, that Two of *Coins* (a dime, in this case), we both futilely turn to sex looking for surcease from dread. We try to go *back* to our lives before she fell, and this is not so very different from all those "lost worlds" I've belabored in my unfinished manuscript: Maple White Land, Caprona, Skull Island, Symzonia, Pellucidar, the Mines of King Solomon. In our bed, we struggle to fashion a refuge from the present, populated by the reassuring, dependable past. And I am talking in circles within circles within circles, spiraling inward or out, it doesn't matter which.

I am arriving, very soon now, at the end of it, at the Saturday night – or more precisely, just before dawn on the Saturday morning – when the story I am writing here ends. And begins. I've taken too long to get to the point, if I assume the validity of a linear narrative. If I assume any one moment can take precedence over any other or assume the generally assumed (but unproven) inequity of relevance.

A large rose-tree stood near the entrance of the garden; the roses growing on it were white, but there were three gardeners at it, busily painting them red.

We are as intimate in those moments as two women can be, when one is forbidden to touch a dime-sized hole in the other's body. At some point, after dark, the rain stops falling, and we lie naked and still, listening to owls and whippoorwills beyond the bedroom walls.

On Wednesday, she comes downstairs and catches me reading the dry pornography of mathematics and relativity. Wednesday is the Seven of Clubs. She tells me there's nothing to be found in those books, nothing that will change what has happened, what may happen.

She says, "I don't know what will be left of me when it's done. I don't even know if I'll be enough to satisfy it, or if it will just keep getting bigger and bigger and bigger. I think it might be insatiable."

On Monday morning, she sips her coffee. We talk about eleven-year-old boys and BB guns.

But here, at last, it is shortly before sunup on a Saturday. Saturday, the Four of Spades. It's been an hour since Charlotte woke screaming, and I've sat and listened while she tried to make sense of the nightmare. The hole in her side is as wide as a softball (and, were this more obviously a comedy, I would list the objects that, by accident, have fallen into it the last few days). Besides the not-quite-ozone smell, there's now a faint but constant whistling sound, which is air being pulled into the hole. In the dream, she tells me, she knew exactly what was on the other side of the hole, but then she forgot most of it as soon as she awoke. In the dream, she says, she wasn't afraid, and that we were sitting out on the porch watching the sea while she explained it all to me. We were drinking Cokes, she said, and it was hot, and the air smelled like dog roses.

"You know I don't like Coke," I say.

"In the dream you did."

She says we were sitting on the porch, and that awful shadow came across the sea again, only this time it didn't frighten her. This time I saw it first and pointed it out to her, and we watched together as it moved rapidly towards the shore. This time, when it swept over the garden, she wasn't standing there to be knocked down.

"But you said you saw what was on the other side."

"That was later on. And I would tell you what I saw, if I could remember. But there was the sound of pipes, or a flute," she says. "I can recall that much of it, and I knew, in the dream, that the hole runs all the way to the middle, to the very center."

"The very center of what?" I ask, and she looks at me like she thinks I'm intentionally being slow-witted.

"The center of everything that ever was and is and ever will be, Em. The *center*. Only, somehow the center is both empty and filled with..." She trails off and stares at the floor.

"Filled with what?"

"I can't *say*. I don't *know*. But whatever it is, it's been there since before there was time. It's been there alone since before the universe was born."

I look up, catching our reflections in the mirror on the dressing table across the room. We're sitting on the edge of the bed, both of us naked, and I look a decade older than I am. Charlotte, though, she looks *so* young, younger than when we met. Never mind that yawning black mouth in her abdomen. In the half light before dawn, she seems to shine, a preface to the coming day, and I'm reminded of what I read about Hawking radiation and the quasar jet streams that escape some singularities. But this isn't the place or time for theories and equations. Here, there are only the two of us, and morning coming on, and what Charlotte can and cannot remember about her dream.

"Eons ago," she says, "it lost its mind. Though I don't think it ever really *had* a mind, not like a human mind. But still, it went insane, from the knowledge of what it is and what it can't ever stop being."

"You said you'd forgotten what was on the other side."

"I have. Almost all of it. This is *nothing*. If I went on a trip to Antarctica and came back and all I could tell you about my trip was that it had been very white, Antarctica, that would be like what I'm telling you now about the dream."

The Four of Spades. The Four of Swords, which cartomancers read as stillness, peace, withdrawal, the act of turning sight back upon itself. They say nothing of the attendant perils of introspection or the damnation that would be visited upon an intelligence that could never look *away*.

"It's blind," she says. "It's blind, and insane, and the music from the pipes never ends. Though they aren't really pipes."

This is when I ask her to stand up, and she only stares at me a moment or two before doing as I've asked. This is when I kneel in front of her, and I'm dimly aware that I'm kneeling before the inadvertent avatar of a god, or God, or a pantheon, or something so immeasurably ancient and pervasive that it may as well be divine. Divine or infernal; there's really no difference, I think.

"What are you doing?" she wants to know.

"I'm losing you," I reply, "that's what I'm doing. Somewhere, some*when*, I've *already* lost you. And that means I have nothing *left* to lose."

Charlotte takes a quick step back from me, retreating towards the bedroom door, and I'm wondering if she runs, will I chase her? Having made this decision, to what lengths will I go to see it through? Would I force her? Would it be rape?

"I know what you're going to do," she says. "Only you're *not* going to do it, because I won't let you."

"You're being devoured."

"It was a dream, Em. It was only a stupid, crazy dream, and I'm not even sure what I actually remember and what I'm just making up."

"Please," I say, "please let me try." And I watch as whatever resolve she might have had breaks apart. She wants as badly as I do to hope, even though we both know there's no hope left. I watch that hideous black gyre above her hip, below her left breast. She takes two steps back towards me.

"I don't think it will hurt," she tells me. And I can't see any point in asking whether she means, *I don't think it will hurt me*, or *I don't think it will hurt you*. "I don't think there will be any pain."

"I can't see how it possibly matters anymore," I tell her. I don't say anything else. With my right hand, I reach into the hole, and my arm vanishes almost up to my shoulder. There's cold beyond any comprehension of cold. I glance up, and she's watching me. I think she's going to scream, but she doesn't. Her lips part, but she doesn't scream. I feel my arm being tugged so violently I'm sure that it's about to be torn from its socket, the humerus ripped from the glenoid fossa of the scapula, cartilage and ligaments snapped, the subclavian artery severed before I tumble back to the floor and bleed to death. I'm almost certain that's what will happen, and I grit my teeth against that impending amputation.

"I can't feel you," Charlotte whispers. "You're inside me now, but I can't feel you anywhere."

Then.

The hole is closing. We both watch as that clockwise spiral stops spinning, then begins to turn widdershins. My freezing hand clutches at the void, my fingers straining for any purchase. Something's changed; I understand that perfectly well. Out of desperation, I've chanced upon some remedy, entirely by instinct or luck, the solution to an insoluble puzzle. I also understand that I need to pull my arm back out again, before the edges of the hole reach my bicep. I imagine the collapsing rim of curved spacetime slicing cleanly through sinew and bone, and then I imagine myself fused at the shoulder to that point just above Charlotte's hip. Horror vies with cartoon absurdities in an instant that seems so swollen it could accommodate an age.

Charlotte's hands are on my shoulders, gripping me tightly, pushing me away, shoving me as hard as she's able. She's saying something, too, words I can't quite hear over the roar at the edges of that cataract created by the implosion of the quantum foam.

Oh, Kitty, how nice it would be if we could only get through into Looking-glass House! I'm sure it's got oh! such beautiful things in it! Let's pretend there's a way of getting through into it, somehow, Kitty.

Let's pretend the glass has got all soft as gauze, so that we can get through...

I'm watching a shadow race across the sea.

Warm sun fills the kitchen.

I draw another card.

Charlotte is only ten years old, and a BB fired by her brother strikes her ankle. Twenty-three years later, she falls at the edge of our flower garden.

Time. Space. Shadows. Gravity and velocity. Past, present, and future. All smeared, every distinction lost, and nothing remaining that can possibly be quantified.

I shut my eyes and feel her hands on my shoulders.

And across the space within her, as my arm bridges countless light years, something brushes against my hand. Something wet and soft, something indescribably abhorrent. Charlotte pushed me, and I was falling backwards, and now I'm not. It has seized my hand in its own – or wrapped some celestial tendril about my wrist – and for a single heartbeat it holds on before letting go.

...whatever it is, it's been there since before there was time. It's been there alone since before the universe was born.

There's pain when my head hits the bedroom floor. There's pain and stars and twittering birds. I taste blood and realize that I've bitten my lip. I open my eyes, and Charlotte's bending over me. I think there are galaxies trapped within her eyes. I glance down at that spot above her left hip, and the skin is smooth and whole. She's starting to cry, and that makes it harder to see the constellations in her irises. I move my fingers, surprised that my arm and hand are both still there.

"I'm sorry," I say, even if I'm not sure what I'm apologizing for.

"No," she says, "don't be sorry, Em. Don't let's be sorry for anything. Not now. Not ever again."

TIDAL FORCES

As I've noted elsewhere, quite some time after I finished writing this story I realized that I'd written almost precisely the same story twice already, first with "The Bone's Prayer" (2009) and then with "Sanderlings" (2010), two other tales of seaside personal apocalypse. There was clearly something lodged deeply in my mind that I was trying to work through, and I believe the third time was the charm. Occasionally, I finally get it right.

And the Cloud That Took the Form

The memories wash over me like sunlight through the window of a moving car, a car moving swiftly along a wooded road so that the warm light is regularly divided by the cold shadows of intervening trees. Increments of sunlight measured out – shadow, sunlight, shadow – a chiaroscuro, train-track rhythm tapping itself into being upon my face. She whispers, "How quickly a metaphor replaces the real thing," and I shut my eyes, wishing dusk had already come and gone, and there were no light, at all. Well, perhaps the moon, but that light is only borrowed, and the moon spins more honest conceits. For a few moments, it *is* that day on the road to Abington, speeding along the too-colorfully named Wolf's Den Road. We're pressed here between the pages of rustling autumn forest and an autumn sky so blue you'll go blind if you stare into it too long. And then the trees and the greenbrier underbrush and their dappled rhythm are behind us, and there are only yellow-brown fields waiting for the snow and then spring and the plow. The fields are partitioned by dry-stone walls of granite, those postcard clichés of New England fitted together just so two hundred, two hundred and fifty years ago. Out here, clear of the woods, we'll find no shelter from the sky, and it wraps around, from horizon to horizon. When I glance up I see a few stray white wisps like pinfeathers.

"Penny for your thoughts," she says, smiling.

"I was remembering that day on the road," I tell her, and her smiles fades, but slowly, by increments. Not all at once.

"The day after you told me about Jupiter, and the floaters and the sinkers and the hunters. The day after you showed me those pictures."

"They were only paintings," she says. "A thought exercise, what the Germans call a *Gedankenexperiment*." I say I didn't know she spoke German, and she informs me that she doesn't, that she picked the word up in a seminar on Schrödinger's cat and Maxwell's demon, that sort of thing. "Intellectual masturbation," she adds.

She frowns and waves a dismissive hand, meaning we should move along to another topic of conversation, because we're getting too, too near whatever did or didn't happen that day on Wolf's Den Road. But those paintings, they're fixed here in my mind's eye, and it's obviously easier for her to move along than it is for me. I can't say why. Maybe she's stopped having the dreams. I don't ask, though, because if she has, I'd rather not know that I'm alone with them now.

She's behind the wheel, and I'm sitting beside her, my face pressed to the window. The glass is chilly. Glancing up, it doesn't seem so unlikely that someone might open her eyes wide enough to choke to death on a November sky.

"The idea's very simple, really," she said, the night she showed me Adolf Schaller's paintings, printed in one of Carl Sagan's books. "We tend to assume life needs a terrestrial matrix to evolve, because that's the way it happened here on earth. But that assumption follows from a single data point, which makes it highly suspect." I'm lying on the floor, staring at the paintings, and they're strange and terrible and beautiful. "Jupiter may have a rocky core, or it may not. It may have had one that was lost long ago, due to the convection of hot metallic hydrogen."

She talks, and I take it for granted that she knows what she's talking about. I don't exactly tune her out, but I'm more interested in the paintings than the theories behind the paintings. Here are vast canyons and rivers of ammonia, methane, water vapor, helium, hydrogen, and through them sail the hypothetical floaters, living gasbags the size of cities. More than balloons, they remind me of mushrooms, and specifically the fruiting bodies of puffballs. They drift in herds a thousand kilometers across, or they drift alone, passively subsisting on whatever organic molecules come their way. Or they might be photosynthetic creatures, autotrophs converting sunlight into the nutrients they need. There are also the predatory hunters, tiny by comparison, sleek-winged things that put me in mind of manta rays and B-2 stealth bombers.

"It's a lazy habit," she says, "always describing an unfamiliar object by recourse to familiar ones."

The herd of floaters is buoyed by updrafts above titanic storms depicted by the artist in all the shades of autumn leaves.

"It may not be a matter of finding an earth-like planet," she says, speaking to me the way she speaks to her students, "but of broadening our expectations of alien life." It's not a condescending voice, but it's confident and wears an air of authority.

The road isn't asphalt, but it isn't dirt, either. I have to ask what it's called, this sort of paving, and she tells me it's called tar and chip. So, the wheels whir loudly as we race along the ribbon of tar and chip below all that blue. I finally look away, turning to watch her, instead, and I wonder how much farther to Abington and the intersection with U.S. 44. It seems to me as though we should have already reached the end of Wolf's Den Road.

"Not much farther," she assures me, though I catch a nervous wash of doubt across her face. I start to ask if we might have taken a wrong turn somewhere, if maybe we should go back and try again, or stop and consult the map. But I don't. I don't know *why* I don't, except that the car is moving very fast, objects in motion tending to remain in motion, and we've been down this road so many times before. She knows the way, and I know the way, and the dry-stone walls are there on either side to prevent our straying from the path. We're not wayward fairy-tale children, no matter what the name of the road might suggest. We're in no danger of being roasted alive by witches in gingerbread houses, or being offered tainted apples, or gobbled up by a big bad wolf. We're merely driving along a road in eastern Connecticut beneath an autumn sky.

In the painting, the enormous floaters are almost the same color as the clouds they inhabit, grey-brown camouflage hues to hide them from the hunters. She describes how the floaters might be capable of expelling heavier gases, somehow separating helium and methane deep within those billowing anatomies, keeping only the useful, buoyant hydrogen. Hunters, she says, wouldn't only attack the floaters for their flesh, but also for the reserves of pure, refined hydrogen stored within the conjectural bladders that keep them aloft.

"It's an eloquent scenario," she says.

"Don't you mean *elegant?*"

"Do I?" she asks.

Late one night when I was six years old, just as I was drifting off to sleep, I heard a sound like a car backfiring. It dragged me to wakefulness again, and I lay waiting for it to be repeated. But it wasn't, and finally I sat up and looked out the window, peering at the stars. We lived far enough out from the city that the light pollution only hid the dimmest stars, and I'd learned to recognize a number of constellations: the Big Dipper, Ursa Major and Ursa Minor, Cassiopeia and Cepheus. But the night I heard the sound like a backfire, there was an unfamiliar light in the sky, to the east, hanging low above the rustling trees. It didn't twinkle, and so I imagined it might be a planet. It was the color of ripe cherries, and its glow grew fainter as I watched. After only half an hour or so, it had vanished entirely.

The tires against that chip-and-tar pavement, the smothering blue overhead, and the nagging sense that we should have already reached Abington.

"It's called *ouranophobia,*" she says, not the night she showed me Adolf Schaller's aliens, but some other night. It's August, and we've gone to the beach to watch the Perseids, but the moon's almost full, and we aren't having much luck. We've spotted only seven or eight meteors in a couple of hours. This is the first time I tell to her how the sky makes me uneasy, how sometimes it makes me more than uneasy. I watch for falling stars and try to explain the anxiety I often feel at the sight of a clear sky.

"I didn't know there was a word for it," I reply.

"From the Greek," she says. "*Ouranos,* meaning heaven."

"I'm not afraid of Heaven. I don't even believe in Heaven," and she tells me to stop being so literal.

"Only in the daytime," I tell her. "And it's much worse in the autumn. Though, the sky above the sea never seems to bother me."

"That's a lot of provisos," she laughs. "Maybe there should be a special sub-phobia erected just for you."

"It's not funny. I can get dizzy, genuinely dizzy, staring directly up at the sky." I don't admit to her that sometimes it's a lot worse than just the dizziness, that sometimes it's also a shortness of breath, nausea, sweating, a racing heart. That sometimes it's so bad that I can hardly speak, and my hands shake, and I'm convinced that if I don't sit down and dig my fingers into the ground or hold onto something sturdy I'll tumble upwards.

I've had dreams wherein I fall into the sky, the laws of gravity reversed or negated, and I fall away from the world, plunging through the stratosphere and mesosphere and exosphere and on and on until the earth is no larger than a baseball, a glimmering azure baseball I can eclipse with the palm of a hand.

"So they drift," she says, "and float, rise and fall. They skim through thunderheads of ammonium hydrosulfide and ammonia crystals. They prowl the tropopause, able to survive only within that vertical column of clouds, which is no more than fifty kilometers, top to bottom. They may be struck down, incinerated, by flashes of lightning a thousand times more powerful than any lightning flash on earth. They skirt the edges of hurricanes larger than our planet. They die, one way or another, and tumble into the pyrolytic depths of the atmosphere."

"But there's no actual evidence," I say.

"Not yet," she replies, and smiles, and talks awhile about sending probes to explore what she calls the "habitable zone" of the Jovian firmament.

I was six, and I stood at my bedroom window and watched a shining crimson star or planet I would never see again. Maybe others saw it that night; I have no idea whether they did or not. I can't say either way.

"Really, it's sort of a chauvinist attitude," she says, "thinking biogenesis and evolution can only occur in lakes and oceans and muddy, stagnant pools of water."

And later, on *this* day, I'm listening to the drone of the tires against the tar and chip, trying hard to keep my mind off the sky and the way Wolf's Den Road seems longer than it ever has before, how it seems we'll never find Abington and the highway. I wish I'd brought a book with me, and I'm about to reach into the backseat for the map, when she tells me to look at the sky, when she asks if I see what *she* sees. I don't look right away. I don't want to *see,* but she slows down and pulls over into the narrow, weedy strip between the road and the dry-stone wall. The car idles, and when I glance at her she's shielding her eyes with her right hand, blocking out the glare of the sun, and her left index finger is pointing towards all that unbearable, suffocating blue.

"Good fucking god," she whispers. "Please tell me I'm not hallucinating. You see that, too, right?"

I hesitate for a last precious handful of seconds, and then, when it would be obvious that I'm afraid to look, my eyes follow her pointing finger to the sky. And yes, I see it, too, just like I knew that I would. I tell her that it's really there, which I imagine is no less difficult than admitting to murder or rape or to having vandalized a church or graveyard.

"Get the camera," she says.

"We didn't bring it," I tell her. My mouth has gone dry, and I feel sick. I'm speaking so quietly I think maybe she won't hear me. "Remember? We left it on the counter in the kitchen," and she curses again, so I know that she's heard me, after all.

It hovers directly above the tar-and-chip slash of Wolf's Den Road. In some ways, it reminds me of a wolf, even though it bears not even the faintest resemblance to a wolf. It reminds me of the emotions the word *wolf* can evoke in a child at her bedroom window, staring out into the night. I can't take my eyes off it now, and she cuts the engine and shifts the car into park. I'm afraid she's going to open the door, and I ask her not to, please. I insist we can see it just as well from where we're sitting, that there's no point in getting out of the car.

Above the road, it seems to roll to one side, then right itself again. It shines dully in the sunlight, and makes me think of cherries. She's hazarding guesses about how high up it is – a hundred feet, a hundred and twenty-five – and about its diameter and circumference. To me it looks as big as a whale.

"And not only Jupiter," she says, that night I see the painting for the first time. "There's also Saturn to consider." Then she takes down another book, a science-fiction novel by an author I've never heard of, and she reads a passage aloud to me:

Birds that have never seen land, living out their entire lives aloft. Gossamer spider-kites that trapped microscopic spores. Particles of long-chain carbon molecules that form in the clouds and sift downward, toward the global ocean below.

We sit there, alone and together, gazing breathlessly through the windshield at the abomination hovering above the road. We watch, hardly speaking, she in wonder and I in silent terror. I keep hoping that another car will come along, or a truck, and someone else will stop and watch it with us. I want to ask her to start the car again, but I don't dare. It's a windy day, but the same wind that disturbs the trees and the tall grass, the thickets of goldenrod and ragweed, doesn't seem to disturb the thing above the road in the least. I tell myself maybe it's high enough there's no wind up there, but I know better.

And then there's a sound, not so unlike an automobile backfiring, and we both jump, startled out of our respective trances. I do more than jump; I cry out, and she takes her eyes off it just long enough to glare at me. She looks disappointed, I think. But it's begun to move away, slowly and with no evident goal, drifting as a jellyfish drifts on the tide, or a derelict ship, or maybe only the way herds of floaters drift through gas-giant skies. Neither of us says anything until after it's out of sight, and then she asks me to turn on the radio, and I do. She starts the car again, and it only takes us five minutes more to reach the end of Wolf's Den Road.

AND THE CLOUD THAT TOOK THE FORM

An exposition on my *ouranophobia*. My fear of cloudless blue skies, of either falling upwards or being crushed by the weight of Heaven. Of being devoured. Of becoming untethered. In 2006, I coined "wide carnivorous sky," a conscious inversion of Paul Bowles' title, *The Sheltering Sky* (1949) and a very personal phrase that so perfectly describes my dread, which I've wrestled with since I was a small child. It was shortly thereafter – appropriated, let's say – by two other authors who shall here remain nameless, but *they* know who they are. They might at least have asked. In the cold April of 2010, I visited these Connecticut backroads, and it truly was a terrible, terrible sky laid out above the bare branches, fields, and dry stone walls. See also R.E.M.'s "Fall on Me" (1986).

The Prayer of Ninety Cats

In this darkened theatre, the screen shines like the moon. More like the moon than this simile might imply, as the moon makes no light of her own, but instead adamantly casts off whatever the sun sends her way. The silver screen reflects the light pouring from the projector booth. And this particular screen truly *is* a silver screen, the real deal, not some careless metonym lazily recalling more glamorous Hollywood movie-palace days. There's silver dust embedded in its tightly-woven silk matte, an apotropaic which might console any Slovak grandmothers in attendance, given the evening's bill of fare. But, then again, is it not also said that the silvered-glass of mirrors offends these hungry phantoms? And isn't the screen itself a mirror, not so very unlike the moon? The moon flashes back the sun, the screen flashes back the dazzling glow from the projector's Xenon arc lamp. Here, then, is an irony, of sorts, as it is sometimes claimed the *moroaică*, *strigoi mort*, *vampir*, and *vrykolakas*, are incapable of casting reflections – apparently consuming light much as the gravity well of a black hole does. In these flickering, moving pictures, there must surely be some incongruity or paradox, beginning with Murnau's Orlok, Browning's titular Dracula, and Carl Theodor Dreyer's sinister Marguerite Chopin.

Of course, pretend demons need no potent, tried-and-true charm to ward them off, no matter how much we may wish to fear them. Still, we go through the motions. We *need* to fear, and when summoning forth these simulacra, to convince ourselves of their authenticity, we must also have a means of dispelling them. We sit in darkness and watch the monsters, and smugly remind ourselves these are merely actors playing unsavory parts, reciting dialogue written to shock, scandalize, and unnerve. All shadows are carefully planned. That face is clever make up, and a man becoming a bat no more than a bit of trick photography accomplished with flash powder, splicing, and a lump of felt and rabbit fur dangled from piano wire. We sit in the darkness, safely reenacting and mocking and laughing at the silly, delicious fears of our ignorant forbearers. If all else fails, we leave our seats and escape to the lobby. We turn on the light. No need to invoke crucified messiahs and the Queen of Heaven, not when we have Saint Thomas Edison on our side. Though, still another irony arises (we are gathering a veritable platoon of ironies, certainly), as these same monsters were brought to you courtesy of Mr. Edison's tinkerings and profiteering. Any truly wily sorcerer, any witch worth her weight in mandrake and foxglove, knows how very little value there is in conjuring a fearful thing if it may not then be banished at will.

The theatre air is musty and has a sickly sweet sourness to it. It swims with the rancid ghosts of popcorn butter, spilled sodas, discarded chewing gum, and half a hundred varieties of candy lost beneath velvet seats and between the carpeted aisles. Let's say these are the top notes of our perfume. Beneath them lurk the much fainter heart notes of sweat, piss, vomit, cum, soiled diapers – all the pungent gases and fluids a human body may casually expel. Also, though smoking has been forbidden here for decades, the reek of stale cigarettes and cigars persists. Finally, now, the base notes, not to be recognized right away, but registering after half an hour or more has passed, settling in to bestow solidity and depth to this complex *Eau de Parfum*. In the main, it strikes the nostrils as dust, though more perceptive noses may discern dry rot, mold, and aging mortar. Considered thusly, the atmosphere of this theatre might, appropriately, echo that of a sepulcher, shut away and ripe from generations of use.

Crossing the street, you might have noticed a title and the names of the players splashed across the gaudy marquee. After purchasing your ticket from the young man with a death's head tattooed on the back of his left hand (he has a story, if you care to hear), you might have paused to view the relevant lobby cards or posters on display. You might have considered the concessions. These are the rituals before the rite. You might have wished you'd brought along an umbrella, because it's beginning to look like there might be rain later. You may even go to the payphone near the restrooms, but, these days, that happens less and less, and there's talk of having it removed.

Your ticket is torn in half, and you find a place to sit. The lights do not go down, because they were never up. You wait, gazing nowhere in particular, thinking no especial thoughts, until that immense moth-gnawed curtain the color of pomegranates opens wide to reveal the silver screen.

And so we come back to where we began.

With no fanfare or overture, the darkness is split apart as the antique projector sputters reluctantly to life. The auditorium is filled with the noisy, familiar cadence of wheels and sprockets, the pressure roller and the take-up reel, as the film speeds along at twenty-four frames per second and the shutter tricks the eyes and brain into perceiving continuous motion instead of a blurred procession of still photographs. By design, it is all a lie, start to finish. It is all an illusion.

There are no trailers for coming attractions. There might have been in the past, as there might have been cartoons featuring Bugs Bunny and Daffy Duck, or newsreels extolling the evils of Communism and the virtues of soldiers who go away to die in foreign countries. Tonight, there's only the feature presentation, and it begins with jarring abruptness, without so much as a title sequence or the name of the director. Possibly, a few feet of the opening reel were destroyed by the projectionist at the last theatre that screen the film, a disagreeable, ham-fisted man who drinks on the job and has been known to nod off in the booth. We can blame him, if we like. But it may also be there never were such niceties, and that *this* 35mm strip of acetate, celluloid, and polyester was always meant to begin *just so.*

Likewise, the film's score – which has been compared favorably to Wojciech Kilar's score for Campion's *Portrait of a Lady* – seems to begin not at any proper beginning. As cellos and violins compete with kettledrums in a whirl of syncopated rhythms, there is the distinct impression of having stumbled upon a thing already in progress. This may well be the director's desired effect.

EXT. ČACHTICE CASTLE HILL, LITTLE CARPATHIANS. SUNSET.

WOMAN'S VOICE (fearfully):

Katarína, is that you?

(pause)

Katarína? If it is you, say so.

The camera lingers on this bleak spire of evergreens, brush, and sandstone, gray-white rock tinted pink as the sun sinks below the horizon and night claims the wild Hungarian countryside. There are sheer ravines, talus slopes, and wide ledges carpeted with mountain ash, fenugreek, tatra blush, orchids, and thick stands of feather reed grass. The music grows quieter now, drums diminishing, strings receding to a steady vibrato undercurrent as the score hushes itself, permitting the night to be heard. The soundtrack fills with the calls of nocturnal birds, chiefly tawny and long-eared owls, but also nightingales, swifts, and nightjars. From streams and hidden pools, there comes the chorus of frog song. Foxes cry out to one another. The scene is at once breathtaking and forbidding, and you lean forward in your seat, arrested by this austere beauty.

WOMAN'S VOICE (angry):
It is a poor jest, Katarína. It is a poor, poor jest, indeed,
and I've no patience for your games tonight.

GIRL'S VOICE (soft, not unkind):
I'm not Katarína. Have you forgotten my name already?

The camera's eye doesn't waver, even at the risk of this shot becoming monotonous. And we see that atop the rocky prominence stands the tumbledown ruins of Čachtice Castle, *Csejte vára* in the mother tongue. Here it has stood since the 1200's, when Kazimir of Hunt-Poznan found himself in need of a sentry post on the troubled road to Moravia. And later, it was claimed by the Hungarian oligarch Máté Csák of Trencsén, the heroic Count Matthew. Then it went to Rudolf II, Holy Roman Emperor, who spent much of his life in alchemical study, searching for the Philosopher's Stone. And, finally, in 1575, the castle was presented as a wedding gift from Lord Chief Justice Ferenc Nádasdy to his fifteen-year old bride, Báthory Erzsébet, or Alžbeta, the Countess Elizabeth Báthory. The name (one or another of the lot) will doubtless ring a bell, though infamy has seen she's better known to many as the Blood Countess.

The cinematographer works more sleight of hand, and the jagged lineament of the ruins is restored to that of Csejte as it would have stood when the Countess was alive. A grand patchwork of Romanesque and Gothic architecture, its formidable walls and towers loom high above the drowsy village of Vrbové. The castle rises – no, it sprouts – the castle *sprouts* from the bluff in such a way as to seem almost a natural, integral part of the local geography, something *in situ,* carved by wind and rain rather than by the labors of man.

The film jump cuts to an owl perched on a pine branch. The bird blinks – once, twice – spreads its wings, and takes to the air. The camera lets it go and doesn't follow, preferring to remain with the now-vacant branch. Several seconds pass before the high-pitched scream of a rabbit reveals the reason for the owl's departure.

GIRL'S VOICE:

Ever is it the small things that suffer. That's what they say, you know? The Tigress of Csejte, she will have them all, because there is no end to her hunger.

Another jump cut brings us to the castle gates, and the camera pans slowly across the masonry of curtain walls, parapets, and up the steep sides of a horseshoe-shaped watchtower. Jump cut again, and we are shown a room illuminated by the flickering light of candles. There is a noblewoman seated in an enormous and somewhat fanciful chair, upholstered with fine brocade, its oaken legs and arms ending with the paws of a lion, or a dragon.

Or possibly a tigress.

So, a woman seated in an enormous, bestial chair. She wears the "Spanish farthingale" and stiffened undergarments fashionable during this century. Her dress is made of the finest Florentine silk. Her waist is tightly cinched, her ample breasts flattened by the stays. Were she standing, her dress might remind us of an hourglass. Her head is framed with a wide ruff of starched lace, and her arms held properly within trumpet sleeves, more lace at the cuffs to ring her delicate hands. There is a wolf pelt across her lap, and another covers her bare feet. The candlelight is gracious, and she might pass for a woman of forty, though she's more than a decade older. Her hair, which is the color of cracked acorn shells, has been meticulously braided and pulled back from her round face and high forehead. Her eyes seem dark as rubies.

INT. COUNTESS BÁTHORY'S CHAMBER. NIGHT.

COUNTESS (tersely):

Why are you awake at this hour, child? You should be sleeping. Haven't I given you a splendid bed?

GIRL (seen dimly, in silhouette):
I don't like being in that room alone. I don't like the shadows in that room. I try not to see them –

COUNTESS (close up, her eyes fixed on the child):
Oh, don't be silly. A shadow has not yet harmed anyone.

GIRL (almost whispering):
Begging your pardon, My Lady, but these shadows mean to do me mischief. I hear them whisper, and they do. They are shadows cast by wicked spirits. They do not speak to you?

COUNTESS (sighs, frowning):
I don't speak with shadows.

GIRL (coyly):
That isn't what they say in the village.
(pause)
Do you truly know the Prayer of Ninety Cats?

By now, it is likely that the theatre, which only a short time ago so filled your thoughts, has receded, fading almost entirely from your conscious mind. This is usually the way of theatres, if the films they offer have any merit at all. The building is the spectacle which precedes the spectacle it has been built to contain, not so different from the relationship of colorful wrapping paper and elaborately tied bows to the gifts hidden within. You're greeted by a mock-grand façade and the blazing electric marquee, and are then admitted into the catchpenny splendor of the lobby. All these things make an impression, and set a mood, but all will fall by the wayside. Exiting the theatre after a film, you'll hardly note a single detail. Your mind will be elsewhere, processing, reflecting, critiquing, amazed, or disappointed.

Onscreen, the Countess' candlelit bedchamber has been replaced by the haggard faces of peasant women, mothers and grandmothers, gazing up at the terrible edifice of Csejte. Over the years, so many among them have sent their daughters away to the castle, hearing that servants are cared for and well compensated. Over the years, none have returned. There are rumors of black magic and butchery, and, from time to time, girls have simply vanished from Vrbové, and also from the nearby town of Čachtice, from whence the fortress took its name. The women cross themselves and look away.

Dissolve to scenes of the daughters of landed aristocracy and the lesser gentry preparing their beautiful daughters for the *gynaeceum* of ecsedi Báthory Erzsébet, where they will be schooled in all the social graces, that they might make more desirable brides and find the best marriages possible. Carriages rattle along the narrow, precipitous road leading up to the castle, wheels and hooves trailing wakes of dust. Oblivious lambs driven to the slaughter, freely delivered by ambitious and unwitting mothers.

Another dissolve, to winter in a soundstage forest, and the Countess walks between artificial sycamore maples, ash, linden, beech, and elderberry. The studio "greens men" have worked wonders, meticulously crafting this forest from plaster, burlap, epoxy, wire, Styrofoam, from lumber armatures and the limbs and leaves of actual trees. The snow is as phony as the trees, but no less convincing, a combination of SnowCel, SnowEx foam, and Powderfrost, dry-foam plastic snow spewed from machines; biodegradable, nontoxic polymers to simulate a gentle snowfall after a January blizzard. But the mockery is perfection. The Countess stalks through drifts so convincing that they may as well be real. Her furs drag behind her, and her boots leave deep tracks. Two huge wolves follow close behind, and when she stops, they come to her and she scratches their shaggy heads and pats their lean flanks and plants kisses behind their ears. A trained crow perches on a limb overhead, cawing, cawing, cawing, but neither the woman nor the wolves pay it any heed. The Countess speaks, and her breath fogs.

COUNTESS (to wolves):
You are my true children. Not Ursula or Pál or Miklós.
And you are also my true inamoratos, my most beloved,
not Ferenc, who was only ever a husband.

If tabloid gossip and backlot hearsay is to be trusted, this scene has been considerably shortened and toned down from the original script. We do not see the Countess' sexual congress with the wolves. It is only implied by her affections, her words, and by the lewd canticle of a voyeur crow. The scene is both stark and magnificent. It is a final still point before the coming tempest, before the horrors, a moment imbued with grace and menacing tranquility. The camera cuts to Herr

Kramer in its counterfeit tree, and you're watching its golden eyes watching the Countess and her wolves, and anything more is implied.

INT. ČACHTICE CASTLE/DRESSING ROOM. MORNING.

The Countess is seated before a looking glass held inside a carved wooden frame, motif of dryads and satyrs. We see the Countess as a reflection, and behind her, a servant girl. The servant is combing the Countess' brown hair with an ivory comb. The Countess is no longer a young woman. There are lines at the edges of her mouth and beneath her eyes.

COUNTESS (furrowing her brows):
You're pulling my hair again. How many times must I tell you to be careful. You're not deaf, are you?

SERVANT (almost whispering):
No, My Lady.

COUNTESS (icily):
Then when I speak to you, you hear me perfectly well.

SERVANT:
Yes, My Lady.

The ivory comb snags in the Countess' hair, and she stands, spinning about to face the terrified servant girl. She snatches the comb from the girl's hand. Strands of Elizabeth's hair are caught between the teeth.

COUNTESS (tone of disbelief):
You wretched little beast. Look what you've done.

The Countess slaps the servant with enough force to split her lip. Blood spatters the Countess' hand as the servant falls to the floor. The Countess is entranced by the crimson beads speckling her pale skin.

COUNTESS (whisper):
You…filthy…wretch…

FADE TO BLACK.

FADE IN:

INT. DREAM MIRROR.

The Countess stands in a dim pool of light, before a towering mirror, a grotesque nightmare version of the one on her dressing table. The nymphs, satyrs, and dryads are life-size, and move, engaged in various and sundry acts of sexual abandon. This dark place is filled with sounds of desire, orgasm, drunken debauchery. In the mirror is a far younger Elizabeth Báthory. But, as we watch, as the Countess watches, this young woman rapidly ages, rushing through her twenties, thirties, her forties. The Countess screams, commanding the mirror cease these awful visions. The writhing creatures that form the frame laugh and mock her screams.

FLASH CUT TO:

EXT. SNOW-COVERED FIELD. DAYLIGHT.

The Countess stands naked in the falling snow, her feet buried up to the ankles. The snowflakes turn red. The red snow becomes a red rain, and she's drenched. The air is a red mist.

FLASH CUT TO:

INT. DREAM MIRROR.

Nude and drenched in blood, the Countess gazes at her reflection, her face and body growing young before her eyes. The looking glass shatters.

FADE TO BLACK.

The Hungary of the film has more in common with the landscape of Hans Christian Andersen and the Brothers Grimm than with any Hungary that exists now or ever has existed. It is an archetypal vista, as much a myth as Stoker's Transylvania and Sheridan Le Fanu's Styria. A real place that has, inconveniently, never existed. Little or nothing is said of the political and religious turmoil of Elizabeth's time, or of the war with the Ottoman Turks, aside from the death of the Countess' husband at the hands of General Giorgio Basta. If you're a stickler for accuracy, these omissions are unforgivable. But most of the men and women who sit in the theatre, entranced by the light flashed back from the screen, will never notice. People do not generally come to the movies hoping for recitations of dry history. Few will care that pivotal events in the film never occurred, because they are happening *now,* unfolding before the eyes of all who have paid the price of admission.

INT. COUNTESS' BEDCHAMBER. NIGHT.

GIRL:
If you have been taught the prayer, say the words aloud.

COUNTESS:
How would you ever know such things, child?

GIRL (turning away):
We have had some of the same tutors, you and I.

The second reel begins with the arrival at Csejte of a woman named Anna Darvulia. In hushed tones, a servant (who dies an especially messy death farther along) refers to her as "the Witch of the Forest." She becomes Elizabeth's lover and teaches her sorcery and the Prayer of Ninety Cats to protect her from all harm. As Darvulia is depicted here, she may as well have inhabited a gingerbread cottage before she came to the Countess, a house of sugary confections where she regularly feasted on lost children. Indeed, shortly after her arrival, and following an admittedly gratuitous sex scene, the subject of cannibalism is introduced. A peasant girl named Júlia, stolen from her home, is brought to the Countess by two of her handmaids and partners in crime, Dorottya and Ilona. The girl is stripped naked and forced to kneel before Elizabeth while the handmaids burn the bare flesh of her back and shoulders with coins and needles that have been placed over an open flame. Darvulia watches on approvingly from the shadows.

INT. KITCHEN. NIGHT.

COUNTESS (smiling):
You shouldn't fret so about your dear mother and father. I know they're poor, but I will see to it they're compensated for the loss of their only daughter.

JÚLIA (sobbing):
There is never enough wood in winter, and never enough food. We have no shoes and wear rags.

COUNTESS:
And haven't I liberated you from those rags?

JÚLIA:
They need me. Please, My Lady, send me home to them.

The Countess glances over her shoulder to Darvulia, as if seeking approval/instruction. Darvulia nods once, then the Countess turns back to the sobbing girl.

COUNTESS:
Very well. I'll make you a promise, Júlia. And I keep my promises. In the morning, I will send your mother and your father warm clothing and good shoes and enough firewood to see them through the snows. And, what's more, I will send you back to them, as well.

JÚLIA:
You would do that?

COUNTESS:
Certainly, I will. I'll not have any use for you after this evening, and I detest wastefulness.

This scene has been cut from most prints. If you have any familiarity with the trials and tribulations of the film's production, and with the censorship that followed, you'll be surprised, and possibly pleased, to find it has not been excised from this copy. It may also strike you as relatively tame, compared to many less controversial, but far more graphic, portions of the film.

COUNTESS:
When we are finished here...
(pause)
When we're finished, and my hunger is satisfied, I will speak with my butcher – a skilled man with a knife and cleaver – and he will see to it that your corpse is dressed in such a way that it can never be mistaken for anything but that of a sow. I'll have the meat salted and smoked, then sent to them, as evidence of my generosity. They will have their daughter back, and, in the bargain, will not go hungry. Are they fond of sausage, Júlia? I'd think you would make a marvelous *debreceni*.

Critics and movie buffs who lament the severe treatment the film has suffered at the hands of nervous studio executives, skittish distributors, and the MPAA often point to Júlia's screams, following these lines, as an example of how great cinema may be lost to censorship. Sound editors and Foley artists are said to have crafted the unsettling and completely inhuman effect by mixing the cries of several species of birds, the squeal of a pig, and the steam whistle of a locomotive. The scream continues as this scene dissolves to a delirious montage of torture and murder. The Countess' notorious iron maiden makes an appearance. A servant is dragged out into a snowy courtyard, and once her dress and underclothes have been savagely ripped away, the woman is bound to a wooden stake. Elizabeth Báthory pours buckets of cold water over the servant's body until she freezes to death and her body glistens like an ice sculpture.

The theatre is so quiet that you begin to suspect everyone else has had enough and left before The End. But you don't dare look away long enough to see whether this is in fact the case.

The Countess sits in her enormous lion- (or dragon- or tigress-) footed chair, in that bedchamber lit only by candlelight. She strokes the wolf pelt on her lap as lovingly as she stroked the fur of those living wolves.

"We've had some of the same tutors, you and I," the strange brown girl says, the gypsy child who claims to be afraid of the shadows in the small room that has been provided for her.

"Anna's never mentioned you."

"*She* and I have had some of the same tutors," the child whispers. "Now, My Lady, please speak the words aloud and drive away the evil spirits."

"I have heard of no such prayer," the Countess tells the girl, but the actress' air and intonation make it's obvious she's lying. "I've received no such catechism."

"Then shall I teach it to you? For when they are done with me, the shadows might come looking after you, and if you don't know the prayer, how will you hope to defend yourself, My Lady?"

The Countess frowns and mutters, half to herself, half to the child, "I need no defense against shadows. Rather, let the shadows blanch and wilt at the thought of me."

"That same arrogance will be your undoing," the child replies. Then all the candles gutter and are extinguished, and the only light remaining is cold moonlight, getting in through the parted draperies. The child is gone. The Countess sits in her clawed chair and squeezes her eyes tightly shut. You may once have done very much the same thing, hearing some bump in the night. Fearing an open closet or the space beneath your bed, a window or a hallway. In this moment, Elizabeth Bathory von Ecsed, Alžbeta Bátoriová, the Bloody Lady of Čachtice, she seems no more fearsome for all her fearsome reputation than the child you once were. The boyish girl she herself was, forty-seven, forty-six, forty-eight years before this night. The girl given to tantrums and seizures and dressing up in boy's clothes. She cringes in this dark, moon-washed room, eyelids drawn against the night, and begins, haltingly, to recite the prayer Anna Darvulia has taught her.

"I am in peril, O cloud. Send, O send, you most powerful of Clouds, send ninety cats, for thou are the supreme Lord of Cats. I command you, King of the Cats, I pray you. May you gather them together, even if you are in the mountains, or on the waters, or on the roofs, or on the other side of the ocean...tell them to come to me."

FADE TO BLACK.

FADE UP.

The bedchamber is filled with the feeble colors of a January morning. With the wan luminance of the winter sun in these mountains. The balcony doors have blown open in the night, and a drift of snow has crept into the room. Pressed into the snow there are the barefoot tracks of a child. The Countess opens her eyes. She looks her age, and then some.

FADE TO BLACK.

FADE UP.

The Countess in her finest farthingale and ruff stands before the altar of Csejte's austere chapel. She gazes upwards at a stained-glass narrative set into the frames of three very tall and very narrow lancet windows. Her expression is distant, detached, unreadable. Following an establishing shot, and then a brief close up of the Countess' face, the trio of stained-glass windows dominates the screen. The production designer had them manufactured in Prague, by an artisan who was provided detailed sketches mimicking the style of windows fashioned by Harry Clarke and the Irish cooperative *An Túr Gloine*. As with so many aspects of the film, this window has inspired heated debate, chiefly regarding its subject matter. The most popular interpretation favors one of the hagiographies from the *Legenda sanctorum,* the tale of St. George and the dragon of Silene.

The stillness of the chapel is shattered by squealing hinges and quick footsteps, as Anna Darvulia rushes in from the bailey. She approaches the Countess, who has turned to meet her.

DARVULIA (angry):
What you seek, Elizabeth, you'll not find it here.

COUNTESS (feigning dismay):
I only wanted an hour's solitude. It's quiet here.

DARVULIA (sneering):
Liar. You came seeking after a solace that shall forever be denied you, as it has always been denied me. We have no place here, Elizabeth. Let us leave together.

COUNTESS
She came to me again last night. How can your prayer protect me from her, when she also knows it?

Anna Darvulia whispers something in the Countess' ear, then kisses her cheek and leads her from the chapel.

DISSOLVE TO:

Two guards or soldiers thread heavy iron chain through the handles of the chapel doors, then slide the shackle of a large padlock through the links of chain and clamp the lock firmly shut.

Somewhere towards the back of the theatre, a man coughs loudly, and a woman laughs. The man coughs a second time, then mutters (presumably to the woman), and she laughs again. You're tempted to turn about in your seat and ask them to please hold it down, that there are people who came to see the movie. But you don't. You don't take your eyes off the screen, and, besides, you've never been much for confrontation. You also consider going out to the lobby and complaining to the management, but you won't do that, either. It sounds like the man is telling a dirty joke, and you do your best to ignore him.

The film has returned to the snowy soundstage forest. Only now there are many more trees, spaced more closely together. Their trunks and branches are as dark as charcoal, as dark as the snow is light. Together these two elements – trees and snow, snow and trees – form a proper joyance for any chiaroscurist. In the foreground of this *mise-en-scène*, an assortment of taxidermied wildlife (two does, a rabbit, a badger, etc.) watches on with blind acrylic eyes as Anna Darvulia follows a path through the wood. She wears an enormous crimson cloak, the hood all but concealing her face. Her cloak completes the palette of the scene: the black trees, the white of the snow, this red slash of wool. There is a small falcon, a merlin, perched on the woman's left shoulder, and gripped in her left hand (she isn't wearing gloves) is a leather leash. As the music swells – strings, woodwinds, piano, the thunderous kettledrum – the camera pans slowly to the right, tracing the leash from Darvulia's hand to the heavy collar clasped about the Countess' pale throat. Elizabeth is entirely naked, scrambling through the snow on all fours. Her hair is a matted tangle of twigs and dead leaves. Briars have left bloody welts on her arms, legs, and buttocks. There are wolves following close behind her, famished wolves starving in the dead of this endless Carpathian winter. The pack is growing bold, and one of the animals rushes in close, pushing its muzzle between her exposed thighs, thrusting about with its wet nose, lapping obscenely at the Countess' ass and genitals. Elizabeth bares her sharp teeth and, wheeling around, straining against the leash, she snaps viciously at this churlish rake of a wolf. She growls as convincingly as any lunatic or lycanthrope might hope to growl.

All wolves are churlish. All wolves are rakes, especially in fairy tales, and especially this far from spring.

"Have you forgotten the prayer so soon?" Darvulia calls back, her voice cruel and mocking. Elizabeth doesn't answer, but the wolves yelp and retreat.

And as the witch and her pupil pick their way deeper into the forest, we see that the gypsy girl, dressed in a cloak almost identical to Darvulia's – wool dyed that same vivid red – stands among the wolves as they whine and mill about her legs.

Elizabeth awakens in her bed, screaming.

In a series of jump cuts, her screams echo through the empty corridors of Csejte.

(This scene is present in all prints, having somehow escaped the same fate as the unfilmed climax of the Countess' earlier trek through the forest – a testament to the fickle inconsistency of censors. In an interview she gave to the Croatian periodical *Hrvatski filmski ljetopis* [Autumn 2003], the actress who played Elizabeth reports that she actually did suffer a spate of terrible nightmares after making the film, and that most of them revolved around this particular scene. She says, "I have only been able to watch it [the scene] twice. Even now, it's hard to imagine myself having been on the set that day. I've always been afraid of dogs, and those were *real* wolves.")

In the fourth reel, you find you're slightly irritated when film briefly loses its otherwise superbly claustrophobic focus, during a Viennese interlude surely meant, instead, to build tension. The Countess' depravity is finally, inevitably brought to the attention of the Hungarian Parliament and King Matthias. The plaintiff is a woman named Imre Megyery, the Steward of Sávár, who became the guardian of the Countess' son, Pál Nádasdy, after the death of her husband. It doesn't help that the actor who plays György Thurzó, Matthias' palatine, is an Australian who seems almost incapable of getting the Hungarian accent right. Perhaps he needed a better dialect coach. Perhaps he was lazy. Possibly, he isn't a very good actor.

INT. COUNTESS' BEDCHAMBER. NIGHT.

Elizabeth and Darvulia in the Countess' bed, after a vigorous bout of lovemaking. Lovemaking, sex, fucking, whatever. Both women are nude. The corpse of a third woman lies between them. There's no blood, so how she died is unclear.

DARVULIA:
Megyery the Red, she plots against you. She has gone to the King, and very, very soon Thurzó's notaries will arrive to poke and pry and be the King's eyes and ears.

COUNTESS:
But you will keep me safe, Anna. And there is the prayer...

DARVULIA (gravely):
These are men, with all the power of the King and the Church at their backs. You must take this matter seriously, Elizabeth. The dark gods will concern themselves only so far, and after that we are on our own. Again, I beg you to at least consider abandoning Csejte.

COUNTESS:
No. No, and don't ask again. It is my home. Let Thurzó's men come. I will show them nothing. I will let them see nothing.

DARVULIA:
It isn't so simple, my sweet Erzsébet. Ferenc is gone, and without a husband to protect you...you must consider the greed of relatives who covet your estates, and consider, also, debts owed to you by a king who has no intention of ever settling them. Many have much to gain from your fall.

COUNTESS (stubbornly):
There will be no fall.

You sit up straight in your reclining theatre seat. You've needed to urinate for the last half hour, but you're not about to miss however much of the film you'd miss during a quick trip to the restroom. You try not to think about it; you concentrate on the screen and not your aching bladder.

INT. COUNTESS' BEDCHAMBER. NIGHT.

The Countess sits in her lion-footed chair, facing the open balcony doors. There are no candles burning, but we can see the silhouette of the gypsy girl outlined in the winter moonlight pouring into the room. She is all but naked. The wind blows loudly, howling about the walls of the castle.

COUNTESS (distressed):
No, you're not mine. I can't recall ever having seen you before. You are nothing of mine. You are some demon sent by the moon to harry me.

GIRL (calmly):
It is true I serve the moon, Mother, as do you. She is mistress to us both. We have both run naked while she watched on. We have both enjoyed her favors. We are each the moon's bitch.

COUNTESS (turning away):
Lies. Every word you say is a wicked lie. And I'll not hear any more of it. Begone, *strigoi.* Go back to whatever stinking hole was dug to cradle your filthy gypsy bones.

GIRL (suddenly near tears):
Please do no not say such things, Mother.

COUNTESS (through clenched teeth):
You are not my daughter! This is the price of my sins, to be visited by phantoms, to be haunted.

GIRL:
I only want to be held, Mother. I only want to be held, as any daughter would. I want to be kissed.

Slowly, the Countess looks back at the girl. Snow blows in through the draperies, swirling about the child. The girl's eyes flash red-gold. She takes a step nearer the Countess.

GIRL (contd.):
I can protect you, Mother.

COUNTESS:
From what? From whom?

GIRL:
You know from what, and you know from whom. You would know, even if Anna hadn't told you. You are not a stupid woman.

COUNTESS:
You do not come to protect me, but to damn me.

GIRL (kind):
I only want to be held, and sung to sleep.

COUNTESS (shuddering):
My damnation.

GIRL (smiling sadly):
No, Mother. You've tended well enough to that on your own. You've no need of anyone to hurry you along to the pit.

CLOSE UP – THE COUNTESS:

The Countess' face is filled with a mixture of dread and defeat, exhaustion and horror. She shuts her eyes a moment, muttering silently, then opens them again.

COUNTESS (resigned):
Come, child.

MEDIUM SHOT – THE COUNTESS:

The Countess sits in her chair, head bowed now, seemingly too exhausted to continue arguing with the girl. From the foreground, the gypsy girl approaches her. Strange shadows seem to loom behind the Countess' chair. The child begins to sing in a sweet, sad, lilting voice, a song that might be a hymn or a dirge.

FADE TO BLACK.

This scene will stay with you. You will find yourself thinking, *That's where it should have ended. That would have made a better ending.* The child's song – only two lines of which are intelligible – will remain with you long after many of the grimmer, more graphic details are forgotten. Two eerie, poignant lines: *Stay with me and together we will live forever./Death is the road to awe.* Later, you'll come across an article in *American Cinematographer* (April 2006), and discover that the screenwriter originally intended this to be the final scene, but was overruled by the director, who insisted it was too anticlimactic.

Which isn't to imply that the remaining twenty minutes are without merit, but only that they steer the film in a different and less subtle, less dreamlike direction. Like so many of the films you most admire – Bergman's *Det sjunde inseglet,* Charlie Kaufman's *Synecdoche, New York,* Herzog's *Herz aus Glas,* David Lynch's *Lost Highway* – this one is speaking to you in the language of dreams, and after the child's song, you have the distinct sense that the film has awakened, jolted from the subconscious to the conscious, the self-aware. It's ironic, therefore, that the next scene is a dream sequence. And it is a dream sequence that has left critics divided over the movie's conclusion and what the director intended to convey. There is a disjointed, tumbling series of images, and it is usually assumed that this is simply a nightmare delivered to the Countess by the child. However, one critic, writing for *Slovenska Kinoteka* (June 2005), has proposed it represents a literal divergence of two timelines, dividing the historical Báthory's fate from that of the fictional Báthory portrayed in the film. She notes the obvious, that the dream closely parallels the events of December 29, 1610, the day of the Countess' arrest. A few have argued the series of scenes was never meant to be perceived as a dream (neither the director nor the screenwriter have revealed their intent). The sequence may be ordered as follows:

The Arrival: A retinue on horseback – Thurzó, Imre Megyery, the Countess' sons-in-law, Counts Drugeth de Homonnay and Zrínyi, together with an armed escort. The party reaches the Csejte, and the iron gates swing open to admit them.

The Descent: The Palatine's men following a narrow, spiraling stairwell into the depth of the castle. They cover their mouths and noses against some horrible stench.

The Discovery: A dungeon cell strewn with corpses, in various stages of dismemberment and decay. Two women, still living, though clearly mad, their bodies naked and beaten and streaked with filth, are manacled to the stone walls. They scream at the sight of the men.

The Trial: Theodosious Syrmiensis de Szulo of the Royal Supreme Court pronounces a sentence of *perpetuis carceribus,* sparing the Countess from execution, but condemning her to lifelong confinement at Csejte.

The Execution/Pardon of the Accomplices: Three women and one man. Two of the women, Jó Ilona and Dorottya Szentes, are found guilty, publicly tortured, and burned alive. The man, Ujváry János (portrayed as a deformed dwarf), is beheaded before being thrown onto the bonfire with Jó and Dorottya. The third woman, Katarína Beniezky, is spared (this is not explained, and none of the four are named in the film).

The Imprisonment: The Countess sits on her bed as stonemasons brick up the chamber's windows and the door leading out onto the balcony. Then the door is sealed. Close ups of trowels, mortar, callused hands, Elizabeth's eyes, a Bible in her lap. Last shot from Elizabeth's POV, her head turned away from the camera, as the final few bricks are set in place. She is alone. Fade to black.

Anna Darvulia, "the Witch of the Forest," appears nowhere in this sequence.

FADE IN:

EXT. CSETJE STABLES. DAY.

The Countess watches as Anna Darvulia climbs onto the back of a horse. Once in the saddle, her feet in the stirrups, she stares sorrowfully down at the Countess.

DARVULIA:

I beg you, Erzsébet. Come with me. We'll be safe in the forest. There are places where no man knows to look.

COUNTESS:
This is my home. Please, don't ask me again. I won't run from them. I won't.

DARVULIA (speaking French and Croatian):
Ma petite bête douce. Volim te, Erzsébet.
(pause)
Ne m'oublie pas.

COUNTESS (slapping the horse's rump):
Go! Go now, love, before I lose my will.

CUT TO:

EXT. ČACHTICE CASTLE HILL. WINTER. DAY.

Anna Darvulia racing away from the snowbound castle, while the Countess watches from her tower.

COUNTESS (off):
I command you, O King of the Cats, I pray you.
May you gather them together,
Give them thy orders and tell them,
Wherever they may be, to assemble together,
To come from the mountains,
From the waters, from the rivers,
From the rainwater on the roofs, and from the oceans.
Tell them to come to me.

FADE TO BLACK.

FADE IN:

INT. COUNTESS' BEDCHAMBER. NIGHT.

The Countess in her enormous chair. The gypsy girl stands before her. As before, she is almost naked. There is candlelight and moonlight. Snow blows in from the open balcony doors.

GIRL:
She left you all alone.

COUNTESS:
No, child. I sent her away.

GIRL:
Back to the wood?

COUNTESS:
Back to the wood.

You sit in your seat and breathe the musty theatre smells, the smells which may as well be ghosts as they are surely remnants of long ago moments come and gone. Your full bladder has been all but forgotten. Likewise, the muttering, laughing man and woman seated somewhere behind you. There is room for nothing now but the illusion of moving pictures splashed across the screen. Your eyes and your ears translate the interplay of light and sound into story. The old theatre is a temple, holy in its way, and you've come to worship, to find epiphany in truths captured by a camera's lens. There's no need of plaster saints and liturgies. No need of the intermediary services of a priest. Your god – and the analogy has occurred to you on many occasions – is speaking to you directly, calling down from that wide silk-and-silver window and from Dolby speakers mounted high on the walls. Your god speaks in many voices, and its angels are an orchestra, and every frame is a page of scripture. This mass is rapidly winding down towards benediction.

GIRL:
May I sit at your feet, Mother?

COUNTESS:
Wouldn't you rather have my lap?

GIRL (smiling):
Yes, Mother. I would much rather have your lap.

The gypsy girl climbs into the Countess' lap, her small brown body nestling in the voluminous folds of Elizabeth's dress. The Countess puts her arms around the child, and holds her close. The girl rests her head on the Countess' breast.

GIRL (whisper):
They will come, you know? The men. The soldiers.

COUNTESS:
I know. But let's not think of that, not now. Let's not think on anything much at all.

GIRL:
But you recall the prayer, yes?

COUNTESS:
Yes, child. I recall the prayer. Anna taught me the prayer, just as you taught it to her.

GIRL:
You are so clever, Mother.

CLOSE UP.

The Countess' hand reaching into a fold of her dress, withdrawing a small silver dagger. The handle is black and polished wood, maybe jet or mahogany. There are occult symbols etched deeply into the metal, all down the length of the blade.

GIRL:
Will you say the prayer for me? No one ever prays for me.

COUNTESS:
I would rather hear you sing, dear. Please, sing for me.

The gypsy girl smiles and begins her song.

GIRL:
Stay with me, and together we will live forever.
Death is the road to awe –

The Countess clamps a hand over the girl's mouth, and plunges the silver dagger into her throat. The girl's eyes go very wide, as blood spurts from the wound. She falls backwards to the floor, and writhes there for a moment. The Countess gets to her feet, triumph in her eyes.

COUNTESS:
You think I didn't know you? You think I did not see?

The girl's eyes flash red-gold, and she hisses loudly, then begins to crawl across the floor towards the balcony. She pulls the knife from her throat and flings it away. It clatters loudly against the floor. The girl's teeth are stained with blood.

GIRL (hoarsely):
You deny me. You dare deny me.

COUNTESS:
You are none of mine.

GIRL:
You send me to face the cold alone? To face the moon alone?

The Countess doesn't reply, but begins to recite the Prayer of Ninety Cats. As she does, the girl stands, almost as if she hasn't been wounded. She backs away, stepping through the balcony doors, out into snow and brilliant moonlight. The child climbs onto the balustrade, and it seems for a moment she might grow wings and fly away into the Carpathian night.

COUNTESS:
May these ninety cats appear to tear and destroy
The hearts of kings and princes,
And in the same way the hearts of teachers and judges,
And all who mean me harm,
That they shall harm me not.
(pause)
Holy Trinity, protect me.
And guard Erzsébet from all evil.

The girl turns her back on the Countess, gazing down at the snowy courtyard below.

GIRL:
I'm the one who guarded you, Mother. I'm the one who has kept you safe.

COUNTESS (raising her voice):
Tell them to come to me.
And to hasten them to bite the heart.
Let them rip to pieces and bite again and again...

GIRL:
There's no love in you anywhere. There never was.

COUNTESS:
Do not say that! Don't you dare say that! I have loved –

GIRL (sadly):
You have lusted and called it love. You tangle appetite and desire. Let me fall, and be done with you.

COUNTESS (suddenly confused):
No. No, child. Come back. No one falls this night.

INT./EXT. NIGHT.

As the Countess moves towards the balcony, the gypsy girl steps off the balustrade and tumbles to the courtyard below. The Countess cries out in horror and rushes out onto the balcony

EXT. NIGHT.

The broken body of the girl on the snow-covered flagstones of the courtyard. Blood still oozes from the wound in her throat, but also from her open mouth and her nostrils. Her eyes are open. Her blood steams in the cold air. A large crow lands near her body. The camera pans upwards, and we see the Countess gazing down in horror at the broken body of the dead girl. In the distance, wolves begin to howl.

EXT. BALCONY. NIGHT.

The Countess is sitting now, her back pressed to the stone columns of the balustrade. She's sobbing, her hands tearing at her hair. She is the very portrait here of loss and madness.

COUNTESS (weeping):
I didn't know. God help me, I did not know.

FADE UP TO WHITE.

EXT. CSEJTE. MORNING.

A small cemetery near the castle's chapel. Heavy snow covers everything. The dwarf Ujváry János has managed to hack a shallow grave into the frozen earth. The Countess watches as the gypsy girl's small body, wrapped in a makeshift burial shroud, is lowered into the hole. The Countess turns and hurries away across the bailey, and János begins filling the grave in again. Shovelful after shovelful of dirt and frost and snow falls on the body, and slowly it disappears from view. Perched on a nearby headstone, an owl watches. It blinks, and rotates its head and neck 180 degrees, so it appears to be watching the burial upside down.

In a week, you'll write your review of the film, the review you're being paid to write, and you'll note that the genus and species of owl watching János as he buries the dead girl is *Bubo virginianus,* the Great Horned Owl. You'll also note the bird is native to North America, and not naturally found in Europe, but that to fret over these sorts of inaccuracies is, at best, pedantic. At worst, you'll write, it means that one has entirely missed the point and would have been better off staying at home and not wasting the price of a movie ticket.

This is not the life of Erzsébet Báthory.

No one has ever lived this exact life.

Beyond the establishing shot of the ruins at the beginning of the film, the castle is not Csejte. Likewise, the forest that surrounds it is the forest that this story requires it to be, and whether or not it's an accurate depiction of the forests of the Piešťany region of Slovakia is irrelevant.

The Countess may or may not have been Anna Darvulia's lover. Erzsébet Báthory may have been a lesbian. Or she may not. Anna Darvulia may or may not have existed.

There is no evidence whatsoever that Erzsébet was repeatedly visited in the dead of night by a strange gypsy child.

Or that the Countess' fixation with blood began when she struck a servant who'd accidentally pulled her hair.

Or that Erzsébet was ever led naked through those inaccurate forests while lustful wolves sniffed at her sex.

Pedantry and nitpicking is fatal to all fairy tales. You will write that there are people who would argue a wolf lacks the lung capacity to blow down a house of straw and that any beanstalk tall enough to reach the clouds would collapse under its own weight. They are, you'll say, the same lot who'd dismiss Shakespeare for mixing Greek and Celtic mythology, or on the grounds that there was never a prince of Verona named Escalus. "The facts are neither here nor there," you will write. "We have entered a realm where facts may not even exist." You'll be paid a pittance for the review, which virtually no one will read.

There will be one letter to the editor, complaining that your review was "too defensive" and that you are "an apologist for shoddy, prurient filmmaking." You'll remember this letter (though not the name of its author), many years after the paltry check has been spent.

The facts are neither here nor there.

Sitting in your theatre seat, these words have not yet happened, the words you'll write. At best, they're thoughts at the outermost edges of conception. Sitting here, there is nothing but the film, another's fever dreams you have been permitted to share. And you are keenly aware how little remains of the fifth reel, that the fever will break very soon.

EXT. FOREST. NIGHT.

MEDIUM SHOT.

Anna Darvulia sits before a small campfire, her horse's reins tied to a tree behind her. A hare is roasting on a spit above the fire. There's a sudden gust of wind, and, briefly, the flames burn a ghostly blue. She narrows her eyes, trying to see something beyond the firelight.

DARVULIA:

You think I don't see you? You think I can't smell you?

(pause)

You've no right claim left on me. I've passed my debt

> to the Báthory woman. I've prepared her for you. Now, leave me be, spirit. Do not trouble me this night or any other.

The fire flares blue again, and Darvulia lowers her head, no longer gazing into the darkness.

DISSOLVE TO:

EXT. ČACHTICE CASTLE HILL. NIGHT.

The full moon shines down on Csejte. The castle is dark. There's no light in any of its windows.

CUT TO:

The gypsy girl's unmarked grave. But much of the earth that filled the hole now lies heaped about the edges, as if someone has hastily exhumed the corpse. Or as if the dead girl might have dug her way out. The ground is white with snow and frost, and sparkles beneath the moon.

CUT TO:

EXT. BALCONY OUTSIDE COUNTESS' BEDCHAMBER. NIGHT.

The owl that watched Ujváry János bury the girl is perched on the stone balustrade. The doors to the balcony have been left standing open. Draperies billow in the freezing wind.

CLOSE UP:

Owl's round face. It blinks several times, and the bird's eyes flash an iridescent red-gold.

The Countess sits in her bedchamber, in that enormous chair with its six savage feet. A wolf pelt lies draped across her lap, emptied of its wolf. Like a dragon, the Countess breathes steam. She holds a wooden cross in her shaking hands.

"Tell the cats to come to me," she says, uttering the prayer hardly above a whisper. There is no need to raise her voice; all gods and angels must surely have good ears. "And hasten them," she continues, "to bite the hearts of my enemies and all who would do me harm. Let them rip to pieces and bite again and again the heart of my foes. And guard Erzsébet from all evil. *O Quam Misericors est Deus, Pius et Justus.*"

Elizabeth was raised a Calvinist, and her devout mother, Anna, saw that she attended a fine Protestant school in Erdöd. She was taught mathematics and learned to write and speak Greek, German, Slovak, and Latin. She learned Latin prayers against the demons and the night.

"*O Quam Misericors est Deus. Justus et Paciens,*" she whispers, though she's shivering so badly that her teeth have begun to chatter and the words no longer come easily. They fall from her lips like stones. Or rotten fruit. Or lies. She cringes in her chair, and gazes intently towards the billowing, diaphanous drapes and the night and balcony beyond them. A shadow slips into the room, moving across the floor like spilled oil. The drapes part as if they have a will all their own (they were pulled to the sides with hooks and nylon fishing line, you've read), and the gypsy girl steps into the room. She is entirely nude, and her tawny body and black hair are caked with the earth of her abandoned grave. There are feathers caught in her hair, and a few drift from her shoulders to lie on the floor at her feet. She is bathed in moonlight, as cliché as that may sound. She has the iridescent eyes of an owl. The girl's face is the very picture of sorrow.

"Why did you bury me, Mother?"

"You were dead…"

The girl takes a step nearer the Countess. "I was so cold down there. You cannot ever imagine anything even half so cold as the dead lands."

The Countess clutches her wood cross. She is shaking, near tears. "You cannot be here. I said the prayers Anna taught me."

The girl has moved very near the chair now. She is close enough that she could reach out and stroke Elizabeth's pale cheek, if she wished to do so.

"The cats aren't coming, Mother. Her prayer was no more than any other prayer. Just pretty words against that which has never had cause to fear pretty words."

"The cats aren't coming," the Countess whispers, and the cross slips from her fingers.

The gypsy child reaches out and strokes Elizabeth's pale cheek. The girl's short nails are broken and caked with dirt. "It doesn't matter, Mother, because I'm here. What need have you of cats, when your daughter has come to keep you safe?"

The Countess looks up at the girl, who seems to have grown four or five inches taller since entering the room. "You are my daughter?" Elizabeth asks, the question a mouthful of fog.

"I am," the girl replies, kneeling to gently kiss the Countess' right cheek. "I have many mothers, as I have many daughters of my own. I watch over them all. I hold them to me and keep them safe."

"I've lost my mind," the Countess whispers. "long, long ago, I lost my mind." She hesitantly raises her left hand, brushing back the girl's filthy, matted hair, dislodging another feather. The Countess looks like an old woman. All traces of the youth she clung to with such ferocity have left her face, and her eyes have grown cloudy. "I am a madwoman."

"It makes no difference," the gypsy girl replies.

"Anna lied to me."

"Let that go, Mother. Let it all go. There are things I would show you. Wondrous things."

"I thought she loved me."

"She is a sorceress, Mother, and an inconstant lover. But I am true. And you'll need no other's love but mine."

The movie's score has dwindled to a slow smattering of piano notes, a bow drawn slowly, nimbly across the string of a cello. A hint of flute.

The Countess whispers, "I called to the King of Cats."

The girl answers, "Cats rarely ever come when called. And certainly not ninety all at once."

And the brown girl leans forward, her lips pressed to the pale Countess' right ear. Whatever she says, it's nothing you can make out from your seat, from your side of the silver mirror. The gypsy girl kisses the Countess on the forehead.

"I'm so very tired."

"Shhhhh, Mother. I know. It's okay. You can rest now."

The Countess asks, "Who are you."

"I am the peace at the end of all things."

EXT. COURTYARD BELOW COUNTESS' BALCONY. MORNING.

The body of Elizabeth Báthory lies shattered on the flagstones, her face and clothes a mask of frozen blood. Fresh snow is falling on her corpse. A number of noisy crows surround the body. No music now, only the wind and the birds.

FADE TO BLACK:

ROLL CREDITS.

THE END.

As always, you don't leave your seat until the credits are finished and the curtain has swept shut again, hiding the screen from view. As always, you've made no notes, preferring to rely on your memories.

You follow the aisle to the auditorium doors and step out into the almost deserted lobby. The lights seem painfully bright. You hurry to the restroom. When you're finished, you wash your hands, dry them, then spend almost an entire minute staring at your face in the mirror above the sink.

Outside, it's started to rain, and you wish you'd brought an umbrella.

THE PRAYER OF NINETY CATS

A story that began with a recurring dream of a demonic child visiting an old and ailing woman who struggled to protect her secrets from the child. On moonless nights, the child would climb the walls of a stone tower and slip in through an open window. That was the nucleus about which accreted this exploration of my fascination with cinema, lost films, and the Countess Elizabeth Báthory de Ecsed. Brit Mandelo writes, "Kiernan's 'The Prayer of Ninety Cats' has a curious, seductive structure that leads the reader ever deeper into the *experience* of viewing a film, on a metatextual level and a literal level. The film that the protagonist is watching for review is one layer of story; the actual world outside the film and the protagonist's experience of it is another. Yet, somehow, it is this fictional film that lingers – the film that I feel, having read this story, I *have* seen myself. That Kiernan manages evoke this visceral and visual memory in a purely textual story, when giving us the film only in snippets of script and description as the protagonist relays them, is nothing short of stunning. The layer of story about the theater, the often-inexplicable immersion of the artificial screen and what is displayed on it – that layer, for a watcher of movies, is breathtaking in its simple, concise, and *real* observations about the nature of the medium and the nature of the time spent indulging in it." The story was nominated for the 2014 Locus Award in the novelette category and also won the 2014 World Fantasy Award for best short fiction.

Daughter Dear Desmodus

If there were any proper name for her specific teratism, the deformity that determined the course of her life, Ileana never learned it. Her life was not filled with doctors or medical researchers to poke and prod, chart genetic abnormalities, to erect a new syndrome in her honor, and publish their exacting findings for all the world to see. That is what did *not* happen. Instead, she was only abandoned by horrified parents, suspecting some imp, succubus, or minor devil might have played a role in the gestation of their child. It *was* duly noted, with some irony, that her parents' small farm was located within a few miles of the nowhere-in-particular crossroad burg of Batson, Mississippi. Late one night, Ileana's mother and father (who did not bestow that name upon her) visited a carnival passing through the relative metropolis of Hattiesburg and sold the infant for the princely sum of five-hundred dollars, tax free. And so Ileana was raised by a dwarf in a rusty, battered 1966 Airstream Overlander trailer, which the dwarf (a clown) shared with the "human blockhead," a fellow paid to insert an ice pick and nails through his sinus cavities. She grew up "where the barkers called the moon down," among the smell of cotton candy, the reek of lion piss, the sweet perfume of camel dung, and the casual profanity of roustabouts. The owner of the carnival didn't dare unveil her to the cake eaters who lined up for his sideshow of anatomical wonders and nightmares until she was eighteen, for fear of various and sundry child-labor laws, deviating as they do from state to state. Besides, as Ileana entered, then passed through puberty, her malformations became markedly more pronounced, and so the carnival owner considered his investment and patience a wise move, indeed.

Three nights after her birthday, after the carnival set up outside the Lawrenceville, Kansas city limits, she took her place among the other freaks. A tall section of bally canvas was painted with a somewhat less than accurate – but undeniably sensational – portrait of DESMODIA: THE BAT GIRL!!!! The name had been suggested by the fat lady, who'd once read a book on bats and remembered that some vampire bats belong to the genus *Desmodus*. This was plenty good enough for the owner of the carnival, and so Desmodia it was (though her dwarf foster father had long since christened her Ileana, after his grandmother, who'd died in a German concentration camp). Outside the canvas flaps, the talker shouted his blind-opening rant to every soul within earshot and then some: "Gonna have to *see* it to believe it! Flapper the seal boy, the Lady Mariah so corpulent she needs a forklift to get from place to place, Siamese sisters – Bethany and Bathsheba – joined at the backside, Mr. Shattertongue the Glass Eater, and Electra, the Lightning Girl! The *horror and the thrill*, spread out before you're very eyes! Yesssiree! All pregnant women refused entry – apologies, show policy, and all members of the fairer sex, be warned and you take your chances! But you ain't heard the best and worst of it yet! We've something new and this something beats the rest *hands down*, for the *very first time* on *this very night!* [pause, voice descending into a sorrowful tone] Truth be told and in all honestly, ladies and gentlemen, I do wish I'd never set eyes on this pitiful creature, found in the tropical wilds of Indonesia. Rumored to be the offspring of an unspeakable congress between a native witch and a flying fox, I wish to the Good Jesus hisself *I'd* never seen her, and I'll tell you *that* for free. Gentlemen and mothers, when you get home, look at *your* dear, dear children. *Love* them, hold them to your *bosom*, and give thanks to God that *you* have not been cursed with a child like this! [voice rises again with former enthusiasm] Come one, come all! See the freaks of humanity!"

He went on like this for almost ten minutes, while the penny whistles and calliope, the drums and glockenspiel cacophony from the midway and the thunderous clatter of machinery and a hundred other voices filled the air. In that ten minutes (or so), sufficient tickets were sold, and incredulous, fearful, skeptical, and amused rubes filed into the darkened tent. By the light of bare electric bulbs strung overhead, they saw what they had been promised, a little more or a little less. But plenty close enough no one asked for his or her money back.

Ileana, in her first appearance as Desmodia, was the last of them all, the penultimate oddity. They'd built a sturdy wooden cage for her, and over long months she'd learned to hang upside down from a steel rod that ran from one side to the other, hanging by her three-toed feet, an accomplishment of which she was more than a little proud, and one that had made her bony legs strong and lean. So, there she dangled, almost nude as the night she was squirted from betwixt her mama's thighs, her "wings" spread wide, teeth bared in a perpetual snarl. It hardly mattered that she was incapable of flight; the rubes didn't know that, and what they don't know, don't tell them. The membranes of flesh (a patagium so thin as to be translucent) extending from her ribcage all the way to the tip ends of her long two-fingered hands; seeing that was quite enough *without* any aerial demonstration, thank you very much. The overall effect was significantly enhanced by the addition of scarlet contact lenses and strips of fake fur glued here and there onto her body with spirit gum. But the jaws and teeth, *those* were her own, that fearsome malocclusion of maxilla and dentary, plus unnaturally sharp incisors protruding at least half an inch below her rouged lower lip. A few in the crowd caught a glimpse of the short tail, sprouting from the end of her spine, no longer than a pinkie finger. Her jet-black hair (dyed from its natural brown) hung down all the way to the straw dust covering the floor of the cage. She spat and hissed as effectively as any movie vampire ever had hissed and spat.

On cue, a terrified *looking* man (who usually sold candy apples) entered the enclosure and held out to her a bowl of "blood" (in actuality, a mixture of cherry Kool-Aid and a dash or two of black food coloring). She craned her neck at what seemed a completely impossible angle and lapped greedily at the liquid. Then she snarled an extra loud snarl, and the vendor of candy apples dropped the bowl of fake blood and dashed to "safety."

Women turned away at the grisly sight and men gasped. How could such an abomination be real, and yet, there she was, and there was no denying the truth of her. Ileana had turned a trick – damned enough near to magic – to put her fellow freaks to shame: she had entered the depths of her audience's unconscious minds, to plague their thoughts for months and even years to come. The most rational among them left the tent impressed and scrambling for a reassuring, soothing, and *scientific* explanation for what they'd just witnessed.

And once five more crowds had filed past, and the talker counted out the night's bunce, and Ileana's compatriots grumbled about "Little Miss Flutter" and "Dracula's Daughter," the Yale padlock on Ileana's cage was unlocked. and she was helped into a bathrobe, then hoppled on her crutches back to the Airstream trailer. The dwarf was still busy with the nightly walkaround that was expected of all the clowns if they wished a check come payday (which, by the way, did not always come). She let herself in the trailer, and was relieved that the blockhead was also out, most likely getting drunk with the shanty and the sledge gang. Of late, he'd taken to looking at her with a desirous eye, and neither she nor the dwarf were equal to fending off his advances. She removed the contacts – which had begun to smart halfway through the show – stripped away the fake fur, and wiped away grease paint with cold cream and tissues. She worked the stiffness from her legs, which had begun to cramp after half an hour, and combed the saw dust from her pretend-ebony hair. Then she went to bed, scrambling clumsily into her upper berth above her dwarf stepfather's lower. There she looked at photographs of beautiful women in a year-old Parisian fashion magazine (stolen from a dentist's office) until she drifted off to sleep with the dim reading light still burning.

She dreamt the sorts of dreams that bat girls dream. She dreamt of normalcy, and she dreamt of flying. She dreamt of a phonograph playing

Twinkle, twinkle, little bat!
How I wonder where you're at!
Up above the world you fly.
Like a tea-tray in the sky.

again and again and again (as a child, the dwarf had frequently read to her from *Alice in Wonderland*). But she also dreamt the familiar dream of a handsome young man who didn't work for any carnival whatsoever, and how he told her, repeatedly, that "What is different is beautiful." In that dream, Ileana had five fingers and five toes on each hand and on each foot, respectively, and she didn't need crutches to walk. As always, he led her away across a summer field festooned with black-eyed Susans and lavender and Queen Anne's Lace.

DAUGHTER DEAR DESMODUS

I believe that I often do my best work when I free myself from the tyranny of Plot, from the artifice of Story, from reader expectations of what constitutes a *proper* short story. I read this tale aloud at KGB Bar in Manhattan on the evening of October 16, 2013. I think it was among the best readings I've ever given. The phrase "where the barkers call the moon down" is borrowed from the Decemberists and Colin Meloy.

Goggles (c. 1910)

1.

Eleven-year old Samuel is sitting alone at the entrance to the Confluence Park bunkers, huddled against the hot, stinking wind, ruffling his hair even though they've all been forbidden to go alone to the entrance. It's long past midnight, and the dreams have been keeping him awake again. The ruins and the storm-wracked sky outside are less frightening than the dreams - all of them taken together as a whole, or any single one of dreams. Better he sit and stare out through the gate's iron bars, fairly certain he can be back in his berth before Miss makes her early morning rounds. He always feels bad whenever he breaks the rules, going against her orders, the dictates that keep them all alive, the children that she tends here in the sanctuary of the winding rat's maze of tunnels. He feels bad, too, that he's figured out a way to pick the padlock on the iron door that has to be opened in order to stare out the bars, and Samuel feels worst of all that he thinks often of picking that lock, too, and disobeying her first and most inviolable rule: never, ever leave the bunker alone. Still, regret and guilt are not enough to keep him in his upper berth, staring at the concrete ceiling pressing down less than a metre above his face.

Outside, the wind screams, and sickly chartreuse lightning flashes and jabs with its forked lightning fingers at the shattered, blackened ruins of the dead city of Cherry Creek, Colorado. Samuel shuts his eyes, and he tries to ignore the afterimages of the flashes swimming about behind his lids. He counts off the seconds on his fingers, counting aloud, though not daring to speak above a whisper – sixteen, seventeen, eighteen full seconds before the thunder reaches him, thunder so loud that it almost seems to rattle deep down in his bones. He divides eighteen by three, as Miss has taught them, and so he knows the strike was about six kilometres from the entrance to the tunnels.

Sam, that's much too close, she would say. *Now, you shut that door and get your butt back downstairs.*

He might be so bold as to reply that at least they didn't have to worry about the dogs and the rats during a squall. But that might be enough to earn him whatever punishment she was in the mood to mete out to someone who'd not only flagrantly broken the rules, but then had the unmitigated gall to sass her.

The boy opens his eyes, blinking at the lightening ghosts swirling before them. He stares at his filthy hands a moment, vaguely remembering when he was much younger and his mother was always at him to scrub beneath his nails and behind his ears. When she saw to it he had clean clothes every day, and shoes with laces, shoes without soles worn so thin they may as well be paper. He stares at the ruins and half remembers the city that was, before the War, before men set the sky on fire and seared the world.

Miss tells them it's best not to let one's thoughts dwell on those days. "That time is never coming back," she says. "We have to learn to live in *this* age, if we're going to have any hope of survival."

But all they have – their clothing, beds, dishes, school books, the dwindling medicinals and foodstuffs – all of it is scavenged remnants of the time before. He knows that. They all know that, even if no one ever says it aloud.

There's another flash of the lightning that is not quite green and not quite yellow. But this time Samuel doesn't close his eyes or bother counting. It's obvious this one's nearer than the last strike. It's obvious it's high time that he shut the inner door, lock it, and slip back through the tunnels to the room where the boys all sleep. Miss always looks in on them about three, and she's ever quick to notice an empty bunk. That's another thing from the world before: her silver pocket watch that she's very, very careful to keep wound. She's said that it belonged to her father who died in the Battle of New Amsterdam in those earliest months of the War. Miss is, Samuel thinks, a woman of many contradictions. She admonishes them when they talk of their old lives, yet, in certain melancholy moods, she will regale them with tales of lost wonders and conveniences, of the sun and stars and of airships, and her kindly father, a physician who went away to tend wounded soldiers and subsequently died in New Amsterdam.

Walking back to his bed as quietly as he can walk, Samuel considers those among his companions who are convinced that Miss isn't sane. Jessamine says that, and the twins – Parthena and Hortence – and also Luther. Sometimes, when Miss has her back to them, they'll draw circles in the air about their ears and roll their eyes and snigger. But Samuel doesn't think she's insane. Just very lonely and sad and scared.

We keep her alive, he thinks. *Because she has all of us to tend to she's still alive, against her recollections.* He knows of lots of folks who survived the bombardments, and then the burning of the skies and the storms that followed, and whom the feral dogs didn't catch up with, lots of those folks did themselves in, rather than face such a shattered world. Samuel thinks it was their inescapable memories of before that killed them.

He crawls back into bed, and lies on the cool sheets and stares at the ceiling until the dreams come again. In the dreams – which he thinks of as nightmares – there's bright sunshine, green fields, and his mother's blonde hair like spun gold. In his dreams, there's plenty of food and there's laughter, and no lightning whatsoever. There is never lightning, nor is there the oily rain that sizzles when it touches anything metal. He's never told Miss about his dreams. She wouldn't want to hear them, and she'd only frown and make him promise not to dare mention them to the others. Not that he ever has. Not that he ever will. Samuel figures they all have their own good-bad dreams to contend with.

2.

The storm lasts for two days and two nights. Miss reads to them from the Bible, and from *The Life and Strange Surprizing Adventures of Robinson Crusoe,* and from Mark Twain. She feeds her filthy, raw-boned children the last of the tinned beef and peaches, and Samuel has begun to resign himself to the possibility that this might be the occasion on which they starve before an expedition for more provisions can be mounted.

But the storm ends, and no one starves.

Early the morning after the last peals of thunder, after a meager breakfast – one sardine each and tea so weak that it's hardly more than cups of steaming water – Miss calls them all to the assembly room. They know it was not originally *intended* as an assembly room, but as an armory. The steel cabinets with their guns, grenades, and sabers still line the walls. Only the kegs of black powder and crates of dynamite have been removed. The children line up in two neat rows, boys in front, girls behind them, and she examines them each in their turn, inspecting gaunt faces and bodies, looking closely at their shoes and garments, before choosing the three whom she will send out of the bunker in search of food and other necessaries.

Once, there were older kids to whom this duty fell, but with every passing year there were fewer and fewer of them. Every year, fewer of them survived the necessary trips outside of the bunker, and, finally, there were none of them left at all. Finally, none came back. Samuel suspects a brave (or cowardly) few might have actually run away, deciding to take their chances in the wastelands that lie out beyond Cherry Creek, rather than return. However, this is only a suspicion, and he's never spoken of it to anyone else.

The lighter sheets of rain that fall towards the end of the electrical storms are mostly only water, and after an hour or so it will have diluted most of the nitric acid. It'll take that long to hand out the slickers and vulcanized overshoes and gloves, the airtight goggles and respirators, and for Miss to check that every rusty clasp is secure and every fraying cord has been tied as tightly as possible. Samuel imagines, as he always does, that the others are all holding their breath as she makes her choices. There have been too many instances when someone didn't return, or when they returned dying or crippled, which is as good as dead, or worse, here in their bunker in the world after the War. Samuel also imagines he's one of the few who ever *hopes* that he'll be picked. He doesn't know for certain, but he strongly suspects this to be the case.

If volunteers were permitted, he would always volunteer.

"Patrick Henry," says Miss. Patrick Henry Olmstead takes one step forward and stares at the toes of his boots. His hair is either auburn or dirty blond, depending on the light, and his eyes are either hazel green or hazel brown, depending on the light. He's two years younger than, Samuel. Or, at least he thinks he might be; a lot of the younger children don't know their ages. Patrick Henry has a keloid scar on his chin, and he's taller than one might expect from his nine years. He's shy, and speaks so softly that it's often necessary to ask him to please speak up and repeat himself.

"Molly," says Miss.

"Please no, Miss." Molly Peterson replies.

"You have good shoes, Molly. Your shoes are the best among the lot."

"I'll let someone else wear my shoes. I won't even ask for them back afterwards. Please choose another, Miss."

Molly is only eight, and her hair is black as coal tar. She's missing the pinkie finger from her left hand, from a run in with the dogs before they found her at the corner of East Bateman and Vulcan Avenue. Before an expedition brought her back to the bunker two years ago. The dogs got her sister, and she's only left the bunker once after her arrival. Molly has nightmares about the dogs, and sometimes she wakes screaming loudly enough that she startles them all from sleep, as her cries echo along the cavernous corridors. Her skin is very pale and freckled. She's small for her age. Samuel fancies if he were to ever court a girl, Molly would do just fine.

"You will go, Molly. Your name has been read, my choice has been made, and we will not have this argument. No one will go in your stead."

Molly only nods and chews at her lower lip.

"You will have eight hours," Miss tells them, just like always. "After eight hours..."

Samuel tunes out her grim and familiar proclamations. No one's ever come back after eight hours, and that's all that matters. The rest, Miss only says to be sure his two companions fully understand the gravity of their situation, and Samuel understands completely. This will be his fifth trip out in just the last year. He's good at scavenging, and Miss knows it. He enjoys entertaining the notion he's the best of them all.

"Eight hours," Miss says again.

"Eight hours, Ma'am," the chosen three repeat in perfect unison, and then she shepherds them away to the room where the outside gear is stored. She gives them each a burlap sack and a Colt revolver and a single .44 caliber bullet; the bunker's munitions cache is running too low to send them off with any more than that single round. She once whispered in his ear, "For yourself, or for one of the dogs. That has to be your decision." He has no idea whether or not she's ever said the same thing to any of the others. He doesn't actually *want* to know, because maybe it's a special acknowledgement of his bravery and approaching manhood, and if it's a jot of wisdom she imparts to one and all, Samuel would be more than a little disappointed.

3.

As almost always, Samuel is given the responsibility of carrying the map. It's a 15-minute topographic map of the Cherry Creek metropolitan area. It's folded and tucked into a water-tight leather-and-PVC case, so he can see it, yet there's minimal danger of its getting wet. But Samuel knows exactly where he's going today, even through the dense fog, so he hardly needs the green and white topo sheet, with its black squares marking buildings and all its contour lines designating elevation. He and Patrick Henry and Molly are heading to what's left of the Gesellschaft zur Förderung der Luftschiffahrt's Arapahoe Station dirigible terminal. A few months back, he and two others were rummaging about in one of the airships that crashed when Cherry Creek was hit by the first wave of blowbacks from Tesla's teleforce mechanism. Deck B was still more or less intact, which meant the kitchen was also mostly intact, along with its storerooms. The two boys with him hadn't wanted to enter the crash, so Samuel had climbed alone through a ragged tear in the hull. He spent the better part of an hour picking his way through the crumpled remains of the gondola, always mindful of the hazards posed by rusted beams overhead and the rotting deck boards beneath his feet. But, at last, he found the storeroom, the shelves still weighted down with their wealth of cans and crates of bottles and jars, a surprising number of which hadn't shattered on impact, thanks to having been carefully packed in excelsior.

Samuel had retraced his steps, marking the path with debris placed *just so,* then cajoled his two fellows to follow him back inside. The three of them had returned with enough food to last several weeks, including fruit juice that had not yet spoiled. The discovery had earned Samuel one night of double rations.

"Are you certain we're not lost?" asks Patrick Henry, his already quiet voice muffled by the respirator covering the lower half of his face.

"I don't get lost," Samuel replied, then tossed half a brick against a lamppost. Someone had long ago shattered the globe crowning the post, or, more likely, a lightning storm had taken it out. "I've never gotten lost, not even once."

"Everyone gets lost sometime," says Molly. "Don't be such a braggart." She was so scared that she jumped at the thud of the brick hitting the lamppost.

"Then maybe I'm not everybody."

"Now, you're not even making sense," mutters Molly.

"Are you sure we're going west?" Patrick Henry asks.

Samuel stops and glares back at the younger boy. "Holy hell and horse shit, I wish Miss had let me come alone. Why are you asking me? *You're* the one with the Brunton."

No one – not even Samuel – is ever allowed to carry both the map *and* the Brunton compass. Just in case. Patrick Henry blushes, then digs the compass from the pocket of his overalls.

"Waste our time and take a reading if it'll make you feel better, but we ain't lost."

"Aren't," whispers Molly.

"But we *aren't* lost," Samuel sighs and rolls his eyes behind the smudgy lenses of his old blowtorch goggles

"It won't take long," says Patrick Henry, and so Samuel kicks at the dirt and Molly frets while he squints into the compass' mirror and studies the target, needle, and guide line, finding the azimuth pointing 270° from true north.

"Satisfied?" Samuel asks after a minute or two.

"Well, we're off by…"

"We're *not* lost," Samuel growls, then turns and stalks away, as though he means to leave the other two behind. He never would, but it works, and soon they're trotting along to catch up.

"It's not as though we can see the sun," Molly says, a little out of breath. "It's not as if we can see the mountains."

"I know the way to the station," Samuel tells her. "That's why Miss picked me, because I know the way."

"It pays to be sure."

"Fine, Molly. Now we're sure. Shut up and walk."

"You don't have to be such a bloody, self-righteous snit about it," she tells Samuel.

"Yes he does," sneers Patrick Henry, and Samuel laughs and agrees with him.

The going is slower than usual, mostly due to deep new washouts dividing many of the thoroughfares. Patrick Henry takes a bad tumble in the one bisecting Davies and Milton streets, where the dead city's namesake waterway has jumped its banks and carved a steep ravine. But he doesn't break or even sprain anything, only almost loses the revolver Miss has entrusted to him. Samuel and Molly pull him free of the mud and helped him back up to street level, Samuel admonishing him for being such a clumsy fool every step of the way. Patrick Henry doesn't bother to say otherwise. The three sit together a few minutes with Molly, catching their breath and staring upstream at the wreckage that had once been Beeman's Mercantile before the building slid into the washout.

It's afternoon before they reach the airship, and Samuel has begun to worry about getting back before their eight hours are up, before Miss writes them off for dead. Besides, with the dogs on the prowl, he knows from experience that every passing minute decreases their chances of not meeting up with a pack of the mongrels.

"It's enormous," Molly says, gazing up at the crash, her voice tinged with awe. All three were too young to recall the days when the Count von Zepplin's majestic airships plied the skies by the hundreds. And this was the first time that either Molly or Patrick Henry had actually seen a dirigible, other than a couple of pictures in one of Miss' books.

"It's like a skeleton," says Patrick Henry, and Samuel supposes it is, though the comparison has never before occurred to him. Once, almost a year ago, he'd crawled through the ruins of the late Professor Jeremiah Ogilvy's museum on Kipling Street. He'd seen bones there, or stones in the shape of bones, and Miss had explained to him afterwards that they were the remains of wicked sea monsters that lived before Noah's Flood and which were not permitted room on the Ark (he was polite and didn't ask her why sea creatures had drowned in the deluge). The petrified bones had much the same appearance of the crushed and half-melted steel framework sprawling before them.

Samuel points to the narrow vertical tear in what's left of the gondola. It's black as pitch beyond the tear. "The larder isn't too far in, but it's rough going. So, we'd best – "

"I'm not going in there," declares Patrick Henry, interrupting him.

"Hell's bell's you ain't," says Samuel, whirling about to face the other boy.

"Aren't," Molly says so quietly they almost don't hear her. "You *aren't* going in there."

"You shut up, Molly, and yes he is most certainly does. I don't care if he's a damned yellow-bellied coward. there ain't no *way* I can carry all the food we need out alone."

"I *won't* go in there, Samuel."

Samuel shoves Patrick Henry with enough force that the younger boy almost loses his balance as falls to the tarmac.

"You will, or I'll kick your sorry ass to Perdition and back again."

"Then you do that, Samuel. 'Cause I *won't* go in, no matter how hard to beat me, and that's all there is to it."

"You slimy, piss-poor whoreson," snarls Samuel between his teeth, and then he knocks Patrick Henry to the ground and gives him a sharp kick in the ribs.

There's a click, and Samuel turns his head to see Molly pointing her Colt at him. With both thumbs, she drawn back the hammer and cocked the gun, and has her right index finger on the trigger. The barrel gleams faintly in the dingy light of the day. Her hands are trembling, and she's obviously having trouble holding the revolver level.

"You leave him alone, Samuel. Don't you dare kick him again. You step away from him, right this minute."

"Molly, you wouldn't dare," Samuel replies, narrowing his eyes, trying hard to seem as if he's not the least bit afraid, even though his heart's pounding in his chest. No one's ever held a gun on him before.

"Is this the day you want to find out if that's for true, Samuel?" she asks him, and her hands shake a little less.

Samuel turns away from her and stares down at Patrick Henry a moment. The boy's curled into a fetal position, and is cradling the place where the kick landed.

"Fine," says Samuel. "If you're lucky, maybe the dogs will find the both of you. That'd be better than if Miss hears about this, now wouldn't it."

"You just don't hit him no more."

"You just don't hit him *again,"* Samuel says, and the act of correcting her makes him feel the smallest bit less scared of the gun. "You might be a slattern, but you don't have to sound like one, Molly Peterson."

Patrick Henry coughs and squeaks out a few unintelligible words from behind his respirator.

"May the dogs find you both," Samuel says, because there aren't many worse ways left to curse someone. He puts his back to the both of them and climbs into the dark gondola. It'll take time for his eyes to adjust, and he leans against a wall and listens to Molly consoling Patrick Henry. Samuel grips the butt of his own Colt, tucked into his waistband.

If I had another bullet, he thinks, but leaves it at that. Miss will take care of them, and oh, how he'll gloat when the coward and the turncoat bitch get what's coming to them. Unless, like he said, the dogs find them first. He thinks, *Molly knows all about the dogs firsthand,* then chuckles softly at his unintentional pun, and begins making his way cautiously, warily, through what's left of the passengers' observation deck.

4.

As has been said, Miss has told all her charges there's no point dwelling on what was, but has been forever lost.

"That time is never coming back," she said, on the occasion Samuel ever asked her about how things were before the War. "We have to learn to live in *this* age, if we're going to have any hope of survival."

"I only want to know *why* it happened," he persisted. "Didn't everyone have everything they wanted, everything they needed? What was there to fight over?"

She smiled a sad sort of smile and tousled his hair. "Some folks had everything they needed, and a lot more besides. You might look up at the dirigibles, or see the brass and silver clockworks, or the steam rails, or go to a great city and wonder at the shining towers. You could do that, Samuel, and imagine the world was good. You could listen to the endless promises of scientists, engineers, and politicians and believe we lived in a Golden Age that would last forever and a day, where all men were free from want. But those men and women were arrogant, and we all swallowed their hubris and made it our own. Ever wonder why folks who never went near a foundry or flew an 'thopter, people who never even got their hands dirty, used to wear goggles?"

"No," he told her, after trying very hard to figure out why they would have. Admittedly, it didn't make much sense.

"Because wearing goggles made us feel like we were more than onlookers, Samuel. It made us feel like we all had our shoulder to the wheel, that we'd all *earned* what we had. We wanted to believe there *was* finally enough for everyone, and everyone did, indeed, *have* everything they needed."

"But they didn't?"

"No, Samuel, they didn't. Not by half. We didn't talk about Africa, the East Indies, or the colonies elsewhere. They didn't talk about the working conditions in the mines and factories, or the Red Indian reservations, the people who suffered and died so that a few of us could live our lives of plenty. Most of all, though, they didn't talk about how *nothing* lasts forever – not coal, not wood, not oil or peat – and how one nation turns against another when it starts to run out of the resources it needs to power the engines of progress. They didn't tell us about the weapons the Czar and America and Britain, China and Prussia and lots of other countries were building. Our leaders and scholars and journalists didn't talk about these things, Samuel, and very few of the lucky people never bothered to ask why."

"So, we weren't good people?"

She stared at him silently for almost a full minute, and then she said, softly, "We were *people,* Samuel. And that's as good an answer as any I can offer you," she told him, then said they'd talked quite enough and sent him away to bed. He paused outside the room where the boys sleep and looked back. She was still sitting on the concrete bench, and had begun to weep quietly to herself.

5.

Lugging his bulging burlap bag loaded with cans and bottles back through the perilous gauntlet of Deck B, Samuel isn't thinking about the conversation with Miss. The sweat stung his eyes, and his head ached from having bumped it hard against a sagging I-beam. His back aches, too, and he's lost track of time in the darkness of the gondola. He isn't thinking about much at all except getting back before their eight hours has passed, and how many they might have left. He has room to worry about that, and he has energy to fume about Molly Peterson and Patrick Henry Olmstead, the dirty cowards shirking their duty and leaving him to do all the hard work. He takes satisfaction in knowing what Miss will do to them back at the bunker, how they'll go a day and a night without meals, how everyone will be forbidden to speak to them for a week. Miss doesn't tolerate deadbeats and cowards.

Samuel's footsteps and breath are so loud, and he's so lost in thought, that he's almost reached the tear in the hull before he hears the dogs. He eases the burlap bag to the floor and slowly draws the Colt from inside his jeans and his slicker. His hand is sweaty, and feels loose on the gun's stock. All at once, the snarling and barking and low, threatful growls are so loud that the dogs might as well be inside the dirigible with him. He knows better, knows it seems that way because he wasn't listening before. He was breaking another of Miss' rules: never, ever lower your guard. But he had. He'd become distracted, and here was the cost.

"Damn it all," he says, but the words are no more than the phantoms of words riding on a hushed breath. He knows well enough how sharp are the ears of the packs. He puts his back to the wall and edges towards the breach. Samuel knows he should retreat and seal one of the hatchways behind him, then pray the dogs go on about some other business before too long. But Molly and Patrick Henry are out there. He *left* them out there, and all his anger is dissolved by the fierce, hungry noises the dogs are making.

As cautiously as he can, Samuel peers through the tear, and sees that the dogs are wrestling over what's left of his dead companions. The pack is a terrible hodgepodge of timber wolves, coyotes, the descendants of dogs gone feral, and hybrids of all these beasts. In places, their fur has been burned away by the rain, and some are so scarred it's difficult to be sure they are any sort of canine at all. Two of the smaller dogs are wrestling over one of Molly's legs, and a gigantic wolf is worrying at a gaping hole in Patrick Henry's belly.

Samuel wants to vomit, but he doesn't. He almost cocks his revolver, but, instead, he drags his eyes away from the sight of the massacre and quietly returns deeper into the bowels of the crashed airship.

I never heard a gunshot, he thinks, wiping at his eyes and pretending that he isn't crying. He's too old and too brave to cry, even at the horror outside the gondola. *I never heard even a single shot, much less two.*

But he knows the dogs are fast, and it's likely as not that neither Molly nor Patrick Henry had time to get a shot off before the animals were on them. Not that it would have made any difference, unless they'd used the guns on themselves. Which is what a clever, clever scavenger does, when a pack finds them. *For yourself, or for one of the dogs. That has to be your decision,* Miss had told him, as she always did. But he'd always understood she *meant* the former, and the second half of her instructions were only an acknowledgment of his choice in the matter.

With the hatch sealed, the corridor is completely black, and Samuel sits down on the cold steel floor. At least he can't hear the dogs any longer. And at least he won't starve, unless he can't find his way back to the storeroom and manage to fumble about in the dark kitchen until he finds a can opener. Not that he dares stay long enough to grow hungrier than he is already. Miss' silver pocket watch is ticking, and for the first time it occurs to Samuel to wonder why she only allots the expeditions beyond the bunker only eight hours. Why not nine, or twelve, or fifteen?

Maybe she's not much saner than the men and women who started the War, he thinks, then pushes the thought away. It's easier to dupe himself and credit her with *some* reason or another for the time limit. *Like all those people who never got their hands dirty, but wore goggles,* he thinks, tugging his own pair from off his face. He does it with enough force that the rubber strap breaks. Samuel drops them to the floor, and they clatter noisily in the darkness. Then he sits in the lightless corridor, and he listens to the beat of his heart, and he waits.

For Jimmy Branagh, Myrtil Igaly, Loki Elliot,
and for the New Babbage that was.

GOGGLES (c. 1910)

I almost titled this "The Last Steampunk Story," a combination of wishful thinking and hubris. It is, in large part, a response to the subgenre's dogged determination to ignore the socioeconomic and ecological consequences of its rose-colored alternate history. Jonathan Strahan chose it for *The Best Science Fiction and Fantasy of the Year (Volume Seven)*. I might have changed my mind about the title, but it is definitely *my* last steampunk story.

One Tree Hill (The World as Cataclysm)

1.

I am dreaming. Or I am awake.

I've long since ceased to care, as I've long since ceased to believe it matters which. Dreaming or awake, my *perceptions* of the hill and the tree and what little remains of the house on the hill are the same. More importantly, more perspicuously, my perceptions of the hill and the house and the tree are the same. Or, as this admittedly is belief, and so open to debate, I cannot imagine it would matter whether I am dreaming or awake. And this observation is as good a place to begin as any.

I am told in the village that the hill, the tree on the hill, was struck by lightning at, or just after, sunset on St. Crispin's Day, eleven years ago. I am told in the village that no thunderstorm accompanied the lightning strike, that the October sky was clear and dappled with stars. The Village. It has a name, though I prefer to think, and refer, to it simply as The Village. Nestled snugly – some would say claustrophobically – between the steep foothills of New Hampshire's White Mountains, within what geographers name the Sandwich Range, and a deep lake the villagers call Witalema. On my maps, the lake has no name at all. A librarian in The Village told me that Witalema was derived from the language of the Abenakis, from the word *gwitaalema*, which, she said, may be roughly translated as "to fear someone." I've found nothing in any book or anywhere online that refutes her claim, though I have also found nothing to confirm it. So, I will always think of that lake and its black, still waters as Lake Witalema, and choose not to speculate on why its name means "to fear someone." I found more than enough to fear on the aforementioned lightning-struck hill.

There is a single, nameless cemetery in The Village, located within a stone's throw of the lake. The oldest headstone I have found there dates back to 1674. That is, the man buried in the plot died in 1674. He was a born in 1645. The headstone reads *Ye blooming Youth who fee this Stone/Learn early Death may be your own*. It seems oddly random to me that only the word *see* makes use of the Latin *s*. In stray moments I have wondered what the dead man might have *feen* to warrant this peculiarity of the inscription, or if it is merely an engraver's mistake that was not corrected and so has survived these past three hundred and thirty-eight years. I dislike the cemetery, perhaps because of its nearness to the lake, and so I have only visited it once. Usually, I find comfort in graveyards, and I have a large collection of rubbings taken from gravestones in New England.

But why, I ask myself, *do I shy from this one cemetery, and possibly only because of its closeness to Lake Witalema, when I returned repeatedly to the hill and the tree and what little remains of the house on the hill?* It isn't a question I can answer; I doubt I will ever be able to answer it. I only know that what I have seen on that hilltop is far more dreadful than anything the lake could ever have to show me.

I am climbing the hill, and I am awake, or I am asleep.

I'm thinking about the lightning strike on St. Crispin's Day, lightning from a clear night sky, and I'm thinking of the fire that consumed the house and left the tree a gnarled charcoal crook. Also, my mind wanders – probably defensively – to the Vatican's decision that too little evidence can be found to prove the existence of either St. Crispin or his twin brother, St. Crispinian, and how they survived their first close call with martyrdom, after being tossed into a river with millstones tied about their necks, only to be beheaded, finally, by decree of Rictus Barus. Climbing up that hill, pondering obscure Catholic saints who may not ever have lived, it occurs to me I may read too much. Or only read too much into what I read. I pause to catch my breath, and I glance up at the sky. Today there are clouds, unlike the night the lightning came. If the villagers are to be believed, of course. And given the nature of what sits atop the hill, the freak strike that night seems not so miraculous. The clouds seem to promise rain, and I'll probably be soaking wet by the time I get back to my room in the rundown motel on the outskirts of The Village. Far off, towards what my tattered topographic map calls Mount Passaconaway, there is the low rumble of thunder (*Passaconaway* is another Indian name, from the Pennacook, a tribe closely related to the Abenakis, but I have no idea what the word might mean). The trail is steep here, winding between spruce and pine, oaks, poplars, and red maples. I imagine the maple leaves must appear to catch fire in the autumn. Catch fire or bleed. The hill always turns my thoughts morbid, a mood that is not typical of my nature. Reading this, one might think otherwise, but that doesn't change the truth of it. Having caught my breath, I continue up the narrow, winding path, hoping to reach the summit before the storm catches up with me. Weathered granite crunches beneath my boots.

"Were I you," said the old man who runs The Village's only pharmacy, "I'd stay clear of that hill. No fit place to go wandering about. Not after..." And then he trailed off and went back to ringing up my purchase on the antique cash register.

"...the lightning came," I said, finishing his statement. "After the fire."

He glared at me and made an exasperated, disapproving sound.

"You ain't from around here, I know, and whatever you've heard, I'm guessing you've written it off as Swamp Yankee superstition."

"I have a more open mind than you think," I told him.

"Maybe that's so. Maybe it ain't," he groused and looked for the price on a can of pears in heavy syrup. "Either way, I guess I've said my piece. No fit place, that hill, and you'd do well to listen."

But I might have only dreamt that conversation, as I might have dreamt the graveyard on the banks of Lake Witalema, and the headstone of a man who died in 1674, and the twisted, charred tree, and...

It doesn't matter.

2.

I live in The City, a safe century of miles south and east of The Village. When I have work, I am a science journalist. When I do not, I am an unemployed science journalist who tries to stay busy by blogging what I would normally sell for whatever pittance is being offered. Would that I had become a political pundit or a war correspondent. But I didn't. I have no interest or acumen for politics or bullets. I wait on phone calls, on jobs from a vanishing stable of newspapers and magazines, on work from this or that website. I wait. My apartment is very small, even by the standards of The City, and only just affordable on my budget. Or lack thereof. Four cramped rooms in the attic of a brownstone that was built when the neighborhood was much younger, overlooking narrow streets crowded with upscale boutiques and restaurants that charge an arm and a leg for a sparkling green bottle of S. Pellegrino. I can watch wealthy men and women walk their shitty little dogs.

I have a few bookshelves, crammed with reference material on subjects ranging from cosmology to quantum physics, virology to paleontology. My coffee table, floor, desk, and almost every other conceivable surface are piled high with back issues of *Science* and *Physical Review Letters* and *Nature* and...you get the picture. That hypothetical you, who may or may not be reading this. I'm making no assumptions. I have my framed diplomas from MIT and Yale on the wall above my desk, though they only serve to remind me that whatever promise I might once have possessed has gone unrealized. And that I'll never pay off the student loans that supplemented my meager scholarships. I try, on occasion, to be proud of those pieces of paper and their calligraphy and gold seals, but I rarely turn that trick.

I sit, and I read. I blog, and I wait, watching as the balance in my bank account dwindles.

One week ago tomorrow my needlessly fancy iPhone rang, and on the other end was an editor from *Discover* who'd heard from a field geologist about the lightning-struck hill near The Village and who thought it was worth checking out. That it might make an interesting sidebar, at the very least. A bit of a meteorological mystery, unless it proved to be nothing but local tall tales. I had to pay for my own gas, but I'd have a stingy expense account for a night at a motel and a few meals. I was given a week to get the story in. I should say, obviously, I have long since exceeded my expense account and missed the deadline. I keep my phone switched off.

It doesn't matter anymore. In my ever decreasing moments of clarity, I find myself wishing that it did. I need the money. I need the byline. I absolutely do not need an editor pissed at me and word getting around that I'm unreliable.

But it *doesn't* matter anymore.

Wednesday, one week ago, I got my ever-ailing, tangerine-and-rust Nissan out of the garage where I can't afford to keep it. I left The City, and I left Massachusetts via I-493, which I soon traded for I-93, and then I-293 at Manchester. Then, it will suffice to say that I left the interstates and headed east until I reached The Village nestled here between the kneeling mountains. I didn't make any wrong turns. It was easy to find. The directions the editor at *Discover* had emailed were correct in every way, right down to the shabby motel on the edge of The Village.

Right down to the lat-long GPS coordinates of the hill and the tree and what little remains of the house on the hill. N 43.81591/W -71.37035.

I think I have offered all these details only as an argument, to myself, that I am – or at least was once – a rational human being. Whatever I have become, or am becoming, I did start out believing the truths of the universe *were* knowable.

But now I am sliding down a slippery slope towards the irrational.

Now, I doubt everything I took for granted when I came here.

Before I first climbed the hill.

If the preceding is an argument, or a ward, or whatever I might have intended it as, it is a poor attempt, indeed.

But it doesn't matter, and I know that.

3.

I imagine that the crest of the hill was once quite picturesque. As I've mentioned, there's an unobstructed view of the heavily wooded slopes and peaks of Mount Passaconaway and of the valleys and hills in between. This vista must be glorious under a heavy snowfall. I have supposed that is why the house was built here. Likely, it was someone's summer home, possibly someone not so unlike myself, someone foreign to The Village.

The librarian I spoke of earlier, I asked her if the hill has a name, and all she said was "One Tree."

"One Tree Hill?" I asked.

"One Tree," she replied curtly. "Nobody goes up *there* anymore."

I am quite entirely aware I am trapped inside, and that I am writing down anything *but* an original tale of uncanny New England. But if I do not know, I will at least be honest about *what* I do not know. I have that responsibility, that fraying shred of naturalism remaining in me. Whether or not it is cliché is another thing which simply doesn't matter.

I reach the crest of the hill, and, just like every time before, the first thing that strikes my eyes is the skeleton of that tree. I'm not certain, but I believe it was an oak. It must have been ancient, judging by the circumference and diameter of its base. It might have stood here when that man I have yet to (and will not) name was buried in 1674 near the banks of Lake Witalema. But I don't know how long oak trees live, and I haven't bothered to find out. It is a dead tree, and all the "facts" that render it *more* than a dead tree exist entirely independently of its taxonomy.

Aside from the remains of the one tree, the hilltop is "bald." The woods have not reclaimed it. If I stand at the lightning-struck tree, the nearest living tree, in any direction, is at least twenty-five yards away. There is only stone and bracken, weeds, vines, and fallen, rotten limbs. So, it is always hotter at the top of the hill, and the ground seems drier and rockier. There is a sense of flesh rubbed raw and unable to heal.

Like all the times I have come here before, there is, immediately, the inescapable sense that I have entered a place so entirely and irrevocably defiled as to have passed beyond any conventional understanding of corruption. I cannot ever escape the impression that, somehow, the event that damned this spot (for it *is* damned) struck so very deeply at the fabric of this patch of the world as to render it beyond that which is either unholy *or* holy. Neither good *nor* evil have a place here. Neither are welcome, so profound was the damage done that one St. Crispin's Night. And if the hill seems blasphemous, it is only because it has come to exist somewhere genuinely *Outside*. I won't try to elaborate just yet. It is enough to say *Outside*. Even so, I'll concede that the dead tree stands before me like an altar. It strikes me that way every time, in direct contradiction to what I've said about it. Or, I *could* say, instead, it stands like a sentry, but then one must answer the question about what it might be standing guard over. Bricks from a crumbling foundation? The maze of poison ivy and green briars? A court of skunks, rattlesnakes, and crows?

The sky presses down on the hill, heavy as the sea.

From the top of the hill, the wide blue sky looks very hungry.

What is it that skies eat? That thin rind of atmosphere between a planet and the hard vacuum of outer space? I'm asking questions that lead nowhere. I'm asking questions only because it occurs to me that I have never written them down, or that they have never before occurred to me so I *ought* to write them down.

A cloudless night sky struck at the hill, drawing something out, even if I am unable to describe what that something is, and so I will say this event is the author of my questions on the possible diet of the sky.

Even after eleven years, the top of the hill smells of smoke, ash, charcoal, cinder lingers – all those odors we mean when we say, "I can smell fire." We cannot smell fire, but we smell the byproducts of combustion, and that smell lingers here. I wonder if it always will. I am standing at the top of the hill, thinking all these thoughts, when I hear something coming up quickly behind me. It's not the noise a woman or a man's feet would make. A deer, possibly. An animal with long and delicate limbs, small hooves to pick its way through the forest and along stony trails. This is what I think I hear, but, then, most people *think* they can smell fire.

I take one step forward, and a charred section of root crunches beneath the soles of my hiking boots. The crunching seems very loud, though I suspect that's only another illusion.

"Why is it you keep coming back here?" she asks. The way she phrases the question, I could pretend I've never heard her ask it before. My mouth is dry. I want to remove my pack and take out the lukewarm bottle of water inside, but I don't.

"It could open wide and eat me," I say to her. "A wide carnivorous sky like that."

There's a pause, nothing but a stale bit of breeze through the leaves of the trees surrounding the lightning-struck ring. Then she laughs, that peculiar laugh of hers, which is neither unnerving nor a sound that in any way puts one at ease.

"Now you're being ridiculous," she says.

"I know," I admit. "But that's the way it makes me feel, hanging up there."

"What you describe is a feeling of dread."

"Isn't that what happened here, that St. Crispin's Day? Didn't the sky open its mouth and gnaw this hill and everything on it – the tree, the house?"

"You listen too much to those people in the village."

That's the way she says it, *the village*. Never does she say *The Village*. It is an important nuance. What seems, as she has pointed out, dreadful to me is innately mundane to her.

"They don't have much to say about the hill," I tell her.

"No, they don't. But what they do say, it's hardly worth your time."

"I get the feeling they'd bulldoze this place, if they weren't too afraid to come here. I believe they would take dynamite to it, shave off the top until no evidence of that night remains."

"Likely, you're not mistaken," she agrees. "Which is precisely why you shouldn't listen to them."

I wish I knew the words to accurately delineate, elucidate, explain the rhythm and stinging lilt of her voice. I cannot. I can only do my best to recall what she said that day, which, of course, was not the first nor the last day she has spoken with me. Why she bothers, that might be the greatest of all these mysteries, though it might seem the least. Appearances are deceiving.

"Maybe there were clouds that night," I say. "Maybe it's just that no one noticed them. They may only have noticed that flash of lightning, and only noticed that because of what it left behind."

"If you truly thought that's what happened, you wouldn't keep coming here."

"No, I wouldn't," I say, though I want to turn about and spit in her face, if she even has a face. I presume she does. But I've never turned to find out. I've never looked at her, and I know I never will. Like Medusa, she is not to be seen.

Yes, that was a tad melodramatic, but isn't all of this? The same as it's cliché?

"It's unhealthy, returning to this place again and again. You ought to stop."

"I can't. I haven't..." and I trail off. It is a sentence I never should have begun and which I certainly don't wish to finish.

"...solved it yet? No, but it is also a riddle you never should have asked yourself. The people in the village, they don't ask it. Except, possibly, in their dreams."

"You think the people in The Village are ridiculous. You just said so."

"No, that is not exactly what I said, but it's true enough. However, there genuinely are questions you're better off not asking."

"Ignorance is bliss," I say, almost mangling the words with laughter.

"That is not what I said, either."

"Excuse me. I'm getting a headache."

"Don't you always, when you come up here? You should stop to consider why that is, should you not?"

I'm silent for a time, and then I answer, "You want me to stop coming. You would rather I stop coming. I suspect you might even need me to stop coming."

"Futility disturbs me," she says. "You're becoming Sisyphus, rolling his burden up that hill. You're become Christ, lugging the cross towards Calvary."

I don't disagree.

"Loki," I add.

"Loki?"

"It hasn't gotten as bad as what happened to Loki. No serpent dripping venom, which is good, because I have no Sigyn to catch it in her bowl." The story of Loki so bound puts me in mind of Prometheus, the eagle always, always devouring his liver, a symbol for the hungry sky. But I say nothing of Prometheus to her.

"It is the way of humans," she says, "to create these brilliant, cautionary metaphors, then ignore them."

Again, I don't disagree. It doesn't matter anymore.

"But it *did* happen, yes?" I ask. "There were no clouds that night?"

"It did happen." She is the howling, fiery voice of God whispering confirmation of what my gut already knew. She has been before, and will be again.

"Go home," she says. "Go back to your apartment in your city, before it's too late to go back. Go back to your life."

"Why do you care?" I ask this question, because I know it's already too late to go back to The City. For any number of reasons, not the least because I have climbed the hill and looked at the silent devastation.

"There's no revelation to be had here," she sighs. "No slouching beast prefacing revelation. No revelation and no prophecy. No מנא, מנא, תקל, ופרסין (*Mene, Mene, Tekel u-Pharsin*) at the feast of Belshazzar." She speaks in Hebrew, and I reply, "Numbered, weighed, divided."

"You won't find that here."

"Why do you assume that is why I keep coming back?"

This time she only clicks her tongue twice against the roof of her mouth. Tongue, mouth. These are both assumptions, as is face.

"Not because of what I might see, but because of what I've already seen. What will I ever see to equal this? Did it bring you here?"

"No," she says, the word another exasperated sigh.

"You were here before."

"No," she sighs.

"Doesn't it ever get lonely, being up here all alone?"

"You make a lot of assumptions, and, frankly, I find them wearisome."

It doesn't even occur to me to apologize. A secret recess of my consciousness must understand that apologies would be meaningless to one such as her. I hear those nimble legs, those tiny feet that might as well end in hooves. There are other noises I won't attempt to describe.

"Is it an assumption that it is within your power to stop me?" I ask.

"Yes, of course that is an assumption."

"Yet," and I can't take my eyes off what's left of the charred tree, "many assumptions prove valid."

She leaves me then. There are no words of parting, no good-bye. There never is; she simply leaves, and I am alone at the top of the hill with the tree and what little remains of the house on the hill, wondering if she will come next time, and the time after that, and the time after that. I pick up a lump of four-hundred-million-year-old granite, which seems to tingle in my hand, and I hurl it towards far off Mount Passaconaway, as if I had a chance of hitting my target.

4.

One thing leads to another. I am keenly aware of the casual chain of cause and effect that dictates, as does any tyrant, the events of the cosmos.

A lightning-struck hill.

A house.

A tree.

A Village hemmed in by steep green slopes and the shadows they cast.

A black lake and a man who died in 1674.

I had a lover once. Only once, but it was a long relationship. It died a slow and protracted death, borne as much of my disappointment in myself as my partner's disappointment *in* my disappointment of myself. I suppose you can only watch someone you love mourn for so long before your love becomes disgust. Or I may misunderstand completely. I've never made a secret of my difficulty in understanding the motives of people, no matter how close to me they have been, no matter how long they have been close to me. It doesn't seem to matter.

None of it matters now.

But last night, after I climbed the hill, after my conversation with whatever it is exists alone up there, after that, I made a phone call from the squalid motel room. I have not called my former lover in three years. In three years, we have not spoken. Had we, early on, I might have had some chance of repairing the damage I'd done. But it had all seemed so inevitable, and any attempt to stave off the inevitable seemed absurd. In my life, I have loved two things. The first died before we met, and with my grieving for the loss of the first did I kill the second. Well, did I place the second forever beyond my reach.

If I have not already made it perfectly clear, I have no love for The City, nor my apartment, and most especially not for the career I have resigned myself to, or, I would say, that I have *settled* for.

Last night I called him. I thought no one would pick up.

"Hello," I said, and there was a long, long silence. *Just hang up*, I thought, though I'm not sure which of us I was wishing would hang up. *It was a terrible idea, so please just hang up before it gets more terrible.*

"Why are you calling me?"

"I'm not entirely certain."

"It's been three years. Why the fuck are you calling me tonight?"

"Something's happening. Something important, and I didn't have anyone else to call."

"I'm the last resort," and there was a dry, bitter laugh. There was the sound of a cigarette being lit and the exhalation of smoke.

"You still smoke," I said.

"Yeah. Look, I don't care what's happening. Whatever it is, you deal with it."

"I'm trying."

"Maybe you're not trying hard enough."

I agreed.

"Will you only listen? It won't take long, and I don't expect you to solve any of my problems. I just need to tell someone."

Another long pause, only the sound of smoking to interrupt the silence through the receiver.

"Fine. But be quick. I'm busy."

I'm not, I think. *I may never be busy again. Isn't that a choice one makes, whether to be busy or not? I have, in coming to The Village, left busyness behind me.*

I told my story, which sounded even more ridiculous than I'd expected it to sound. I left out most of my talks with the thing that lives atop the hill, as no one can recall a conversation, not truly, and I didn't want to omit a word of it.

Whether or not each word is of consequence.

"You need to see someone," he told me.

"Maybe," I said.

"No. Not maybe. You need to see someone."

We said goodbye, and I was instructed to never call again.

I hung up first, then sat by the phone (I'd used the motel phone, not my cell).

A few seconds later, it rang again, and I quickly, hopefully, lifted the receiver. But it was the voice from the hill. Someone else might have screamed.

"You should leave," she said. "It's still not too late to leave. Do as I have said. It's all still waiting for you. The city, your work, your home."

"Nothing's waiting for me back there. Haven't you figured that out?"

"There's nothing for you here. Haven't *you* figured *that* out?"

"I'm asleep and dreaming this. I'm lying in my apartment above Newbury Street, and I'm dreaming all of this. Probably, The Village does not even exist."

"Then wake up. Go home. Wake up, and you will be home."

"I don't know how," I said, and that was the truth. "I don't know how, and it doesn't matter any longer."

"That's a shame, I think," she said. "I wish it were otherwise." And then there was only a dial tone.

You can almost see the hill from the window of my motel room. You can see the highway and a line of evergreens. If the trees were not so tall, you *could* see the hill. On a night eleven years ago, you could have seen the lightning from this window, and you could have seen the glow of the fire that must have burned afterwards. Last night, I was glad that I couldn't see the hill silhouetted against the stars.

5.

The three times I have visited the library in The Village, the librarian has done her best to pretend I wasn't there. She does her best to seem otherwise occupied. Intensely so. She makes me wait at the circulation desk as long as she can. Today is no different. But finally she relents and frowns and asks me what I need.

"Do you have back issues of the paper?"

"Newspaper?" she asks.

"Yes. There's only the one, am I correct?"

"You are."

"Do you have back issues?"

"We have it on microfiche," and I tell her that microfiche is perfectly fine. So, she leads me through the stacks to a tiny room in the back. There's a metal cabinet with drawers filled with yellow Kodak boxes. She begins to explain how the old-style reader works, how to fit the spools onto the spindles, and I politely assure her I've spent a lot of time squinting at microfiche, but thanks, anyway. I am always polite with her. I ask for the reel that would include October 26th, 2001.

"You aren't going to let this go, are you?" asks the librarian.

"Eventually, I might. But not yet."

"Ought never have come here. Can't nothing good come of it. Anyone in town can tell you that. Can't nothing good come of prying into the past."

I thank her, and she scowls and leaves me alone.

I press an off-white plastic button, and the days whir noisily past my eyes. I have always detested the sound of a microfiche reader. It reminds me of a dental drill, though I've never found anyone else who's made the association. Then again, I don't think I've ever asked anyone *how* they feel about the click-click-click whir of a microfiche reader. One day soon, with so much digital conversion going on, I imagine there will be very few microfiche archives. People pretend that hard drives, computer disks, and the internet is a safer place to keep our history. People are fools. At any rate, the machine whirs, and after only a minute or so I've reached October 26th, the day after the lightning strike. On page four of the paper, I find a very brief write up of the event at the crest of the hill. One Tree, as it seems to be named, though the paper doesn't give that name. It merely speaks of a house at the end of an "unimproved" drive off Middle Road, east of The Village. A house had recently been constructed there by a family hailing from, as it happened, The City. The world is, of course, filled with coincidence, so I make nothing of this. I doubt I ever shall. The house was to be a summer home. Curiously, the family is not named, the paper reporting only that there had been three members – father, mother, daughter – and that all died in the fire caused by the lightning. Firefighters from The Village had responded, but were (also curiously) said to have been unable to extinguish what must have been a modest blaze. I will only quote this portion, which I am scribbling down in my notebook:

Meteorologists have attributed the tragic event to "positive" lightning, a relatively rare phenomenon. Unlike far more commonly occurring "negative" lightning, positive lightning takes place when a positive charge is carried by the uppermost regions of clouds – most often anvil clouds – rather than by the ground. This causes the leader arc to form within the anvil of the cumulonimbus cloud and travel horizontally for several miles before suddenly veering down to meet the negatively charged streamer rising up from the ground. The bolt can strike anywhere within several miles of the anvil of the thunderstorm, often in areas experiencing clear or only slightly cloudy skies, hence they may also be referred to as "bolts from the blue." Positive lightning is estimated to account for less than 5% of all lightning strikes.

The meteorologist in question is not named, nor is his or her affiliation given. I do find it odd that far more space is devoted to an attempt to explain the event than to any other aspect of it. Also, it appears to have been cribbed from a textbook or other reference source, and deviates significantly from the voice of the rest of the article. There is, reading over it again and again, the sense that explaining the nature of lightning was far more important to whoever wrote the piece than was reporting the deaths of the family or even the general facts of the case. A single anonymous source is quoted, a resident of High Street (in The Village) as a witness to the lightning strike. There is also mentioned a "terrific booming from the sky" that occurred an hour *after* the strike, and I can't help but wonder why the paper went to so much trouble to make plain that there was nothing especially peculiar about the lightning, but records another strange incident in passing which it makes no attempt to explain.

"Did you find what you were looking for?" the librarian asks, peering into the small room. I notice for the first time that the room smells musty. Or maybe it's the librarian who smells musty.

"I did," I reply. "Thank you. You've been very helpful."

"I do my job. I do what the town council pays me to do."

"Then you do it well," I say, determined to inflict upon her a compliment.

She grumbles, and I leave while she's busy removing the spool and returning it to its yellow Kodak box. I step out onto the tiny courtyard in front of the library, and it's just begun raining. Cold drops pepper my face. I stand, staring up into the rain, and consider calling the editor, apologizing, and asking for a second chance. Telling him there really is no mystery here, so it could be a great little piece debunking a rural myth, a triumph of science over the supposedly miraculous. I could return to The City, to my apartment, and wait for other jobs. I would find a way to forget about whatever lives at the top of the hill. I would tell myself I'd imagined the whole affair, mark it up to weariness, depression, something of the sort.

The rain almost feels like needles.

6.

I awake from a nightmare. I awake breathless to sweaty sheets. I think I may have cried out in my sleep, but I don't know for sure. Almost at once, I forget most of the particulars of the dream. But it centered on the charred tree. There was something coiled in the branches of the tree, or perched there. It was gazing down at me. A shapeless thing, or very nearly so, clinging somehow to those charcoal branches.

I wanted to turn away, to look away, but was unable. I felt the purest spite spilling from it, flowing down the gnarled trunk and washing over me. I have never believed in evil, but the thing in the tree was, I knew, evil. It was evil, and it was ancient beyond any human comprehension. Some of the eldest stars were younger and the earth an infant by comparison. Mercifully, it didn't speak or make any other sound whatsoever.

I awake to a voice, and I recognize it straightaway. It's the voice from the hill. Near the door, there's the faintest of silhouettes, an outline that is only almost human. It's tall and begins moving gracefully across the room towards me. I reach to turn on the lamp, but, thankfully, my hand never touches the cord.

"Have you seen enough?" she asks. "What you found at the library, was that enough?"

She's very near the foot of the bed now. I would never have guessed she was so tall and so extraordinarily slender. My eyes struggle with the darkness to make sense of something I cannot actually see.

"Not you," I whisper. "It hasn't explained you."

"Do I require an explanation?"

"Most people would say so."

If this is being read, I would say most *readers* would certainly say so. There, I *have* said it.

"But not you?"

"I don't know what I need," I say, and I'm being completely honest.

Here there is a long silence, and I realize it's still raining. That it's raining much harder than when I went to bed. I can hear thunder far away.

"This is the problem with explanations," she says. "You ask for one, and it triggers an infinite regression. There is never a final question. Unless inquiry is halted by an arbitrary act. And it's true, many inquiries are, if only by necessity."

"If I knew what you are, why you are, how you are, if there is any connection between you and the death of those three people…" I trail off, knowing she'll finish my thought.

She says, "…you'd only have another question, and another after that. *Ad infinitum.*"

"I think I want to go home," I whisper.

"Then you should go home, don't you think?"

"What was that I dreamt of, the thing in the tree?"

Now she is leaning over me, on the bed *with* me, and it only frightens me that I am not afraid. "Only a bad dream," she sighs, and her breath smells like the summer forest, and autumn leaves, and snow, and swollen mountain rivers in the spring. It doesn't smell even remotely of fire.

"Before The Village, you were here," I say. "You've almost always been here." It isn't a question, and she doesn't mistake it for one. She doesn't say anything else, and I understand I will never again hear her speak.

She wraps her arms and legs about me – and, as I guessed, they were delicate and nothing like the arms and legs of women, and she takes me into her. We do not make love. We fuck. No, she fucks me. She fucks me, and it seems to go on forever. Repeatedly, I almost reach climax, and, repeatedly, it slips away. She mutters in a language I know, instinctively, has never been studied by any linguist, and one I'll not recall a syllable of later on, no matter how hard I struggle to do so. It seems filled with clicks and glottal stops. Outside, there is rain and thunder and lightning. The storm is pounding at the windows, wanting in. The storm, I think, is jealous. I wonder how long it will hold a grudge. Is that what happened on top of the hill? Did she take the man or the woman (or both) as a lover? Did the sky get even?

I do finally come, and the smells of her melt away. She is gone, and I lay on those sweaty sheets, trying to catch my breath.

So, I do not say aloud, *the dream didn't end with the tree. I dreamt her here, in the room with me. I dreamt her questions, and I dreamt her fucking me.*

I do my best to fool myself this is the truth.

It doesn't matter anymore.

By dawn, the rain has stopped.

7.

I have breakfast, pack, fill up the Nissan's tank, and pay my motel bill.

By the time I pull out of the parking lot, it's almost nine o'clock.

I drive away from The Village, and the steep slopes pressing in on all sides as if to smother it, and I drive away from the old cemetery beside Lake Witalema. I drive south, taking the long way back to the interstate, rather than passing the turnoff leading up the hill and the house and the lightning-struck tree. I know that I will spend the rest of my life avoiding the White Mountains. Maybe I'll even go so far as to never step foot in New Hampshire again. That wouldn't be so hard to do.

I keep my eyes on the road in front of me, and am relieved as the forests and lakes give way to farmland and then the outskirts of The City. I am leaving behind a mystery that was never mine to answer. I leave behind shadows for light. Wondrous and terrifying glimpses of the extraordinary for the mundane.

I will do my damnedest to convince the editor to whom I owe a story – he took my call this morning and was only mildly annoyed I'd missed the deadline – that there is nothing the least bit bizarre about that hill or the woods surrounding it. Nothing to it but tall tales told by ignorant and gullible Swamp Yankees, people who likely haven't heard the Revolutionary War has ended. I'll lie and make them sound that absurd, and we'll all have a good laugh.

I will bury, deep as I can, all my memories of her.

It doesn't matter anymore.

ONE TREE HILL (THE WORLD AS CATACLYSM)

This story is one of those very rare times when I feel like I got it just right. A whisper, instead of a scream. If I were wise, I'd never write another weird tale set in New England, because I'll never do a better job of it than this story. Anyone familiar with T. E. D. Klein's classic *The Ceremonies* (1984) will note my very conscious nod to that novel.

Black Helicopters

~ A Novel ~

One measures a circle, beginning anywhere.

~ Charles Fort

Sometime the questions are complicated and the answers are simple.

~ Dr. Seuss

For Sixty Six

1.

Radio Friendly Unit Shifter (Dublin, 12/10/2012)

Here's the scene: Ptolema sits alone in the booth at Bewley's Oriental, sipping bitter black coffee. The October morning sun makes hard candy of Harry Clarke's stained-glass windows, and she checks her watch, and she stares into her coffee cup, and she looks at the stained glass, in that order, over and over again. The two agents are late, and late could mean anything. Or it could mean nothing at all. She's surrounded by the clamor of Trinity students and faculty, locals, tourists, latter-day bohemians. Ptolema hasn't been in Dublin in almost twenty years now, and it made her angry and sick to her stomach to see the fucking Starbucks that's opened almost directly across the street from Bewley's. This thoroughfare is no longer the Dublin of James Joyce and Oscar Wilde, not the Dublin of Mícheál Ó Coileáin and the Easter Rising. Grafton Street, she thinks, might as well be a Disney World reconstruction of the city. It was not so far along, this cancer, the last time she was here. But, again, that was almost twenty years ago. This is Dublin *attempting* to remake and sanitize itself for the World At Large, the travelers who want history as exhibit, local color free of anything that would make them uneasy. Plastic Paddy souvenirs. Leprechaun and shamrock tchotchkes. But, Starbucks or no Starbucks, the McDonalds at the intersection with Wicklow Street or no, Burger fucking King or no, a block or two in almost any direction, and that, that is still Ewan MacColl's "Dirty Old Town."

Heard a siren from the dock.
Saw a train set the night on fire.
Smelled the spring on the smoky wind.
Dirty old town, dirty old town.

And even here on Sráid Grafton, there's still the buskers, the street preachers, the children sent out by their parents to beg for spare change. Stand on Ha'penny Bridge, and the Liffey still brings to her mind Murdoch and how "No man who has faced the Liffey can be appalled by the dirt of another river." The tourist-friendly cancer is kept hemmed in by the disagreeable, living city that will never have its face scrubbed up presentable for company. So, good for you, Dirty Old Town.

I want to give a picture of Dublin so complete that if the city suddenly disappeared from the earth it could be reconstructed out of my book.

Ptolema checks her watch again: 10:38, which puts the X agents almost a half hour tardy. She's already called her handler in London once, and if she calls again Ptolema knows she'll be pulled. Because it could be a set up. Because it might be. She turns off her phone, just in case Barbican Estate decides to ring her. There's too much riding on this meeting, and she's not about to see three month's work swirl down the shitter because someone can't tell time. Or can't be bothered. This is, of course, to be expected from the X motherfuckers, and she knew that going in. She leans back in the booth, wanting a cigarette, and the air smells like frying eggs and dry little disks of black and white pudding.

Watch face. Coffee. Stained glass.

She bought the watch from a Munich pawnshop in 1963. The steaming coffee reminds her of the mist rising from that bay in Maine that's disgorged Hell's own derelicts. The windows hint at an unfamiliar world.

Ptolema notices four students at a nearby table staring. Laughing amongst themselves. Sniggering boy-men. Muttering German. One jabs a thumb her way. To those pasty, pale bastards, she must cut a strange sight, sure: bald head smooth enough it glistens in the sun through the windows, her brown Egyptian skin, the ugly scar over her left ear, and, to them, she probably appears no older than thirty, thirty-five. She smiles and shows them her middle finger, and they shut the fuck up and mind their breakfasts. Perhaps it was the impatience in her eyes. Maybe they caught sight of all the secrets there, all the necessary evils of her station, all the men and woman she's sent to Charon – by her own hand or the obedient hands of her subordinates.

Ptolema stares at the door, as though she can will the Xers to show up.

The coffee steams, and she tries not to think of Deer Isle. She hasn't entered the quarantine zone herself, and she won't if she can help it. Thank you very much, but there's plenty enough ugliness this side of the pond without going abroad in search of more and better. Let the CDC handle it, the NSA, that Other American Group that has no official or unofficial title, but is ever on standby when this sort of shit goes down – which seems to be happening more and more often, and fuck all if she even wants to know why. It's not even her *job* to know why. It's only her job to monitor the comings and goings of the X. To fathom the unfathomable, as it were, because how do you understand the goals of an organization so secretive 99.9% of its operatives have only the faintest idea of the big picture and are let loose to make up the do's and don'ts of a mission or experiment as they go along. Anarchy leaves almost as bad a taste in Ptolema's mouth as would the crap they sell at that McDonalds across the way.

The four German kids depart, surly and still muttering amongst themselves. She checks her watch again; 10:45. And she's just about two centimeters away from *Screw these idiots, and screw Barbican* when she catches sight of two faces that match the photos tucked into the dossier in her satchel beneath the table. These expats, supposedly cast out by their own designs. Fallen from their brethren quasi-Buddhist, mongrel Hindu, cyber-Shinto, Gnostic Thelemite worshippers at the shrines of Castaneda, Crowley, Camus, Blavatsky, Robert Anton Wilson, Velikovsky, Berlitz, Charles Fort, *ad infinitum,* a congregation based, possibly, in Saigon, or Calcutta, or Kyoto or, more likely, nowhere at all. Anyway, this pair of ladies, they look like the rough end of flattened shit. Even more tattered than in their photographs. A wonder someone didn't turn them away at the door, because they sure as fuck look more like panhandlers than anyone who could afford a meal or a pint. Between them, probably not even the two pounds twenty for a side of potato farl. Oh, but how looks can be deceiving, and for all she knows, these two might be goddamn stockbrokers or solicitors on the bum. Still, no one's going to touch an X. Not anyone who isn't deep in the know. Won't have the foggiest *why,* so call it instinct. In their rags, genuine or carefully cultivated, these two weave their way between the tables, untouchable because *that's the way it is.* Fucking ghosts, the whole lot of them. Even rogue agents like these two – assuming they actually *are* rogues, and that's not just another layer of some other ghost's one-dimensional logistic map or what have you. Ptolema sits up straighter and straightens the lapels of her leather blazer – force of habit from years when the Y didn't send her out to do business with sketchy cocksuckers, when the Bureau's resources were not stretched so bloody thin, and Ptolema was held back for shadow dignitaries and face-to-face sitdowns with those occupying *unquestionable* power, for whom appearances actually mattered.

They reach her booth, there below Harry Clarke's windows. One of the women is a tall redhead with a buzz cut and a ring in her nose. The other's not so tall, and her black hair's pulled back in two long braids. Right off, it's obvious neither of them are Irish. Ptolema doesn't even have to hear them speak to know that much. Americans, the both of them, and she'd bet half her Swiss bank account on that. They slide into the seat across from her.

"You P?" the redhead asks.

"When the need arises," Ptolema replies, "but not in my fucking trousers."

The girl with the braids laughs. "Cute," she says. "Real cute."

"Told you," says the redhead, "that she'd be like this. Every one of them, they're all cheeky, smart-mouthed cunts."

Ptolema checks her watch again. "I assume tardiness is a point of pride with you."

"Close enough," says the redhead. Beneath her biker jacket, she's wearing an oatmeal-and-mud-colored sweater that might once have been white. The array of buttons festooning the jacket is just a little too deliberate. But only subtly so, not the sort of affectation one would notice unless one were trying to spot affectations, which Ptolema can't help but do. It keeps her on her toes. It's kept her alive more than once. Even the selection of buttons – a red anarchy symbol on a black field, the Sex Pistols, a skull and crossbones, the Dead Kennedys, the Clash – and the array of spikes and studs set into the shoulders and collar and sleeves. It all comes off prefab. Their accents are a Manchester put-on.

"Didn't whoever holds your leash bother to inform you of the current decade?" Ptolema asks and points at the jacket. "The X must be even more desperate than usual."

The one in braids (who isn't wearing a biker jacket, just a ripped-up Bauhaus t-shirt and a ratty faux fur leopard-print coat) leans over and whispers in the redhead's ear. The redhead laughs.

"I'm not going to ask your names, because I neither need nor want to know them," says Ptolema.

"Good, because we weren't planning on tellin' you," the redhead replies.

"Always convenient to be on the same page."

"If you fuckin' say so," shrugs the redhead.

Ptolema removes an early model iPod from the inner pocket of her blazer, complete with earbuds. She sets it on the table between them.

"You've both assured me you're turncoats," she says, "but policy is to treat all defectors and moles as re-doubled agents. Ergo, I am proceeding on the assumption that this will, sooner or later, get back to Julia Set."

"We don't parlay with JS no more," says the redhead. "Bridges burned good and fuckin' proper."

"Bureau policy. Not my call. Also, we know the X routinely factors traitors into its equations. Free variables, as it were. But, as I've said, that's our working assumption, and we've taken it into account. Nonetheless, I am instructed to proceed on good faith."

"Which means *you* lot are desperate," smirks the woman with braids, and she reaches for the iPod. "What's this then?"

Ptolema lets her have it, though she'd intended the redhead to hear the recording first. There's the second deviation from Barbican's itinerary.

"That's reason Number One that we're having this conversation," she says. "Our people in Manhattan and Boston are picking it up all over the place. A twenty-four second transmission broadcasting on pirate stations. On FM, it's popping up at ninety to ninety-one megahertz, and on mediumwave exclusively at 1710. We've spotted it on single sideband modulation, as well, and shortwave. And we have five instances thus far of it having been embedded in pop and country songs on several Top 40 FM stations."

The redhead glances suspiciously at Ptolema. "Thought this was about – "

"We'll get to that. But first, we're getting to this. Consider it prologue, okay?" And Ptolema taps the iPod.

"Whatever you say, sister."

The redhead takes the iPod from her companion, so, hey, a smidge of realignment, one less red mark. She puts the buds in her ears and presses her thumb against the click wheel. Immediately, she frowns and shakes her head.

"Just fuckin' static," she mutters.

"That passes. Shut up and listen."

The redhead shuts up, and Ptolema watches her closely. The first tell could come right here, the very first hint the X might be lying. Long, long ago, Ptolema learned to read body language like it was words on a printed page. But the redhead's reactions are genuine. Thirty seconds pass, and she yanks out the earbuds and silently stares at the iPod a moment before she says anything. The woman with black braids watches her closely.

"Yeah, well, that is the dog's bollocks of mental, I'll give you that."

Ptolema takes a sip of her coffee, gone cold now, then asks the redhead, "Where'd they find you two, anyway? Nebraska? Oklahoma?"

The woman with black braids snickers and elbows her companion.

"So, tell me what you heard," Ptolema says, setting down her cup.

"Nothin' much. The static, yeah. Then a little girl, kid's voice, creepy, innit?"

"What'd she say?" asks black braids.

"Six words. Just six words. 'Black Queen white. White Queen black.'"

"What the feck does *that* mean?"

The redhead stares at Ptolema, as if waiting for an answer to black braids' question. Instead, she has questions all her own.

"First time you've heard it? Either of you?"

"Sounds like chess shite to me," the redhead mutters.

"Okay, fine, so I'll take that as a no."

"Take it however you want. That's all you got?"

Ptolema reaches underneath the table for her satchel. The worn leather is camel hide, and there are cracks here and there. She unfastens the strap and removes a manila folder. She lays it on the table next to the iPod.

"The phrase you heard is also turning up as graffiti, but the taggers we've questioned don't know shit about it. Or if they do, they won't say. A week ago, Xeroxed fliers started appearing in both cities, Boston and New York, just those six words, always on canary-yellow paper."

"Canary," says black braids. "Like the bird?"

Ptolema ignores the question, but does note that the woman no longer seems to have an interest in hearing the recording for herself. Which might mean several things or might mean nothing at all. But worth noting, regardless.

"It's nothing from our cell," the redhead says, then glances over her shoulder towards the doors and the big windows fronting Bewley's. "Can't speak for the others, but you know that."

"Of course," Ptolema tells her. Then she opens the folder, and on top there's a glossy color photo of a woman standing on a street corner. There's nothing especially remarkable about her appearance, and if that's deliberate she's mastered the art of blending in. A little frowzy, maybe. She's wearing a windbreaker the color of an artichoke.

"This was taken here in Dublin three days ago, up on Burgh Quay. I'm not going to ask if you know her, because all three of us already know the answer. She goes by Twisby."

"Yeah," says the redhead, and she doesn't say anything else about the photo. She takes out a cigarette, but doesn't light it. She just holds it between her fingers. Ptolema can see she's getting nervous, but anyone could see that.

"And now this woman," Ptolema says, pushing aside the first photo to reveal a second. The woman in this one is as striking as the first was plain. She's sitting on a park bench reading a paperback. Her white hair is cut in a bob. "I snapped this on St. Stephen's Green yesterday."

"The twins," says black braids and chews at a thumbnail. "The albinos. One of them. Think that's the one calls herself Ivoire. That's her mac, yeah? Always wears that thing, if it's rainin' or not. Yeah, that's Ivy."

"Ivy?"

"Yeah, Ivoire," says the redhead.

"But Ivoire – Ivy – and the Twisby woman, you've never seen the two of them together, have you?"

"No," replies the redhead. "That's not the way it works."

Ptolema sets aside the second photo, and there's one below it that could be the same person. Same face. Same cornsilk hair and haircut, same pale complexion, same startling blue eyes. She's sitting beneath a tree, also reading a paperback. They are, in fact, both reading the same book, which is plain upon close inspection: Kurt Vonnegut's *Cat's Cradle*.

"No. Yeah. That one's the other. Bête, I mean," black braids says around her thumb. "Feckin' bitch, in on what they're doin' to her own sister. Just wrong, by anyone's standards. Not just her sister, either. But guess you – "

" – already know the twins are also lovers?" interrupts Ptolema. "Yes. We know that. And the two of you have spoken with all three of these individuals?"

"That's why we're here, innit?" asks black braids.

Ptolema returns the photos to the folder, the folder to the satchel, and she fastens the strap again. She returns the iPod to her pocket.

"That all?" asks the redhead.

"No," Ptolema says. "That's us just getting started. But it's enough for this morning. We'll talk again tomorrow night. I trust you two know Beshoff's, on O'Connell."

The redhead nods. "We know it."

"Eight o'clock. And at least *consider* being on time, will you?"

The redhead moves the unlit cigarette between her fingers the way a magician might a coin. But then, she is a magician, isn't she? "My associate and I will take it under consideration, guv'ner." She's trying to sound cocky, but she's rattled. That's good.

Ptolema pays them both, even if it's only a formality and she doubts either of them needs the money. Then again, if they aren't lying and they've actually severed ties with Julia Set, they could be poor as fucking church mice.

"Eight. Beshoff's. Don't you keep me waiting again."

They slide out of the booth, one after the other. Before the pair turn to leave, the redhead grins and says, "Like you have a choice."

When they've gone, Ptolema considers getting another cup of coffee, maybe even something to eat. Instead, she keeps her seat and lets her eyes trace the angles and drink in the backlit colors of the stained-glass windows until her phone rings.

2.

Anybody Could Write a True Story (9/28/2012)

It's dawn, unless it's sunset. I'm sitting on the mattress, and Sixty Six is sitting on the other side of the room listening to me. It isn't true to say that she never speaks, but it's true to say that she very rarely ever speaks. I talk enough for the both of us, and if it bothers her she has never said so. Watching the sun rise, or set, I've been talking, this time, about expectation effects, straying into the Gettier problem, propositional knowledge, epistomology, observer-expectancy and subject-expectancy effects. I will not say that she is enduring my rambling patiently, or politely, because Sixty Six is not blessed with an over-abundance of either of these qualities. I am the nattering; she the hush-hush. Yeah, and then, without warning, she reaches for the rifle on the floor, rises to her knees, rests the gun on the attic windowsill, and fires five shots – *bang, bang, bang, bang, bang* – in quick tattoo succession. I don't have to look to know that she's dropped one or two or several of the demons that have marched out of the sea. *Battalions of the accursed, captained by pallid data that I have exhumed, will march...Some of them livid and some of them fiery and some of them rotten.* Who wrote that? I cannot remember now. The pain, the dope, the way horror can turn to the mundane, to existential shock, it's all made a sieve of my mind, and now memories slip straight through. You'd never know, Bête, that I was who I was two months ago. You'd never know me, I fear. Sixty Six lingers a moment at the window, then sets her gun aside and goes back to her place on the floor. She's not unpretty, despite the darkness like bruises that surrounds her oddly golden eyes. Her ebony hair hangs in unkempt dreadlocks, except when she ties it back. Almost always she keeps it tied back, out of her face. (The lead in my pencil breaks, and I have to stop to sharpen it again with my pocket knife.) There are days and nights (though the two are now, here, hardly distinguishable, one from the other) when I fancy her my shaded, sooty twin. But don't think me unfaithful, Bête. The air in the attic is still jangling from the gunfire, but I ask her if she'd like me to stop nattering; she knows it's what happens when I get nervous. And I'm almost always nervous, unless I'm on the street or on the beach and those things are coming at us and I don't have to think about anything but the sword in my hand cutting them down. Then I am calm, and the pain fades away, no matter how long it's been since my last fix. Sixty Six shrugs. She shrugs a lot, but I do try to talk less. I'm getting on my own nerves. Down on West Main, I hear more shots, other soldiers sent here to do no good whatsoever, unless we are actually holding the line and the demons haven't made it off Deer Isle to the mainland. But, how is that even possible? We can barricade the bridge and shut down the fishermen and ferries, and the CDC and DOD and X and Y and the Sons and Daughters of Machiavelli can all do their very best, even the endlessly circling patrol boats we have been told patrol Eggemoggin Reach and the rest of the bay. We can do all that, but we can't see what's going on *below* the sea, now can we? Below the *surface* of the sea. So, I think there are the usual lies, though I try to pretend otherwise. I'm here to do the job I'm here to do, to flap my wings and set distant hurricanes in motion. That's what I'm here to do, to mind *sensitive dependence on initial conditions,* the voyeur of utter destruction as beauty, marking micro-changes in deterministic non-linear, non-random systems. No, no. Not marking them. Setting them in motion. Whatever it was out there Sixty Six just put down, well, the death or deaths sent ripples, as did the bullets, and her every move during the act, and the weight of the gun on the sill, and my interrupted words and thoughts. And a million other variables that will have so many repercussions to echo down history to come. History of the future, that's what we are making. Maybe the rest are fighting the scourge, but not us. We only *seem* to be soldiers against these interlopers; we are actually instigators, toppling dominoes, setting in motion. "Deterministic Nonperiodic Flow," 1963, *Journal of the Atmospheric Sciences,* 20 (2): 130–141, Dr. Edward Norton Lorenz (also author of the concept of strange attractors, near and dear), an MIT alumnus just like Father. I have written equations on the attic wall, for old time's sake and more for comfort.

I've stopped trying to explain them to Sixty Six, because I'm pretty sure it bores her almost enough to turn that rifle on me. There's no theory in *her* chaos. She doesn't need theory when she's so adept at the practice. The magic I do not believe in swirls around her, before my very eyes, but I'm not ever again going to believe what I see, and I know that. I sometimes wonder if behind her dirty face and smudgy eyes Sixty Six harbors an intelligence to put us both to shame, dearest Bête. If she has any other name – and she must – she's never going to let it slip. A time or two, she's whispered this or that about her past, and, by the way, she can't be more than, I don't know, twenty. Twenty-two. Her mother sent her away to...a hospital? I'm not sure, but it shows. I check my wristwatch, which tells me that *is* sunset out there. Well, if watches even work in this event horizon that was once an island off the coast of Maine, notable only for its granite quarries, the Haystack craft school, lobsters, the one-time home of Buckminster Fuller. In *Travels with Charley,* Steinbeck wrote, "One doesn't have to be sensitive to feel the strangeness of Deer Isle." So, how long *has* this place been wrong, and was it always set to be the epicenter for this plague? Was it always damned? Have we – all the shadow people – been sitting back for centuries or millennia waiting for this to begin? Or did a butterfly only recently flap its wings? Sixty Six is staring at the window and eating from a bag of stale Funyuns. We eat what we can find in what is left of the grocery stores and convenience stores and restaurants. That's not much, but the heroin has mostly killed my appetite, and Sixty Six, she doesn't seem to mind the slim bill of fare this ruin offers. I believe she could live off candy bars and Skittles. A wonder she has any teeth left. She looks away from the window and says to me, "We should go soon." By which she means, I understand, that if we wait much longer I might miss the drop, my week's supply of dope to keep the agony at arm's length. The pain they gave me so I'll be a good marionette, as if taking you away from me weren't enough. I think it's cancer, but there's no way to know. Not like I can get to a doctor. There were a couple here in Stonington, but they died shortly after the first wave rose up and slithered across the sand and docks and over the seawalls. I got only Vicodin and Percoset at first, then oxycodone, then the heroin. The stations of my walk to addiction to make of me a junkie. Anything to dull the pain. The needle and the blade, because I haven't mentioned (or have I?) that the pain fades completely away – I mean *entirely* – whenever the killing starts. Numbness is my reward for being a good tin soldier, a dutiful agent with initiative, who only rarely receives direct orders, who acts on her own recognizance. And, Bête, here's the rub, I am becoming precisely that, and I mean without worrying about your safety, without the carrot-on-a-stick, without any coercion. I am beginning to feel as though I was almost meant to come here and to be what I have become, these days and this island and Ivoire set on an inevitable intersecting path from the birth of the universe, Planck Time, zero to $\sim 10^{-43}$ seconds, and there was never any doubt that this is how it would go. Sixty Six is up, pulling that pink filthy hoodie over her head, reaching for her coat. She tosses me my coat, too. And my pack. So, sorry Bête, that's all now. *What rough beast slouches* time. Time to fight the thunder and the lightning and the obscuring mists that roll in from the wicked, wicked sea.

3.

A Wolf at the Door/It Girl. Rag Doll (5/7/2112)

The village barge moves listlessly south, and Johnson has spent the past fifteen minutes gazing out a starboard porthole, towards the vast salt marshes cradling the ruins of Old Boston. His grandfather was a meteorologist who served on the Intergovernmental Panel on Climate Change, but, long ago back then, the IPCC's direst predictions never went so high as seven goddamn meters of new ocean by the turn of the century. Surprise, motherfuckers. The air through the open porthole smells of the poisoned sea, and for one whose spent too much of his life cowering amongst industrial squalor, it's a welcome smell. A comforting smell. Out here, a man can still be free, or he may at least manage to *pretend* he is still free. All this water is under the jurisdiction of the Far Shore Navy, expanded U.S. territorial since a quarter century ago. But, this far north, mostly they have their hands too full up with contraband from the cross-Arctic smugglers out of Russia and the Northern European Union to spare much time for drifters. Ahmed says something, something that he makes sound urgent. Ahmed makes almost everything sound urgent. Johnson closes the brass hatch. The hinges squeak. There's an undeniable melancholy to the skeletal remains of those distant, marsh-bound skyscrapers, only half visible through the haze. Melancholy, but hypnotic, and so it's sort of a relief, whatever Ahmed's on about.

Ahmed is sitting in front of one of the antique QD-LED monitors, data streaming down the screen like amber rain, bathing his face in amber light. Ahmed Andrushchenko is not a man who is well in the head, and lately his periods of lucidity have grown fewer and farther between. But Johnson doesn't mind his company. Plus, the man's obsessions with all the ways history might have gone, but didn't, help to pass empty hours when the comfort of the sea and the village sounds drifting down from above and up from below, the motion of the barge on the waves, are not sufficient. Almost always, he's harmless enough, is Ahmed Andrushchenko, and when he begins drifting towards the bad days, Johnson always manages to keep him from tearing up the cabin they share below the markets. Different rhythms soothe different people, and Ahmed says that Johnson's voice soothes his tattered mind.

"It won't last very long," Johnson tells him, "before a backtrace snips you."

"Fuck them," barks Ahmed, without daring to take his eyes off the screen. These fleeting uplinks to one or another satellites are too precious to him.

"One day, they'll trail you, and the entire village is gonna lose input and output, all because one man couldn't keep his eyes on the now and tomorrow."

Johnson, whose first name is Bartleby, but no one's called him that since he was a boy, he sits down in his bunk and sighs. "You can be one selfish prick," he says.

"And *you* can be a nearsighted cunt," Ahmed says.

Johnson shakes his head and stares at the walls of the cabin, decorated with Ahmed's collection of pinned Lepidoptera, almost every one of these species extinct fifty years or more. He buys them off the merchant skiffs, or, more often, barters his mechanical and process skills for the butterflies. No questions ever asked, naturally, but Johnson knows most have been looted from the unreclamated ruins of museums or stolen from other collectors' private vaults.

These butterflies, at least, will never again flap their wings.

Today, Ahmed is chasing the twin again, the one who proved dominant, the one who proved the force with which to be reckoned when push came to shove all the world off its foundations. He spends as much time chasing the albino as he spends mulling over the taxonomy of his bugs, picking through conspiracies printed on decades-old buckypages and teslin sheets. As much time – more, really – than he spends muttering at inattentive Johnson about the Martian refugees and their dead air since the war, or the lights over Africa and Argentina, or the strategic excise bioweapons that are rumored to have been deployed over India when it withdrew from the Global Population Control Initiative.

"She's here," says Ahmed. "You have to read between the undercode, then filter that through a few archeo El Gama and syncryption algorithms, but she's here all over. Shitbirds didn't think she could spin chess, but they were sorely mistaken, my skeptical friend."

"I never said I was a skeptic," Johnson mumbles, no matter how little of Ahmed's absurdities he doesn't believe; he says it any way.

"See, now that's all middlegame," Ahmed says, and taps on the screen. "You never get much of her middlegame. Most of it's sunk too deeply in the sats. But, fuck me, this is only '26, and she's already got king safety down to an art. She's hitting the internationals so hard even their material advantages have been pummeled into irrelevance. Oh, she's moving to a very violent position. That strategy is beautiful."

"Give the devil her due," Johnson says.

"Goddamn right."

"You best spool and close it down now, Ahmed. I'm not kidding. I'm the one who'll catch fuck and back if you get the ordinances on us."

"My friend, you ought to see this. I wish you could appreciate – "

"C'mon, Ahmed."

Ahmed's fingers are dancing over the keys fast as a screw from a ten-penny whore, but Johnson's been counting and Ahmed's gone over the eight-second mark. Johnson might as well be a gust of wind seven miles away.

Ahmed calls out the moves, tongue almost as fast as his fingers.

"42.cxd4+ exd4 43.Kd3 Kb4 44..." and he trails off.

"Okay," Johnson says, getting up, crossing the cabin while Ahmed is still too caught up in the twin's mythical corporate game of chess to see him coming. "I try to play nice, and you know that." Johnson presses the downlink key, and the screen goes a solid wash of amber light. He braces himself for the full fury of Ahmed thwarted. The man's brown eyes are all at once choked with anger.

"You don't *do* that, Ahmed," Johnson warns. "You don't even *think* it. How many teeth you got left you can afford to lose?"

And there's a good argument. The fire in Ahmed's eyes begins to flicker out, and he sits staring at the monitor.

"I was getting close," he says disconsolately.

"Yeah, you were. Getting close to buying the whole barge a pudgy good fine." And Johnson pulls the cover down over the cabin's wall unit. Then he goes back to his bunk.

"You think they don't want us to think she was never real?" asks Ahmed.

"Who's 'they'?" Johnson asks back, even though he knows the answer perfectly well. This is their own game of chess, the one the two men play every few days. *Huge sea-wood fed with copper Burned green and orange, framed by the coloured stone, In which sad light a carvèd dolphin swam. Isn't that the way it goes? "What shall we do tomorrow? What shall we ever do?"*

"They, you idiot. *They*."

"Don't call me an idiot, Ahmed. I don't like it when you call me an idiot."

"You think I am a lunatic."

Johnson rubs his eyes. He didn't know, until this moment, how tired he was.

"I think you need another route to time displacement, that's all. This ain't healthy. In fact, this is dangerous, cutting into the feeds like that. And Jesus, I'm tired of telling you this. How many times have I told you that?"

"She was a genius," Ahmed says, almost whispering. "But that does not mean someone could not have interceded *before* she reached middlegame."

"Your book says someone did. A whole several someones, if I recall."

Ahmed has two books, actually. Two genuine analog books from back before: *A Field Guide to Eastern Butterflies* and *The White Queen*.

"I mean to say..." but then it's as if he forgets what he's saying, loses his train of thought before the sentence is hardly begun.

"I know what you mean to say, Ahmed. Don't let it eat at you. I know what you mean, so don't worry."

"Here is the day," says Ahmed, and this time he actually is whispering, and Johnson almost doesn't catch the words. Also, just as he says it, the *Argyle Shoestring* takes a rogue wave across her bow and rocks to port, so there's another distraction. But *Here is the day*, that's a folk hand-me-down, a scribble in the margin of paranoia, what some believe were the last words from the twin before the sky went black and the night came crashing down so, so long ago. Read that bit as you will, literally or figuratively.

"Right, well," Johnson tells his cabin mate. "This is what I've heard."

And then Johnson turns back to the porthole glass and watches the sun sinking over the Massachusetts horizon while Ahmed goes to his trunk to get the plastic chess set.

4.

Black Ships Seen Last Year South of Heaven (Dublin, 13/10/2012)

As an American colleague of Ptolema's has said to her on several occasions, *There is late, and then there is not fucking coming, so give it up and go home.* She's sitting alone picking over the sad remnants of her €7.50 plate of smoked cod and chips. Her mouth tastes of beer, malt vinegar, and fried fish. She pokes at the rind of a lemon slice with her fork, then her eyes wander once more to the tall windows facing out onto Upper O'Connell Street. No sign of either the anonymous redhead nor black braids. She knows their names, of course, all of it right there in the dossier, and, sure, they know that she knows, but this is how the game is played. She stops stabbing at the lemon slice and pushes the plate away. Late was an hour ago.

Maybe, maybe, she thinks, *I should ditch them both. They're playing me, or they think they are. It's all a goddamn puppet show for the X. It's never much of anything else, now is it?*

She finishes the dregs of her second pint of the evening and briefly considers ordering a third Guinness. But her head's already a hint of cloudy, and it's not completely beyond reason to suppose that the pair, or one or the other of them, might yet turn up. So, no more alcohol. When she gets back to the hotel, she'll turn to the bottle of Connemara and let the whiskey do its job good and proper.

Enough is goddamn enough, she thinks. *No one can blame me for canceling on a tête-à-tête that's never coming. I'll call Barrymore and lay it all out, start to finish, and, if I'm lucky, he'll tell me to take the next plane the fuck out of Ireland.* She leaves a generous tip, then abandons the warm sanctuary of the restaurant and steps out into the raw and windy night. Before crossing the bridge, she stands at the edge of Aston Quay, watching the dark waters of the peaty Liffey sliding past on their way to the sea. She folds up the collar of her coat and winds her scarf more tightly about her face. This wind'll strip the skin right off your bones, and here it's not even November. The freezing air smells like the river. It smells like the algae clinging to the constricting stone channel through which the river flows. On the opposite shore, Eden Quay is a garish spray of neon signs.

Ptolema isn't aware the redhead is standing only a couple of feet away until the woman speaks. "I'd say I'm sorry about that," she says. "Only I'm not, and I'm not in the mood for lies, if you catch my drift."

"You might have let me know." Ptolema unwinds the scarf from her face, so her voice won't be muffled by wool.

"Might have, but I did not. Bury the past. Move on. Keep on truckin'. Here we are now, and now we can conduct our business beyond the attentions of any we desire not to know our business."

The redhead has dropped the phony accent, so at least there's that.

"You think I don't have other problems besides you?" Ptolema asks her. "You think you're at the very fucking top of my list of priorities?"

"I do," the woman says, and she lights a cigarette. She exhales smoke and the fog of her breath. "At the very tippy top, or near enough. I thought you wanted me to drop all the deceits, Miss P."

"So, we're going to stand out here in the cold and have this conversation? I'm going to placate you and freeze my ass off because you're afraid someone might overhear us in a fish-and-chips shop?"

"If you actually want to hear whatever it is I have to say. I know you Y sorts. I know if there's one of you, then there's two, and I know if there's two, there's four. I'm keen to your exponential support protocol."

"Our what? You just fucking made that up."

The redhead takes another drag on her cigarette and shrugs.

"Are you here to listen, or are you here to talk, Miss P?"

Ptolema takes a Punt Éireannach from a pocket and tosses it into the Liffey, a shiny red deer cast in nickel and copper for goddesses forgotten or goddesses who never were.

That there, that's not me – I go where I please – I walk through walls, I float down the Liffey...In a little while, I'll be gone. I'll be gone. I'll be gone. Must then my fortune be...wake by the trumpet's sound... and see the flaming skies. I'll be gone.

Her random thoughts, that come and go, talking of Michelangelo.

O O O O That Shakespeherian rag.

"Fine," Ptolema tells the redhead. "Twisby and the twin, the twin named Bête."

"You don't like what I got to say, if you think I'm bullshittin' you, you got orders don't you? Terminate. Terminate, with extreme prejudice, just like Jerry Ziesmer tells Martin Sheen in *Apocalypse Now*. That's how it is, I know."

Ptolema chews at her chapped lower lip, smothering impatience.

"And we shall play a game of chess?" The woman asks her and laughs.

"No more games. No more stalling."

"But your tape, Miss P. Your creepy child's voice from out the ether. Is it not commanding that we do just that?"

Ptolema wonders how many years or centuries the coin will lie lost among the rocks and silt on the river bed. After even she's dead. Long after this crisis has come and gone and is only an ugly shred of occult history. The X would build an entire equation around the consequences of her having tossed a punt into the river.

"Twisby and the twin," she says and leaves no room in her voice for any more nonsense from the redhead.

"As you like it," she replies. "Yeah, I saw 'em both. I talked with 'em both, but that's the part you already know, and fuck all if I dare waste your precious time."

"This was after you met Ivoire."

"You know that, too. Yeah, it was after, down at Kehoe's pub, but you also already know that. So, fast forward. Total cunt of a day, so mostly I was just wanting to get drunk, but I have friends who hang out there, so I was hoping to see them. Two birds, one stone. But that night, none of them showed, which was a bummer – "

"I'm not here to discuss your social life. Twisby and the twin."

"Jesus fuck, lady. I'm getting to them, okay?"

The October wind is a wailing phantom through the bare limbs of the few skinny trees lined up along the quay. Ptolema shivers at the sound, though she knows perfectly well there's nothing the least bit ominous about it. There's nothing at work but her exasperation, exhaustion, and imagination. Nothing but the reports and rumors from Maine. That, and this Twisby person and the twins to set her nerves on edge.

A red deer on a coin.

Cervus elaphus scoticus.

Deer Isle.

Odocoileus virginianus.

Barrymore warned her not to let it get inside her head, that miasma, the muddling aura that surrounds every last agent of the X. But Ptolema knows it's exactly what she's done. The redhead is talking; Ptolema curses and wonders how much she's missed in the lapse.

"…not the same shade as mine, but more like an auburn. Tied back. She wasn't drinking anything, and she hardly said one word the whole time. It was mostly the twin, mostly this Bête girl said what was said. It wasn't all that much, mind you, but it was enough. Frankly, more than I wanted to hear, seeing as how Ivoire and I were already close enough to friends. Well, as close as you get to making friends these days, right?"

Ptolema quit smoking nearly fifteen years ago, but she almost asks the redhead for a cigarette. She's still shivering and tries to stop. It's a sign of weakness, and you never let an Xer see that kind of shit. They drink it up like nectar.

"I can't recite it word for word, but the gist of it was Bête *knows* it was someone on our side made her sister sick, someone on our side set up this whole masquerade about her sister having been kidnapped. Put it in Ivoire's head – brainwashing, menticide, thought reform, hypnosis, don't ask me – that she'd lend her not inconsiderable talents to the cause and march off to that unholy fucking shitstorm in Maine, or else her sister would be tortured, raped, ravaged, tagged and bagged, whatever. That it was the X sending Ivy the goods."

"The drugs?" Ptolema asks her, and the redhead nods.

"Ivoire, she told me it was just Vicodin at first, but that wasn't enough. The pain was way beyond vikes, you know. And, from what she said, it was like whoever was in back of this operation, like they knew that, which is when the oxy started coming, instead."

"But Ivoire's never seen who delivers the packages?"

"Nope. They just show up. Sitting on a fence post with her name written neatly on the brown-paper wrapping. Or tucked into a knothole in a tree she just happens to pass. Shit like that. Happenstance. But every time she's running low, the deliveries show up like clockwork. Tick tock."

"And now it's heroin."

"Yeah. Not as if she had any say in that. She told me when they cut off the oxy, she scoured the whole goddamned island, top to bottom. But after the looting and the fires, wasn't nothing left. Piddley-shit, one-whore place only had, what? Two chemists to start with. Fuck it."

Ptolema rubs her hands together. The gloves aren't helping at all. If the cold bothers the redhead, she's doing a good job of pretending it doesn't.

"And her sister knows all of this? Bête?"

"Miss P, I'm pretty certain that's what I just said. We've…they've… got her buyin' into that whole utilitarian, greater-good crapola. Hook, line, sinker. There's her sister out there, her fucking *lover*, sick as a dog and probably dying, and now she's a junkie, and there's hardly ever a moment she doesn't seem terrified about what's happening to Bête, but Bête, this Twisby woman has her full fucking cooperation, wrapped around her pinkie finger. Nothing's going too far."

Ptolema stops rubbing her hands together – it's pointless anyway – and she says, "This can't be the first time you've seen them pull this level of shit on someone." The redhead is quiet. She doesn't answer the question that, to be fair, wasn't really a question. She doesn't say whether she has or hasn't seen this sort of shit before. Which, Ptolema knows, means that of course she has. It's *de rigueur*, business as usual in the trenches of a war that's never had honor or a code of conduct or a Geneva Convention and never fucking will.

"Go on," Ptolema says.

"That sounds an awful lot like an order to me," says the redhead.

Now, Ptolema rubs her eyes. They feel as if they're turning to ice. "I didn't mean it to."

"You watch that tone, then. Where was I?"

"Twisby appears to be controlling Bête, and somehow they're both controlling Ivoire."

"Right, so at first the Bête twin, she was all puffed up, pleased with herself and these sick machinations, pure, undiluted braggadocio. But then she mentions someone called Sixty Six, apparently another good lil' factotum shipped off to the Pine Tree State. That was about the first time Twisby perked up. Shot Bête this ugly stare, reproach, you know. Disapproval. But not like it was a secret that Bête shouldn't have let slip. More like Twisby is carrying a beef of some sort with this Sixty Six. More like that. Maybe. I don't know."

Ptolema stops rubbing her eyes. She's afraid they might shatter if she keeps it up, the way a rose dipped in liquid nitrogen shatters when struck against a hard surface.

"You know who this Sixty Six character is?" she asks the redhead.

"I got some intel. Not a lot, 'cause her profile is buried in lock-down. But I fished up some tidbits. She was deployed shortly before

Ivy. They met afterwards. Sixty Six's not much older than the twins. Twenty-ish, so about the same age as the twins. She spent some time in a mental hospital in upstate New York. Her parents had her committed when she was just a kid. But the X sprung her."

"You know why?"

The redhead looks annoyed and flicks the butt of her cigarette at the river. A trail of embers follows it down.

"How the hell would I know a thing like that? I'm sure there was some reason deemed sufficient and necessary to keep everything moving smoothly."

"Okay, so Twisby doesn't like Sixty Six."

"Not if that glare meant anything. But after she gave Thing Number Two that nasty look, Bête's whole demeanor changed. You'd have thought someone flipped a light switch in her soul. So, right off, seems to me Twisby has Bête on a short tether. But, as I said, this twin gets all twitchy, flinching, not half so talkative. Went virtually autistic, then and there. I'm not ashamed to admit, gave me the willies even more than I had them already. That's when the taciturn Doc Twisby begin speaking directly – "

"Doc? Twisby's a doctor?"

The redhead mumbles something Ptolema can't make out over the wind.

"I strongly dislike being interrupted," the redhead says, and she fishes another cigarette from a pocket and lights it. "Almost as much as I dislike taking orders."

Ptolema apologizes.

"I figured that much out just watchin' her, yeah. But afterwards I tapped a contact of mine at Cal State, and yes, she is a doctor. Neurology. Biopsych. Oxford and Yale alumnus. High profile in the APA. But then, plop, she drops off the academic radar, only to pop up on *another* radar. Three years, she was cryptologic, No Such Agency, Never Say Anything, black ops, clandestine research feces had her bouncing back and forth between the NSA and Homeland Security and OSIR. Mostly OSIR. Some highly weird goings-on, from what I was told. She – "

"How did your contact learn anything at all? If 'Twisby' is only her alias – "

"Two strikes, lady. Three, you're out, and I'll take my chances with your wrath."

This time, Ptolema doesn't bother apologizing. The redhead continues.

"*As I was saying*, if you will please fucking recall, Madam Doc Twisby was up to something unpleasant with covert funding from these various sources, shadow phenomenology bushwa, way above top secret. I'm guessing, obviously, some manner of next-gen weaponizing."

"It's better if you refrain from guessing," Ptolema says. The lights across the Liffey have her thinking of a carnival now. The redhead is silent long enough that Ptolema begins to believe she's not going to get anything else out of her.

"We...they...pulled her. Not sure when, but, near as I can suss, no one in Washington raised a hand to prevent her departure. Even for the X, that's kind of ballsy, dipping into TPTB with such complete confidence. Which sets me thinking there's an arrangement in place, tit for tat, an exchange of information in the offing. Naturally, those fucks in the States won't get anything but a stingy fraction of whatever comes of Twisby's mouse in a maze experiment. Whether or not they know this, bugger all if I can tell you."

"Okay," Ptolema says, when she's sure she isn't interrupting the redhead. Yeah, she has orders to kill her. But she doesn't want it to come to that, not with an informant that could still prove valuable down the line. Not just yet. This could, of course, change in a matter of seconds. "We have a former high-profile psychiatric wiz using these two twins for fuck only knows what. The X have Ivoire – reluctant soldier – convinced her sister will be killed unless she follows orders, and, as added insurance, extra control, they've infected or poisoned her and have her dependent upon them for painkillers. Have you considered she might only *think* she's sick?"

"I have," the redhead replies. "But pain is pain."

"Her twin," Ptolema continues, "with whom she's been involved in an incestuous relationship for seven years, since the two were thirteen, not only has no problem with this, she's helping out." Ptolema is suddenly, and, she thinks, unaccountably seized with a need to lean over the rail and vomit her dinner and all that beer into the river.

"Sorry," the redhead says. "The nausea will pass. Probably. My focus has never been spot on. Chaos can be goddamn chaotic and all."

"Fuck you," Ptolema mutters and tries to concentrate, but she can taste bile. "After your confab with these two sweethearts, did either of them say they'd be in touch again?"

"Nope. She did not."

"She?"

"Doc Twisby. Got hostile there at the end. I ought to mention that. Stopped just short of making full-on, out-and-out threats. But close enough the hairs on the back of my neck were prickling. Sufficient tension in the air I was wondering if I could reach the Glock in my shoulder holster before she pulled some sort of telekinetic nonsense or what have you. Pyro- or cryokinesis. Quantum tunneling. Doesn't matter if you wind up on the wrong end of the stick, now does it?"

"She's TK?"

"That's the vibe I got. Same with Thing Number Two, and, I'd bet a hundred large, same with Ivy."

Ptolema pinches the bridge of her nose, hard enough her eyes water, because sometimes that helps when she's motion-sick. And whatever inadvertent energy has sloughed off the redhead and onto her feels more like motion sickness than anything else.

"But she didn't do shit. Little staring match there between me and the Doc, and Bête doing some sort of origami shit with a bar napkin. Oh, hey, I haven't mentioned that, have I. See, the twin, she kept making an origami swan. They looked top notch to me, but every time Twisby would nod her head and Bête would get all hangdog and start over. Fuck me in the ear if I know what *that* was all about. By the way, Miss P, is it true the twins are some sort of prodigies? Geology, some sort of something of the sort?"

"Evolutionary biology," Ptolema replies. The nose-pinching remedy has done no good whatsoever, and her stomach rolls. "Paleontology. They were both grad students before this began."

"So we've a crop of brainiacs all round, don't we. Yeah, Ivy dropped hints to that effect. But I don't always know what's crap and what's for true. But, here's what I still don't get. Why is it you lot are chasing after this Twisby and her pale riders? Or is that need-to-know?"

Ptolema shuts her eyes, then opens them again. She truly is going to puke. And it comes to her this isn't an accident. This is the redhead's safety net, just in case the meeting went sideways and she needed an exit strategy. "You heard the recording," she says quietly and swallows.

"Black Queen white, White Queen black," says the redhead, sounding amused. "You don't look so hot there, Miss P. Gone a little green around the gills. But, the recording. Gotta admit, don't see how it hooks up with the twins."

"Then you're dumber than I've given you credit for. Think. Ivoire and Bête?"

"Yeah, and?"

"Ivory beast," says Ptolema. It's only seconds now until she loses it.

"*Damn*, yeah. Dude, how did I *not* see that? White queen. Two white queens. *Dangerous* white queens. So, you're thinkin' the message refers to those two? You know, if the gods send worms, that would be kind, if we were robins."

"And just what does *that* – " But Ptolema doesn't finish. Instead, she rushes to the railing and hurls into the Liffey. And when the cramps and dry heaves finally pass, there's no sign whatsoever of the redhead. She may as well have been a ghost. An hallucination. A false memory.

5.

How Ghosts Affect Relationships (1/1/2001; 12:01:01 a.m.)

It is everything but an understatement to call this room white. It is white in so absolute a sense that it is almost impossible for the eye to detect the intersection of angles where the four walls meet ceiling, where ceiling meets walls, where walls meet floor, to pick out each individual object placed within the room, for all of these are completely white, as well. The furnishings are few and plain: a bed, a nightstand, a white lamp with a white lampshade, a blank white canvas within a white frame, a white table and two white chairs – one placed at the north end of the table and one at the south. On the southern wall, there is a window, one window with white drapes. Outside, snow is falling so hard the land and sky blur together, white-out conditions. The white door with its white marble knob is set into the eastern wall. However, any sense of direction would be lost as soon as one were to dare enter the white room. Indeed, even the ability to tell up from down would be jeopardized. *That* is how achromatic is this room.

Though Lizbeth Margeride has no recollection of ever once having entered the room, she has been here many, many times, and, in its way, each time has been different. But always her awareness of being here begins with her seated in the white chair at the southern end of the table, facing her sister, Elle, who sits at the northern end, facing her. Both of them are wearing nothing but white camiknickers that would have been fashionable in the 1930's, with matching white stockings and Mary Janes. There is a chessboard on the table between them, and it, too, is entirely white, every one of the sixty-four squares precisely identical, and yet unmistakably distinct.

The first violation of the room's immaculateness are the sixteen and sixteen chess pieces themselves, as there are both white and black pieces. The black pieces are arranged before Lizbeth, and the white before Elle. It is appropriate, Lizbeth thinks, as Lizbeth always thinks, that her sister will make the opening move, as is ever the privilege of white, in keeping with the color scheme of the white room.

The second violation is the sisters themselves. Though their hair and eyebrows are almost as pale as the room, their milky skin seems just shy of pink in this place, and their blue eyes are as radiant as star sapphires. Their twenty fingernails have been polished crimson.

White.

This is the illusion of a single "color" perceived by the three sorts of cone cells present in the human eye when confronted simultaneously with all the wavelengths of the visible spectrum at once. White isn't the absence of color, as many mistakenly believe. It is, rather, the perfect reflection and perception of all colors, therefore the *antithesis* of black – black being perfect absorption, which is the perception of the absence of color.

Elle moves her Queen's white knight ahead two spaces and one space west.

Lizbeth studies the move. It may seem hours before she counters.

One must move with the utmost care.

Too much is always at stake.

Always.

Sometimes, even the gods themselves are merely pieces in a higher game, and the players of this game, in turn, are merely pieces in an endless hierarchy of larger chessboards.

"My move," Lizbeth says.

"Take all the time you need, love," answers Elle, as she always does. "What matter if you take a hundred years?"

She speaks with neither malice nor restlessness.

"A slow sort of country," said the Queen. "Now, here, you see, it takes all the running you can do, to keep in the same place. If you want to get somewhere else, you must run at least twice as fast as that."

Beyond the white door lies an endless white hallway. Lizbeth knows this instinctually, though she has never once stood, crossed the room, and dared to open the door. There is a soft horror in all this white that would be increased a hundredfold, she suspects, if the door were ever opened.

I don't think it's a hallway at all.

It's a maze.

The white hands of the white clock on the white wall count off the seconds, minutes, and hours. There is too much time here, and there is no time at all. In all this white, Lizbeth's thoughts inevitably begin to blur, which is unfair, as one needs clarity for chess, and her sister always gets the first move, being always white, and so still has clarity before the onset of the blur. *This room is*, Lizbeth thinks, *a cathedral to…*

To what? Closed systems where entropy prevails? A permutation of the Second Law of Thermodynamics? Quantum mechanical zero-point energy? Dissolution? The Nernst heat theorem?

Insanity?

Faultless sanity?

"If you're cold, love," Elle says to her, "you may open the window."

I may, yes. No one and nothing is stopping me.

Then comes the third violation. Her name is not Twisby, but that's the only name she has ever provided the twins. Or, not Thisby. There is sometimes contention between the sisters on this point, but the woman has never offered a definitive answer, no matter how many times they've inquired. *She is someone we will meet.* Lizbeth knows that, just as she knows that her first move will involve a pawn, no matter how much she wishes otherwise. She knows that the woman is threat and shelter, peril and deliverance. A future catalyst. When the woman speaks, the air shimmers and the twins turn towards her in unison. The legs of their white chairs scrape, in unison, as a single sound, against the white floor.

"There is but one evil," the woman named Twisby (or Thisby) tells them. "Only a single sin. It is waste. Were it not for me and what I will teach you when you are ready, you would be wasted. I cannot abide that. I will come to light the fuse. To provide the push that will be necessary to begin the – " She pauses. "To begin the cascade."

The woman opens her hands. Her left palm has been painted as red as the twin's fingernails. Her right is the color of Lizbeth's chess pieces, which is to say *all* colors.

"Quietness is wholeness at the center of stillness," says Twisby (or Thisby). "But this is only your cocoon, Lizbeth. This is only your cocoon, Elle. Such a metamorphosis awaits you. You will see. There will be no waste. No sin. No evil."

And then she's gone.

"Your move," says Elle.

"Yes," replies Lizbeth. "My move."

When at last she wakes from the dream of the white room, Lizbeth Margeride lies very still, smelling her own sweat on the damp sheets, and she keeps her eyes trained on her sister, still fast asleep in her own bed. She watches Elle until dreams come again.

6.

The Way Out Is Through (9/30/2012)

It was almost an hour past dark by the time we made it back to the attic. I can only be sure of the transition by recourse to my watch. In its current condition, the sky is hardly a help. But so late in the day, we shouldn't have been that far from the attic, not so far as the docks at the end of Seabreeze Avenue. But we needed food. I'm sick as a sick dog today. The pain has been a hammer pounding my entire body, glass and razors in my joints and lungs and belly, but I didn't dare fix until we got back here. The dope is as good as any toxin out there in the turmoil at the end of the world. Sixty Six hates when I call this that, the *End of the World.* She never says so, but she makes the face she makes whenever she disapproves of something I've said. I think of it as her Disapproving Face. Anyway, I fixed almost an hour ago, and now there's only the music of Hell seeping in through the walls and the open window. Never mind the season, tonight it is too warm to shut the window. Still, despite the heat, Sixty Six keeps her hoodie on. I've stripped down to my bra and panties, and I'm still sweating. Drips of me, of my internal ocean, splashing against the dusty floor as I write this. *My* ocean is clear, though, not the sloshing putrescence of the bay, of all the sea surrounding Deer Isle. We found a tidy cache of food in the harbormaster's office – cans of meat and vegetables, mostly. We filled our packs, and it should keep us fed a week, at least. *If* we live another week. Sixty Six seems indifferent to survival, and, at times, fuck but I wish I were, too. Then there would only be the monotonous rhythm of pain and the freedom from pain the dope brings, the heroin's euphoria, our days on the street hunting down the demons (I do not mean this word in any conventional sense; no other seems to fit, that's all), gun fire, the hilt of my khukuri in my hand, slashing the air, slashing flesh that isn't flesh. Matter, protoplasm, *Urschleim*, but not flesh. The stink of ozone when I have no choice but to resort to those intangible weapons folded up inside me. The howling, capering abominations. But we're "home" again, "home" again. Me and taciturn Sixty Six. There's a crooked stack of books beside her mattress. She reads. She reads as much as I did, before. We found the public library our first week here, not long after we found each other, and it was one of the few instances when she's seemed happy. She used a shopping cart to haul away dozens of books. Now, I think they keep her company much more than I do. *They* are her solace. I want to talk about what we saw down there this afternoon, how we found ourselves hemmed in and almost did not make it back. But that is the one subject I can rest assured Sixty Six will never discuss: whatever's happening here. The sea is the color of semen. The sea is the consistency of jizz. *The scrotumtightening sea.* It smells like sewage. It steams and disgorges demons. "Demons." All but shapeless shapes that burst when shot or cut, their constituent molecules thereafter slithering back into the semen sea to reassemble and gather themselves for a new assault. Sixty Six calls them *shoggoths*, a word she's taken from old horror stories, turns out. I don't care what the fuck they are. They pop and slither off. There's a pretty picture drawn nice as nice can be, isn't it, Bête? I spend my days hoping you are safe, that they are doing you no harm. I spend my days in slaughter, in a charade meant to convince the few survivors in Stonington that we have their irrelevant interests at stake. That we are more than two lost souls, refugees ourselves, sent here to topple the dominoes just so, perpetuating calculated chaos, perhaps for no other reason than because curious men and women desire to see the pretty fractals that will follow from our efforts. Last night, Sixty Six was reading *The House at Pooh Corner*, and since she doesn't seem to mind my talking while she reads, so long as I don't expect replies, I rattled on for a while about Tuscaloosa and mine and your time at the university. Oh, she did find it odd that we chose to go to school in Alabama, when she knows (I do not know how) that we might have had our pick of Ivy Leagues. Anyway, yes, I talked about blastoids – how we were the first to find *Granatocrinus granulatus* in the Fort Payne Chert; how, as undergraduates, we named *Selmasaurus russelli,* a new genus and species of plioplatecarpine mosasaur; the papers we delivered together on mosasaur biostratigraphy at annual meetings of the Society of Vertebrate Paleontology (Ottawa, Austin, Cleveland, then

Bristol and our first trip to England); taking part in the dig that produced the tyrannosauroid *Appalachiosaurus*, our small role in some of the preliminary examination of the skeleton while it was still in the matrix and plaster field jackets; the mess with FHSM VP-13910, how *we* prepared it and first saw it for what it was, a second species of *Selmasaurus,* but the credit going to others and our work unacknowledged; collecting Oligocene fossils in the White River badlands of Nebraska; standing in the wooded gully at Haddonfield, New Jersey, where, in 1858, the first dinosaur described from America was discovered; how we were the first to happen upon and describe the remains of a velociraptorine theropod from the Gulf Coast (even if it was only one tooth). I went on and on like that – *Ditomopyge*, Little Stave Creek, *Globidens alabamaensis*, the Pierre Shale and Pottsville Formation, that skull of *Megalonyx jeffersoni* we prepared but were afraid we'd screw up and so didn't finish (one of many failures, I admitted), freezing strip mines in the winter and blistering quarries and chalk washes in July…and on and on and on. She *heard*, but I'm pretty sure she didn't *listen* to a word of it. She is a master of compartmentalization. Anyhow, I don't care what William Faulkner said, Bête. I think the past *is* the past, for us, and we can recall those days, but we'll never go back to that life we cherished. Will we. No. Science and reason are being demolished around me. Paradigms are being reduced to matchsticks, to splinters. Topsy-turvy. I hope you are safe, sister, and that they are keeping their promises. I'm doing everything I'm told. To the letter. I am obedient. But that's always come easily to me. Not like you, sweet Bête. But I know even if I do not die here, if we ever are reunited, there is no going back. Now, returning to the matter of the Semen Sea, here is what we think we know, pieced together from hearsay, frightened confessions, newspaper and other local periodical accounts printed in the weeks before it began (*Commercial Fisheries News, Compass Classifieds, The Deer Isle Chronicle, Island Ad-Vantages,* et al.) from captains' logs we've recovered off derelict fishing boats: on the night of August 20th, a chartreuse light fell screaming from the sky. It is agreed the light did scream, or whatever cast the light screamed, as it fell into the bay somewhere beyond Burnt Cove. But the sun and the stars were still visible until the 27th, when the visibility zero-zero began rolling in *from the east*, so not from the direction of Burnt Cove. Empty boats, dead fishermen found floating or washed up to make a feast for crabs and gulls and maggots. The greasy rains and the sickness that came after them, the plague that killed 78%+ of Deer Isle's population before we arrived, the whatever it was the CDC couldn't even slow down before it claimed most of their team, too. The stars coming back…wrong; unrecognizable, alien constellations spinning overhead. Yes, I do sound like a mad woman, and I don't expect any of this will ever be made public. If it is contained, if it ever ends – The Event – they'll be sure no one talks, I think, even if it means murdering everyone who survives. There will be a mock-rational explanation. Mock science everyone will want to believe, because believing the truth – even were it not concealed – would be intolerable. But enough for now. Sixty Six has dog-eared a page and put her book away. She wants me to turn off the Coleman lantern. I need the sleep. Tomorrow will be at least as bad as today, as bad as yesterday, as bad as day after tomorrow. Or worse. Night, sister. Sweet dreams.

7.

Golgotha Tenement Blues/Counting Zeroes (11/15/1966)

Wait. Let's not get ahead of ourselves. Shun a premature narrative, lacking necessary background exposition. Ergo, the future, which will shortly be spoken of as the past, the *future* of the past (as all futures are), 1973 and the intergovernmental hysteria rightly triggered by the indiscretions at the Watergate Hotel. The steps hastily taken to destroy records of *previous* indiscretions, and among them the efforts of CIA Director Richard Helms to annihilate all evidence of Project MKUltra. Between the early 1950's and 1973, the CIA's secret efforts at behavioral engineering in humans. This fell to the members of the Scientific Intelligence Division, who dutifully employed "chemical, biological and radiological" agents to accomplish their ends, along with a buffet of torture, sexual abuse, sensory deprivation, prolonged verbal assaults, and so forth.

LSD was popular.

Had Helms been successful, MKUltra would have managed to disappear. No mean feat, that would have been. But spooks are notoriously fine magicians. Only, Helms was the cut-rate sort of magician who makes a living at children's birthday parties. That is, if we evaluate him solely on his failure to erase the two plus decades of *this* project.

Now. Then. Before.

Here is a woman named Madeline Noble. One day, she, unwed, will have a child who will be named Patricia Elenore. In time, Patricia Elenore at age twenty, also unwed, will give birth to a daughter to be christened Olivia Estrid "Sixty Six" Noble.

Link to link to link.

Dot to dot to dot.

LSD, amphetamines, barbiturates, ergine, temazepam, psilocybin, mescaline, heroin, 3,4-methylenedioxy-*N*-methylamphetamine, et alia. And the researchers were especially proud of their superhallucinogenic glycolate anticholinergic dubbed "BZ." Words that roll off the tongue like pretty pharmacological poetry. In 1964, Madeline Noble enrolled at Bowling Green State University, undecided on her course of study, though, ironically, leaning towards psychology. Madeline was one of five students unknowingly administered multiple doses of BZ *via* cafeteria food. Seven doses, over fourteen weeks, culminating in a psychotic breakdown. Solid data for the studious number crunchers and keepers of albino lab rats to mull over. Control the mind, control the will. Control the soul. Render malleable strategic individuals, armies, the populous of an entire city malleable, or insensible. Useful.

That upon the wings of a super-bat, he broods over this earth and over other worlds, perhaps deriving something from them: hovers on wings, or wing-like appendages, or planes that are hundreds of miles from tip to tip – a super-evil thing that is exploiting us.

By Evil I mean that which makes us useful.

Madeline. Here she is, in a white, white padded cell, kept safe from herself, in the sense that she may not now do herself bodily harm, may not end the nightmare of her life. The hurricane within her amygdala, its inability to imagine an end to the storm and send an all-clear to the medial prefrontal cortex. This cyclone puts the [anti] cyclonic Great Red Spot of Jupiter to shame. She is divorced from this place and this time, thrown forward, backwards, and she watches the sky fall whenever she shuts her eyes.

Catch a falling star and put it in your pocket.

Never let it fade away.

Catch a falling star and put it in your pocket.

Save it for a rainy day.

In every way, Madeline Noble is a success story for the geeks and bureaucrats of MKUltra. She is a shining star, falling or not. Hard work pays off and has been rewarded with manna from Heaven, as it were.

As she is.

In her head, the sky falls. There, it bleeds over the waters of Penobscot Bay, above and upon Deer Isle, where her parents have a summer home. Where she spent her summer vacations, before college. When she is visited by psychiatrists from McGill University, happily serving their CIA manipulators, when they question her for voice recordings and meticulous notes, she recites blasphemies written down and published more than four decades earlier, though none of them will ever make the connection with *his* damned book. How the brilliant are often blind.

They press the record button, pencils held at the ready, ears perked like alert hounds, and sometimes she will sing for them: "When You Wish Upon a Star," "Stars Fell on Alabama," "Catch a Falling Star," "I Only Have Eyes For You." They scribble, and *she* says:

"A thing the size of the Brooklyn Bridge. It's alive in outer space."

"Something that big? Wouldn't we have seen it?"

"*Shhhh*, Logan. Don't interrupt her."

Madeline is silent for a moment, glaring at the three men in her cell. And then, again, she says, "A thing the size of the Brooklyn Bridge. It's alive in outer space.

"Something the size of Central Park kills it.

"It drips."

"Jesus," Logan whistles to himself.

"Showers of blood," she says. "Might as well *be* blood. One especial thing, a thing the size of the Brooklyn Bridge, as there are vast living things in the oceans, there are vast living things in the sky. Leviathans. Fleets of Leviathans. Our whole solar system is a living organism, and showers of blood are its internal hemorrhages." There are no italics here because every word she says is emphatic.

"Rivers of blood that vein albuminous seas."

"Dreiser, how do you spell 'albuminous'?"

"The phosphorescent gleam seemed to glide along flat on the surface of the sea, no light being visible in the air above the water. Though...disruption may intensify into incandescence, apart from disruption and its probable fieriness, these things that enter this earth's atmosphere have about them a cold light which would not, like light from molten matter, be instantly quenched by water. They still burn. They can't stop burning."

She names asteroids that have not yet been discovered.

She describes, in great detail, Saturn's north polar hexagon, which will not be observed until the year 2005.

She also describes Io's volcano Tvashtar, the frozen seas of Europa, the September 18th, 2006 discovery of a supernova 240 million light years away.

She asks them, "Who are the twins?"

She asks, "Who is the Egyptian? Have you any idea how long she's been alive?"

She asks, "What is the Ivory Beast?"

"What is the meaning of 'Black Queen white, White Queen black'?"

And after a prolonged silence, followed by a fit of laughter that not a man among her watchers does not find disconcerting, she turns her head towards the ceiling. And taking great care to enunciate each syllable so that they will not mistake these words for any others, she says, "Gentlemen, we have arrived at the oneness of allness. A single cosmic flow you would label disorder, unreality, inequilibrium, ugliness, discord, inconsistency."

"Jesus *Christ*," Logan mutters. "Haven't we heard enough of this shit for one day?"

"Don't make me tell you to shut up again."

"Checkmate," says Madeline. "Because this is the meaning: Black Queen white, White Queen black. A game of chess played in the temples of Eris, the halls of Discordia. There will be murders on *La manzana de la discordia*. You know, or may learn of Omar Khayyam Ravenhurst, not his real name, but let that slide. The gods were not pleased, and so, of course, all were turned into birds. Even the birds will rain down upon the bay and upon the island. Eris tosses the Golden Apple, and the sea heaves up her judgment upon us all. Watch for the Egyptian and the arrival of the twins and my daughter's daughter. Watch for Strife, who, warns Homer, is relentless. She is the sister and companion of murderous Ares, she who is only a little thing at the first, but thereafter grows until she strides on the earth with her head striking heaven. She then hurls down bitterness equally between both sides as she walks through the onslaught, making men's pain heavier.

"The calla lilies are in bloom again. Such a strange flower – suitable to any occasion."

"Be still," she says. "The chaos rains around you now."

She tells them very many things, and these things Richard Helms *will* succeed in expunging from the knowledge of man. In that, at least, he will be successful. There are those *outside* the CIA who will see to that.

Later, on the flight back to Montreal, Dr. Allan Logan examines their notes. "Thank fuck we know that woman will never have a daughter, much fucking less a granddaughter. Whatever Washington is aiming for, I believe they overshot the mark with that one."

"Ours is but to do or die," replies Dr. Dreiser.

"That's not how it goes."

"Not how *what* goes?"

"That poem. 'The Charge of the Light Brigade.' Tennyson. It goes, 'Theirs not to reason why, theirs but to do *and* die.'"

"Fuck you, Logan." With that, Dr. Dreiser shuts his eyes and concentrates on the rumble of the Boeing 707's turbocompressors. He dislikes air travel almost as much as he dislikes Logan.

But a daughter will be born to Madeline Noble.

And a daughter to her daughter.

Eris plays a mean game of chess.

8.

Bury Magnets. Swallow the Rapture.
(17 Vrishika, 2152)

She sits on a bench in the main observation tier of the *Nautilus-IV*, her eyes on the wide bay window set into the belly of the station, the icy spiral of the Martian northern pole filling her view. She being the White Woman. *La femme albinos. Ca-ng bâi de. Blancanieves.* More appellations hung on her than all the words for God, some say. But if she has a true name – and doesn't everyone? – it is her secret and hers alone. A scrap of knowledge forever lost to humanity. So, her blue *eyes* are fixed on the Planum Boreum four-hundred kilometers below, yes, but her *mind* is on the Egyptian – Ancient of Days, El Judío Errante, Kundry, Ptolema – she has many "names," as well. The Sino LDTC ferrying her is now less than eight sols out. The Egyptian racing towards her. An unforeseen inconvenience. In no way at all a calamity, no, but still an unfortunate occurrence to force the White Woman's hand. It tries her patience, and patience has been the key for so long that she cannot even recall a time before she learned that lesson.

In less than eight sols, the transfer vessel will dock, and they will speak for the first time in…

Ça fait combien de temps déjà?

She answers the question aloud, "Cent trente-neuf ans."

"Vraiment?" asks Babbit. "Autant que ça?"

When she arrived on the station two months ago, Babbit was assigned the task of seeing to her every need. As has been her wish, he hardly ever leaves her side. The company of anyone is a balm for her sometimes crippling monophobia. A medicine better than any she has ever been prescribed. It doesn't matter that this tall, thin, towheaded man is only mostly human. Many times, she's resorted to and relied upon the companionship of splices. Besides, Babbit's fast borrow capabilities saved her the trouble of telling him all the tales he needs to know to carry on useful conversations. And there will be much less fuss when she orders his death, before her flight back to Earth. Easy come, easy go.

"Vous n'êtes jamais allé à Manhattan," she says.

"Madame, c'était perdu avant que je sois né."

"Bien sûr," she replies, and the White Woman holds up her right hand, absentmindedly running fingertips along the window, tracing the serpentine furrow on the Chasma Boreale. It seems almost as long as her long life, and almost as aimless. *Possédé de direction*, she thinks, *n'est pas être possédé d'intention*.

"En tout cas," she says to Babbit, "nous étions à Manhattan. Je venais juste de rentrer de la Suède. Il y a si longtemps. Presque au tout début."

"Autant que ça," he says again.

"Je ne pourrais pas commencer à comprendre ce qu'elle espère accomplir en venant ici me poursuivre comme elle le fait."

"Moi non plus, Madame."

"Il se peut que le vaisseau soit armé. Ça serait bien son style: une attaque préventive, sacrifier le poste entier et tout le monde à bord afin d'accomplir ses objectifs."

"Ces fanatiques sont extrêmement dangereux," says Babbit.

"Ce n'est pas possible qu'elle espère *argumenter* avec moi. Elle ne peut pas imaginer l'idée que nous partageons un concept commun de Raison."

"Des vrais croyants, je veux dire," Babbit says.

"Je sais ce que vous voulais dire."

"Bien sûr, Madame."

"Peut-être elle ne souhaite que d'être témoin," the White Woman says. "Être présente quand le cavalier de mon roi prend son dernier fou."

Babbit clear his throat. "Je m'attends à ce que le capitaine aura prévu la possibilité d'une attaque," he says, then clears his throat once more.

She laughs. "Il n'a rien fait de la sorte. Il n'y a pas eu d'alerte, pas de préparation pour intercepter ou protéger. Il reste assis et attend, lui, comme un petit animal peureux qui se recroqueville aux sous-bois."

"Je ne faisais que de supposer," admits Babbit.

The White Woman pulls her hand back from the window, and she seems to stare at it for a few seconds. As if in wonder, maybe. Or as if, perhaps, it's been soiled somehow. Then she turns her head and watches Babbit. He lowers his head; he never meets her gaze.

"J'ai considéré retenir le lancement jusqu'à ce qu'elle embarque," she says to him. "Jusqu'à ce qu'elle soit assez proche."

"Alors vous avez pris votre décision? Le lancement, je veux dire."

"J'ai pris cette décision avant de quitter Xichang. Ce n'était qu'une question de quand."

"Et maintenant avez-vous décidé du quand?"

No one on the *Nautilus-IV*, no one back on Earth, no one in the scattered, hardscrabble colonies below, none of them know why she is here. Few enough know that she *is* here. She was listed on no passenger manifest. They do not know she's ready to call the Egyptian's gambit and move her king's knight. To cast a stone on the still waters. Not one of them knows the nature of her cargo. No one but Babbit, and he won't talk.

"Maintenant, j'ai décidé quand," she tells him, and the White Woman shuts her blue eyes and pictures the vial in its plasma-lock cradle, hidden inside a shipment of hardware and foodstuffs bound for Sharonov. The kinetic gravity bomb will detonate at five hundred feet, and the contents of the vial will be aerosolized. The sky will rain corruption, and the corruption will take root in the dome's cisterns and reservoirs.

הנעל.

Wormwood.

Apsinthion.

...and a great star fell from heaven, blazing like a torch...

"Madame," says Babbit, not daring to raise his head. "Êtes-vous sûre d'obtenir les résultats desirés? Il y a de règles d'évacuation, des procédures de confinement environnemental – "

...the waters became wormwood...

"Babbit, toute ma vie je n'ai jamais été sûre de rien. Ce qui en est en cause."

She turns back to the window and can almost feel the wild katabatic winds scouring the glaciers and canyons. The White Woman pulls her robes more tightly about herself. She's glad that Babbit is with her. She wants to ask him if he might take for granted that she has never loved, if no one has ever been dear to her. But she doesn't.

Instead, she says again, "Ce qui en est en cause."

"Oui, Madame," he says. "Bien sûr."

9.

A Plague of Snakes, Turned to Stone (11/4/2012)

It is difficult to believe this can continue much longer. The seasons are not changing. It seems as though it will always now be late summer, earliest autumn, here in Stonington, as though this horror has frozen time. And yet we move through time, and we speak, and our thoughts occur, and that which bears a vague resemblance to day and that which bears a vague resemblance to night comes and goes. We get hungry. We run out of ammunition. We kill. We forage. All these factors assure me there must continue to, at the least, exist some *facsimile* of time. It's like a forgery by an unskilled counterfeiter. God makes a copy, but he gets it wrong. Or, he gets it different. *The world I have known is lost in shadow.* That shit from the sea, it warps time. Invokes a time dilation that exists between here and, possibly, all the rest of the world. Or – if not a gravitational time dilation, not us beyond the perimeter of a Schwarzschild radius where time comes to a grinding halt on the singularity of a collapsed, frozen star, then a subjective time dilation, happening in my mind. Have I written that already, on some other page? Does it matter if I have? *And the stars are black and cold. As I stare into the void.* Tonight is tonight, and I sat down and opened my notebook and took up my pen to write about tonight. Today, tonight. Both. About how they have been peculiarly quiet. That happens sometimes, the quiet days. The lulls. In a way, they're worse than the day-to-day war we are not here waging upon foes we have not come to defeat. Not in the strictest sense. No. Not the way the few remaining survivors of Deer Isle are fighting. The way the military and the CDC are fighting. You, Bête, you will know what it is

I mean. And the pain, it's getting so much worse. There are days now when Sixty Six has to venture out alone. She never seems to resent my inability to accompany her. Is she relieved? Would she rather do her work alone? Can't say, haven't asked, won't even hazard a guess. Stepping outside today, slinking from our attic because we needed to restock our provisions, because somewhere another domino needed toppling to a faraway effect, we left the attic and realized at once it would be a Quiet Day. I walked along behind Sixty Six, keeping up as best I can despite the pain in my legs and stomach. She found two cans of Heinz baked beans and a can of brown bread in the looted shell of the Fisherman's Friend Restaurant on Atlantic Avenue. This is very close to the public library, and she'd stopped for a couple of new books. We sat at the end of one of the wharves and ate. She read and ate. I only ate and watched the sticky sea which was so still today that it seemed almost to have solidified. How and why do I force myself to observe those waters, bereft of so much as even the suggestion of waves? I do not know, Bête, my love. The tides do not rise and fall here any longer, so the horror holds a greater sway than does the moon. Up there where the constellations shift about, might be there is not longer a moon, or never *was* a moon. Consider that! But, we sat together, eating. Me, chewing but not tasting. Just grinding my jaws. Her reading *David Copperfield*, between plastic sporkfuls of baked beans. (*I had considered how the things that never happen are often as much realities to us, in their effects, as those that are accomplished.*) There was a cramp, an especially bad one, and I vomited everything I'd swallowed into the sea. No. Onto the sea. My puke spattered across that pearly surface and lay there. Not sinking. I think it's alive. Have I said that? That I think what the bay has become is alive? I wiped my mouth and stared up at the resilient buttermilk August-September-in-November sky. *We had the sky, up there, all speckled with stars, and we used to lay on our backs and look up at them, and discuss about whether they was made, or only just happened.* Sixty Six turned a page. She did not seem to notice I'd been sick, but I am sick a lot. Old hat. Like bullets and blades and blood and ichor. We no longer find the remarkable at all remarkable. I wiped my mouth and said, very softly, "What out there do you miss? Do you miss anything at all?" She continued reading, not raising her eyes from the novel. "What *would* I miss? No." I wiped my mouth again and spat. "Where did you learn to shoot?" I asked, and I admit I was talking just to hear my voice. The world here grows more silent every day. "Nowhere," she replied. She told me how she'd never held a gun before the X came to her and sent her here. "What was there to learn?" she asked. "It's all mathematics. Nothing but a sort of trigonometry." For no reason I can now recall, I then recalled that it was Thursday. On Thursday nights there are films in the National Guard armory. Sixty Six likes to go. Mostly they screen – yeah, Bête, this part is bizarre – these fucked-up old Disney cartoons, Donald fucking Duck in the army, in World War II. *The Vanishing Private*; there's the only title I remember. Jesus, I'm making less sense than usual, but I had to use more of the dope than usual to so much as sit up and hold the pen. Maybe *you* know why my being made sick is necessary to this experiment – if that is the word – but it is lost on me. Back to the wharf. Sixty Six sat her empty can aside, and I asked if she were going to the movies tonight. She shrugged. All of this was playing out through the fog of pain and drugs dream-like. I don't question that sensation anymore. I reached into a pocket of my jacket, the variegated camouflage one I took from the aforementioned armory (no one tries to stop me from doing anything, not here). A small ammonite like the one you wear on the silver chain around your neck, sister. My tiny black *Hildoceras bifrons* from our trip to Whitby. I held it out to her, its whorl shining dully in my palm. She set her book down and stared at it, seeming truly and totally mystified. "Why?" she wanted to know. Suspicious. "I don't know. I want you to have it, that's all. Maybe because you keep saving my life out here." She took it; I hadn't thought she would. "People don't give me things," she said. "I just did," I said. "You miss things," she said. "You miss what you had before, you and your sister. Your science. The fossils." Practically a sermon, that many words from Sixty Six all at once. It actually made me smile. "Yeah, I do. I miss Bête, and I miss what we did." Sixty Six let the ammonite tumble from one hand to the other. "Not just the sex," she said. "Not just the sex," I replied. Have I mentioned that, sometimes, the internet is still accessible from the island? Just now and then. One of the terminals in the city hall hasn't been smashed, and I've sat and used it a few times. "I see what you read online," Sixty Six said to me. "You want to go back." "Don't you?" "Back to what?" There was a long silence then. I heard sirens off towards town proper. I don't know why they still bother with those, but the sound was a welcome interruption on a Quiet Day. "Okay," I said. And then I talked about the last thing I'd read online. Others might have been scouring the web for news of the outside world and whether it has any fucking idea what's happening here. I don't. Last time (and Sixty Six was with me, searching through old file cabinets, though I cannot say for what) I read *PLoS One* and an article on a newly discovered freshwater mosasaur from Hungary, *Pannoniasaurus inexpectatus*, and sitting on the wharf I explained to Sixty Six that paleontologists hadn't thought that mosasaurs lived in freshwater. Only, here's the thing, Bête. You'll not have read this article, I don't think. Because *this* was the December 19, 2012 issue of *PLoS One*. And we're back at time dilation. "Look at this," Sixty Six said, and that she was talking so much, it was starting to freak me out. "Look at this," and she pointed at the little ammonite in her hand. At the center of its whorl. "It begins *here*, and it goes round and round and round, and it's always growing larger from the center. What begins as a point becomes very wide before it ends." I didn't know what to say, so I didn't say anything at all. She understands the heart of it, doesn't she? Every minute action, or omission of an action; every breath we breathe; the shedding of every dead skin cell; every trigger pulled; every man and woman on this island who crosses our path – it all echoes through eternity, growing larger and larger in its consequences as the whorl goes round and round about. Oh, oh. What did I just write? I should not have, should have kept that bottled. I ought to *destroy* this page. I ought to *burn* it and swallow the ashes. Don't follow me, Bête. Whatever happens, don't follow me. *Fais que ton rêve soit plus long que la nuit.*

10.

Throwing a Donner Party at Sea (5/13/2114)

Today is Friday, though for many aboard the village barges scattered about the globe, and so on the *Argyle Shoestring*, the distinctions between days and weeks and months tend to blur. But not for Ahmed Andrushchenko, who obsessively marks off each date on calendars he makes himself. Bartleby Johnson has never seen the point of it. Sure, the tier farmers and hydroponics need to know the growing seasons, and there are still those who celebrate Christmas, Ramadan, Easter, Chanukah, all the host of High Holy Days, Boxing Day, Launch Day, goddamn May Day and St. bloody Valentine's Day. There is that peculiarly nostalgic minority. Johnson, he figures it's the norm ashore, that the terrestrials rejoice as a matter of course. But it's raw on the waves, and most old ways have been set aside for the monotony of the deep. Today is Friday, and he's repairing the aft solar-sail array. It's tedious work – especially with such jerry-rigged replacement parts – but it beats to hell and back passing the afternoon with Ahmed. His latest tiresome obsession is the trans-Neptunian object 90377 Sedna, which by his calculations (and century old astronomical charts) has recently overtaken the dwarf planet Eris as the farthest known celestial body orbiting the sun. That, and news of the civil unrest in the Greater Republic of India.

Better, thinks Johnson, *that I spend however many hours dangling from this catwalk, suspended above the abyss with a wrench and spanner.*

He is undeniably fond of Ahmed. They've been quarter mates for eight years now, ever since Johnson came aboard in Portugal. But the prattle wears on one's nerves and wears thin. So, times like this he is grateful to be a mechanic, frequently called out to keep this ramshackle cobble-together from breaking apart to scatter across the waves and send them all to the drowning.

Johnson is replacing a shot rivet at the base of the heliogyro when the sirens sound that mean another vessel is coming alongside. He uses both feet to shove off the hull, swinging his harnesses around for a better view. It's an FS Navy ship, a high-speed trimaran wearing the name *Silver Girl.* Never a good sign, the Navy bothers sending a trimaran this far from littoral. A voice booms from the *Silver Girl's* loudspeakers, notifying the barge that it will be boarded in five minutes and to ready the ramp right quick. Johnson curses, takes a firm hold of the crisscross network of safety lines, and hauls himself back up onto the widowmaker. By the time he's unbuckled, navigated the jibboom and bowsprit, then climbed down to Red Tier, through his spyglass, across two hundred yards, he can see the Navy men are filing onto the barge, two abreast, armed so that it will be obvious to everyone in the village that they mean business. This isn't some sort of routine inspection (not that they'd ever send a littoral trimaran for an inspection).

It might be that crate of black market quinoa, flax, and soy they bartered for a while back. Or it might be the two fugitives they (very unwisely) gave sanctuary down on the Houston wharves, on a Texas run six months ago. Or it might be...

Ahmed.

Johnson shoulders through the throng of worried, frightened, and curious onlookers blocking his way. He moves as quickly as he possibly can, and once there's almost a scuffle when he overturns a melon cart. But by the time he's made it to the front of the crowd, one of the Navy men has hauled Ahmed from below decks and is leading him in cuffs towards the ramp. Ahmed's head is down, and he doesn't see Johnson. They take Ahmed Andrushchenko away, and not once is there eye contact between him and Johnson. Two midshipmen in hard-shell hazmat suits are carrying Ahmed's footlocker with as much care as they would handle a nuke. A major reads off the charges to anyone who cares to hear them, and before half an hour has passed the *Silver Girl* is rapidly putting distance between them, tacking westward towards shore. In another fifteen minutes, it's only a glint on the horizon.

On his way back to his quarters, Johnson is intercepted by another mechanic – a hulking Scotsman named Galbraith – who wants to know what the fuck *that* was all about.

"He was *your* bunkmate, yeah? Figure you gotta have a notion, yeah? What was in that fucknut's footlocker?"

Johnson shakes his head, and he tells Galbraith, "No idea. His business was his own. But you swim quicktime, you can ask 'im for yourself, yeah?"

"You are a lying cocksucker!" the Scotsman shouts after him.

Yes, I am. Yes, I most surely am. But so are we all.

Ahmed traded a box of chips and circuits for it almost a year back, so long Johnson can't even recall the name of the barge he found the trunk on. But he does remember the contents. Nothing he'd conjured on overly long, and, truth told, he'd not ever thought of the trunk in quite a long while. But now, now, now it was fresh in his mind as that busted rivet on the sail. Mostly there'd only been an assortment of musty old books, a case of roundabouts no machine on a dump like the *Argyle Shoestring* would ever be able to spin, and an assortment of motion cubes – equally fucking useless. Among the books was a volume on advanced chess tactics and another on cosmological inflation theory, and Johnson, at first, had assumed those were the reason Ahmed had bothered haggling for the lot. Until he'd pulled a shiny lead cylinder from the jumble. There was a Category A UN 2814 biohazard designation pressed into one side and also the lid of the cylinder, along with a date: 18-2-13.

"No," Johnson had told him, grabbing for the cylinder, no matter how it was scaring him shitless. "That goes right the fuck overboard."

"Screw you, Bartleby," Ahmed said. "It's mine. It cost dear, and it is mine." There had ensued a tussle that ended in Johnson sporting a newly chipped incisor and Ahmed an eye that would go black and blue as storm clouds. But Bartleby had given up. He threatened to report Ahmed to the selectmen, but that hadn't made any difference. He threatened never to play chess with Ahmed again, and, again, no dice. Johnson sat on the floor below the porthole, sweating and teasing the damaged tooth with the tip of his tongue.

"You ain't gonna open that, you crazy son of a bitch. Even you're not that daft."

But then Ahmed did pop the seal. There was an audible hiss, and a subsequent series of clicks as the cylinder released the inner capsule. A fog of liquid oxygen or nitrogen billowed from the violated artifact, and when it cleared Johnson saw what had been shut away more than one hundred and one years: clamped firmly in place between steel rods, a glowing tube, maybe thirty-five, maybe forty milliliters. Whatever was in the tube had a pearlescent quality about it, and it glowed ever so slightly in the twilight filling up the cabin.

"You got no inkling what that shit is," Johnson said.

"Isn't that the marvel of it?"

"I ought to murder you in your sleep, you bastard. Slit your throat, toss that shit overboard myself." Johnson hadn't meant it, but he was frightened, and his tooth hurt, and he has always been apt to blurt such threats in the heat of the moment.

"If you gotta, then you gotta," Ahmed shrugged, and he gazed in wonder at the pearly tube before shutting and sealing the cylinder again.

So, thinks Johnson, sitting on the edge of his bunk, *so somehow the military got word and come for it. Might be they've been doggin' that can around for tens and tens, and Ahmed gets it, and they get Ahmed. Fuck. Fuck. Fuck.*

"Fuck."

That's when Johnson happens to glance at the shelf that holds Ahmed's books, and right off he notices one, and only one, is missing. *The White Queen*.

"Fuck us all," he whispers and lies down and stares at the underside of Ahmed's bunk. Soon enough, it'll be someone else's bunk.

11.

The Spider's Stratagem (London, 12/12/2012)

Ptolema taps ash, ash from her first cigarette in fifteen years, onto the polished floor of the Commissioner's study. The tiles are cut from beds of lithographic limestone near Langenaltheim, Germany, the same quarry where the first specimen of *Archaeopteryx* was discovered in 1861. If the Commissioner objects to cigarette ash on his Jurassic floor, he's kept it to himself. Maybe he's too absorbed in their game of chess to notice, or it may simply be that he doesn't care. Ptolema takes a long drag, exhales, and considers her next move. The Commissioner takes chess very seriously, and it wouldn't do to let on that she truly has no interest in whether she wins or loses. It wouldn't do to put the man in a disagreeable mood this evening, not with her report still freshly landed on his desk.

Ptolema sees that she can win in eleven moves and tries to decide whether or not to throw the game, whether or not it's necessary, and if he'd know. He is a strange man, even among this bevy of strange men and women, and she has long since learned that second-guessing the Commissioner is a perilous undertaking, indeed.

"That disagreeable woman in Dublin…" he begins and trails off, lifts his black knight, then returns it to the board. "I do trust that you were quite thorough before taking care of her?"

"I'm certain of that, Sir."

"Ptolema, my dear, no one is ever fucking certain of anything. In all the wide world, there is not a scintilla of certainty."

Ptolema keeps her eyes on the board.

"I put two bullets in the back of her head, and another in her chest. I weighted the body and sunk it in the river. Unless the Xers have mastered necromancy, you may rest assured she's out of the picture."

"I never rest assured of anything," he sighs, lifts the knight a second time, and, a second time, returns it to the board.

"She's dead, Sir."

"And that other one?"

"Her, too. Three bullets, same as the redhead. With all due respect, meting out death is one of the few things at which I excel. I've been doing it…seems like almost forever."

"It wasn't an insult, Ptolema. You ought to know enough to know that. But I like to hear these things delivered directly from the horse's mouth, as it were. Paperwork is all well and good, but it cannot replace my ability to glean the truth of a situation from the timbre, the tonality, of a human voice."

She has heard it said that the old man is a living, breathing polygraph machine. She's heard it said he's as good as a syringe of sodium pentothal or thirty seconds of waterboarding. Only an idiot would lie to the Commissioner, but, even within the ranks of their organization there are very many idiots, though their tenure inevitably proves short.

"Understood, Sir."

"Is it a fact that you once played Wilhelm Steinitz?" he asks her, studying the board, clearly aware of her advantage. "I have heard that, but one hears so many fairy tales."

"I did," she replies. "In 1892, before he lost his title to Lasker."

"And you beat him?"

"No, Sir. Stalemate, after fifty-two moves. Queen versus pawn, but his pawn had advanced to its seventh rank."

"Still," he said, "Steinitz. What I would have given just to have *seen* that game. Now, what about the Twisby woman?"

"It's in the report – "

"Bugger the ruddy report, woman. I asked *you*, did I not? Where do we stand as regards to that slippery bitch?"

"No one's seen her since the seventh of December when she was spotted in Paris."

He swears and dithers over his one remaining knight.

"You knew that already," she says, and he looks away from the board only as long as it takes him to scowl at her. "But, at this stage, she hardly matters," the Egyptian continues. "Not with a double agent in place on site. We give the kill order, and it's over. To be frank, I don't understand why it wasn't given a month ago. The longer we wait..."

He shakes his head and leans back in his chair, as if ready to surrender the game.

"Complications," he sighs. "Protocol."

"Since when do we acknowledge even the *existence* of protocol among terrorists?"

"Since, my dear, no one wants to see these parlor games escalate into all out war. *That's* since when. Also, the twins' PK potential is so far off the goddamn charts – we have no idea *what's* going to happen when your agent is activated. I'm not going to have this affair blowing up in my face."

Ptolema nods and sends a series of smoke rings towards the ceiling. The third time Ptolema met with the redhead, fifteen minutes before her execution, she'd said, "What Twisby told me, and I quote – more or less, so maybe I should say 'paraphrase,' instead – 'What if Einstein had needed a small push to get him moving? What if, say, Oppenheimer or Fermi had needed a bit more motivation? That's all this is. Bête and I providing her sister a bit more motivation, so her skills are not wasted among petrified bones and dusty museum drawers. That's all.'"

The Commissioner says, "Also, it would be preferable, would it not, if our cryptographers made sense of that message before we dispatched the twin?"

"Right," Ptolema says, hardly bothering to hide her sarcasm. "The twin."

"Clearly this Thisby person has washed her hands of the girl, the way she's on the move."

"Twisby, Sir. And that may be true. Or it may be true that she's accomplished her mission, and there's nothing left to do but wait."

The Commissioner mutters, then picks up his knight, and quickly, before he can change his mind, moves it to the king's second square. Ptolema immediately takes it with her one surviving white knight. She has him in four more moves.

She's thought before, and here she thinks again, how much the Commissioner looks like John Tenniel's interpretation of the White Knight from *Through the Looking Glass*. The same absurd mustache. The beak of a nose. All he needs is a sway-backed horse and spiked anklets to guard against shark bites. *He said "I look for butterflies, that sleep among the wheat..."*

Only, he always plays black. Or maybe only when he pits himself against her.

"Blast," he mutters and pours himself another brandy from the decanter on the table. "Blast your arse. You might at least have pretended to be taken off your guard."

"Apologies, Sir. Your move."

He takes a sip of the brandy. "In your expert estimation, Ptolema, am I both imbecilic *and* blind? I can *see* the bloody board."

"Neither," she replies. "A question, though. Have you considered that there's no code to crack?"

He looks at her as if she's the imbecile.

"I mean," Ptolema continues, "hasn't anyone considered the…outside chance…that the message is meant to be taken *literally*?"

His expression doesn't change, and he doesn't answer her. For a few seconds, the study is so quiet she could hear a mouse fart, were one to choose just then to do so.

"More a sort of roundabout, cockeyed sort of exposition, Sir. 'Black Queen white, White Queen black.' And then the second part, the Trenton transmission, 'To see themselves, they're gazing back.'"

"I *know* the blasted rhyme, Ptolema."

"Of course. But it seems to me everyone's been so busy assuming it's the usual cryptic shit we get from the Xer's, no one's even paused to – "

"This is in your report?" he asks. He drains his glass and watches her.

"No," she says. "It isn't."

"Odd, given it appears to have aroused some considerable passion."

"It only occurred to me just this morning. I was standing in front of my bathroom mirror, brushing my teeth, and – really, it was the mirror that set me thinking there might – "

"You have me in four," he says. "And I despise futility."

"Do you want to hear this, Sir? Because, if you don't, I'll shut the fuck up. I know I'm out of line. I don't have to be told this isn't my department."

"I would have thought, my dear, that in all those centuries you've seen come and go, you'd have learned to stand your ground. I have until a quarter of," and he points at the immense grandfather clock occupying one corner of the study.

The Commissioner pours himself another drink. And Ptolema tells him what's on her mind, a hunch that might be nothing more than that, but a hunch that succeeds in explaining almost, but not quite, everything they know. While she speaks, she contemplates the cross-section of a fossil ammonite, its logarithmic spiral, preserved in the polished limestone floor. The spiral echoes across the universe: the arms of the Milky Way; a moth to a flame; the configuration of corneal nerves; the bands of a typhoon; a fractal seahorse tail of a Misiurewicz point.

Ptolema talks.

The clock rings the hour, and he doesn't interrupt her. As she goes on, his expression changes from skepticism to disbelief to the very last thing she ever expected to see him show, something she'd wager her left hand is fear.

12.

Thunder Perfect Mind/Judas as a Moth (undated)

Estrid Noble sits naked and alone on the wet concrete floor of the small room that, though it *is* a small room, seems to stretch on forever in all directions. Forever and forever and forever. The towering, rumbling Waxen Men have all two gone, but she couldn't say how long since they left her, were she to say anything at all. Which she won't. There is no light in the room save the miserly flicker glow of a naked twenty-five-watt bulb. One of the Waxen Men bumped his head against the dangling fixture on his way out. He snarled obscenities, not noticing and, surely, not caring how he'd set the light to swinging pell-mell so that it became the arm of a luminous pendulum. It sways from side to side, pushing at the four murky corners of the room that is surely much too small to *have* four murky corners. The shadows are indignant and push right back. The light is a bully. And, if that's so, the darkness is a counter-bully. Or, it is the other way round. Or, such a black-and-white dualism cannot even exist here. But this is where they left her, sick of her again – sick of, they say, her bullshit, and so they left her in this room where the walls seem to stretch on forever. Estrid, her back pressed against freezing, slippery ceramic tiles and mildewed grout. Once upon a time, back before the ghosts of all these imprisoned lunatics, those walls were white as snow, white as the uniforms of the Waxen Men who dragged her howling from Room 66 and left her here. First, they took her clothes and turned the spigots on her, water so cold it would freeze a polar bear in its tracks.

A line, a white line, a long white line…

Her honey-colored eyes do the math, calculating angles, the dilapidated geometry of the inside of this cube, the velocity and acceleration vectors of that swinging bulb. Before anyone knew she was insane, she was called a prodigy, carrying the burden of π to 67,393 digits, NaN x 10-4 around in her booming, insomniac skull. In this place, hospital, institutional blue, asylum (which does not mean *sanctuary*), neither the doctors nor the nurses nor the Waxen Men will take mercy and give her paper to put the numbers on. She has to keep them all in her head. This she will learn to do forever more.

Four walls that once were white. You can only scrub so much shit, mold, and, yes, even blood off four walls. Probably, she believes, it has been a thousand years since these walls were genuinely clean. They will never be clean again, for so befouled is their soul, the soul of the walls of this dripping room. A tenth circle of the Inferno. Or an annex to a lesser circle. It is cold as the Arctic here, and she shivers. Hence, it might be the antechamber of the Ninth Circle, possibly the foyer. *Obscure they went through dreary shades, that led along the waste dominions of the dead.*

Xibalba be. A unillumined path through the stars. Six calamitous houses: Dark House, Cold House, Jaguar, Bat, Razor, and Hot House.

She lies down, feels anxiety descending, a person who loses a name (for all the Waxen Men will call her is 66). Now, right cheek, right shoulder, right side come to rest against the smooth concrete, she stares across that grey manufactured plain towards the faraway door, locked, like Hell, against her escape. Like Hell, no one escapes. No one. She recalls snow and knows all too well that this is the sort of plain that ought to be smothered under a blizzard.

"Tell me, when was the war over?" I asked.

"The war is not over," he answered. "Millions are being killed. Europe is mad. The world is mad."

Not only me. The world is mad, and the we of I, the wee of eye, we will fight in unknown wars.

A line, a white line, a long white line…

Through the window of her room, the glass trapped behind a screen of steel diamonds, every winter she watches the snow. It brings more comfort than any of the pills or injections or the sizzling, sparking electrodes to her temples.

This is Hell, and her mother is the Queen of Heaven who damned her.

The Waxen Men are only devils.

The snow is redemption, eternally out of reach.

A line, a white line, a long white line…

In this room, no snow, just rain to set her to shivering, teeth to clattering, the uncrystallized water from the spigots. Uncrystallizable.

I have mingled my drink with weeping,

And my days are like a shadow.

"You have no one to blame but yourself," said Mother. "You're not sick, you're lazy. You just want the attention. You're not sick, but you can damn well be *treated* as if you are. See how you like that. I've had enough, you hear me?"

So Estrid has her room and the dayroom, never outside, never anything but the glimpse of snow outside, the shower when she's filthy or when the Waxen Men, like Mother, have had too much of her bullshit.

For my days vanish like smoke.

I am like an owl in the desert

Among the ruins.

A wall, a barrier, towards which we drove.

My God, man. There's bears on it.

Are there? Three bears? A wolf in a red riding hood?

I know numbers, but the walls are high, and I can't climb over.

Estrid Noble lies on the concrete floor, and she lies in snow softly drifting down from a leaden winter sky. Both are true, a particle *and* a wave. That, or, instead, the flawed observer, her, the mad-woman observer, an emergent, second-order consequence, madness and quantum, madness disbanding paradox. *I don't know what I mean, Mother. I don't know what I mean, anymore.* Has she believed there is no escape, when she can go to the snow globe of her unconscious where the Waxen Men cannot follow?

However, lying in the snow, there is blood in the sky mixed with the snow, and she reaches for the shotgun at her side, and she feels the magic welling up within her, which means this cannot be then, then consigned to a dustbin of her past, and so this must be now.

She sits up in the small room where the Waxen Men have left her.

She sits up in the snow, where the Waxen Men do not know she can go, which means they cannot stop her and cannot find her when she's here.

She sits up in the small room, realizing someone is watching her from the shadows. Someone indistinct to the left of the door, tucked into that corner, only half revealed when the bulb's glow happens to swing that way.

The someone is another woman, white as a ghost, blue eyes, hair same as the snow.

"I know you," Estrid says, and the pale woman says, "I know you, too."

"How did you find me here?" Estrid asks.

"It wasn't hard. You split your head wide open. You let me in."

"They don't let anyone in."

"How could they have stopped me?"

Estrid has no answer for that question, but the shotgun feels very good in her hands. At such close range, this is no job for the Kalashnikov, her favorite engine. No. So, her finger's on the trigger of the gasoline-powered, 28 gauge Remington 1100; this close, she couldn't miss if she tried.

"Sixty Six," the pale woman says, the albino whose name is Ivoire. Okay, not her name – because the Waxen Men and X stole *all* their names – but the sole name that anyone knows to call her. "Sixty Six, I would ask you who wants me dead, who's making you do this, but you wouldn't tell me. I know you'd never tell me. You can't."

"Where are we really?" Estrid asks Ivoire. "Ivoire, when are we really?"

"Don't you usually call me Ivy?" the albino asks. "When you bother to call me anything at all? Why are we so formal now?"

The air is bruised with questions.

"Star fall, phone call, no one gets out of here alive," Estrid whispers, hating the way she whimpers like a rabbit in a snare. Isn't she the one holding the shotgun? Doesn't *she* have the upper hand?

"Your poor spirit," Ivoire sighs. "Shattered, piled up with equations, snippets of song, memories broken apart like twigs. Aren't you tired of being used?"

Estrid lies on the concrete floor, and she holds the barrel of the Remington beneath Ivoire's chin. She blinks, and wishes, just once, the Waxen Men had forgotten to lock her in with the grout and the dirty wet tiles. The light swings, and Ivoire's blue eyes twinkle, a flash before the light swings away again, a flash like a falling star plummeting, screaming as it tumbles towards Penobscot Bay.

"I know your secret," she says to Ivoire, and Estrid smiles a vicious Cheshire grin. It's all she has, the secret and the shotgun. *If I'd had the shotgun then, I'd have lain low the Waxen Men. If I'd had the gun then...*

"But you didn't, Sixty Six," says the voice from what is momentarily only darkness. "There in the showers, you were naked and helpless. You didn't have anything at all but a dream of snow."

Outside the window of the attic where they sleep, demons are marching out of the sea. Outside the attic window, hardly anyone is left to scream at the sight.

"Tell me the secret," Ivoire urges her, though she doesn't sound the least bit desperate to know. There is no hint of urgency in her voice. "Then we'll both know. If I'm about to die, where's the harm in my knowing?"

"I am now, and I am then," Estrid whispers.

The light shows Ivoire's face, and Estrid thinks she looks a little sad, like whatever's coming is something she doesn't want to arrive.

"A particle and a wave. You are the paradox, Sixty Six. Free and a prisoner. At now and at then. I know."

Well, I went down in the valley,
You know I did over there ever stay.
You know I stayed right there all day.

"A broken record, that's you," says Ivoire. Estrid tightens her grip on the trigger, and she stares up into the bloody snow falling all around her. "And the paradoxical fruitcake, two places and two times at once, if only in your mind."

"Not like you," Estrid says. "Maybe I'm a metaphor, but not *you*."

"Is that your secret, Sixty Six," and now, ah, now the woman in the corner of the shower room looks nervous. *Dread*, that's the word for her expression.

"Twin," Estrid growls.

"Yes, Sixty Six, I am a twin. I have a sister."

In five seconds, Estrid Noble will squeeze the trigger and spatter Ivy's brains across the attic wall. That's already happened.

"Twin," says Sixty Six. "It's not a noun. It's a verb."

She grits her teeth and closes her eyes and fires two rounds. Someone has told her this will save the world. One instant. One action. A butterfly flaps its wings.

13.
Soft Black Stars
(12/21/2012)

Stop me if you've heard this one. Good and Evil walk into a bar...

Here: At precisely eight hundred ten hours, the directive came down from – it matters not where, but D.C. is a good enough supposition. Effective immediately, cease all evacuation efforts. Additional civilian and military casualties an acceptable loss. Mourn the coming dead *after* zero-zero-thirty of the twenty-first day of December, but blow the goddamn Sedgwick suspension bridge spanning Eggemoggin Reach, blow it this very night, bury it on the muddy bottom of the leprous bay.

Theirs not to reason why...

Finally, all other avenues and efforts and fools' hopes exhausted, they will follow orders, press the red button, implement Operation Umbilicus. Yes, in fact, until this evening the name has seemed hilarious to more than a few. *Who the hell came up with that one, anyway? Don't ask me. I just fucking work here.*

The writing has been on the wall since August, but no one has wanted to read it. No one wanted to believe it would ever go this far, because we are not goddamn Neanderthals huddling in caves by firelight, trembling at the eyeshine Outside, lions and tigers and bears, oh my. Because we are not savages. Because a shoulder to the wheel, and all our technology, and all our beautiful weapons, and all our careful planning, and brave men can solve any situation, no matter how dire. Isn't that motherfucker bin Laden dead? Have we not eradicated smallpox? Are we not making the world safe for democracy? Well, are we not? Do we now leave men and women to die deaths more horrific than any ever imagined by Hollywood, the RAND Corporation, science-fiction fucking authors, the alarmists, survivalists, the Book of Revelation, supersecret think tanks, et cetera and et cetera and et cetera?

"Doesn't seem that way," replies the Major General with his two stars on his shoulder. One named Wormwood. The other left unchristened.

A sergeant barks orders, and his men cannot allow themselves to think about the consequences; three have gone rabbit since yesterday, and all three were shot as deserters. Not arrested. Shot. The rest will do their job and see to the explosive charges, the dynamite, nitroglycerin – the catalysts before the detonation of the linear shaped charges. The demolition team stands at the ready, and have stood so since dusk. Executioners, who are also saviors, watch the clocks, ticking off the bits and pieces of seconds until the implosion of the suspension bride connecting Little Deer Isle to the mainland. The bridge uniting Deer and Little Deer will be left intact. No one knows why. Theirs is most emphatically not to wonder why. The deities and demi-gods in Washington and the Command Center in Brooksville have those answers, which has to be good enough. Good enough for government work.

Good enough to shove a cork in an apocalypse.

הנעל.

The third angel blew his trumpet, and a great star fell from heaven, blazing like a torch, and it fell on a third of the rivers and on the springs of water. The name of the star is Wormwood. A third of the waters became wormwood, and many died from the water, because it was made bitter.

"Buck up, little buckaroo. We're saving the world tonight."

"Does anyone believe for a minute this is going to stop…that?" And the corporal points at the glistening sheen smothering the reach, the foulness slick in the Solstice moonlight. "Assholes may as well shoot at an elephant with a BB gun."

Bows and arrows against the lightning.

The air is being chopped apart with the noise from the rotors of the vigilant Sikorsky UH-60 Black Hawks patrolling overhead. Angles of harsh angels and flat surfaces, terrible swift swords. Do not look at the face of god. Padre, say a prayer for me: *We'd circle and we'd circle and we'd circle, she a laughing giggling whirlybird, my final days in company, the devil now has come for me, and helicopters circling the scene, this is the end, my beautiful friend, this is the end, that's Charlie's point, except you – you were talking about the end of the world, Lord hold our troops in your loving hands, protect them as they protect us, bless them and their selfless acts they perform for us in our time of need, Sed libera nos a malo hosanna, amen, amen.*

"Now, my child, go and sin no more."

Below the bridge, a lumpy round mass more vasty than Leviathan or ten humpback whales is rising from the slime, slime rising from the slime, the star-fall corruption taking shape. It opens one eye.

On the granite boulders north and south of the bridge, the shamans, the witches, the archimages all have begun their chants and sacrifices. Black books have been opened. The first shockwave is their magic...

T-minus three minutes and counting.

...and the second is the Blacks Hawks' barrage of armaments, laser-guided AGM-114 Hellfire missiles, Hydra 70 rockets, the *chut-chut-chut* bursts from machine and Gatling guns enough to wake the dearly departed. The thing below the bridge bleeds and howls and surges forward. There is no reckoning the anger in that eye. No reckoning whatsofuckingever. It howls, and now other shapes are rising from the dead waters, answering the call.

"You can't kill Old Gods with shotguns."

"You may as well grab a pointy stick."

Write *that* on the shithouse wall.

T-minus one minute.

T-minus forty-five seconds.

Two of the Black Hawks come apart in the air and trail flaming debris across the Maine night sky and raise fireballs from the haunted forests of Little Deer Isle. Nothing touched the choppers. Nothing at all. They simply came apart.

T-minus...

"I'm tellin' you, man. You can't kill fuckin' Cthulhu with a shotgun. Ain't you seen *Godzilla?* Ain't you ever seen *Cloverfield?*"

"Dude, I saw *Aliens*, okay? And guns and nukes worked just fine in *Aliens*."

"Those ain't nukes, you stupid fuckin' hick. Those *ain't* nukes."

Rotten waves slop against the shore below the bridge, beneath either shore at either end of the bridge – northeast, southwest. The lantern beams of lighthouses carve white clefts across the battlefield, shooing away any who would dare wander near in these last seconds. Lighthouses that still stand and still shine and fuck all knows how that can be. Because the gods have a flair for the cinematic? Deer Isle Lighthouse. Pumpkin Island Lighthouse. Some that ought not even *be* visible from this vantage point, but the abominations rising from the reach have begun to warp the fabric of the world, triggering a cascade of gravitational lensing, photons deflected by arcseconds. Mirage.

"Jesus Christ. I see around corners."

T-minus one second.

Boom.

Men and women turn away. Fall to their knees, are knocked flat on their asses by the blast. Cross themselves. Weep and wail and cover their ears as the bridge announces its deafening death throes and tumbles into the slime, concrete and steel and whipping cables slicing apart monsters, if only for a few heartbeats. If only for the time required for them to coalesce again.

But the bridge is down.

And now it's up to the wards raised by the practitioners of forgotten sorceries, the priestesses who have called out to indifferent heavens, the marshaling of chaotic alchemical elemental Babylonian ninja motherfuckers.

With a little luck and elbow grease, this has only been the *beginning* of the end.

Punchline: But, then, so is every day. (Rimshot/Sting) (Cue laugh track)

14.

Where I End and You Begin (The Sky Is Falling In) (21/12/12)

"Well, in our country," said Alice, still panting a little, "you'd generally get to somewhere else – if you run very fast for a long time, as we've been doing."

"A slow sort of country!" said the Queen.

"Yes, Sixty Six, I am a twin. I have a sister."

Alice becomes Queen.

Black Queen white, White Queen black.

Adaptation, counter-adaptation, reciprocation, system instability, runaway escalation.

"Twin. It's not a noun…"

This is not the when and certainly not the where that the woman who calls herself Twisby (whose true name, now it can be told, is Lane Dunham, Ph.D., MD) would have chosen for extraction and reintegration, for the experiment's endgame terminus. Pretty fucking far from optimal conditions. But she's been warned by both Karachi and Kathmandu of two Brit assassins who've been on their asses since the plane touched down at Munich International. And, much worse still, the subgnosis pipeline is humming fit to burn with a most ominous forecast: Endgame has been triggered prematurely. The suggestion buried in the subconscious abyss of a hyper-suggestible, third-gen schizophrenic X sleeper agent is surfacing three hours ahead of schedule. Three goddamn hours. So, fuck the architects' itinerary; there isn't time to reach the Arstagagan safe house in Uppsala. The architects aren't on the run from bullets. If the trial goes south, they'll just toss the project back to R and D for turnaround at the next best opportunity.

Not that a shitstorm like Deer Isle comes along but maybe once a century. Once a century, at best. The architects have nothing if not the luxury of second, third, and fourth chances. So, this abandoned warehouse on the outskirts of Knivsta will have to do. If she tries to make those last sixteen kilometers to Uppsala before retrieving the package, the risk of failure skyrockets to 78%.

"…it's not a noun."

Her phone rings as she's inserting the IV needle into Bête's forearm, and the twin's trying not to show how scared she is, but the psychiatrist knows her too, too well not to recognize the fear in her eyes.

"Dream," the psychiatrist sweetly murmurs, and the twin immediately falls asleep on the bedroll spread out on the dusty floor.

Second ring.

Third ring, and she "answers," but you do not say *Hello* when the incoming communiqué has all those zeroes and nothing else *but* zeroes. This call from Julia Set riding piggyback through the mundane transmissions of hacked and repurposed communication satellites, you do not say *Hello*; you hold the phone to your ear and you listen.

Mac OS X speaking for whoever is on the other end of the line, a voice filtered or a contingency recorded weeks ago, and here are the words stiffly relayed by "Victoria," one-way digital instructions – "And we shall play a game of chess?"

In an attic in Stonington, Maine, a shotgun is pressed to Ivoire's left temple, and the numerical mad woman is about to make love to the trigger.

The psychiatrist drops the phone and it skitters across the floor. Bête's eyelids flutter with the illusion of REM sleep. The portable electroencephalograph converts impulses from the low-density electrode array attached to the twin's scalp, cheeks, and forehead to a tidy display of spike and wave discharges. The IV drips, and the psychiatrist fills a syringe and injects Bête with 0.125 cc's of triazolam. A single, bright crimson bead leaks from her skin. The psychiatrist pops the yellow lid on a mobile automated external defibrillator and powers it up. Just in case. Just in fucking case.

Alice castles. Bête seizes.

"It's not a noun…"

"…it's a verb."

Black Queen white, White Queen black.

Six months in the field, and it ends here. Redaction commencing. The EEG beeps, and the sound seems almost deafening inside the empty warehouse. The psychiatrist pulls back the plunger of a second hypo and draws five cc's of diazepam. But precious seconds pass, and the twin doesn't seize after all. By now, Sixty Six has done her job and done it well, no matter how far ahead of schedule. A soul is careening along the predetermined, nonesuch, ethereal nowhere highway between two continents, simultaneously crossing the Atlantic and an unnamable dreamtime gulf.

"…it's a verb."

The psychiatrist leans close and whispers in Bête's left ear, "Checkmate, love. You're home now. Wake up."

"…a verb."

And the twin opens her blue eyes.

"You can hear me?" the psychiatrist asks, her voice shuddering with relief. "Bête?"

"Ivoire…" the twin croaks, *her* voice raw and groggy.

"Ivoire?" the psychiatrist asks.

"Bête."

The psychiatrist brushes sweaty bangs away from the twin's face. "Now, now…full name, love."

Only a heartbeat's hesitation, and the twin replies. "Lizbeth Elle… Lizbeth Elle."

"And surname, please?"

Lizbeth Elle coughs, and the psychiatrist wipes at her forehead again.

"Margeride. Lizbeth Elle Margeride."

The psychiatrist laughs softly, a nervous, relieved laugh. "Good and Evil walk into a bar…" she begins.

"But, then, so is every day," answers Lizbeth Elle Margeride. "So is every fucking day." The twin smiles for the psychiatrist; Elle opens her left hand to reveal a vial of liquid from Penobscot, a pearly vial that glows like sickly, trapped fireflies.

15.

ἀποκαλύπτω
(1/5/2013)

Here's the scene: The G-line crosstown local, rattling along the underground throat connecting Queens and Brooklyn. Ptolema sits near the rear of the subway car. She isn't quite alone. There's a black kid at the opposite end, plugged into his iPod and oblivious to all else. There's an elderly Hispanic woman, her purse clutched close to her chest. A man whom Ptolema has taken for either Greek or Turkish sits across from the old woman, reading the *Times*. So, four, only four, and she can live with four. She shuts her laptop and returns it to its carrying case, then stares at the blackness beyond the train's window, which, unfortunately, means staring into her own reflection, which unkindly stares back at her. The negotiations in Albany didn't go well, too many concessions when she can't understand why they've made any at all. Moreover, the cover story that would attribute the Deer Isle Incident to a reactor meltdown aboard a *Seawolf*-class nuclear submarine, to the ensuing explosion and quarantine, is just short of absurd. Perhaps the wipes were potent enough no one much, military or civilian, Y or X, quite remembers the events of the twenty-first of December, but she seriously doubts the Navy patrol, the US Army, and one collapsed bridge is going to keep that secret a secret forever. Fortunately, everyone was too busy freaking out over Maine to even broach the subject of "Twisby's" twinning experiment. There isn't the least sense of vindication knowing that the theory Ptolema passed along to the Commissioner more than three weeks ago, the theory he then handed up to the Council, appears to have been correct. Lucky fucking guess. Intuition come too late to intervene.

Reflected in the safety glass, her eyes look every bit as ancient as they are, every bit as weathered as her spirit. At the meeting, no one dared use her name. Only the Egyptian, two words to signify and summarize all the ages of an inexplicably long life. She lowers her head, hiding from the window, too much there to despise. Maybe she'll shut her eyes and try to sleep. Maybe she'll be lucky, and there will be no dreams.

Maybe pigs will fly.

"Stop me if you've heard this one," says the white-haired woman standing in the aisle, the woman who definitely *wasn't* there only a minute and a half before. She's wearing a cream-colored Gore-Tex parka, ragged jeans, black wraparound sunglasses. Cheap sunglasses. There's a polished, cross-sectioned ammonite on a silver chain around her neck. She glances towards the other three passengers, nods, then turns back to Ptolema. The albino, the twin who is not now and never *was* a twin, the cipher, the Black Queen who is the White Queen, and vice versa.

To see themselves, they're gazing back.

"See," says the albino, taking the seat on Ptolema's right, "In the beginning, God created the heavens and the earth. But, right off, he was hit with a class-action suit for failure to file an environmental impact statement."

"I've heard it," Ptolema tells her. "Probably before you were born."

The albino pretends to look disappointed. "Damn it. I was afraid of that."

"Bête," Ptolema says, whispering as softly as a falling leaf. "Ivoire. Lizbeth Elle. The Ivory Beast. What am I supposed to call you?"

"Elle's fine," the albino says. "But you can speak up. It's not like they can hear us. Hell, they can't even see me, unless the mojo coming out of Harlem these days isn't what it used to be."

"Do I talk, Elle?" asks Ptolema. "Or do I listen?"

"Some of both, though that wasn't my decision. Anyway, we don't have too long before the next station, so, you know. Choose your words wisely."

"Still a lot of unanswered questions, Elle. A lot of people in your own organization pissed off for being left out of the loop regarding Dr. Dunham's enterprise."

"Too bad there isn't ever going to be time for all those answers."

"You're not sick."

"Nope," Elle replies and smiles. "Crazy lady with a shotgun back in Stonington, she was good enough to dispatch that malignancy."

"I don't get the elaborate cloak-and-dagger, dog-and-pony show," Ptolema says, watching both their reflections now. "The bread crumbs. The informants. The meetings in Dublin. No one ever had to know shit about what you fuckers were up to."

"You'd have to ask Twisby about that," sighs Elle. "I didn't even know myself. That is, during the procedure, so far as I knew, every bit of it was gospel. We were two. The we of I and all that. Quietness is wholeness at the center of stillness, et cetera, blah, blah, blah."

"Both personae were real? Both were corporeal?"

"Abracadabra."

"The particle and the wave."

"Exactly. But we're almost out of time, like I said. And I suspect your people are already busy running every imaginable computer simulation to determine every imaginable outcome to all these ripples. That is, if they're not too busy with the shoggoths."

"The what?"

"Oh, right. Sorry. The girl who killed me, that's what she called that nasty crap kept crawling out of the bay. Shoggoths."

"You and Deer Isle," Ptolema says. "We don't think that was a coincidence. We don't think it was only a happy, convenient coincidence. We think – "

" – a lot of crazy shit, and only time will tell. Maybe Twisby built herself the Second Coming of Jesus Christ. Or, it may be I'm the *Anti*-Christ. Shiva. Maitreya. Take your pick. Or only a trial run, a dress rehearsal for the *Big* Show, so nobody of consequence. Nothing at all but a nerdy girl who wants to go back to her stones and bones."

"That would be a waste," Ptolema says.

What if Einstein had needed a small push to get him moving? What if, say, Oppenheimer or Fermi had needed a bit more motivation?

Waste is the only evil.

"Okay," Elle says. "My turn." She digs a thumb and index finger into a pocket of her jeans and pulls out a single 45-caliber cartridge. It gleams dully beneath the subway car's fluorescent lights. "This was meant for you."

Ptolema gazes down at the bullet.

"Then why am I still alive?"

"Ripples," says Elle Margeride. "I think it's about time I began making a few of my own. Twisby's a sweetheart, and she means well, but she's also the one went and made a queen out of a pawn. She needs to start taking that into account."

And then Elle slips the cartridge into Ptolema's hand and stands up.

"Is this the last time we'll meet?" Ptolema asks, trying not to think about how heavy the bullet feels.

Elle shrugs. "We'll know if it happens, maybe about a trillion dominoes from now."

Ptolema tastes metal, and she licks her dry lips. "There are people looking for you and Dr. Dunham. You know that, right? They catch up with you, they won't be merciful. You've made an impression."

"Introduced a new variable," says Elle, and she pokes a finger at the bridge of her cheap sunglasses.

"One last question?"

"One last question."

Ptolema sits up straighter, glancing at the bullet and then back to the albino.

"Do you miss her? Your sister? Your lover? If both of you *were* real – "

But then Lizbeth Elise Margeride is gone, as unceremoniously as she appeared, and, once again, there are but four other people in the car. Ptolema shuts her eyes and leans her head back and tries to concentrate on nothing but the throb of steel wheels on the rails.

∞

8.

[*les Anglaise* Remix]
Bury Magnets. Swallow the Rapture.
(17 Vrishika, 2152)

She sits on a bench in the main observation tier of the *Nautilus-IV*, her eyes on the wide bay window set into the belly of the station, the icy spiral of the Martian northern pole filling her view. *She* being the White Woman. La femme albinos. *Ca-ng bâi de. Blancanieves.* More appellations hung on her than all the words for God, some say. But if she has a true name – and doesn't everyone? – it is her secret and hers alone. A scrap of knowledge forever lost to humanity. So, her blue eyes are fixed on the Planum Boreum four-hundred kilometers below, yes, but her mind is on the Egyptian – Ancient of Days, El Judío Errante, Kundry, Ptolema – she has many "names," as well. The Sino LDTC ferrying her is now less than eight sols out. The Egyptian racing towards her. An unforeseen inconvenience. In no way at all a calamity, no, but still an unfortunate occurrence to force the White Woman's hand. It tries her patience, and patience has been the key for so long that she cannot even recall a time before she learned that lesson.

In less than eight sols, the transfer vessel will dock, and they will speak for the first time in…

How long has it been?

She answers the question aloud, "One hundred and thirty-nine years."

"Truly?" asks Babbit. "As long as all that?"

When she arrived on the station two months ago, Babbit was assigned the task of seeing to her every need. As has been her wish, he hardly ever leaves her side. The company of anyone is a balm for her sometimes crippling monophobia. A medicine better than any she has ever been prescribed. It doesn't matter that this tall, thin, towheaded man is only mostly human. Many times, she's resorted to and relied upon the companionship of splices. Besides, Babbit's fast borrow capabilities saved her the trouble of telling him all the tales he needs to know to carry on useful conversations. And there will be much less fuss when she orders his death, before her flight back to Earth. Easy come, easy go.

"You've never been to Manhattan," she says.

"Ma'am, it was lost before I was born."

"Of course," she replies, and the White Woman holds up her right hand, absentmindedly running fingertips along the window, tracing the serpentine furrow on the Chasma Boreale. It seems almost as long as her long life, and almost as aimless. *Possessed of direction,* she thinks, *is not to be possessed of purpose.*

"Anyway," she says to Babbit, "we were in Manhattan. I'd only just returned from Sweden. It was that long ago. Almost all the way back at the start."

"As long as all that," he says again.

"I can't begin to understand what she hopes to accomplish, coming here, chasing after me this way."

"Nor can I, Ma'am."

"The vessel may be armed. It would be like her, a preemptive strike, sacrificing the whole station and everyone aboard if she believes doing so would accomplish her ends."

"Zealots are extremely dangerous people," says Babbit.

"It can't be that she hopes to *reason* with me. She cannot entertain the notion that she and I have ever shared in common a concept of Reason."

"True believers, I mean," Babbit says.

"I know what you meant."

"Of course, Ma'am."

"Maybe she only wishes to bear witness," the White Woman says. "To be present when my king's knight takes her remaining bishop."

Babbit clear his throat. "I expect the Captain will have anticipated the possibility of an attack," he says, then clears his throat once more.

She laughs. "He has done nothing of the sort. There has been no alert, no preparation to intercept or shield. He is sitting and waiting, like a small and frightened animal cowering in the underbrush."

"I was only supposing," admits Babbit.

The White Woman pulls her hand back from the window, and she seems to stare at it for a few seconds. As if in wonder, maybe. Or as if, perhaps, it's been soiled somehow. Then she turns her head and watches Babbit. He lowers his head; he never meets her gaze.

"I have considered holding off on the launch until she boards," she says to him. "Until she is that near."

"Then you've made your decision? To make the drop, I mean."

"I made that decision before I left Xichang. It was only ever a question of when."

"And now you have decided when?"

No one on the *Nautilus-IV,* no one back on Earth, no one in the scattered, hardscrabble colonies below, none of them know why she is here. Few enough know that she *is* here. She was listed on no passenger manifest. They do not know she's ready to call the Egyptian's gambit and move her king's knight. To cast a stone on the still waters. Not one of them knows the nature of her cargo. No one but Babbit, and he won't talk.

"Now I have decided when," she tells him, and the White Woman shuts her blue eyes and pictures the vial in its plasma-lock cradle, hidden inside a shipment of hardware and foodstuffs bound for Sharonov. The kinetic gravity bomb will detonate at five hundred feet, and the contents of the vial will be aerosolized. The sky will rain corruption, and the corruption will take root in the dome's cisterns and reservoirs.

הנעל.

Wormwood.

Apsinthion.

... and a great star fell from heaven, blazing like a torch...

"Ma'am," says Babbit, not daring to raise his head. "You are certain you will obtain the desired results? There are evacuation protocols, environmental containment procedures – "

...the waters became wormwood...

"Babbit, I have never in all my life been certain. Which is the point."

She turns back to the window and can almost feel the wild katabatic winds scouring the glaciers and canyons. The White Woman pulls her robes more tightly about herself. She's glad that Babbit is with her. She wants to ask him if he might take for granted that she has never loved, if no one has ever been dear to her. But she doesn't.

Instead, she says again, "Which is the point."

"Yes, Ma'am," he says. "Of course."

ACKNOWLEDGEMENTS

I do not write in a vacuum, and I should note the more important influences that played a role in my conception and execution of *Black Helicopters*: T. S. Eliot's *The Waste Land*; Lewis Carroll's *Through the Looking Glass, and What Alice Found There*; the works of Charles Hoy Fort; more books on chess than would be practical to list, but notably Martin Gardner's examination of the "chess problem" in *Through the Looking Glass, and What Alice Found There*; Twain's *The Adventures of Huckleberry Finn*; David Bowie's *Outside*; Poe's *Haunted*, Funcom's *The Secret World*; J. J. Abrams, Alex Kurtzman, and Roberto Orci's *Fringe*; Grant Morrison's *The Invisibles*; Current 93's *Black Ships Ate the Sky* and *Soft Black Stars*; James Joyce's *Ulysses*; the music of Radiohead; various works on chaos theory, astronomy, and quantum physics, including Kip S. Thorne's *Black Holes and Space Time: Einstein's Outrageous Legacy*, John Briggs and F. David Peat's *Turbulent Mirror: An Illustrated Guide to Chaos Theory and the Science of Wholeness*, and P. J. E. Peebles' *Principles of Physical Cosmology*; Leigh Van Valen and others biologists' writings on the Red Queen's Hypothesis; and Edward Gorey's *The Other Statue*. Very special thanks to Denise L. Davis (Brown University) for the French translation in the eighth section ("Bury Magnets. Swallow the Rapture. [17 Vrishika, 2152]"), to my comrade in virtual arms and conspiracy, Vic Ruiz, and to my niece, Sonoye Murphy. The paleontological exploits, misadventures, and disappointments of the "twins" mentioned in the text are my own, a sharp jab of autobiography.

BLACK HELICOPTERS

Jonathan Strahan said, upon beginning *Black Helicopters,* "This story opens like Radiohead doing a cover version of a Pogues song about a John le Carré novel." *Black Helicopters* has received some wonderful reviews, but somehow that remark pleased me more than any of them. I do, by the way, consider *Black Helicopters* – like *The Dry Salvages* before it – a novel, *not* a novella. At approximately twenty-six thousand words, it's almost as long as *Of Mice and Men* (29,160 words) and *Animal Farm* (29,966 words), and it's about the same length as *The Old Man and the Sea* (26,610 words). Frankly, I dislike the term *novella,* though it's hardly as silly as *novelette.* But then, as a taxonomist I was always a "lumper," never a "splitter." Nonetheless, *Black Helicopters* was nominated for the 2014 Locus and World Fantasy awards in the best novella categories. It was written over the course of thirteen days during December 2012.

Epilogue
Atlantis

With me older and grown less whole.
With me weary and self-soiled.
And admittedly unaccountable.
Far here from home that never was my home.
Down dull yellow strands,
down roiling yellowed beaches.
That grinding, elder flywheel of shattered memory.
The liminal tumult that breaks hope and dreams alike,
indifferent and in equal measure,
as if only so much granite.

Between the stone and the whirlpool
would I betray myself
in a guise a little less than shunned Circe's ire.
I would so sink the world.
But I alone would go a-foundering.
Swine and a woodpecker and heads of seven snarling dogs.
Too, these oddly placid lions
and wolves that show their throats.
I am all those, witch and bewitched.
Drowned and, likewise, drowning brine.
I am all those.

12 August 2010

Publication History

Original publication dates appear first, followed in parentheses by the year each story was written. Most of the stories have been reprinted multiple times since their initial appearance. First reprint publication history is included for those stories first published in *Sirenia Digest.*

"Bradbury Weather" *Subterranean Magazine* #2, 2005 (2004)
"Pony" *Sirenia Digest* #2, 2006 (2006); reprinted in *Tales from the Woeful Platypus* (2007)
"Untitled 17" *Sirenia Digest* #3 2006 (2006); reprinted in *Tales from the Woeful Platypus* (2007)
"A Child's Guide to the Hollow Hills" [as "Untitled 23"] *Sirenia Digest* #10, 2006 (2006); reprinted in *The Ammonite Violin & Others,* 2009
"The Ammonite Violin (Murder Ballad No. 4)" *Sirenia Digest* #11, 2006 (2006); reprinted in *Dark Delicacies II,* 2007
"A Season of Broken Dolls" *Sirenia Digest* #15, 2007 (2007), *Subterranean*, Spring 2007
"In View of Nothing" *Sirenia Digest* #16, 2007 (2007); reprinted in *A is for Alien,* 2009
"The Ape's Wife" *Clarkesworld Magazine* #12, 2007 (2007)
"The Steam Dancer (1896)" *Sirenia Digest* #19, 2007 (2007); reprinted in *Subterranean: Tales of Dark Fantasy,* 2008
"In the Dreamtime of Lady Resurrection" *Sirenia Digest* #20, 2007 (2007); reprinted in *Subterranean,* Fall 2007
"Pickman's Other Model (1929)" *Sirenia Digest* #28, 2008 (2008); reprinted in *Black Wings: Tales of Lovecraftian Horror,* 2010
"Galápagos" *Eclipse Three,* 2009 (2009)

"The Melusine (1898)" *Sirenia Digest* #31, 2008 (2008); reprinted in *Confessions of a Five-Chambered Heart,* 2011
"As Red as Red" *Haunted Legends,* 2010 (2009)
"Fish Bride" *Sirenia Digest* #42, 2009; reprinted in *The Weird Fiction Review* #2, 2011
"The Mermaid of the Concrete Ocean" *Sirenia Digest* #43, 2009; reprinted in *The Drowning Girl: A Memoir,* 2012
"The Sea Troll's Daughter" *Swords and Dark Magic,* 2010 (2009)
"Hydrarguros" *Sirenia Digest* #50, 2010 (2010); reprinted in *Subterranean: Tales of Dark Fantasy II,* 2011
"Houndwife" *Sirenia Digest* #52, 2010 (2010); reprinted in *Black Wings II: New Tales of Lovecraftian Horror,* 2012
"The Maltese Unicorn" *Supernatural Noir,* 2011 (2010)
"Tidal Forces" *Sirenia Digest* #55, 2010 (2010); reprinted in *Eclipse Four,* 2011
"And the Cloud That Took the Form" *Sirenia Digest* #59, 2010 (2010)
"The Prayer of Ninety Cats" *Sirenia Digest* #60, 2010 (2010); reprinted in *Subterranean,* Spring 2013
"Daughter Dear Desmodus" *Sirenia Digest* #70, 2011 (2011)
"One Tree Hill (The World as Cataclysm)" *Sirenia Digest* #80, 2012 (2012); reprinted in *The Ape's Wife and Other Stories,* 2013
Black Helicopters, Subterranean Press, 2013 (2012)
"Atlantis" *Strange Horizons*, 3/5/12 (2012)

The author wishes to note that the text for each of these stories, as it appears in this collection, will differ, often significantly, from the originally published texts. In some cases, stories were revised for each reprinting (and some have been reprinted numerous times). No story is ever finished. There's only the moment when I force myself to stop and provisionally type THE END.

The stories in this volume were written at the Kirkwood School Lofts, 138 Kirkwood Road NE #2, Atlanta, Ga. (2004); 1193 Mansfield Avenue NE, Atlanta, Ga. (2004-2008); and in Providence, R.I. (2008-2014). The stories in Volume One were written at "Burt's Bohemian Bear Garden," #5 1619 16th Avenue S., Birmingham, Ala. (1993-1994); the Carriage House, 279 1/2 Meigs Street, Athens, Ga. (1994-1997); #303 Liberty House, 2301 1st Avenue N., Birmingham, Ala. (1997-2001); #302 Liberty House, 2301 1st Avenue N., Birmingham, Ala. (2001-2002); and the Kirkwood School Lofts, 138 Kirkwood Road NE #2, Atlanta, Ga. (2002-2004)

Appendix

Bibliography (1985-2015):

Compiled by Caitlín R. Kiernan, Kathryn A. Pollnac, S. T. Joshi, and Sonya Taaffe (20-28 January 2015)

First Publications:

As Kenneth R. Wright:

"The Burning" 1985 *The Freshman Sampler*, ed. Peggy B. Jolly, University of Alabama at Birmingham, Kendall/Hunt Pub. Co.

"Another Christmas Carol" 1985 *The Freshman Sampler*, ed. Peggy B. Jolly, University of Alabama at Birmingham, Kendall/Hunt Pub. Co.

Short Fiction (by date of first publication; for *Sirenia Digest* first *print* reprint noted)

"Between the Flatirons and the Deep Green Sea" 1995 *High Fantastic: Colorado Fantasy, Dark Fantasy, and Science Fiction*, ed. Steve Rasnic Tem, Ocean View Books (First fiction sale.)

"The Comedy of St. Jehanne d'Arc" 1995 *Dark Destiny: Proprietors of Fate*, ed. Edward E. Kramer, White Wolf Publishing

"Hoar Isis" 1995 *The Urbanite* (#6), ed. Mark McLaughlin, Urban Legend Press

"Persephone" 1995 *Aberrations* (March #27), ed. Richard Blair and Michael Andre-Driussi, Sirius Pub. (First published short story.)

"Anamorphosis" 1996 *Lethal Kisses*, ed. Ellen Datlow, Orion Books,

"Escape Artist" 1996 *The Sandman: Book of Dreams*, ed. Neil Gaiman and Ed Kramer, HarperPrism

"Giants in the Earth" 1996 *Michael Moorcock's Pawns of Chaos: Tales of the Eternal Champion*, ed. Ed Kramer, White Wolf Publishing

"Stoker's Mistress" 1996 *Dark Destiny III: Children of Dracula*, ed. Ed Kramer, White Wolf

"Tears Seven Times Salt" 1996 *Darkside: Horror for the Next Millennium*, ed. John Pelan, Darkside Press

"To This Water (Johnstown, Pennsylvania 1889)" 1996 *Dark Terrors 2*, ed. Stephen Jones and David Sutton, Victor Gollancz Ltd.

"Bela's Plot" 1997 *Love in Vein II*, ed. Poppy Z. Brite, HarperPrism

"Breakfast in the House of the Rising Sun" 1997 *Noirotica II*, ed. Thomas S. Roche, Masquerade Books

"Emptiness Spoke Eloquent" 1997 *Secret City: Strange Tales of London* (World Fantasy Souvenir Book), ed. Stephen Jones

"Estate" 1997 *Dark Terrors 3*, ed. Stephen Jones and David Sutton, Victor Gollancz Ltd.

"The Last Child of Lir" 1997 *The Urbanite* (#8), ed. Mark McLaughlin, Urban Legend Press

"Superheroes" 1997 *Brothers of the Night*, ed. Michael Rowe and Thomas S. Roche, Cleis Press

"A Story for Edward Gorey" 1997 *Wetbones* (#2), ed. Paula Guran

"Two Worlds and In Between" 1997 *Dark of the Night*, ed. Stephen Jones, Pumpkin Books

"Found Angels" 1998 (with Christa Faust) *In the Shadow of the Gargoyle*, ed. Nancy Kilpatrick and Thomas S. Roche, Ace Books

"The King of Birds" 1998 *The Crow: Shattered Lives and Broken Dreams*, ed. Ed Kramer, Del Rey

"Postcards from the King of Tides" 1998 *Candles for Elizabeth*, Meisha Merlin Publishing Inc.

"Salmagundi (1981)" 1998 *Carpe Noctem* (Vol. IV, #4), ed. Tom and Catia Carnell, CN Publishing LLC

"Glass Coffin" 1999 *Silver Birch, Blood Moon*, ed. Ellen Datlow and Terri Windling, Avon Books

"The Long Hall on the Top Floor" 1999 *Carpe Noctem* (#16), CN Publishing LLC

"Rats Live On No Evil Star" 1999 *White of the Moon*, ed. Stephen Jones, Pumpkin Books

"Salammbô" 1999 *Palace Corbie* (#8), ed. Wayne Edwards, Merrimac Books

"Angels You Can See Through" 2000 *Tales of Pain and Wonder*, Gauntlet Press (removed from 3rd edition, 2007, Subterranean Press).

"Between the Gargoyle Trees" 2000, *Tales of Pain and Wonder*, Gauntlet Press

"By Turns" 2000 *Strange Attraction*, ed. Edward E. Kramer, Bereshith Publishing
"In the Waterworks (Birmingham, Alabama 1888)" 2000 *Tales of Pain and Wonder*, Gauntlet Press
"Lafayette" 2000 *Horror Garage* (#1), ed. Paula Guran
"Pædomorphosis" 2000 *Tales of Pain and Wonder*, Gauntlet Press
"A Redress for Andromeda" 2000 *October Dreams: A Celebration of Halloween*, ed. Richard Chizmar and Robert Morrish, Cemetery Dance Publications
"San Andreas" 2000 *Tales of Pain and Wonder*, Gauntlet Press
"Spindleshanks (New Orleans, 1956)" 2000 *Queer Fear*, ed. Michael Rowe, Arsenal Pulp Press
"Valentia" 2000 *Dark Terrors 5*, ed. Stephen Jones and David Sutton, Victor Gollancz
"Onion" 2001 *Wrong Things*, Subterranean Press
"The Rest of the Wrong Thing" 2001 (with Poppy Z. Brite) *Wrong Things*, Subterranean Press
"So Runs the World Away" 2001 *The Mammoth Book of Vampire Stories by Women*, ed. Stephen Jones, Carroll and Graf
"In the Garden of Poisonous Flowers" 2002, Subterranean Press; reprinted 2006, *Alabaster*, as "Les Fleurs Empoisonnées," Subterranean Press; reprinted 2011, *Two Worlds and in Between: The Best of Caitlín R. Kiernan (Volume One)*, as "Les Fleurs Empoisonnées, or Dans le Jardin des Fleurs Toxiques," Subterranean Press
"Night Story 1973" (with Poppy Z. Brite) 2002 *From Weird and Distant Shores*, Subterranean Press
"Nor the Demons Down Under the Sea" 2002 *The Children of Cthulhu*, ed. John Pelan and Benjamin Adams, Del Rey
"Rat's Star (A Fragment)" 2002 *From Weird and Distant Shores* (lettered edition only), Subterranean Press
"The Road of Pins" 2002, *Dark Terrors 6*, ed. Steve Jones, Victor Gollancz
"Standing Water" 2002 *Darker Side: Generations of Horror*, ed. John Pelan, Roc/NAL
"Andromeda Among the Stones" 2003 chapbook accompanying *Embrace the Mutation*, ed. William K. Schafer, Subterranean Press
"The Drowned Geologist (1898)" 2003 *Shadows Over Baker Street*, ed. Michael Reaves and John Pelan, Del Rey
"Mercury" 2003, Subterranean Press (chapbook)
"The Dead and the Moonstruck" 2004 *Gothic! Ten Original Dark Tales*, ed. Deborah Noyes, Candlewick Press

"La Mer des Rêves" 2004 *A Walk on the Darkside: Visions of Horror*, John Pelan, Roc/NAL
"Riding the White Bull" 2004 *Argosy Magazine* (#1), ed. Lou Anders, Coppervale Intl.
"Waycross" 2004 Subterranean Press (chapbook)
"Apokatastasis" 2005 *To Charles Fort, With Love*, Subterranean Press
"Bradbury Weather" 2005 *Subterranean Magazine* (#6), ed. William K. Schafer, Subterranean Press
"Faces in Revolving Souls" 2005 *Outsiders*, ed. Nancy Holder and Nancy Kilpatrick, Roc/NAL
"Flicker" 2005 *Frog Toes and Tentacles*, Subterranean Press
"From Cabinet 34, Drawer 6" 2005 *Weird Shadows Over Innsmouth*, ed. Stephen Jones, Fedogan & Bremer
"La Peau Verte" 2005 *To Charles Fort, With Love*, Subterranean Press
"Los Angeles 2162 (December)" 2005 *Frog Toes and Tentacles*, Subterranean Press
"Madonna Littoralis" 2005 *Sirenia Digest* (Dec. #1), Goat Girl Press; reprinted 2006 *Fantasy Magazine* (#2), ed. Sean Wallace, Wildside Press;.
"Ode to Katan Amono" 2005 *Frog Toes and Tentacles*, Subterranean Press
"Pages Found Among the Effects of Miss Edith M. Teller" 2005 *Frog Toes and Tentacles*, Subterranean Press
"Pump Excursion" 2005 *Frog Toes and Tentacles*, Subterranean Press
"Untitled 4" 2005 *Frog Toes and Tentacles*, Subterranean Press
"Untitled 7" 2005 *Frog Toes and Tentacles*, Subterranean Press
"Untitled 11" 2005 *Frog Toes and Tentacles*, Subterranean Press
"Untitled 12" 2005 *Frog Toes and Tentacles*, Subterranean Press
"Untitled 13" 2005 *Sirenia Digest* (Dec. #1), Goat Girl Press
"Alabaster" 2006 *Alabaster*, Subterranean Press
"The Ammonite Violin (Murder Ballad No. 4)" 2006 *Sirenia Digest* (Oct. #11), Goat Girl Press; reprinted 2007, *Dark Delicacies II: Fear*, ed. Del Howison and Jeff Gelb, Carroll & Graf
"Bainbridge" 2006 *Alabaster*, Subterranean Press, revised 2014 for *Alabaster: Pale Horse*, Dark Horse Books/Dark Horse Comics
"The Black Alphabet (Part One)" 2006 *Sirenia Digest* (May #6), Goat Girl Press
"The Black Alphabet (Part Two)" 2006 *Sirenia Digest* (June #7), Goat Girl Press; reprint 2007, parts One and Two collected as ***The Black Alphabet (A Primer)***, Subterranean Press
"Bridle" 2006 *Sirenia Digest* (Feb. #3), Goat Girl Press; reprinted 2010, *The Ammonite Violin & Others,* Subterranean Press

"The Cryomancer's Daughter (Murder Ballad No. 3)" 2006 *Sirenia Digest* (July #8), Goat Girl Press; reprinted 2010 *The Ammonite Violin & Others*, Subterranean Press
"Eisoptrophobia – A Sketch" 2006 *Sirenia Digest* (Feb. #3), Goat Girl Press
"For One Who Has Lost Herself" 2006 *Sirenia Digest* (April #5), Goat Girl Press; reprinted 2010, *The Ammonite Violin & Others,* Subterranean Press
"In the Praying Windows" (with Sonya Taaffe) 2006 *Sirenia Digest* (Sept. #10), Goat Girl Press
"The Lovesong of Lady Ratteanrufer" 2006 *Sirenia Digest* (Nov. #12), Goat Girl Press; reprinted 2010 *The Ammonite Violin & Others*, Subterranean Press
"Metamorphosis A" 2006 *Sirenia Digest* (Nov. #12), Goat Girl Press; reprinted 2010 *The Ammonite Violin & Others*, Subterranean Press
"Metamorphosis B" 2006 *Sirenia Digest* (Dec. #13), Goat Girl Press; reprinted 2010 *The Ammonite Violin & Others*, Subterranean Press
"Ode to Edvard Munch" 2006 *Sirenia Digest* (May #6), Goal Girl Press; reprinted 2008 *The Mammoth Book of Vampire Romance,* ed. Trisha Telep, Running Press
"Orpheus at Mount Pangæum" 2006 *Sirenia Digest* (Jan. #2), Goat Girl Press; reprinted 2010 *The Ammonite Violin & Others*, Subterranean Press
"pas-en-arrière" 2006 *Sirenia Digest* (April #5), Goat Girl Press; reprinted 2007 *Tales from the Woeful Platypus*, Subterranean Press
"The Pearl Diver" 2006 *Futureshocks,* ed. Lou Anders, Roc/NAL
"Pony" 2006 *Sirenia Digest* (Jan. #2), Goat Girl Press; reprinted 2007 *Tales from the Woeful Platypus*, Subterranean Press
"Portrait of the Artist as a Young Ghoul" 2006 *Sirenia Digest* (Aug. #9), Goat Girl Press
"Untitled 17" 2006 *Sirenia Digest* (Feb. #3), Goat Girl Press; reprinted 2007, *Tales from the Woeful Platypus*, Subterranean Press
"Untitled 20" 2006 *Sirenia Digest* (March #4), Goat Girl Press; reprinted 2007 *Tales from the Woeful Platypus*, Subterranean Press
"Untitled 23" 2006 *Sirenia Digest* (Sept. #10), Goat Girl Press; reprinted 2010 as "A Child's Guide to the Hollow Hills," *The Ammonite Violin & Others*, Subterranean Press
"The Voyeur in the House of Glass" 2006 *Sirenia Digest* (Dec. #13), Goat Girl Press; reprinted 2010 *The Ammonite Violin & Others*, Subterranean Press
"The Well of Stars and Shadow" 2006 *Alabaster,* Subterranean Press
"Anamnesis, or the Sleepless Nights of Léon Spilliaert" 2007 *Sirenia Digest* (Jul. #20), Goat Girl Press; reprinted 2010 *The Ammonite Violin & Others*, Subterranean Press

"The Bed of Appetite" 2007 *Sirenia Digest* (Oct. #23), Goat Girl Press; reprinted 2012 *Confessions of a Five-Chambered Heart*, Subterranean Press

"The Collector of Bones" 2008 *Sirenia Digest* (Jan. #26), Goat Girl Press; reprinted 2012 *Confessions of a Five-Chambered Heart*, Subterranean Press

"The Crimson Alphabet (Part One)" 2007 *Sirenia Digest* (Dec. #25), Goat Girl Press

"The Daughter of the Four of Pentacles" 2007 *Thrillers 2*, ed. Robert Morrish. Cemetery Dance Publishing

"Daughter of Man, Mother of Wyrm" 2007 *Tales from the Woeful Platypus*, Subterranean Press

"Excerpt from *Memoirs of Martian Demirep*" 2007 *Tales from the Woeful Platypus*, Subterranean Press

"Flotsam" 2008 *Sirenia Digest* (Apr. #29), Goat Girl Press; reprinted 2008 *Not One of Us* (Sept. #40), ed. John Benson, Not One of Us Publications

"Forests of the Night" 2007 *Tales from the Woeful Platypus*, Subterranean Press

"The Garden of Living Flowers" 2007 *Tales from the Woeful Platypus*, Subterranean Press

"In the Dreamtime of Lady Resurrection" 2007 *Sirenia Digest* (Jul. #20), Goat Girl Press; reprinted 2010 *The Ammonite Violin & Others*, Subterranean Press

"In View of Nothing" 2007 *Sirenia Digest* (Mar. #7), Goat Girl Press; reprinted 2009 *A is for Alien*, Subterranean Press

"The Madam of the Narrow Houses" 2007 *Sirenia Digest* (Oct. #23); reprinted 2010 *The Ammonite Violin & Others*, Subterranean Press

"Night Games in the Crimson Court" 2007 *Sirenia Digest* (Apr. #17), Goat Girl Press

"Outside the Gates of Eden" 2007 *Sirenia Digest* (May #18), Goat Girl Press; reprinted 2010 *The Ammonite Violin & Others*, Subterranean Press

"Salammbô Redux (2007)" 2008, *Tales of Pain and Wonder* (3rd edition), Subterranean Press

"A Season of Broken Dolls" 2007 *Sirenia Digest* (Feb. #15), Goat Girl Press; reprinted 2009 *A is for Alien*, Subterranean Press

"Scene in the Museum (1896)" 2007 *Sirenia Digest* (Aug. #21), Goat Girl Press; reprinted 2010 *The Ammonite Violin & Others*, Subterranean Press

"Skin Game" 2007 (*Sirenia Digest* (Feb. #15), Goat Girl Press; reprinted 2010 *The Ammonite Violin & Others*, Subterranean Press

"The Sphinx's Kiss" 2007 *Sirenia Digest* (Jan. #14), Goat Girl Press; reprinted 2010 *The Ammonite Violin & Others*, Subterranean Press

"The Steam Dancer (1896)" 2007 *Sirenia Digest* (June #19), June 2007; reprinted 2008 *Subterranean: Tales of Dark Fantasy*, ed. William K. Schafer, Subterranean Press
"Still Life" 2007 *Tales from the Woeful Platypus*, Subterranean Press
"Untitled 26" 2007 *Sirenia Digest* (Mar. #16), Goat Girl Press, reprinted 2010 as "The Hole with a Girl in Its Heart," *The Ammonite Violin & Others*, Subterranean Press
"Untitled 31" 2007 *Sirenia Digest* (Dec. #25), Goat Girl Press, reprinted 2012 as "Subterraneus," *Confessions of a Five-Chambered Heart*, Subterranean Press
"Untitled Grotesque" 2007 *Sirenia Digest* (Sept. #22), Goat Girl Press
"The Wolf Who Cried Girl" 2007 *Sirenia Digest* Nov. #24), Goat Girl Press; reprinted 2012, *Confessions of a Five-Chambered Heart*, Subterranean Press
"Zero Summer" 2007 *Subterranean Magazine* (#6), ed. William K. Schafer, Subterranean Press
"Beatification" 2008 *Sirenia Digest* (Feb. #27), Goat Girl Press; reprinted 2012 *Confessions of a Five-Chambered Heart*, Subterranean Press
"Concerning Attrition and Severance" 2008 *Sirenia Digest* (Apr. #29), Goat Girl Press; reprinted 2012 *Confessions of a Five-Chambered Heart*, Subterranean Press
"The Crimson Alphabet (Part Two)" 2008 *Sirenia Digest* (Jan. #30), Goat Girl Press; reprint 2011, parts One and Two collected as ***The Crimson Alphabet (A Primer)***, Subterranean Press
"Dancing With the Eight of Swords" 2008 *Sirenia Digest* (Nov. #36), Goat Girl Press; reprinted 2012 *Confessions of a Five-Chambered Heart*, Subterranean Press
"Derma Sutra (1891)" 2008 *Sirenia Digest* (Jul. #32), Goat Girl Press; reprinted 2012, *Confessions of a Five-Chambered Heart*, Subterranean Press
"I Am the Abyss and I Am the Light" 2008 *Sirenia Digest* (Oct. #35), Goat Girl Press; reprinted 2012 *Confessions of a Five-Chambered Heart*, Subterranean Press
"Lullaby of Partition and Reunion" 2008 *Sirenia Digest* (Dec. #37), Goat Girl Press; reprinted 2012 *Confessions of a Five-Chambered Heart*, Subterranean Press
"The Melusine (1898)" 2008 *Sirenia Digest* (June #31), Goat Girl Press; reprinted 2012 *Confessions of a Five-Chambered Heart*, Subterranean Press
"Murder Ballad No. 6" 2008 *Sirenia Digest* (Dec. #37), Goat Girl Press; reprinted 2012 as "Murder Ballad No. 7," *Confessions of a Five-Chambered Heart*, Subterranean Press

"Pickman's Other Model" 2008 *Sirenia Digest* (Mar. #28), Goat Girl Press; reprinted 2010 *Black Wings: New Tales of Lovecraftian Horror*, ed. S. T. Joshi, PS Publishing

"Rappaccini's Dragon (Murder Ballad No. 5)" 2008 *Sirenia Digest* (May #30), Goat Girl Press; reprinted 2012 *Confessions of a Five-Chambered Heart*, Subterranean Press

"Unter den Augen des Mondes" 2008 *Sirenia Digest* (June #31), Goat Girl Press; reprinted 2012 *Confessions of a Five-Chambered Heart*, Subterranean Press

"Untitled 33" 2008 *Sirenia Digest* (Sept. #34), Goat Girl Press, reprinted 2012 "Fecunditatum (Murder Ballad No. 6), *Confessions of a Five-Chambered Heart*, Subterranean Press

"The Z Word" 2008 *Sirenia Digest* (Aug. #33), Goat Girl Press

"The Alchemist's Daughter (a fragment)" 2009 *Sirenia Digest* (June #43), Goat Girl Press

"At the Gate of Deeper Slumber" 2009 *Sirenia Digest* (Apr. #41), Goat Girl Press; reprinted 2012 *Confessions of a Five-Chambered Heart*, Subterranean Press

"The Belated Burial" 2009 *Sirenia Digest* (Jan. #38), Goat Girl Press; reprinted 2012 *Confessions of a Five-Chambered Heart*, Subterranean Press

"The Bone's Prayer" 2009 *Sirenia Digest* (Feb. #39), Goat Girl Press; reprinted 2010 *The Year's Best Dark Fantasy & Horror 2010,* ed. Paula Guran, Prime Books

"A Canvas for Incoherent Arts" 2009 *Sirenia Digest* (Mar. #40), Goat Girl Press; reprinted 2012 *Confessions of a Five-Chambered Heart*, Subterranean Press

"Charcloth, Firesteel, and Flint" 2009 *Sirenia Digest* (Sept. #46), Goat Girl Press; reprinted 2011 *A Book of Horrors*, ed. Stephen Jones, PS Publishing

"The Dissevered Heart" 2009 *Sirenia Digest* (Oct. #47), Goat Girl Press

"Exuvium" 2009 *Sirenia Digest* (Nov. #48), Goat Girl Press

"Fish Bride" 2009 *Sirenia Digest* (May #42), Goat Girl Press; reprinted 2011 *The Weird Fiction Review* (#2), ed. S. T. Joshi, Centipede Press

"January 28, 1926" 2009 *Sirenia Digest* (Jul. #44), Goat Girl Press

"Last Drink Bird Head" 2009 *Last Drink Bird Head*, ed. Jeff VanderMeer, Ministry of Whimsy Press

"The Mermaid of the Concrete Ocean" 2009 *Sirenia Digest* (June #43), Goat Girl Press; reprinted 2012 *The Drowning Girl: A Memoir*, Roc/NAL

"Paleozoic Annunciation" 2009 *Sirenia Digest* (Aug. #45), Goat Girl Press

"The Peril of Liberated Objects, or the Voyeur's Seduction" 2009 *Sirenia Digest* (Apr. #41), Goat Girl Press; reprinted 2012 *Confessions of a Five-Chambered Heart*, Subterranean Press

"Shipwrecks Above" 2009 *Sirenia Digest* (Sept. #46), Goat Girl Press; reprinted 2015 *Blood Sisters: Vampire Stories by Women,* ed. Paula Guran, Skyhorse/Night Shade Books
"The Thousand-and-Third Tale of Scheherazade" 2009 *Sirenia Digest* (Jan. #38), Goat Girl Press; reprinted 2012 *Confessions of a Five-Chambered Heart*, Subterranean Press
"Untitled 34" 2009 *Sirenia Digest* (Dec. #49), Goat Girl Press
"Vicaria Draconis" 2009 *Sirenia Digest* (Jul. #44), Goat Girl Press
"Werewolf Smile" 2009 *Sirenia Digest* (Aug. #45), Goat Girl Press; reprinted 2012 *The Drowning Girl: A Memoir*, Roc/NAL
"– 30 –" 2010 *Sirenia Digest* (Dec. #61), Goat Girl Press; reprinted 2014 *Magic City: Recent Spells*, ed. Paula Guran, Prime Books
"And the Cloud That Took the Form" 2010 *Sirenia Digest* (Oct. #59), Goat Girl Press; reprinted 2013 *World Horror Convention Souvenir Book*, ed. Norman Rubenstein, Horror Writers Association
"The Ape's Wife" 2010 *Realms: The First Year of Clarkesworld Magazine*, ed. Neil Clarke, Wyrm Publishing
"Apsinthion" 2010 *Sirenia Digest* (Feb. #51), Goat Girl Press
"As Red As Red" 2010 *Haunted Legends*, ed. Ellen Datlow and Nick Mamatas, Tor
"The Eighth Veil" 2010 *Sirenia Digest* (Feb. #51)
"Fairy Tale of the Maritime" 2010 *Sirenia Digest* (Aug. #57), Goat Girl Press
"Houndwife" 2010 *Sirenia Digest* (Mar. #52), Goat Girl Press; reprinted 2012 *Black Wings II*, ed. S. T. Joshi, PS Publishing
"Hydrarguros" 2010 *Sirenia Digest* (Jan. #50), Goat Girl Press; reprinted 2011 *Subterranean: Tales of Dark Fantasy 2*, ed. William K. Schafer, Subterranean Press
"John Four" 2010 *Sirenia Digest* (Sept. #58), Goat Girl Press; reprinted 2014 *A Mountain Walked,* ed. S. T. Joshi, Centipede Press
"On the Reef" 2010 *Sirenia Digest* (Oct. #59), Goat Girl Press; reprinted 2011 *Halloween*, ed. Paula Guran, Prime Books
"Persephone Redux (A Fragment)" 2010 *Sirenia Digest* (Feb. #51), Goat Girl Press
"The Prayer of Ninety Cats" 2010 *Sirenia Digest* (Nov. #60), Goat Girl Press; reprinted 2015 *The Year's Best Dark Fantasy and Horror 2014*, ed. Paula Guran, Prime Books
"The Sea Troll's Daughter" 2010 *Swords and Dark Magic*, ed. Jonathan Strahan and Lou Anders, Subterranean Press/Harper Voyager
"Tempest Witch" 2010 *Sirenia Digest* (May #54), Goat Girl Press

"Three Months, Three Scenes, With Snow" 2010 *Sirenia Digest* (Apr. #53), Goat Girl Press

"Tidal Forces" 2010 *Sirenia Digest* (June #55), Goat Girl Press; reprinted 2011 *Eclipse Four*, ed. Jonathan Strahan, Night Shade Books

"Workprint" 2010 *Sirenia Digest* (Apr. #53)

"The Yellow Alphabet (Part One)" 2010 *Sirenia Digest* (July #56), Goat Girl Press

"The Yellow Alphabet (Part Two)" 2010 *Sirenia Digest* (Aug. #57), Goat Girl Press; reprint 2012, parts One and Two collected in ***The Yellow Book,*** Subterranean Press

"Another Tale of Two Cities" 2011 *Sirenia Digest* (Nov. #72), Goat Girl Press

"Blast the Human Flower" 2011 *Sirenia Digest* (Dec. #73), Goat Girl Press

"The Carnival is Dead and Gone" 2011 *Sirenia Digest* (Apr. #65), Goat Girl Press

"The Collier's Venus (1898)" 2011 *Naked City: Tales of Urban Fantasy*, ed. Ellen Datlow, St. Martin's Press

"Daughter Dear Desmodus" 2011 *Sirenia Digest* (Sept. #70), Goat Girl Press

"Down to Gehenna" 2011 *Sirenia Digest* (June #67), Goat Girl Press

"Evensong" 2011 *Sirenia Digest* (Sept. #70), Goat Girl Press

"Figurehead" 2011 *Sirenia Digest* (May #66), Goat Girl Press

"The Granting Cabinet" 2011 *Sirenia Digest* (June #68), Goat Girl Press

"A Key to the Castleblakeney Key" 2011 *The Thackery T. Lambshead Cabinet of Curiosities*, ed. Ann and Jeff VanderMeer, Harper Voyager

"Latitude 41°21′45.89″N, Longitude 71°29′0.62″W" 2011 *Sirenia Digest* (Oct. #71), Goat Girl Press

"The Lost Language of Littoral Mollusca and Crustacea; Part the First" 2011 *Sirenia Digest* (Dec. #73), Goat Girl Press

"The Maltese Unicorn" 2011 *Supernatural Noir*, ed. Ellen Datlow, Dark Horse Books/Dark Horse Comics

"Random Thoughts Before a Fatal Crash" 2011 *Sirenia Digest* (Mar. #64) Goat Girl Press; reprinted 2013 *The Ape's Wife and Other Stories*, Subterranean Press

"Slouching Towards the House of Glass Coffins" 2011 *Sirenia Digest* (Aug. #69), Goat Girl Press; reprinted 2013 *The Ape's Wife and Other Stories*, Subterranean Press

"Untitled 35" 2011 *Sirenia Digest* (May #66), Goat Girl Press

"Blind Fish" 2012 *Sirenia Digest* (Dec. #85), Goat Girl Press; reprinted 2014 *Searchers After Horror: New Tales of the Weird and Fantastic*, ed. S. T. Joshi, Fedogan & Bremer

"Cages I" (with David T. Kirkpatrick) 2012 *Sirenia Digest* (Mar. #76), Goat Girl Press
"Cammufare" 2012 *Sirenia Digest* (Jan. #74), Goat Girl Press
"Fake Plastic Trees" 2012 *After*, ed. Ellen and Terri Windling, Hyperion
"Goggles (c. 1910)" 2012 *Steampunk III: Steampunk Revolution*, ed. Ann VanderMeer, Tachyon Publishing
"Here Is No Why" 2012 *Sirenia Digest* (Feb. #75), Goat Girl Press
"Hauplatte/Gegenplatte" 2012 *Sirenia Digest* (Apr. #77), Goat Girl Press
"Our Lady of Tharsis Tholus" 2012 *Sirenia Digest* (Aug. #81), Goat Girl Press
"Love is Forbidden, We Croak and Howl" 2012 *Sirenia Digest* (May #78), Goat Girl Press; reprinted 2014 *Lovecraft's Monsters*, ed. Ellen Datlow, Tachyon Publications
"A Mountain Walked" 2012 *Sirenia Digest* (Sept. #82), Goat Girl Press; reprinted 2014 *The Madness of Cthulhu: Volume 1*, edited S. T. Joshi, Titan Books
"One Tree Hill (The World As Cataclysm)" 2012 *Sirenia Digest* (Jul. #80), Goat Girl Press; reprinted 2014 *Black Wings III: New Tales of Lovecraftian Horror*, ed. S. T. Joshi, PS Publishing
"Quiet Houses" 2012 *Sirenia Digest* (June #79), Goat Girl Press
"Tall Bodies" 2012 *Sirenia Digest* (Jul. #80), Goat Girl Press; reprinted 2013 *The Ape's Wife and Other Stories*, Subterranean Press
"The Transition of Elizabeth Haskings" 2012 *Sirenia Digest* (Jan. #74), Goat Girl Press; reprinted 2015, *Weirder Shadows Over Innsmouth*, ed. Stephen Jones, Fedogan & Bremer
"Whilst the Night Rejoices Profound and Still" 2012 *Sirenia Digest* (Oct. #83), Goat Girl Press; reprinted 2013 *Halloween: Magic, Mystery, and the Macabre*, ed. Paula Guran, Prime Books
"Elegy for a Suicide" 2013 *Sirenia Digest* (Jul. #90), Goat Girl Press
"Mote[L] 2032" 2013 *Sirenia Digest* (Nov. #94), Goat Girl Press
"The Peddler's Tale, Or Isobel's Revenge" 2013 *Sirenia Digest* (Dec. #95), Goat Girl Press; reprinted 2015 *The Mammoth Book of Cthulhu*, ed. Paula Guran, Prime Books
"Pickman's Madonna" 2013 *Sirenia Digest* (Oct. #93), Goat Girl Press; reprinted 2015 (revised and in part) *Cherry Bomb: A Siobhan Quinn Novel* (as Kathleen Tierney), Roc/NAL
"Pushing the Sky Away (Death of a Blasphemer)" 2013 *Sirenia Digest* (Aug. #91), Goat Girl Press
"Sea-Drift" 2013 *Sirenia Digest* (Mar. #87), Goat Girl Press
"Study for *The Witch House*" 2013 *Sirenia Digest* (Sept. #92), Goat Girl Press

"Turning the Little Key" 2013 *Sirenia Digest* (Apr. #88), Goat Girl Press
"What Dread Hand? What Dread Grasp?" 2013 *Sirenia Digest* (Feb. #86), Goat Girl Press
"Ballad of an Echo Whisperer" 2014 *Fearful Symmetries*, ed. Ellen Datlow, ChiZine Publications
"The Beginning of the Year Without a Summer" 2014 *Sirenia Digest* (Apr. #99), Goat Girl Press; reprinted 2015, *The Monstrous,* ed. Ellen Datlow, Tachyon Publications
"A Birth in the Wood of Self-Murderers" 2014 *Sirenia Digest* (Sept. #104), Goat Girl Press
"Black Glass, Green Glass" 2014 *Sirenia Digest* (Aug. #103), Goat Girl Press
"The Cats of River Street (1925)" 2014 *Sirenia Digest* (Jul. #102), Goat Girl Press; reprinted 2015 *Innsmouth Nightmares*, ed. Lois Gresh, PS Publishing
"Chewing on Shadows" 2014 *Sirenia Digest* (Feb. #97), Goat Girl Press
"Far From Any Shore" 2014 *Sirenia Digest* (June #101), Goat Girl Press
"The Green Abyss" 2014 *Sirenia Digest* (Nov. #106), Goat Girl Press
"Idyll for a Purgatory Dancer" 2014 *Sirenia Digest* (Jan. #96), Goat Girl Press
"Interstate Love Song (Murder Ballad No. 8)" 2014 *Sirenia Digest* (May #100), Goat Girl Press; reprinted 2015, *The Best Science Fiction and Fantasy of the Year (Volume Nine),* Solaris/Rebellion Publishing, Ltd.
"The Jetsam of Disremembered Mechanics" 2014, *The Book of Silverberg: Stories in Honor of Robert Silverberg*, ed. Gardner Dozois and William K. Schafer, Subterranean Press
"Black Ships Seen South of Heaven" 2015 *Black Wings IV*, ed. S. T. Joshi, PS Publishing
"Bus Fare" 2015 *The Year's Best Weird Fiction (Volume 2)*, ed. Kathe Koja and Michael Kelly, Undertow Publications
"The Cripple and the Starfish" 2015 *Sirenia Digest* (Jan, #108), Goat Girl Press
"The Aubergine Alphabet (Parts 1 & 2)" 2015 *Sirenia Digest* (Feb.–Mar. #109–110), Goat Girl Press
"Dancy vs. the Pterosaur" 2015 *Sirenia Digest* (Apr. #111), Goat Girl Press
"Le Meneur des loups" 2015 *Sirenia Digest* (May #112), Goat Girl Press
"Dead Letter Office" 2015 *Sirenia Digest* (June. #113), Goat Girl Press
"Dry Bones" 2015 *Sirenia Digest* (Jul. #114), Goat Girl Press

Novellas (by year of first publication)

The Dry Salvages 2004, Subterranean Press
Black Helicopters 2012, Subterranean Press

Collections

Tales of Pain and Wonder 2000, Gauntlet Press; 2002, Meisha Merlin (2nd edition); 2008, Subterranean Press (3rd edition, definitive text)

"Anamorphosis"
"To This Water (Johnstown, Pennsylvania 1889"
"Bela's Plot"
"Tears Seven Times Salt"
"Superheroes"
"Glass Coffin"
"Breakfast in the House of the Rising Sun (Murder Ballad No. 1)"
"Estate"
"The Last Child of Lir"
"A Story for Edward Gorey"
"Salammbô"
"Pædomorphosis"
"Postcards from the King of Tides"
"Rats Live on No Evil Star"
"Salmagundi"
"In the Water Works (Birmingham, Alabama 1888)
"The Long Hall on the Top Floor"
"San Andreas"
"Angels You Can See Through"*
"Lafayette (Murder Ballad No. 2)"
"Between the Gargoyle Trees"
"Zelda Fitzgerald in Ballet Attire"
* Not included in 3rd edition; "Mercury" and "Salammbô Redux (2007)" added to 3rd edition.

Wrong Things (with Poppy Z. Brite), 2001, Subterranean Press

"Onion"
"The Rest of the Wrong Thing" (with Poppy Z. Brite)

From Weird and Distant Shores 2002, Subterranean Press

"Escape Artist"
"The Comedy of St. Jehanne d'Arc"
"Stoker's Mistress"
"Emptiness Spoke Eloquent"
"Giants in the Earth"
"Found Angels" (with Christa Faust)
"Two Worlds and In Between"
"The King of Birds"

"By Turns"
"Persephone"
"Between the Flatirons and the Deep Green Sea"
"Hoar Isis"
"Night Story (1973)" (with Poppy Z. Brite)
"Rat's Star (A Fragment)" (lettered edition only)

To Charles Fort, With Love 2005, Subterranean Press

"Valentia"
"Spindleshanks (New Orleans, 1956)"
"So Runs the World Away"
"Standing Water"
"La Mer des Rêves"
"The Road of Pins"
"Onion"
"Apokatastasis"
"La Peau Verte"
"The Dead and the Moonstruck"
The Dandridge Cycle:
"A Redress for Andromeda"
"Nor the Demons Down Under the Sea"
"Andromeda Among the Stones"

Frog Toes and Tentacles 2005, Subterranean Press

"Pages Found Among the Effects of Miss Edith M. Teller"
"Untitled 4"
"Untitled 7"
"Flicker"
"Pump Excursion"
"Untitled 11"
"Untitled 12"
"Ode to Katan Amono"
"Los Angeles 2162 (December)" (lettered edition only)

Alabaster 2006, Subterranean Press; expanded edition reissued 2014 as *Alabaster: Pale Horse*, Dark Horse Books/Dark Horse Comics

"Les Fleurs Empoisonnées"
"The Well of Stars and Shadow"
"Waycross"
"Alabaster"
"Bainbridge"
"Highway 97" (in *Alabaster: Pale Horse*)

Tales from the Woeful Platypus 2007, Subterranean Press

"Untitled 17"
"Pony"
"Forests of the Night"
"Daughter of Man, Mother of Wyrm"
"Untitled 20"
"Still Life"
"pas-en-arriere"
"The Garden of Living Flowers"
"Excerpt from *Memoirs of a Martian Demirep*" (lettered edition only)

A is for Alien 2009, Subterranean Press

"Riding the White Bull"
"Faces in Revolving Souls"
"Zero Summer"
"The Pearl Diver"
"In View of Nothing"
"Ode to Katan Amono"
"A Season of Broken Dolls"
"Bradbury Weather"

The Ammonite Violin & Others 2010, Subterranean Press

"Madonna Littoralis"
"Orpheus at Mount Pangæum"
"Bridle"
"For One Who Has Lost Herself"
"Ode to Edvard Munch"
"The Cryomancer's Daughter (Murder Ballad No. 3)"
"A Child's Guide to the Hollow Hills"
"The Ammonite Violin (Murder Ballad No. 4)"
"The Lovesong of Lady Ratteanrufer"
"Metamorphosis A"
"The Sphinx's Kiss"
"The Voyuer in the House of Glass"
"Metamorphosis B"
"Skin Game"
"The Hole With a Girl In Its Heart"
"Outside the Gates of Eden"
"In the Dreamtime of Lady Resurrection"
"Anamnesis, or the Sleepless Nights of Léon Spilliaert"
"Scene in the Museum (1896)"
"The Madam of the Narrow Houses"

Two Worlds and In Between: The Best of Caitlín R. Kiernan (Volume One) 2011, Subterranean Press

PART ONE (1993–1999)

"Emptiness Spoke Eloquent"
"Two Worlds, and In Between"
"To This Water (Johnstown, Pennsylvania 1889)"
"Tears Seven Times Salt"
"Breakfast in the House of the Rising Sun (Murder Ballad No. 1)"
"Estate"
"Rats Live on No Evil Star"
"Salmagundi (New York City, 1981)"
"Postcards from the King of Tides"
"Giants in the Earth"
"Zelda Fitzgerald in Ballet Attire"

PART TWO (2000–2004)

"Spindleshanks (New Orleans, 1956)"
"The Road of Pins"
"Onion"
"Les Fleurs Empoisonnées"
"Night Story 1973" (with Poppy Z. Brite)
"From Cabinet 34, Drawer 6"
"Andromeda Among the Stones"
"La Peau Verte"
"Riding the White Bull"
"Waycross"
"The Dead and the Moonstruck"
"The Daughter of the Four of Pentacles"
The Dry Salvages
"The Wyrm in My Mind's Eye"
"Houses Under the Sea"

Confessions of a Five-Chambered Heart: 25 Tales of Weird Romance 2012, Subterranean Press

"The Wolf Who Cried Girl"
"The Bed of Appetite"
"Subterraneus"
"The Collector of Bones"
"Beatification"
"Untitled Grotesque"
"Flotsam"
"Concerning Attrition and Severance"

"Rappaccini's Dragon (Murder Ballad No. 5)"
"Unter den Augen des Mondes"
"The Melusine (1898) "
"Fecunditatum (Murder Ballad No. 6)"
"I Am the Abyss, and I Am the Light"
"Dancing With the Eight of Swords"
"Murder Ballad No. 7"
"Lullaby of Partition and Reunion"
"Derma Sutra (1891)"
"The Thousand-and-Third Tale of Scheherazade"
"The Belated Burial"
"The Bone's Prayer"
"A Canvas for Incoherent Arts"
"The Peril of Liberated Objects, or the Voyeur's Seduction"
"Pickman's Other Model (1929)"
"At the Gate of Deeper Slumber"
"Fish Bride (1970)"

The Ape's Wife and Other Tales 2013, Subterranean Press
"The Steam Dancer (1896)"
"The Maltese Unicorn"
"One Tree Hill"
"The Collier's Venus (1898)"
"Galápagos"
"Tall Bodies"
"As Red As Red"
"Hydraguros"
"Slouching Towards the House of Glass Coffins"
"Tidal Forces"
"The Sea Troll's Daughter"
"Random Notes Before a Fatal Crash"
"The Ape's Wife"

Beneath an Oil-Dark Sea: The Best of Caitlín R. Kiernan (Volume Two) 2015, Subterranean Press
See this volume.

Chapbooks

Candles for Elizabeth 1998, Meisha Merlin Publishing, Inc.
Study for "Estate" 2000, Gauntlet Press
On the Road to Jefferson 2002, Subterranean Press

Trilobite: The Writing of Threshold 2003, Subterranean Press
Waycross 2003, Subterranean Press
Alabaster 2003, Camelot Books and Gifts, Inc.; expanded 2006 for *Alabaster*, Subterranean Press
Embrace the Mutation (with J.K. Potter) 2003, Subterranean Press
The Worm in My Mind's Eye 2004, Subterranean Press
Mercury 2004, Subterranean Press
False/Starts: Being a Compendium of Beginnings 2005, Subterranean Press
The Merewife (a prologue) 2005, Subterranean Press
The Little Damned Book of Days 2005, Subterranean Press
Highway 97 2006, Subterranean Press
The Black Alphabet (A Primer) 2007, Subterranean Press
Tails of Tales of Pain and Wonder 2007, Subterranean Press
B is for Beginnings 2009, Subterranean Press
Sanderlings 2010, Subterranean Press
The Crimson Alphabet (Another Primer) 2011, Subterranean Press
The Yellow Book 2012, "Ex Libris" and "The Yellow Alphabet," Subterranean Press
False/Starts II: Being Another Compendium of Beginnings 2015, Subterranean Press

Novels

The Crow: The Lazarus Heart (writing as Poppy Z. Brite) 1998, Harper Prism
Silk 1998, Roc/NAL
Threshold 2001, Roc/NAL
Low Red Moon 2003, Roc/NAL
The Five of Cups 2003, Subterranean Press
Murder of Angels 2004, Roc/NAL
Daughter of Hounds 2007, Roc/NAL
Beowulf 2007 (film novelization), Harper Entertainment
The Red Tree 2009 Roc/NAL
The Drowning Girl: A Memoir 2012, Roc/NAL

As Kathleen Tierney:

Blood Oranges 2013, Roc/NAL
Red Delicious 2014, Roc/NAL
Cherry Bomb 2015, Roc/NAL

Poetry

"Zelda Fitzgerald in Ballet Attire" 2000, *Tales of Pain and Wonder,* Gauntlet Publishing
"Aperçu" 2008, *Tales of Pain and Wonder*, Suterranean Press
"Atlantis" 2012, *Strange Horizons* (online publication); reprint 2015, *Beneath an Oil-Dark Sea: The Best of Caitlín R. Kiernan (Volume Two)* 2015, Subterranean Press

Comics and Graphic Novels

The Dreaming (DC Comics/Vertigo; October 1997–May 2001)
The Dreaming #17–19, **"Souvenirs"** (October '97–December '97)
The Dreaming #22–24, **"An Unkindness of One"** (March '98–May '98)
The Dreaming #26, **"Restitution"** (July '98)
The Dreaming #27, **"Stormy Weather"** (July '98)
The Dreaming #28, **"Dreams the Burning Dream"** (August '98)
The Dreaming #30, **"Temporary Overflow"** (September '98)
The Dreaming #31, **"November Eve"** (coauthored with Peter Hogan; December '98)
The Dreaming #33, **"Dream Below"** (February '99)
The Dreaming #34, **"Ruin"** (March '99)
The Dreaming #35, **"Kaleidoscope"** (April '99)
The Dreaming #36, **"Slow Dying"** (May '99)
The Dreaming #37, **"Pariah"** (June '99)
The Dreaming #38, **"Apostate"** (July '99)
The Dreaming #39, **"The Lost Language of Flowers** (August '99)
The Dreaming #40, **"New Orleans for Free"** (September '99)
The Dreaming #41, **"The Bittersweet Scent of Opium"** (October '99)
The Dreaming #42, **"Detonation Boulevard"** (November '99)
The Dreaming #43, **"The Two Trees"** (December '99)
The Dreaming #44, **"Homesick"** (January '00)
The Dreaming #45, **"Masques & Hedgehogs"** (February '00)
The Dreaming #46, **"Mirror, Mirror"** (March '00)
The Dreaming #47, **"Trinket"** (April '00)
The Dreaming #48, **"Scary Monsters"** (May '00)
The Dreaming #49, **"Shatter"** (June '00)
The Dreaming #50, **"Restoration"** (July '00)
The Dreaming #51, **"Second Sight"** (August '00)
The Dreaming #52–54, **"Exiles"** (September '00–November '00)

The Dreaming #56, **"The First Adventure of Miss Catterina Poe"** (January '01)
The Dreaming #57–60, **"Rise"** (February'01–May '01; series finale)
Vertigo: Winter's Edge #1, **"The Dreaming: Deck the Halls"** ('98; coauthored with Peter Hogan)
Vertigo: Winter's Edge #2, **"The Dreaming: Marble Halls"** ('99)
Vertigo: Winter's Edge #3, **"The Dreaming: Borealis"** ('00)
The Girl Who Would Be Death (four-issue miniseries; 1998–1999)
The Sandman Presents: Bast: Eternity Game (three-issue miniseries; 2002)
Alabaster: Wolves (ed. Rachel Edidin, Dark Horse Comics; five-issue miniseries, 2012; hardback collection, 2013)
Alabaster: Boxcar Tales (ed. Rachel Edidin, and Daniel Chabon, Dark Horse Presents; November 2012–December 2013; hardback released as *Alabaster: Grimmer Tales*, April 2014)
Alabaster: The Good, the Bad, and the Bird (ed. Daniel Chabon, Dark Horse Comics, five-issue miniseries, 2015)

Scientific Publications

Wright, Kenneth R. 1985a. **A New Specimen of *Globidens alabamaensis* from Alabama.** *Journal of the Alabama Academy of Science* **56(3):102.**

Wright, K. R. 1985b. **What (If Anything) is *Tylosaurus zangerli*?** Society of Vertebrate Paleontology 45th Annual Meeting, Rapid City, SD, poster session with abstract.

Kiernan, K. R. 1985c. **A New Specimen of *Globidens alabamaensis* from Alabama.** Society of Vertebrate Paleontology 45th Annual Meeting, Rapid City, SD, platform session with abstract.

Wright, K. R. 1986a. **A Preliminary Report on the Biostratigraphic Zonation of Alabama Mosasaurs.** *Journal of the Alabama Academy of Science* 57:146.

Wright, K. R. 1986b. **On the Stratigraphic Distribution of Mosasaurs in Western and Central Alabama.** *Abstracts, North American Paleontological Convention IV*, Boulder, CO: A51.

Wright, K. R. 1986c**. On the Stratigraphic Distribution of Mosasaurs in Western and Central Alabama.** Society of Vertebrate Paleontology 46th Annual Meeting, Philadelphia, PA, platform session with abstract.

Wright, K. R. 1987. **The Mosasaur *Clidastes*: The Specimens and New Problems.** *Journal of the Alabama Academy of Science* 58:99.

Wright, K. R. 1988a. **The First Record of *Clidastes liodontus* (Squamata, Mosasauridae) from the Eastern United States.** *Journal of Vertebrate Paleontology* 8:343-345.

Wright. K. R. and Shannon, S. W. 1988b. ***Selmasaurus russelli,* a New Plioplatecarpine Mosasaur from Alabama.** *Journal of Vertebrate Paleontology* 8:102-107.
Wright, K. R. 1988c. **On the Taxonomic Status of *Moanasaurus mangahouangae* Wiffen (Squamata: Mosasauridae).** *Journal of Paleontology* 61(1):126-127.
Wright, K. R. 1988d. **A New Specimen of *Halisaurus platyspondylus* (Squamata: Mosasauridae) from the Navesink Formation (Maestrichtian) of New Jersey.** *Journal of Paleontology* 8(3):A146.
Wright, K. R. and Varner, Daniel 1988. **Fleshing-Out the Mosasaurs (Squamata: Mosasauridae).** *Journal of Paleontology* 8(3): A147.
Wright, K. R. and Williams, G. Dent 1989. **Vertebrate Fossils of the Blufftown Formation.** *Journal of the Alabama Academy of Science* 60(3):
Kiernan, C. R. 1992. ***Clidastes* Cope, 1868 (Reptilia, Sauria): proposed designation of *Clidastes propython* Cope, 1869 as the type species.** *Bulletin of Zoological Nomenclature* 49:137–139.
Schwimmer, D. R. and Kiernan, C. R. 2001. **Eastern Late Cretaceous theropods in North America and the crossing of the Interior Seaway.** *Journal of Vertebrate Paleontology* 21(3):99A.
Kiernan, C. R. 2002. **Stratigraphic distribution and habitat segregation of mosasaurs in the Upper Cretaceous of western and central Alabama, with an historical review of Alabama mosasaur discoveries.** *Journal of Vertebrate Paleontology* 22(1):91-103.
Kiernan, C. R., and Schwimmer, D. R. 2004. **First record of a velociraptorine theropod (Tetanurae, Dromaeosauridae) from the Eastern Gulf Coastal United States.** *The Mosasaur* 7:89-93.

Miscellany (Non-Fiction)

"Transmeditations" 1992-1993, *The Alabama Forum* (monthly column), Lambda, Inc.
"Approximately 2,000 Words About Poppy Z. Brite" 1997 *World Horror Convention Program Book,* Horror Writers of America
"...And in Closing (For Now)" 1998 afterword for *Are You Loathsome Tonight*, Poppy Z. Brite; Gauntlet Press
"Foreword" to *Gloomcookie Vol. 1* 2001, Serena Valentino and Ted Naifeh, Slave Labor Graphics Pub.
"Introduction" to *Kissing Carrion* 2003, Gemma Files, Prime Books
"*Skin* by Kathe Koja" 2005 *Horror: Another 100 Best Books*, Carroll & Graf
"Notes From A Damned Life" 2007 *Weird Tales* (Apr.-May #444)

"Awful Things" 2007 *Locus* (May #556)
"The Most Beautiful Music I've Ever Read" 2008 Introduction for Ray Bradbury's *The Day It Rained Forever*, PS Publishing
"Lovecraft and I" 2011 *Lovecraft Annual* (August #5), Hippocampus Press

Copyright © 2015 by Caitlín R. Kiernan

Acknowledgements

As I said in the acknowledgements to *Volume One,* given the scope of a book of this nature, there really is no way to thank everyone who ought to be thanked or to recognize the efforts of everyone who should be recognized. But here's a special thank you to the editors and publishers who solicited a number of these stories and first gave them homes: Lou Anders, Neil Clarke, Ellen Datlow, and Jonathan Strahan. And *very* special thanks to the many subscribers of *Sirenia Digest,* as most of these stories would not exist without you. Indeed, it is worth noting that twenty of the twenty-eight stories in the book were written for and first appeared in *Sirenia Digest.* Once again, Lee Moyers has provided a portrait of a truer me than is visible with the naked eye (and has given me *Selmasaurus kiernanae,* realized). Neil Gaiman lent me a beautiful cabin in the Catskills in which to hang with the ghost of Bob Dylan and survive the editing and proofreading of this volume; thanks also to Augusta Ogden and Philip Marshall, who together insured that my two stays in Woodstock during the winter of 2014-2015 were comfortable. I am beholden to S. T. Joshi for his introduction, as I simply could not seem to pull one together for this book. Vince Locke, Richard Kirk, Steve Lieber, and Dark Horse Comics permitted me to reprint the artwork in the limited edition. Thanks to my agent, Merrilee Heifetz of Writers House, for sticking with me all these years. Greer Gilman read an early draft of "Atlantis" and offered valuable criticism. Sonya Taaffe assisted with the proofreading. A special thanks to the Jenks Society for Lost Museums, Brown University and to Christopher Geissler of the John Hay Library, Brown University. And of course, I am grateful to Bill Schafer at Subterranean Press who suggested and published these two volumes. But above all, thank you, Kathryn, still my bear, my goat girl, my cranky, melancholic love.

About the Author

The New York Times recently called Caitlín R. Kiernan "one of our essential writers of dark fiction" and S. T. Joshi has declared "...hers is now the voice of weird fiction." Caitlín's novels include *Silk, Threshold, Low Red Moon, Daughter of Hounds, The Red Tree* (nominated for the Shirley Jackson and World Fantasy awards), and *The Drowning Girl: A Memoir* (winner of the James Tiptree, Jr. and Bram Stoker awards, nominated for the Nebula, World Fantasy, British Fantasy, Mythopoeic, Locus, and Shirley Jackson awards). To date, her short fiction has been collected in thirteen volumes, including *Tales of Pain and Wonder, From Weird and Distant Shores, Alabaster, A is for Alien, The Ammonite Violin & Others, Confessions of a Five-Chambered Heart, Two Worlds and In Between: The Best of Caitlín R. Kiernan (Volume One),* and the Fantasy Award winning *The Ape's Wife and Other Stories.* She has also won a World Fantasy Award for Best Short Fiction for "The Prayer of Ninety Cats." During the 1990s she wrote *The Dreaming* for DC Comics' Vertigo imprint, and has recently completed *Alabaster* for Dark Horse Comics. The first volume, *Alabaster: Wolves,* received the Bram Stoker Award. She lives in Providence, Rhode Island with her partner, Kathryn Pollnac.

But all she ever *wanted* was to be a paleontologist...

About the Font

This book was set in Garamond, a typeface named after the French punch-cutter Claude Garamond (c. 1480–1561). Garamond has been chosen here for its ability to convey a sense of fluidity and consistency. It has been chosen by the author because this typeface is among the most legible and readable old-style serif print typefaces. In terms of ink usage, Garamond is also considered to be one of the most eco-friendly major fonts.